# *More* TOTALLY HEROTICA

# More TOTALLY HEROTICA

## A Collection of Women's Erotic Fiction

### EDITED BY MARCY SHEINER

Quality Paperback Book Club
New York

# CONTENTS

## HEROTICA 4

# Contents

## HEROTICA 5

## HEROTICA 6

*Contents*

# HEROTICA 4

*This book is dedicated to my teachers,*
*Marco Vassi and Susie Bright.*

# ACKNOWLEDGMENTS

I am grateful to Leigh Davidson for her unflagging sense, sanity, and support.

If she ever gets the time, I owe Linnea Due a Chinese lunch for her generous feedback.

Shar Rednour, treasure of the Bay Area sex scene, provided editorial assistance, literary acumen, lessons in diplomacy, and fashion expertise. She calls me her mentor, but really she's mine.

One of the bonuses of editing this book was working with the extraordinary Joani Blank. Without her vision and energy, there would be no *Herotica*®, no Down There Press, no Good Vibrations, no Open Enterprises.

A smile for Phyllis Christopher, the only photographer who can make me do it.

Everyone thanks their partners for putting up with them, so . . . I thank mine, although seeing me through the process of *Herotica*® has probably been one of the more pleasurable aspects of Jamie's life with me.

# INTRODUCTION

The first time I wrote a pornographic story, I was amazed to find my pen flowing across page after page in a nearly seamless movement from beginning to middle to end. In twenty years of writing fiction and journalism, this had never happened to me. It seemed that the freeing of my sexual voice had loosened my creative voice as well. I learned, on a kinesthetic level, about the connection between sexuality and creativity. Not only do the creative and sexual impulses emanate from the same source, but the two are also synergistic.

In writing fiction suffused with sexual content, I became more prolific and proficient at my craft. This kind of symbiosis between creativity and sexuality is not limited to writing; it's the reason that so many artists—dancers, actors, photographers, painters—inevitably delve into the sexual arena.

Still, while pornography provided a fountain of creative inspiration for me, after a hundred or so stories I began to wonder just how many ways I could possibly continue to say "They (or we) did it." In editing women's erotic fiction, I've learned that the number of ways to say "They (or we) did it" are in fact infinite.

Since the first *Herotica®* collection appeared in 1988, a supportive atmosphere has developed in which women can express and communicate exactly what arouses us sexually—but until this recent explosion of women-created erotica, our sexual voice had been largely silent. Men, of course, were permitted, even encouraged, to articulate in graphic and loving detail the myriad ways of getting it on, and so the pornography industry inevitably reflected their sexual tastes and behavior. More significantly, the parameters of male sexual expression widened to fill the space it was accorded, while we women remained in the dark about one another's, and often even our own, erotic proclivities.

We are rapidly moving out of these dark ages; although there are still some who question whether or not it's all right for us to write, much less read and get off on, sexual words and images, women's erotic writing has become a fact of life and a hot item in the publishing industry. Our stories are sold in national chain bookstores, promoted at international book fairs, and distributed through mainstream book clubs. The more we publish, read, and talk about what we think and feel concerning sex, the more the boundaries of our sexual imagination expand.

The *Herotica* series continues to lead the way in mapping the still largely uncharted landscape of female desire. The subjects in this, the fourth collection, range from a precocious student's seduction of her English teacher to an evening with a couple of high-class call girls. What strikes me most about the collection is the richness and complexity of the plot lines surrounding or interwoven with the sexual encounters. Some of the work in this collection is as literary as anything you'll find in *The New Yorker* or *The Paris Review*, but because overt sex is largely compartmentalized in our culture, you can bet your multiple orgasms these stories won't be winning any Pushcart Prizes.

And literary quality, as these authors prove, does not have to be sexless: "I take his cock in my mouth, sip from it, drink from it in the same fashion that I consumed the beer in the bar." "Wet, wet, so very wet, the delicious friction made me erupt volcanic, shuddering against her, inside her, through her." These lines are eloquent without being euphemistic; the erotic charge is clearly the springboard for the writing.

In other ways as well *Herotica* stories differ from the kind of wham-bam pornography that focuses primarily on the physical act. What exactly is it that distinguishes these stories?

## Context

From the moment she lays eyes on the electrical repairwoman, the heroine of "Electricity in My Bed" wants to sleep with her—but this desire is rooted in the context of a long-standing wish to make love with another woman. At the other end of the relationship spectrum, sex in "Giving and Receiving" occurs within the context of a long-term affair.

Judging from the way women write about sex, one of the most important paths to our arousal is the context in which sex occurs. Some might cite this as proof of women's long-alleged inability to enjoy sex outside of a relationship. But context does not equal relationship; context simply means there's a dynamic between the characters that gets expressed sexually. Whether our heroine is sneaking a furtive hump in the ladies' room or riding the emotional waves of a long-term relationship, the sexual encounter is but one thread in a tapestry that may incorporate various aspects of her history. As the Parisian lover in "Real Pleasure" puts it to her obtuse American counterpart, "Just because I have emotions doesn't mean I want a relationship. It only means I'm not a machine."

This is the reason so many women remain unmoved by porn videos: there's rarely any kind of tension between the characters, or any context for the sex act. Mainstream porn videos tend to focus on organs and orgasms rather than on people and their interactions. Analysts have concluded that women simply don't respond to visual stimulation. Well, it's not that we don't respond to visual stimulation—it's that we don't respond to vapidity. How else to explain the uproar among *Playgirl* subscribers when the magazine decided to put clothes on its male centerfolds: their readership demanded that the models disrobe immediately!

Erotic literature leaves room for the reader to reshape the specifics to her own tastes, something that's more difficult to do with moving pictures on a screen. And from what I've heard women say about the ways they use pornography, we seem to be less immediate—an image "lifted" from porn might come back to us months later, sliding right into our fantasy to send us a notch wetter and wilder. If *Herotica* stories don't always fall under the heading of "one-handed reading," that's because women generally don't read porn one-handedly. Rather, we raid pornography for images and ideas, then adapt them to suit our own sexual quirks. We want mental as well as sensory engagement.

Thus, *Herotica* authors take their time developing plot, character, and setting before inviting us into bed. They tease us with the promise of arousal and satisfaction, then leisurely go about creating a universe, whether it's centered in Hollywood or in Victorian England, in a city's red-light district or on another planet. This exquisite attention to detail plays an essential role in the sexual schema: the authors create an erotic environment, and they don't quit at what may be a crucial moment for either the characters or audience. They don't leave us hanging just outside the bedroom door.

## *The Forbidden Zone*

Pornography is not polite—that's one of the reasons it's continually under attack. To be effective, sexually explicit writing must break society's rules. That's why most attempts to create sweet egalitarian erotica are misguided; sure, some gals or even guys may get off on sunset-drenched scenery, but for most people very soft-core stuff just doesn't pass the wet test. Sex is about exploration and discovery, and that frequently involves entering some forbidden zone.

What's forbidden depends on who you're talking to. For some women, fantasizing while with a partner feels wrong—so guess what? The very act of fantasizing turns them on like nothing else. For many women, thoughts about physical or emotional mistreatment during sex seem politically if not morally incorrect—and so violence and humiliation fill their fantasies. The element of danger—physical or emotional—is a powerful aphrodisiac. Fear of social censure is another, so anything verboten in the culture is guaranteed to excite. Interracial sex. Intergenerational sex.

Adultery. As every teenager knows, any situation requiring secrecy is inherently exciting.

Since lesbians have been historically stigmatized, the very portrayal of two women making love defies a taboo, and the act itself is imbued with a sense of danger, as well as rebellion—another potential aphrodisiac. For a Japanese woman, the public expression of female sexuality is such a no-no that when the narrator of "My Dance at Juliana's" displays herself in public, "a surge of power rushes through my body and I feel high." For a heterosexual American college girl the ante gets upped considerably: in "Make Me," the young heroine's attraction to a father figure skirts around the territory of incest.

But while these stories shine a light into some dark corners, the door to the female forbidden zone is only slightly ajar. The *Herotica* series is part of a movement still in its infancy. We're only beginning to explore, much less speak publicly about, these hidden areas of desire. We have barely begun to articulate the interior processes we undergo during sex and in our fantasy lives.

Exactly what goes through her head and heart when he grips her shoulder and pushes her to her knees? What complex combination of jealousy and excitement inspires her to orgasm when she watches her lover fucking her best friend? What psychic shift occurs when, for the first time in her life, she has her way with a passive man? What familial or cultural ghosts hover around her bed when she surrenders totally to a dominating partner? These are the kinds of questions that women, at this stage of our sexual evolution, still frequently shy away from.

If we're not willing to look at our own responses and share them with one another, we'll do a better job of limiting our sexual expression than any censor. It's ironic that women, notorious for consulting therapists about everything from insomnia to failing relationships, don't do the same when it comes to sexual behavior. We're going to have to crawl as deeply into our sexual psyches as we do into other aspects of our lives. We're going to have to look honestly at the reality, rather than the ideology, of sex, even if what we find turns out to be humiliating, mundane, or—*surprise!*—politically incorrect.

We are beginning to see glimmers of this kind of exploration. "My Mother's Body," for instance, looks at a woman's childhood erotic feelings toward her mother and how they affect her adult sexuality:

> Your breasts are beautiful, like my mother's. . . . I was fascinated by her breasts. They were large and very dense with nipples in perpetual erection. The thought that my body might one day look like hers thrilled me. I watched in awe as she put her bra straps over her shoulders, bent over and shook all of that pink flesh into the white cotton cones of her 36C Maidenform.
>
> Bend over and shake for me.
>
> Freud had it all wrong. It's the mother-daughter relationship that's so titillating. Women are either lesbian or bisexual; how can we be anything but, when our first and primary love object was our mother?

Entering another forbidden zone, the narrator in "Night Talk" admits a penchant for hearing abusive, even misogynistic, language during sex:

> "They were being way too polite. I had to tell them to talk filthy to me. They started out pretty tame, but they ended up whispering things like 'Come on, bitch, come for us. You know you want to. Let's hear you come. You like having two cocks in you, don't you? You like getting fucked by two dicks at once, you slut. Oh, you're such a little whore. What a sweet little snatch you have. Your ass is so hot and snug. You better come soon, bitch, 'cause I can't hold back much longer.' Once they started talking like this, I totally lost it."

## *Women's Love Affair with Words*

My passion for language developed around the same time as my passion for sex. In high school I began writing essays that knocked my teacher's socks off: during that same time period I began making out with boys in the backseats of cars. The day after one of those steamy encounters, I'd recall delicious details that made my stomach flop—but it was not the remembered feel of an erection through layers of clothing, or even the occasional hand on my breast that I conjured up to turn myself on. No, what I turned over and over in my mind, savoring them like precious jewels, were the *words* he had whispered in my ear. Whether he'd promised eternal love or begged permission to unsnap my bra, his words moved me on a deeper level than his touch.

A popular song at that time, "Things I Wanna Hear," resonated with the girls and instructed the boys in the art and importance of sweet talk. That quintessential "girl group," the Shirelles, insisted they needed a constant barrage of "pretty words" if their lovers expected to get to first base with them. That song told me I was not alone in my hunger for erotic or romantic words.

*Herotica 4* authors do the same. Sometimes they create a subtle undertone of language as foreplay. At other times they allude explicitly to the erotic power of words, as in "Amazing Grace," where a lover's sweet talk is "one of the best parts, the slow run of his voice like sugar syrup, over her head and around her ears." Then there's the metaphorical "Tasting the Sky," in which a woman hides in a library cubicle and squeezes a book full of words between her legs. Sometimes, as in "Coming and Cumming," two little letters can mean the difference between long, leisurely sex and quick release:

Cum . . . is the short form of the verb, for boys who bounce up and down on you and cum in three minutes. . . . Women are built for the long haul—watch what comes.

Pornography, like sex itself, has a way of revealing us to ourselves, and as you read *Herotica 4* you may find yourself responding to images and situations you've never thought about, or dismissed as out of bounds. Just be sure to watch what comes.

*Susan St. Aubin*

# Coming and Cumming

I was nineteen and the oldest senior in my high school when I found my first lover. Because I was slow learning to read, I'd repeated first grade, but once I caught on, nothing could hold me back. By the time I was a freshman, I had a reputation for intelligence: history teachers would check their facts with me; English teachers would ask me obscure points of grammar. *Lay* or *lie*? I always knew the appropriate form.

In my senior year I took an honors course called Early English Literature, a survey that covered everything from *Beowulf* to Milton's *Paradise Lost*. The teacher, Miss Wilson, probably wasn't more than three or four years older than I was. This was her first job, and in her short skirts, flat shoes, and little gold earrings, she looked younger than most of us.

I wanted to shine for Miss Wilson. She was brilliant: she could recognize a line from the most obscure Elizabethan sonnet and tell you the name of the poem and who had written it. Though I knew I was no match for a mind like hers, I was hopelessly in love. I was sure she'd never guess what a girl like me could feel, hiding in the fortress of my body: fat face, stringy blond hair, hunched and rounded shoulders, heavy legs. Even my feet were fat in their sandals, the white straps cutting into the abundant flesh on my heels and toes.

In Miss Wilson's class I put out. I kept class discussions going when no one else would say two words, and I worked hard on my essays, though I could easily get As in most English classes just by plopping down words on paper.

It was late May, two weeks before graduation. No teacher would admit it, but we knew our grades were decided before final exams. It was a time of movies in all our classes: films on the periodic tables in chemistry or on the digestive system in biology—stuff we already knew, but our teachers liked to pretend there was a great danger that we'd forgotten. One day, Miss Wilson showed an old black-and-white film of *Romeo and Juliet*, a condensed version in just two reels. Now they'd have a color video, but this was back in 1965, when all we saw in school was old movies, the reels spinning, the black-and-white images flickering, and the whole class half asleep in the dimness of the lowered blinds.

When the bell rang, everyone stood up at once. The first guy out the door hit the lights, flaring the room into brightness. I stayed in my seat next to the projector, watching the shadows of Romeo and his lover continue to glide across the screen. I was the projectionist, which girls never were in those days; running movie projectors was considered highly technical. But I'd taught myself how to thread one (which wasn't all that different from threading a sewing machine), how to fix it when it jammed, and how to rewind the films when class was over. I shut the projector off and watched the image freeze as the film stopped mid-reel, then turned off the projector light, loosened the film from its wheels and pulleys, and moved the reel to the rewind position. Miss Wilson still sat at her desk staring blindly at the screen above her head.

"Patricia?" she said, as if awakening from a dream. My zombie hands continued their motions. In the hall, lockers banged. It was Friday, last period of the day, so everyone was leaving as fast as they could. I put the reel of film into its metal can and snapped the lid shut, then slowly wheeled the projector to the door. Alone with my idol, I was speechless.

"Patricia," she said again. "I'd like to talk to you a minute."

"Yes," I answered, "of course."

I locked the classroom door so no one could interrupt our conversation, which I imagined would be so intellectually esoteric I'd remember it forever, and went to the front of the room to stand before her desk.

"It's about your paper," she said.

Then I saw she'd been correcting our essays while the movie was running.

"It's really quite remarkable."

For extra credit I'd written about slang as a sort of shanty language that grows up around the established city of the main language. I was daring: I talked about sexual slang, especially about the word "to come," spelled "cum" the way the boys wrote it on the walls, in the gym, and on the door of the girls' bathroom, sometimes along with "fuck" and "cunt."

In gym class, I'd be down on the floor doing those silly leg lifts they made girls do to reduce the size of their hips, and there it would be, carved into the expensive wood floor we weren't even supposed to walk on in our street shoes: CUM. Though I couldn't find this word in my pocket dictionary, I had an idea what the boys meant. I knew the suspense as my fingers danced over my crotch, the waiting and waiting and wondering, is it going to happen this time, is it? And then it comes, yes, there it is.

In the school library I'd found an edition of the *Oxford English Dictionary* in two volumes, with the hand-held viewing glass you had to use because the print was so tiny. Some guy had actually scratched "CUM FUCK" into the plastic handle in minuscule letters right under the name of the optical company. It must have taken him hours.

Why did I assume it was a guy? Because back then I didn't think girls did what I did. No one ever said anything. Girls were there for guys, as the objects of their desire. It seemed strange to me that girls never seemed to like each other much, because they were also the objects of *my* desire, and, I assumed, each other's.

I ran the viewer down the miniature columns of the *O.E.D.* "Cum: Latin, meaning 'together with.'" Yes, that made sense, though I always did it alone, but how much better it would be with another girl like myself. Beneath that was "Cum, obs. form

of come." A verb, cum as in come. Obsolete. Old English. I pictured generations of Anglo-Saxons and their heirs cumming and
cumming. While the rest of the language moved ahead, into
coming, the sex part stayed back in the more primitive, obsolete
form. That was how I pictured it.

I wondered if Miss Wilson was a woman who knew what she
was waiting for, who knew about cumming, who knew in a rush
what that word meant when she passed it on the walls of our
school; a woman who wouldn't cover her mouth and giggle when
she saw it, like the girls did, or run to get the janitor to clean it
off, like Miss Richardson, the Dean of Girls. I guessed that Miss
Wilson might be like me because she was so smart. Most of the
girls I knew, even the other two in the honors English class, just
didn't seem very bright. I had some idea that it might be plain
intelligence that made a person "cum."

In my paper I explicated the verb "to cum," and the noun,
too, because yes, this versatile word had become a noun, though
I didn't know quite how. Once someone dropped part of an ice-
cream bar in the hall under my locker, and wrote "Jim's cum"
with an arrow pointing down at the viscous puddle the melted
ice cream had left. Jim had the locker next to mine, but I never
had a class with him because he was a real genius who took
nothing but advanced chemistry and math.

I had some vague idea that when boys came, something came
out of them. In biology class, this was called the orgasm, or so
I thought. I was remarkably ignorant for someone who knew so
much about language and literature, but there it was: I believed
men had orgasms, which I defined as stuff coming out, but when
women came (which few did), they just got a little wet, like I
did. As usual, men had more of what we had.

Now Miss Wilson was shaking her head. I wasn't worried; my
solid A in her class couldn't be destroyed by one extra-credit
paper.

"It's very good," she said, "but I think you're wrong about several things."

Did she know how wrong? She ran her tongue over her lips
and shuffled the pages.

"I don't think you can assume high school boys are in fact using Old English," she said, laughing. "That's too much. I think they just can't spell. Do you know how often I've seen 'cum' for 'come' in an ordinary misspelled paper?"

I smiled. "They could be teasing you," I suggested.

"Not much chance that would work," she said, and her eyes locked with mine.

She stood up, letting my paper fall back onto the desk, and stretched her arms over her head. Her breasts lifted beneath her thin cotton blouse. I saw for sure that the rumors I'd heard were true: she didn't wear a bra. She was so small and firm you couldn't tell from a distance. Blushing, I lowered my eyes. She put a hand on my shoulder.

"I didn't mean to laugh," she said. "I like the way you think about language, even about what you see written on walls. But I still think 'cum' is more of a cute spelling, like 'thanx' with an 'x,' or dotting your 'i's' with circles. Kids tend to do those things. I always spell it 'come,' the modern way. I'm not sure I believe your theory of sexual 'cumming' dating back to Old English, though it's true most people are so backward about sex it's logical that the words they use for it wouldn't have evolved with the rest of the language. 'Fuck,' as you know, goes straight back to Anglo-Saxon, and so does 'cunt.'"

As we stood side by side I felt something coming to both of us. In my mind, I spelled it the modern way. Come on, I silently prayed. I willed her to move closer to me, and she did.

"Come," I think she whispered, and her lips were on my shoulder next to her hand.

Our arms slid around each other, easy as cream; her mouth on mine had the sharp sweetness of berries. We slid to the floor under the desk as though we'd dissolved to water, our basic body fluid. There we were, liquefied, flowing into each other. The liquefaction of our clothes: Robert Herrick, seventeenth century. I remembered at once everything and nothing; the liquefaction of my brain.

Suddenly I felt her body solidify against me. "I locked the door," I whispered into the short curls above her ear, and felt the tension flow out of her.

"You think of everything," she whispered back. She didn't

know the half of it. My brain and body were both ready to explode.

Her expert fingers slid down my sides, massaging and squeezing my flesh. "So nice," she murmured.

Nice? I thought I was just fat. Guys followed me in the hall, laughing. "Look at Pat's ass," they'd say, coughing and wheezing into their clenched fists.

She was so light on top of me, with her hands underneath me, inside my underpants, on my ass, rippling across my flesh, massaging and teasing. She spread my legs with one hand on my mound, two fingers rubbing between my lips.

Cumming, I thought. It's coming. I felt as though a tidal wave would burst through the classroom door.

Her fingers stopped and the tide receded. I gasped in disappointment.

"Not yet," she said. "I want you to wait for it."

Once again she brought me to the edge of that rough ocean, then stopped.

"Wait," she hissed.

Each time, what was coming felt larger and rounder.

"Do you feel it coming?" she asked. "Patricia, tell me, is it coming?"

"Yes, yes," I panted.

"And not 'cumming' with a 'u'?" she asked.

This was certainly the most vivid grammar lesson I'd ever had.

"No, no, it's round, like an 'o,' " I wailed.

And then it came, like wings flapping high over the sea, then swooping under the waves.

"It came," I laughed. My "a" was round and liquid on my tongue. Not the short hum of "cum," which had no past tense, but "came," as in something that certainly happened.

When my breathing slowed, she moved herself over my body, unbuttoning my blouse and removing my bra so skillfully I hardly felt her. She was like a small animal—a cat or a dog or even a human infant, crawling over my soft belly, which beat like a drum, my thighs, and my breasts, which she took, one after the other, into her generous mouth, kneading them with all her fingers spread as she sucked, like a kitten kneads its mother.

Her skirt was off, and her underpants and shoes. It was so hot neither one of us wore stockings. I reached up inside her blouse to feel her small breasts, the tiny nipples hard as seeds beneath my fingers.

She lowered her wet crotch onto my knee and moved up and down, her lips spread so wide it almost felt like my knee was inside her. I moved it back and forth, following her rhythm. I could feel her cunt start to twitch, but then she stopped.

"Why?" I asked. She sat still on my knee, looking down at me, and put a finger to her lips. A hot rain of sweat dripped from her forehead onto my breasts. I was afraid the windows of the classroom were steaming behind the blinds, and that someone would notice and break in, but the halls were quiet.

" 'Cum,' " she said, "is the short form of the verb, for boys who bounce up and down on you and cum in three minutes. The noun for that is also 'cum'—that's the stuff they spurt out before they know it's arrived. Women are built for the long haul—watch what comes."

She drew the vowels out long and liquid. "Long," she whispered as she moved herself on my knee. "Long and longer. Let me show you how long."

She moved forward then, until her cunt was over my breast. Carefully she lowered herself until her soft wetness surrounded my nipple. I felt something rising in me, coming. My nipple was a hard knot inside her while her pubic hair tickled my breast as she pressed herself upon it. Everything I'd ever felt between my legs was concentrated in one wet, engaged nipple. When I twisted beneath her she held me firm, not stopping now but riding up and down on the saddle her weight had made of my breast. Both of us were hanging from the same wave, suspended over the ocean.

Whenever I took my breast in my hand to push it deeper inside her, she put her hands firmly on my shoulders and murmured, "Wait, wait."

"I can't!" I nearly screamed. She put one hand over my mouth and then screamed herself, so loud I was sure every teacher and hall monitor would be instantly upon us. But over an hour had passed since I'd locked that door, so the school was deserted.

I felt a throbbing in my breast, and an echoing pulse between my legs. I was wet all over my chest, as though my breast had leaked. My teacher had fallen forward on me so that my nose was in her navel. I reached beneath her to wipe the clear, sticky liquid off my breast. What was it? Did it come from me or from her? Was it what the boys called "cum"?

She pushed herself up and sat beside me. "See what can come if you wait long enough?" she said, wiping my breast with one hand. "I don't always do this, but it's wonderful when it comes."

"Is all that from you?" I asked.

She looked into my eyes. "It can come from women, too, you know, from deep inside." When she brushed her fingers across my lips, I tasted her rich sour cream.

" 'Cum,' " she said, her "u" short and clipped, "is for boys who never want to wait. We come, we arrive, and come again," she murmured in her round voice, moving her hands down my body, expanding with her fingers that timeless afternoon, that lesson in the grammar of the body.

We were in no hurry.

# Night Talk

Madison had gotten her tiny hands on Jack's cuffs again. She held them near her ear. Clickclickclickclickclick. They sounded like glass or ice.

"Tonight?" Madison asked.

"Tonight we are going to sleep."

"I'm not sleepy."

"But I am." Jack padded around to his side and eased between the flannel sheets. "Tell me a story."

Madison took up his challenge. She had been carefully escalating their bedtime ritual. "You want to hear a true one tonight?"

"Madison," Jack gently chastised. He had taken to using her name casually. A command, a plea, a silly comfort noise.

"Mace and Danny came over last week," she began.

"Who are they?"

"Friends. Like you."

"Right," Jack quickly conceded. "We are friends. I don't want to get involved right now. It's not you, I just need to remain autonomous—"

"You're obviously on your own," Madison interrupted. She wouldn't be snared in his dramatics. Madison realized then that when they finally parted, decency would compel Jack to smear the blood around. He had not yet learned that abandoning a person takes nothing. Any threadbare phrase would do.

The inevitable grated at her, so she hollowed out a nook between Jack's arm and chest. She furrowed her brows at his milky skin and swallowed the impulse to desecrate it with hickeys.

"Madison? Tell me your story."

"All right. Mace and Danny had come over to study *Frankenstein* for our English exam."

"What were you wearing?" Jack interrupted. He was the most aesthetically inclined man Madison had ever fucked.

"I was wearing sweats when they came in, but Mace asked me to change. He told me to put on that white eyelet gown you gave me. He and Danny were in smoking jackets. They had gotten this wacky idea that we'd all do better if we really got into the material. You know, kind of study in the novelist's own style."

"Uh-huh."

"So I changed and made jasmine tea. Mace had brought chocolates and oranges. We lit every candle I had and then sat on the rug in a nest of books and food.

"Since we were playing at romance, I had Mace lie down with his head in my lap. I fed him slices of orange while Daniel read us the important passages. Every time he finished a paragraph, I rewarded him with a chocolate.

"We studied that way for a while until only wrappings and peels were left. Then Danny read us some notes reporting that Shelley and her consorts prided themselves on their liberal sexuality. So Mace up and says, 'Why not take off our clothes?' And he strips."

"Not one to miss an opportunity, is he?" Jack asked.

"Are you?" Madison countered.

Jack kissed Madison behind her ears, smirking into her charcoal curls. "But this was all to enhance your studying."

"Presumably."

"You and Dan were still dressed?"

"Uh-huh. But soon we began to feel left out. Mace was having more fun. So I told Danny to undress me.

"The buttons on my gown ran from the collar down to the hem. He stood behind me and started at the top. I could feel his cock straining at my ass through his trousers. He kept asking me if he was doing it right, placing his mouth close enough to my ear for me to feel his lips moving. His breath on my neck made my nipples hard. He began rubbing them gently with the insides of his wrist.

"Mace knelt in front of me and started unbuttoning where Danny had stopped. His fingers against my stomach tickled. Once he got to my panties, he forgot to keep going. He let his hands rest against my thighs and bent his head toward my pussy. While Danny was still fondling my nipples, Mace started kissing my panties. He ran his tongue under the elastic and cuddled his whole head against my crotch. He went on and on like this until I asked him to stop. I thought I was going to fall over."

Madison caught Jack squeezing his balls. He met her gaze. He was brave and intent, like an enthralled child. Madison smiled. She loved to watch him. His Santa Claus eyes looked foreign against his biting features. She traced them with one finger as she talked so he could better hold himself quiet. Jack knew better than to interrupt these stories.

"Mace started kissing my pussy through my panties," Madison continued. "They were soon soaked through with my wetness and his saliva. Danny uncupped my tits and shoved his hand into the back of my panties. He reached around with his other hand and pulled my panties up completely so that I was exposed to Mace's scrutiny.

"Mace looked up at me and asked if he could play with it. He put one finger inside me and prodded and poked until he found my G-spot. He pressed on it while Danny's finger slid quickly in and out of my ass. He leaned into my pussy and began kissing it very softly. After caressing every inch of my lips, his tongue began massaging my clit. His circles got faster and smaller and I felt an orgasm welling up inside of me, but just as I was about to go over the edge, Danny said, 'Slow down, man. I can feel her ass muscles tightening up. She's about to come.' So Mace went back to his slow deep sucking and kissing. I tried to keep quiet and still, I tried to come without their noticing, but every time I was about to, my ass muscles clenched involuntarily, and

Danny told Mace to ease up. I knew the only way I was ever going to get to come was if I got one of their cocks into me."

Madison suddenly felt overwhelmed. She let her heavy lids fall and ground her pelvis into Jack's favorite pillow. "When Mace started flicking my clit again," she continued, "I begged him to put his cock in me. Danny said he wanted to put his in too. I thought he meant my mouth, and I nearly squealed when he sat down on the sofa, pulled his pants and briefs down to his ankles, and told me to ease his cock into my asshole. I wanted to shove it in, but Danny made me go slow because he was worried I'd hurt myself. It took about five minutes. When I had him completely in me, Mace knelt in front of the sofa on a pillow and put his cock into me too.

"I started to giggle because I wasn't sure how we could move with two cocks in me like that. But Mace told Danny to hold me around the tummy while he held the small of my back. Then they both started moving me up and down their cocks. It was a little clumsy at first, but they soon matched each other's rhythm. I felt like I was flying. I let my body totally relax as they lifted me up and down their pricks."

Madison faltered. She wondered whether she ought to describe their cocks to Jack. Men were so weird about their dicks. She loved Jack's; it was, in fact, exactly the size of her favorite vibrator. Danny's was perfect for ass-fucking: small. But Mace's was as thick as her delicate brown wrist.

Jack must have thought her mouth was dry because he handed her their bedside water glass. "Go on," he urged sweetly.

"Where was I?"

"You were flying, I believe."

"Oh yes. I wanted to come so bad by now I could have cried. I begged them not to stop. I knew I was going to start coming if they kept it up, and I started moaning. I worried they might slow down to tease me again, but I couldn't keep quiet.

"They started talking to each other about how they thought I was about to come all over their cocks. They were being way too polite. I had to tell them to talk filthy to me. They started out pretty tame, but they ended up whispering things like 'Come on, bitch, come for us. You know you want to. Let's hear you come.

You like having two cocks in you, don't you? You like getting fucked by two dicks at once, you slut. Oh, you're such a little whore. What a sweet little snatch you have. Your ass is so hot and snug. You better come soon, bitch, 'cause I can't hold back much longer.' Once they started talking like this, I totally lost it. I came so hard and long. I guess my pussy and ass clenching around their cocks sent them over the edge, too. They both had come by the time my orgasm subsided."

Madison was jolted from her reverie by Jack's finger working its way up her ass. She had almost forgotten him.

"What happened next?" he prodded.

"Isn't that enough?"

"Uh-uh, I want to hear everything."

"I took a shower and the guys ordered pizza."

"That was out of period," Jack said.

"I thought the very same; after they had eaten, I suggested studying, but Mace and Danny started going on again about how good my pussy felt and how tight my ass was. Soon they both had hard-ons."

"Were you turned on too?"

"Yeah, but I didn't want to let them know it. I wanted to mess with them for a while. I told them to stand up about a foot apart. Then I ordered them to look directly at each other and not let their eyes wander, no matter what. I knelt between them.

"It got me hot to imagine how deliciously awkward Mace and Danny must have felt. Two straight boys staring bravely at each other while a girl they knew only vaguely knelt between their engorged cocks. I bet that turns you on too."

"You know I love your taste for atrocity," Jack conceded.

"I told them to keep their eyes open and tell me how they felt at each moment. Then I began sucking Mace's balls."

"Did you press on that little spot right behind them?" Jack asked. "That's my favorite."

"You don't want to spoil the plot, now."

"Never," he laughed. "Tell your story." Jack pulled Madison on top of him and ground his cock into her.

"I thought you were exhausted."

"I *am*." He yawned theatrically. "You better tell me what happens next before I fall asleep on you."

"Well, Mace did exactly as he was told."

"What did he say?"

Madison giggled. "First he said, 'Oh Jesus, I'm gonna fail English.' "

Madison dragged in her breath and tried to send up an accurate delivery. "Then he said, 'Oh, girl, you really know how to make me want you. My balls are starting to tighten up. Your mouth feels all slick and spongy. I hope you start licking my cock soon.' "

"What did Danny say?"

"Danny begged me to do him too. But I told him to shut up and wait his turn."

"How vicious." Jack grinned.

"I made him listen to Mace describe how good I was making his cock feel while he waited."

"And what did Mace say after you started playing with it?"

"Let's see . . . 'Lick my cock all over, baby. Yeah. That's it. I love the way you hold my balls for me. They feel so safe. You cradle them just right. Oh god yeah work your finger up my ass. Uh-huh. You got it nice and wet first. What a sweet girl. Ooo, not so fast baby. Yeah like that. Put it in your mouth now. I need to get inside. Come on. Please, baby. I can't stand it. Come on, bitch, suck me. Oh yeah. Oh yeah. Ah Jesus. You really know how to suck cock, don't you, girl? You can really take it in. Follow your mouth with your hand now. It's so slippery. You squeeze just right. Oooo. Make it last, baby. Slow down. Slow down now. Yeah. Lick my balls some more. Mmm-uhm. That's it, girl. Uhhh. Get your hand real wet and run it up and down the shaft. Oh god. That's good. That's how I like it. You're a good girl. You're gonna make me come, aren't you baby? Oh yeah. Come on. Put it in your mouth again. I want you to swallow it for me. Suck it, whore. Oh yeah. Make me come now, bitch. Harder. Harder.' "

Madison took Jack's index finger into her mouth.

"Then what did he say?"

"Then," Madison smiled, "he didn't say anything at all."

"Madison!" Jack slapped her ass playfully. "What a nasty girl you are."

"I know. My name is Madison Vasquez and I am a sex addict."

"The first step is admitting you have a problem."

"The second?"

"Telling me more."

"And corrupt you with this filth?"

"You need to work through it."

"Such an altruist! Well, Mace had to brace himself against Danny while he came. When I looked up, I saw that he had collapsed onto Danny's shoulder.

" 'You stopped looking at Danny,' I said. He told me he was sorry, but that wasn't good enough. I asked him what he thought he should do to make up for it."

"What did he say?"

"He told me he would help me get Danny off."

"Mace said that?" Jack scooted up against his pillows.

"If you had seen how pretty Danny's cock was, you would have wanted to help too. His balls had already drawn up and little beads of semen were dripping off the end. Besides, we were still honoring the Romantics' daring sensibilities."

"Oh yeah. I had almost forgotten about those."

"Well, Mace hadn't. He knelt behind Danny and started stroking his ass while I kissed the inside of his thighs. Before I had even touched his cock, Danny started to moan."

"My god. What was Mace doing to him?"

"While I had been kissing him," Madison explained eagerly, "Mace had spread Danny's cheeks and was licking his asshole. I reached my finger behind his balls and felt Mace's tongue darting across it like it was a girl's clit. It was so slippery that I just eased my finger in and out while Mace kept tonguing around the edge."

"Then you went back to sucking his balls," Jack offered.

"Yeah. Just like I suck yours."

"But you weren't mean. You didn't make him wait too long. When he started to beg you took his cock in your mouth. You put it in all the way and took it to the back of your throat. You didn't move, you just held it in your mouth for a while."

Madison took up the thread. "But then I moved up to the head and sucked on it while I tugged gently at his balls. Before long he laid his hand on the back of my hair and started pushing against my lips in earnest. I could tell he really needed to come."

"So do I."

"But this was supposed to be your bedtime story, Jack. Aren't you ready to go to sleep?" Madison reached to turn off the light.

Jack grabbed her arm. "Hey!"

"But baby, you're so tired."

"Don't tease. Sophie used to tease."

Madison rolled onto her tummy and let her lips brush the head of Jack's cock. She thought of Mace. She thought of Danny. She flicked her tongue across his opening and thought of her other lovers. Jack pushed himself into her mouth and she thought of all the men who had found solace there.

Madison loved nothing more than giving head. It made her feel secure for a little while. She knew that as long as her mouth held his cock, Jack needed her. Her lips held him captive. His cock was heavy with blood. No man would float away while she was sucking him.

Jack wasn't thinking about Sophie anymore, but Madison was. Sophie was Jack's excuse. He thought he had to get over her. I need time to recover, he would say. Whenever he spoke that way, Madison wanted nothing more than to say, I won't do those things. Let me hold you. Be my baby. I will never, never leave.

But Madison's sense of decorum kept her silent. The dignity she had assumed would not let her succumb to the banalities of passion. Neither would it let her haggle in flea markets or ask for autographs.

Madison's most biting desire was thus her most humiliating secret. She dreamed that Jack would dissolve her identity, crush her faults, distill her down to a small pure lump he could slip into his pocket with his keys. She wanted him to fall on her and eat until all that remained was her hair and her rings.

Madison swallowed back her longing like she had swallowed Mace's insistent semen. When Jack blundered into Sophie, all Madison could allow herself was, "Yes, baby, I know, I understand." Then she would spread her legs to him. This was all the comfort he could accept. It was all she would spare.

"Open your legs for me."

Madison drew her lips up the length of Jack's cock, sucked the head for a few moments, and released him. Then she did as she was told.

"Oh yes," Jack sighed. "What a beautiful little pussy you have. May I kiss it?"

"Handcuff me first," Madison pleaded. He had been promising for a week.

Clickclickclickclickclick. Her hands froze to the wrought iron behind her.

"Who am I tonight?" he murmured into her pussy.

"Daddy."

He couldn't help laughing. "That's sick!"

"I know, Daddy. You should spank me."

Jack drew himself up onto one elbow and began massaging her clit. It pushed out from its hood to meet his fingertips. He liked how it was hard and soft at the same time.

"Now why would a good daddy ever spank his little girl?"

"For fucking two boys at once!"

"That was naughty," Jack agreed with mock disapproval.

"Yes, Daddy. Spank me, please."

Jack hooked Madison's knees behind his arm and pulled her legs up. Her thighs were now on the same plane as her stomach and her ass was bared to Jack's fancy.

He nudged his tongue between her lips until it met with her clit. She felt it rest there as he positioned himself. Then he began to let his fingers caress her Renaissance ass. Just when she was afraid she'd start giggling, he brought his hand down hard against her right cheek.

"Daddy," Madison ventured. "Would you suck my nipples please?"

Jack brushed his lips against Madison's nipple. It tightened against his chapped lip, and he began teasing it lightly with his tongue. Madison tilted her pelvis hopefully. Her clit throbbed with blood.

"Daddy?" Madison crooned.

"Hmm?"

"Play with my pussy, Daddy. Just for a little." Madison sighed with gratitude when she felt Jack manipulating her clitoris. She started to moan. The handcuffs cut into her wrists.

"Come for me," Jack encouraged. He rubbed her more vigorously. "Go ahead, baby—oh yeah. That's it. Stay with it, baby. That's my girl . . . Madison . . . Oh no, baby. Don't stop now. Keep coming for me. Don't you still feel a little tense up in your pussy? Don't my fingers feel good? Oh yeah. I knew they did."

After Jack had licked the last of Madison's come from his fingers, he asked ritualistically, "How did you like it?"

"I didn't think I was going to come twice," she said. "You can unlock me now."

Jack complied, rotating her wrists slowly. "Don't make me start liking you."

Madison took his familiar prick in her hand. "I won't."

*Cecilia Tan*

❧

# Porn Flicks

The first porn flick I ever watched was with the first woman I ever dated. I know, I know, you'd think to look at me now, perched on my bike in my leathers, that I'd been licking pussy all my life. But not so long ago I had just one foot out of the closet and was living a sheltered life. Mona taught me the right way to appreciate porn movies, among other things.

I met her at a bar. Not a dyke bar, just a regular smoky loud rock and roll club where my friend Derby's band was playing. I first caught sight of Mona in the back of the crowd, talking with some other women who hooted out comments toward the stage from time to time. Derby's band wasn't that popular, so the crowd was thin. I wandered by, trying to get a good look without being too obvious.

She wore all black, biker boots, with a loop of dog chain hanging from her neck. Now that I think of it, that's how most people in those bars dressed, but something about the way she stood or the look in her eyes tipped me off, I don't know—I wanted to go home with her the minute I saw her.

It wouldn't have been the first time I wanted to: I had been an avowed bisexual for years. That is to say, it had been at least six years since I told my parents I might bring home someone of the same gender for Thanksgiving. But I never had. I'd had my crushes, my flirtations, my passing acquaintances—but I just didn't know how to meet women.

I still hold that the only way to meet women is through Fate. And that night Fate was with me. I went backstage after the show to congratulate Derby and the band on another searing rendition of "The Brady Bunch Theme," and there she was. A friend of hers was a friend of Derby's too, and that's just the way Fate works. Mona and I talked at the bar until they threw us out and then we ended up at her place.

She lived in a one-room studio apartment, which means that the kitchen and the bathroom are only a few convenient steps away from the bed. We spent all the next day in that bed, getting up only to answer the various calls of nature and to pay the pizza delivery man. After the workout she gave me, it was heaven.

At first I hadn't been real keen to reveal that I'd never slept with a woman before. But after I found out that she'd never been on a motorcycle, nothing was held back. She grinned evilly as she pressed me down into her futon. "I'll be happy to teach you everything I know. But you have to promise . . . promise that you'll do everything I say from now to sunrise."

I promised. She kissed me, her smile wide open, and hugged me. I remember thinking, wow, women are so curvy.

She was, as she put it, a big girl. I loved the shape of her hips, her jiggly thighs, her mounds of breasts; I couldn't wait to get my hands on them.

"Strip for me," she said, lying back against the pillows.

I stood up, my striptease abbreviated by the fact that I was wearing a one-piece catsuit and not a lot else. I stood in front of her naked, and turned myself around for her to see.

"Not bad. Now come here."

She enveloped me in softness, her hands like silk all over my arms, my back, my breasts. She felt me all over like a veterinarian would a cat.

"I like your nipples," she said, circling them with her fingers so they stood at attention. "Nice and dark." She slid her hands down over my pubic hair.

"Now let's see what you like." She searched over the hood of my clit, so hot it felt like it was burning. As her fingers slid down into the wetness, her eyes lit up. I gasped and clutched at her as she put two fingers deep inside me.

"Ooh, you like penetration." She wiped her hand on a bedside towel and pulled my mouth to her breast. She coached me very strictly on nipples.

"No teeth to start with," she said. "And don't suck too hard. Now, about your tongue . . ." Near the end I bit her and she gasped. "Hey, you promised."

"I promised to do what you said, but not to not do what you didn't."

"Smart ass. For that you get the Het Chick Torture. Stay right where you are." She stood on the mattress and clicked on the television set in the alcove at the foot of the bed.

"What's the Het Chick Torture?" My stomach filled with butterflies.

"You'll see." She put a tape into the VCR. "Here are the rules. We're going to watch a het porn flick. Every time a woman gets something in her cunt, you get something in yours. Every time someone comes, you have to come."

If I had to tell you the plot of the film today, I couldn't, but it involved several men and women in various combinations in various rooms of a house. Maybe there was no plot and it just involved the same actors and actresses over and over.

I was surprised to find out that the film was much more comical than I'd thought it would be. I had always heard, of course, that porn videos were dark, evil, misogynistic affairs of a seedy underworld. But then again, I had always heard that lesbians were women who really wanted to be men—and we know how well that story holds up. So much for stereotypes and assumptions. This movie was silly; in one scene a guy getting sucked off by the pool fell into the water when he came.

And the women in this thing, I had to admit, weren't as bad as I'd feared. Sure, they all had bigger tits than their waists would suggest, but I decided I liked a lot of tits, especially Mona's. In fact, I decided that from their necks to their ankles, all the women in the film were damn hot, if only they'd lose the stupid shoes, the makeup and the Farrah Fawcett hair. At least they looked like they were enjoying themselves.

In the first sex scene the blonde and her boyfriend did it in about ten different positions, none of which I had ever seen before, much less tried in the privacy of my own home. They had no attention span, constantly switching from one position to another, with her sucking him in between. I started keeping my head near Mona's crotch, since at unexpected moments the actress would suddenly start gobbling. I would bury my face in Mona's pubic hair, my tongue learning the way through her folds better and better every time. With my face there I couldn't watch the screen, so Mona had to say "Fingers," when it came time to put her fingers inside me. For a long time the couple fucked on the floor of their living room and I floated away while Mona pumped me and tickled my G-spot. We both laughed when the guy's roommate came in, and with a shrug of his shoulders threw off his clothes and joined in. The actress began sucking him without climbing off the other guy.

"Put your own fingers in," Mona said, pushing my head down between her knees.

I moaned while I licked her. I was close; it was hard not to make myself come. But I knew if I was going to come once for every orgasm in the film I had better save them up. Lucky for me, while my head was down there the first guy came all over the actress's back.

"Come now," Mona said, luxuriating underneath my tongue. My nostrils filled with her salty smell, I came, my noises muffled by her muff.

The next big scene involved the women in the bathroom. Mona pulled me up beside her saying, "Watch this, you may learn something."

The two women rubbed each other's breasts, sucked each other, fingered each other. Mona put her fingers inside me whenever one of the actresses did it to the other, and told me to do it myself whenever they were doing themselves. Like the male/female couple, they switched positions and activities faster than a cable TV junkie switches channels. Now they were cunt to cunt, bumping and grinding against each other.

"Will we do that?" I asked.

"Maybe later, if you're good," she said, kissing me on top of the head. Now they were sixty-nine, side by side.

"That?" I asked.

"Definitely," she answered. The women came simultaneously and she made me come twice in a row, not letting me pause in between to catch my breath or rest my clit.

"Why is the music so cheesy?" I asked later, during the big orgy scene in which every actor and actress was involved, and the cuts from one shot to another were fast and furious. By then I had come about seven or eight times. I was on top of her, my head between her legs, pausing in my licking to talk.

"Who knows?" she said. "If you wrote good soundtracks, would you sell them to porn flicks?"

"Ah," I agreed, letting my tongue fly. By the time the credits rolled we had forgotten the game and were just licking and fingering and sucking each other as much as we could.

Two days later I got a membership at the local video store. And I took Mona for her first motorcycle ride. Neither of us has been the same since.

## Jo Manning

# By the Rivers of Babylon

Musky sweet, pungent, the bar of hand-milled sandalwood soap released its fragrant oils as I unwrapped it from its bed of crinkled brown tissue. Amazing! After all these years, the smell still brought forth memories. I laid it against my cheek and closed my eyes.

The Government Sandalwood Oil Factory in Mysore, India, sold its wares in a large, airy room redolent with the pervasive scent of sweet heartwood. Displayed on oddly bare-looking wooden shelves were vials of the oil itself, bars of soap, incense, sachets, perfume in glass bottles, hand-carved beads and other jewelry.

I inspected them all languidly that morning, like every morning I had so far spent in India: hot, indolent, tropical hours, full of nothing to do. Jake had his research and writing; I had Jeff to look after—no, not really—Ayah looked after Jeff. I looked after myself, gave orders to the cook, the gardener, the *dhobi* who did our laundry.

I was bored to distraction.

Mysore was a small, quiet Indian city. It had been a princely state before independence, ruled over by a fabulously wealthy maharajah. The south of India is beautiful and green, blessed with abundant wildlife and lushly forested. We were lucky to be here rather than in the dry desert city of Hyderabad, another former princely seat in central India, or in noisy Bombay, crowded with the dregs of piteous humanity, oppressively humid. Delhi could be cold in winter; Calcutta was a mess, by any objective standard. The only place I would rather have been was Kashmir, in the Hindu Kush, a Himalayan paradise to the north.

Or home. Yes, I would rather have been home. But I'd come, in the wake of my best-selling novelist husband, Jake Fuller, who was here gathering material for his next blockbuster, trailing our three-year-old son behind me, hoping to save my marriage.

After six months, the marriage was no closer to being saved. And having nothing to do was driving me out of my mind. I knew no one here—few Europeans or Americans passed through—and Indians were private people, shy of strangers. So I did nothing. I was simply here, waiting my husband out.

It had been 1,100 days since we had last made love.

Jake hadn't touched me since Jeffie's birth. After a normal vaginal delivery a woman is supposed to abstain from sexual intercourse for six weeks, to give those sensitive, birth-traumatized parts a chance to heal. When I came back from the hospital with Jeffie, I discovered that Jake had moved all his things out of our bedroom and was sleeping on the convertible sofa in the living room. He never moved back. Worse, he claimed he was impotent.

I was mystified, then hurt, then angry, pleading with him to see his internist, a psychiatrist, anyone who could help. His retort was that it was his problem and he would deal with it himself; he made it clear that he wanted to hear nothing from me on the subject. I retreated in pain, lavishing the attention that was once his on Jeffie.

Result: one extremely spoiled son. Poor Ayah! He gave her a run for the few rupees we paid her each month.

Now he had broken away from her grasp and was hurtling through the showroom of the sandalwood factory. Terrific! He'd collided with a tall stranger whose back was to me, and had conked himself on the head. He let out a loud, peevish wail. I sighed, gesturing to Ayah to pick him up while I apologized to

the man, who'd been almost knocked over by the surprise missile attack of a three-year-old—I had to admit it—a three-year-
old brat.

"I'm very sorry. Please accept my apologies. Jeffie gets a little
rambunctious sometimes."

The young man turned. He was broad-shouldered, handsome,
dark-haired, and sported a dapper mustache. "Maybe you should
carry him around in a cage, madam," he replied, smiling. "But,
no harm done. And . . . my condolences."

I winced at his cutting reply. Some people clearly did not like
children. Well, I understood. I was rapidly becoming one of
those people myself.

"Do you know where I could get that cage—cheap?" I asked
him.

Surprised by my rejoinder he began to laugh, shaking his
head. "If I knew, I'd be glad to buy one for you myself." He extended his hand. "Tony Borden. And you are . . . ?"

"Camilla. Camilla Fuller. Nice to meet you, Tony, and to hear
those American vowels. Not too many of us pass through this
town." His hand was warm and he had a good, firm grip. I liked
that in a man. With a pang, I realized how long it had been
since Jake had even touched me. How infinitely long it had
been since . . . I let the thought die, stillborn.

Tony pointed in Ayah's direction. "Can your servant deal with
your child so I can buy you a cup of coffee? I'm beginning to
miss American English too."

I nodded, walking over to Ayah and instructing her, in my basic untutored memsahib Kannada, to take Jeffie home, feed him,
and put him down for a nap. Let her deal with it. She took off
on her slightly bowed legs (a relic of childhood rickets? I'd often
wondered), the end of her ragged green cotton sari trailing in
the dust of the factory floor. Jeffie was still crying. What a terrific
mother—I could care less.

We walked to the Kwality Restaurant and Coffee Shop, a few
doors down from the factory on the dusty main road, and ordered steaming cups of frothy sweet Mysore coffee. Chai is the
drink of choice everywhere else in India, but coffee plantations

ring the low hills surrounding Mysore, and their beans are among the best and most highly prized in the world.

In the background a tape was blasting out the latest Boney M. hit, "Rivers of Babylon." The popular black singing group—we heard this song everywhere and saw posters of the two women and one man in all the shops—was either African or British, depending on who you asked. When Boney M. sang "Babylon," it sounded as though they were saying "Bobby-lon." Interesting, and annoying, too, because it was one of those tunes that stuck in your mind.

I caught myself humming it several times a day. It tended to sneak up on your mind when it was otherwise unoccupied, which, in my case, was most of the time. *By the rivers of Bobby-lon . . . where we sat down . . . Oh, yah, yah, yah . . . and there we wept, when we remembered Zion.*

I sipped at the foam on my hot coffee and studied Tony Borden. He was a fox. Or was it just because I was sex-starved? I had to face it, I was embarrassingly horny. No, he really was a very handsome man, around my own age—thirty-one—or younger. He was taking a full, detailed inventory of me, too. The interest in his dark eyes was beginning to warm me up. I shifted in the hard wooden seat and parted my thighs slightly. I felt moist where I hadn't been moist for a very long time. Was it the humidity? It was disconcerting.

"Why are you here, Tony?" I asked.

"I was just about to ask you the same thing, Mrs. Fuller. I'm an architect on a Fulbright travel grant. I got here a few days ago to teach a three-week seminar at the college on Indian architecture and its influence on the western tradition. I work in New York City for Berrill Skidings, the firm that did the Paxmore Building at Battery Park City. Perhaps you know it?"

The Paxmore was a controversial office building that had raised quite a few of the more conservative eyebrows in our own Gotham City. I personally thought it was one of the most innovative structures I had seen in a long while. At nightfall, the setting sun blazes over its taut aluminum skin in dark purples and orange; sunrises are even more spectacular, gold striking the building in an epiphany of shuddering light.

"Yes," I answered. "I really love it. We live near there, in an old loft building in TriBeCa. I saw the Paxmore going up. Did you have anything to do with its concept?"

"A little." He shrugged modestly. "It was the first project I worked on when I joined the firm, just after I graduated from Harvard."

Oh, dear, he was young! The Paxmore had been up a year, under construction for almost two. Even given the extended period of study the discipline of architecture demands, Tony Borden wouldn't see thirty-anything for a while. A baby. A damned good-looking baby. I sighed.

"Pardon?" He'd heard my too-audible sigh. I had to watch it; I was alone too much, sighing out loud, talking to myself.

"Nothing," I lied, trying to cover up, "I was just wondering what time it was."

"Time for me to take you to lunch. Is the food here any good? Or can I treat you to a meal at my hotel, The Majestic?"

I admired his decisiveness. It was an admirable trait in one so young. He seemed used to organizing, planning, giving orders. He certainly could give me a few, I fantasized. Yeah, I could take quite a bit from him. I wondered, rigidly willing my gaze not to seek out the area of his crotch, how much he had to give. Stop it, girl! I admonished myself. Stop it before you make yourself crazy.

Recovering my equilibrium and responding quickly, pushing aside my hot, naughty thoughts, I answered. "They have good Chinese food here, steaks, too. However, there are a few items on the menu I would watch out for—for instance, their cream of chicken and corn soup tastes and smells like freshly squeezed piss. But, otherwise, it's okay."

Tony chuckled. "I like you, Camilla Fuller. What in hell is a sharp girl like you doing in Mysore?"

"You've heard of Jake Fuller, the novelist?"

He nodded. "Who hasn't?"

"Well, Jake's my husband. He's here to research a book about the glorious and colorful last days of the former maharajah, his conflict with the British, his eccentricities, and so on. He spends a lot of time in the archives of the old royal palace and is actively seeking out people to interview who remember those days of glory and empire. I had the choice of staying home and perhaps advancing my own career—I used to edit young-adult fiction at Dell—or coming here and going crazy. As you can so clearly see, I made the wiser decision."

I was being blunt and reckless in my speech and manner with a stranger, a man I didn't know at all, but funny things happen to you when you're living in a Third World country, where so much that goes on seems bizarre and foreign to your very nature. You tend to confide in anyone who sounds as though he or she could be someone you knew from back home. It was happening with me and Tony Borden, except, of course, he had not been in India long enough to foolishly confide his deepest secrets to me.

"Jake Fuller." Tony couldn't seem to get over the connection. A new look came into his eyes. It does tend to floor everyone, my being Jake Fuller's wife. "I read one of his books, the first one, I guess, *Savage Sinner*." He shook his head in amazement. "All that graphic sex and gratuitous violence. I guess it sells a lot of copies, but he must be hell to live with."

I traced two esses absentmindedly on the scarred wooden tabletop as I replied to his frank comment. "He saves up all the violence for his books. The sex, too." I looked steadily into Tony Borden's appraising eyes, blatantly spelling it out for him. He was a smart boy. I wagered he would catch on quickly, but the thought both terrified and excited me. I couldn't blame the moisture between my upper thighs on the humidity anymore.

"Lunch at The Majestic sounds fine to me," I heard myself saying in a voice almost alien—low-pitched, husky, last heard in Jake Fuller's bed in the early days of our once sexually exciting marriage.

The Majestic Hotel is at least a hundred years old. It's small, in a style I'd loosely describe as Victorian Gingerbread, with its many cornices and pillars painted white. It's so airy and spacious on the ground floor of The Majestic that the room seems to float and shimmer in the hot sun. The few tables in the dining area are set apart; waiters and majordomos hover everywhere you look. The tablecloths and napkins are stiffly starched, and someone had taken the trouble to fold the napkins into fanciful shapes resembling birds or flowers.

Our lunch was light: masala dosai, those south Indian pancakes made of sour, fermented whole wheat batter stuffed with hot, spicy vegetables, a side order of dal and chutneys, and two large glasses of chilled Eagle brand beer. The icy liquid quenched my thirst but could not cool me off.

Tony Borden invited me to his room after lunch. "But I have no etchings to show you," he warned, smiling. He had a nice smile, good teeth, and a very sexy mustache. Ever since I fell in love with Clark Gable at age eleven watching the uncut version of *Gone With the Wind* on television, I've been a sucker for a man with a dark, full mustache. What followed was inevitable.

Looking back on my state of mind that day, I can justify everything that happened. I was bored; I hated my life; I was fed up with my child; I had been roundly rejected by my husband. Tony Borden was tall, dark, handsome, and, best of all, interested. There was no way I could have changed any of it. Nor would I have wanted to.

Tony latched the door to his suite, locking it securely, and took off all my clothes, then all of his. They made a small, soft heap on the polished hardwood floor of his bedroom. "You're beautiful," he told me.

Maybe not beautiful enough for Jake Fuller but, yes, I still had enough self-confidence to take pride in my looks—my long, curly hair and my small but curvaceous body with great legs. I get my fiery auburn hair and green eyes from my Irish parents.

Meanwhile, I was having my fill looking at the unclothed Tony Borden. My wanton gaze devoured him, inch by promising inch. His crotch area was no disappointment, not in the least. And growing even more interesting by the second. "Well-hung" didn't begin to describe the majesty of his groin. I trembled at the thought of all that tantalizingly engorged flesh inside my body, those heavy balls batting and rubbing between my legs. Subconsciously, I was already opening to receive him, so excited I could barely stand.

I thought Tony would take me to bed immediately, before my

trembling legs gave out, but he had other ideas. Interesting ones. He pressed me against the wall of the bedroom, raising my legs so that they encircled his waist. With his two strong hands he shifted my buttocks and slowly, teasingly, rubbed my crotch against his hot, stunningly erect cock. His mouth found mine and our two eager tongues grappled wetly and fiercely; he won, swallowing me up entirely. I had not been kissed that way in a long, long time.

We didn't say a word. Our eyes, fixed on each other, said it all. His were smoldering, passionate, heavy with desire, as he lifted my hips and impaled me on his stiff shaft, penetrating me to the very core of my being, taking possession as if it were his right. I cried out with the suddenness, the wonder of it, but he hadn't hurt me. I had the fleeting image of a hot knife cutting through butter; I was the butter, melting on impact.

Tony was in complete control of the situation, watching my face intently as he lifted my hips up slowly and brought them down in a rhythm that increased in tempo, his tempo. He moved away from me a bit so he could lick my aching nipples with his warm, wet tongue. Ecstatic to be brought back to life after such a long, cold hiatus, my nipples became as rock hard as his cock. Waves of feeling ran down my torso, from my breasts to my cunt, hard tingles of excitement I could barely contain. My long pent-up passion rocked me from within. I felt as if I was falling into a void, my only reality the strong arms and legs of this exciting stranger.

I swooned in ecstasy and started to come. I came, and came, and couldn't stop coming. My hands, in a frenzy, clawed at his shoulders and raked his broad back. And still I came, and came, and never wanted to stop coming. I trembled and shook and couldn't stop, not even when, finally, he did. He held me close and tight as the last wave crashed over me and I cried out against his hand cupping my mouth, fulfilled, filled to bursting. I had waited such a long time.

When it was over, I wept with relief and abandon.

Tony Borden cradled me in his arms and carried me to his bed. The linen sheets were cool against my perspiration-filmed back. I sighed contentedly. It was so peaceful, so quiet. I dozed for a few minutes.

My lover woke me. Balanced on one elbow, he was licking a long, wet, sensuous trail from my throat to my belly. He looked up at me and smiled. I smiled back, lazily, shifting slightly, raising my knees.

"Don't stop," I whispered, my voice a soft purr.

He needed very little direction. Grinning mischievously, he teasingly licked my belly button, causing my stomach muscles to tighten involuntarily.

"Oh," I whispered, half to myself, "that feels so good."

His talented tongue continued south, slowly, snail-like, through my nest of tight red curls. Suddenly, the tip of his tongue flickered against a small, sensitive nubbin of flesh. I jumped.

"Easy, easy," he cautioned, his free hand stroking my breast, causing the nipple to stand to attention. He shifted to my other breast and did the same. I was quivering in anticipation. His mouth, his hands, his cock, all of him, were sources of immeasurable delight. This time, in contrast to our initial fierce, tempestuous coming together, he was taking it slowly, so slowly I thought I would die.

"Easy, love," he crooned. "No need to rush. We have so much time." He went back to lavishing his attention on my clit, licking, sucking, stroking, squeezing, until I could barely stand it. I was whimpering shamelessly.

"Oh, please, Tony, please."

"Patience," he admonished, shifting his weight onto both his elbows and nuzzling my aroused nipples. They were so hard they hurt, and I groaned, my hips moving under his.

"Shush, darling, hold on," he whispered, his breath warm and sweet against my temples. He laid his mouth across mine to stifle my moans. His thick mustache tickled. I sucked on the soft hairs and opened myself to him. His tongue sought mine again and this time I could taste myself, hot and salty, on his tongue. It made me insane with desire. His body strained against mine.

Tony slid two long fingers inside me, and I arched my body in quick response, my hips grinding against his. He chuckled softly at my impatience as he probed my slickness, reaching deeply, making my insides ripple. I reached for his cock and squeezed; he groaned as I rubbed his shaft, feeling the silky skin pulling against the bulging vessels encased within. He withdrew his sopping fingers and gripped my buttocks. I guided him into me, gasping as again he pushed to the hilt and filled me.

I grabbed at his hair and offered him my mouth. He pressed his mouth on mine and plunged his tongue between my lips, as deep as his cock was between my legs. The outside world didn't exist for me any longer. There was just this man, this stranger, pumping between my feverish thighs and possessing my hot mouth.

I forgot everything: Jake, Jeffie, India, my unhappiness and boredom. They weren't real, not now, perhaps not ever. My pulse raced, my heart thrummed loudly in my chest, and my screams would surely have woken up half of downtown Mysore if Tony hadn't swallowed my cries in his throat as he came with me.

Later, spent but exhilarated, we had a last cup of coffee at the Kwality Restaurant. I perched gingerly on the edge of the cheap wooden chair, all too conscious of the lovely tenderness of my long-unused female parts. My body was alive again, alive and singing. I had loved every fierce, exciting, adulterous minute of it. I tingled and sang with the knowledge that my body had been well and deeply pleasured. The feeling would last a long, long time.

Tony Borden, my skillful young lover, looking not much the worse for wear, his dark eyes full of the knowledge of me, of my body, perhaps of my soul, took one of my hands and turned it palm up, kissing it passionately. His voice was low, throaty, soothing, and he made me an offer no sane woman could refuse.

"I start teaching this seminar tomorrow, Camilla, every day from ten to one. I want to see you again, make love to you again, hear you make all those delicious noises just for me. Can you arrange to be at The Majestic every afternoon at two o'clock? I'll get you a key to my rooms. We'll order in room service. And you can get home in time for dinner. Every afternoon, for three weeks. Are you game?"

I thought of my trim little Raj-era bungalow on the Old Palace Road, competently run by Ayah, Cook, and the *mali* who cared for the extensive rose gardens. Every Monday and Thursday the *dhobi* came for our wash. Jake left the house at six A.M. and returned at seven or eight in the evening. Some nights he didn't come home at all. He had been after me for some time to do something with myself, annoyed at the way I moped about the house with a long, unhappy face every day.

I would make Jake happy and tell him I had signed up for an architecture seminar at the college from two in the afternoon until seven at night. It would keep me busy. And the readings for the course—which I'd have to do in the college library—would occupy my weekends, when he was rarely home. It would make both Jake and me happy that I finally had something to do.

Such an incredibly lovely, pleasurable something to do.

"Three weeks," I agreed, nodding, "three weeks." I squeezed his hand, then kissed it. We were coconspirators, partners in crime, coupled for the nonce.

And after the three weeks? What then?

No. I wasn't going to spoil this idyll for myself. I refused to think that far ahead. I would live for the moment, in the moment. The future would have to take care of itself. The present was more, so much more, than I had ever ventured to dream.

Boredom, deadly, soul-draining boredom, would be held at bay. Tony Borden had come along at just the right moment, saving my life. For that alone, I knew I would never forget him.

Behind us the overworked tape deck blared on: *Oh, yah, yah, yah, when we remembered Zion.*

I took a last deep breath of the brown oval of sandalwood soap, remembering that sweet, short, faraway time. Oh, yah, yah, yah, how well I remembered Zion.

# C. A. *Griffith*

# Necessary Lies

Where do I begin? Here? It's 5:27 A.M. and I can see a few cars, cabs mostly, from my terrace. Twelve stories above the city and you can still hear the sound of horns honking and the wind trying to find its way. After a while, you forget what the night and crickets sound like and the cacophony of New York at night seems almost quiet.

There are nothing but secrets and dreams at this hour of the morning. I cannot sleep, therefore there will be no dreams. That leaves secrets. Tomorrow, I will cancel lunch with Ashley, again. We've been friends for years and she still wonders if it is to my memory that Michael makes love, if I was the woman who kept him away from his daughter's birth. All the while smiling, confiding, crying, "Angela, Angela. What would I do without you?"

Walking arm in arm with Ashley, I have often felt the harsh admonition of other black people, especially black men, the luxurious warmth of soft, old church ladies, and the fascinated envy of strangers. We are frequently mistaken for sisters, sometimes for twins. Often for lovers. It is easier to let people believe what they will. We are the closest of friends, but sometimes seeing her is painful. We both know that in some perverse way, we are implicated in too many lies.

And Michael. Still hoping for absolution in my voice. Still trying to make it up to me—because I am only godmother to his daughters, because I can't hurt Ashley by confirming her suspicions any more than I can forgive him for hurting her with his affairs. Because our friendships hang in the balance, everything is too complicated. One day, it will be too late.

I woke up this morning singing the blues. I woke up this morning with the blues wrapped around my heart, and scattered all around my bed. Thinking about things I should have done, should have said.

I have a photograph of Ashley and Michael's girls, my godchildren. These two beautiful brown angels smile at me from atop a shelf full of books I've reread too many times on sleepless nights such as this.

I also have a photograph of my ex-husband, Roberto, that I keep tucked away in a drawer. I take it out when I wake up with the blues all around my bed—not so much to look at him, or at a happy time, but to remember happiness itself. It was the only time in my adult life that *anything* seemed possible. I didn't have a care in the world. And it was the only time he wasn't fucking a very wide circle around me while I pretended not to know. It's amazing how small that circle became in five years. On paper, we stand together, dry, colorful leaves whipping around our ankles. He is kissing my neck. We look directly into the camera, wondering if the self-timer will take the picture before the wind knocks the tripod over. I don't recognize the woman as myself.

I close my eyes. I am in California, eighteen years ago, in the dorm library. It's very early in the morning and I am laughing out loud, reading St. Augustine's *Confessions*. I am startled by the voice behind me; I thought I was alone.

"That's the first time I've ever heard you laugh," a guy says, leaning against the door. I am annoyed by his grin and arrogant good looks. I don't have time for another rich white boy trying to flirt with me. I'm too busy trying to finish the book before I go to work.

"How am I supposed to respond to that?" I ask.

"Good morning, Angela, my name is Michael Sloan." He sits on the table, takes the book from my hands. "I lived down the street from you. I just moved off campus." He tries again. "I helped you move your trunk upstairs a couple months ago. Remember?"

If he tries to ask me out and looks deep into my eyes before he asks what I am—black and what?—or tells me I'm interesting looking, I don't know what I'll do. I wait for him to flash his perfect teeth at me and say, *Excuse me, but I just have to ask you something* . . . but he doesn't say a word. He's waiting for me.

"Do you want me to thank you again?" I ask.

"No. I wanted to thank you. For what, right? Well, I'm in your Western Civ class, the one where you got up in front of five hundred people to ask the professor why he—what did you say— 'consciously and maliciously skipped the fact that St. Augustine, one of *the* major contributors to Western thought and civilization, was a black man from Africa.' " He looks at me, waiting. Where the hell is he going with all of this, I wonder. I just stare at him, waiting. "Well," he says, "I was one of the few pale faces applauding you."

"And I'm supposed to thank you for that?"

"Did you know that your nickname around here is Ice Princess? Of course not. Well," he says sarcastically, "I guess anybody who can risk the scorn of a pompous, malicious, tenured professor and find *anything* humorous in St. Augustine can't be all that bad."

He hands my book back to me and I open it, reading aloud. "Lord, grant me salvation, but not yet!" He looks at me skeptically and I show him the words on the page. Laughing, he extends his hand.

The memory fades there, after I shake his hand and go back to being busy. I remember that he was not easily fooled, or put off by my coldness. From that day on he made a point of saying hello, visiting me at work in the library, trying to make me stop and talk, even when he could see I was in a rush. Eventually we became friends.

Another memory. We are in my bedroom. He has filled it with plants, made an aquarium for my bookshelf, and put fat, black goldfish in it. A piece of stained glass we found at an abandoned house in town covers the tank and catches the afternoon light.

But it is night now and he is reading *The Great Gatsby* aloud to
me as I rest my eyes. I have an exam in the morning and am
fighting sleep. He toys with the belt of my robe and says that we
should sleep together. I tell him that we do sleep together and
he explains the difference between falling asleep on the same
bed and sleeping together. I poke him in the belly button.

"I don't fuck my friends," I say, and he pretends to be
shocked, drops his jaw. I tell him, *"En boca cerrada no entran
moscas."* It was something my mother used to tell me. "The
closed mouth swallows no flies." Mrs. Johnson, my pretend
grandmother, told me the day I left for college, "Not too much
academics, not too much beach, and not too much courtin'.
Them's your ABCs." I think of my mother and Mrs. Johnson as
I smile at Michael.

"Speaka-da-English." He frowns, raises one eyebrow.

"Goodnight, sweet prince." I kiss him on the cheek.

"Here." He points at his lips, puckers them. Laughing, I kiss
him on the lips.

"I want another." I give him another.

"Satisfied?"

"Never." And every night after that, and whenever we first see
each other, the same dance.

Several weeks later, I am approached in the girls' shower.
Friends, and others, want to know why I don't "stick with my
own kind," why I have "betrayed the race." Those who know
me, or simply know better, want to know why I am not jealous
of his other women. Still others are jealous because it is pre-
sumed that I am the "other woman." I am not sure how I would
respond to their questions even if I cared to do so.

Do I insist upon fidelity to my class, my race, my people, and
say that Michael and I are not lovers to appease them, knowing
that they still won't believe me? Or do I tell them in a hushed,
confidential whisper of the day I borrowed his car and came
back well after nightfall to return the keys, unlocked the door to
his apartment, called out his name softly—and heard another
woman's voice echo my words in a deep, sensual moan?

"Umm . . . Mi . . . chael."

Do I tell them that I left the keys on the table and quietly closed the door behind me and walked home? Or do I tell them the truth? That I found myself outside Michael's bedroom, staring at another woman's breasts through the veil of her long, black hair as she leaned forward. How I stood mesmerized by the soft light of a bedside candle illuminating her taut stomach and gently rocking hips as she moved slowly up and down, her strong, smooth thighs tensing and releasing, Michael's body beneath her, almost imperceptible in the shadows but for the outline of his thigh, his hands moving around to hold her waist, the base of his cock slowly moving in and out of sight? Do I dare tell them how I longed to see her face, that the sweat glistening from between her breasts and along the curve of her neck was not enough? I had to see the lips that made that sound that washed over and through me, leaving me wet and trembling and afraid. Not afraid of being caught watching them; I was camouflaged by the darkness of my skin and the shelter of the shadows.

Yes. There. Those are his hands moving into the light to stroke her arms, dig his fingers into the soft flesh of her breasts, squeeze her hard, dark nipples together as she tosses her head back, her eyes closed tight, her hips jerking in tight, tight circles. Yes. That is her, calling out to God with the face of an angel, wearing a vivid mask of pleasure and pain, her eyes suddenly wide, her breathing a deep staccato as she looks in my direction, looks right through me, as her body shudders and a moan escapes our lips and we come together. Michael rises up, embracing her in the light. He cries like a wounded beast, breaking the spell.

I close the door behind me, walk home, and lie down between cool sheets. I tell myself that it was Michael I wanted between my thighs, not her. That is what I tell myself, over and over, until sleep comforts me and helps me believe it.

Over the next few months I keep myself very busy. I have to work. I have to catch up on reading. I don't have time to waste.

I don't see much of Michael. When he calls, I tell him that nothing is wrong, I'm just busy. I bury myself in my studies and work. By the time I come up for air, freshman year is over and I am free.

At home in Chicago, I miss Michael more than I can admit.

I miss his hello kisses. I miss him playing his guitar, keeping me company in that spooky dormitory basement as I did my laundry. I am wondering if he thinks of me, if he misses me also, when the phone rings. My mother picks it up and hands it to me. It's Michael.

He asks how I'm doing. I talk about everything except how I miss him. He tells me that he has made four thousand dollars in profits on investments he made a couple of months earlier. I tell him he is turning into a capitalist bastard and he says that I'm too ambitious to still be such an idealist. I ask him if he used his daddy's money and if he's sitting with his feet up on his daddy's desk. In the background, I hear the chair squeak loudly as he tells me that it takes money to make money, but he doesn't an-swer the part about whose desk his feet were on. I say that I love him and there is silence. I want to tell him that I love him as a friend, as a brother, but I am no longer sure that is true.

Several weeks later he calls again and ends the conversation whispering, "I love you." I am afraid to ask him what he means.

At the end of the summer, I visit him in his parents' New York apartment. The cab stops in front of a large Upper West Side building—very West End Avenue, very regal, complete with a uniformed, elderly black doorman who opens the cab door for me and offers me his hand.

"Michael told me you were real pretty, Angela. My name is Smiley." He reaches out to take my bags and I give him the lighter of the two. I stand there, feeling utterly lost. He touches my arm lightly and leads me inside. A short, round man with a ruddy face holds the elevator door open for me.

"I've forgotten the apartment number. I'm sorry."

"Don't worry, he knows the way," he says, handing my bag to the elevator man.

"Thank you, umm . . . I can't call you Smiley."

"Then don't you call me that, Sistah. Call me Benjamin. My friends call me Benjamin." The elevator man pulls the iron gate closed and Benjamin leans forward.

"It'll be okay, Angela," he whispers.

The wood-paneled doors close and the elevator man takes me up past the numbered floors to level P in silence. He opens the gate and the elevator doors open directly into the Sloan family's foyer. He deposits my bags at the edge of the living room as a grinning Michael opens his arms to hug me. Behind him are his parents—their smiles drop flat. Michael picks me up and swings me around wildly, the two of us laughing and laughing. I have to beg him to let me down. I am dizzy, and the room is still spinning around me as Michael introduces me to his parents, but I am certain that I see Mr. Sloan nudging his wife. She tries to smile. It looks like a muscle spasm at the corners of her mouth.

Later, I am in the shower. Steaming, soothing heat. I turn off the water, expecting silence. I am not so fortunate.

*Mr. Sloan: . . . how to live your life. We're glad you're so close. So, she's not Jewish, she's a lovely girl, but—*

*Mrs. Sloan: But nothing! You talk about her constantly and forget to mention she's a Negro? She's lovely, but friends, you're not. Don't you lie—I'm not stupid. It's bad enough you bring this* schvartza *into my house.*

Oh, how I wish I hadn't turned off the shower just in time for that. I also wish I could come out and ask Mrs. Sloan why she is so obtuse, and so damned middle-aged. How could a woman who survived the war and escaped with nightmares and numbers tattooed on her arm *dare* to call me a *schvartza*? Instead, all I do is brush my teeth. As I exit the bathroom, Mrs. Sloan is in the hallway, a bowl of melting pink ice cream in her hand. I smile.

"You're keeping the guest room so neat and clean, Michael's room is such a mess! I wish I could find a girl to clean this apartment as well as you do." I smile, convinced of her ignorance—she couldn't *possibly* look me in the eye and say what she said. But she *did* say it. And before I have a chance to tell her how offensive it is, she disarms me.

"You have such a beautiful smile, dear. Have some ice cream. There's plenty in the freezer."

I decline.

"Goodnight, Angie. Sleep well."

In a few steps I am at the threshold of Michael's door. He stares at me for a moment, then says, "You heard." He takes my hand and sits me down on the bed. Looking down at his hands, he apologizes for his parents, then abruptly rises and closes the

door. Barefoot, bare chested, bare legged; his rugby shorts fit
him too loosely.

"You're losing too much weight, Miguelito," I say. He rubs my
shoulders. "I should get going to bed. Goodnight, sweet prince,"
I whisper, leaning back against him. I start to get up but he hugs
me. He won't let go. "I love you too," I tell him. "It doesn't matter. Really."

"It does matter," he says. "Sometimes, I really hate them, I
do." He stands, walks across the room, and looks out the window. I call him, and he comes to me. I hold his face in my
hands, waiting until his tears stop. I lie down and his fingers, hot
and guitar-callused, massage my hands, arms, shoulders. Ten
years of music stroke my back, from the nape of my neck to the
curve of my spine. I try very hard to stay awake. I know I have
to comfort his parents with the click of my door.

I awaken near 5 A.M. to the sound of cars whizzing by below
on West End Avenue, and the pattern of Michael's aquarium
light playing on the ceiling. Michael's head is on my stomach.
The towel his mother gave me, red, with an ornate *S* stitched in
white, is draped over the back of his chair. I do not attempt to
cover my nakedness or to escape quietly into the guest room until morning. Will I have lox and bagels, averted glances, silence,
or a little talk, perhaps an early return home to Chicago for
breakfast? No. I simply let my hands twist and part the soft, full
head of hair upon my stomach. I let my fingers trace the curve
of his ear, neck and shoulder. He stirs, and looks at me, unsure.
I see my fear reflected in his eyes. What can I do but silence his
question with a kiss? He says, "I want another." And the dance
begins.

I am not dreaming. Nor do I offer his parents the click of the
guest room door. I offer them a song. Not an old Negro spiritual,
but something entirely different. I sing in a voice so sweet and
deep, a voice they could only dream of and hope for their only
son.

But they won't understand this song. They will hear this song
and turn it into something dirty, something raw and distorted, a
challenge, a dare, a phase . . . something it's not, anything but

what it is. I stretch, gripping the stereo dial, turning it on. This song is not for them.

As I bring my hands back to Michael's head, he begins to lick tiny circles around my nipples and suck from each breast.

Soon his head is where it began when I awakened and in a moment it will be lower. He makes a trail of wet kisses along my hips, inside my thighs, teasing me with the secrets he whispers between my legs, stroking my lips in a language we have spoken only with others, a language we have never shared as friends.

He asks me if he should stop, and I moan, my hands pushing his head lower and deeper, my hips rocking, my clit hard against his tongue and lips in response. He moves his fingers inside of me and my mind goes blank. When I begin to tremble, he whispers, "Not yet." Tossing my head back, I close my eyes.

Suddenly, there is no bed, no night, no music, no sound. I see him, not much bigger than my two hands, a tiny Michael, premature, sliding out from between his mother's pale legs. And now, with my honey thighs guiding him in the darkness, I gasp and the warm weight of his body covers me as I urge him deeper, back into my womb—back to the beginning, back to where I too longed to rest. Before the ignorance of hatred, to the safety of home.

A month or so later, in the amber light of the darkroom, I watch my image taking shape under water. On paper, Michael stands behind me, his face nestled against my cheek, his arms around my waist. He doesn't know that I am pregnant and scared, but it shows on my face. I switch on the light and the photograph turns black in the tray.

That brief moment, when the image was sharp and clear, just before the silver reacted to the light and turned it jet black, still haunts me all these years. I had seen my mother's face in my own and it frightened me. I had seen her *"No hablo inglés"* eyes, her "Baby, *estoy cansada"* eyes. I'd seen that look in the eyes of every too young, too tired, poor and desperate teenage mother. I didn't want to have their eyes or my mother's eyes. I could not have this baby. I did what I had to do. I aborted her ghost. I graduated from college three years later and laid her tired body to rest the next year.

The telephone rings and startles me. It's Ashley, apologizing for waking me before ten on a weekend. I tell her I've been awake for hours and she is concerned. I make it easy for us both and tell her that I'm fine. She reminds me about lunch tomorrow and I tell her that I have to cancel. She is disappointed.

"Angela," she says softly, "I have to see you." I want to tell her that I'm not good company, that I have work to do, and my own shit to deal with. Instead, I ask what's wrong. She tells me that they ran into Michael's parents that morning, coming back from breakfast with the girls.

"They kept walking as they looked at us, and then down at the girls," she says bitterly. "Not one word. They just walked right by as if we were total strangers." She tells me of her rage and Michael's silence. I ask if the girls are okay, if they knew what was going on.

"They had no idea. And—" Suddenly, she is crying.

"And what?" I ask softly. "Ashley, try and tell me what happened."

"He just left."

I tell her I don't understand.

"We walked home, he called somebody—some woman—and said he'd be back later."

I resent having to say it, but I know she needs to hear that I'm not the other woman and that Michael hasn't told me who she is.

"Do you still love him?" she whispers.

"Michael? Yes, I love him. I love you all."

"No. I mean Roberto. Do you still love him? After everything?"

"Yes," I said quietly. "But I'm over it."

I don't want to think about these things so I tell Ashley that my relationship, separation, and divorce didn't make me an expert on any of those matters, but I did learn something of use to her. I tell her that she must get out of the house, come here, or do something—anything but wait for him to come home. I tell her that I can take care of the girls for a while, if needed. When her tears have stopped and she is calmer, I ask her what she wants, what she needs, and for a long time, there is silence.

"I want to be happy, Angela. Is that too much to ask?"

I have no answer for my sister. I have no magic to scatter the lingering pain of unbearable truths, necessary lies, deep rage, heartbreak, or the blues.

"No. It's not too much to ask," I tell her, my voice cracking with emotion. And this is what I tell myself as I hang up the phone and step outside to lie in the warmth of the sun. I close my eyes to the city rising up around me, just beyond the sanctuary of this terrace garden. No, happiness is not too much to ask for.

I am haunted by the simple, elusive promise of these words. I say them over and over again, until anger comforts me, and helps me believe.

## Jolie Graham

❧❧❧

# Tasting the Sky

I don't want to starve to death, she thought, when she first made the decision to rent the room in the library. I feel like I could starve to death. She nodded to the man who was leaving his cubicle as she entered hers for the first time.

The next day the carpet had changed colors. It was woodsy green instead of gray. She didn't notice. She wanted the right book.

She touched the cookbook tentatively, as if making some big decision. He noticed the way her hands held it and turned it over, examining the binding. While she was in the reference section a river sprang up between them, so he reluctantly returned to his little room next to hers. He could hear her door lock click. He could detect subtle movements coming from their shared wall.

She pulled more books into her cubicle every day, creating a mountainscape within it. The READ poster on the wall now said EAT. As she became more engrossed in her search for sustenance, he became more engrossed with her. She was a thin and plain-looking young woman, with a serious face. She usually wore jeans and a T-shirt. But whenever she was near he caught a whiff of something, some perfume or aura that made him want to climb the big oak tree now growing in the middle of the library. Or climb her.

Climbing. Climbing up her body. He contemplated it as he leaned back in his chair. There was a row of narrow windows near the ceiling between their rooms. They hadn't been there before. With trembling eagerness he climbed on top of the table. The light was off in her room. But with the light streaming through those upper windows he could see her. She was naked, examining a fresh stack of books.

She selected a large volume, one with a rough leather binding and no dust jacket. *Tasting the Sky: A History of Flowers As Food.* She squatted on the grassy carpet, her legs spread. As he watched, she slowly rubbed the spine of the book between her legs. He could hear the sound of moisture, smell the heavy scent of rain in the air. She moaned. The room was becoming darker. Night was falling despite the light in his room. In a few moments he would lose sight of her entirely. He could hear her little grunts and groans as she pushed herself onto the book.

Quickly he shed his clothes and climbed through the open window, dropping from the stack of books to the ground beside her. She looked up in surprise. A naked man in the paper mountains.

"Oh," she whispered, "I've been so hungry." She opened her mouth to him. The book fell open to some unseen recipe.

She licked his balls, sucked his cock until he came, until he thought he would never stop coming. Like a silent rain, rose petals, violets and chamomile fell steadily from the dark sky. They rolled in the flowers, becoming drunk on the scent, drunk on the liquids from their bodies. He ate her, ate the flower that bloomed between her legs. With joy and laughter, their voices echoed off the walls of this banqueting hall. The room had grown spacious as their bodies moved, opened, and consumed each other in every way. They tasted exotic fruit and created new books about it.

When the flowerfall ceased they stepped out into the now darkened library. From all around them came the whisper of pages being turned in the dark, the sigh of volumes of naked bodies being opened. Some inarticulate choral music rose in concert from the floors, tables, chairs, and shelves. And everywhere, ankle-deep flowers bathed the arching bodies as they sang and sighed and tasted the sky.

## Emily Alward

❦

# Honeymoon on Cobale

They had sauntered through her dreams ever since she could remember, these handsome and confident Cobalean men who existed to give her pleasure. Melerie struggled fitfully to remind herself of those dreams, while her nerves screamed and the wedding guests babbled on around her.

"You don't really want dessert, do you?" she heard her cousin Nikalla ask. "You'll be getting lots of honey later." Nikalla grinned at Melerie and, without waiting for a reply, waved away the server.

Melerie stared longingly at the rich pastry with its golden crust and toppings of fragrant honey and spiced cream. Finally she decided her cousin was right: she was too nervous to enjoy it.

*And that's all right,* she told herself, echoing her upbringing on faraway Earth. *Brides are supposed to be nervous on their wedding night.*

But not on Cobale. Here, in this culture that comprised the other half of her heritage, women were self-confident and sexually assertive.

"Everything is for the woman's pleasure here, you'll see," her aunts had said when they'd first started making marriage plans for her. Melerie was willing to grant the theoretical truth of their statement—at least no one had suggested that she give up her graduate studies or anything else to conform to a husband's whims—but it hardly helped reassure her about tonight. Her nerves were jangling with apprehension and her stomach was so clenched that she wished she hadn't eaten anything at all during this interminable wedding banquet. It wouldn't do to be sick in the arms of one of her new husbands.

She ventured quick glances toward them now, masking her interest by pretending to watch the musicians. Dillin aq Dubraiz sat at the table nearest hers, his slate black eyes jewels of intensity. She wondered how he worked that trick, of following her steadily with his gaze while carrying on a serious conversation with the friend at his side. Tall, dark-haired and urbane, he clearly was not a man to be trifled with. When he noticed her studying him, he raised his goblet in a silent toast. Melerie nodded in polite recognition, but the exchange brought her no further knowledge of the man: mystery was wrapped around him like his elegant cloak.

She looked around for the other two men to whom she had just pledged her bond and body. Simen mir Gower stood in a corner of the hall, his hand resting lightly on the hilt of the ornamental dagger on his belt. For comfort, she guessed—Simen looked as if he'd rather be anywhere else but here at his wedding feast. The forest green suede he wore and the copper circlet in his dark brown curls were suitable enough garb—yet they subtly conveyed that he belonged in the woods and open spaces, not in an ancient hall where politics and revelry thickened the air. When he felt Melerie's attention on him, he shifted his lithe body uneasily.

Across the room a clump of followers surrounded Rafe xi Torrin; they were tossing dice and coin-jewels in insouciant disregard of the more sober guests. Rafe looked up and grinned when he felt her scrutiny, then turned back to settle a squabble among his henchmen. Blond, broad-shouldered and convivial, he radiated an easy mastery that knocked Melerie's poise into the violet Cobalean stratosphere.

Three men, as different as the separate fields of stars that marked their shields. They shared nothing beyond the pledges they had offered her this day, pledges originating in the need for a truce among three powerful families. Each man was strong and determined in his own way. She need not try to bring them together; simply by their sons each having bonded with the same woman, the families were expected to reach a degree of amity.

But that assumed that she, Melerie, would attain some degree of attachment to each man. Could she do it? Doubts crowded her mind; she shivered at the daunting task before her. Her new husbands were not known to her except by their pedigrees and the formal meeting held before the announcement of the match. And they were not men she would have picked had she done the choosing.

Not that she had ever been so lucky or knowledgeable about choosing men: she had gone for sex or for friendship, but never both from the same man, a common custom of the culture she'd grown up in. The friendships had proved less disappointing than the sexual encounters. But never had she felt an inclination to evaluate a male as "husband material," by either society's standards. So when it came time to do so, she had been willing to defer to the Cobalean tradition and let her maternal relatives make the choices.

Still, she could not let go of the notion that one should find rapport with a husband—or even husbands. She had no clue as to how to go about establishing a relationship with any of these formidable men, let alone what to expect of the formal Cobalean sexual ritual.

"He's supposed to bring some game or art to entertain you," Nikalla had told her, and chuckled as she added, "but you won't need it."

Her cousin nudged her now. "Do you like what you see?"

Melerie blushed; Nikalla had probably been watching her all along, entertaining the bawdy speculations that were standard observations of a Cobalean bride. She stole another quick glance around the room, pausing at each of her new husbands.

"Yes," she said reluctantly, admitting to herself that all three were very attractive. The flush spread from her face to suffuse her body in a soft sheen of desire. She took one more look, but really looked this time, first at Rafe, then at Dillin, and finally at

Simen, and an urgent emptiness tingled in her cunt. She found herself wondering which of them might best fill it.

Melerie reached out to take a sip of the golden ale, to steady herself and mask the excitement she suddenly felt. To have three attractive men legitimately make love to her—for once to have as many delights as her body craved—there *were* some advantages to the Cobalean family system beyond the obvious political ones. How was it she had not thought of them before?

*Because I don't know how things will go with any one of them,* she reminded herself, *and rightly so.* Pursuing her periodic desires had always brought more trouble than pleasure. Why would pledges make it any different?

Despite her part Cobalean heritage and having lived on the planet for half a year, there were moments when it seemed incredibly alien to her. Especially the men.

She took another sip of mead. Its tiny bubbles tickled her throat. Her sensory boundaries were falling. As she leaned across the table to put her mug down, the gems decorating her gown's bodice brushed her nipples with promises.

Shaken by the flood of sensory input, she knocked over a candle. Nikalla and two guests leaped up to smother it, and Melerie stood, apologizing in half-coherent phrases for her awkwardness.

"Never worry," Nikalla told her. "No one expects a new bride to be a model of poise."

"I think I'll go now," she murmured, picking up another candle to light her way. Nikalla's eyes widened, but she gave her cousin an understanding smile. It was only when a cheer went up from the crowd that Melerie realized the implications of her sudden flight. Scalded by embarrassment, she fled down the ancient stone hallways.

She sat in her darkened suite, gazing out on a lake through the tall windows. Tiny points of light glinted on its onyx surface, reflections of the torches set into the castle walls. They called this place the Lake of Dreams, and it was famous in Cobalean history and legend. It seemed as good a backdrop as any to face down the haunting questions and gather courage.

How had she ever gotten herself into this incredible situation?

Three new husbands, and absolutely no idea what to do with them—beyond the obvious, of course.

*Maybe the obvious is enough,* said a mocking little inner voice.

*Impossible!* She sighed. If that were true, her whole life would have gone differently. And better.

*But maybe Cobalean men are different.*

*Impossible,* she snapped at the inner imp. But then, because it held out a hope she sorely needed, she entertained that possibility.

They had been in her dreams ever since she could remember; as a small girl she had known that somewhere, circling another star, was her other family, with uncles and brothers who would give her toys and patiently play long games of chance or strategy with her. As she grew, the delights offered in her dreams changed.

Melerie's mixed-race heritage brought her more than the usual teenage troubles. Taunts of "alien" gave way to uneasy male attention; on certain days the bolder boys followed her with doggish persistence, like hounds trailing prey.

"Bitch," the other girls called her. For all her efforts to stay modest and invisible, her stubborn body, with its pheromones and gossamer shimmer, kept proving them right. Even worse were her impulses, which built relentlessly, until every few months she would go off with any agreeable mate and fuck and fuck, until her cycle burned itself out and she slunk home.

Her father and grandmother had greeted these episodes with hurt and sympathy. Knowing how she hated the biological double bind their culture put her in, they did not scold or shame her. Both became adept at apologizing to the outraged mothers of teenage boys. It was only when she returned home with a black eye and cord burns on her neck that they sent her to a renowned xenogynecologist who gave Melerie drugs to suppress her cycles.

No longer did Melerie send out tantalizing signals once a month, and her body's impulses lost their urgency. For the first time she was able to concentrate on her studies. The next year she went to university and majored in planetary ecology with the vague idea of visiting Cobale and claiming her other heritage—her mother's half—some day.

Most of her fellow students in the course were men. Without the threat of cyclic hormonal demands, she was able to befriend several of them. They'd take long walks through the subtly tinted exhibits in the holographic gardens, talking about the Meaning of Life and the new horizons they intended to explore. Melerie never took it beyond friendship, nor did she want to. Even if her body had been willing—and it hardly was—her past bewilderment at being rejected after sharing pleasure haunted her. She wasn't going to risk that hurt again.

Then she attained her dream; she traveled to this planet and met her Cobalean relatives. An important and protective noble family, they showered her with so much warmth that she naturally fit herself into their culture—which included, she discovered with mixed shock and fascination, polyandry to cement political alliances.

The details blurred in her mind now; all that mattered was that she'd ended up with three of those handsome and confident men dreamed of long ago. They were supposed to give her pleasure. Would they? All she knew for sure was that as an adult the games would be played on her body—and theirs. And the next move was hers.

She must have drifted off, because suddenly thunder was booming across the lake and through the massive castle walls, then receding to a loud pounding on her door. Nikalla eased the door open and whispered, "Melerie, are you all right? Everyone's saying that you have no liking for your new husbands."

Melerie moaned softly. She saw, with wonder, that her skin was radiating a slight glow into the room. Between her legs she felt warm and damp and faintly throbbing.

"*Nyai*, that's not true. One of them can come in."

"Which one should I call?"

She wasn't sure about the proper etiquette; she truly didn't know which one to call. With a mix of fear and delight she realized that she didn't really care.

"Um, I don't know. Why don't you have them draw lots?"

Nikalla scurried away. Melerie stretched lazily, leaned over the casement to make sure the two moons had risen above the Lake of Dreams, and waited in a strange world for a husband she didn't know.

He came in to her in the darkness. She felt the tension in his shoulders when he embraced her, and was relieved that he shared her anxiety about this first encounter.

But his touch was sure and stirring. Strong hands tangled in her hair. Lips found hers and brushed a quick tantalizing kiss across them before sliding down to trace her body. Fingers caressed her throat. Hands gently cupped her shoulders. As they reached her fingertips she muffled a ripple of laughter and delight: his technique was exquisite. Her cells were tingling with excitement and desire—how long must she wait while he paid homage to her fingertips and other assorted body parts?

She turned her face and pressed her lips searchingly against his, then burrowed in and claimed the velvety welcome of his tongue. He tasted like salt and honey.

She felt the swell of his erection. Her hips circled in response and she pushed against him. His hands found her breasts and scribbled questions across her nipples; she answered with small wiggles that teased his penis. She shrugged off her loose gown; a moment later his tunic and trousers tumbled to the floor. She leaned into his embrace and their bodies touched, all along the line from shoulder to thigh. Against her heat his skin was cool and warm and smooth and rough all at once.

Then her arms were holding empty darkness. Kisses parted her legs and flickered over her clitoris, growing ever stronger, his mouth becoming the driver and Melerie the giddy rider. Just as she melted under his tongue, he gave her a last slow lick and stopped. His hands released her buttocks and traced their way down her body as they had done earlier.

He went all the way to her feet this time, then stood and reached out his hand. Her desire flared higher than ever, but this interruption of their love game seemed right. As she followed him to the bed she looked back to where they had just embraced. A faint light shimmered in the night air.

He paused to make sure she was ready, then plunged into her, sure and intense. She rose to meet his thrusts with her own, seeking, matching his intensity. The world faded away and the darkened room blurred into insubstantiality; all that remained was her body and his, rocking across the chasms that had separated them.

On the brink she cried out. He paused; a shade of uncertainty hung between them. But it was joy, not pain, that had elicited her cry. She clutched him tightly, letting her soft throbbing cunt caress his cock.

He came a moment after she did. Melerie, still basking in the sweet descent, felt ripples of aftershock stir her womb. She smiled. The ripples were pleasant, a quiet bonus to their lovemaking. Exaltation drenched her, spreading like amber honey through her veins, bubbling into every cell like the points of light dancing over the inky lake outside.

The promises she had heard about Cobalean men were true.

In the early morning Dillin stirred and spoke to her for the first time. "Were you pleased?"

"Oh, yes," she murmured. Still groggy with sleep and satiation, she tried to find words to express her wonder. "I didn't expect—I mean, there are so many differences between us."

He stroked her cheek tenderly. "My dear, don't you know that's why the Creatrix made us this gift? So the differences can bring us together?" He put an arm around her and trailed kisses across her face and shoulder.

Melerie had to remind herself twice that it was all right to enjoy the kisses and still look forward to encounters with her other husbands.

That afternoon she was unpacking her books and holodiscs when she suddenly felt a hand tracing the flare of her hips. Surprise and sudden new desire rippled through her. She turned to look into the warm brown eyes of Simen mir Gower.

"Oh. Can you stay?" she asked, feeling awkward.

He nodded, and took the cup of licochat she offered, saying nothing. Melerie began to worry that she'd broken a taboo. Was silence a required part of foreplay? Then Simen muttered, "It won't work here, not this time," and grabbed her by the hand.

He led her down the castle's corridors until they found a door leading to a lakeside path.

Birdsong like merry glass bells followed them. Simen pointed out the tiny crystal birds, almost transparent, revealing themselves as their wings flashed silver through the air. He picked delicate blue flowers for her hair. He called to a strange furry creature, who came right onto the path and snuggled up to Melerie while Simen explained how it fit into the life of the forest. Melerie's heart warmed, but at the same time she burned with reawakened need. Was he going to give her a course in Cobalean ecology before he made love to her?

Finally he pushed aside a veil of leaves and pulled her into a glade. Sweet herbs and grass were strewn across the ground, walled off by interwoven branches; obviously he had gone to a great deal of effort to make this place comfortable. Once inside, Simen's diffidence fell away. With a lightning flick of his dagger he cut the fasteners from her gown.

Shocked, Melerie stood perfectly still. He drew her up against him. His chest was smooth and tautly muscled, his penis suddenly enormous: it fit into the triangle between her legs as if it had always belonged there. To her delight she felt herself wet and quivering, and opened up to him, leaning against a tree while he thrust inside her cunt. He moved back and forth just enough to tease, coaxing her to lead him on. Melerie's every nerve screamed; she wiggled and circled until he stabbed deeply within her, touching the center of her need, jarring layers of tension loose so that she felt herself dissolving. She shuddered; for a brief moment she worried that she was coming too fast—but she didn't care.

On the walk back to the castle he said, "Next time we'll do it your way."

"I have no complaints about this time," she said, reaching out for his hand. Simen beamed, no longer the worried young man who'd lurked in a corner at his wedding feast. Melerie suddenly noticed the cacophony of birdsong and animal sounds surrounding them, and wondered what new secrets their next time might reveal.

✧   ✧   ✧

They met Rafe xi Torrin on the threshold to her quarters. The two men exchanged a quick suspicious look, but Simen relinquished her. Once inside, Rafe unloaded an armful of objects: a flask of bubbly wine, a wheel of cheese, a large box and a small one. The small box turned out to hold an exquisite necklace of rare chromatic gold. Rafe fastened it around her neck with a flourish, ruffling her honey brown hair. Then he stood back and admired her, making faces as though he had personally put her together and wasn't quite sure what finishing touch he wanted to add.

Melerie giggled. She was already thinking *I know what you should do for a finishing touch,* but her bold thoughts astounded her and instead asked, "Did you expect me to have two heads or something?"

"Aret's hounds, no. Just two extra husbands. It's not much fun to wait until last." He shrugged, as if dismissing the other men from his mind. "Don't you want to know what's in the other box?"

"Of course." She reached out for it, but he held it back.

"Aren't you supposed to bring me games and entertainment?" She felt an urge to challenge him.

"Only if you're gracious. I can tell you don't have much patience for the rituals. That's all right, but at least we can eat first." He poured wine into two glasses and cut wedges of cheese, holding one out to her.

*Three men within the same twenty-five-hour day,* Melerie marveled. Her Earth memories kept telling her it was not quite seemly, but her body kept purring in delight.

Rafe finally unwrapped the package. It was a version of *kini,* a Cobalean game that mixed imaginary quest with truth or consequences. But what a version! Most of the questions were on preferences, sensory or sexual, and Rafe insisted on checking out each answer. He explored her outer ear. He fingered the lingerie in her dresser drawer. He skimmed kisses across the nape of her neck, and tongued her nipples until she gasped. Somehow no opportunity arose for her to explore him—until he drew a card that made him choke with laughter. He waved it at her. "It says you're supposed to chase me to get your way with me."

She sprang up, but he'd already had a head start. Around the room he ran, and into the enclosed private yard with its grotto pool. Melerie ran after him, cut across to the gate, and slipped on a wet rock. She wasn't hurt, but she seethed with anger. Husbands weren't supposed to behave this way!

A moment later he dashed by. She reached out and grabbed him by the ankle. He fell down beside her and they rolled over and over, tangled in each other's arms.

"I have you!" she cried. "But Rafe," she said, her voice falling, "I won't make you do anything. You're supposed to want me just as much."

"Don't you think I do?" he growled. It was the first time he had been serious. "Is there any reason we can't have fun and love each other too?"

He'd uttered the magic word, the word that supposedly didn't exist on Cobale, or in its marriages. He must have gone to a lot of trouble to look it up.

"So tell me what you want me to do," he said. She tried another word—an obscene word on Earth, but it translated as "joy" on Cobale.

"Fuck me. Oh, fuck me," she cried.

Rafe held her tightly, caressing her arms, her breasts, her labia, letting her put an arm around his broad strong back and do nothing else while he pleasured her. When she was shaking with anticipation he entered her. His tongue explored her mouth so that her glad cries bubbled up like the sweet wine they had drunk. One hand was still doing crazy things to her nipples, while his cock moved deliberately inside her, almost meeting her need, giving it time to build and build. She raged and smiled and simmered silently, knowing she could change that if she wanted to. Finally she could stand it no longer, and responded, challenging him to match the rhythms. He took a few oblique strokes to tell her he'd picked up the challenge, then confronted her moves with hard thrusts. She careened with him through somersaults of ecstasy, until they shuddered to a breathless stop.

Her skin soaked with sweat and the planetary night mist, her womb drenched from lovemaking, Melerie decided she had never been so happy before.

Three husbands! Long after Rafe fell asleep, she was still day-dreaming about the next round with each of them.

## Stacy Reed

❦

# Holiday

They always met for lunch at *Coeur Carré*—Elizabeth hated the steaming mounds of meat and slippery cabbage dished up in most other Berlin restaurants. She grinned at Drew around a mouthful of *crêpes d'épinard*.

"And how's Jeremy?" she asked.

Drew tongued the rim of her thick-glassed mug. "Very accommodating."

"I can't imagine any man could accommodate you."

"I wouldn't have come here if he couldn't," Drew replied.

"Yes. New Orleans is overflowing with the merely adequate."

Drew cautiously set down her mug, as if the heavy glass might splinter in her pale hands. "This is ridiculous, Elizabeth."

"What? You actually falling for some guy?"

Drew sucked in her lower lip and teethed it lightly. "Elizabeth, have you ever seen me like this before?"

"You were like this about Noel."

"And since him?"

"No. It's true. I haven't seen you this unrestrained in years. You have yet to offer me a battery of reasons why you ought to be with Jeremy."

"I can't think of any."

"Well," Elizabeth began methodically, "there's the sex."

"Yes, there is that."

"And then there's compatibility."

"You're making us sound like a personal ad."

"And finally there's this completely inexplicable fondness he has for you."

Drew smiled openly at Elizabeth so the small space between her teeth showed. "That's easy to explain," Drew countered. "He's after my best friend."

"That's another thing! Three weeks I've been in Berlin and he hasn't so much as flirted with me."

"I'm so sorry," Drew laughed. "I had no idea he would be this unswerving."

"He's very focused, this one."

"I know," said Drew ruefully. The thought of Jeremy's simplicity quieted her. She tossed back the last of her beer and watched the city traipse by.

"Whatever will we do?" teased Elizabeth.

Drew reached across the debris of their lunch and smoothed her friend's rebellious black curls. "We'll have to do what's only decent."

Elizabeth leaned forward conspiratorially. "Yes?"

"Approach him on his own terms."

Jeremy stared intently toward the window at a point suspended approximately five feet in front of the blurred U-Bahn wall. The advertisements swished by him too rapidly; they might as well have been American. Only the angry graffiti inside the subway car distinguished the train as German.

With his weak grasp of the language, it was easy for Jeremy to ignore the monotonous calls for the various stops. He fantasized about Drew. It embarrassed him that she had become his favorite transit material. Wasn't he supposed to be dreaming of some woman who didn't want him?

He looked across the aisle at a young woman in a sundress. Her breasts moved easily against the floral print as the train bumped around corners. He imagined what her nipples might look like after he had sucked them hard. He tried to think of how she might taste, what she might whimper as she came.

He laughed at his contrivances and looked back out the window. Drew loved to come. He had made love to her this morning before leaving for the firm, as he had every morning since they'd immigrated. Their life together had uncoiled along a series of rituals, rituals that never disintegrated into unruly habits.

During the past week Drew had taken to hiding herself just before he arrived home from work. The first time, he had assumed she was out with Elizabeth, until he'd stumbled across her crouching behind his woolen suits, wearing nothing but the leather gloves she'd given him for Groundhog Day. She gave him some quiet gift on every holiday she remembered.

He exited at Thielplatz and strode up Habelschwerdter. It was a long walk. He studied the crumbling remnants of the older buildings and imagined how they might have looked before the war. He saw their simple row of new apartments down the block and imagined them cut at a cross-section, their interiors exposed. He envisioned all the rooms and nooks where she might be. He thought of her scurrying naked through the flat, looking for a new hiding place. He tried to remember all the places he had found her.

He greeted the downstairs tenant and loped up the three flights to their flat. He fumbled his key into the hole, turned the stubborn lock, and kicked the base of the heavy door lightly with the toe of his shoe.

"Hi, baby." Drew pressed herself against him.

"You're not hiding."

She took his awkward portfolio from him and with a pointed finger traced his jaw, willful beneath its gauzy cloak of olive skin. "You're not disappointed in me?" she asked.

He shook his head slowly and knelt in front of her. He petted her fine-threaded cotton dress reverently. He closed his shadowed eyes and leaned his head against her crotch.

"Jeremy, Elizabeth has come over for dinner."

He furrowed his brows dramatically but held his eyes shut. "Tonight?"

"Yes. She's here now."

He nuzzled Drew's thighs, inhaled patiently, and rose. "Where?"

"In the dining room."

He quietly kissed Drew's flaxen strawberry hair. "Let's not have dessert tonight."

The three sat around the table. Jeremy chewed purposefully, resolved to either take Drew or work on his drawings, depending on what time Elizabeth left.

He watched Elizabeth and Drew exchanging glances. They were more like an old married couple than best friends. They talked to amuse themselves, but it was extraneous to their communication.

When Drew left New Orleans, she had promised Elizabeth that she would be gone no longer than the year Jeremy took for his preceptorship. In the winter, she and Jeremy would return to New Orleans and he would join an architecture firm in the city. They had invited Elizabeth to come to Berlin with them, but her grant at Tulane kept her in the States most of the time.

Jeremy set his fork prongs down at the edge of his plate, propped his chin against the heel of his hand, and looked quizzically from Drew to Elizabeth.

"Look at him," giggled Elizabeth. "I told you he'd know."

"He's quite astute," Drew conceded, looking not at Elizabeth but at Jeremy.

"You say that's what you like about me," said Jeremy.

"So I do." Drew raised her fine eyebrows and spoke to her glass of wine. "We have a proposition for you, Jeremy."

"You're blushing."

"Elizabeth would like to fuck you and I would like to watch. Does that strike you as an agreeable way to pass the evening?"

"Why, yes. It does." Jeremy smirked affably at Elizabeth. He cut his eyes sideways toward Drew. "But I thought you planned to finish Chapter Six tonight."

"She finished it this afternoon," Elizabeth interjected. "She even began outlining Chapter Seven."

"How industrious you are."

"You should reward her, Jeremy."

"Come here, then." Jeremy pushed his chair back from the table. Elizabeth went to him. "Now sit down so that Drew can see you."

She sat down cautiously on Jeremy's lap, resting her back across his shoulder so that Drew could see them both. She leaned her head back and whispered something in Jeremy's ear. Drew smiled proudly.

Jeremy drew Elizabeth's short pleated skirt up so that her white mesh panties showed. Holding Elizabeth's waist with one hand, he stroked the insides of her thin tan thighs with the other. He looked directly at Drew while breathing into Elizabeth's ear.

"Pull her panties aside," said Drew. "I want to see her pussy."

Jeremy pulled Elizabeth's panties over so that her lips were exposed. "Like this?"

"Yes. Now ask her what she wants."

"Tell me what you want me to do to you, baby."

"Tease my nipples," said Elizabeth.

Jeremy pushed Elizabeth's burgundy silk blouse up over her full round tits and pulled down the cups of her lacy bra. He flicked his thumb and forefinger against his tongue for moisture before rubbing them over her eager dark nipples. She squirmed helplessly against his hardening cock.

"You're doing beautifully," said Drew. "I think she's enjoying this. I bet she wants you to play with her pussy."

Jeremy politely ran his hand down Elizabeth's smooth tummy and over her black curls. He scooted back in his chair, propping Elizabeth's legs further open. Drew could see how wet her friend had gotten; a spot appeared on the dress slacks she'd bought Jeremy for St. Patrick's.

"You're making a mess on Jeremy's favorite pants," Drew chided.

"Isn't Labor Day coming up soon?" asked Jeremy.

"I promise I'll find something special for you if you play with Elizabeth's pussy for a little while."

Jeremy flashed Drew his finest little-boy grin and placed an index finger at Elizabeth's opening. "How should I touch her?"

"Like this," Drew whispered, scooting her chair into an especially viable angle beside Jeremy's. She placed her hand over his poised finger and moved it up the length of Elizabeth's lips to her engorged clit. She moved his finger around in tiny circles until Elizabeth moaned plaintively against Jeremy's neck.

"I think that means she wants you inside her," Drew advised, furtively tracing Elizabeth's slippery opening with her red-tipped finger.

Still holding Elizabeth by the waist, Jeremy stood and backed her onto their dining room table. She caught herself with her hands and looked up at him expectantly.

From her chair Drew unbuckled Jeremy's belt and eased his pants down. She pulled his boxers gently over the head of his cock and ran her tiny hand over it, pulling insistently to the right, then squeezing as she went back down the shaft. He braced himself against the polished wood and laid his head on Elizabeth's shoulder as Drew tugged impatiently on his hard cock.

"Now put it in her," Drew instructed.

Jeremy held up Elizabeth's ass and bent his knees so that the head of his cock nuzzled against her yawning pussy. Elizabeth arched her back and whimpered for him to push inside her. He exhaled sharply at the feel of her wet lips dragging over his cock.

"Please," someone murmured. Jeremy complied, driving his thick cock into Elizabeth until his balls were nestled softly against her contracting ass muscles.

Drew pressed her hand firmly against the curve of Elizabeth's spine. "Now fuck her very slowly while I watch," she whispered.

She leaned her pixie chin on the edge of the table, right in front of their arching pelvises. It thrilled her to see Jeremy's cock plunging in and out of her best friend's cunt. His dick was slicked in Elizabeth's wetness. She wanted to take it out and suck it, but Elizabeth's cries dissuaded her.

"Fuck me harder, Jeremy," Elizabeth begged.

"Hold on." Jeremy braced himself against her abundant ass. He rolled back his sharp shoulder blades ceremoniously and sighed.

"Are you coming, baby?" Elizabeth asked.

"Don't move," Drew hissed to Jeremy. "Don't come yet."

Elizabeth was desperate to come. "Drew," she pleaded, "please let him fuck me."

"In a minute," Drew said, holding fast to Jeremy's gaunt hips. "I'm kind of enjoying this. You can wait, can't you?" Drew kissed Elizabeth on the lips. They felt thin and tight. After Jeremy's appetite had abated slightly, Drew released him. "Go ahead. I want to see her come now."

Each time the base of Jeremy's cock bumped up against Elizabeth's clit, she felt herself getting closer to orgasm. Drew slipped her finger into Elizabeth's pursed asshole. "Do you like getting fucked by Jeremy's cock?" she asked.

"Yes, Drew." The words came out staccato, shattered by Jeremy's oblivious ramming.

Drew scrutinized Elizabeth's contorted features; the slightest prompting could push her to orgasm or throw her completely. She'd take her chances.

"Come on, Elizabeth. You like to get fucked by my boy, don't you? You like getting your pussy and your asshole fucked at the same time. Show me, baby. Show me how good his cock feels."

Drew's persistent encouragement drove Elizabeth to a spasmodic climax. Every muscle in her body seized up against each of Jeremy's compelling thrusts and she cried out in ecstasy.

Jeremy shuddered. "Oh, Drew, baby, I'm gonna come if I keep fucking her."

"Do you want to come now?" asked Drew.

"God, yes."

"Give me your cock."

Obediently, Jeremy pulled out of Elizabeth's satiated cunt and turned to Drew. "Please suck me."

Drew opened her mouth very wide, inserting Jeremy's cock without really touching it, then fastening her Cupid lips near the base and sucking deeply. She drew her mouth up the shaft and paused at the head, licking the tip quickly with her probing tongue. Cradling his heavy balls in one hand, she sucked and lapped at the head of his cock for long minutes while her other hand pulled at the skin of his shaft.

She let his balls go and pressed her hand against his thigh when he began pushing himself persistently into her mouth. Her thong panties were soaking wet from the thought of his tossing off in her mouth.

Drew moaned gratefully when she felt Elizabeth's hand slip down her panties. She concentrated feverishly on pleasing Jeremy as Elizabeth steadily massaged her protruding clit. Elizabeth's slick fingertips pinched Drew's stiff clitoris, coaxing out one intense orgasm after another.

Drew's muffled cries combined with the sight of Elizabeth manipulating her pussy finally overwhelmed Jeremy. He grabbed Drew's hair, thrust his dick against the back of her throat, and came. He kept thrusting until the last racking blows of his orgasm had subsided.

Drew smiled at Jeremy and licked her lips. "Happy Bastille Day."

## Erin Blackwell

༓

# Real Pleasure

I had a dildo in my hand when I answered the phone and I nearly spoke into the wrong instrument.

The voice issuing from the receiver belonged to my ex-girlfriend, Candace, the one who got away. We can go months without speaking, but it's always worth the wait.

"How would you like a two-week, all-expense-paid trip to Europe?" she asked.

"What's the catch?"

"I'm giving some safer-sex workshops for women, and Jan, my regular partner, is tied up. Literally. Some dominatrix has her in bondage in Berkeley. So I thought of you."

"I think about you a lot, Candace," I said.

"This is business, not pleasure," she reminded me.

"Can't it be a little of both?"

"With you, it'll have to be."

"Should I bring my hardware?" I asked.

"Hardware?"

"Dildos. Vibrators. Ass plugs. I was just putting one away when you called. They travel in their own customized leather carrying case. Those Europeans ain't never seen nothin' like it."

"As long as you can get them through customs."

"They never look in your bags."

*       *       *

First stop: Paris. I was so excited, the airplane food tasted like *haute cuisine* and the sleepless night made me feel years younger. Arriving at Charles de Gaulle Airport was so *chic* that even the moving sidewalks looked *exotique*. Candace and I pinched each other and laughed. We were going to have fun.

We got our passports stamped, then stood waiting for our bags to emerge from the belly of the plane. We were schlepping them toward the exit doors when a woman in quasi-military drag motioned me to a counter under a sign marked DOUANE. I complied, hoisting up my big plaid suitcase.

So this was France: clear brown eyes, skin like cream and cheeks like peaches, glossy chestnut hair swept off her face in a *chignon* and lips in a pout. Was she in a bad mood or was she being sultry? Or was this the prescribed national expression? She gestured to the leather case.

Uh-oh. I didn't mind her looking through my underwear, but my sex toys were off limits: I may be an exhibitionist but I'm not into humiliation. I unzipped the large plaid suitcase but she only pointed again to the leather case. Oh well, I guess this was an erotic moment like any other. Too bad I couldn't videotape it for the gals back home.

Lovingly, I undid the straps and lifted the lid. There, snug in their leather restraints, were thirteen vibrators and thirteen dildos, plus assorted ass plugs in varying shapes, sizes and colors. A real rainbow coalition. I was proud to be an American, proud to be a dyke, and very proud to be an impeccably accessorized butch top.

Mademoiselle Douane seemed not to know what she was looking at, but she clearly didn't like the look of whatever it was. I grinned at her and she sneered. I started miming what they were used for, but she closed her eyes. A facial tic seized her upper lip and nose, which jiggled like a hungry rabbit's. When she opened her eyes, she wouldn't look at me or my collection.

I caught a glimpse of Candace walking through the double doors to freedom. I waved to her but she seemed not to see me. Uh-oh. The last thing we needed was to lose each other at the airport.

Mademoiselle slammed down the lid. She held up a finger, which could have been a criticism of my collection, but was in fact a signal to another woman, a senior officer. A few counters down, a woman broke into a smile that gave me that home-cooked feeling: I couldn't help smiling back any more than a strip of bacon can resist being fried.

Her brown skin heated up her white shirt. Solar disk earrings and beaten gold bracelets played off the regulation *épaulettes*. A mountainous cascade of tiny braids ending in drops of gold defied the colonialist bureaucracy she served. She looked like Cléopatre in uniform, her gait as stately as any Nile River barge.

With a single deep red fingernail, she lifted the lid on my dildos. Shaking her head as if she was having trouble believing what she was seeing, she gestured to her sister officer to pick up the case and follow her. I picked up the plaid and we made our way to a small glass-walled office. Cléopatre dismissed her inferior and told me in exotic English to make myself comfortable. Coming from her that was quite an invitation, but I wouldn't have known where to start. Besides, she was on duty.

She took a printed form out of a drawer and asked, "What do you do with these . . . *gadgets?*"

"I fuck women," I said.

Her eyelids fluttered, then batted themselves half open. That old U.S. charm had her in its grip.

"You may not bring your paraphernalia into France. However, if you will sign this paper," she said, handing me a form, "we will hold your property until you leave Paris on a plane back to your country. Until then the suitcase will remain in my personal care."

However moved I was at the thought of her personally caring for my paraphernalia, I had to put up some kind of a fight. "It's not as if I'm smuggling drugs," I said. "It's not as if I'm running guns. I came to Paris to taste the joys of *l'amour*." She smirked. "Why take from me the very thing guaranteed to give pleasure to the women of France and inspire their love?"

She moved her lips in the most amazing way. "I wonder why you think you need these *accessoires* to inspire the love of *femmes françaises*. You are cheating yourself. You need a *femme française* to show you what real pleasure is."

*Real* pleasure? What'd she think I'd been having all these years—*fake* pleasure?

As a matter of formality she asked for my address during my stay in France. When we stood up, I felt like I was still sitting down: this woman was tall. She made an un-Frenchlike offer to shake hands. Her palm was dry and warm. I felt like butter on hot biscuits. I melted out of her office and picked up my plaid suitcase. Walking through the exit doors, I looked around for Candace, whom I found sitting at a small marble-top table.

"You're all right!" she said when she saw me.

"Cléopatre took away my toys."

"We'll just have to do without them," she said, trying to get a waiter to acknowledge our existence.

"It won't be the first time," I sighed.

"We never used those things. When did you start?"

"When was the last time we made love?"

"Twelve—no, thirteen years ago."

"Thirteen years ago, then."

"You started the minute you left me?"

"*I* left *you*?"

"Let's not get into it."

"I was broken-hearted, Candace, you know that. Well, I wasn't going to let any other woman get to me the way you had. Literally. I wasn't going to let anybody else inside."

"But you used to love that."

"I was hooked, but I managed to kick the habit and become emotionally independent."

"You sure you don't mean emotionally dead?"

"Let's just say I grew up."

"And no one's been in there since?"

"I've got my sexuality where I want it: under control. I get pleasure from giving pleasure. My technique is flawless. Just wait till you see me in action."

"Too bad about your collection," she said, turning to the waiter. "*Deux cafés, s'il vous plaît.*"

"Oh my goddess. What am I going to use?"

o   o   o

Next morning we ate *baguette* for breakfast and visited a *cathédrale* that felt like a public library installed in an antique spacecraft. All the tourists took each other's pictures, grimacing beside the gargoyles that crouched on the uppermost balustrades.

We *rendezvous*ed with the workshop organizers at a small restaurant near the *hôtel*. A sad-looking woman named Véro, who made English sound like Danish, outlined the day's *programme*: lunch, a two-hour workshop using volunteers from the audience, a break for coffee and cake followed by a *débat* on the theoretical implications of the demonstration, then dinner and dancing. Sounded like my kind of *programme*.

Lunch was an inspiration. Everything was *au* something else: *pâté au saumon, canard à l'orange, fromages aux fines herbes*, washed down by a *château au vent*. We all giggled a lot. They stared at us like we were visitors from another planet and maybe we stared at them the same way. The table got very *chaleureuse*, which is to say warm and friendly. If this kept up we'd be asking for volunteers from the audience before dessert: *glace au marron avec sauce au chocolat*.

After a slug of that tar they call *café* we paid and left the restaurant. Sauntering up the narrow one-way street to number 68, we ducked into a doorway designed for carriages and crossed a small cobblestone courtyard dripping with ivy. Up a flight of spiral stairs, we passed through a high doorway into an airy room with plaster molding and *chandelières*.

About forty women were seated in folding chairs, talking and laughing. They calmed down when we walked onstage. Véro introduced us and the audience applauded. Candace started her spiel, explaining why safer sex was necessary even if some *lesbiennes* fantasized themselves immune to AIDS. Véro's translation made everything sound refined but sexy. Candace held up dental dams, gloves, condoms and finger cots. We pantomimed using them and passed out samples.

The audience tested the give-and-take of the latex and discussed the ins and outs of safer sex. Candace asked for questions, but there weren't any. Until the door opened at the back of the room and Cléopatre walked in with my suitcase.

Uh-oh, a raid. Before we'd even gotten started. Couldn't she have waited until the coffee break?

"*Bonjour,*" she said. "I'm Marie-Antoinette de Retour and I have a question."

She had a nerve. I'd signed that form in her office—what was she doing dragging my suitcase all over Paris? Whatever it was, she looked great doing it. A red leather bolero jacket set off a black silk blouse tucked into zebra-striped stretch pants that snuggled her *mont de Vénus* and the curves of her *derrière.* Watching her stride to the foot of the stage made my legs quiver.

Candace asked what was the nature of her question. Marie-Antoinette set the suitcase down and slid open the straps, musing, "Is it true you *américaines* use these things? That you can't make love without them?"

When she opened the lid the audience craned its collective neck and jumped to its feet. Candace looked at me as if I'd planned this little *divertissement.* A few of the women were horrified, most were amused and some couldn't be bothered. Those who got a close look described what they saw to those who'd remained seated. When the aftershocks were over, Candace looked at me like I was supposed to do something. I decided to make Marie-Antoinette squirm.

"What a fine collection," I said. "Is it yours?"

"*Non,*" she confessed. "My Uncle Marcel, a member of the *Résistance,*" she lied, with a tremolo, "was caught and tortured by Vichy swine. After the war, he required a synthetic means of expressing his passion. This," she laid a familiar hand on my case, "is the result. On his death, my aunt Madeleine built a chapel to house these *réliques plastiques.* She claimed that touching them had cured her rheumatism." The audience giggled in disbelief.

"I don't claim my uncle was a saint," said Marie-Antoinette. "*Au contraire.* If the workshop is *d'accord,* I will show my uncle's triumph over Vichy's antieroticism. I will inaugurate his legacy of pleasure for a new generation of *femmes françaises.* At the same time, I will demonstrate French proficiency in what is considered a *technique américaine.*" There was scattered applause. "If I could have a volunteer."

About six women left the room, yelling what sounded like "Day-Glo ass!" but turned out to be "*dégueulasse!*" meaning "to vomit!" Someone in the back grumbled, "*Typiquement américain*" but stayed. Those in the front laughed as if this U.S. *comédie* wasn't worth the effort of a political analysis. Marie-Antoinette stepped onstage and, when nobody else volunteered, asked me to help her into the harness.

I looked at her like she must be kidding. She looked at me like she wasn't. I didn't have an answer for that. Lest things degenerate, I removed the pad that would massage her clit from inside the harness. She put a hand on mine to convince me otherwise and I felt as if I'd stuck my finger into a light socket. Trembling, I reinserted the pad.

Candace began a running commentary which Véro did her best to translate accurately. The audience was on the edge of their folding chairs as I liberated a midsize dildo from its leather stall, but Marie-Antoinette pouted her lips doubtfully. Pointing a recently trimmed fingernail at a model twice the size, she winked. The largest in my collection, that monster had been given to me as a joke. It was never intended for actual use—least of all on me.

"The back row has to see, too," she murmured.

Just a simulation, I reminded myself.

Fitting the unwieldy dildo into the harness, I handed the thing to Marie-Antoinette, who wouldn't take it. That meant I had to move in to where I could smell her body through the silk and leather. Her breath on my ear burned like a desert wind. She leaned a broad palm on my shoulder and I went down on my knees. Her hand slid onto my neck as she stepped through the legholes. I pulled the belt up over her zebra stripes so that the dildo was poking me in the face. Was this real pleasure? I strapped her in.

The sight of her wearing my damn dildo would've been funny if I hadn't felt a little woozy. Probably the wine at lunch. I made the mistake of standing up too fast. My cunt went liquid and started to throb like hot sulphur springs. She, *au contraire*, looked like a long-distance runner at the starting block.

Candace handed me a condom, thereby adding insult to

injury—or was she trying to save my life? That's what we were
there for, after all: safer sex. The workshop must go on.

I held up the rubber for everyone to see, then fumbled
around on the head of Marie-Antoinette's dick. I couldn't get the
thing on. I just couldn't. I mean, those things only stretch so far.
I was relieved when the latex tube split, since we could now
move on to something else, but Candace produced another condom. Marie-Antoinette slipped it over her member before I
could say, "Let 'em eat cake." She grinned at me with the largest, most ferocious teeth I'd ever seen. Then she asked for a
glove, which she pulled onto her right hand.

"Close your eyes," she told me.

"Why?" I gasped.

"I'm just a poor *femme française*," she purred. "We aren't
used to high-tech sex. If I know you're watching me with all your
superior U.S. know-how, I'll be too timid to try." The audience
found this funny and clapped their encouragement, chanting in
unison, *"Fermez vos yeux!"* I closed my eyes and imagined myself in the *cathédrale* we'd seen this morning. What was its
name? Like the football team. That huge, cluttered, candlelit
barn seemed like the perfect place to hide.

Her hands are on my shirt, undoing my buttons. My pounding
heart is probably visible through my chest. She pulls my bra up
over my breasts and just leaves them there, hanging. I cover
them with my hands. *O-là-là.*

Her hand slides down to my belt buckle and I feel a tug and
hear a clink and the belt's open. I feel another tug and I know
Customs is taking care of me. Customs is looking into it. Customs is unzipping my pants.

"This is just a simulation," I remind her.

"But it has to be believable," she murmurs.

My pants are pulled down in my very first striptease for a
French audience. Candace can't think what to say and Véro
doesn't feel the need to translate. I can hear the door open and
close. Are they coming or going? I don't want to know.

The dildo knocks up against my hipbone before being redirected so it's bending into my thigh. She sighs. I guess that's her clitoris getting its massage.

Something brushes my pubic hair. Latex. Preparing the area for entry. Her hand moves down to my lips. I shudder. She kisses me suddenly on the mouth. She's so moist and warm. She sticks her finger in. One finger? Two? She twirls them around as I rock my pelvis. I want it. The whole nine yards.

*Notre Dame*, that's it! Only they pronounce it differently. Our Lady of Paris. Our Lady of Pleasure. Do it again, do it again. I like it, I like it.

"*C'est si bon*," she tells me. Her mouth travels down my neck to my breasts, to my nipples. She sucks and she bites.

"*C'est si bon*." Everything she does is so good. So fast, so soft, so hard, so slow. I want her in there. She's in there. I want her to stay. She's gone. Where is she? If she doesn't come back I'm going to scream.

"Relax," she says. She's back and she's bigger than ever. It's not her—it's that dildo! This can't be happening. She'll never get it in. She's insane to try. I'm insane to let her. First she takes away my toys, then she fucks me with them—I've never been so excited in my life! I see stained glass windows depicting blood-engorged labia. A customs officer is examining the contents of my cunt. Instead of stamping my passport, she stamps my clit—with lipstick. That's it! I come and I keep on coming, sweating and crying, and she holds me. We stand there exchanging waves of vital energy. I open my eyes and I can barely focus but I can see her smile.

After a stunned silence everyone in the audience started babbling at once. We were a hit if the idea was to give them something to talk about.

Marie-Antoinette peeled off her glistening glove and threw it to the crowd, who dove for it, shrieking like seagulls. Véro gestured to a long table covered with fruit tarts and announced, "Mesdames, there's coffee in the back." That got them moving.

I started to button my shirt. Marie-Antoinette interceded. "I can do it," I told her.

"*C'est un plaisir pour moi.*"

Oh. Well then. Who was I to begrudge Marie-Antoinette a *plaisir*, after what she'd put me through? She dressed me in silence and I unbuckled her harness. The condom on the dildo was dry.

"Wait a minute," I said. "If you didn't use the dildo, what did you use?"

"These," she said, wiggling her fingers.

"All of them?" I said hopefully.

"Just these two," she said.

"Two? That's all? Are you sure?"

"There are plenty of witnesses."

"It felt so big!" I said.

"As big as your imagination," she laughed. "As big as your desire."

"Two fingers is nothing," I mumbled.

"Two fingers is all that's needed if you know how to use them."

"I thought for sure you'd used the dildo," I muttered.

"Did you want me to?"

"Of course—I mean, of course not. But when I thought you were going to, I got ready to take it. And then the feeling was so intense, I was sure I was doing the impossible."

She stared at me. "Why should making love be impossible?"

I didn't know how to explain. "You wouldn't understand," I said. "It doesn't matter. Let's go get some coffee."

"How long are you in Paris?" she asked.

"Two more days."

"That's not enough."

"The workshop must go on."

"I'm serious," she said.

"So am I," I said.

"When can I see you again?" she asked.

"Look, we just met. We don't know each other. I'm not your type."

"What do you mean?"

"I can't speak French," I said. "You don't know me."

"I know *me*," she said. "I know what I want."

"You can't always have what you want."

"Does that mean you don't want me?" she asked.

"I didn't say that."

She turned away from me and something splashed on the floor. Uh-oh.

"Marie-Antoinette, you're crying."

She turned around to hiss and spit at me. "Do you think I do this for a living? Do you think public sex is part of my job as a French customs officer? Do you think I'm a professional dominatrix? Don't you know, if I wanted to teach you a lesson, it's because I care about you? Do you think because it's *érotique*, it can't be *émotionnel*? Do you think—at all?"

Uh-oh, emotions. Where was she getting all this passionate dialogue? Don't tell me she was confusing a casual sexual encounter with the love of her life. I may be cute, but this was ridiculous. I didn't know what to say to calm her down without hurting her feelings more than I already had. Somebody shoved a plateful of berry *tarte* in my hand and I was frankly grateful for the interruption. Sex is one thing, but complications are a drag. Marie-Antoinette could dish it out, all right, but then she wanted what she'd dished out back. Sex doesn't work that way. If you want to play, fine, but leave your emotions in your bathrobe pocket.

I looked down at the pastry on my plate. It's times like these I wonder why I bother with women at all, why I don't just eat my way to ecstasy. The *tarte* was a vision of red and purple berries sunk into a firm but creamy custard separated from the crispest of *millefeuille* by a layer of almond paste. Pretty as it was, the *tarte* was even better on the tongue, where the various layers of flavor did a culinary version of the dance of the seven veils. I closed my eyes and moaned.

When I opened my eyes, I found myself surrounded by audience members sharing theories and rattling off long-winded questions. They were all cute, they were all excited, and they were all trying to seduce me—so why wasn't I enjoying myself? I couldn't understand what they were talking about. When I looked around for Marie-Antoinette to translate, she was gone. Seeing her suddenly not there made me feel as if one of those gargoyles had sunk its claws into my chest. I choked on the forest fruit and custard, which is how I knew I was being a jerk.

I handed the *tarte* to someone, ran out of the room and down the spiraling staircase, threw open the door to the courtyard and flew over the cobblestones into the shadows of the entranceway. Out on the street, I swung my head wildly from right to left hoping to catch a glimpse of her, but all I could see were women in high heels carrying carefully wrapped packages of *charcuterie*.

"*Chérie,*" said a low voice behind me.

I turned and saw her, leaning up against the heavy wooden door.

"You're still here!"

She held out her hand and when I came over, drew me to her.

"I'm sorry I forgot to be cool," she said, looking into my eyes with a smile. "I know you *américaines* like things to be cool. Otherwise, you get very *émotionnel*. It was silly of me to make a crisis. We don't know each other well enough for that. Forgive me."

I stared at her. How had she gotten so reasonable so fast? Was this a French trick? "I forgive you," I said.

"We had a nice time together and now you have a *souvenir* of Paris. That's all." She squeezed my hand and tried to let go, but I held on.

"Marie-Antoinette," I whispered, thinking the whole street must be staring. "Nobody's ever fucked me like that. And nobody's fucked me at all for a long time. I wouldn't let them. I didn't want them to. But you—I don't know—you're making me feel things I don't know if I want to feel. I'm kind of out of my mind right now, but I don't see how we could have a relationship when I'm only here for two days. You see what I mean?"

"Just because I have emotions doesn't mean I want a relationship. It only means I'm not a machine. That shouldn't scare you, it should reassure you—unless you fantasize about robots."

I was starting to like this woman. "You don't want a relationship?"

"You please me," she said, like someone addressing a chocolate *éclair*. "I want to take advantage of your presence in Paris. *Voilà, c'est tout.*"

"Really?"

"More or less," she said, extending her lips in an ambiguous pout. "The important thing for me is to see you again."

"Why?"

She brought my hand to her lips and with her eyes closed, slowly traced between my fingers with her tongue. She opened her eyes as if she were returning from another world. "I want you inside me."

Now I know how an electric blanket feels when somebody plugs it in with the dial on high. "Where do you live?" I'd explain to Candace later.

"The *métro's* right there—it's only three stops—or we can walk. It's so beautiful out."

I wanted every moment to last.

"Let's walk," I said.

*Martha Miller*

❧❀❧

# Hormones

It was the hormone replacement therapy that caused the weight gain. Alexis had always been plump, but the estrogen/progestin treatment did her in. As a child she remembered trips to the doctor—she'd leave with a 1,000-calorie-a-day diet and a grape Tootsie pop. She remembered suppers of broiled hamburgers, cottage cheese and canned peaches. As an adolescent she had been heavy until she'd discovered diet pills and for several years went up and down like a yo-yo. After the children came she settled into a comfortable size 18. Now the kids were almost grown. Billy was working his way through college. Alex was still in high school—he'd lost a year in drug rehab and all that had led up to that.

It sort of happened overnight. One morning she woke up and felt like hell: hot flashes, depression, fatigue and irritability. She thought she had the flu or had eaten something spoiled. When the symptoms didn't go away, she decided to see a doctor. She chose a female gynecologist, thinking that with a woman she'd at least find compassion. She hadn't. The only thing the medical profession seemed to have to offer was a twenty-pound weight gain that sent her already sinking sense of self-esteem over the edge. The doctor, who was probably ten years younger than Alexis and called all her female patients "ladies," minimized her

complaints with an "Oh, don't be a baby" look on her face. The
hormones she prescribed did help with many of the symptoms,
but they also created new symptoms—like the weight.

Alexis finally had to stop wearing even her largest rings. She
gave up on blue jeans and bought jerseys and sweat pants.

"I don't have any medication that will make you feel like
you're eighteen years old again," said the doctor when she com-
plained. Alex remembered the scene from *Gone With the Wind*
where Mammy told Scarlet she'd never have an eighteen-inch
waist again—only it was a *size* 18 that Alexis had lost forever.

"I'm gaining weight," she said.

"Are you eating more than usual?" the doctor, a plump
woman herself, asked. "Sometimes depression . . ."

"I'm eating the same as I have for the last twenty years!"

"How about exercise?" The doctor's hair lay in damp ringlets
on her forehead; her face was rosy and flushed. She looked like
a frustrated cherub. What the hell did an angel know about real
life anyhow?

"I injured my back when the kids were little," Alexis said. "I
used to walk in the park, but last year I got mugged."

The doctor turned away and shuffled through some papers.
"A massage will help with the edema. I'm going to give you a
booklet about our wellness clinic. They have an exercise program
there."

Alexis considered it, then repeated, "Look, I have a bad back.
Exercise programs just get me injured."

"There's a trained professional who will monitor what you do.
Brian hasn't let anyone get hurt yet."

Oh, great. A man, thought Alexis. "Can't you just give me
some hormone that doesn't do this?" she persisted.

"How's your sex life?"

"What?"

"Sex." The doctor turned to face her. "Vaginal dryness? Painful intercourse?"

Alexis felt sweat break out on her forehead and she thought
she might be having her first hot flash in weeks. "I'm lesbian."

"Yes?"

"Actually, I'm single," Alexis confessed. "I don't have much of anything." Sweat dripped out of her hair, onto her collar.

"Well," said the doctor with a weak smile. "You lucked out on that one. Many women have problems in that area too."

Alexis pulled a tissue from a box on the white counter and sponged her forehead.

"It was the children that threw me," the doctor said, shaking her head. "And, of course, you don't look lesbian."

"Am I supposed to say thank you?" Alexis picked up a magazine and fanned herself. She was angry. Her body felt out of control. She hoped that she was at least losing some water weight. "What does a lesbian look like, anyway?"

"I'm sorry. I didn't mean to offend you." The doctor stammered slightly, then regained her composure. She handed Alexis a booklet and a yellow sticky note with a phone number and name on it. "This should help. I've written down the name of a good massage therapist. You won't need another appointment with me for six months unless you have some medical problem."

"When I hit three hundred pounds, will you consider it a medical problem?" Alexis shot back.

The doctor was at the door. She turned and said, "Try to get some exercise. Get refocused."

"Are you going to tell me to get a lover too?"

"That wouldn't hurt a thing," the doctor said over her shoulder.

Alexis tossed the magazine at the closing door. It thudded and slid downward, pages fluttering.

The following Tuesday Alexis left work early to keep an appointment with a massage therapist. She sat in the waiting room on a wicker chair, reading a magazine. The lighting was soft, relaxing. The curtains on the windows were sheer and ruffled, like the ones her favorite aunt Midge had when Alexis was a child. A small desk held a phone and an appointment book cluttered with scraps of paper. The desk was the cheap kind you get at Kmart and put together at home; her kids had had them and usually dismantled them within a year. A couple of two-drawer filing cabinets with a door across the top sat against the opposite wall, serving as a desk for a small printer. A metal office chair that looked like it came from the Dumpster was stacked with thick manila file folders. Hanging plants and a large potted palm added a homey touch.

A woman came in. Alexis smiled. She looked a little older than Alexis. Plump. Attractive. She sat on a wicker love seat across the room. It snapped and gave slightly under the woman's weight.

Alexis looked at her watch. The woman had pulled a book from her purse and started to read.

"My doctor sent me," Alexis said. The woman looked over the top of her glasses, smiled and nodded, then returned to her book.

"Hormones," Alexis said.

The woman looked up again. Was she annoyed?

"I started gaining weight." Alexis realized the woman was larger than she was and probably wasn't interested. "Every day another pound." Why was she talking? Why couldn't she shut up? It was probably the progestin; it was that time of her cycle.

The woman closed her book and set it in her lap. "Isn't it hell, what we have to put up with?" she said.

Alexis nodded. "If someone had told me ten years ago, I wouldn't have believed them. A lot of the time I don't even feel like myself."

The woman smiled. Not a big smile, but a small smile of acknowledgment. She said simply, "I know."

Alexis's heart leapt—they had connected.

Late-afternoon sun slanted through the window, falling across the woman's shoulders. Alexis noticed her graying hair, long, salt-and-pepper-colored. She felt some envy. She'd started coloring her own dark hair a year ago. She hated it, but couldn't seem to make the decision to stop. "My name's Alexis," she said at last.

"Rose," the woman said.

They were quiet for a minute. Alexis checked her watch again. Her appointment was for ten minutes ago. "She usually runs late," Rose said. "She takes extra time with someone who really needs it, and that screws up her schedule for the rest of the day." Rose shrugged. "No one really minds. Especially when they're the one who needs the extra time."

"Are you here to see Sandra?" Alexis asked.

"Her daughter Dana," Rose said. "They're in together. I usually try to get Sandra, but this is an emergency. I took what I could get."

"You had a massage emergency?"

Rose smiled. "Sounds silly, doesn't it?"

"No sillier than a hormone emergency."

"Now, a hormone emergency," Rose said. "That's a real emergency."

Alexis liked Rose—so much, in fact, that her nipples were getting erect. Damn progestin.

A young man walked through the waiting room, and a barefoot girl in cut-off jeans and a red T-shirt that said "Chicago Bulls" followed. "Did you want to make a next appointment?" the young woman asked.

The man seemed groggy. "I'll call later in the week," he said.

"Okay." The girl smiled. Her teeth were white. Perfect. She turned to Rose. "I'll just be a minute. I need to change the sheets." She left the room at the same time the man went out the front door.

Alexis stared after the girl.

"Dana's very pretty, isn't she?" Rose said softly.

"Takes my breath away," Alexis said. "God, I'm salivating."

In Rose's silence Alexis realized what she'd said. How could she have forgotten herself? She looked across the room. Particles of dust swirled in the sunlight, and Rose's face was in shadow. Alexis wasn't sure, but she thought Rose was smiling.

"My, my," Rose said, clicking her tongue. "You *are* having trouble with hormones, aren't you?"

Alexis slid down in her seat. Sweat broke out on her forehead and ran down the side of her face. When Dana returned to call Rose to the back room, Alexis couldn't look at her.

The massage was wonderful. The room was dim, with soft light and music. Sandra was a big blond woman who spoke in soft tones and had strong hands. Alexis had to excuse herself to pee halfway through the treatment and stopped at the bathroom again on the way out. When she got home she shut herself in her bedroom, threw off her clothes and masturbated. For the first time she noticed that her vagina *was* dry. She needed K-Y jelly even for self-pleasure. Was this her body? The one she'd known all these years? What the hell was happening to her?

The exercise room had emerald green carpets and several shiny chrome machines. Alexis chose the early morning class that met twice a week at 6:00 A.M. Most days the slightest exertion caused sweat to drip from her forehead and run down the valley between her breasts, but the hot flashes were subsiding; they were fewer and farther between. The hormones were working.

Brian, a middle-aged gay man, hovered over her. Alexis hated it. The first day of class there were four women and two older men. Brian favored the men and fussed over them in a way they seemed to love. At the second class two of the women didn't come and a new woman started. It was Rose.

Alexis was thrilled: now there was someone in the class larger than she was. Also, she was happy to see Rose again.

At first Rose didn't recognize her. How could that be? Their meeting had meant so much. They had shared so much. Hadn't they? She gave Rose a big smile, which Rose politely returned. At the end of the class, sitting in the bubbling hot tub with the other two women, Rose asked, "Do I know you?"

"The massage therapist," Alexis answered. "You were seeing Dana that day."

"Oh, yes." Rose laughed. "Menopause."

The other two women, who were probably in their twenties, stared at Alexis as if Rose had mentioned leprosy. Alexis sat in silence, the water bubbling around her, a smile pasted on her face. Was it her imagination or did the women actually slide a little farther away from her?

Weeks passed and though Alexis watched the scale religiously, her weight didn't drop. It did stop increasing, though, and she felt a little better. She started looking forward to the morning workouts. She was always glad to see Rose. Everyone in the class except Alexis and the two men, Paul and Richard (who she was soon convinced were lovers), had a terrible attendance record. Rose missed at least every third session. Alexis hadn't missed a class, but the morning of the storm she almost stayed in bed.

She awoke with a slight headache. She could hear thunder and rain. The room was cool. She pulled the covers up and turned over on her belly, opening one eye. It was 5:30. She had just enough time to brush her teeth, pull on her shorts and T-shirt and get to class.

She lay there for a minute, calculating. Rose would probably miss today. Alexis could use the sleep. She wanted to lie in bed and listen to the storm. But first she needed to pee.

On her way out of the bathroom she stepped on the scale. She was five pounds lighter. She blinked. Stepped off and on again. Five pounds less.

She put on her shorts, pulled her tie-dyed T-shirt over her head and grabbed her gym bag and umbrella. Rain beat down noisily, splashing in puddles. Lightning streaked across the dark gray morning sky. The wind blew her umbrella inside out as she ran from her car to the door. By the time she was inside, her wet hair was plastered to her head, and the shoulders and back of her T-shirt were soaked.

There were four of them that morning: Paul, Richard, Alexis and Rose. Alexis was glad she'd come.

"I lost five pounds," she mouthed to Rose during the warm-ups. Rose put her thumb and forefinger together in an "okay" sign. Alexis felt a warm rush. Was it a hot flash? She waited for the sweat to start pouring. It didn't.

Halfway through the workout Alexis realized that she and Rose would have the women's hot tub and sauna all to themselves. She put extra energy into the workout that morning, feeling good for the first time in months.

Brian had to slow her down at one point. "Have you forgotten your bad back?" he said, patting her damp shoulder.

"Fuck off, Brian. I've lost five pounds!"

"Just be careful, honey," he said. "We don't want you to be the slimmest person in traction."

At the end of the workout Alexis rushed into the dressing room, grabbed her gym bag and unzipped it.

"Shit!" she shouted.

"What's wrong?" Rose was behind her.

"My swimsuit. I left it at home." Alexis pictured the black suit hanging over the shower rod.

"You don't need it."

"What?" Alexis turned. Rose was closer than she'd thought.

"It's just the two of us," Rose said. "You don't need it. Hell, I'll leave mine off too."

"Do you think?"

"Sure. Come on."

Alexis stepped into a changing stall and slowly pulled off her damp clothes. She looked in the narrow mirror. Her body was full. White. Glistening. She was scared and excited. She wanted to get into the water before Rose. Peeking out the door, she saw no one and made a dash for the hot tub.

Rose was standing there, testing the water with her toe. Her body was round, her breasts full with pale brown nipples. Her pubic triangle was dark and feathery. "Water's fine," she said, and stepped in.

Alexis sat in the tub with the warm water bubbling around her. "I can't believe I'm doing this," she said.

"There's no one here but us. Brian and the boys are busy. And you can bet they're not in *their* suits."

"Really?"

"Why the hell do you think they're so religious about attendance?"

Alexis laughed nervously. "Do you think they're making it over there?"

"We can hope."

"Boy, I haven't done anything like that for ever so long," Alexis said wistfully, breathing in the steam from the noisy, churning water.

"Well, you should." Rose moved closer.

"That's what my doctor said."

"Sounds like a smart doctor." Rose was right next to her.

Alexis exhaled slowly. Purple shadows gathered in the corners of the locker room. Rose's gym bag sat on a bench, two white towels folded beside it. Waiting. Alexis felt her muscles relax. "This is nice," she said.

Rose pushed a strand of hair off her damp forehead. "When I was a kid, the neighbor girl and I played in a wading pool in the backyard. On hot days we swam naked. I guess our mothers thought we were too young for that to matter. We'd play out there for hours. Get sunburned all over. I was always a fat, healthy-looking kid."

Alexis tried to imagine the wading pool. Hot summer days. The cool water. Two naked children.

"We'd touch ourselves," Rose went on. "It was great. By the time I was nine I was coming. I think that's early. But we had that pool."

Alexis leaned her head back and let her body float slightly off the marble bench.

"When I was twelve, I was coming with the shower massage in my mother's bathroom. Spraying it at my cunt."

"Didn't you run out of hot water a lot?" Alexis asked, thinking of her own teenaged kids' long showers. Her youngest would stay in there as long as the hot water lasted.

"Oh, no," said Rose. "It didn't take long."

Alexis laughed.

"Sometimes even now I like to position myself under the running water in the bathtub," Rose said. "Of course, I'm older. Fatter. I must look a sight with my legs in the air like that. But what the hell?"

Alexis closed her eyes and tried to imagine Rose in the bathtub. "Sex was always easy for me," she sighed. "These last few years have been hard. A big breakup. Menopause. I feel like I've lost my place. Like I have to start all over again."

As if from a long way off, just over the sounds of the bubbling water, Alexis heard Rose say, "We could touch ourselves here. We could use these jet streams."

Alexis opened her eyes. Rose already had one hand working under the water.

Something deep in Alexis's middle ached. She slid her hand down her belly, separated her folds, touched the flowery edges of her labia. The water was swirling. She pushed and kneaded her swollen lips. She held her breath.

"I'd like to kiss you," Rose said softly. She had moved very close.

Alexis nodded.

Rose's mouth was warm and moist. Alexis leaned into the kiss as Rose embraced her, pressing her soft flesh against her. The kiss lasted a long time, moving, soft pressure, moist tongue. At last Alexis pulled away to breathe. A low moan escaped her throat.

"Turn around, move this way," Rose whispered.

Alexis turned sideways on the bench and pulled one knee up. A jet stream of air flooded against her cunt. Rose cradled her from behind, reached around, and gently moved Alexis's fingers away, replacing them with her own. Slowly Alexis moved her head luxuriously from side to side. She stretched and wiggled against Rose's fingers. A tingling sensation spread. How could anyone touch like that? How did Rose know just what was needed and give just that, no more?

Alexis willed herself to let go and with a rush of exhilaration her climax, a mixture of pleasure and pain, beat through her. She felt one with the churning water, spilling, flowing, warmly melting.

Alexis turned to Rose. Sweat dripped off her face and she was panting. "Wow," she said.

"You're so articulate." Rose smiled.

Alexis kissed her and touched her voluptuous breast. "Come sit on my knee," she said.

Rose shifted her body. The warm water made her light, buoyant. With her arms around Alexis's shoulders Rose straddled her thigh and moved in a gentle fucking motion. Alexis felt the water sucking and swirling, the pressure of Rose's cunt, somehow warmer, wetter, more slippery than the churning water. Rose was right. It didn't take long.

The jet stream timer ended and the room was suddenly quiet. Rose cried out, clinging to Alexis. She rested her head on Alexis's shoulder and whimpered softly

After a minute Rose said, "We'd better go. Brian will think we've drowned in here."

Rain was coming down vigorously as the two women walked through the gym. The window behind Brian's desk looked like a gray waterfall.

"You girls look beat," Brian said.

Alexis nodded. "I think this is helping, though."

"You *look* like it's helping." Brian smiled.

"Thanks." She winked at Rose.

Alexis opened the door and hesitated. Rain splashed on the sidewalk and street. Rivers of water ran to the parking lot.

"Damn," she said. "I just got dried off."

Then she plunged into the downpour.

# Debbie Esters

# My Nail Broke: A Story in Four Scenes

### *Prologue*

I broke a nail. Who cares? Well, maybe you need to hear how it happened. I wish you'd have been there to see for yourself.

It all began when I decided that life is too short for me to be walking around as a horny bitchy down-at-the-mouth celibate and I went off the wagon, sexually speaking, in a big way. One issue that had been on my mind during my celibacy was getting it on with more than just one other person. I'm not the type of person who initiates much, but I'll do almost anything once if I'm asked—so when Michael asked me if I wanted to go to a sex party that he saw advertised in a magazine, I said okay.

Now, Michael had been to one such party with another friend of his, but she got cold feet and decided not to participate. Michael told me all about that first party so I knew what to expect when I got there.

### *Scene One*

We drive to Hayward. I guess you got to go to the burbs to find anyone who's bored enough to pay for a sex party. I'm sure there's plenty happening in the city, but by invitation only.

So we go to this house painted green with a neglected front yard. Inside we're greeted by this skinny broad in a robe who asks us to sign in. It doesn't take two seconds to sum up that I'm one of the best-looking broads there and Michael is number one for guys. But he sees one pretty lady he likes, and I'm enjoying all the attention I'm getting so we decide to stay.

We walk to the kitchen and each pour ourselves a glass of the Chardonnay we'd brought along. We meet our hostess, Sophia, and take a tour. I haven't seen so many mattresses in one house since that movie where a mafia gang all live in one place during a mob war. It's a bit too cheap and tacky for my taste: I mean black lights and fluorescent posters are cool, but a sexy scene, in my opinion, must have matching sheets and incensed air, candles and erotic knickknacks on low tables. This was more like plastic flowers and faded prints of blondes with big tits on cars, country western music and stick-on-the-wall mirror squares. But everything was very clean. I like that. Cleanliness makes me less inhibited.

### Scene Two

After changing into a towel, the attire of preference at the party, I go back to the deck where there's a hot tub. I have to squeeze my way into the circle of naked strangers, plus Michael who's already there. *New meat* must be emblazoned on my forehead, but hey, that's what I'm here for, meat. I'm not in the tub ten seconds and the guy next to me has his hand up my cunt. An old geezer he is, but his sixty-odd years have taught him a thing or two about hand jobs.

I can't stay in hot water too long—the heat wrinkles my skin and ruins my acrylic nails; remember, this is a story about a broken nail. So I say, "My nails can't take the water," and slide myself off of Mr. Sixty-something to go dry off.

I sit down to finish my glass of wine and smoke a cigarette in the living room. Not much happening. Two TVs going simultaneously; one with the Olympics and the other showing a video of a cock being sucked by painted lips. There may or may not have been people attached to these body parts; I never saw any. You know the type of video I mean.

Michael appears and tells me there's something hot going on upstairs so I extinguish my cigarette and follow him.

### Scene Three

It turns out that Sharon, a pretty, tan lady Michael saw earlier, is getting it on with her husband Larry. Michael loves to watch, so we go join them on the adjacent mattress. I don't quite know what to do. Being new to the scene and not much into visuals, I begin to give Michael a massage. I figure that if rubbing those hard, tight runner's legs of his doesn't get me in the mood, nothing will.

Sharon speaks first, addressing us with a simple "Hello, is this your first time?"

It takes us a minute to clarify that it is my first party but that Michael had been to one before because most folks who come to these parties are married couples or at least in long-term relationships. We, being just casual partners, are unusual. After a weird pause Larry asks me if I want Sharon to give me a massage.

I think I need to describe Sharon to you at this point. One very sexy lady. Caucasian. Deep, deep tan with white tan-line breasts that shine in the black light. Very slender, the body type that when turned sideways sort of disappears, but with an unusually soft round ass. And skin: smoothest skin I have ever felt, on anyone. She is like soft brown silk crepe, the kind that floats through your fingers.

I guess she and Larry think that of the four of us I'm the one needing the most attention, being new meat and female; I know the situation of a foursome where the other girl gets cold feet. Must be what they anticipate, because Sharon gets to rubbing me and Larry joins in and Michael takes me in one hand and Sharon in the other—I think. At some point I just close my eyes and start drinking in all these sensations. I mean, six hands rubbing me, three mouths sucking on my tits, licking my ears. I reach out my hands; it's cock to the right of me, cock to the left and pussy in the middle. My first pussy, other than my own. I think I'm developing an appreciation for pussy. It's fun to compare shapes and sizes and then it's like driving someplace familiar—the car, you know, drives itself. I mean, you just know how to move your hands on the wheel to take the vehicle home. A clit is a clit and I've spent enough time with my own to know exactly how she feels and what "ooh" means and what "ahh" is. We're talking easy. See, with men it's always a bit tricky the first few times until you figure what does it for them. But Sharon—a piece of cake, or should I say, coffee mousse.

There is something very sweet about a foursome. You reach out and your hands find parts and you don't know right away which is whose but the textures blend; silky skin here, coarse chest hair there, a slippery cunt, a hard smooth cock, hard balls, soft balls, tits, nipples of various shapes and sizes. A flesh cocktail; each tasty morsel blends in with the flavor of the next.

Nothing lasts forever. Sharon wants to eat me but I don't consider cunnilingus to be safe sex so I say no thanks. Now, Michael wants to eat me too and had been asking me for it all week but I tell him no for the same reason, so he goes down instead on Sharon. Right about here I contemplate asking Larry to suit up—put on a condom—and fuck me but I don't know if being demanding is correct etiquette so I don't say a word. Mistake. He starts watching Sharon but sort of moves away from the scene, dejected. She notices this and manages to drag herself off of Michael's face to ask him what's up. He says he's feeling left out and sure enough his cock is flaccid. Being such a loving wife, Sharon sets to sucking him back into shape. Now, watching her suck him is all Michael wants to really get him going so he suits up and drags my ass to where he wants it so he can fuck me, which is fine because I'd been wanting it for ten minutes or so while he was busy with lunch and Larry was feeling sorry for himself.

Well it gets good because she takes Larry from her mouth to her cunt and I put my head down and my butt up so Michael can watch them while he pounds me. But no one's coming yet. Larry gets to talking about whether he wants to continue at all, so I climb up on his chest and rub my drooling cunt on him, figuring that's got to make him feel good, which it does, but he says, "I can't feel anything with a condom on."

And I say, "I don't fuck without them."

I do want to fuck the man, so we're at an impasse. Then Sharon says, "I'm not fixed. I mean, my tubes aren't tied and I won't let anybody but Larry fuck me because he is fixed and we have two kids and that's plenty. I don't trust condoms not to break."

I'm still holding to my safe-sex standards. So Michael goes back to eating Sharon and Larry and I just sort of sit back and watch.

It is fun to watch. She obviously is getting off, and getting on and getting off again, just writhing there under Michael's face. At some point I join in, sucking her tits or fondling them. Then Michael moves from sucking her to fucking me full force. She moves on to me too and Larry starts fingering my clit. I think, oh goody, my turn again, and all of a sudden I know it's towel-time. I start giggling this giggle that always needs to be explained because it's not that I'm laughing *at* anything or anybody but just that I'm having a good time and if I don't get something under me I'm going to ejaculate all over the bed and make puddles on the mattress.

Anyway, Michael is fucking me, they are fondling me and the three of them are making me come all over the towel. Larry is finger-fucking me and Michael is back on Sharon and every time I giggle I dribble some more onto the towel and it is getting so I can still laugh but I can't ejaculate anymore and Larry hasn't figured out yet that what I'm doing is coming all over his hand.

So I can't come anymore and Sharon's having orgasms on Michael's tongue again and I glance at Larry, who's looking dejected, like a beached seal. I take that as a challenge. I remember reading about a woman who puts condoms on cocks with her mouth. First she practices with bananas, then works her way up to cucumbers until she finally gets the guts to ask a friend if she can practice on him.

Well, it's one of those times when I know I should have practiced when I was reading the book, because I want to use the

technique on Larry. I think, Can you do it, girl? Hell yes! I answer myself. But this is going to be trial by fire.

So I say, "Larry, I want to suck your cock, but I'm not going
to do it without a condom, do you mind if I put one on you with
my mouth? You don't have to do anything."

"You can try," he says, "but I just don't get off that way."

Well, I pick one of Michael's condoms out of his variety pack
figuring that I ought to use the best, and I suck the reservoir tip
into my mouth with the edge around my lips and head for Larry.

"Hey, doesn't she look like one of those inflatable dolls," he
says.

Wham! I grab his cock in my mouth, suck him in and push
down on the condom edge. He's deep in my throat and I want
to gag, but voilà! He's dressed!

I suck his cock hard. He's big and not easy to eat. I still want
to feel him in my cunt so I straddle him. He grabs my ass and
starts pumping from underneath. He thrusts and twists and
makes me want to pump back. He's one of those fucks that can
fill your cunt and rub your clit with his pelvis at the same time,
no hands needed. Then he comes. Really quickly when you think
of it.

"Gives you some respect for latex," I say sarcastically. Sliding
off him the condom sticks in my cunt and I have to take it out
carefully and carry it to the bathroom, where I wash my hands.

It's pushing midnight. Larry and Sharon have to split; Wednesday is, after all, a workday. They hand their phone number to
Michael; it reads *Jean and Arnold* . . .

### Scene Four

I'm feeling pretty good about myself. I mean, I always feel good
when I come buckets-full, don't you? But I think about Michael
and how he sure is a tough nut to crack sometimes. What do you
expect from a man who runs six miles just for fun? So I'm not
surprised at all when he asks me to go with him upstairs to the
*Big Room* for some more action. It's big all right, with about six
mattresses all pushed together and a big screen TV continuously
running videos.

The room is vacant when we get there. Michael and I get started one on one. But honey will draw flies: the ratio of men to women had been about 2:1 when we'd arrived but by this time many women had left. So a small crowd of guys comes in to watch us. I hear a strange voice say, "I'm next, I . . . I mean if you want to."

I don't answer but I feel hands on my breasts again and mouths on my thighs and I'm feeling too relaxed, too good not to enjoy it all. Now, Michael, he does like to watch, but I'm really surprised when he dismounts and moves aside. Then he whispers to me, "Is this what you want?" and I answer in the affirmative.

The first guy goes to eat my cunt and I stop him and tell him I won't have that without plastic wrap or latex. That gets some laughs from the others but I close my eyes, lying on my back, and what follows is the fulfillment of one of the few fantasies I've ever had: one after the other these four (or five) men line up to fuck me. I keep my eyes shut and it creates a mystery: see, I don't know which cock belongs to what voice or what hand belongs to which face. Michael is right there, jacking himself off, letting me jack him off too. Michael's sweet; even as I'm getting him off he keeps an eye on all the goings (and comings) for me. At first I try to touch each cock to check for dress code, but Michael tells me he's watching them so I can just relax.

A lineup of men, each just waiting his turn to fuck me—that was my fantasy. But the reality is better. I mean, each one is like his own short story. The old guy from the hot tub shows up. He starts something but never finishes and I never see him again. I feel one light touch on my thigh and hear a heavy Pakistani accent: "Oh, I came before I even touched her."

I guess he did because I hear all the other guys laugh. Then someone flips me over, enters me and with one hand on my clit, fucks me and makes me come again. One after the other they sort of come and go. Michael too—only after he comes he goes to the bathroom and is nice enough to bring me a glass of water on his way back. Because, you know, I feel like just lying there, still, for a moment. I reach up for the cup, maybe too fast, and my middle finger jams into the porcelain mug, and my nail breaks.

## *Epilogue*

On the way home, after one last dip in the hot tub and some homemade lasagna, Michael and I talk about how we should have been paid to go to that party instead of paying to be there. But this morning I wake up relaxed and think to myself, Gee whiz, I fucked about eight people last night, including a woman, and I had an honest-to-goodness fantasy fulfilled for real. I might not have given any of these guys the time of day in another situation, I sure didn't give anyone my phone number, but each one was part of my *lineup*, just waiting his turn for me. I mean, this is not something that one or two friends can do for you. It takes a whole bunch to form a line, right?

Anyway, I got to go now and get this nail fixed.

*Angela Fairweather*

❧❧❧

# My Dance at Juliana's

*Juliana's was a Tokyo disco where women were admitted free to perform erotic dances onstage. In its heyday as many as 3,000 people watched the amateur dancers. Juliana's closed in September 1994, after three years in business, under pressure from an outraged public.*

When I start dancing a surge of power rushes through my body and I feel high. I love that feeling; I live for nights at Juliana's. I open my feathered fan and undulate to the music, moving my fan real slow—two big flutters above my waist, two below. I pretend not to notice the men staring up at me; I keep my eyes discreetly lowered, at least at first. But I notice who's looking and who isn't, and when I have an audience, I make small gestures to further entice them.

Machiko and I discovered Juliana's about a year ago. "Kaoru," she said, "let's go see what it's like." "Sure," I said, "we can check it out." The first night there we realized this was the place for us—it made us feel alive.

Machiko and I are secretaries in the same office. We hate our jobs, hate the way the men treat us in the traditional way, as if we were foolish, dispensable objects. Sometimes we talk about it over tea, but really, there's no solution. Mostly we find ways to escape.

I wear my skirts skin-tight, what we call "body con," body conscious. At first I didn't; I was afraid to be too provocative and maybe get thrown out of the club, like Hatsuka did when she wore no underwear. But once I caught on, I knew what was okay and what was too much. We've stretched the rules a lot this year and we have much more freedom now. Machiko says I push the limits and should be more careful, but I think we should rebel, let them know that we have feelings and desires that matter too.

Two months ago I bought a bustier. My breasts are full for a Japanese girl, and the bustier emphasizes them even more. I can't believe how much this attracts the men.

I wear sheer bikini panties that often ride up my hips when I dance. Sometimes I pull the front of my panties tight so the men can see more when they stare up at me from the dance floor. I get wet when I see someone staring; it makes me hot to see how much power I have. I'm tempted to put my fingers down there and let them watch, or even get crotchless panties so they can see me better.

When I was seventeen I was voted the prettiest girl in our school in Osaka, where I come from. Also the most sexy. It's an all-girls school and each year the students vote on the cutest, prettiest, smartest, and so forth. They also voted me the most brash—because one warm spring day when we were in English class, I decided to tease our teacher, who was American. I knew he had a crush on me; actually, we all knew it. He was facing the blackboard, so I stood up on my chair real quietly. When he turned around I lifted my skirt over my head. He was only a few feet from me and he had no choice but to look. He got really red and said, "Kaoru, sit down at once." We all laughed.

Japanese men like their women cute and pert, but also sub-missive. At least the traditional men do, but frankly I want nothing to do with tradition. Maybe it's because my name is modern, and they say we're affected by our names just like we're affected by astrology. I don't think my parents know about the incident at school and why I was voted most sexy and brash, but my brother does. He heard about it from Reiko's brother, Takeshi. He wasn't happy about it and told me I'd better watch out, but at least he kept his mouth shut to the rest of our family. Being rebellious gets me in trouble, but I don't intend to change—at least not yet.

When I came to Tokyo I was a typical girl from a respectable family. I was trained as a secretary, and since I did well in my studies it wasn't hard for me to get a good job. I found an apartment that I share with my friend from school, Reiko, who also breaks rules, so I'm in safe company. I don't tell on her and she doesn't tell on me. We go home once a month to visit our families and we keep ourselves subdued at work. We don't want to give our families cause for alarm.

I'm starting to socialize with the men who watch me, and I've let a few of them take me home. Frankly, I was uneasy the first time—actually, a little scared—because you never know if they're just going to be a little pushy, or if they might actually force you. After all, they figure you're fair game if you're flaunting yourself on stage.

But the big worry is the Yakuza. They run the gambling and prostitution rings. They abduct women and force them to work for them, especially the American prostitutes who come here to work because Japanese men think they're exotic. But the Yakuza sometimes blackmail Japanese girls. They frequent the clubs to check us out. I can usually tell them from the guys who are just there to cruise; you learn after a while. Besides, the guys at the door are my friends and they watch out for me.

I'm getting bolder. I love how it feels to mix with the men, all the time pretending to be demure. Now that I've had several lovers, I know what to do and how to act to make them crazy for me.

Let me tell you what it's like to be a secretary in Tokyo. We wear dresses or suits to work, sometimes even slacks, but it's always pretty straight and formal. I wear my hair tied back at the neck and not much makeup, just a little blusher, eyeliner and lipstick.

The men expect me to make tea first thing before they come in and I have to serve them while I bring them their phone and fax messages. All day it's "Kaoru, take a letter," or "Kaoru, I

need you to call Aishi at the brokerage right away, hurry now,"
or "Kaoru, I need 30 copies of this," and it's just before the time
to go home and they know I'll miss my train. They make jokes
all the time, often rude, always sexist, but I pretend not to notice. It isn't lost on them that I'm pretty—maybe even sexy—but
I play it down and act like nothing is on my mind except waiting
on them while I look for a good husband.

Inside I feel all nerves and frustration. I don't know how we
keep ourselves so composed. I guess it's because of how we're
raised. You have to hide your feelings from the time you're
little—that's just how it is. By the weekend all this tension has
built up inside and I feel like I'm going to explode. That's when
I go to Juliana's.

First I take a long bath and then I oil my skin and mousse my
hair so it's all tousled as it hangs over my shoulders and down my
back. I stand naked in front of the mirror and admire myself
while I dress. When I wear the bustier I don't do this, but when
I have on my leopard skin dress, I pinch my nipples several
times to make them stand out and rub against the fabric. Then
I put on my bikini panties and a belt that hangs on my hips, or
I wear my skirt that's so short it almost breaks club rules.
Hiroshi's in charge, though, and he's got this crush on me, so he
never says anything; I make sure to talk with him a few times
each night, and sometimes I brush my body against his so he
feels my breasts through my dress. I make it look like an accident, but he's on to me.

I put on my makeup carefully so I don't look washed out in
the light, and then gold spike heels, a pair of long earrings and
a few bangles on my wrists. Most of the girls who go to Juliana's
change clothes in the bathrooms at the train station because
they're too embarrassed to be seen dressed like that in public. I
think that's silly, but I have to admit I do wear a full coat.

I go to Juliana's with Reiko and Machiko. The stage at
Juliana's is three feet above the dance floor. We dance on the
main floor if it's too early and not many of the women who
dance are there, but soon enough we climb up on the stage because that's where you're bound to get noticed.

When I do go home alone afterward, I tease myself with fantasies. Sometimes I stand in front of the mirror in a demi-bra and bikini panties and act out my part of the fantasy. Other times I lie in bed in the dark and watch the scene as if it was a movie in which I star.

My favorite fantasy takes place at Juliana's. I am on the stage dancing. I am wearing my tightest, most revealing dress with the low top and the short, short skirt. Other women are dancing too, but the men are all looking up at me. Slowly, one by one the other women disappear, until only I remain in the spotlight dancing.

I am not demure, nor do I keep my eyes downcast. Instead, I look directly at each man, my eyes hard, my mouth in a sultry pout, as I move my hips in rhythm with the music. I put my fan down, and sensuously fondle my breasts, accentuating each one, pulling on my nipples. My hands follow the contours of my body down my hips. I let my skirt ride up so it's resting on the tops of my thighs and the edges of my panties show. Then I slowly look from man to man, pulling my panties apart so they can see they're crotchless and I am open to them.

I slip my fingers inside where it's fragrant and wet like a flower at dawn. My other hand plays with my breasts, and I arch my back, my face toward the ceiling, so they can see how good it feels to have my fingers inside, how hot and wet I am. I bring my fingers to my mouth and slowly suck them, all the time staring blatantly at the men's crotches. They are all growing very hard. Good. That is just what I want.

I ease my dress up over my hips and my waist, then pull it over my head. My hair drops back as I dance, my arms are high in the air, my dress is falling to my feet. I look through the audience and see my bosses standing there, their faces all shock and amazement. Then there's the cute guy down the hall from my office, the arrogant one who flirts with us brashly, thinking we must be dying for his attention. And there in the crowd is Hiroshi, Reiko's brother, Takeshi, and oh, even my brother Riota! I wink at Riota and he stares back, shocked. He wants to drag me off the stage but he is frozen in place—and what? Yes! He is very aroused too.

Some of the women, even my friends, are in the audience.

They admire my total control, the flouting of everything we have been taught to be. They are mesmerized. And, too, they are very aroused. Aroused in the way that our genitals tingle when we are repulsed by but also drawn to something truly scandalous. The way I felt when I saw a picture of a beautiful transsexual.

I am heady with power. I say to my audience, "Expose yourselves to me. Show me what you have that I might want." They all comply, unbuckling belts, unzipping flies, pulling up skirts and discarding panties. The men bring themselves out for me to see; they are hard and moist. I study each one carefully. And the women too.

"Come up on stage with me and spread your lips," I say. "I want to see you unfold like roses." The women boldly come onto the stage, encircle me, and open their lips. I pull my breasts out over the fabric of my bra, then kneel down to look at each beautiful pussy, blushing deep, surrounded by a mantle of black silk. I slip my tongue into each woman, one at a time, balancing myself with my hands on each woman's hips. I run my tongue over their clits as they hold themselves open to me, some sighing, some crying out a little as I lick. I bring one of my breasts up and rub it between their aching lips. I slip my fingers deep inside them. The men are going wild, stroking themselves, eyes glued to the spectacle.

After I lick each beautiful pussy, I turn the women around and they play with themselves for the men. They do it not to please the men but to be totally in control, wearing haughty looks on their faces. This makes the men even more crazy. Yes!

I come down from the stage and walk through the audience. I study each of the men, holding their cocks to see how they feel, cupping their balls in one hand and gently scratching my long nails along the inside of their thighs. Even my Hiroshi, Takeshi, and yes, even my brother! I am so bold, even I am shocked . . . well, actually, I'm shocked only to be telling you this fantasy.

I choose one man and I bring him on stage. I have never seen his face before. And he is very big, especially for a Japanese man. He follows me with his hard cock leading his body.

There is a bed now on stage too; the women have brought it

there, and they flank it on both sides. I lead him to one side and he removes his clothes for everyone to see. The women remove my bra and panties, and then they lay me on the bed, spread my legs open, and caress and lick me all over. The man I have chosen and those in the audience ache so badly they can hardly bear it.

The women stroke me and lick me until I am so hot I must have him to ease the throbbing inside. Two women lead him to me, and another two hold my legs open. He enters me hard, thrusting into me again and again until I come very hard and I scream.

Sometimes I allow him to come, other times, not. It is my choice, after all, my pleasure. The women now may have whomever they choose from the audience, men or women, whatever they want. We are the pagan goddesses, the deities of fertility, and they are simply our vassals. The music returns, loud, and I grab my fan and dance naked in the spotlight as everyone applauds and begins to dance again.

You know, there is one more component to all of this, and that is what will happen next—what will happen to our lives. My girlfriends, even Reiko and Machiko, may talk freedom, but what do they really want? A boyfriend who will spend time with them and take them to the beach. In the next five years they expect to marry and settle down and be good wives and mothers.

There is nothing wrong with that; in fact it is a good thing to aspire to. I wish that could be me as well, but I have a deep secret. I have already told you so much that I will confide this to you too, though now I must say I find it hard to look you straight in the eyes; my head is downcast and I feel submissive.

I have a love for women. Yes, I crave having power with men and I sleep with them. But what I really want is a woman. And that is not something a Japanese girl can speak of. In fact, it is even more unspeakable than my fantasies with men, more even than my desire for power and control.

It wasn't always this way. The pillow books of women in the courts of the Samurai tell of how the women provided comfort and erotic pleasure for one another. Of course, it was within the context of men being away at war. Nevertheless, they could touch and love each other, woman to woman, at least part of the time.

I am not sure of what I should do. But I have read that in America it is different, that the women can love each other there. I found a magazine that tells about it, but my English isn't good, especially to read. Machiko reads English better, but I am afraid to speak to her of this as I don't want to risk losing our friendship. Perhaps someday.

In the meantime I will continue to dance. A short dress and gold spike heels, my fan slowly moving, two flutters above the waist, two flutters below.

*Calla Conova*

❧

# Electricity in My Bed

At 5:00 P.M., dressed in the standard brown Pacific Gas & Electric work clothes, she stood in my doorway, responding to my service request. At first I only noticed her short sandy hair, wire-framed glasses and a toolbox in one hand. I had been too involved in moving to even think about sex. But it didn't take long for her to bring me back to my senses.

I watched her make her routine check of pilot lights, her competent fingers lighting matches, tools clattering in her toolbox. I had once been an electrician, so I felt some camaraderie. Or was it something else?

"This isn't right." She pointed threateningly to the water heater vent. "Gonna have to turn it off till it gets corrected."

Shocked at this disruption of my plans, I protested, "I've been moving and cleaning for two days. I was counting on a shower tonight."

Her eyes swept me down and back up again so quickly I might have dismissed it. But then they settled on my breasts, assessing me. I started wishing I was wearing something more revealing, something that would tell her I wasn't wearing a bra, that my breasts were real nice with talented pink nipples that stand out with only a whisper of attention. I'd never had a woman check me out like that. Men, plenty of times. It was familiar, that look, but this was a whole new context.

She retreated coolly down the stairs, looking over her shoulder as she spoke. "All right, take it now before the water cools off. I'm working this area all night. Here's my emergency number." She came back up the stairs and shoved her card at me. "Call if the landlord gets it fixed tonight."

She was almost mean. So why was my crotch so excited? I called the landlord right away.

Was I going to pursue this attraction? I was shaking as I hurried into the bathroom to undress. She dominated my thoughts as I stood beneath the blessedly hot water. Mmm, I *am* beginning to think about sex again. After all these months celibate, and now turned on by a woman! *That's* different.

I shampooed and soaped everything, and then shaved my legs, wondering if lesbians liked legs shaved or au naturel. Well, I liked them smooth. This was my fantasy; I was going to have it any way I wanted. Was she lesbian, bi or like me—attracted for the first time? She seemed strong and in control. I'd always envisioned it that way—someone dominant to tell me how to do it all. But what was I thinking? This was a PG&E service person!

Hot water all used. I relished moving through the fresh paint-scented air completely nude. These thoughts of dangerous possibility would last me for days.

My answering machine showed one message: the landlord coming over in a few minutes. Got to get dressed. I put on some baggy jeans, a sweatshirt and tennis shoes. Forget all this; back to my nonrevealing protection.

After three hours of the landlord's huffing and puffing with the water heater and boring me with stories of his six grandkids, it was fixed. I was alone and getting juicy again, just imagining what might happen if I called her. I did, and while the phone rang I flung off my sweatshirt. I wanted her to know, over the phone, that my nipples were standing at attention. Her radio phone crackled, her voice sounded very distant and professional. My voice was kind of squeaky; I couldn't help it.

"This is the person who has the water heater that you turned off. I'm on 16th Avenue . . . Yeah, right. Landlord fixed it. Could you . . . uh . . . come over now and . . . uh . . . turn it back on?"

I laughed nervously, waiting for some signal in her voice. God, I was getting hot, and about to chicken out. There was silence as she checked her list. Still revealing nothing she said, "I can be there in an hour. Did you get your shower?"

That was all she said. My heart was beating hard, and my face was flushed. I wished she would come stomping up the stairs right now, saying something, even something cold—saying it with a look that would take the doubt away.

I tried clothes on, checking myself out in the mirror. I put on the flowered drop-waist dress. Too coy and feminine. How about the black cleavage-creating bra and sheer white blouse? No. What if she wasn't even interested, or had some other woman? What if I was making this whole thing up? Come on now, you know what you felt. I finally settled on black cotton leggings and a black, oversized button-down shirt, unbuttoned a little more than usual. No bra. I told myself I would be wearing this no matter who was coming to the door. But the truth was, I often stood alone in front of the mirror, wearing this shirt completely unbuttoned, my hands sliding over my body. It was my turn-on shirt.

Half an hour left. Earrings? Lipstick? I decided to just go plain, but to add sandalwood lotion.

In the bathroom again, I yanked down my leggings, no panties. I never needed an excuse to smooth the scented lotion onto my hips, butt, and inner thighs, all the way to my pussy. My pussy: maybe I should give it a little attention before she came, just to get the musk in the air. Fifteen more minutes, there was time. If it turned out to be a false alarm I would at least have had my fantasy bubble before it burst.

Getting the lubricant out of my bedroom dresser, I took it, my vibrator and *her* to bed. *She is right here watching me, then helping me, her commanding hands pulling my clothes off, her intense eyes inspecting and approving of my breasts. I'm naked—she is still dressed in her brown uniform. She authoritatively pushes my legs wider. Then her tongue is flicking and sucking. She is looking up from between my legs and asking if I*

*like her doing it. I beg her for more. I am swooning, thrilled to
have her push me around. My hips buck up for her access, for
her viewing, for her poking fingers and tasting, sucking tongue.
She teases me, "I think you want to come in my face. I can make
you come so hard you'll never want a man again."*

*And I beg her, "Yes . . . God . . . Fuck me . . . Woman-fuck me
. . . oh yeah." Screaming. "Oh yeah . . . I'm . . . shit yeah . . .
coming . . ."*

The doorbell rang. I wiped my hands on the sheets, pulled up
my leggings and half-closed the door on the unmade bed. My
face was burning when I opened the door. "So you got your
shower, eh?" she asked, checking me over, almost sniffing to see
how clean I'd gotten. She was not wearing her glasses or her
jacket. I tried not to be conspicuous as I eyed her small breasts.

Our eyes met again. "Yeah, nice and hot, too." I smiled, stepping aside for her. She brushed my arm as she passed. I followed
her to the water heater. She did her check in silence; I wondered what she was thinking.

"Okay. You've got hot water now. It's according to regula-
tions." She filled out a form in triplicate on a clipboard.

"Is there anything else you want . . . uh, I mean, want to
check?" My heart was racing, my cunt aching, and my tone
slightly desperate; I felt wetness starting to soak the crotch of my
leggings. Did she notice?

"Well, you're the last house on my schedule tonight." She put
down her clipboard. "Do you mind if I wash my hands?" She
moved toward the kitchen sink.

"Sure, but I've got some nicer soap in the bathroom. Smells
like sandalwood."

"Oh, this will do just fine," she said as she picked up the bottle of dish soap.

The fluorescent ceiling light was buzzing. "I hate this light," I
said. "I never turn it on. I only had it on for your work. Are you
done now?" I flipped the switch and the buzzing stopped, leaving a dim light over the stove. She studied me as she dried her
hands on a dish towel.

She seemed to be taking her time so that I wouldn't miss her
drift. "There *are* some other things I'd like to check," she said.

"Care for a soda?" I turned to the refrigerator and began talk-ing rapidly. "How long have you worked this job? Do you enjoy it? Do you always work at night?" She answered in short replies that I didn't even hear.

We had definitely stepped over the line of a PG&E service call. She lifted the bottle to her lips, tipping it up but keeping her gaze on me. Around the third sip her eyes began roving over me again. Yeah, I was right! I leaned on the refrigerator across from her, resting my head back.

"You changed out of your moving clothes. Bet that feels nice." Why didn't I greet her at the door with no clothes on, still wet from my shower? I thought. She jolted me into the next level of intensity by taking two steps toward me, saying, "Yes there is definitely something I need to check. What kind of shirt is this, a girl's shirt, a guy's shirt?" Her clean hand fingered the light fab-ric of my sleeve. Looking down, I saw the gaping spaces be-tween the buttons, my flesh darkly visible.

"It's comfortable. Feels good with nothing under it. What do you wear when you aren't working?"

"Oh, I like jeans and T-shirts. But you look great in this."

We found ourselves staring alternately at each other's lips and breasts. Her nostrils were flared. I looked away, suddenly shy. Her hand smoothed its way up my arm, across my shoulder. Holding my breath, I watched her hand proceed boldly to my breast. She took my nipple between her thumb and index finger, very intentionally pinching and releasing. I exhaled loudly through my mouth. Heat flashed to my crotch.

"You like girls? Yeah, you are cute with your gumdrop nip-ples." My knees almost gave out. "You like girls, don't you? You don't have to answer. Test the merchandise first."

Full mouth, juicy kiss, our tongues very involved with each other. Deep throat moans, her hand cupping my breast. Dizzy, I loved her pressing me against the refrigerator.

Amazingly, my hand went to her crotch first. *I know what to do with this. I know what I like.* She unzipped her pants and I reached in, feeling her as wet as I was. It was so easy to find her clit and finger it in hard circles. Her breath heaved.

"Yeah, you like girls," she said as she gingerly caught my nipple with her teeth. Pulling off the rest of our clothes, we stumbled to the mussed bed, where my vibrator lay on the pillow.

"Ooh la la, girl, I am so glad you got over your shyness," she said, reaching for the white plastic vibrator. " 'Cause you are gonna get girl-fucked the right way your first time. Yeah, I can tell it's your first time. You just relax." She pushed me down and pinned one of my hands to the mattress.

Her turn-on patter was doing its trick. "Let me just slide this toy up inside you. I want to watch you. Just slow. Just a little bit at a time. You want this much?" She looked up to watch my face. "How 'bout this much?" Another inch of plastic. "You want a little more?" I spread my knees wider in answer. The vibrator twisted further inside me, sliding easily with my juices. Succumbing to her excited me more than anything ever had.

Without warning she roughly pulled the slippery toy out of me and pushed my legs together. Shocked and desperate, I tried to grab the thing. She calmly held it out of my reach, placing it to her face and taking in its thick aroma.

"More, please," she had me begging pitifully. I would do anything now. I admired her discipline even as I squirmed.

With the vibrator against her clit, she whispered, "Let me have a few plunges." I watched her expert maneuvers. Her eyes told me to look but don't touch. I watched her fucking herself, her eyes closed. The fingers of one hand attacked her clit, the other hand was grinding the thing inside her. The wet sucking sound drove me wild. She opened her eyes halfway and eased off. "Ah . . . yeah . . . Now what else do I need to check?"

A lusty picture of her going down on me gave me a rush. She caught the picture. "I gotta check this part."

Her fingers combed through my triangle of hair. Her breath and fingers became inspectors. Fingers and shivering tongue went sliding, pressing, flicking, entering, probing. A hum from her mouth full on my vulva transmitted a fine vibration that caused my eyes to roll. I clutched her head, encouraging her, and impulsively nuzzled my face into her aromatic and sweaty crotch.

Finally! The act I had always wondered if I could actually do. I started lapping at this woman like I was in a watermelon eating contest. So sweet and soft. We matched tongue thrusts in a rhythm of deep sucking. She made sure I came first, then she exploded in her own orgasm.

But she wasn't done. Commandingly she rolled me around until we were lying face to face, breasts pressing. Her mouth and chin were smeared wet and loose. My prayers were answered when I felt her fingers purposefully separating my labia. She whispered in my ear, "Here's your dessert," her low voice buzzing. "What a sweet slit you have. Bet I can put something in there you never felt before." Two heavily lubricated fingers screwed into me. My nostrils flared, I nodded, my pelvis opened like a flower in the sun. *Do anything to me. I'm your plaything.* Two more fingers joined the others inside. They stretched me, opened me, fucked me. *Make me shiver and squirm like a puppet on the ramming rod of your expert hand.*

"Can you handle it? You want it all?"

"Yes, yes, fuck yes."

"Okay, your initiation awaits." Thumb folded in. Hand in up to wrist. Everything exploded orange and yellow behind my eyelids. Inside me. *I can't hold on.* My body jerking in contortions. I screamed, fire raging to the top of my head.

Sobbing loudly, I gave up with a shuddering breath. Her hand relaxed and withdrew. She held me, cupping my crotch as my crying subsided. A warm stillness enveloped us and she whispered, "Now you know."

The next day I answer the phone. It's a TV cable company representative. Her voice is healthy, athletic, boyish. She is offering discount installations in my neighborhood. I undo my top shirt button as I give a musky call with my voice.

"Sure, can you come install it today?"

# Susanna J. Herbert

# Breaking and Entering

How I got into his apartment doesn't matter. Curiosity, not necessity, can be the true mother of invention.

Finding myself outside his front door at 3 A.M. surprised me. I had seen him once or twice before, but always at a strict professional distance. I had no knowledge what, if anything, he knew about me.

Opening the door I was struck by a lightning bolt of sanity. What if he's wide awake? What if he's not alone? What if he has a gun?

For once in my life, pure bravado won out over logic. I took a quick gulp of Cuervo 1800 from a sterling flask in my coat pocket and fingered the doorknob. Cold. After all, even L.A. gets chilly in November at 3:02 A.M. The fact that I was wearing nothing underneath my leather coat but seamed stockings, a lace garter belt, and scraps of silk and lace that someone had the imagination to call a brassiere, didn't help raise my temperature.

I didn't mind. Somehow I knew I wouldn't be cold for long.

Miraculously, I got the door open and no security alarms were tripped. I carefully shut it behind me, smiling at my success, considering a potential career as a second-story woman.

The room was dark. Pitch black to be precise. Even after my pupils had acclimated, I could not see an inch in front of me, proof positive that this entire journey was to be fueled on instinct. With a strong sense of direction that came from I-don't-know-where, I walked through the main room. I decided to remove my five-inch heels, lest they make too much noise.

I crept into the bedroom. The blinds were cracked just enough to paint the room in James M. Cain moonlight.

He was sound asleep in the majestic king-sized bed, beautifully deep in sleep. I took a long look at him, courtesy of my accomplice, the moonlight. His body was naked, only partially covered by a pure white goosedown comforter.

Quietly I removed my coat and let it fall to the floor. My heart stopped as he stirred in slumber. Miraculously, he merely turned onto his side. I drank in the line of his back, the drape of his neck, the lush, masculine curve of his ass.

Women are not trained to enjoy the power of voyeurism toward the male body. Forget the childish gyrations of boy-toy dancers; I followed the waves of his breathing, the strong, quiet beauty igniting a heat that began in my cheeks and quickly flowed to my pussy. His cock, half-hard, undulated, and I tried to imagine what dreams were spinning in his head, how they would measure up to what I had in mind.

My hand moved to my nipples; not difficult since they peeked through the tips of my lacy bra. My little pebbles enjoyed the caress. My other hand slowly slid between my legs and my familiar middle finger found its way into my silky, slippery cunt.

Wild! Here I was, standing in a strange man's bedroom, only steps away from his delicious naked body, masturbating like a hot little schoolgirl!

This luscious voyeurism paled in comparison with what happened next. Slowly, sinuously, I crept into his bed, curling spoon fashion behind him, my nipples pressing into his back, my barely covered pussy snug against his ass. As I'd hoped, he moaned contentedly but didn't awaken.

I let a full minute pass, allowing our bodies to touch, allowing the pulse in my pussy to throb. His ass began to tighten almost imperceptibly and I knew this meant he had grown fully hard.

When I'd removed my coat I had taken a wispy silk scarf from the left pocket and placed it beneath the bed: my initial plan had been to bind his hands. But now I knew that wouldn't do. I wanted his hands all over me—and soon.

Besides, I came up with a far better use for the scarf. Gently, quickly—before he grew fully conscious—I wrapped the fragrant pastel silk around his eyes. In sleep he smiled, enjoying the fabric's caress. His eyes were fully covered.

My hands reached around his chest and gently pinched his ripe nipple. Still more asleep than awake, he reached for my hand to pull it to his throbbing cock.

No. Without saying a word I made it clear we were not going to rush. He seemed content to enjoy the waking dream while I explored his body. His shoulders were firm, his arms muscular. The hollow in his ass cheek—now wet from my pussy—was made to be kneaded, needed and enjoyed. When I moved my finger to his face, he took my hand and licked the inner palm, his tongue darting between my fingers as though licking hot cunt. I fed him my pussy-covered fingers and he sucked hungrily, his ass gyrating against my cunt.

Finally I reached for his cock.

Oh, his cock! Gloriously thick, sensuously full, every vein pulsing against my touch. His balls were magnificent; full and lush and fluid. Wetting my palms I pulled and stretched and scratched the skin, letting his guttural moans conduct my movements.

When he reached his arm around me and thrust his finger into my quivering cunt, I knew he could no longer distinguish what was reality and what was a dream. Still unable to see, he turned his body so we were face-to-face, lying on our sides. Our arms clutched each other and we fell into a kiss or series of kisses that were soft and wet and searching and hot. My hand was squeezing, rubbing his turgid cock; he was wildly fingering my lips and cunt as the kiss went on and on and on. Lips and tongues and teeth created their own language. I could feel drops of cum, hot cum, from the tip of his cock.

I moved him slightly and he turned onto his back. I straddled his legs and leaned forward. His hands traveled across my bra. He seemed surprised—and pleased—when he realized my nipples could be had without removing the seductive lace surrounding them. He licked and sucked their sweetness, moaning. "Cherry hot nipples. Sweet baby titties." I wanted to douse them in rum, dip them in sparkling champagne, dot whipped chocolate cream on the very tips to surprise and assault his taste buds. He was wild, out of control, his every movement telling me I was the hottest fuck in the world.

There was no stopping our accelerating pace. He let loose a moan as I pulled my breasts away from his hungry mouth, but before he could move I buried his cock deep into my hot pussy. We shook and rocked and I rode his cock like a wild woman. My sweet swollen clit, my baby-girl dick, met the base of his cock with every stroke. One of us was gasping, maybe both of us. The equation floated back and forth, hour after hour, as pussy met cock met lips met balls met finger met ass met tongue and back again.

The window let a sliver of daylight into the darkness. I had to go. We had both been dozing. Quickly I got up, threw on my clothes, and left the room. He moaned "come back" in semisleep, but I ran out, got in my car, and drove away.

Back home I had a moment to reflect on all that had occurred before I fell into a deep sleep. Too deep. Reliving everything in my dreams, I overslept, and had to rush to prepare for a business meeting that logic kept telling me to cancel. If I had listened to logic, though, the previous night would never have occurred. So I kept my appointment, foregoing my pink-and-black-checked Chanel suit for coral pants in a cool linen and matching turtleneck.

I arrived, miraculously enough, a few minutes early. I entered the building and looked around for the suite I needed. No one to ask; I was the only one in the lobby.

At that moment a man emerged from the elevator. I'd ask him. We made eye contact and—oh my God!—I felt my cheeks instantly burn. "You're . . ." I said, half-saying, half-asking his name. "Yes," he replied. "You must be Linda."

I nodded, the absolute professional. He extended his arm. "My office is this way."

I followed him, smiling slyly, wanting to burst out laughing. I'd no idea *he* was the man I'd had an appointment with. I loved the fact that I had a secret on him. And *what* a secret!

We sat in his office and reintroduced ourselves. He was impressed with my résumé, my designs, my ideas about how the project should go. We talked and talked and talked, finally ending the meeting knowing we wanted to work together. I rose to leave. I held out my hand in a gesture of farewell. He pulled his hand from his pocket and squeezed something into my palm.

My silk scarf.

"I believe you left this at my house," he said. I smiled. So did he.

"Thank you," I said. I turned to leave. His voice stopped me.

"I'd like you to begin tomorrow," he said.

My reply was swift and assured. "I'd like *you* to start tonight."

*Eve Mariposa*

# Back to the Future with a Vibrator

It's time for another family visit to the suburbs.

From the moment I step off the plane, despite the fact that I came equipped in my uniform of individuation—combat boots, defiantly deteriorated jeans, and as much black as I can manage to cram into one outfit (Mom prefers me in pastels)—I always seem to get swept up in the tide of daughterly duties and expectations. I am everyone's "little girl" who looks "so sweet"—at least from the left side of my face, where you can't see the nose ring.

Mom and Dad are both here to pick me up this time, divorce and all. Mom has the metallic helium "Welcome Home" balloon which I am years beyond being embarrassed about, and Dad is beaming from ear to ear. A strange ritual has evolved around my visits. My parents, who otherwise have little to do with each other, come together in their long-rehearsed role as the ubiquitous, indestructible "Parents"—so that everything can be "like it used to be." Throughout my stay we all play the big happy family game and pretend that nothing has changed. Dad comes to the house, Mom cooks dinner, both sets of in-laws come over, and at the end of the night Dad quietly slips out of the house while Mom and I pretend not to notice.

I like to think of my entire visit as an exercise in make-believe.

I am not really the struggling-to-be-a-poet Generation X funk/ folk neophyte who lives in San Francisco, but rather a prepubescent girl with a Farrah Fawcett haircut and braces who wears whatever she's told and smiles even when she's feeling lousy. I refer to my oversized pink suitcase—a bad choice made in seventh grade—as the time travel machine that links the Rachel of yesteryear to the tall, unpredictable woman with attitude who invades her room a few times a year.

The relatives are waiting for me as we lug my excess of luggage into the hallway. As I wrestle the backpack off my shoulders, Grandpa Hymie pulls me aside and gives me a resounding slap on the rump. "What's the story with this *tuchas*?"

"It doesn't tell stories, Grandpa."

"I mean how'd it get so big?"

"Yes, I know what you mean," I say, and I go to the kitchen to get a drink.

When I return to the living room with a Diet Coke and a piece of pita bread, Grandma Lilly crowds me into a corner of the couch and presses a finger into my chest. "Do you have any boyfriends, Rachel?" As if they come in sets.

"No, Grandma, not currently." They wouldn't approve of my live-in situation—not to mention the convulsions of horror I'd have to endure if they ever discovered that he's not Jewish. I've learned to keep my love life to myself.

"You know why the boys don't like you? Because you're so skinny. You don't have enough curves. Boys like curves." She raises her eyebrows in the direction of my breasts, apparently indicating that they will grow if I eat more.

"I don't date boys, Grandma. I'm twenty-five years old—I prefer men. And who said the boys don't like me?" I give her a devilish wink, and she frets off to the kitchen with pursed lips.

After dinner I clear the table and wipe the place mats while Mom does the dishes and Grandma Shirley wanders around the kitchen trying to remember what she came here to do, asking me again and again what my name is and where I live. I answer her questions while Mom sighs heavily from the sink. Mom's hair is in her eyes, and she looks smaller than I remember.

As the sun lowers over the deck the grandparents decide they are tired and ready to drive home. I kiss everyone good-bye, get some money stuffed into my pockets (along with another re-sounding slap on my oversized *tuchas*), and we stand at the door waving as the cars pull away. Dad turns on the game and I run up to the bathroom where I sit for about fifteen minutes, staring out the window, answering "Yes" every time Mom yells up to see if I'm okay.

When Dad has gone "home" to the apartment we never men-tion, Mom takes off her makeup and I feign exhaustion and shut myself in the pink room that has been preserved as a shrine to my adolescence. It immediately envelops me with its cutesy cross-stitched proverbs pockmarking the walls, the mirrored "Rachel," which I'm beginning to find redundant, and my once-prized Bat Mitzvah gift—a satin cloud with my name hand-painted in rainbow colors dangling its silver gauze over my twin bed.

The bed's headboard, pink and white with large wooden knobs on either end, is a significant landmark in my brief history of re-bellion. As the story goes, one night I got angry at my parents for letting my brother sleep with them but not letting me, so I chewed on the knobs of the headboard in protest. To this day the knobs remain chipped and scarred, and I smile remembering the gutsy girl who dared misbehave in this suffocating pink room.

I spend a few minutes examining the plants that Mom has been watering in my absence for six years. As always, they are drooping, but alive. I pull off all the dead leaves and water them. Then I browse through the bookshelf that holds an unusual con-glomeration of childhood books crammed in alongside college texts; *Shahat the Egyptian* is bedside mates with *Ramona the Brave*. Squished in next to a stack of Cliffs Notes on *Moby Dick*, *Ulysses*, and other such memorable works, I uncover an old diary.

I used to sneak this particular diary into the bathroom to write, leaning the book against the tub while kneeling solemnly on the floor mat and recording my secrets. Now I reread with fascination my epic high school tragi-comedy of failed romance. Was it really this complicated and painful? Interspersed are some elementary rhymed poems about tragedy and loss, two subjects of which I knew close to nothing. Then I come across the following entry addressed to no one in particular:

> I want to tangle flowers in your hair and lead you to the
> river. I want to ambush you with kisses and move through
> you like trains. I would like to singe your mind with
> the hunger of your hands, get you sloshed in my vodka
> poetry. I would like to part your lips over my breasts' enduring
> pink. Send you reeling like the seagulls. I would have you
> jellied and raw, the sting pulsing through me the way
> your guitar travels the floorboards and suffuses my feet
> with wanting. I would flute you through my silver wand
> and drink the last kiss of breath from your mouth.

Eat your heart out, Grandma Lilly.

This entry, which could have been referring to any number of passing crushes, looks like it's speaking to the guitar player in the band I sang with during senior year. I loved the way he bent seriously over his guitar, and I also remember liking his bushy hair. His name was Dave and he was very quiet. I deciphered his silences as mysterious. I would invent scenarios in which I would catch him completely off guard and seduce him, thereby revealing his true passion. I imagined that secrets lurked beneath the serene blue of his absent eyes that never seemed to really focus on me. But after months of fruitless advances, I realized that Dave was not dying to be probed or discovered, and that in all probability he was not only uninterested but just plain boring.

Then there was Alec. And Jonathan. And Paul. All recorded faithfully down to the last detail: the small space between Paul's front teeth and his enormous high-top sneakers that were never laced, the red number 12 that was peeling off Jonathan's football jersey, the fact that Alec used to cut eighth period to watch *The Addams Family* in his friend's basement. All of these were invented romances that amounted to at most a few kisses, a ridiculous grope or two, many unreturned phone calls, and endless nights in the bathroom recording the minute details of each interaction.

Rereading the teenage Rachel, I am very sad. So many eloquently voiced urgent desires thwarted and frustrated by the limitations of the clique infrastructure at school, ignorance of my body, and an unwillingness to deviate from the "good girl" persona. Closing the diary, I find I am walking the delicate tightrope between Rachel of past and present. Tingling with all the missed opportunities, all the conquests I did not conquer, all the unnamed stirrings that kept me awake on winter nights, I realize that I am wildly horny.

I rummage through my suitcase and come up with a long narrow felt bag with a drawstring at the top that accompanies me on every trip home. I stick my head out the door of my room. Mom's lights are out. I turn out the lights, extract my vibrator from its bag, and plug it in.

Using a vibrator in my childhood room is one of my most cherished activities. I imagine the sensation is akin to what race car drivers feel when they race—maneuvering a tiny, confining vehicle around some tricky turns and then taking off at a million miles an hour. It is at once irreverent, wild, ridiculous, and intoxicatingly dangerous. After all, Mom is just around the corner. The truth might get out that I'm a sexual human being, and then our family's little world of make-believe would spontaneously combust, leaving me a regular ol' adult and everyone else at a complete loss.

As I switch the vibrator on and position it in its well-worn spot just below my clitoris, my head fills with the smell of a damp football jacket. I am nuzzling soft stray hairs curling behind pink fleshy ears. Must be Jonathan. I think I still have that jacket in the basement closet. That's what he gets for dumping me: I keep the goods. They collect mold in the basement.

I run my hands over my body. I am slightly damp with exertion, buried under three blankets to mute the sound of the vibrator. Jonathan is pressing me up against the rough brick wall behind my high school. My sweater is unbuttoned but I don't notice the cold, though I can see my breath fogging the air. Girls are coming out of the locker room, ponytails bobbing and field hockey sticks in hand. We are in an alcove hidden behind a brick partition. The girls don't notice us.

I am panting. Jonathan is whispering something urgent in my ear, his forehead lowered to my shoulder, which he bites with the same urgency. His hand is pressed hard against my jeans between my legs. His face is thinner and sadder in my reinvention than it probably was. And I give him a little more scruff for this go-round. Scruff turns me on, though I couldn't have known it at the time.

Jonathan has just triumphed over the button to my jeans when, against all odds, Sebastian—the French guy I met in Radio Shack one summer when he was trying to sell my mom a set of speakers—walks out the doors we are leaning against. Jonathan does not appear surprised or concerned, and I certainly don't complain when Sebastian reaches into my unbuttoned sweater and firmly grasps a warm breast with his chapped hand, sending chills up my spine. My breasts are always larger in my fantasies than in real life—they aren't big enough to really be mobile, and I like to fantasize the jiggling that real life doesn't make possible. So Sebastian hefts my enormous lobe of breast in his hand, squeezes the nipple into a solid tip, then fills his mouth with me.

Meanwhile, Jonathan has worked his hand down the narrow passageway between jeans and skin into the steamy crevice of my cotton flowered underpants. He has my legs spread open against the wall and is trying to shimmy the jeans down my thighs for a better range of motion between my legs. Unfortunately, these are the days of skin-tight jeans, and Jonathan is hardly graceful, muttering "Fucking shit!" under his breath, and with a tremendous effort yanking both my jeans and me to the ground.

Sebastian goes with the flow, following us to the ground where he lifts the hair from my neck and breathes his milky breath over the goose bumps on my shoulders. I straddle Sebastian, take him by the throat and fill his ear with my tongue, working the dainty lobe with my lips and teeth. My ass is to Jonathan, who places his pointer finger just inside my underpants and traces the indentation of the elastic all the way around my thigh. I gasp as his finger glances over the lips of my pussy and then pinches my clitoris with unexpected force. I fasten Sebastian's hands on my breasts from behind and climb onto Jonathan. His erect cock springs up from behind the zipper as I lower it. My eyes water with nostalgia at the familiar aroma of Zest soap and clean sheets as I surround the tender flesh of his cock with my mouth. He smells like a fresh, well-groomed little boy, and I am going to suck the cum out of him.

I have all but forgotten about Sebastian when I feel my gloriously weighty breasts scraping the pavement. It feels like scruff but even better. Rougher. Sebastian is pressing me to the ground, still with Jonathan's cock in my mouth. He spreads the lips of my labia open to the wind. Then he does nothing—just holds me open and exposed. I wait. Jonathan waits. I notice I am trembling more in anticipation than from the cold. He is doing this exactly as I like it to be done—I have remade him with a profound knowledge of all my preferences. Ah, the advantages of fantasy.

When my lungs are thick with suspense and I can hardly breathe, Sebastian slowly slips inside. He's got on that ever-ready spare tire condom that melts in a teenage boy's wallet for a year or two and is perfectly useless by the time it's called into action. I am so thrilled to have my mouth and pussy full at the same time that I don't object. The three of us merge into a seasick swamp of motion. My hair is sticking to my face, my clothes lie in a rank pile on the cold cement, and I am screaming like I never screamed at those mandatory pep rallies for the goddamn football team. I am screaming because I am getting laid bigtime. They are biting and scratching me. I am thrashing and pumping and grasping and yanking somebody's hair.

We all come at the same time—another luxury of the world of make-believe. Jonathan shoots his sweet cum into my mouth and I swallow hungrily while rocking back onto Sebastian in heaving tides of loose silk. Sebastian is holding onto my breasts with gusto, moaning his final thrusts into my ear.

I get up matter-of-factly and gather up my rumpled clothes. Sebastian and Jonathan are flushed and sweaty, and neither will look me straight in the eye. "Go home and do your homework," I tell them. They duck their heads sheepishly, dig their hands deep into their pockets, and kick small pieces of gravel across the pavement as they saunter off in different directions.

As I return my vibrator to its carrying case my eye catches the chewed knobs of my headboard. I smile deviously. "Good night, Mom," I whisper.

## Jane Handel

❧

# In Flagrante Delicto

We sat around a table sipping cocktails in the late afternoon, chatting casually about everything and nothing, waiting for the waiter to return and take our food orders. During a momentary lull in the conversation, my friend Gloria turned to the woman on her left, a new acquaintance, and asked, "Do you have a sexual preference?"

The eyes of each of us quickly focused on the beautiful young woman to whom the question had been addressed, and it almost seemed as though we held our breath collectively in anticipation of her answer. We didn't have to wait long; after the briefest of pauses she replied with a firm, unequivocal "No."

"Good," said Gloria, in her inimitably straightforward manner. "We must seize desire where we find it."

Following this rather show-stopping bit of dialogue, our conversation proceeded along a more general path, but a provocative door had been opened. And when, several times throughout the course of the meal, the eyes of the woman who had answered no met mine, I felt they did so with a new implication. Of course, this could very well have been wishful thinking on my part and it's a moot point in any case since I did not see her again.

o   o   o

But I remember the incident now while lying on a sun-drenched hill in the Napa countryside—reveling in the sultry heat of summer and enjoying a much-needed respite from the stress of urban living. My body, naked and still moist from its shower, is gently dried by a breeze as I massage lotion onto its parched surface. A hawk circles overhead searching for a field mouse or a rabbit, and I wonder if it might also be voyeuristically eyeing me and my nakedness. But no, it suddenly swoops down with lightning quickness and then flies off into the distance with a snake dangling from its beak. Nearby, a lizard is doing push-ups. It reminds me of the ones I used to catch as a child, keeping them in coffee cans and pretending they were pets. Inevitably, they made a dash for freedom in the middle of the night, and the next morning I would be desolate when I discovered the empty can. As I raise my hand to massage another dollop of lotion onto my belly, this one stops his calisthenics, eyes me warily and then scurries under a bush, thus bringing my fantasy of voyeurism to an abrupt end.

To a city dweller this California hilltop undoubtedly seems serene and still, devoid as it is of technology's pervasive hum. It seems that way to me, but as I listen and look more closely, I become aware that it is, in fact, alive with noise and activity: yellow jackets, horseflies and crickets buzz; birds chatter; leaves and grass rustle in the wind; children's voices ring out from the valley far below. I become acutely aware not only of this continuous symphony of sound, but of a drama being acted out all around me, the main character being the light that shifts constantly as the sun journeys overhead; the clouds that change shape and move from here to there; the dust devil in the distance swirling aimlessly and then vanishing mysteriously. In this landscape of flux the only mute and static element is myself—the observer. But no, I too am contributing to this lively interchange: with each intake of breath my chest rises slightly, then collapses as I exhale. And if someone were to press an ear to my heart they would surely hear its beat.

But there is no one to press an ear, no one to observe the rise and fall of my chest. Even the lizard and the hawk have long since moved on.

Another breeze comes up and I catch a whiff of lavender and rosemary and again hear Gloria's voice in my ear. Feeling as though I am being seduced by the insistent caresses of the sun and the wind, languorously and subtly my body begins to awaken. Alone on this oak-studded hilltop, my lovers are the four elements, the four directions, the flora and fauna. Myself. I revel in the purity and simplicity of this moment as my hand joins the wind and the sun and I seize desire where I am finding it.

My hand reaches between my legs and probes the wet, dark place it finds there. As I lick the sticky, pungent wetness from my fingers, my back arches and my breath quickens. With tender precision I press and massage the tiny pink clitoris in a rhythmic, circular motion. I am suddenly oblivious to my surroundings—to the fact that I am naked and exposed and that the gardener may drop by to water the newly planted squash and tomato plants, or a hiker might mistake the driveway for a trail. I am simply immersed in the ruthless, single-minded activity of bringing myself to orgasm. At first it seems elusive and I shift my hips slightly, raising them so that the pressure is at a different angle. My fingers move faster and more insistently until the miraculous explosion occurs and I cry out in spite of myself. When the convulsions subside, I lie still for a moment, catching my breath. Then I quickly look around and am relieved to find that no intruders have witnessed my moment of abandon.

The sun begins to sink below the horizon and another breeze comes up but this time there is a slight chill to it, so I gather up my towel and lotion and wander down to the house. Inside, I put on a tape of John Coltrane's ballads, fix myself a margarita and sit on the couch, wrapped in the towel, watching the last bit of orange and pink light fade. I feel content and relaxed.

But my reverie is soon interrupted by the intrusive ring of the telephone. At first I debate whether or not to answer. After a few more irritating rings I do.

"Hi," says a familiar male voice. "How are you?"

A conflicting wave of anxiety and happiness collide inside me when I hear this voice, but I try to answer in my most confident and relaxed manner. "I'm wonderful. How are you?"

He tells me about his work, we chat about a mutual friend. I avoid any potentially volatile topics. Over the past few months our relationship has taken a turn for the worse, and the foundation is now strewn with hair-trigger time bombs. The slightest jostle could set one off and blow me to smithereens.

"I miss you," he says, and I detect a slight tremor in his voice.

"I miss you, too—in fact, I was just thinking about you." I continue to try to affect casualness in my tone, a bravado I don't feel.

"Oh?" he says with a nervous laugh. "Nothing bad, I hope."

"Quite the contrary. I am sitting here watching the sunset, listening to Coltrane, and thinking about how much I desire you. Sometimes the desire I feel for you is so overwhelming it scares me and I become paranoid about scaring you with its intensity . . . overwhelming you with my overwhelming desire."

I pause for a moment but there is only silence on the other end. Chances are he is feeling equally awkward and self-conscious, maybe even more so, but consumed as I am with my own anxiety, this never occurs to me. So I try to fill in the void with a stilted monologue, attempting rather foolishly to explain the inexplicable: irrational, primal lust.

"Sometimes, I feel such a rush of desire, emotion and terror all mixed up together that I panic. I'm afraid you'll be repulsed by its excessiveness. When I was a child, I learned by necessity to be stoic; I come from very stiff-upper-lip British stock, you know."

I chuckle at my own joke, but again, the silence on the other end is almost deafening. "Are you still there?" I query, starting to feel a bit annoyed.

"Yeah, I'm here," he answers tersely. I think I detect a subtle change in his breathing but I am not sure. Wondering to myself why I am doing all the work in what is becoming an increasingly one-sided dialogue, nevertheless I plunge fearlessly ahead.

"Well, anyway, as I was saying, at an early age I learned to tone down my ardor—god forbid anyone should find me undignified. Little girls are to be seen—preferably with their legs crossed at their ankles and their hands folded demurely in their laps—and not heard. That's why I've never revealed to you just how much I long to caress every part of you, to lick and penetrate every orifice, to merge all of me with all of you . . . but that's what . . ."

Suddenly I'm out of breath and my voice falters. I'm feeling too agitated to continue—in fact, if I weren't still wrapped in a towel, I'd be sitting in a pool of liquid that would undoubtedly leave an embarrassing stain on my friend's white sofa. Once again, I wait for him to say something to relieve the tension. It is quiet for what seems like an eternity. Then, in a voice barely audible, he asks, "Can I come see you?"

Slowly exhaling, I skip a beat before responding with a perfunctory, "Please do."

An hour has passed and his mouth now has me in its thrall, could probably keep me mesmerized indefinitely: the shape of the lips, delicate yet full, elegant and succulent like a tropical fruit begging to be eaten. With the tip of my tongue I trace the edges, memorizing the shape, probing under the lips inside the moist, warm cavity, feeling the smooth, even teeth; tasting his saliva, inhaling his breath into my lungs, sucking and licking, delirious with sensuous pleasure. I continue the journey with my tongue, exploring the crevices of his throat, his clavicle, marveling at the silky texture of his skin as he lies beneath me, passive and subdued yet alert and watchful. Every so often a groan resonates from the deep cavity of his chest and his eyes roll back in his head. I too am watchful, measuring his response, attuned to the intake and exhalation of breath, the rapidity of pulse beating faster and faster. My tongue and mouth probe every orifice, travel to all the nether regions, again memorizing all the details. I am hungry for this memory as if I am about to go to the electric chair and this is my last supper. I am anxious to carry this memory to my grave, to eternity.

For a moment, I revel in the grandiose notion that I am in command of my own destiny and maybe even his. But it doesn't take long for this reverie to be turned inside out, for him to grow tired of the passive role. In one quick motion he roughly throws me off him and onto my back, pinning my arms behind my head and pushing his groin hard into mine. I gasp for air. His body covering mine, his mouth to my ear, his deep, resonant voice murmurs, "Submit to me."

"Submit to me," the voice repeats with grave insistence, and the man who is making this demand presses his groin even more roughly against my pubic bone.

"Yes," I whisper. "Yes, I will submit to you. Completely."

"But you don't even know what I want yet," he says, his temple pressed hard against mine, his groin continuing its relentless grinding, rubbing raw the skin of my pubis.

"That is true submission," I say with calm assurance. "If I say I will do anything you want without knowing yet what it is."

His breathing intensifies; my unquestioning acquiescence clearly excites him.

"Yes, it is," he groans, biting my earlobe so hard I gasp at the pain. "You're right. Not to know but . . ." I can no longer make out his words. He yanks my arms harder behind me and continues in a voice I can now decipher. "While you were talking to me on the phone I was masturbating."

This is the most arousing and provocative thing anyone has ever said to me. I suddenly feel faint.

"Whatever you want I will do it," I say again. And as I speak these fateful words, a shiver of fear runs up my spine. I don't know why I reveal my desire to be dominated by this man, nor do I understand it, but somehow I instinctively know it is time to give myself up. I have been waiting for this moment for what seems like a lifetime.

# Serena Moloch

❦

# Behind the Mask

## I. Maid and Mistress

Sometimes it begins like this.

I follow my mistress as she makes her way through a crowded train station. I carry her bags for her. Her bags are very heavy, so heavy they dig into my hand, and later, when I look at it, there will be a rough red mark where the bag bit my hand with its toothless mouth. My mistress is dressed in a pale travel costume, the latest style with billows and ruffles that come right down to her heels, and she is clean, so clean that I can track her even in this mass of people simply by following in the wake of her stupendous shining cleanliness. Her hair glows with it, her skin gleams with it, her clothes remark loudly on the absence of any disfiguring spot.

I, on the other hand, am dirty, so dirty that even in this filthy crowd I can feel people turning to stare at me. I am remarked upon. Perhaps, I imagine, someone will mistake me for a spittoon or a rubbish tip and absentmindedly make me the receptacle for some choice piece of garbage. I feel the impulse to protest: it's not my fault, it's my duty that coats me in dirt. The servant's life: up at 5:30 to clean the grates and fill the coal scuttles, out on the steps at 7:00, bucket and soap and brush in hand, to wash the house clean, to kneel on their marble and try not to imagine how everyone who passes can look at my legs, will look up my skirts, insult me in language as foul as the chamber pots it is my duty to clean at 9:00.

Nine o'clock, when I must attend on my waking mistress. I bring up her breakfast tray, I sniff the aromatic chocolate steaming in the dainty, oh so dainty china cup, as thin as her calla-lily neck and just as easy to snap if one doesn't take the proper care. I carry the hot rolls and the linen napkins; gingerly, I bring her the chamber pot and watch her piss and shit into it and then I prepare to wash her clean. First she tosses off her sheets and grabs her chocolate, sucks it greedily down—there are times I've seen when I can tell you, she's no lady—and then she points at the tub. She isn't ready to speak, yet. I trudge up and down and up then down again to get enough hot water to satisfy her and then she undoes her night frock and I know my duty, I pick her up (like a stack of pillows, she's so light) and lower her gently into the tub, so gently she'd never suspect how easily I could crack her head against its edge.

Then I get to work, I know my task: with a bar of the best French soap I begin to clean every bit of her body, sliding the soap under her armpits, down along her back, by the sides of her neck, in between each one of her toes, skimming along her downy calves, up to her heavy breasts where I take special care, sliding the soap round and round, down to her belly, rubbing it up into a fine lather, until she shows how impatient she is with me by arching her back and thrusting her cunt toward my face. Because even she has a cunt, my mistress, though certainly it's pinker and pearlier than mine or any other one I've seen, and quite, quite clean, thanks to my daily labors.

So I begin, soaping her fleecy hair, rubbing my fingers between her lips, pulling up the hood of her little knob to clean beneath that, prodding her opening with the soap, cleaning her little brown hole until I feel it open beneath my fingers so that I can reach in and clean deep, deep inside. And if I dared to look up to her face I know I'd see her eyes hooded with mean enjoyment of the pleasure she feels when I kneel outside the tub and my hands swarm all over her and my fingers probe inside her and she wallows in the sweet hot water. And when the pleasure gets too strong and I feel the heat in her asshole penetrating to my finger's very bones and the skin around her pearly little cunt goes taut and tense, I hear the voice that always comes: "What's the matter with you, you sluttish thing? Don't you know your work? Get this soap off me, now."

I do know my work. I lower my head and begin to lick her soapy cunt, lapping up the lather with my tongue, which is as strong and muscular as the rest of me, dipping my head into the water to spit out the soap and fill my mouth with fresh hot water so I can pour it out of my mouth and over her mound. My finger is still up her ass, I push her buttocks up so I can lick her cleaner and cleaner, and as I clean she thrusts herself toward me so that her lips smack into my teeth, oh, I've come to learn she likes it a bit rough, so I rasp my tongue harshly across her until she convulses, smothering the sides of my face with her greedy thighs, then pulls away from my fingers and my face so she can loll back in her bath and throw her washcloth at my still-bowed head so as to let me know that she wants me to fetch the towels and dry her off.

What I wish for more than anything during my mistress's bath is to take my hand, my soapy hand with the dirt well worked in under the nails, and ram it up her foaming cunt, my whole hand right up her, clean up to the top of her head, show her what a real going-over is, not these pretty little games with soap and water and scented oils, but she knows better than to give me a taste of her insides. The one time I tried to put my fingers in her cunt instead of her bum she slapped my hand hard and said, "Filthy thing. You know your hands are too dirty to go in there—and anyway, that's for master, not for you. I'm afraid we'll have to have words about this later."

Words from her always mean one thing, of course—me, kneeling on all fours with my face touching the floor and my hands tied together in front of me, my skirts lifted up and my knickers pulled down, being whipped by my mistress's pretty lash or hairbrush, or worse, one of master's belts, all to remind me of my place. Then I'm forced to gawk at my red and welted bum in the mirror behind me while I tell her how sincerely I repent of my sinful, soilful ways.

But I do know my place and when I've finished dutifully cleaning my mistress with my tongue I wrap her in clean white towels and help her to dress. And on days like today, when she is about to make a voyage, I pack her clothes and toilet things and I scurry around trying to finish my household tasks—washing, dusting, scrubbing and oiling—so that I might at least snatch time to do up my hair and wash off my arms before I accompany her through the streets to the station. It's a race we run, she and I. I know she wants me to look as filthy as possible as I follow her through the streets, so that people will remark on us, my shameful grime lagging behind her haughty self, and it's a race she always wins.

And so here we are, as we began, in Victoria Station, waiting for the train to accept passengers. I stand by her luggage, my hands clasped before me and my head bowed low, while my mistress scornfully looks over the crowd and then prods the ground with the tip of her umbrella. I quiver and turn hot and cold when I feel people stop near me and whisper to each other. I can imagine the spectacle I must make for them, standing in the middle of the station, my face and hands streaked with coal marks and dust, greasy strands of hair flying about, my dress hopelessly soiled, my shoes caked in dirt, and as I imagine their eyes, some skimming over me and turning away in disgust, others staring in fascination at my impossible dirtiness, I hear my mistress hiss, "You hopeless wench! Look, look, *look* at that!"

I keep my head down but turn in the direction to which her umbrella points, at her feet, her boots, made of the finest kid leather with pointed toes and a high heel sharpened almost to a stiletto point. And what she points at are little specks of dirt, splattered on no doubt as we walked through the streets, but the umbrella points accusingly first at her feet, then toward me, as if to say—which she soon does—"Is this how you work for me?"

I know what comes next. I pick up my mistress's bags and follow her to the place we've always used in this situation, a retired part of the station where there is just enough danger of being seen and just enough certainty that we won't be. I gently place

her bag on the floor and admire her endless spirit, the nobility
and panache with which she pulls a handkerchief from inside
her sleeve and drops it so that it flutters to the floor beside me.
She lifts her skirts just above her ankles and says to me, "On
your knees, and be quick about it. I want these shoes spotlessly
clean before I board my train."

And so I kneel, and as I've always done, I pick the handkerchief up from the floor with my teeth and bring my head down
so that I can move the cloth about her shoe with my mouth. But
there is so little, little time that very quickly I let the cloth drop
and simply go to work with my tongue, taking all the little spots
off and working the soft leather into a respectable shine with my
spit, all the time wondering how soon someone might come
along and find us at our shameful game, so I work even faster,
grabbing my mistress's leg just above the heel so that I can lick
the bottom of her boots clean, as both she and I love, feeling the
bits of grit work down my throat, and then the moment of supreme bliss for us both as I suck her heel into my mouth and
gently, so gently, she slides it in and out of my slippery hungry
mouth, and as I think of how useful and obedient I am, how I
would do anything for my mistress, even take her dirty boot
proudly into my mouth, I feel my cunt contracting, its slimy
juices squirting out of me as I come and come and come, so
hard I don't even notice how brusquely my mistress's foot has
been jerked from my mouth.

Then I hear the voice. It's what we've always dreaded—the
educated and indignant voice of a young man come to interrupt
our seedy pleasures with his outrage and his testimonials. A
poorer man we could bribe, an older rich man would be
charmed and in any case hardly shocked, old rich men being
what they are, a woman would merely scurry away—or stay to
join us. But this man, I can see, will not be nearly as simple to
handle, as I stand up and smooth down my dress. His sandy
mustache is quivering with conceited pleasure at having someone to save, and that someone is me.

"What do you mean, my good woman, performing such an
abominable act in the middle of Victoria Station?"

"My dear sir, I would hardly call this the middle of the station and any act I may be performing is certainly no concern of yours."

"I should think it is," he said. "I'm an active member of the Domestic Reform League and this past month we've been particularly concerned with the abuse of servants. Why, I've been on the committee that's been drafting a bill to present to Parliament on this very question. And I won't stand by and see this poor woman abused without interceding." He turned to me. "Can I help you, my dear?"

Before I could answer, my mistress laughed and said, "I would love to draw you out more on the subject of servant abuse, but I really must run to catch my train. Do stay here with Hannah and rescue her, by all means, if you see fit. I wish you all the best in the endeavor. Good-bye, Hannah dear." And with that, she leaned over, kissed me full on the mouth, picked up her heavy bags and teetered away unsteadily. I wiped my mouth and turned to my sputtering savior.

"It's unspeakable," he said. "Unthinkable. Never have I seen such a thing. Most of our young women's troubles are with the masters of the house, not the mistresses. But such, such . . . perversity is simply unheard-of. My dear young woman," he said to me forcefully, each word a wedge, "you must let me help you. Follow me to my club, and perhaps from there I can find new accommodations for you."

And having nothing better to amuse myself with, since my lover, my playmate, my pretend mistress, my beloved partner in crime had fled, follow him I did.

## II. *The Offending Member*

For the third time that day—though by now it was night—I was kneeling, this time inside a tub rather than outside one, and the person I was cleaning was none other than myself. Some strange circumstance had dictated that my rescuer's club was closed for the evening, though he had a key and let himself in. He had led me to the basement, to a marvelous tiled bathroom, the latest in sanitary reform and engineering feats, he assured me, with hot water and cold water both running out of taps into a deep and delicious tub that drained into pipes laid underground.

It had been a pleasure to wash myself once he left me to my own devices with a bar of scented soap and some rough cloths. I watched dirty water run down the lustrous copper drain and clean, hot water fill the tub up again, I felt my skin begin to pucker up and the room fill with aromatic steam. I cleaned beneath my nails, scrubbed under my arms, washed my hair, soaped my breasts carefully, tended to every hidden fold. And then he knocked, my crusading hero. I snatched up a towel and tied it around my breasts to cover them, then called to him to enter.

He came and sat in a chair, an enormous stuffed chair, by the tub.

"Do you have everything you need?" he asked solicitously.

"It's wonderful," I sighed. "Delicious. Luxurious. Absolutely continental."

"Continental?" He looked startled but avoided looking at me directly. Under cover of his bashfulness, I stared at him hard. He seemed transformed from the earnest prig at the station to something more dissolute, looser about the mouth. Had he been drinking?

"Missus always says her bath makes her think of France and such, sir."

"Your mistress," he said, "seems to be all too familiar with the sorts of viciousness that we know tend to insinuate themselves into this country from abroad. Particularly from France." He rose from his chair and knelt by the tub. How pleasant it was to float in the water while someone lowered himself before me.

He took my hands, keeping his eyes averted from my face. "May I?" he asked.

"Lord, whatever for?" I tried to pull them away. He held fast.

"You can tell so much about a person from their hands," he murmured, a touch maliciously it seemed to me. "Their future . . . their past." He turned my hands palm up and began to trace lines on them with his finger. "Here is the path of love, and here is the path of life. I can see that you've loved loyally up until now, that your line of life is curiously . . . ruffled. I can see a difficult past . . . a troubled future . . . and here," he said, suddenly raising his eyes to mine and digging his nails into my hand, "here we have the unmistakable sign of the deceiver. Because these," he said, shoving them away from himself, "these are not the hands of a servant. These hands are not calloused, these hands are not hard, these hands are not marked with years of labor. These are the hands of a lady. A lady given to strange amusements and curious pleasures."

"That is correct," I said, leaning forward in the water, "and very penetrating of you. And now," I said, undoing the damp towel I had knotted about my breasts, dropping it along with all pretense of modesty, "if you permit me, I will demonstrate how very amusing those pleasures can be." And while his eyes were riveted on my now exposed breasts, I pressed on his mouth a hot and very hungry kiss. I climbed out of the tub, pushed him onto the capacious chair, and straddled him, water streaming down my body onto his, raising a musty but not unappealing odor from his suit.

"You're fascinated by these, aren't you," I murmured, bringing his hands to my breasts and to the rings that pierced my nipples. "You're staring at them. Go on, touch them. Pull on them." Tentatively, he tugged at the golden hoops. "Hard," I ordered before bruising his mouth again, sucking his tongue between my lips, gently biting him, running my hands under his jacket, loosening his tie, unbuttoning his shirt. I pulled away from him to better feel the strain on my breasts. A tense thrill ate me up. I ran my hands over his face as he put his hands flat up against my breasts. He grasped the nipple rings and pulled, as though guiding a horse by a bridle. I opened my legs so that I could rub my cunt and clit against his trousered thigh. I let my weight fall on him. Now I was riding him; my breasts led his body. I shoved his head against my tits and forced him first to suck one ringed nipple, then the other. I grunted with pleasure, grunted because he didn't deserve to hear me moan or cry out. When his licking, pinching and pulling had excited me as far as they could, I roughly opened his trousers and took out his cock. It was hard enough for me to be able to push it inside me, and so I did. Then I began to ride him in earnest, diving up and down on his prick, one hand grasping his shoulder, the other busy working my clit into a frenzy, until, almost too quickly, I came in resisting spasms. I pushed his mouth and hands away from me then, and got off him though he tried to keep me in place. I rose and stood before him and watched while he wrapped his own hand around his cock and frantically pulled a climax out of it.

I reached into the tub and pulled the stopper to let the water drain. There is nothing I detest more than a tub filled with cooling, dirty water.

"Take off your clothes," I told him. "I would like some company in my nudity."

He stood up and wrestled out of his costume. Then he pulled me to him and back down on the chair, in a parody of a domestic embrace. He stroked my hair and planted a kiss on the top of my head.

"I too have a confession to make," he murmured.

"I have made no confession for you to add to," I haughtily corrected him. "You made a surmise which I have as yet done nothing to confirm. But by all means, do confess."

"I am not a reformer. I am a scoundrel. I did not bring you here to rescue you."

"How refreshing." I smiled, trying to duck out from under the hand that held my head down.

"In fact, I brought you here on a wager."

I stiffened beneath the increasingly strong pressure of his hand.

"You see, every week the chaps, the members, bet on whether one of us can lure a woman into the club and have our way with her. That's why it's shut. To leave the field clear. Not everyone wins, but I always have. Though this time my trophy is of extraordinarily unusual—shall I say quality? interest? What word would you use, Miss . . . ?"

I snapped my head away from his heavy hand. "Wouldn't you rather have to say that it is I who have had my way with you?" I looked coldly into his face.

"Ultimately it's immaterial. Evidence, ocular evidence, is what counts, and in the end, that evidence never reveals who took who. My fellow members are not particularly imaginative men, my dear Miss—shall I call you Hannah? Such an unsuitably plebeian name for one so perniciously refined. And when my fellow members see you buried up to the hilt on my stalwart tool, they certainly won't hesitate to hail me as the conqueror."

"And what is this ocular evidence to which you refer, pray tell? Do you have spies hidden in the next room? Trick mirrors on the walls?"

"Oh, nothing so primitive," he said. "The club has a camera, the latest thing, doesn't require that one stay still for nearly so long as those old daguerreotypes did. Almost instant. And you're going to pose for some pictures. With those lovely rings of yours. I'd heard they were all the rage among society women lately, but this is the first time I've had the pleasure. Tell me, did it hurt? How and where did you get it done?"

Hoping to disarm him, I said, "The woman you saw me with at the station is my lover. You caught us, I'm afraid, playing one of our favorite games—maid and mistress. But when we're not at play, we're New Women. I take courses in political economy at the University of London, and my friend studies medicine. She is also the daughter of an eminent surgeon, whom she often assists in his operations. She obtained the necessary instruments and anesthetics and performed the piercing herself."

"Capital," he said, rubbing his hands, "absolutely capital. I knew right away you were no serving girl. A veritable decadent, that's what you are. Tell me, did she use ether? I've heard women become the absolute devil when they're under the influence of ether."

My swain was beginning to reveal a most annoying incorrigible disposition.

"Aren't you," I asked, taking his hand, "going to show me your picture camera?"

The photographic apparatus was in a miniature laboratory, filled with flasks, retorts, acrid vapors, heaps of papers, scraps of material, mineral specimens and odd fleshy objects floating about in jars like last season's pickles. I had wrapped myself in a robe that had been lying about in the bathroom, and stood by while my hero, now metamorphosed into a young man eager to prove himself to someone more advanced than he in the school of corruption, rustled about looking for old photographs to show me. He pounced on a pile in a corner. "Here they are!" He waved a sheaf of thick paper at me. "Come look."

I stood by him while he flipped through an apparently endless series of pathetic portraits, each girl looking more embarrassed and put out than the next, breasts flapping to one side, legs awkwardly parted to reveal a hairy slit, one arm stretched before a face in a wretched attempt at anonymity, the other arm stretched forward toward the camera as though to balance an eminently precarious act.

"That's Helen," he said enthusiastically. "She was a virgin and we paid her mother ten pounds to have her. She lost her virginity twenty times in that one night! And each time screamed as though it hadn't just happened before. By the time I had her, the jism was pouring out of her. Fred, he's the president of the club, he wanted to etherize her like they do in the specialty brothels, but we couldn't get hold of any. Maybe *you* could get us some," he mused. "And that's Kitty. You see the stripes on her legs? That was Harold, he likes to whip them. Has a special cat-o'-nine-tails for it. That's what comes of too many beatings at Eton. He's a regular devil. But Kitty was a sport, she was always happy to suck on one gentleman's member while getting fucked by another. She brought a friend along, too, where's her picture"—more furious flipping—"there, Phoebe, I think her name was. Phoebe was terribly fond of Greek love, if I remember rightly. Had three or four of the members' cocks up her asshole that night. You see," he said, "on the outside we call this the Sportsman's Club, but amongst ourselves we're the Randy Bohemians. Most nights it's a collective proposition, but Wednesdays, as I told you, it's more of an individualistic endeavor. Are you ready for your pose, Lady Hannah?"

"Soon," I said, leaning into him. "Show me some more so I have an idea of how to arrange myself."

"Of course," he obliged. "Lovely of you to be so agreeable. Most girls put up a horrible fight, we usually have to threaten to turn them into the police for prostitution. Well, that's if they're working girls. In your case I suppose blackmail would be more the trick."

"Won't be necessary, dear," I answered breezily. "Do show us some more."

He returned, engrossed, to his pretty pictures. "There's an awfully good one of an old hag named Hermione. She seemed pleased to have someone taking such an interest." As he searched, I undid my robe, working loose the belt that tied it. I wrapped each end tightly around my hand and stood poised, ready to seize my moment.

When it came, I had the belt tied round him quicker than even I could apprehend, and soon I had his arms completely immobilized, pinned tight against his sides. A pained expression overtook his features.

"I say, this isn't very sportsmanlike of you."

"Well, darling—what did you say your name was?"

"Arthur," he pouted.

"Dear Arthur," I hissed, pulling some rope from a mound of odds and ends, turning him round to secure each of his legs to the handles of the drawers behind him, "I am many things, but I am not a sportsman and have never claimed to be one." I took the pictures off the table and dropped them in front of his feet. "And neither, by the looks of *these*, are you." A match came easily to hand and I used it to set the pile aflame. "I'm afraid these have to go. And you'd better not move to save them, or you'll get a nasty burn."

"The work of years," he moaned, "years and years of planning, research . . ."

"They're easily replaced, Arthur."

"They are not."

"Oh, yes, they are," I said, "by some stunning portraits of you, a martyr to your own lust and your too, too trusting nature. Do maintain that look of agony, and strain at your bonds a little bit more." I picked up his camera and stood at the requisite distance, fiddling with the various knobs and buttons. Emma had attended the Ladies' Photographic School for a bit to learn about medical pictures and she'd told me some of what she'd learned. How amused she'd be when I showed these to her and told her everything that had happened after she left me at the station. "If you'd arch your back and turn your head to the left, you'd look

very much like that delightful Spanish oil of Saint Sebastian in
the National Gallery. With the fire blazing at your feet it's really
quite wonderful." I shot and shot until the flames went out.
Then I stepped through the ashes and delicately took hold of Arthur's prick.

"Why, here it is," I said, clasping his limp cock. "The offending member." I tugged at it a bit. "You really should be more
careful, Arthur, whom you pick up in Victoria Station. I could be
anybody. I could be that mad Ripper who keeps cutting people
open. Of course, he's only been cutting open women till now,
but one can never be sure . . . perhaps that's all been a ploy to
make fools like you feel safe." I wanted him to tremble. Instead,
of course, I only made his cock swell and rise up in my hand. I
dropped it in disgust, then began to slap it from side to side.
"You see, Arthur, you're terribly unaware of your true nature.
You think you want to come between women, to conquer and
capture them as trophies and possess them for all eternity, but
really what you've always wanted is just this, to be tied up with
some female bandying you about"—I slapped harder—"holding
the power of life and death over you." My robe had opened and
my breasts brushed against his shirt front. I grabbed his cock
and squeezed it hard. "Don't you love the helplessness, the danger?" Silence. I squeezed harder. "Don't you?"

"Yes," he gasped. "It hurts."

"Good," I said. "I like that. And so do you, don't you?"

"Yes," he choked, "yes. Please."

I relaxed my grip. "Such a good boy. So obedient. Perhaps
you're not really a boy at all." His cock got harder than ever in
response to these taunts. "Perhaps you're a girl. Perhaps you'd
like me to perform a little operation on you to help you be a
girl." I pressed against him so that his cock was smashed between us. "Would you like that, Arthur? Would you like me to
cut off that offending member?" I gestured toward the preserved specimens. "We could put it in a jar for you to look at
from time to time." I felt his hips straining as he writhed against
me. I let him. I even helped him along. "Take it out to play with
now and then. And you'd be free to be the girl you really are,
wouldn't you?" He was pushing faster, and whimpering. "Why, if

you weren't so dirty and I weren't so nice and clean, I'd turn you around and fuck you right now, just to get you in the habit, Arthur." I pulled away and his cock bobbed helplessly up and down. "But I must go now, Arthur. I'm sure some trustworthy club member will find you here tomorrow and set you free. And an evening spent in bondage is an invaluable lesson in submission. You'll only thank me later. And you'll think of me every time you look at our photographs of tonight, which I promise to send to you here." I leaned over and kissed him on the forehead. "You will remember me, Arthur?"

"Yes," he gasped.

"Yes, ma'am."

"Yes, ma'am."

"And you won't interfere anymore when you see girls playing out of doors?"

"No, ma'am."

"Well," I said, gathering my robe regally about me and sweeping out the door, "good night then."

And I descended once again to the basement, where I found and donned my clothes. I assumed a grand gray mantle pillaged from the cloakroom and stepped out through the club's ornate and narrow doors. I stood poised for a moment on its marble steps, then made my way into the waiting city square, radiant in the misty, illuminated night.

# Christine Beatty

## The Secret of Her Success

The gutter was a grotesque mixture of the repulsive and crude, a microcosm of this blighted neighborhood. Along this stretch of curbside was an assortment of cigarette butts in varying lengths and stages of decay. One of them was still smoldering. Shattered glass from bottles of cheap wine and hard liquor lay strewn in the pitted and stained concrete channel. Spent condoms, wrinkled and rotted from exposure, peeked out from beneath charred and tattered newspapers, junk-food wrappers and defiantly discarded parking tickets. In a clear section of gutter lay a used syringe clogged with blood, its spike askew, testimony to the lack of needle exchange in the city.

Lifting away from the dying cigarette was a pristine red leather pump, size eight. This shoe held a well-shaped foot clad in shiny new support hose surrounding an equally attractive leg. A red spandex miniskirt fell just an inch below the woman's firm, round buttocks.

She was a striking woman, apparently in her early twenties, with long straight black hair worn with no styling. Her hips and butt molded the tight skirt into an excruciatingly attractive curve that tapered into a thin waist and almost perfectly flat stomach. Firm, high breasts strained maddeningly at a white, pucker-knit tube top that showed off her smooth pale torso. Her face was devoid of foundation, but she wore heavy eye makeup, blush and lipstick. She could have posed for any men's magazine she wanted to—she was that kind of beautiful. Other women envied and hated her.

Her eyes were the most unusual thing about her—alive and sparkling with mischievous energy, greener than the glass of a Seven-Up bottle. But her most striking features were also her best-kept secrets.

She idled along this stretch of downtown sidewalk, illuminated by the multicolored neon of the shops and the yellowish orange of the sodium-vapor streetlamps. Her eyes scanned the approaching traffic warily, searching for the police cars she was trying to avoid and the customers she hoped to attract.

A dusty old Nova slowed for her; it was at least ten years old and wheezed blue smoke. The driver was not a day under fifty; even in this light she could see how disheveled he looked, as if he'd slept in his clothes. His eyes were wide and his mouth leered.

She tossed her head and looked away. A guy in a car like that wouldn't be good for more than a twenty, and he didn't look like he was worth taking for less than her usual fifty or sixty. Besides, a guy that creepy sometimes made her physically ill. There were plenty of fish in the sea on a Friday night, Tanya didn't have to settle. There had been times when she was so desperate that anyone would do—but tonight she was able to hold out for what she wanted.

Tanya passed two other hookers walking in the opposite direction and smiled to herself at the change in their conversation. She was the new mystery woman on the stroll, and everyone was trying to figure her out. She didn't mind if they talked about her. Everywhere she had ever gone, people had done that.

No one had seen her arrive: she'd just turned up in the Tarrington one day. She'd registered in that dismal lobby just before dawn several months ago, so her neighbors hadn't seen her check in. Tanya hadn't made a secret of her existence, but it took more than a week for the other residents to even notice that someone was living in 212. Nobody had even known her name for almost a month. She was polite when spoken to, but very close-mouthed. Mostly she didn't stay in a conversation long enough for anyone to learn anything about her.

It was hard for people to figure out what she was all about. She had no obvious needle tracks on her arms, legs or neck, so people assumed she smoked the pipe or did pills or drank. Oddly, she never seemed loaded. She hadn't asked anybody about getting drugs, which gave rise to the theory that she had her own connection. Most everyone in her hotel believed she had to be *some* kind of addict. After all, why would a girl *that* pretty be hooking *on the street* if not for a fix? And, like some addicts, you only saw her at night.

Ten minutes after she brushed off the Nova, Tanya's patience paid off. A metallic blue BMW pulled up. The guy, apparently a professional of some sort in his early thirties, dressed for success, rolled down the passenger side window. She favored him with a wide-lipped smile as he signaled for her to come over.

"What can I do for you this evening, darling?" she asked in a light, almost musical voice.

"Are you dating?" he returned.

"Most certainly," she replied in her cultured voice.

"How much?"

"Let me in and we'll talk about it."

He pulled up the lock and cracked the door for her. Tanya looked left and right out of habit to make sure no cops would witness this, then gracefully slid into the passenger seat and shut the door. Soon they were cruising down the street at fifteen miles an hour.

"I can't believe a girl as pretty as you is working the streets."

"I like being my own boss," Tanya said, "and I'm not cheap."

"How not cheap are you?"

"Well, we can do a quickie right here for a sixty, or you can get us a room and spend a hundred for half an hour."

Staring at her luscious cleavage and firm young thighs, he licked his lips and, with a slight quaver to his voice, asked what they could do for that long.

"Anything you want to do, honey," she smiled. "I'm open-minded."

"All right," he said. "Where do we go?"

In only a few minutes he had the car parked in one of the slots of a budget motel on the edge of the neighborhood.

"I'll wait for you out here. Okay, baby?" she said as he got out. "I'd prefer not to disturb the management. They'd frown at the idea of me plying my trade in their rooms."

"Good thinking, doll. I'll be right back."

After a few minutes he returned, jingling the keys triumphantly. With a generous, knowing smile she smoothly left his car and strolled over to take his proffered arm. He escorted her discreetly up the stairs to the second-floor balcony.

"So how long you been dating?" he asked quietly as they searched for the room.

"Couple of years," she replied.

"Why?"

"As I said, I like being my own boss. Nobody tells me what to do and I come and go as I please. I can pick and choose who I date, and I do quite well for myself."

"Where are you from? I notice you have an accent—Eastern European, I'd say."

"I don't know. My people have been on the road so long, I really have no idea where. We really kept to ourselves. I'd probably still be with them, but a girl can't stay at home forever, you know?"

"I guess," he said, and let it go at that.

With trembling fingers, the guy opened the door and ushered Tanya into the motel room. Intoxicating fantasies played through his mind as he began taking off his clothes. Tanya sat on the edge of the bed, slowly peeled down her pantyhose and wriggled out of her tube top. Her high pert breasts popped forth, nipples already swollen.

She sat there waiting for him in her red spandex skirt. His libido in overdrive, his cock astir in his shorts, he sat next to her and buried his tongue in her mouth. She eagerly, passionately returned his kiss and ground her bosom into his furry chest. His hands flew to her breasts and the crotch of her panties.

He slid his fingers beneath the hem of her underwear and found her vagina moist and open. Tanya sighed loudly, feeling his finger snaking into her lubricated pussy, and she sucked eagerly at his mouth, writhing her crotch against his hand.

The trick stood and pulled off his shorts while Tanya wiggled out of her skirt and G-string and lay back on the bed. She drew her thighs wide open to part her labia for him. The pink wet lips glistened slightly, and she wiggled her hips sinuously. She was a little taken aback by herself: it wasn't often that a client affected her like this.

Tanya wasn't a hooker because she liked anonymous sex. The best tricks came and went, and the sooner the better. Like most whores, her motto was "get 'em in, get 'em off and get 'em out." Of course, she occasionally had a john who was a good lover, but that created other problems for her.

As the trick pulled himself onto the bed he couldn't resist a closer inspection of Tanya's pussy. Her scent, wild and musky, sent a heady wave of desire through him, and before he knew what he was doing he found his lips poised over her cunt.

Tanya knew what was coming, but for some reason she didn't mind; in fact, she was primed for it. Maybe it was just something about this guy, but she responded to his touch almost immediately. The feel of his breath on her mound made her want to thrust her crotch into his face.

Tanya groaned in delicious surprise at the sensation of his tongue sliding up her juicing vagina, and she gasped when it brushed her electrified clit. She felt a heat growing in her belly, and knew it was about to happen. Quickly she grabbed him from beneath his arms and pulled him up so they were face to face.

"Wow! You work out or something?" His face registered surprise as well as passion.

"Let's do something else," she said, hoping it wasn't too late, that he hadn't aroused her too much. She scissored her legs together and tried to think about bank vaults, about blank brick walls—anything to distract herself.

"Hey, baby, c'mon," the trick said, insinuating a hand between her clenched thighs. "We're just getting warmed up here!"

Suddenly he froze. His fingers had encountered something unexpected. But he had *seen* her pussy—had *tasted* it. Maybe she was some kind of transsexual or hermaphrodite? He wasn't really sure, but he knew the hard cock he now felt in his hand was definitely attached to this beautiful . . . woman?

Now he knew one of her secrets, and he tried to pull back.

Knowing she had been discovered and that he wasn't into it at all, Tanya grabbed his arms and held fast. The trick felt her inhuman strength as he tried to struggle from her grasp, and became horrified. No woman—not even a man—should be this strong. And while he was trying to comprehend his powerlessness, he suddenly felt the stubble of heavy whiskers grate against his face. Where had *they* come from?

Tanya's trick fought to get away, struggling to free himself, preparing to shriek out in fright. Then she opened her lips wide, showing him her full smile for the first time, and he almost fainted. He tried to make sense of her other secret—her inch-long incisors—as she sank them into his shoulder.

He kicked and flailed, but she held fast, sucking greedily at the blood that pumped into her waiting mouth. Dizzy and weak, he noticed that the five o'clock shadow that had rasped against him had disappeared. As he felt his consciousness beginning to ebb, he reached back down to her crotch and recoiled in shock: he knew he'd felt a penis there just a moment ago, but there was only smoothness now.

Tanya stood unsteadily over the trick's lifeless body and collected herself. She shimmied back into her pantyhose, tugged her top back on and tiptoed out the door. She was in luck; there was nobody outside on the balcony. She headed for the stairs.

There were times when Tanya almost regretted being the way she was, even though she couldn't help it. She'd hated leaving her clan five years ago, but they couldn't abide her sex-changing ways.

There were definite advantages to being a shapechanger. The other transsexuals out here relied on all kinds of hormones, silicone and surgery to become women, but all Tanya needed was fresh blood.

By the time she reached the street, she was ready for another trick.

## Annalisa Suid

❧

# After the War

I notice him as soon as I walk into the lobby, sitting there at the far corner of the bar. He has very short hair, almost a crew cut, bristly like an animal's fur. It works well with his eyes, and though I can't tell their color, they glitter like a tiger's in the early jungle evening, glitter and shiver in the gold dim light of the hotel bar.

I sit down, diagonally across from him, and watch the band, but I turn back to the counter when I feel a soft tug on my sleeve—the bartender trying to get my attention.

"Miss, this gentleman," he says, pointing to my animal man, "this gentleman would like to buy you a drink."

I smile, first at the bartender, and then, graciously, at my short-haired friend, and I say, "A beer would be wonderful." The bartender places an ice-cold bottle in front of me, and I lift it in a quick toast, my head bowed, and sip.

He watches me hold the bottle, watches my hand slip down its long, icy neck. I swallow the foam of the first sip, and he watches my throat contract on the cool liquid.

When the band takes a break, I wend my way through the throng to where he's seated.

"Thank you," I say. He nods.

We talk. I learn that his name is Jesse Miller, that he's a

twenty-seven-year-old air force lieutenant, was divorced after the war, and has no children. I learn that he hangs out at this bar and drinks tonic water every Friday night, and that in his year and a half as a regular, he has bought exactly one drink for one woman: me.

I notice how his green eyes catch the light from the chandelier above us, how the music, once the band starts again, seems to vibrate through his body, and he rocks, gently but right with the beat, in rhythm to the large black singer's whiskey voice.

I notice.

At two a.m., when we've done all the chit-chat you can do at a bar, I ask if he will walk me up the stairs to my hotel room. He seems happy that I've asked, and agrees, but he doesn't take my hand or touch me. In my room, we sit on the sofa and talk some more. Then, in the middle of a sentence, he leans over and brushes a wisp of hair out of my eyes. His cool skin chills me deliciously. I notice again how his eyes glitter in the dimmest light.

"Are you frightened?" he asks at the first pause in our conversation. I know he's trying to read my expression, the slight worry lines that have wrinkled my forehead as I fight within myself.

"You want to be with me, don't you?" he continues when I remain silent.

I smile and nod, because I do, but shouldn't.

"I promise that we won't 'go all the way,' to use a phrase from high school," he says, interrupting my thoughts.

I sigh, relieved. Now we can play.

Jesse kisses me softly on the lips, and I'm surprised at how excited this makes me. I shift slightly, feeling my panties clinging, thrillingly wet, and Jesse watches me move. He says in a voice like a lullaby, "You are the sexiest woman I've ever met."

I laugh. I don't see myself as sexy, though I know that men do, and while my lips are still curved in a grin, he pins my body back against the sofa and ravishes my neck and shoulders. I shudder as he pulls my blouse aside and covers my collarbones in hot, feverish kisses, slides his lips along my shoulders, bites me. I shudder again, and he understands instantly, knows that I want him to overpower me. He holds onto my hands, keeping them flat on the sofa while he suckles my breasts through my blouse, nips and bites the tender skin.

Then he moves his fingers up the split of my body, trying to touch my clitoris, but I don't want his hands there yet. I struggle until I can arch my back and press crotch to crotch with him. His cock throbs against me and grows harder still when he leans in to nibble my earlobe. He whispers to me, "What's the kinkiest thing you've ever done?"

"Ever?"

"Uh-huh." His lips are against my neck, so I feel his words more than I hear them.

"I was tied up once," I say.

"Yes?"

"Tied and mastered."

His grip on my wrists tightens.

"You?" I say in a rush of breath.

"I shaved her." He's husky. "Have you ever been shaved?"

I nod.

"I shaved her and then ate strawberries and whipped cream off her naked pussy. Would you like that?"

I nod again.

"Would you like to feel my flat tongue on your clit, licking you, probing you, then moving up to kiss your lips?"

"Yes."

"Don't you love the taste of sex, the smell of sex on your skin?"

"Yes."

"Do you like it if a guy eats you after he cums inside you?"

"I've never done that," I sigh. His hands wander over me, his hands and his eyes, and his lips and his breath, and his smell, and his sex.

He runs his fingernails all the way down the inside of my legs, setting my skin on fire. Then, with his hands on my nylons, he says, "Take these off."

I do, and he presses his sweet lips to the lips of my pussy, sheathed in damp white cotton.

"Would you like me to eat you through your panties?" He does this as he asks and I wriggle and squirm and stroke his short hair, like animal fur, that rubs against my thighs. He licks me and bites me, rips my underpants aside, and slips two fingers deep inside me. He spreads my juices over the tattoo on my ankle and sucks it clean. Then he pulls my panties down all the way and licks in circles around my clit until his lips are slick with my honey. He reaches up and grabs my shoulders, forcing me to bend and kiss him.

"Do you like the way you taste?" he says into my mouth.

"Yes."

"I do too."

I shift on the sofa to turn off the light, and while my back is toward him he picks me up and carries me to the bed. The lamp is still on, and I leave it, wanting to see his glittering eyes, to watch his serious face change as he cums.

Quickly, I pull off my blouse and undo my bra while he takes off his oxford shirt and jeans. He's wearing silk boxers, decadent for a lieutenant I think, though I have no experience with members of the air force. The silk caresses my naked skin as we press our bodies together, joined from the chest down.

"I want to taste you again," he whispers, and I lie back on the pillows and let him. This is something he's good at, something he's obviously had practice doing.

He eats me slowly and effortlessly, moving his tongue in and out of me like ocean waves, kissing and licking and sucking until the rhythm of his mouth becomes the rhythm of my blood, of my body.

Probably because we've decided not to "go all the way," I am dying to feel him inside me, and I tell him.

He lifts his mouth off my pussy just slightly. "Do you want my cock here?" he asks, rubbing the right spot. "I'd like to tease you until you beg me to fuck you."

But he's not going to, and that fact, along with his words, makes me even hotter. I slither down on him and unbutton his boxers to reveal his cock. I leave his boxers on, and open, while I take his cock in my mouth, sip from it, drink from it in the same fashion that I consumed the beer in the bar. He talks to me while I perform magic tricks with his cock, making more and more of it disappear down my long, cool throat, while my tongue flicks out to kiss his balls.

His voice caresses me while his hands smooth and stroke my hair, press firmly on the nape of my neck to help me release that catch that opens my throat even wider.

"You are sweet," he tells me, his voice husky again. I rub my cheeks against his silk-clad thigh in answer. "A kitten," he says, and then, when I swallow hard and take the last inch of his cock down my throat, "A panther."

I like that he sees me as feline and I wonder if my brown eyes glitter as hungrily as his. I look up at him, a question in my eyes, and he tries to answer by opening his wider. I feel that I might lose myself in his eyes, and I look away, concentrating again on that hard, pulsing rod deep in my throat.

"After the war," he says, in a sad voice that makes my skin tingle, "After the war I stopped sleeping."

"Mmmmm?" is all I can manage, too filled to respond appropriately.

"Just an hour or two a night—no dreams, no colors, just an hour or two."

I keep my motion steady, working him, drinking in his heady pre-cum.

"I couldn't make love to her," he continues, and his voice sounds as if he's crying, though when I glance up quickly, I see that he's not. His eyes are hard now, shiny and sad.

"She didn't understand." He shrugs with his entire body, and the movement pulls his cock from my mouth. I am quick to re-capture it, and he strokes my cheek very gently as I start my steady beat again.

"But I understood, and I let her go."

I am watching him now while he talks to me. His eyes are hypnotic, his voice sad but urgent, as if he is forcing himself to tell me this, as if he has told no one but himself, over and over again. The words are simple, the pain most certainly intensifying the pleasure I'm giving him.

"I came home two years ago," he says. "And I only sleep an hour or two a night. I'd like to make love to you, but I haven't been able to do that, either."

Suddenly he moans, and I feel the first delicious drops of his cum slip down my throat. I'm startled enough to back away, letting the rest shower his chest and flat belly. He has an amazing amount of semen, and I rub it into his skin, delighting in the warm satiny glaze it forms on my hands and fingers. I bend to taste the salty-sweet cider, and he strokes my hair again, as if petting an animal.

"So much," I whisper.

"I haven't been able to cum." He pauses, and shakes his head as if angry at himself before continuing. "Not for a long time."

When I look up, hearing the tears in his voice again, I see that they are real, sliding crystal-like down his fine cheekbones. His grip on my shoulder is exceedingly firm, as if he needs something to hold on to. I move up his body into his embrace, but somehow it shifts, it turns, and I'm the one holding him. He lets me, resting his head on my naked breasts. He falls asleep in my arms.

I watch peace steal across his features, watch from beneath the black panther hair that falls over my eyes. I stroke his tiger fur and run the tips of my fingers up and down his cheeks, wiping away the tears. Then, hardly moving, I click off the light on the bedside table. I, too, feel peaceful as the first rays of sun filter in through the blinds and dance over the bed, slowly warming the body of the still, sleeping soldier cradled in my arms.

## Mary Maxwell

❦

# The Café of the Joyous Women

The restaurant was tucked away on a side street, just a block away from the school that Jennifer's two children attended. On her way to a PTA meeting late one afternoon, she noticed the newly painted facade, the gold lettering on the door. The sign read LE CAFÉ DES FEMMES JOYEUSES. She had taken two years of French in high school and she remembered just enough to translate: The Café of the Joyous Women.

It was a tiny place: no more than a dozen small marble-topped tables set quite close together. On each table, a white candle burned beside a bud vase that held a single red rose.

The first time she passed the restaurant, she noticed a woman sitting alone at the window table—the one that commanded the best view of the street. Jennifer was struck by the expression on the woman's face—a broad and contented smile. That smile intrigued Jennifer. What delicious food, she wondered, could inspire such an expression.

For special occasions, Jennifer's husband, Kevin, usually took her to dinner at the country club. But for her twenty-fifth birthday, Jennifer suggested that they go to Le Café des Femmes Joyeuses. "It would be fun to try something a little different, don't you think?"

He frowned. "That's not one of those places where they serve fish raw, is it?"

"No, dear. You're thinking of sushi. This is a French restaurant."

Kevin shrugged good-naturedly and agreed. From his expression, Jennifer knew that he would have preferred the country club—where he knew that his steak would be well done and the portions would be generous—but he was willing to indulge her.

Kevin had been her high school sweetheart; they had married shortly after graduation. Right out of high school, Kevin had assisted in his father's plumbing business. Now he owned his own business—a successful plumbing supply store. They had two children—Nicole and Jason.

Jason, the younger of the two, had just entered kindergarten, leaving Jennifer, for the first time in seven years, with time to herself. In the afternoon, when Jason was at school, Jennifer sometimes found herself afflicted with a strange restlessness. There were many things she could do—wash clothes, make a cake, read a book—but none of them seemed worth the time. It was on just such an afternoon that she had ordered new lingerie from a mail-order catalog: a white lace teddy and matching garter belt, sheer white stockings. The lace, a glorious impracticality, was her birthday present to herself.

On the night of her birthday, she dressed carefully, starting with the new lingerie. For years, she had worn practical cotton underwear and Maidenform bras that could stand up to machine washing. The silk and lace of the teddy felt so fragile, as soft as rose petals. She slipped the teddy over her head and fastened the snaps at the crotch. The silk felt strange against her skin—so light, as if she wore nothing at all. She pulled the garter belt over her hips and gently pulled on the stockings. So sheer, so delicate.

She stood before the full-length mirror, studying the effect. Her full breasts pushed against the teddy, the rosy nipples visible through the lace. Between the tops of the stockings and the teddy was a band of naked flesh.

"Honey, the babysitter's here," Kevin called through the bedroom door.

"Okay! I'll be ready in a minute!"

She thought about wearing a slip, but all her slips seemed wrong with the simple elegance of the silk and lace. Instead, she pulled on the blue silk dress that she had worn to her sister's wedding three years before. She strolled to the vanity to get her evening bag. Without a slip to hamper it, the silk caressed her legs as she walked.

They had reservations for eight o'clock. A smiling waiter greeted them at the door. "Welcome to *Café des Femmes Joyeuses*. My name is Jacques, and I will be your waiter tonight."

It was early and only a few tables were occupied. The candles were lit and a fire burned behind the grate in the fireplace. He seated them at a table by the window.

"Isn't this beautiful," Jennifer said. "Candlelight and roses."

"The tables are kind of small," Kevin commented. He opened the menu and his frown deepened.

Jennifer opened the menu. The dishes were listed in French, with no English translations. "Oh, it's no problem, dear. I got an A in French in high school, remember?"

While Jennifer was examining the menu, Jacques returned, leading another diner: a self-assured young woman wearing a black silk dress. Her hair was short and dark, cropped close to her head. He seated her at the table beside them, just a few feet from Jennifer's elbow.

Jennifer glanced at her, curious. It seemed odd for a woman to be dining alone in such an elegant restaurant. The woman caught Jennifer staring and smiled. Her eyes were dark and they reflected the candlelight. Jennifer quickly looked away, embarrassed to be caught looking.

Kevin was puzzling over the menu. "So what's this?" he asked, tapping his finger on an entree: *Le Lapin au Thyme Frais.*

Jennifer frowned. "Well, I know what thyme is, but I'm not sure about the rest. I wonder if the waiter would help . . ."

"Perhaps I can be of some assistance?" said the woman at the next table. "I could not help but overhear. The food here is delicious, but the seating . . ." She laughed softly and waved her hand in a gesture of helplessness.

"I'm not sure," Jennifer began, but the woman was already leaning toward her.

"*Le Lapin au Thyme Frais*—oh yes! That is the rabbit cooked with cream and thyme. Quite nice, I think. And this—" She reached out and tapped a selection on the menu. "*Ris de Veau en Croûte*—that's veal sweetbreads cooked with vermouth, mushrooms, and cream in a pastry crust. A specialty of the house."

Kevin made a face and the woman laughed. Her hand fluttered and then came to rest, just for a moment, on top of Jennifer's hand. Her skin was cool and smooth, and Jennifer caught a slight whiff of perfume, but then the woman was pointing again.

"*Le Filet Mignon au Béarnaise*—that is, perhaps, more to your liking. A simple cut of steak, with a delicious sauce." She smiled at Kevin, but her hand once again rested on Jennifer's. "It sounds so much better in French, don't you think?" Her voice was soft, as if she were whispering secrets.

"Well," he said, softening a little. "I do like a menu I can read."

"Of course," she said. "But the food is exquisite. I come here often. It's truly worth these small inconveniences. I promise that you will both be pleased that you decided to come."

"It was Jenny's choice." Kevin shifted his eyes to Jennifer, perhaps realizing that he sounded rather rude. "Happy birthday, honey."

"It's your birthday. How wonderful!" She smiled at Jennifer. "Jenny—is that short for Jennifer? Such a romantic name," she said. "My name's Maria. Very plain and ordinary."

The waiter returned with a bottle of red wine and two baskets of rolls. He showed Maria the label and she lifted her hand from Jennifer's to wave toward the wineglass. "And some for my friends," she said. "This is an occasion to celebrate. It's Jennifer's birthday and, I think, her first visit to the restaurant." The sensation of her touch lingered on Jennifer's hand.

"I don't ordinarily drink," Jennifer began, but Jacques had already poured the glass.

"It's your birthday, Jenny," Kevin said. "Go ahead and have a glass." He was already buttering a roll, happy that the food had arrived.

"Of course," Maria said. "This is not an ordinary occasion. I regard it as a personal responsibility to welcome you to my favorite restaurant."

Maria helped them order: filet mignon for Kevin and, after some discussion, sweetbreads for Jennifer and herself. While Kevin was examining the wine list, Maria leaned close to Jennifer once again. "You must be careful with sweetbreads," she mentioned in a confiding whisper. "Some say that they are an aphrodisiac." She lifted her eyebrows and smiled to indicate that she was joking.

The food was, as Maria had said, excellent. And Maria was a fine dining companion. She asked Kevin about his business and he was quite willing to explain recent innovations in plumbing fixtures. "I used to have three kinds of kitchen faucets, and now we stock over fifty. And you've got your choice of pipe: your polyurethane, your copper . . ."

Jennifer was content to listen to Kevin's recitation, a familiar litany of hardware. She found herself looking out over the restaurant, admiring the way the flickering candlelight reflected in the tabletops, in Maria's dark eyes. Maria kept Jennifer's wineglass filled.

Jennifer was sipping her wine when Maria touched her hand unexpectedly, making some point about the value of plumbing. Startled, Jennifer jumped, splashing a few drops of wine on her dress.

"Oh, I'm so sorry," Maria said.

"It's my fault," Jennifer said. "I'm so clumsy."

"Come." Maria stood up and reached out for Jennifer's hand. "We must take care of this immediately, or it will stain. You will excuse us," she said to Kevin. "Women's business."

Without thinking, Jennifer put her hand in Maria's. Maria led her toward the restroom. As they made their way between the tables, she called out to Jacques in French too rapid for Jennifer to follow. He disappeared into the kitchen, then reappeared with a bottle of club soda. Maria took the bottle and waved Jacques away.

She escorted Jennifer into the powder room. There were two rooms: a small outer room with a vanity, a sink, and a single upholstered chair; an inner room with a toilet.

"Come, come," Maria said. "No time to waste. Turn around." Jennifer obeyed automatically, and felt Maria's cool fingers on her neck as she unzipped the dress. "Take it off now." Jennifer slipped the dress over her head. The air was chilly, and she clutched her dress, feeling foolish and exposed.

"Here," Maria said, taking the dress from Jennifer. "A quick rinse with club soda and the stain will come right out." She turned to the sink and busied herself and then turned back with a damp but unstained dress. "Now, we must give it a moment to dry." She blotted it with the towel and draped it over the towel rack. "There now." She turned back to Jennifer with a rustle of silk. "Sit down, *ma chérie*. No need to stand. You look cold."

Jennifer had crossed her arms over her breasts, partly for warmth and partly for modesty. "It's a bit chilly," she said.

"Sit," she said, and again Jennifer obeyed. She caught a glimpse of her reflection in the mirror. Her nipples had hardened, and were pushing against the thin lace of the teddy. She felt exposed, vulnerable.

"It is my fault you are cold, and I must help to warm you," Maria said. She knelt on the carpeted floor beside the chair. "And how might I do that?" she mused, as if to herself.

"I'm fine," Jennifer protested. "It'll just be a few minutes."

"What lovely stockings," she murmured, as if she hadn't heard a word. "So pure and white." Jennifer felt her touch, a hand running down her leg from the thigh to the ankle. "Beautiful legs in beautiful stockings."

"I don't think . . ." Jennifer started to say, but Maria's touch on her leg stopped the sentence before Jennifer could finish it.

"Of course you don't," Maria said. "This is no time to think. Don't think at all. We have a few minutes now, while your dress dries. But no time to think." With a rustle of black silk, she shifted her position so that she knelt at Jennifer's feet, looking up at her with a sweet smile. One hand held Jennifer's foot, gently yet firmly, encircling the ankle. The other hand traced a path up the inside of her leg. Her touch was very soft. At the top of the stocking, her fingers hesitated, playing with the reinforced edge. "There is nothing more romantic than a garter belt and stockings," she said. "Panty hose are so . . . pedestrian, I think. Don't you agree?"

"I think . . . perhaps . . . we should . . ." Jennifer was finding it difficult to speak. She knew she should stop this, but she said nothing as Maria's fingers delicately caressed the sensitive skin of her inner thigh just above the stocking's edge.

"Oh, don't worry, *ma chérie*," she said. "I have already locked the door."

"I mean we shouldn't . . ." She stopped, unable to say exactly what they shouldn't do.

Maria's fingers had moved higher. They played now with the silk crotch of the teddy, sometimes pressing against Jennifer and sometimes toying with the small curls of hair that had escaped around the cloth. "I'm afraid that . . ." Jennifer didn't finish the sentence, unable to sum up her fears while Maria's fingers continued their teasing.

"You are afraid that I will run your lovely stockings." She finished the sentence for Jennifer. "Oh, no, I would not do such a thing. I will be very careful. Very careful." One careful finger had slipped past the silken edge of the teddy and was softly stroking the outer lips of Jennifer's cunt. "But perhaps we had best undo these snaps. What do you think, *ma chérie?*"

She did not give Jennifer time to respond. Jennifer heard the click, click, click of the three snaps in the crotch of the teddy.

"Ah—no need to think. They are undone." She had moved closer, and Jennifer felt the warmth of Maria's head resting against her inner thigh. The air was cool on her exposed cunt.

"And here is a treasure," Maria said softly. Her breath warmed Jennifer's cunt. "Such beautiful curls you have," she murmured, parting the pubic hair. Jennifer felt both hands now, teasing the outer lips of her cunt, stroking down in an insistent rhythm.

"You are not thinking now, are you, my sweet? Not thinking at all." Maria's fingers explored the inner lips. When one questing finger stroked her clitoris, Jennifer's hips moved involuntarily, pushing toward the hand, and she exhaled suddenly.

"Not thinking at all," Maria murmured, and the finger traced tiny circles with the clitoris at the center. For a moment, the finger dipped into Jennifer's cunt and she moaned.

"Softly, *ma chérie*. Very softly." Her finger, now wet with the juices from Jennifer's cunt, returned to its place, rubbing harder. "Here now, this will help." One hand left Jennifer's crotch to lift her foot so that it rested on the vanity before her. Jennifer's other foot came up of its own accord. Her legs were spread wide. In the mirror, she could see her face and two high-heeled blue shoes. The rest was hidden by the vanity.

Maria's hand returned to Jennifer's cunt. While one finger continued teasing her clit, another finger pushed between the lips. Jennifer raised her hips to meet it, but the finger withdrew as she pressed toward it.

"What do you say, *ma chérie?*" Maria's voice was as rhythmic as her rubbing. "What do you say?"

"Yes," Jennifer moaned. "Oh, yes."

"You want this now, *ma chérie?* You want this."

Jennifer's nipples rubbed against the lace of the teddy. Her clitoris was a hard knot under Maria's finger. Her cunt was aching to be filled. "Please . . . oh, please."

"So polite," Maria whispered. "Are you still afraid?"

"No. Not afraid. Please."

"Good," she whispered. "That's very good." Jennifer felt Maria's mouth on her clitoris, kissing her, her tongue teasing the hard knot of flesh. Gently, she slid a finger into Jennifer's cunt. "Yes," she whispered. "This is what you want, isn't it, darling?" She looked up at Jennifer with those beautiful dark eyes. The scent of her perfume filled the small room. "You want me to fuck you."

"Yes, fuck me. Please fuck me."

Maria laughed and moved her finger slowly, pressing into Jennifer's cunt, then pulling back just a little. Involuntarily, Jennifer's back arched, bringing her hips to meet the hand. "Yes, you like this," Maria murmured, pushing again. Her mouth returned to Jennifer's clit, now sucking hard. Maria pushed a second finger into Jennifer's cunt, pressing hard against her, filling her.

The orgasm took Jennifer in a great rush—a natural force, like gravity, like magnetism, like lust. She was picked up and shaken and tossed back in the chair, limp and exhausted.

"Softly," Maria murmured between her legs. "Softly now." Still kneeling on the floor, she smiled up at Jennifer. Her hair was tousled; her face slick with the juices of Jennifer's cunt. Still smiling, she slipped her fingers from Jennifer's cunt and she stood, looking down at Jennifer. "I think you are warm now."

Jennifer didn't move. Yes, she was warm. Very warm.

Maria shook back her hair and washed her hands and face in the sink. Jennifer watched her dry her hands on the towel and smooth her hair into place. She knelt again and neatly snapped the teddy closed. "A good girl always puts away her toys," she said brightly. "And I am always a good girl." She stood and took the dress from the towel rack.

"Voilà! Your dress is dry, you are warm and happy. And it is your birthday. What could be better? Come now." She pulled Jennifer up from the chair. Jennifer stood passively while Maria dressed her, dropping the dress over her head, zipping it. "There now!" She stood behind Jennifer. "I do love quiet women. They always seem so surprised."

"I am surprised," Jennifer said.

She laughed and kissed Jennifer's cheek. "Come now."

Jennifer followed her back into the warm restaurant, filled with the scent of coffee and pastries. The plates had been cleared from the table. Jacques stood beside the table, chatting with Kevin about basketball scores.

"I ordered coffee," Kevin said as Jacques retreated. It seemed odd that Kevin was still there; it seemed to her that they had been gone for a very long time. He smiled at Jennifer indulgently. "It took you a while."

"Ah, yes," said Maria. "Wine stains can be tricky. But you see . . ." She gestured. "As good as new." She glanced over her shoulder. "And here is Jacques."

Jacques emerged from the kitchen bearing a small cake decorated with candles. "Happy birthday to you," he sang. Maria joined in. "Happy birthday to you!" After a moment, Kevin sang as well. "Happy birthday, dear Jennifer. Happy birthday to you!"

After the cake and the coffee, as Jennifer and Kevin were preparing to leave, Maria took Jennifer's hand in hers. "I hope you enjoyed yourself."

Momentarily flustered, Jennifer glanced at Kevin.

"Sure," he said affably. "The food's fine, once you figure out what it is. Could use bigger portions, but that's all right." He patted his stomach. "I could lose a few pounds anyway."

"We have ladies' luncheons here every Wednesday afternoon at one," Maria said. "Perhaps you'd like to attend, Jennifer?"

Jennifer hesitated. Then Kevin said, "You ought to, honey. It'd do you good to get out of the house more."

Maria smiled and Jennifer nodded. "I'd like that," she said softly.

"Until Wednesday, then," Maria said. She squeezed Jennifer's hand and smiled brilliantly. "I will look forward to it."

On her way to the door, Jennifer caught a glimpse of herself in the mirror. She was smiling like a woman with a secret.

# Francesca Ross

❦

# Giving and Receiving

**Dorset, 1820**

She never let him give her gifts. That disconcerted him, for
ordinarily he was the most generous of lovers. He liked wom-
en, and liked pretty things, and liked giving women pretty
things. And usually they liked accepting them from him; he was
wealthy and had impeccable taste.

But Katerina maintained the edict as fiercely as she maintained her independence, and he not unreasonably became obsessed with disobeying it.

After the first week they spent together in the cottage in the
Dorset hills, he sent her an elegant little bracelet—six hundred
pounds' worth of pearls and sapphires in a white gold setting. It
came back by return post, with a cool note: "Sir. Thank you for
the bracelet. Regrettably, I am unable to accept it. Remaining always yours respectfully, Katerina Garrick." It was not, as he first
thought, a dismissal. No, she would accept his visits, and his
kisses, and his passion, and respond in kind. But she would not
accept his gifts.

"I am not your mistress," she told him once when he had the
effrontery to slip an Indian silk shawl over her shoulders. "I am
not your mistress."

And of course she wasn't, in the sense of being kept by him. Her husband had left her well off; she had a manor home in Devon and a town house in London as well as the little ivy cottage; she had a tragic past in a foreign land, a lost family she couldn't speak of; she had a child, a circle of eccentric artistic friends who knew nothing about him, a life of her own. She was not his mistress.

"What are you then?" he asked.

Folding up the shawl, she gave him that slanted look from those exotic Eastern eyes, the look that told him he would never truly know her. "I am my own. Nothing more."

"Then what am I?"

She had come to him then, her hands gentle on his face, her voice husky with love and longing. "Oh, Eric, you are my joy."

Aye, he was that, and only that. He was not her husband or her protector or her employer, her owner or her friend. He could not live with her or tell his friends about her or take her to meet his children. He was her private diversion, and she was his, and their connection was kept hidden from the world. He was only her joy, a secret reward she allowed herself when she had been very good.

And it was enough for him; he wanted to be no more than that. He had his own life, his own past, a wife he still mourned years after her death. He was as wary as Katerina of that sense of betrayal that would come of greater intimacy. They had both loved before, had learned, somehow, to live with loss. Now they had each other—but only in joy, never in sorrow, never in sadness.

That was enough for him, truly. He didn't want her sorrow; he had enough of his own. He wanted to tantalize her, and be tantalized by the mystery that was the center of her. He wanted to slip into her life as he slipped into her bed, bringing pleasure, reminding her to laugh and tease and love again. It was just—oh, he wanted to leave something with her when he left, something more lasting than the taste of him on her lips, than the trace of his kiss on her skin, something of himself.

Katerina, no less than any other woman, had her inconsistencies. She wouldn't let him give her gifts, but sometimes she would let him give her pleasure. She could not resist French chocolates or French scented soap or French champagne—by the bottle, at least; she refused the case. She was a sybarite of the first order, and she loved delicious things. So he could bring a box of bonbons, bite one in half and put the other half in her mouth, and laugh as she sighed and surrendered. As long as it was momentary, as long as it was mutual, she would shake her head and kiss him and accept.

So when he returned from voyages to the West Indies, he brought her Jamaican coffee for their breakfast. When he came down from London, he brought raspberry jam and crumpets from Gunters. She would taste and close her eyes and he would think, ah, at least you will take pleasure from me, if nothing else.

It wasn't until the third year that he thought of the cottage. After that, he thought of it often, when he was sitting in meetings at the Admiralty, when he walked on his quarterdeck hearing the sails sing in the wind, when he lay alone in his oceanic bed at home. The cottage was not the only place they met; there was a discreet little London flat near the new Regent's Park, where they could walk in the mist at dawn, holding hands like children, and a lodge within an hour's drive of town, where they could ride headlong across the heath. The cottage was reserved for those summer weeks when she took a holiday from the duties of running an estate and rearing a son. Their affair had started there, and he sometimes thought that one day, when he didn't expect it, it would end there. So he thought of it with a mix of longing and loss, of triumph and trepidation.

That third summer he came early, a month, in fact, before their appointed time. The sun was high, the breeze light off the lake, as he circled the little house, his boots leaving crescents in the soft grass. The yard was overgrown and the garden lush with May's abundance. The ivy climbing the old brick walls was glossy now, with tiny white flowers strewn like stars through the green. The windows shone in the sun with that peculiar blankness that said there was no one home. But the memories were there, drifting through the garden where they had their breakfasts, rising from the lake where they swam naked in the moonlight. Would she see the memories if their inconclusive affair concluded this time, or would she, with her gentle ruthlessness, dismiss them as she had dismissed him?

Of course, she had never dismissed him, never spoken of an end, never suggested they might not go on like this for the rest of their lives. She had no other lover, he knew that, and after the first few months neither did he—what point would there be in others? Sometimes he thought they could go on forever in their private world, making love a holiday from care. But they couldn't; he knew it. Joy was all they shared and joy can't last forever, not even with all the goodwill in the world.

He crossed the empty terrace in a few long steps, imagining her here painting at her easel, her brow furrowed in concentration, a spot of paint on her cheek, her sable hair pulled back in a long braid down the sweet curve of her neck.

"My mother painted birds," she told him once, watching the birds fight for space in the bath. Her eyes were opaque, her head tilted to the side, her paintbrush held suspended near the canvas.

Mother and daughter could both have painted the marble birdbath today. It was full of rainwater and white petals from the crabtree, the pedestal a dusty gray against the rich green ground. A motley flock perched on the fluted edge—a finch, a wren, an oriole, a bright and dark collection of song. The birdbath was an oddity in this humble setting, a block of marble elaborately carved like an Ionic column. It must predate the cottage by a half-century, installed when this plot was part of the gardens of a larger estate long since partitioned off when the mortgage couldn't be met. The great house was gone, along with the gardens, but the birdbath remained to testify to some earlier grandiosity.

It came to him then. He would give her something too big to send back, something too impressive to ignore. Something permanent. Something imbedded. Something to make her laugh and give in and accept, because she had no other choice.

A bath. He would make it a Roman bath, because she collected ancient artifacts, and because it would be big enough for them both. He would make it opulent, because he had always been extravagant. He would add on the most newfangled equipment, because he was a man of vision. He would sink it deep into the foundations of her cottage, so she would never be able to make it go away.

He was a navy man, used to acting with dispatch, and he had sources at all the docks. A block of Italian marble and its Florentine carver had just arrived at Southampton, to be used for a pedestal for some garish statue at the Brighton Royal Pavilion. A hundred pounds slipped to the king's contractor was enough to have the shipment condemned as flawed, and the carver was pacified with the promise of better pay. Eric arranged for workmen to meet him at the cottage while Katerina was still in London. Of course, difficult little Katerina had never provided him with a key, so he had to break a pane in the front door to unlock it. The workmen only looked down and shuffled their feet as he committed this felony, then trooped in after him carrying their tools. They excavated the small second bedroom easily, there being only dirt beneath the plank floor, and then the craftsmen moved in.

The plumber, having lately worked at the Brighton Pavilion, blanched when he saw his latest assignment. But like the Italian carver, he swallowed his professional pride and invented on the spot an innovative piping system flowing from a rainwater cistern on the roof, as well water lacked the requisite softness. Of course, the roof had to be reinforced to hold the cistern, and the walls replastered over the pipes, but that was a small price to pay for running water. Most impressive of all was the stove and water-tank contraption, through which a copper pipe traveled. When the stove was lit, the plumber assured him, hot water was only a matter of turning a tap. He produced from his pocket taps fit for just such a purpose; solid gold they were, with rubies in the handles, meant, he assured Eric, for the king's personal bath. The Florentine carver nodded his approval and went back to etching laurel vines in the steps that led up to the bath. And so the copper piping ran to solid gold taps, which spewed hot and cold water at the slightest urging.

Katerina could not refuse this gift.

The last workman swept up the debris and left Monday afternoon. Eric stood in the doorway, surveying the new addition. It was worthy of any Roman emperor, six feet by four, with a marble shelf running along one side, steps leading up and down into it, all of it carved of the creamiest Carrara marble veined in deep purple. Heavy gray towels were stacked on a low bench, a crystal decanter of bath oil nearby. Hand-painted gray and blue tiles covered the walls to chest height. The hearth was tiled in the same colors and stocked with beech logs. A bay window looked out onto the garden—eventually he would have to add a wall, for privacy's sake.

For a moment he sat on the step and let himself imagine Katerina's response when she saw his gift. Would she be angry at his high-handedness, declare that her rustic hideaway had been ruined? No. No. He ran his hand over the curve of the marble, cool and smooth under his touch. She would rise out of the soap bubbles like Venus from the sea, all naked glory, and welcome him home.

Katerina unlocked the front door and let the coachman carry the baggage in and set it down before she entered. As she tipped him, she noted with some distant appreciation that the cottage smelled not at all musty. Perhaps Mrs. Glover, the caretaker, had come in to air it out.

There was a white square on the floor of the tiny foyer, a note that had been pushed under the door. She opened it as she walked into the sun-filled parlor, savoring that sweet fluttering she felt at the familiar bold scrawl, the endearing misspellings:

"Kat—The last time I was here I left something for you in the back bedroom. I shall be there as pledged Tuesday. E." The door to that back room was shut, but an unprecedented amount of light poured through the inch-high crack underneath. Alarmed, she flung it open, then stepped back instinctively, blinded by the sun shimmering through a new window. Once there had been an old four-poster bed here. Now there was an ocean.

An empty ocean. "Oh, Eric," she murmured, rubbing her forehead with her fist, "you are *impossible*."

The tub took up most of the small room. The rest was filled with a merrily burning stove—what a waste of fuel, and in

June—a great expanse of window and window seat, and hundreds and hundreds of exquisite tiles, tiny gray triangles laid in a herringbone pattern. She almost turned and walked out again, but steeled herself and went to touch the shimmering taps. Just as she expected, real gold. No brass for Eric.

It was all new, the walls, the ceiling, the flooring, the window. And it was better suited for some glossy modern town palace than this old cottage. No doubt Eric thought of this as an improvement over the tin bath in the kitchen. But how could she sell this cottage now, if she needed to? Only one bedroom, but an acre of bath. You might have asked, she accused silently, and imagined his injured reply, *But you would have said no.*

With a sigh, she perched on the edge and gazed around. His presence lingered there with his extravagant gift. He had been here recently to light the stove. And the ice in the gold bucket was still melting around the champagne, next to a bouquet of yellow tulips from her own garden, stuffed into a lead crystal vase.

Idly, she turned one tap. First a trickle and then a stream of water emerged, only to pour down the open drain. The waste offended her frugal nature, so she cut off the water and looked about for something to stop up the drain. When nothing more promising revealed itself, she bent over to shove her balled-up handkerchief into the gold-rimmed drain. Like an inquisitive child, she turned on one tap then the other, letting the warming water cascade through her fingers. When it grew too hot to touch, she switched to the other stream, which was pleasantly cool and smelled of rain, like Eric when he came in from sailing.

It was very like a miracle. Katerina had heard, of course, of the advanced plumbing installed in new homes, of nabobs returned from India who insisted on hot running water. She had never expected to see it in her simple holiday cottage. But then, she ought to know better than to underestimate the grandiose Eric Radcliffe.

Extravagance proved contagious. With a generous hand, she poured in the fragrant bath oil, producing billows of suds. It was too inviting to resist, like its giver, and after a moment's struggle, she gave in. Twisting her hair up, tossing her gown and stockings into a heap in the corner, she climbed naked up and then down the marble steps into the welcoming water. The side opposite the taps was curved precisely to fit a woman's body, her body, in fact. Did he take measurements? Or did he know her so well? She slid down the slick marble, imagining Eric's square, capable hands sketching their familiar path along the slight curve of her back, the gentle slope of her hips, the length of thigh, while the stone carver nodded thoughtfully and measured the arcs left in the air.

The water rose, sluiced over her belly, through the valley between her breasts, over her shoulders, the suds tickling the sensitive nape of her neck. The oil made silk of her skin; she ran her hands along her sides, thinking of Eric and his designing ways. He had corrupted her, as she always worried he would, with his extravagance and ardor. He knew too well all her weaknesses.

She always found it hard to let go, to let the tight control slip, to give in to the simple joys of a man, a summer holiday, a love affair. She had always been tempted to live too narrowly, to focus her life too tightly on one source. Since her husband's death, she had not made that mistake again. Painstakingly she built another life, this one strictly apportioned. She had her literary friends in London, and her artistic friends in Devon; she had her charitable works and her paintings and the routine business of running a home and estate. Each part was separate and detachable from the others, replaceable.

Only her child and her lover broke through the boundaries. Her son, of course, was central; she was tied to him with a thousand knots. But she had no illusions; he would slip those knots someday, as he must. The process had already begun. Yesterday she had held her boy tight, seeking a reason not to leave. Once he would have cried and clung to her, and she would have wept too, leaving him. This time Jack had squirmed out of her farewell embrace, taking off after his little cousin without looking back. A child knew no loyalty, only love, and that love was limited no matter how unconditionally it was returned. She knew that, else she wouldn't have let him go; she knew all about the borders to love, and the loss that accompanied their crossing.

Eric didn't know that, she thought. He couldn't help himself;

he had a generous heart and couldn't help giving it away. She could be so generous only in passion, and only because some trick of nature had given her a sensualist's body along with a Puritan's heart. That, at least, she could give him—a passion to match his own. But someday it wouldn't be enough.

She thought hard of him, conjuring him up as if his spirit lurked nearby. She thought of his calloused sailor's hands, felt her nipples harden under her palms. She had left the door off the latch, and soon enough it opened. She heard Eric call her name, heard his footsteps moving surely, too surely, through the hall to her new sanctuary. At the door he halted, his expressive face the picture of surprise. "Kat, what have you done? A Roman bath here? What a sight!"

"You can't fool me, you rogue. Come here."

A little wary, he approached the tub. She reached out a hand to touch his leg, looked up and saw that he wondered if she liked his gift. She curved her fingers around the leather boot, felt the taut calf underneath, wished she could caress his tension away.

"I rather hoped," he said wistfully, "that you would rise to greet me. Like Venus. Merely for artistic demonstration, I mean."

"Like this?" Both hands on the sides for security, she rose, the water streaming off her, soap suds clinging in suggestive places. He was so close she could hear the quick intake of his breath, sense the instinctive flex of his hand toward her. She slipped back into the water, away from him. But then she held out her hand. "Will you join me?"

That merry smile that always lingered at the edges of his mouth broke through, and he yanked off his boots and stripped off his riding clothes. He was a beautiful man, fair-skinned and dark-eyed, restless and lean and mercurial. She wanted to tell him so, to tell him that she loved the laughing curve of his mouth, the sweet boyishness of his slender waist but all his life women had marveled over him, and he disliked it. So instead she waited until he ducked under and came up, soap suds frosting his shoulders, and praised what no one else ever thought to praise in him—his wickedness. "You were very clever, my darling, having all this done without my knowing."

The irony in her voice only made him laugh—he was in the clear, and they both knew it. He stretched out beside her, his long body slippery against hers, his hand sliding sensuously along her hip and up to her breast. He just skimmed the tip, as if by accident, and cupped her face, his thumb going to stroke the bow of her lower lip. Her tongue flicked his thumb; then slowly, tantalizingly she sucked it, her teeth gentle on the callus at the end. He bent close and kissed her, their mouths meeting as his thumb withdrew. "Were you surprised?" he whispered against her lips.

She pulled away to search for signs of guilt in his eyes, but no, they danced with laughter, pride, triumph. "Surprised. Yes, you could say that. I think I have never been so surprised in all my life. The bath, the window—the bath oil, in my favorite scent. How ever did you arrange all this? How did you get in?"

His dark lashes swept down to hide his eyes—he was guilty after all. He was also aroused; she felt him stir, rise warm and intimate against her thigh. But they had time yet for that, time to let the desire gather as they learned each other again. Time to let him explain himself, and absolve himself, and time for her to forgive him his sins and let him sin more.

"I had to break a pane in the door. It worries me, kitten, that it's so easy to get in here. I think my next improvement will be a solid oak door. And bars on the window. Not this window, I don't want to spoil the view—I had a locksmith take a wax impression of the lock and craft me a key." A bit sullen, he added, "I left the key there on the side table in the hall."

"Oh, keep it, Eric, do. This new addition without doubt cost more than I paid for the entire cottage, so I think we must consider you half-owner now."

That impulsive offer surprised them both, because she was never impulsive. But she would not take it back; it was a gift to match his own. He liked that, though he tried to conceal it, shrugging as if it were of no consequence. "It was worth every penny, just to see you surrounded by bubbles." He twined his legs around hers, holding her fast against him, her breasts pressed against his chest, his arms tight about her waist. "You do like it, don't you?"

"Yes. Thank you."

He had the grace to confess, "Oh, I did it for me, too. You know that."

"I still thank you."

"For what?"

"For reminding me of the occasional felicity of the universe."

He didn't want to be thanked, but he didn't want the gratitude going elsewhere either. She traced the sulky droop of his mouth with a tender finger as he said, "I don't know what the universe has to do with it."

"And the felicity of you. Ah, Eric, you remind me every moment—" She couldn't find the words, had to let her hands trace the thought on his chest, her lips trace the sentiment against his.

But he slipped away from her kiss—the bath oil made them slippery, she realized with a shiver of anticipation. "Katerina, my love, do cultivate a bit of patience."

He reached out a long arm for the bottle of champagne. "Let us toast to our Roman pleasure before you start on all that Russian pleasure you have in store for me." Effortlessly he popped the cork, then looked around, frowning. "I forgot the glasses."

"We can drink out of the bottle, Eric."

"But then how will we toast?"

"I can think of a way." She took the bottle from him, tilted it up and let the froth run into her mouth. Then, lying against his chest, she kissed him. His tongue pushed her lips open, slipped inside, made a sensuous circuit of her mouth.

"I love the taste of champagne on your lips," he whispered. "Kat. Kat."

They got through half the bottle that way, Katerina thinking that she could never take another lover after Eric. Surely no other man would waste so much time on lips and mouth and tongue while his hands lay gentle on her back and his erection pulsed patiently against her inner thigh. No other man would settle for just kisses while the water cooled and the champagne warmed, would let his tongue brush rough then soft against hers,

catch her lip in a gentle suck and then release it, let her tease
him with tiny bites and ask for no more than this moment and
these mouths.

It was she finally who ended this coupling of kisses, for her
hands ached to touch him, to trace the hard living form of him.
Her awareness was intense but narrow; she could not kiss him
and touch him too, not if she wanted to experience either. So
she rested her head on his chest and closed her eyes, let herself
be mesmerized by the steady surge of his heart, and detached
her hand from his to touch him.

In the months they had been apart she had forgotten how different a man's body was from her own; now she remembered
that his shoulders broadened where hers left off, that everything
soft in her was taut on him. By memory, not sight, she found the
tattoo on his upper arm, tracing the masts of the ship with three
fingers—his first love, he had told her once, the HMS *Defiant*.
He was entirely alien to her, this man, and entirely familiar now
that she could touch again this body she knew far better than
her own. Up past the hard swell of his chest, with its thicket of
damp curling hair, her hand found out those felicitous para-
doxes—the roughened cheek and the suggestion of velvet on his
eyelids, the silken brush of his long lashes against her wrist, the
generous curve of his mouth. Somewhere under her touch was
the secret of him, some essential knowledge denied to her vision
and reason. All of her followed that quest of sensation her hand
traced, and all of him waited in the silken darkness to be
discovered.

Now he became restive, as she drew her fingers across his
lips, down the square-cut chin, parting the water to trail down
the chest to the heavier tangle of hair below his belly. She closed
her eyes tighter, listening for that quick breath that told her she
had come too close, and traced a circuit around, sliding her fingers into the water-soft curls, feeling under her fingertips the
very pulse of his life. His patience was nearly gone; the muscles
and tendons in his loins were gathered tight under her touch,
ready to spring. She waited, suspended in her search, until he
moved, shifting slightly so that her hand could close gently over
his arousal. "Ah," he whispered, and she could feel, hear, the vi-

brations in his ribs lying ridged against her cheek. She slid her hand along the shaft, not to arouse him, only to explore him, the velvet skin, the pulsing ridge of vein, the power embodied there, the secret of him.

And then his hands were at her waist, pulling her up along his thighs, and she had to let him go to take him another way, her legs going around his waist to tuck against the marble wall. His entry was inevitable in that intimate position, his withdrawal an anguish, this action echoing in the core of her as she slid back and forth across his wet legs, until his strong hands held her there, body to body, her ragged breath mingling with his.

There it was, the border. He drew her across it, and she rested her cheek against his damp neck, her lips on the surging pulse in his throat, her own pulse surging in answer, and she felt the careful construction of her self dissolve. There would be time, she told herself, to build it back up again, time to cross back again that border.

But for now she let him carry her with him, hold her against him until the shimmering stopped, pick her up shivering from the chill water and wrap her in a gray towel, his arms wrapped around her too. The bed linens were cool, but his body was warm.

"Thank you," he murmured against her hair.

"For what?"

"Oh, for that occasional felicity of the universe of yours. And for you."

And for the joy, and the sadness it leaves behind. One day she would accept that too.

# Barbara DeGenevieve

❦

# My Mother's Body

I have this memory. I'm not sure where it came from. I don't know if it's a dream, I don't know if it ever happened. I don't think it did, but I'm not sure. I wonder how you'll feel hearing this. I'd hate to complicate or confuse our relationship, but I'm desperate to talk about it. It frightens me, but it excites me more.

We're in my studio, talking, sharing a bottle of wine. I tell you that you have a perfect body, the body I've always wanted, the one I inhabit in my fantasies, the one I watch in my fantasies, the one I fuck while my lover makes love to my other body. You sit there staring at me, not understanding what I'm talking about.

I ask if I can tie you up. You say yes, but you might resist. I say, good. We know each other. We are in the same body, the same mind, the same fantasy. When we ask each other questions, it is only to confirm what we already know, to play the word game, to hear the desire in each other's voice.

We move from kitchen table to couch. Rather than undressing you, I tell you to take your clothes off, slowly, for me. At first you are uncharacteristically shy about it, but by the time you've slipped off your shoes and jeans, the script begins to interest you. You stand in front of me in a long-sleeved orange velour shirt that fits tightly over your breasts, your black thong underwear barely visible beneath. Watching my eyes watch your body, you unfasten the 14 small buttons and slide the clinging fabric from each of your arms, letting it drop to the floor. As you reach to unhook your bra, I tell you to stop, that I'll do it later. For now I just want you to stand there. I want to take in what I have only been able to imagine. I can be the aggressive voyeur, the solipsistic pervert now. You don't mind. You like it. Your desire to be desired feeds my compulsive fixation on your body. You tempt everyone around you to fantasy. You want everyone to want you. Well, I do.

I ask you if I've ever told you about my mother. Only that she committed suicide, you say.

Oh. Your breasts are beautiful, like my mother's. It's odd when I think about the ease with which she dressed and undressed in front of me. She was so uncomfortable about every other aspect of sex in relation to her daughters, but not her body. I was fascinated by her breasts. They were large and very dense with nipples in perpetual erection. The thought that my body might one day look like hers thrilled me. I watched in awe as she put her bra straps over her shoulders, bent over and shook all of that pink flesh into the white cotton cones of her 36C Maidenform.

Bend over and shake for me.

Freud had it all wrong. It's the mother/daughter relationship that's so titillating. Women are either lesbian or bisexual; how can we be anything but, when our first and primary love object was our mother? Freud never got very far with his ideas about women because he was so hung up on the dick thing. It's the breast that's so powerful—for everyone.

I tell you to close your eyes and I lead you into another part of the studio where two heavy braided leather ropes hang from a ceiling beam. I quickly fasten you into the wrist restraints at the end of each rope, place a thick wooden dowel behind your back, and clamp your wrists close to your waist. In this position, your back is straight and your breasts display themselves to me. Your eyes are open now watching me prepare. I go to the toy box and pull out the blindfold.

Please don't make me wear that, you say. I want to watch you. It's more delicious when you don't know what to expect, I say.

You stop protesting because you are as much into your own pleasure as I am into mine. I put the blindfold over your eyes and tie it behind your head. Touching you for the first time, I run my fingers through your long hair, down your back, down the crack of your ass.

Lightly I kick your feet to spread them almost a yard apart. I walk around to the front of your body. I want to gorge myself on what I see. I move my face within a fraction of an inch of your smooth, browned skin. You can feel my breath as I exhale your scent back onto your flesh. I smell your whole body—up and down each arm, under your hair, around your face, down your back and left leg, across and up your right, circling around your waist to your belly and breasts and finally down to the place where I know you want me to be. I pull your panties away and nuzzle the dark, damp hair, breathing in deeply and blowing out into your separated lips. Your smell is strong and I linger only to tease you with the weight of my breath.

I move away silently as your body chills from the absence of my warm face. Where are you, you ask.

I don't answer, but I press my body into your back as I begin to peel off my clothes. I unbutton my loose, silky pants and let them fall down the back of your legs; I pull my shirt over my head and dangle it between your breasts before letting it slide down the front of your body. You can feel the soft leather corset I'm wearing, my breasts pressed against your shoulder blades. I turn and rub my ass against yours, letting you know that our taste in underwear is similar.

I take another tour of your body, my gaze focusing again on the beautiful breasts quivering inside a black lace bra. My lust embarrasses me and I'm comforted by your blindness to my lechery. I want to work your body into the same frenzy I feel in mine. My cunt is throbbing. I stick two fingers into my wet and swollen hole and bring them up under your nose. You smile and your tongue darts out so quickly that my attempt to tease you is foiled. I wipe my fingers on your chest as I slide my hand down to your breast and pull the bra away. I lick your nipple and you moan, the first indication of increasing heat. I suck hard for a few seconds then move away, leaving you with one breast hanging over the bra, the other still in place. You look quite helpless, an unusual situation for you.

Shake your breasts for me.

I continue the story about my mother. I don't know why I was so focused on her body. I never thought of it as sexual until I started telling you about it. When I was a kid, I compulsively drew breasts and high heeled shoes, usually without attachment to a body. When I got mad at one of my girlfriends, I would draw a picture of her naked and pretend a group of kids gathered around to watch and laugh. My mother found some of my pictures and was so upset she slapped my face and made me kneel in the corner with my hands behind my back for two hours. The next day, she took me to confession and stood outside, listening to make sure I told the priest what I had done.

I pull the other side of your bra down and run my hands across those exquisite tits. I take a nipple between thumb and forefinger of each hand and squeeze. Their immediate erection provokes a tighter pinch. Your head rolls and your shoulders sway back and forth as if teasing an audience in an erotic dance. I squeeze harder and your mouth falls open. I stick my tongue inside, probing the open cavity, then slide it over your lips and chin, licking your cheeks and ears while you squirm to move away. I pull you back by your nipples and with one last rough tweak, I release you.

I make another trip to the toy box.

The scissors are old, the ones my mother kept in her sewing box. They're beautiful—long shiny blades with a delicate incised pattern decorating the finger holes. I press them against your throat and you flinch from the icy coldness. Dragging them down your chest, I open them just as they pass your bra. I catch the fabric between the blades and slice. You draw your breath in through your teeth, making a hissing sound. I've heard it before. I know what it means. I move the scissors across your flesh to one strap—clip, and then the other—clip. The black lace falls to the floor.

Shake your breasts for me. You lean forward this time.

The hallway that connected the three bedrooms in our house was carpeted with an ugly green and brown fake oriental pattern. I knew how to negotiate the design to avoid the creaking of the old floorboards beneath. My mother never closed the door all the way when she undressed for bed at 9:30 every night.

Shake your breasts for me.

Your legs are still spread from my earlier positioning. Another two clips and the small piece of black cloth that covered little more than your pubic hair and cunt is lying on the floor near your bra. I pick it up and bring it to my face. It is as wet and aromatic as I expected. I put the scissors down but within reach and begin to roam your body.

It's not cursory this time; I'm no longer teasing. I take off the corset and cover the front of your body with mine. We move to a center point as if gravity begins where our bodies collide. My hands grab your ass, spreading your cheeks and exposing the puckered hole to night air. Our tongues enter each other's mouths and taste the wetness, feel the teeth, lick and suck lips, cheeks, chin, neck, shoulders, while our bodies remain glued together.

I finally break away to focus again on your breasts.

Take the blindfold off. I want to watch you want me, you say.

Your arrogance and voyeuristic desire arouse my exhibitionism. I slide the mask off your head and say, shake them for me.

You grin and lean forward, enticing me to play. I kneel down to face them, to return to a place of familiarity. I lift them in my hands, study them, and sink my face into their fullness. I learn them with my hands and every part of my face. My nose follows the contour of each, my tongue tastes and makes them wet, my mouth sucks your nipples, my head thrashes back and forth between them. You lean farther into me so I can have as much as I want. You love it—both what I do to your body and the frenzy you see in mine.

I pull away, knowing I can never be satiated but wanting to bring you to this same place of desire. I move the scissors over, place them next to your foot, and sit back on my heels between your legs. You look down and know what I'm going to do. Oh, no, please don't, you say.

Why not? I ask.

I feel so naked and exposed, you say.

That's just how I want you to feel, I answer.

But before I start, I lean into the hair and explore the flesh beneath. I spread your lips with my fingers and my tongue makes a slow deliberate pass over your clit. Your whole body convulses. You've been waiting for it all night. My fingers find the tunnel and burrow in while my tongue continues its slow but firm navigation of the center of the universe. The name of this game is desire. I want you to want me as much as you want to be the object of everyone's lust. My fingers move faster and harder in and out of your slippery cunt. Your whole body is trembling now and you are moaning loudly. The walls of these studios are paper thin, and I like the thought that the people in the three adjacent units are all hearing you.

I stop, leaving you very close to an explosion. You plead, don't stop. Please. Finish me. I want you back inside me, I want your tongue. At least hold me. This is cruel, you cry.

I pick up the scissors and touch them to your cunt lips. The coldness startles you but you are subdued for the moment by any stimulation. I grab some hair between my index and middle finger and shear it away. You wince. I do it again and again, pulling it away from your body but leaving only short stubble. I move a light close to your body so I can see your cunt mouth. The danger of the situation instigates new whimpers and moans. You like it. You like all attention paid to your body.

When I finish cutting, I brush and blow away the loose hair. I'm not going to shave you. This is much more abject, much less tidy, a contrast with the rest of your body. I'm reminded of the photographs of women whose hair was cropped to stubble because they were accused of being Nazi collaborators during World War II. I was fascinated by those pictures; it's only now that I can understand the sexual implications of being held down against your will and having your hair, part of your identity, chopped away. I want to feel the stubble on my face, let it prick my tongue and lips. I want to gag on the hair that gets stuck in my throat.

Shake for me.

My thoughts exhaust me. Your moans fill my head and I plunge back into your nearly bald pussy. This time I don't stop. I don't want to. I'm as close as you are.

I can see what you want me to do. I'm in your head and I understand the three spots that need attention. My fingers, tongue and face move from clit to cunt to anus. I think my heart is going to pound through my chest.

Your voice rises. The couple next door turn on their stereo to drown out the screams. With one hand occupying your clit, I reach up and unclasp the restraint on your right wrist. I hold you to keep your balance while you undo the other wrist, and we both tumble to the floor. You get on your hands and knees and I follow like a male dog after a female in heat.

I lie on my back, head under your cunt, and bring you down on my face. From here I see your breasts moving above me as I lick and suck and penetrate this hot wet mass of sex between your legs. I want to slow down again, to catch my breath, to take a drink of water, but you won't let me.

All my energy now focuses on your clit. Your hands squeeze your breasts and you move yourself rhythmically over my mouth, maintaining just the right speed, just the right pressure. Within minutes your legs start to quiver uncontrollably and you stop rocking. You stop breathing. You become totally unconscious to anything but the sensation that is erupting in your body. I watch it happen. You suck in your breath three or four times. Your screams are feverish. I continue to work your engorged bud until your body jerks away from my mouth and you collapse in convulsive spasms on top of me.

I have this memory. I'm not sure where it came from. I don't know if it's a dream, I don't know if it ever happened. I don't think it did, but I'm not sure.

## Karen Marie Christa Minns

❧

# The Muse Comes

*I felt her before I saw her, the summer blanket whisked from my
sweating body, the cooling night washing over me like fine mist.
Still fog-bound from sleep, I hardly knew what was happening.
Before I could cry out for help, the bed groaned, and then there
was the scent of her, like fresh peaches, like grapes ripened and
ready to burst. I listened as my stomach growled.*

*"Don't worry, honey," she crooned, laughing into my hyper-
sensitive ear. "You aren't the first."*

"It's your own fault." Kim rolled her eyes in deep disgust. She
put the cigarette out in her Diet Coke.

"Give me a break," I pleaded, trying to clean acrylic from a
brush. It kept me from facing my roomie's accusations.

"Orleans, I've sent over at least five students—each of them
has a couple of years of modeling experience. You tell me what
is wrong with any of them, for chrissakes."

I kept stabbing the brush into the cake of Ivory. Kim didn't
relent.

"Just because they don't meet some abstract scale of perfection! Jesus, O, all this shit about your 'muse' is just that. *Merde.*"

The P-town sea breeze of early spring was crisp, tangy, almost
edible. Still off-season, we'd soon enough be invaded by summer

throngs. Then there'd be full-blown, rowdy, ripening flesh a'plenty, all more than willing to pose—but that was later. My deadline for this last portrait was in three weeks. The naked canvas stared blankly at my offended friend. It had long ago tired of looking at *moi*.

"You know, O, you are the biggest looksist pig I've ever met, and that includes the last man I slept with in college. Yuck!" Kim plopped her lithe frame into the overstuffed and much duct-taped easy chair.

"Wanna go for my jugular with an Exacto blade?" I put down the now denuded brush.

"For the past nine months I've watched an entire parade of women pass through this studio, O. And now, the one painting that is of a fictional character, and could, ergo, use anybody at all as a model, you go bonkers—nobody is good enough. C'mon, the other portraits were of real women, O, but this is a made-up character—you know—like the Greek myth books in grammar school. Or your imaginary friend. You did have an imaginary friend, didn't you? Shit, I don't even see why you need an actual model. I think it's the old excuse to get laid—being horny can do strange things to a woman."

"Will you stop already?" I dropped a bottle of Simple Green on my foot.

"See! You can't even talk about it. Put the paint away and come to the club with me tonight. People think I've buried you at sea, it's been so long." Kim stretched and cracked her knuckles, then her entire body, joint by joint, like a giant Tinkertoy.

Wiping the cleaner off my Nikes with the back leg of my jeans, I tried to explain, yet again.

"When men write encyclopedias about the wonder of their muse nobody bats an eye, but let me strive for my little ideal, my little piece of perfection, and I'm a pig. This is the final piece in my first solo show, may I remind you. You're my alleged friend. I'm not supposed to get flak from you. Call that fair?" I leaned heavily against the sink, still rubbing green cleaner from my sneaker laces.

"There's going to be an Etheridge wannabe from Boston at the club tonight. Come with me, O. Lai-Sau is coming, too, and you know how Lai takes it personally whenever anyone tries to cover M. E.'s material. We have to protect the singer—I need help." Kim stood, five feet five inches of loose and beautiful.

"Maybe."

"Yeah, tell me something I don't know. Well, I tried. See you later, roomie."

I watched Kim open the attic door and head downstairs, the sound of her cowgirl boots the most lonesome music I'd ever heard.

Okay, I'm a pig—maybe. Perhaps, I'll admit it then, at least when it comes to this one issue: *The Muse*. Mine. Her first public "out-of-my-psyche" appearance just had to be perfect. It was my metaphorical ass on these canvases, *my* frigging muse. The other portraits were all "Women Close to the Artist"—not exactly a Shakespearean title, but passable. All of them were simply themselves. But the Muse—she was everything I thought, dreamed, felt or hoped about art and life, and most especially, about women. She was "The One" I'd been chasing all of my adult career. How many times had I fallen into heavy thrall with some incredible female only to fall out of love the moment the muse left her body? I'd paint the babe and, boom, muse gone south, affair *finito*. The woman hadn't changed. I hadn't changed. The only difference was the fickle timing by that most fickle of all capricious spirits—*La Muse*. And I honestly never saw it coming until the spirit split.

Not the best way to build a reputation—as an artist or otherwise. So, okay, I'm a pig. And I've racked up major karma. But why did paybacks have to kick in right before my first major exhibit? Kim was right; I'd gone through every beautiful woman in Provincetown who would even remotely consider a sitting.

Word was out—avoid Orleans at all costs. Secretly I blamed Lai-Sau, who was the first to accuse me of being an "unrealistic, unrelenting bitch-painter-in-heat" right after I'd politely turned down her offer to pose. It just wasn't the right look—the four-foot-eleven flat-topped Lai didn't possess much in the way of "musability."

Now I was up the proverbial creek without a paddle.

* * *

"I did warn you. Tell me that I warned you." Kim sipped her Heineken with delicate know-it-all grace.

I was busy stretching canvas, Goddess knew why. I had enough ready for the rest of my no-good life.

"Maybe, well, maybe there is one more student I can bribe." Kim was interrupted by a knock at the studio door.

"Come in, it isn't locked," I shouted across the attic.

The door swung wide. This was a good thing, since the woman standing behind it needed the space. All the space.

"My name's Melina. I heard down at the pharmacy that somebody over here is looking for a model—a painter's model?"

Kim spat up Heineken. She jumped up and ran for the bathroom.

"Asthma," I tried to cover.

"Really? At the beach?" Melina didn't wait for any sort of confirmed invitation. All six feet, two hundred and fifty-plus pounds stepped into the studio.

I backed up into one of the empty easels, knocking over a jar of acrylic glaze.

"Shit! I mean, never mind, sorry," I sputtered, dumping rags into the sopping mess. "Why don't you sit down somewhere."

Melina looked around, decidedly unimpressed. "That's okay. I have a dental appointment in half an hour so I'd like to get through this interview as quickly as possible. Is that realistic?"

Kim emerged, thank Goddess, her golden face tinged with fuchsia. "Hi. I'm the roomie. Sorry about my exit—beer down the wrong pipe, you know." Kim stuck out her slender hand.

"I'd heard it was asthma." Melina's fist swallowed Kim's tiny paw as she shot me a knowing look. I was not on her A-list.

"So, you live here, with her?" Melina dropped Kim's hand, nodding in my direction.

"Yeah. Downstairs. But she's the painter. I'm just a lowly art historian. Really, we aren't related." Kim grinned stupidly.

"Yes, well, I gathered you weren't sisters. Tell me what, exactly, you are looking for—in a model, I mean. I brought my portfolio. Actually, I'm only in town for three and a half weeks. Just finished a big underwear campaign—'Large Lady Fashions'— maybe you've seen my work? I needed a break so I came here to stay at a friend's summer place. Now I'm antsy. Not too much to do off-season, is there? I was talking to the pharmacist and she mentioned there was an artist in town looking for a model—desperate for a model, actually is what she said—said you were legit. Neurotic, but legit. Well, I've never done this type of modeling. Just ads. Well, actually, there is that commercial—'Heavenly Momma Pantyhose'—did you see it? Last fall?" Melina rose to her full height, stretched mightily, and then moved to the line of windows overlooking the sea.

I wondered if I wouldn't have a real asthma attack from lack of oxygen. Desperate, neurotic . . . maybe—but this desperate?

"Wait!" Kim was across the room and by Melina's side. "I did see the commercial! It won all kinds of awards, didn't it?"

"How nice of you to notice. Yes, it did. You *are* an art historian." Melina turned around abruptly.

Like a ballerina gone ballistic, I dove for two canvas panels I was sure she would knock through the windows. But it wasn't Melina's bulk that smashed them; I tried to pick up the broken easels and my own clumsy self.

"Are you sure she's the painter?" Melina looked suspiciously at Kim.

Kim merely smiled, enthralled.

Melina pointed at me again. "Does she do drugs or what?"

"Just caffeine and white sugar." Kim looked disgusted.

"That explains a lot. Well, ladies, do you want a peek at my portfolio? It's getting late."

I crawled to the duct-taped easy chair, my head still spinning from the stupid pratfall.

Melina reached into her tote bag and came up with a leather-bound portfolio. There was more invested in that binder than in one month of our rent. I was gasping and Kim was ready to genuflect. Melina only smiled demurely.

Gingerly, Kim reached for the English bridle-bound book and began to carefully turn the pages.

I was mostly dumbfounded.

Hundreds of Melinas—all in see-through nighties and peek-a-boo bras. Melina, earthbound, pinkly glowing, running rampant amid cherubic children, all sporting shorty p.j.'s; Melina in lace teddy and feather boa, striding wickedly atop stiletto heels. I had to stop.

Kim, however, was emitting a long, low wolf whistle, the likes of which I was sure Lai-Sau had never heard.

Suddenly, from behind us, we heard the soft thump of discarded shoes and clothing. Turning, I found our entire universe had shifted.

Not four feet away stood Melina—stripped. Ready, I suppose, to pose, or to fight. She was an amazing mountainous confabulation of Amazonian wonder, a mighty woman, a woman of might.

Firm as California foothills, buffed, waxed, shaved and shining. Rounded out, thickly ribald, undulating—all Melina. Her flesh was the perfect saturation of roses and cream. It was eggshell sprinkled slightly with golden dust of minute freckles—almost Victorian, and just as provocative because one knew these freckles only a spring sun could bestow upon the most careful of Northeastern skinny-dippers.

O Goddess!

O mother!

Kim and I fell back on top of each other.

Melina, well, she did not stop there; no, she began to "work." I guessed it was years with those hyped-up photographers on fashion shoots that made her move the way she did—or maybe that was just Melina—but she seemed to almost float over the attic floorboards, all the while undulating like the swells off Hawaii's North Shore.

Kim shoved an elbow into my spleen, but even the pain wasn't enough to shut my mouth. Melina was beyond voluptuous, beyond overload, beyond anything I had any contact or words or feelings for. I was in a place of absolute shock and disarray. Was it her pure animal sensual side, or just her size in comparison to any image I'd ever imagined about my muse? At that point, who could tell?

Finally, Kim sputtered, "Melina, really, that's fine. Thank you."

Melina stopped mid-flight, looking mildly surprised. Then she broke into a wide grin.

"It's so nice working with other women," she gushed, picking up her clothing as she went.

Kim dumped me unceremoniously from her lap and jumped forward to help the rerobing model.

"I knew we could work together," said Melina. "Now, here's my card and the number where I can be reached in town. You call me just as soon as you need me, but remember, don't wait too long. I'm only here for three and a half more weeks." She finished dressing, then planted a juicy kiss on Kim's cheek.

"One last thing." Melina turned before her descent to the street. "I've never had a problem with your 'tribe'—I mean, eighty percent of the people I work with are gay. But there are some folks in this town with way too much time on their hands. I know you know what I mean. I told my neighbors there won't be any more over-the-fence comments about 'the lesbos in town.' You both just should know where I stand. Toodley-oo!"

The attic stairs seemed to call out a wooden-voiced chorus as she descended.

"Don't say a word, Orleans. I mean it. This is a gift from heaven and you don't deserve it. You call that woman, you call her right back. You call her or so help me, I'll have Lai-Sau sit on your face."

Kim raved on. "Did you see those hips? That skin? Have you ever seen anyone move like that? Jesus H. Christ! Look at me, I'm sweating. I never sweat. Can you imagine what kissing her must be like?"

I sat back in the duct-taped embrace of the old chair and wondered.

But what about my muse? *My* muse was slender, ebony-tressed, closer to five feet than six. Her eyes were ebony, not delft blue, not shifting in the spring light like Melina's. *My* muse had a rich tan and would never move like that. *My* muse was an angel, a subdued lady, an intellectual who would have to be coaxed, after long hours of growing intimacy, into shedding her clothing. Her basic skin tones were woodsy and earth-infused, not peaches and roses. Kim's ideal (much to my, and I was willing to put money on it, Lai-Sau's surprise) was zaftig. But my ideal?

Kim took one look at my contorted face and shook her head in quiet disdain. Once again I was treated to the cowgirl rendition of "Lonesome Blues," as she clomped downstairs and slammed the door behind her.

I went to the window. I needed a fresh perspective on this strange spin. Across the street, the waves turned from palest peridot to deep emerald. Thoughts of all the women in whom I had seen the muse flashed like the light on the water outside. All the women I had been attracted to—later to find the Muse moving through them, filling them with inspiration to guide my hands, my eyes. There was the Gypsy, and Ginny, Medora and Melissa and Mary Jane, Katharyn and Catherine and Kathryne and Kathy and Cate, Lenore and Liza and Teresa: where did Melina fit?

Half an hour later, with the sun gone down in its celestial sputter, I dialed Melina's machine.

"So this 'muse' stuff, you take it seriously? For real? Kim told me you absolutely believe it. Huh?' Melina was fiddling with the bath towel I insisted she wear.

"Melina, look, if you talk I can't draw your mouth, okay?" I hid behind the canvas, grateful for its small refuge. I was in no way convinced that the experiment of Melina-as-muse was going to succeed.

"Right. Sorry." Melina grinned, then shut her mouth tight.

"You know, Orleans, these portraits of your friends, you've really got something here." Melina moved in that floaty way which defied the laws of gravity and totally unnerved me. She knew the effect it had on me—and relished it.

I was trying to focus on mixing colors before the light changed. She was not helping my concentration.

There was something about her skin—marvelous or terrifying. As an artist I had never had such a challenge presented to me. The light shifted upon her and, within milliseconds, the hue changed. Where there had been an amber cast it was now rose—or rose would cool to lavender, then suddenly, up to a warming gold. Maddening. Complex. Almost as infuriating as she was. She was getting under my skin.

"Have you looked at them?" Melina was insistent.

"Of course. I painted them, didn't I?"

"Look, honey, photographers need art editors to pull one good picture from a hundred rolls they've shot. Just because you drew these women doesn't mean you can see them. Take a break and come here for a second."

I made no move in her direction.

"Look at this one of Kim. I've only just met her but she's becoming a real friend—so smart and funny. I just love her little blush. And her friend, Lai, well, they took me by your club and it was a trip! I had the best time line-dancing. I forget how much fun women are. Anyway, this painting of Kim, just look at those eyes! Not only did you get the exact color of brown there, but you have the, well, the *expectation* of brown. You know what I'm saying?"

Okay, I'll admit it, by this time I peeked. "Expectation of brown?" I was confused.

"I don't know what you artsy-fartsy types call it, but you know, like even if I hadn't met Kim yet I'd still know what her eyes would look like, outside, near the ocean, or inside, at the pool table at your club. You got it down, in the paint, girl, can't you see?"

Melina had crept up and was not more than three or four inches from my face. I felt her hot, sweet, vanilla-scented breath as it poured over me. I noticed, too, the musk of her perfume. Sweat trickled down my sides and across my shoulder blades.

"It's a God-given gift, Orleans. I hope to hell you don't take it for granted." Melina stood there, hands splayed on her hips, like Athena.

I felt the blush burn, bad as Kim's.

"Isn't this what you're supposed to be doing in the first place? Showing people what they can't see for themselves? Like a poke in the eye with a sharp stick? Kim's loaning me some books and that does seem to be their point." Melina moved back. Suddenly, I could breathe regularly again. The air cooled down. I could continue to paint.

❉ ❉ ❉

"Well, it looks like something." Kim moved around the canvas.

"Care to be more specific?" I was swabbing titanium white into cerulean blue, trying for another generation of "Basic Melina Flesh."

"Well, it's just . . . face it, O, she intimidates the hell out of you." Kim stubbed out her cigarette in the empty ashcan.

"What?"

"Even Lai-Sau sees it and she hasn't seen you in a month. You aren't dealing with the real Melina yet—no understructure, no surface tension. What are these supposed to be?" Kim pointed at Melina's hips.

My face burned. I sputtered but couldn't come up with a quick line.

"Aren't you the artist who 'carves paint'? Isn't that what they said at the last juried show in New York? An artist who can go through half a gallon of 'Mars Black' just to get some model's pubes right? What's the matter, O? Is Melina pressing a few buttons back there, or what?"

A sudden image of what it might take to get Melina's pubes right flashed across my deadening mind. Kim was right. I was totally thrown by all my churning reactions to the model. Who the hell was I? All my old standards were being reset and I wasn't ready for it. Wasn't even sure I wanted the overhaul.

"You know, O, if you believe in your muse as intensely as you claim, you should be treating Melina with a whole lot more respect than you have so far. What if she *is* the muse, come down to play with your mind, as well as your other parts, huh? Better tread mighty carefully, Orleans. Listen, if you feel halfway human later, stop by the club. Melina might even be there. I'd say you owe her more than a few drinks."

Almost midnight. I'd cleaned every brush in the place. There was enough canvas for an entire flotilla to set sail. Only the still unformed, unfinished portrait of Melina remained to accuse. I grabbed my denim jacket and fled the haunted attic.

❉ ❉ ❉

The bar wasn't crowded. From the back I heard the high, happy sound of a drunk Lai-Sau and knew immediately where they all were.

I walked up to the bar and ordered a beer. Toni smiled, passing the foaming bottle along with a crack about me coming back from the dead. I took a long swallow.

And then I choked.

There, on the middle of the dance floor, in the arms of the bar owner—probably the most sought-after dyke in Provincetown—twirled and dipped my model, Melina. To the strains of Ronstadt's "Blue Bayou," Katherine Ann Maple, a Sharon Stone look-alike if ever there was one, moved the amazing Melina across the dance floor, totally absorbed and enraptured.

I couldn't catch my breath. Toni banged me on the back, trying to help. Finally breathing, albeit raggedly, I slipped from the bar stool, somewhat dazed. When had all this occurred? The way Melina was holding on to Katherine, this was obviously not the first time they'd locked legs. And it wasn't a "straight girl good-time dance with a friend"—not by a long shot. Score one for our team, right? Another freed-up straight girl finally on the right track. Right? So why did I feel so damned depressed?

I left the bar, meandering my way back to the studio, under the blaze of stars.

It must have been around three a.m. when I awoke, and then I felt her. Like cool air against my feverish skin, like a fine mist washing over me, causing me to shiver, still fog-bound, sleepy, unsure of what was happening.

"Your roomie let me in." Melina's husky voice ripped the remaining shreds of sleep from my consciousness.

I sat upright. She pushed me back down. I stayed there.

Before I could holler for help, the bed sagged and then, like a fine rain, like good light pouring all over and around and into me, her scent—ripe peaches and fresh berries. I listened as my stomach growled.

She laughed. "Don't worry, honey, you aren't the first," she crooned, her ruby lips descending and then locking on my gaping mouth.

The folds of her hot flesh enveloped me, velvet and wet, so

wet against my own moistness. Her leg was thrust harshly, exciting me with the shock, causing new wet to rise from between my thighs. Our breath mingled, then hers overtook mine, like a friendly bellows, feeding me clean air.

My arms came up of their own accord, floating weakly. I felt the large muscles buckle and shift beneath the firm flesh, felt the slick and slithery movement as she squirmed against me, the sliding curl, the happy dance, the gentle moans. She was crying like a dove, like a doe, like a dangerous angel.

As if on an air mattress in a swimming pool, warm, cushioned, suspended between two worlds, I surrendered to this magnetic ride, uncrushed, unrelenting, all hardened nipples and rising clits, all pounding hearts and smashing pulse.

Melina thrust again and again, releasing then recapturing me between the trap of her powerful legs. I was weak and groaning, taken for the third time, almost wrung out and yet she kept on. Wet, wet, so very wet, the delicious friction made me erupt volcanic, shuddering against her, inside her, through her. It was as if she'd been taking lessons on the side, as if she'd learned not only what to do but when to do it. My model turned muselover, beginning the slow, insidious grind that was blowing out into explosive fuck. Her hands reached inside me, kneading me, working me like the first time she worked the studio in front of Kim, and I was as taken—more, Christ, so much more. My throbbing clit, engorged as a cherry, ready to go off yet again, she carefully ignored, maddening me to prayer, praying for just one more touch, one more brilliant caress. But the maniacal nerve-maddened Melina just laughed and huffed and thrust yet deeper, moaning that she would take me the way I'd taken so many women all my bratty butch life. She could take me as deep as I could stand, maybe even deeper, making me burn in that obliterating place of black hole hunger, making me babble and speak in tongues, making me buck like an animal. Her fist almost wholly inside, her mouth only leaving my lips and tongue alone long enough to come up for sobbing gulps of air, she would take me, almost break me until, when I thought surely I would die, she brought me back up, buoyed me and started all over again.

Each act was given with such magnitude. Before I could ask or even groan, almost before I could gasp, I was totally engulfed, encircled, shaken; one with the heaving bed, almost lost to myself; every orifice filled with Melina. All hands and toes and tongue and breasts, fingers churning cunts and cunts lapping at lips and lips bit and reddened and teased into screams; clits ripened in voluptuous suck, bursting as if they could shoot, soaked and swollen and fully engorged, all meltdown, all high and magnificent gush.

Melina, Melina—when had there ever been such a powerful one? Melina my model, my lover. My muse.

"You know I'll never forgive you." Kim passed a glass of cheap Chablis in my direction.

All around us the crowd parted like water between stones in a stream. Nobody knew I was the artist, unless introduced. Nobody but my friends.

"I swear, I didn't make a single pass." I blushed, still thinking of Melina's scalding mouth as she went down on my clit again and again.

"Just this one night, you hear me, you artist hound-dog, you," Melina had whispered.

That's all it had been. She'd slipped away by dawn.

"Well, I'll believe it the day Lai-Sau proposes marriage," said Kim, reaching for the melting Brie. "You have to admit, it's the best portrait in the exhibit. The hit of the show."

My roomie was right—as usual.

I sipped the weak wine and toasted the health of my muse.

*Bonnie Ferguson*

# Amazing Grace

"The harvest is *ripe*, look out in the *field*," Wilette Jefferson sang as she moved among the bean rows toward Ruby Hawkins. She bent down on the word "harvest," her hands seeking out the slender green shafts hanging among the leaves. She picked the string beans, one after another, at the precise place where branch and stem joined, until her hand was full. When she got to "field" in her hymn singing, she straightened her back and re-leased the beans into her bucket.

Wilette moved closer to Ruby, ahead of her in the next row, and continued to sing the song that signaled it was time to run away—to go off and hide, play a game, tell a secret, conspire, ask a question, or confide a fear that only a girl of fifteen could have.

Ruby continued to pick beans until Wilette's voice was just a breath away. She didn't turn her head until their hands brushed, offering beans to the same basket.

"I can't go tonight," Ruby whispered so their mothers in the row up ahead wouldn't hear them.

"Who's going to watch me then?" Wilette whispered back.

"Watch what?"

"What I got to show you," Wilette said, grinning.

Every Wednesday night that summer, each girl left her home at dusk to meet at a certain crossroad, then follow a path to the

Zion Methodist Episcopal Church that bordered the Hawkins property. Before Wilette and Whistler got to courting, the girls would creep to the porch and watch the service through the window together because Ruby was afraid, being a white girl and seeing what went on inside.

Just for devilment, Wilette would sometimes leave her alone and go inside. Then Ruby would have to watch by herself as Wilette raised her arms among the others, all their hands fluttering in the air like low-flying starlings promising rain. Ruby would watch Wilette wail and sway among the men and women caught up in shouting spasms, arching their backs, jerking and swooning.

Sometimes before Wilette came to herself, Ruby would have to run home, her feet stuttering on the path in the dark. There she would slip into bed and lie trembling, in fear of the place where nothing was covered and nothing was still.

"I'm going by myself then and you just have to do without my secret," Wilette said, thinking about Whistler, and about spreading and waving her arms and legs, making angels in wet night grass.

Wilette left her field work and walked down the path below the Hawkinses' house where she and her mother lived as sharecroppers for Ruby's family. She took a bucket of cool water into the bedroom and washed herself by the window, enjoying the little licks of late afternoon sunshine on her body, thinking about Whistler out there waiting for her. She lifted the flowered dress from the nail by her bed, put it over her head, and let it hang like a canopy over her body, thinking of how Whistler could suspend himself above her. She let the dress fall down, past the brushes of her hair, catching at her hips, swirling around her sturdy brown legs. She pulled the top up over her breasts, pausing when the moving cloth made her nipples sing as she had recently discovered they could.

When she was ready, she grabbed a cold biscuit from the kitchen and went out the door, humming and singing. Her mamma was on the way in.

"You going to prayer meeting, don't go sashaying past the Hawkinses'," said Mamma. "Don't go showin' yourself."

Passing the Hawkinses' house, Wilette began to sing "Swing Low, Sweet Chariot," then changed to "When the Roll Is Called Up Yonder" because it was louder. She was gratified when Mrs. Hawkins came onto the porch to hurl a pan of dirty dishwater toward a slip of crepe myrtle, her eyes directing a strong rebuke at Wilette.

Wilette passed by with long strides, unaware of the soft white shape of Ruby slipping along behind her like a shadow. She climbed the hill above the creek, rushing, the blood rising in her face. When she reached the cemetery in the glen behind the church, Whistler was already lying on an unoccupied piece of ground, wiggling his bare toes, whistling a tune that was connected by nothing except cheer. He had gathered pine needles into a thick ground cover.

She ran, laughing, and he turned his head to watch her approach.

He was long on the ground. She towered over him—the only time that she could.

She put her hands on her hips and looked down on him.

"Jesus didn't never look *down* on who He was standin' over!" boomed the preacher's voice from the church. On a night as still as this, the straining voice of the preacher and the congregation's moans and shouts encouraged Wilette and Whistler, and hid their cries. That was why they continued to meet there.

Wilette worshiped him. His head was noble, the way he held it. His neck was thick and tender. The muscles of his arms were complemented by the range of his shoulders. His chest was wide and hard, narrowing to a waist that she could enclose when she circled her arms around him. His pelvis was quick and flat, his legs shafts of tendon and muscle. He was territory, and she claimed him sprawling, finding both with her legs, her arms, and all of her fingers.

As soon as she was settled, Whistler began on her dress, admiring the flowers on the cloth, capturing a scrap near her neck, rubbing it between his thumb and forefinger.

"Waas *blind* but *now* I see," the congregation sang.

Whistler never took his eyes off Wilette's face. When it was open and soft, he began his predictions, studying the shift of her expressions while his fingers moved with soft urgency.

"Your face is going to fall apart first," Whistler promised. "Your eyes are going to brighten and spring forth in tears."

"Amen," someone said inside.

A drift of breeze played across Wilette's back. She let Whistler move her with his hands and with his voice. It was one of the best parts, the slow run of his voice like sugar syrup, over her head and around her ears. When the prodding upon her from inside his britches became more insistent than his fingers, she eased off him and walked away, swinging her hips, knowing he was watching. When she reached the honeysuckle tangle, she slipped off her dress and bloomers and hung them there. She returned to him with her head bowed before his hungry gaze.

She let him take her by the arm, bring her down and back. She let him cup her head with one hand, to pillow it until he had her settled upon the bed of pine needles where his working-man's hand explored her deeper. When he finally reached down to undo his britches, she was ready to help him. He chuckled at her haste to expose his lively coil and let it spring. Astraddle her, he put his hands around his cock and hammered her folds. She raised her pelvis as if her hungry mouth down there could close upon him, take him in, and give suck. He let his cock nuzzle and part her until she moaned.

"I am *climbing!*" the preacher's voice inside asserted. "*You* are climbing!"

Wilette's brown legs climbed Whistler's back as soon as his first glide and thrust filled her. She panted, opening her mouth wider each time he delivered his drive, squeezing around him, sucking and pulling him with the mouth between her legs, eating and drinking him before he could withdraw.

"Enter into His gates now," the preacher inside told the crowd.

Wilette panted, opening her mouth wider and closing tighter around his pounding shaft until she barked as he called up the sharp deep animal woman sound she had inside her, the sound that made him come—filling her, emptying him.

"Lord, Lord," she murmured.

"Oh, mercy," he breathed, his words falling over her like baptism.

A gust of wind whipped up, carrying "Oh, For a Thousand Tongues to Sing" through the trees in peculiar harmonies.

Whistler slipped downward and Wilette caressed his ears as he licked up her wet place, he the mother cat, she the kitten newly born, he making her shudder and cry with pleasure born again.

"Wilette?" The cry on the air sounded like hope. Wilette raised herself up and looked toward the sound. She could almost hear Ruby in that cry, almost see her slipping away from the honeysuckle, hurrying to the churchyard, holding herself the way she did when she was worried or frightened, her arms clutched around her waist.

Wilette rose, gathered her dress, and went to the creek to wash. When she returned, Whistler dried her off with his arms and kissed her mouth before he walked her to the churchyard where the lights beckoned. Leaving her there, he slipped back among the trees.

Wilette walked toward the church where silhouettes swayed on the window and the sounds of singing rose again.

"The harvest is *ripe*," they chanted. "Look out in the *field!*"

Wilette moved closer and looked through the window, half-expecting Ruby to join her. She saw Old Brother Peterson dancing in his own circle in the aisle, his arms spread-eagled, all eyes beholding his ecstasy. She took the chance, and eased herself inside the door to join them, sitting down in the last pew, as if she had been present all the time, waving the fan beside her.

## Lisa Rothman

❧❧❧

# Commuter

I am sitting in the kitchen surrounded by the chaos of splattered tomato sauce and dried-out cooked spaghetti strands courtesy of my considerate roommates when the phone rings. It's David.

"I'm really tired from my bike ride."

Damn, he doesn't want to see me tonight. I guess that's what I have to expect when I go out with a man sixteen years older than I am.

"But I still want to see you."

Ah. Hope springs eternal.

This guy is not exactly a whiz at saying what he means. The first time he invited me to his house he said, "Want to meet my cat, Samson?" Although I'm allergic to cats I said yes immediately—I guess that doesn't make me too straightforward either.

Tonight David asks, "Want to come over to watch *Northern Exposure*?"

What would happen if I told him the truth? David, I don't want to haul my lazy ass to Oakland from San Francisco to watch *Northern Exposure*. I could watch it very easily from the comfort of my housemate's flea-infested bedroom. The real reason I'm going to Oakland is for the privilege of stripping down to my gray lace bra, pushing you against the kitchen counter, unzipping your Levi's Dockers and licking the length of your big cock until it stands up to your navel and you beg me to fuck you.

Instead of speaking my mind, I deal with logistics. How am I supposed to get to Oakland by nine?

"I'll pay for a cab to BART."

Though I am tempted, I take MUNI to the BART station instead. I'm just not comfortable having David treat me. It would feel too Holly Golightly.

My Victoria's Secret underwear slides and tangles as I cross my legs. Can the other passengers tell that I am going to meet my lover? At twenty the thought of having a regular lay still blows my mind. As the train enters the tunnel, plunging us below the bay, my ears pop from the pressure.

I get off the train and hastily tuck my billowy green shirt into my black jeans. David is leaning against the rail in all his six-foot-two-inch glory waiting for me. Taking my hand, he steers me out of the station. He opens the passenger side of his car first. What a gentleman. When David gets inside I stroke his red curly hair. He reciprocates by grabbing my inner thigh. What powerful fingers.

"Did you use the StairMaster today?" he asks.

"Yep. I need to keep in shape for the workouts you give me."

David unlocks the door to his penthouse apartment overlooking Lake Merritt. It's so soothing to leave my messy flat in the lower Haight, where the brown rug in the bathroom is shaggy with soapy water and mildew, where my housemates have been known to leave their dirty casserole dishes in the sink for five days.

We neck while we watch the show. David seems tired. I tell him he should get more sleep. "When?" he asks.

"I get plenty of sleep the nights that I'm not with you," I reply.

"I never have my nights off," he says. "I think about you all the time."

Right answer. As far as I'm concerned, he wins the car, the boat, the all-expense-paid trip to Jamaica and the ceramic dalmations.

But I've had enough of this idle chitchat. I slither my hand down his stomach to his penis, snake behind his balls, and press lightly on his prostate just the way he likes it. Groaning, he slides off the sofa and gets on all fours. I start stroking him from behind, running my hand from his ass to his abdomen. Occasionally I tweak his nipples. He keeps moaning and groaning. Staggering to a standing position, he leads me to his bedroom. "I thought I was just coming over here to watch *Northern Exposure*."

"It's a package deal."

He pushes me down on the bed. As I swing my legs up in the air to wriggle out of my jeans he grabs my cunt with his palm. I gasp and flop my legs over to the side.

"You're so wet."

"It comes with the territory. I'm just a fertile, nubile twenty-year-old sex machine. You should have felt me when I was still a teenage thrill kitten."

David does a somersault off the bed and lands on the floor. I pull him back on the bed and push him onto his back. My tongue begins a long slow journey to his cock. I devoutly outline the ripples of his taut stomach. His penis is soft by the time I reach it. No matter. I cradle it in my hand and slither it into my mouth, using my fingers to lightly scratch his balls. It starts to grow and hits the roof of my mouth. Success.

David begins to pant. "Oh, oh."

I don't want him to get too excited too soon, so I stop sucking. Instead I firmly lick from the base of his cock to its big fat head. I alternate between lightly flicking the head and licking its entire length. Once again I stop. Then I establish a slow steady rhythm and caress his balls. I look up. David's head is thrashing from side to side and he's pumping his pelvis.

"Please, please. Don't stop." I love it when a man begs.

Enough teasing. David's cock is so hard that it slides easily into my mouth. I pulse the inside of my cheeks and start to suck—hard. I feel his penis contract as it goes ramrod rigid and he's coming and coming and coming in my mouth. Cum is in my hair and dripping down my chin.

David lies on his back without moving for a good five minutes. Finally I ask if he's okay. Slowly he lifts his hands and stares at them. Once again I ask him if everything is copacetic. It's all he can do to stare at his hands. Eventually he says, "My fingers are tingling. So are my toes. That was the longest orgasm of my entire life. I have never experienced anything like that. Thank you."

He switches position so that I'm on my back and he's on his side. Slowly he rubs my clitoris with his thumb. Back and forth. Nice and hard. Over and over again. I'm about to come.

And then his hand stops. I can feel his chest steadily rising and falling. He's just plain tuckered out. I guess that's what happens when you have the longest orgasm of your entire life.

Unfortunately, I am one hot and bothered young woman. And, quite frankly, I'm a little resentful. When I decided to date a man sixteen years older than myself, I thought he would go to extreme lengths to please me. Instead, David got the greatest orgasm of his life, and what did I get in return? A comatose lover and the sound of his snoring.

I waited for him to finish his silly bike ride. I waited for him to take a shower. I waited for him to call me. I waited for MUNI. I waited for BART. I waited for the end of *Northern Exposure*. My pleasure has waited long enough, Goddammit. It's high time I claimed what is rightfully mine. As I wriggle my hand between our bodies and start to stroke my clit, I am reminded of the saying, "If you want something done right, do it yourself."

The sound of David's snoring represents his weakness and defeat, I decide, and I am going to mock him by turning it into my own pleasure. I let the volume of his snores set the pace of my hand. It's fairly quiet at first—a quick inhale through his nose followed by a gasping exhale from his lips. I stroke my middle finger up over my clit fast, then slowly slide it down. Up and down. Up and down. I dip my other hand into my wetness and bring it, moist and warm, up to my large breasts and massage my pale pink nipples.

Oh, David, if you hadn't expended all your energy on the ridiculous bike ride, you would be able to revel in my wet cunt right now. I'd let you stick a finger or two inside me, and you would feel the rippling of the walls of my vagina. Instead, you are oblivious to everything, drool gathering in the corners of your mouth, while your voluptuous twenty-year-old girlfriend gradually strokes herself into a frenzy.

Whenever David makes a noise, I move my hand. When he doesn't, I stop. His snoring grows progressively louder. I'm surprised he doesn't wake himself up. I am aware of how hard my nipples and clit feel in contrast to the overall softness of me. My eyelids are half-closed, my head is tilted back exposing my long white neck, and I am panting through my moist lips. Ah, David, you are missing out on what I know, having watched myself in the mirror countless times, is a damned sexy spectacle.

My caresses cross the line from leisurely to urgent, and my legs begin to tremble. What if he shifts position and stops snoring? When I'm this close to coming, holding back is torture. I hover on the edge. Even David's stupid cat Samson jumping on my face can't stop me. My toes curl and my back arches into David's downy chest as I come.

Gradually, I stop moving my hand. David stops snoring. I drift into sleep.

The radio news show *Morning Edition* wakes me up. David is standing in front of me, doing what appears to be tai chi. In the middle of a low lunge he stops to run his hands through his hair.

"What step is that exactly?" I ask. "It doesn't look like red-crane-waiting-at-the-water's-edge."

"It's the Yanni," he says. Then he goes back to the lunge and breaks it up by scampering across the floor like a hermit crab.

"And what move is that?"

"The M. C. Hammer."

Laughing, I get out of bed, amble to the kitchen and take the frozen waffles out of the freezer. David starts the coffee dripping and takes a shower. Midway through, I join him.

"Is it a hair-care product morning?" he asked.

"No, I'm going to the gym before work."

David drives me to the BART station and kisses me good-bye. "I'll call you tonight."

Going down the escalator to begin the tedious trip back to San Francisco, I wonder if I should stop this commuting thing. I'm a resourceful gal. I should be able to find a lover closer to home.

## Sonja Kindley

❧

# Make Me

There is a clammy, remote stairwell that no one thinks of using, and that is where we go, midafternoon, when I am done with classes and he has a coffee break. Today all I'm wearing is a short crepe dress and sandals, and my skin feels warm and steamy. I'm excited to be near-naked. He is wearing tan linen, white cotton, and tortoise shell glasses. He smells like foamy mocha, he smells like heat, he smells like he could screw me—but that is not why we are here. The stairwell is solemn and it is dangerous.

Turn around, he advises. I do, heart stuttering. He raises the hem of my dress and pulls my bare ass to his crotch. I feel his shaft pulse through pleated linen and I get dizzy, flower bulbs opening up inside me, nectar dripping. If I fall, will he catch me?

You have the stench of wench, Angie, he smiles, his dry palms creeping up my inner thighs.

Put your finger in my cunt!

He wraps his arm around my shoulder blade to hold me close and jams it in. My knees give; I am drunk with this; he holds me. He whispers, Your cunt's a little inferno . . . Yeah, I say helplessly, clenching onto the finger which draws me out, spreads me glistening over smooth white.

Tell me you wish we were fucking!

I am bent over the railing and his cock is out now, sliding between my trembling thighs.

I wish we were fucking!

Say it again.

I wish we could do it. I wish . . . I could have you . . . just once . . . inside me . . .

I mean this; my intensity is almost hysterical. I want to shove that erection inside me and have at it, to gasp and laugh and squeal, to get rammed by this brilliant, worldly, wicked fifty-year-old man who is my equal in deviousness and the sport of seduction. Leo, Leo Saxon, who is popular and respected and not unkind.

He will do everything but. Or not even that. He hasn't eaten me, nor I him. We are playing it safer than safe, which means no latex and the wedding ring stays on.

I am straddling the railing and its cold metal feels cruel and kinky. His teeth come down on my right flank and I yelp in surprise. Little peach, juicy thing. He kisses to make it better. I want to leave my mark on you. No, *I* do.

He zips his pants and I turn around, aggressively meeting his eyes. I like to get up close and stare at him because it's interesting how the intimacy unsettles his usually unflinching composure. We separate and watch each other. He is sitting on the steps, I am standing.

So tell me, he says, Why do you want to fuck your dad?

He became my dad when he said he was my mirror reflection, and that my swagger was affected. He saw how I don't trust easily, how I doubt my femininity. He told me I have great potential and will go far because I'm a truth-seeker and an adventuress and that is when I thought: a father. You see, he understands me.

I was tired of boys and their demands, their I-don't-knows, their wonder at warped sex, their fleeing. I was with a boy once who hung onto my back as a papoose, so timid, never voicing opinions. In bed he would thrust away arhythmically as if I were

a blow-up doll, and then come with a whimper and a sigh. Don't
tell me that can't hurt after awhile. I'm tired of boys.

Leo says boys are easy, too easy, when we compare tales of seduction. And: Men are dogs, women are cats. Woof woof, I say.
He smiles at me with curiosity. Who is Angie this time? That
time I was my little self, the one who says nasty words for a giggle, the one who flashes, the one who jumps up on him like an
untrained puppy. Leo thinks all this is a pose, the one I use to
manipulate people with, the sure-fire method for enchantment.
I am afraid he is right.

I thought the ring was a teaser, although I now recognize that
as desperate hope, not insight. I thought, he is the kind of man
who would wear a ring to attract only women who are looking
for trouble. This is still true, but it's not the reason for the ring.
Diane, the jet-setter whom I've never seen, is. She's a buyer for
Saks and hobnobs in Europe much of the time. Leo says their
marriage is quite good. I believe this; I would hate to believe
otherwise and feel destructive. The reason we don't fuck is that
their marriage is quite good.

No kids, thank God. I'm sorry but I could never let a father
of a person older than me grab my butt, it's too sinful.

Leo has all his hair, a strong jaw, and an energetic, fit body.
He was a drug fiend and hyper academic in the sixties. He now
rides a Harley, which he insists keeps him in touch with his feminine side—spread-eagled, a big warm machine between his
legs. He is proud of that feminine side and likes to feel gentle
sometimes. I don't think he knows jack about femininity, but I
won't say that to him yet.

We met because I originally wanted to set up a summer in-
ternship with the magazine but missed the deadline, so we were
just going to rap and he'd look at my résumé and offer advice.
I liked him when he said, "I think that bright, thoughtful, articulate young artists should be cared for." I thought he was referring to me. I knew the rumor about him, though, and wanted to
see if it was true: ladies' man or not? I could tell he was sincere
about his dedication to his work and fostering young talent—I
recognized him as a good man with heart—but I also sensed his

love of mischief, as he teetered between friendly professionalism and artful sleaze during the two hours we chatted.

A month later he revealed, "I had this flash of putting my cock in your mouth, but then went back to the business at hand. There was something about the way your lips curled . . ."

I scolded him—You shouldn't have been thinking about those things so early!—but he was more honest than I: I had had erotic dreams about Mr. Leo Saxon before I'd ever met him, and when he said that, I realized he was the first man I'd met who seemed to be as fascinated by sexual tension and its inner workings as I was.

How do you do it, Leo?

Even on acid he was pulling straight A's at grad school, four hours of sleep a night. He sold his services to a wealthy Mrs. Robinson—satin sheets, honeymoon suite, age eighteen; he had a pleasant and solitary homosexual experience in the early seventies; he has swallowed cum—he is braver than I. Leo, of the *ménage à trois*, the Why Not, the wake-up screaming scene— yes, it's in his past; no, he's never had "safe sex" per se but he might be persuaded to step into the phone booth and become Latex Man if, by chance, we feel compelled to do the deed.

Where are you, Leo? I'm waiting in the lobby, wearing your favorite dress, the narrow purple rayon with the buttons down the front. I want to feel your gruff hands on my hips. I wish I could kiss you but you don't kiss. I like you so much. You challenge me. You want me to succeed in life, to grow up without making your mistakes, to take risks.

See, I brought some photos from my childhood to help you remember me as a kid. My birthday was June 12, 1970. Gemini. I was a weird, ghostly thing before I became more confident and pretty. That is me when I was thirteen and had no real friends. I lived at Gramma's farm that summer and mucked around with the animals. The bandage is on because a horse stepped on my toes. As a baby I had enormous blue eyes and a pouty underlip.

You were twenty-eight when I was born, remember.

I am still looking at the photos when he takes a seat beside me.

Who's the babe?

Oh, I don't know.

Lemme see them.

He goes through the pictures quickly as if speed-reading, looking for a theme, the major points.

Even as a child you were into costumes and drama, he observes. You were cute and coy—enfant terrible. Collusion written all over your face.

He once said that he'd "smelled" it on me when we met. My nasty curiosity. I told him I am really quite inexperienced and he said, "You just think you're more virginal than you are, Slick." When I asked, he said I was neither a succulent nymphet nor a jaded woman of ill repute but a "succulent woman who wants to retain her nymphetishness while becoming more jaded."

He can describe me to me with astonishing accuracy. He knows what kind of transformations I have gone through to deliberately erase my family's influence, from the mild cautious bookworm to the shrewdly flamboyant femme fatale; he knows the image I desire will always elude me until I stop cracking the whip. He calls me a narcissist. He tells me we are made of the same mold, full of too much jive and power trips, only he is a face reader who ignores how he feels and I am a manipulator of faces.

I say these things to you with affection, he says. And I know you are strong and self-aware and will take what you want and chuck the rest.

His hand is on the top button of my dress. He opens it slowly, exposing my throat.

Leo says, I would hate to have you think I took advantage.

And another time: You should never reveal who you really are because people will take advantage.

And then: Why do you want to fuck me? I'm a happily married man.

I say, You are bad and like to get into trouble. You are the first man who has ever seduced me before I seduced him and the first man to make me blush. So, thanks.

I can't explain why I want to fuck him. Maybe I don't really want to go that far.

We're outside on the park bench now and I'm getting that feeling again, that daughter-dad giddiness which makes me act like a goofy girl, munching chips with my mouth open, sitting with my knees pulled to my chest. I'm happy. There is a sweetness between us. He tells me I am a kook; he is stimulated by my stubborn passion. Then he chides me for flashing my snatch—he calls it that; not very dad-like, I might add. I think I'd like to snuggle up to him. But we are across from his building and I understand the situation all too well.

His face does not look like mine. Though light-haired, he has a profile like Clark Kent. How can he be my father? I am soft and wispy and red-haired, with Swedish blood.

I ask him if he has five minutes for a rendezvous in the stairwell. He can't say no. I watch him and he has so much vitality and directness—it amuses me to note what a fine actor he is, looking so courtly and open when he's actually planning sleazy escapades.

I join him thirty seconds later inside. He looks at me sassily when I open the door, as if I had interrupted a meeting.

You want something, he says, knowing I am never satisfied.

I want to kiss you. Can I?

I lean over, put my hands on his shoulders, and try to kiss him but he opens his mouth wide and my lips fall in. He did that on purpose.

I hate you, I say.

I'm sorry. Hey, Angie, don't sulk.

You made me feel stupid.

I apologize. Sometimes I can't control my antagonistic tendencies.

You don't trust people—I trust more than you do. I make myself vulnerable but you're always playing games.

Give me your foot and I'll kiss it.

Yeah, sure.

Give me your foot.

I let my shoe clunk to the floor and he puts my leg across his corduroy thighs and pets it like a sleek eel.

There is something very intense about you, he says. If I were
twenty-two you would scare me. Sometimes I wonder if you are
a spy, sent out to ruin me.

As if your reputation could be ruined!

I drop my leg between his thighs and rub his crotch. I think
corduroy is a funny fabric. He is gazing at me. When I touch
him I feel powerful—it feels like trespassing and I do it with
glee.

Now he's tracing my lips, now he's thrust a finger inside my
mouth and I roll my tongue over this invader and tighten lus-
ciously. I feel a charge in my cunt. He goes in and out slowly.

I would love to slide in from behind and fuck you.

I grab his hand and put it where it should be.

See how wet I am . . . I'm oozing.

I would even love to watch you with another man.

Put it in—please.

He is rough and I am caught off-guard. He forces my walls
open with his index finger and it's not sensual, it's rude and frantic. I take hold of his wrist. I move my hand into his big hand
and when I meet his amused eyes I look away, then brush the
dust off my dress.

His theory is that when you really trust someone nothing they
do to you will feel painful because you're so open to them. I fear
ever reaching that point, even though it's considered good; I
want to always be able to distinguish pain from pleasure. The
lover I trust will not be someone who will ever hurt me.

Leo said, You must not tell a soul. So far I have told a couple
of souls. My reasoning was that they don't really care who he is
and besides, they would not be inclined to talk about this with
anyone who cared. The secret was burning a hole in my stomach. I felt as if I were losing touch with the moral majority in my
degenerate pursuit of intrigue.

I made my friends uncomfortable. I understood then that I
really was all alone in this, that even if I were to confess to every
friend I had it would still be my burden, and I would run the
risk of serious self-incrimination. I hated feeling judged by a
trying-to-be-sympathetic jury. I became defensive, spiritual: I

said he was an angel sent to unnerve me and help me recognize my strength, and my receptivity to the message was contingent upon a sexual rapport. I was breathless. I gave up.

We're in his white, airy office overlooking the park. He has a hollowed skull of red clay on his desk which seems voodoo-ish but he can get away with it; there is nothing weird about him to the public eye. He tells his staff nothing; they can only guess.

So how would you explain my presence to someone? I ask, slyly.

You're an aspiring journalist and I'm taking you under my wing. I don't need to explain it to anyone.

Should we close the door?

Nope, don't need to. We've got an open-door policy here.

I want to show you something.

I lift up my blouse and flash my dainty breasts.

I didn't see anything. Do it again, slower.

I know what he's doing, he always does this: He takes my dare and ups the ante, making me exceed my threshold for scandal, scooting me past an already tainted decorum.

I have so many questions for him in the back of my mind about how he grew up, how he loves, what made him want to get to know me, why he's still with Diane. There never seems to be enough time. There's so much joking.

That's why I typed up the questionnaire. His laughter is a short blast; he can't wait to read it. "This is most excellent," he says. "It's so Angie. Direct, aggressive . . . academic."

Question one: What was your relationship with your mother like?

"I was her surrogate husband. I slept with her from age four to nine when my father would go out with prostitutes. Nothing happened, of course; I would just listen to her cry and complain and try to comfort her."

Question two: Should I trust you?

"You mean am I trustworthy? Yes, I am trustworthy, but I can't tell you whether to trust me or not. The choice is yours. You have to follow your instincts. Somewhere along the line a person you're close to is bound to disappoint you if that kind of promise is made."

After ten more questions to which he responds frankly— almost too frankly (I'd assumed he would laugh at some of them but he took each one seriously, which made me embarrassed for doubting his sincerity)—he puts his coffee mug down and says, I understand you so much better now.

I get off on the pornography my mind whips up, splices and dices; I am sometimes surprised by what I need: I like force, a hissing in my ear, a passion that makes me happy, helpless, a man who knows how to fuck me. Because Leo has me twitching, flipped out with desire, I think of him, always.

I see him following me up the stairwell, smiling and focused. I see him on his knees, licking me, murmuring, *You are so beautiful.* I let him lead. His hands smooth my body my skin tingles I am alert he says *Relax Angie I need to fuck you you're so sexy* and has me lean over the railing and OH he's in he's thrusting I hear him groan my wet walls clutch him hold him I need to come screaming I am losing control he's on the edge his breathing is shallow we will get to the same place at the same time . . .

I meet him for coffee and he asks, Are you wet? and yes, I am.

He's not going to touch me. I can see it in his eyes. He is thinking, "I should be more respectable. Maybe." But it's also possible that there are no shoulds in his vocabulary, as he is a spontaneous man.

He used to say "make love." Now he says "fuck" more than I do. I am inclined to call it "making love" now because I have these reverent feelings for him, but fucking is what we will do. Is this sad?

I tell him I think he has too much power.

No, he says seriously, I don't have any power. Maybe you're just not used to these terms?

Right, I'm not. But you can't deny that you dictated the terms, and that's power.

The choice was yours to accept or reject.

o  o  o

The first time we touched: It was seven-thirty at my apartment and he was half an hour early for our breakfast date. He asked me to dim the lights. He asked me to come over. I went over to him, feeling curious. Closer, he said.

I stood between his legs, a little princess in sky blue silk pajamas, waiting. He breathed me in: His face brushed across my throat, memorizing my natural rumpled bed scent. I remember thinking: I am very young. I was quaking a little from the danger and my lust. His light brown hair was thick, smelling of citrus.

He said, I want to touch and not touch.

He said, If you could feel only one part of my body, what would it be?

I squeezed his thigh as I stared into his eyes and watched him respond. He took his turn and caressed my ass through the silk and I thought: I am younger. I lowered myself onto his thigh.

Look at my breasts.

Just look? He unbuttoned me, watching my face seriously. What would you like me to do?

I answered, in a small voice, shy: Feel me.

When I rubbed his erection it felt sacrilegious—what was I doing, touching an older man's cock?—then deliciously nasty. I felt empowered. I had never related to someone like him in a sexual manner. With each stroke I had my way with every male history teacher, every friend's handsome relative, every actor/musician/politician I have desired from afar. That is some kind of power. I accepted; how could I have refused?

Today I assure him, though, that if the sexual element in our relationship is causing any discomfort I would be happy as a platonic friend. He said the same thing to me the third day after the initiation, I remember.

A flash of relief appears on his face.

"This is good—it's good to have some nice options," he says. "I haven't made up my mind yet but I'm glad we're mutually respectful."

Then he sits back in his chair and describes a "secret position" he knows and he won't tell me what it involves but "one of these

days we'll either find ourselves in it or you'll discover it on your
own."
   So I'm still dangling.

   There have been times when I've wondered about Diane and
felt rotten, but whenever the guilt comes I start feeling disgusted with Leo because he's older and should know better.
Sometimes I want to reprimand him: You think you have the
right to just fuck around with women half your age to do whatever you please when you're married? The thing is, I can't
express this disapproval because I'm benefiting from his degen-
eracy. So we call each other "sleaze ball" affectionately.
   We don't talk much about Diane, but when he brings her up
he has compliments. I'm not jealous of Diane, actually; I think
she's probably a great woman, a hard worker.
   That's enough on Diane.

   I'm blind.
   I'm in his car and a cool, wet wind blows against my face as
we go around curves, up these anonymous hills. A silk scarf is
wrapped around my eyes, our agreement. He asks me if it's too
tight and please tell him if I get too hot or cold. I touch the thick
Pendleton wool of his blazer, I feel the heat of his jean-clad
thigh, the softness of his shaved cheek. I am safe.
   Tonight we are going to make love.
   There is something thoughtful about him, something tentative. He hasn't made many jokes and there are more pauses than
usual. He admits that he is going through a small debate, and do
I understand why? Yes, I understand why. He wonders if the acting upon desire is less important than the desire itself, or the
pursuit. This has all been good fun and I like you a lot . . . he
explains.
   But what happens once we get over the edge? I fill in.
   Yes. I'm afraid of fucking things up in three people's lives,
he says, simply.
   He stops the car. We must be up in the hills where the big
houses are. A minute goes by. A decision is made. He pulls back
onto the road.

How are you doing? he asks.

Good. I love this mystery. I like feeling clueless.

Soon we park and he takes me gently by the hand. I take tiny steps but he will watch out for me. I feel like a gummy-eyed kitten, sniffing wildly, nuzzling. He picks me up and my black velvet coat falls open as he folds me into a furry zigzag. We go up steps. This may be his house, though he said it wouldn't be.

He lowers me onto a futon-feeling surface and spreads me so I'm lying on my back. The softness could continue indefinitely, wall to wall, a moonlit cushy rumpus room. I have no sense of space.

The door clicks and a second later I feel his body next to mine, a warm breath on my neck, a broad hand resting on my hip. I reach for him, purring. He puts his thigh between my legs and I hold on. He is pensive. I want to keep my blindfold on and go by Braille.

Nothing needs to happen, I say.

I know.

But you are serious. This is confusing to you.

Give me a minute.

I wriggle out of my coat. I unzip my dress. I don't know if he's watching me or not and the uncertainty relaxes me. I feel close to him. I strip until I am naked. I reach for him and affix myself to his body, feeling pleasant.

Suddenly he's on top of me, pushing my legs open wide and rubbing hard against me. There is anger in his movement. I try to adjust to it, hoping it is passion. He scrapes his fingernails down my skin, he bites my tits. We are breathing heavily. I pull off my blindfold to see his face and it is agonized: tight jaw, closed eyes. He is harsh. He flips me over and I hear a zipper unzip, pants pulled down. My face is smushed into the pillow and I'm soaking wet, terrified. He yanks my ass up to him and puts his raging hot cock at my cunt, grazing my clit, and I begin to pulse. If he fucks me I will be gone forever.

Leo!

Angie . . . he slurs. Angie . . . let me get to you . . .

But I slither out of his grip and lean back on my elbows.

Tell me you wish we were fucking, I say.

Oh God, not this.

He runs his fingers through his hair, staring at me with disbelief. Without glasses, his eyes look vulnerable and aged.

Say it.

Angie, I won't do games. Don't be a girl.

He rubs my pussy, slicking me down. I feel like collapsing, running wet all over. He slowly drives two fingers inside, his face hovering above my belly, then lowering to kiss my inner thighs.

. . . Because you're not a little girl, Angie . . .

I'm opening to him, I clench his hair in my fist as his tongue flutters on my clit, one firm hand holding my tilting pelvis down. I shudder. Tears begin to pool in my eyes.

. . . and you don't need a father . . .

Leo! I cry, breaking the rhythm, We can stop, we can stop this! I want you to look at me.

I push myself up. I give him my hand, and he takes it. He waits for me to speak, his face softening when he notices the tears. We pause, watching, as the rain knuckles the rooftop.

I want to tell him about the angel. I want to say I got the message, I want to use the word *trust*, to say, Watch me fly from the cocoon, watch me leave you as a daughter. I got the message.

But my mouth is dry. I'm a slippery naked thing with wide spooky eyes, soft bones, and now I'll hold myself, waiting.

## Michelle Stevens

❧❧❧

# Pornophobia

It was already dark by the time Emmy and I got home from the rally. I was carrying all the signs, since both her arms were tired from thrusting her fists in the air. She had a sore throat, too, from screaming so much.

Emmy and I had been together about three years, and these weekend rallies had become a way of life. Emmy was a member of NOW, GLAAD, Greenpeace, Eco-Feminists for a Non-Violent World, and about three thousand other activist groups. In the past six months she'd even added the ASPCA to her list.

Today's rally had been an antipornography sit-in at the Playboy mansion. Actually, it was held two hundred feet away from the street end of Hugh Hefner's driveway. There were about twelve of us sitting in the ivy, chanting slogans and holding up signs.

Hugh never showed.

When we got home, Emmy took off her boots and plopped down on the couch. I dropped my signs by the front door, along with a stack of the magazines we were protesting—used for display and educational purposes.

I sat down beside her and kissed her feet.

"I'm pooped," she said with the little bit of voice she had left.

"Saving the world is hard work," I laughed, and I kissed her feet again.

When she closed her eyes, I took the chance to take a long look at her. Just ninety-seven pounds with those tiny little features: a turned-up nose, little baby lips, and the same pixie haircut she'd had since I met her. With the Levi Strauss jeans and the Eddie Bauer shirt, I imagined she was the perfect genetic mix of k. d. lang and Katie Couric.

The brown eyes opened sleepily. The little baby lips gave me a grin.

"What are you thinking about?" she asked.

"Sex."

She giggled and rolled her eyes. "I'm too tired."

"I know." I got up and kissed her forehead. "I'll make you some tea."

Before I went into the kitchen, I quietly picked up the informative stack of *Playboys* and *Penthouses* and *Hustlers*. Emmy was already asleep.

I went into the kitchen and picked up the kettle, dropping the magazines on the table. The top one opened to Seana.

Seana. Beautiful, long-haired, long-legged Seana with the world's most perfect breasts. *Penthouse* Pet-of-the-Month, September 1992. Many a night had I spent with Seana while Emmy was at a meeting. And Brandy and Lacy and Maxine, Mistress of the Night. Oh, if Emmy only knew!

I was deep into Seana's thighs when the kettle brought me back to reality. I put the tools of women's imprisonment into their rightful drawer and brought Emmy her tea. She was still asleep, and I didn't have the heart to wake her. I put the mug on the coffee table, threw the afghan over her and went back to the kitchen.

Seana was right where I'd left her.

In the bedroom, I pulled out my power-packed Panasonic Massager 2000. It hadn't been designed for this purpose, but it did the job anyway. Emmy had a real vibrating dildo that she'd bought at the West Coast Women's Music Festival. It had two speeds and was shaped like a dolphin.

I lay down on the bed, put the Panasonic on my crotch and opened to the first page of Seana's layout. There she was, in her little white boots with her little white jumpsuit, smiling at me,

flirting with me. "The Luck of the Irish," read the caption. I like
to read the stupid captions.

As I turned the pages, there she was again and again. In her
little purple business suit with the skirt missing. In her bad-boy
leather biker jacket. Oh, Seana, you have the greatest . . .

I heard the doorknob turn. I barely had time to throw Seana
under my pillow. The Panasonic was still on my crotch when
Emmy walked in. She laughed when she saw what I was doing.

"Ah ha! Now I know what you do at night when I'm not
around," she joked.

"I never outgrew puberty." I grinned.

"Why don't you use Flipper?" She grabbed my Panasonic,
which packs a lot more power than our dolphin-shaped vibrator.

"Not enough voltage." I grabbed it back.

Then she jumped on top of me and gave me a long kiss while
she nuzzled her hand between my legs.

"I thought you were tired," I said when we broke for air.

"I got my second wind," she said. She unbuttoned my jeans
and pulled them off. "Let's do it Darwin style."

"Huh?"

"Darwin style. You know. Survival of the fittest." She pulled
off my underwear and kissed me.

"Do you want to eat? Or be eaten?" I asked.

She started to laugh, so I tickled her to keep it going. Then I
grabbed her by the waist and flipped her over. I jumped on top
and started unbuttoning her shirt.

"Hey! What are you doing?" she laughed, as I wrestled with
her bra clasp.

"There's no contest," I answered. "*I* am the fittest."

"Oh, yeah?" She picked up the pillow and hit me with it.

I tried to push the *Penthouse* behind the mattress, but it was
too late.

"Argh!" she cried out, as she looked right into Seana's package. "Chris! What is—? Christine?!"

She looked at me with confused, pleading, angry little brown
eyes—like any wife who has just discovered the other woman.

"Do you—were you *reading* this?"

"No," I tried to joke. "I only buy it for the pictures."

I turned my head away, unable to look Emmy or Seana in the eyes.

"I don't believe this!" She tossed the magazine against the wall. "I don't *believe* this!" She picked up my Panasonic Massager 2000 and threw *it* against the wall. "What were you thinking?"

"It turns me on," I answered feebly.

"It's perverted filth," she screamed.

"But I like it."

Emmy started pacing back and forth in front of our bed. "Chris," she said between gasps, "you cannot *use* that magazine. It's degrading to women."

"But I *am* a woman," I answered quietly. I could look her in the eyes now. I was getting *my* second wind.

"It's a tool of patriarchal oppression!"

"What about *Playgirl*? With all those pictures of naked men? Or the gay ones? *Honcho*? *On Our Backs*?"

"Porn is porn. It takes away the human being and objectifies the body."

"No," I said. "*I* objectify the body when I look at the picture. *It* doesn't do anything. *It's* an inanimate object. The issue is not pornography, Em. The issue is the person looking at the pornography. What's the difference between a naked girl in *Penthouse* or a painting by Manet? They're both just *pictures.*"

"But one is meant for sexual—"

"Emmy," I interrupted her. "It doesn't matter what it was meant for. People will use whatever they want. Some people get turned on by the pictures in *Playboy*, and some get off on *The Wizard of Oz*."

"That's my point," she said. "It's wrong to get off on *things*. People should love each other."

"But everyone gets turned on by things. Everyone objectifies sometimes. It's a natural part of our sexuality."

"Not me." She shook her head and lifted her chin a few more inches into the air.

"Of course you do," I told her. "When we make love, don't you find yourself, sometimes, just focusing on one part of me?

Don't you forget I'm in the bed sometimes when you're sucking
on my breast?"

"No," she said.

"But Emmy, you have to! You must! You're not being honest
with yourself."

She gave me her long, pity-filled look. I hate that look.

I walked over to the far wall of our bedroom and picked up
the crumpled *Penthouse,* brought it back over to the bed and put
it right in front of her. I opened it to page 42. Seana.

"The Luck of the Irish," I started to read.

"What do you think you're doing?" she asked.

"I want to show you."

"No!" She slammed her eyelids closed and started to walk out
of the room. I grabbed her just before she walked into a lamp.

"Emmy," I said, "you protest these magazines every weekend.
But have you ever looked at one?"

"Of course not," she said. "They're garbage."

"How do you know if you've never even looked at one?"

She let out a long sigh and glared at me.

"Emmy," I kept up, "don't you think you should at least look
at one? Just once in your life? You said yourself that these pictures couldn't turn you on."

"Of course they couldn't," she snapped. "Never."

"Then what's the harm in looking?" I grinned. "For educational purposes."

Another sigh and a glare. I opened the magazine.

"The Luck of the Irish," I read. Then I showed her Seana.
Beautiful, long-haired, long-legged Seana. I took extra care to
point out the world's most perfect breasts.

I showed her Seana in her little purple business suit with the
skirt missing. In her bad-boy leather biker jacket. In her lacy little negligee two sizes too small. Then I showed her Brandy and
Lacy and Maxine, Mistress of the Night.

Then I closed the magazine and I started to talk about
Emmy's body. I told her how sometimes, when she was asleep,
I would just stare at her turned-up nose for hours. How I loved
her tiny lips and her pixie haircut. How sometimes when we
made love I forgot who she was or who I was or where either of

us were, because all I could think about were her perfect little breasts. How sometimes I got completely lost in her neck or her elbows or her ears. How I would fantasize about parts of her body. The parts that I loved. And how it made me want to make love to her.

As I spoke, Emmy started to cry. Soft and quiet.

I put my hand on her cheek and wiped a tear away. She put her hand on mine and we looked into each other's eyes.

"I'm sorry," she said, still crying.

"No, I'm sorry," I said. I kissed her forehead and wiped some more tears away.

She finally stopped crying and gave me a kiss. That turned into another kiss. Then another.

Emmy slid her hand down between my legs, and we were off.

*Carol Queen*

# The Best Whore in Hillsboro

"I hope you're available tonight. This call is going to be good."
It surprises Kitty to hear this much enthusiasm from her friend
Corrina. Of course she's available; who can afford to turn down
business the week after Christmas? But Corrina is really tired of
being a whore; she's gotten blasé or negative toward just about
everything, and Kitty can't imagine what she considers a good
trick. Corrina is way past thinking whoring is a grand adventure,
she doesn't like most of her clients, and because she feels like
she has to keep her work a secret from her straight friends, she
doesn't get much support. She ought to just quit the business.
But Corrina got caught by the IRS a few years ago and she's still
paying off the heavy fines. Pimped by the government, the
whores call it. Corrina is stuck, and every little thing that makes
her feel better about still working as a prostitute takes on great
significance. This client must be pretty special; Kitty appreciates
an intriguing sexual adventure almost as much as she appreciates
$350 outcall rates.

Kitty's also glad to be called for a double with Corrina because
she's turned on to her, and the feeling seems to be mutual. Kitty's trained ear can tell by the sounds Corrina makes when they
have sex that she likes it better than being done by a client. This

is a bonus, though. Only a truly homophobic whore would prefer to do a client alone when she could get someone to help.

Kitty gets out a very elegant black suit, high heels, and her most expensive lingerie, the crimson silk with black French lace.

Nice makeup, not too slutty. It didn't take Kitty long in the business to realize that most whores dress up, not down; signaling that your ass is for sale on the night streets of the Tenderloin is one thing, but slipping into the Fairmont to service an out-of-town CEO is quite another, and Kitty's bought more conservative clothes since she began whoring than she's ever owned in her life.

As she dresses she wonders what kind of date could make Corrina so enthusiastic. A wealthy submissive? Corrina would rather dominate clients than fuck them. The only client Corrina ever said she actually liked was a disabled man. Corrina felt happy about bringing him pleasure—she said most guys who paid for pleasure were too fucking rich and spoiled and Republican to appreciate it.

Corrina picks her up at nine.

"So where are we going? Who's so special?" Kitty asks.

"We're going to Hillsboro," Corrina says. A very wealthy suburb. "We're going to see a couple."

A couple! Corrina fills her in. These two called the escort service a couple of months ago looking for "someone intelligent."

"That's a switch!" Kitty squeals, and Corrina says, "Yeah, but they meant it. They're well read and cultured and didn't want to play with anyone they couldn't talk to. When they found out I'd been to law school it was like they were ready to ask me to move in."

"I shoulda worn my Phi Beta Kappa key," Kitty says.

"You should have. Maybe they'd want to pay you more." Corrina giggles. "I already told them you're a writer. If your book was published they'd have bought it already."

Kitty is wondering what to expect. Every new client is like a blind date—doubly so, this time. She's conjuring up well preserved older literary types, just a little bohemian. No wonder Corrina's dropped her customary ill-feeling about her clients. This *is* an adventure.

There's another angle to her excitement: being called to see a woman. Kitty is acutely aware that almost every dollar she makes equals adultery. Maybe two percent of her clients are single; the others don't tell their wives where they go on those long lunch hours. If the Mrs. ever finds out, it's because there's been a stupid slip-up, an indiscretion with alcohol and resentment most likely to blame. Kitty is not particularly devoted to heterosexual monogamy either as theory or as practice, but she gets tired of all the businesslike betrayal, the idea that men have to call her because they think their wives are too pure or too "frigid." Kitty hopes all the wealthy ladies whose husbands she fucks are lustily consorting with their garden boys, but still, it's a weird job, shoring up the illusion that married life is a functional state. It feels more legitimate to do this date, and that makes Kitty think about the fucking whore's stigma that she has to deal with. She wonders if this is the beginning of her own disillusionmnt with working, if this is how Corrina felt at first.

All this is flitting through her head as they walk from the car to the door of the very tony Hillsboro house where the couple lives.

The woman standing at the door is poised and wonderfully attractive. Kitty almost laughs—talk about what she does like about the business, here it is: another stereotype shot to hell! It takes a minute for Kitty to get introduced because the pretty woman has grabbed Corrina and is hugging her and telling her how fabulous she looks. A minute later the woman is embracing Kitty and telling her how much she's been looking forward to meeting her. She takes both their hands and pulls them toward a big living room, where a giant Christmas tree sparkles.

Her name is Pamela and her husband's name is Tom, and Tom has been waiting to meet Kitty too. He has been pouring them all glasses of Remy Martin.

Jesus Christ, Kitty thinks, this is like a Victorian Christmas tale where the whores get rescued by the rich people. Kitty has been in a lot of wealthy houses (usually while the wives were away), but rarely has she been made to feel welcome in them. Pamela is only a little older than Kitty and Corrina. Tom is already offering to loan Kitty a book. They are creating the near-seamless illusion for Corrina and Kitty that they are all affectionate friends, in the same class and enjoying the same life circumstances—that they are equals chatting about Christmas and sipping brandy.

It's the same thing Kitty does with her ordinary clients, in a way—part of what she's paid for is to create the illusion that she's their devoted mistress, even if it's the first time she's met them. They're supposed to feel like it's normal to be with her, that their behavior has an emotional context, certainly not that they're committing a misdemeanor with an expensive whore.

Corrina is eating all this up.

It's certainly understandable—the seduction here has nothing to do with the sex that will get underway once they have all finished their brandy. Maybe with Pamela and Tom, Corrina can feel good about what she's doing. Kitty feels pretty good about it most of the time, which gives her a vantage point to watch this rare situation work its magic on her usually reserved friend. Corrina is sexier than Kitty's ever seen her, laughing and at ease—she's seen these two several times already—and teasing Tom about being ganged up on by three women.

Kitty has already envisioned the bed. King-size, big enough for four to stretch and romp; expensive white linens, already turned down. Books on the carved Chinese nightstands. Pamela says she decorated herself; it took two trips to China to buy the antiques.

Kitty's glad for her silk lingerie. She's glad for the expansive bed and the pretty, lively woman she's being paid $350 an hour to go down on. She's glad they like Corrina so much; maybe they'll adopt her and invite Kitty over on weekends. It's so hard to believe Tom and Pamela are going to drop $1,400 (they will almost certainly go into the second hour) on this. Ironically the perfect illusion of comfort they've created makes it all seem surreal.

So Kitty concentrates on one thing at a time. Slipping half a dozen condoms out of her purse and onto the bedstand. Pamela's soft, pampered skin connecting coolly with hers as she slips up behind her, arms round her waist. Tom's lanky body emerging from his clothes; Pamela's ringed, French-manicured hand stroking his cock, already hard and high from all Corrina's giggled teasing. He'll please three women, he declares, or die trying.

Three women are going to please each other, Kitty thinks. She wonders if Pamela's the one the party was arranged for. Is it easier or harder to be bisexual if you're a married lady in a rich suburb? Why aren't these two throwing parties for all their decadent friends? Why are they hiring prostitutes? Kitty knows if she dwells on this too much she'll miss out on the fun; she'll be too busy deconstructing the best date ever to really appreciate it. So she puts a lid on the analysis.

Tom, Corrina, and now Kitty have Pamela laid out on the bed. Her silk bra and panties have been pulled off. She's wearing nothing but lots of gold jewelry—it gives the scene a slight Roman orgy feel. Her thick blond hair is streaked expertly, her pussy trimmed and starting to swell and get pinker as her husband strokes her body, then sucks on one nipple after the other. Corrina lies by her side and kisses her.

Kitty is never shy in situations like these: she lies between Pamela's slender thighs, breathing on her pussy, hot little blasts of air on Pamela's clit, and smiles when she hears her begin to sigh. At the price this woman is paying to get her pussy attended to, Kitty will lick it very well indeed.

Maybe Pamela's comparing it to a Roman orgy too. She is bucking and thrusting in no time, thoroughly hot from all the attention, being held down, and the wet heat of Kitty's tongue stroking and stroking her clit. Pamela is clutching Corrina and is very close to coming. Tom urges Corrina up onto Pamela's face, Corrina's pussy settling down on Pamela's lips and muffling her sounds in a way that inspires Kitty to lick her even better.

Corrina doesn't come very easily, Kitty knows, but feeling Pamela's mouth on her pussy, coming and gasping and then settling down to lick her as soon as her orgasm is over, has her very close. Kitty scrambles up from between Pamela's legs and reaches for a condom from the nightstand. Tom's erection is straining from rubbing against Pamela while she came. Kitty works the rubber over this cockhead and rolls it down the shaft—a nice big cock, which is what Corrina likes.

"Put it in Corrina's cunt," Kitty urges, "right over Pamela's mouth, Tom, that's right, let her lick your balls while you fuck Corrina." Kitty hopes Tom has a modicum of self-control; lots of her clients would fill a rubber just at the mere suggestion. Of course, most of her clients didn't have wives like Pamela. If they did, business would either die out or be hopping—Kitty isn't sure which.

Tom kneels behind Corrina and rubs his cock up and down her slit, already wet from Pamela's tongue. Kitty slips her hand between them with some extra lube, strokes it onto his cock and then lets go, hearing with satisfaction the very sincere noises Corrina starts making the minute Tom's cock sinks into her. Pamela is going crazy having both a pussy and Tom's cock and balls to lick. She pulls Corrina down to her pussy; now they're sixty-nining. Kitty slips a couple of fingers into Pamela's cunt. Tom's fucking Corrina. Kitty's fucking Pamela. Their faces are buried in each other's muffs. Kitty glances up and grins at the sight of Tom—he's beside himself. Kitty and Corrina both have bodies that look like Pamela's, small-breasted and slender.

But now Kitty loses herself pumping her strong right arm: she can feel Pamela's cunt opening in the last expansive moment before climax. As Pamela starts to come Corrina begins a muffled cry, one Kitty has only heard a few times—her friend's nonfaked orgasm.

Kitty has never faked an orgasm in her life, but she's heard and seen enough phony ones with her whore girlfriends to cherish the real ones. She's even run into a few men who fake it. She's not sure why she lets go into enjoyment more easily than her friends, but she's sure that's what makes it possible for her to like sex work. When Corrina comes it bridges the gap between their experiences as whores.

Tom almost loses himself, connected to two orgasming women, but not quite. He collapses on the bed beside Pamela and Corrina. Now Pamela takes over.

How inspiring, Kitty thinks, to see a pampered, wealthy suburban woman deep-throat like a succubus! In her fantasies women like Pamela never suck dick, but obviously Kitty's had the wrong idea, because Pamela is going to town on Tom. It's pretty to watch partners suck and play with each other—she's seen plenty of paid-for blow jobs up close, but this is very different. Pamela relies less on impressive technique (though her technique is plenty impressive, Kitty notes), and more on her pleasure in making Tom groan and shake. Unlike all the other wealthy suburban housewives (to hear Kitty's clients talk), Pamela *likes* sucking cock.

Kitty lies next to them, propped up on one elbow, and strokes her clit while she watches. Then she remembers how much money Tom and Pamela are going to fork over for the honor of their company and decides she'd better get back to work. "Nice job if you can get it," she reflects. Corrina is lying on the other side of Tom and Pamela. Kitty winks at her and then begins describing what she sees.

"Tom, I wish you could get right down here close to Pamela's hot mouth and watch her lips slide up and down your dick. It's slick with her saliva, baby, and I can see she knows all the places on your cock that make you go crazy. She's sucking your big cock with her eyes open, Tom, she's watching your face to see how much you like it. Give it up to her, baby, go ahead, let her take you, she knows how, let her take you there . . ."

Tom bucks and writhes with the effect of Kitty's words and Pamela's million-dollar tongue. She's slowing down; she won't let him shoot. He's thrashing his head back and forth and saying, "God, yes, honey, please, oh please, oh make me come, oh Pammie . . ."

But Pamela won't. She gets him down her throat one last time and then pulls her mouth all the way off him, hand around his balls and shaft like a cock ring, and says, "No, baby, not yet, don't you come yet, I'm going to fuck you, honey, you wait for me."

She straddles his hugely straining cock, rubs it on her pussy, croons as she slides slowly down his length, "No, baby, you wait for me." Tom is still thrashing.

Kitty watches admiringly. This woman is good. She is fucking him so slowly and with such focus, eyes locked on his, whispering to him, that Kitty wouldn't be surprised if he started to whimper. Pamela's voice gets a little louder, loud enough for Kitty and Corrina to hear.

"I'm going to fuck you so fine, Tom, just like I fucked that man who took me to the top of the biggest hotel in Denver and bought me all that champagne, baby, remember that story? That time he put me in front of the window with nothing but my high heels on, remember? What did he do to me, honey, you remember what I told you."

Tom is mesmerized, and he definitely remembers. "He fucked you where everybody could see, Pammie, he fucked you in front of the window, in the daytime, and everybody could see your tits, honey, and your pussy, and his cock in you, he fucked you."

Pamela is fucking him, oh boy. Kitty briefly considers moving between their legs and rimming Pamela; there's no plastic wrap in sight, though, and even though it may be the hottest trick ever, it isn't worth a possible case of amoebiases. Besides, she wouldn't be able to hear Pamela's story clearly, so she doesn't.

"What else did he do to me, baby? What else did I do in the hotel?"

Tom's having a hard time speaking. "He . . . he ate your ass . . . by the window . . ."

"Uh-huh, honey, where everybody in Denver could look up and see me, everybody could look up and see me holding my asscheeks open wide so he could run his tongue up inside."

Hmmm, Kitty thinks. Synchronicity. She gives an instant of thought to which position she'd rather be in—tonguing a beautiful woman's asshole high above Denver, or spreading her cheeks to the world. She really can't bring herself to pick just one.

". . . And you pissed . . . all over him . . ."

"He drank my piss, baby, he drank it right out of me." She's riding Tom like a galloping polo pony. His eyes are standing out of his head, drinking her in, totally keyed in to this story he's obviously heard many times. "And he paid me for it, too, honey, a thousand bucks for it, a thousand bucks so he could drink my hot piss . . ."

"Uhhhhnnn!" Tom is shooting, lifting Pamela up off the bed with the strength of his thrusts. She rides him like a mermaid on a dolphin. She has his nipples between her fingers, squeezing.

Corrina's eyes are wide. This is apparently a new wrinkle in her relationship with these two.

Kitty is ready to combust. This is just too much. But Pamela isn't finished. As soon as Tom has shot his load into her she pulls off him and spins around, presenting her creamy, cum-filled pussy to his mouth, and he sets to like a starving kitten, licking it all out of her. Pamela is beginning to shudder; now that her performance is over she can come again.

"Jesus, Corrina, fuck me!" Kitty is beside herself. When had she died and gone to porno heaven? She'll have Corrina's whole hand inside her within five minutes. Such kamikaze arousal with a client is rare, but this is no ordinary situation. Corrina's too happy to oblige; she's on another plane of existence herself, completely free of the pall of guilt and withdrawal that she usually carries when she tricks. By the time Corrina works her little hand into Kitty's over-amped pussy, Pamela has recovered from her most recent orgasm and gotten into the act; Tom still lies there panting while she licks Kitty's clit with slow, teasing swipes that build her toward a big explosive one. Kitty dimly hopes she won't break any of the small bones in Corrina's hand. Tom, just back from the over-the-rainbow place where she's about to rocket, reaches over and takes Kitty's hand.

After such a big come Kitty's brain is always a little fluffy. Pamela pads out and returns with the cognac. Afterglow in Hillsboro, Kitty mumbles to herself. Pretty perfect, with her head pillowed on Tom's belly and the hot waft of the Remy in her nostrils.

"Is this what folks out here do all the time?" she asks.

Pamela laughs and says if people were all doing this wouldn't the world *already* be a better place?

Sure would, Kitty says.

Corrina's eyes are sparkly. Kitty has never seen her so happy. Pamela goes off to the big marble master bath for a quick shower. Tom puts his arms around Corrina and Kitty and thanks them for the wonderful time. "It's really good for Pammie to be around girls like you," he says. "With our other friends she just can't really be herself."

He really does loan Kitty the book, a best-seller she'd never have bought on her own. "It's fabulous!" he says. "You have to read it. You'll be on the best-seller list yourself someday."

So will you, Kitty thinks. But no one will ever believe it.

Astonishing, the intimacy that comes with sharing the secrets of strangers. Pamela and Tom fondly kiss them good-bye. Tom has slipped Corrina an envelope. Kitty tucks the fat hardback under her arm and promises to have a critique of it for them next time, even though she knows that, as a whore, she's never guaranteed a next time.

In the car Corrina slits open the envelope. Fourteen hundred-dollar bills and a Christmas card. Kitty gets seven, then gives Corrina one hundred and fifty back—her courtesy fee for the referral. But Corrina is dreamy, not much focused on business.

On the way home they do a postmortem, even stop for coffee so they can linger over it. This is a whore's ritual, precious time for sharing secrets no one else wants to hear.

"Was Pamela really a prostitute once?" They both want to know. How did she get in that big lovely bed with a devoted rich man? Kitty is suspicious of Cinderella stories, though she knows she'll be an ex-whore someday who whispers salacious tales to her lovers. What inspires her about Pamela is that, unlike all the other working girls who graduated to marriage—which looks to her like full-time whoring with one inescapable client—she shares her secret. And Tom loves her for it. Smart man, stiff-dicked over the best whore in Hillsboro.

Kitty says all that to Corrina. She nods, but there's a faraway look in her eyes. She's just beginning to be able to believe what Kitty already knows: there's going to be life after whoring.

# HEROTICA 5

*For Angie, who never dreamed
what she was starting when she showed me
the road to sin and salvation.*

# ACKNOWLEDGMENTS

Thanks to Shar for her brilliance; Jamie for his technological expertise; and Leigh, not only for her hard work but also for pushing me to write about Mick.

# INTRODUCTION

Editing women's erotica is somewhat different from editing other kinds of writing. Sure, the nuts and bolts of spelling, grammar and punctuation, and of helping a writer tell the story in the best possible way, are the same as with any other fiction—but to be involved in the creation of sexually explicit literature by women is to be part of a collective exploration of female sexuality and the evolution of a relatively new literary genre.

Nearly seventy years ago Virginia Woolf put forth a theory of literature as a collective progressive endeavor. "[M]asterpieces," she said, "are not single and solitary births; they are the outcome of many years of thinking in common, of thinking by the body of the people, so that the experience of the mass is behind the single voice."

I can just imagine feminist and literary academics rolling their eyes at my evocation of The Canonized One in a discussion about pornography. Well, add another footnote, dearies—because the ideas Woolf talked about in *A Room of One's Own* are nowhere more applicable than in the field of women's erotica.

Woolf believed that it was solely because women lacked the time and space for writing that they had not developed a body of written expression. She predicted that "the habit of freedom and the courage to write exactly what we think" would lead, in the next hundred years, to the emergence of a female literary canon. And she was not a snob about what form this writing should take: "I would ask you," she exhorted women, "to write all kinds of books, hesitating at no subject however trivial or however vast."

There's no doubt that Woolf's predictions were on target with regard to mainstream women's fiction, feminist theory, and historical works. They are also turning out to be accurate with regard to women's erotica.

Would women be writing truthful stories about their sex lives and fantasies if the only forum for sexually explicit stories was *Hustler*? Not only wouldn't *Hustler* publish the kinds of stories found in *Herotica* and other women's anthologies, but without access to sex stories by other women, we might not feel inspired and/or courageous enough to tell our own.

One of the first pornographic stories I ever wrote was about a sexual encounter with a prisoner in a private room in a prison. Because the story was written for a male-produced magazine geared towards a largely male audience, I wrote it as a purely exciting adventure, omitting any of the fear and ambivalence inherent in such a situation. Were I writing that story today, for *Herotica* or for another women's anthology, it would read very differently.

It would also have my real name, rather than a pseudonym, on it. Recently I wrote a heavy-duty S/M story for a lesbian collection, and I put my real name on it, something I would not have done ten years ago. Were it not for the brave women who've trailblazed the genre of S/M literature, I never would have had the courage to do this. I believe that this is what Woolf was talking about—the influence we exert on one another's work.

The lead story in this fifth *Herotica* collection, "The Knitting Circle," also exemplifies Woolf's theory. The women in this story urge each other to talk about their sex lives, until their stories become interwoven and the knitting circle widens:

> The weeks and months went by, the needles moved steadily through the yarn, and we talked and talked. We branched out from the present and delved into the dim past of wild youthful flings and

into the fantasies of the man next door, the mechanic at the garage, the brawny young hulk who came to repair the roof. Pretty soon more friends began to show up Tuesday evenings. Some of them didn't even knit.

Similarly, working with authors to revise and shape their stories is a vital element in this ongoing sexual dialogue that women are engaged in. Participating in that dialogue is, for me, the most rewarding aspect of editing erotica. Some of the pieces I accept for *Herotica* need little or no revision, but others need that extra push to realize their full potential. Contributors have a wide variety of writing experience: some are professionals, some even specifically professional sex writers. Others have never written any kind of story before. The level of the author's experience, though, has little to do with whether or not the story needs revising.

I've found that when something's missing from a story, what's most often needed is for the author to go deeper. "Wouldn't this narrator feel afraid in this situation?" I might ask, and after a long pause the author confesses that in fact fear was what triggered the woman's arousal. "Write it into the story," I tell her, and we've all moved one baby step further along in our evolution as writers and as honest sexual beings. Each time we take a step towards greater truthfulness, each time a writer journeys deeper inside, she paves the way for more honesty from the next story, the next author, the next collection. And so we build upon our own and each other's work.

"This doesn't ring true," I tell another writer. "I don't understand why the narrator stays with him."

"Funny you should say that," she tells me, "because right after I wrote this story I decided to leave him." And then she'll tell me the tragic real-life saga that inspired the fiction, the details that never made it into the written story, because she thought they were "too heavy"; by the time we're through she can't wait to get to her computer to add another dimension to her piece.

Sometimes asking women to go deeper means pushing them to fully claim their story. As fiction, these stories are already assumed to be fantasies—yet many women are still afraid to present them without some caveat like: *This is a fantasy I made up for my lover*, or: *And then I woke up.* Getting a woman to give up the camouflage is a delicate operation; it's a big step for her to remove the protective veneer she's painted over a story that's probably intensely personal.

Even having been on the other end, and knowing as I do the value of this process, I'm still amazed every time a *Herotica* writer responds with enthusiasm to my suggestions. I'm impressed and grateful when she is willing to rework a story, sometimes for as many as four drafts. Writers of erotica feel a gut-level commitment to this group grope with words.

Even if an author thinks my ideas are off the wall, we're likely to wind up in some pretty interesting conversations, the kind not usually engaged in at your everyday editorial conference. One author was perfectly willing to embellish her story by adding some reflection on the psychic significance of the bondage scene, but she disagreed with my interpretation of exactly what that was. Perfect strangers, we ended up having an intimate phone conversation on "what bondage means to me." Another writer questioned whether or not a sexual position I suggested was technically possible, and our conversation dissolved in fits of laughter when I assured her that I could personally attest to its viability. There are stories where the sexual activity is shrouded in metaphor, and I've had to ask an author exactly whose cunt or cock is doing what to whose. Or I'll ask a writer to clarify her complicated description of a sexual position, and in finding the words to untangle the characters' limbs we'll end up trading sexual secrets and giggling like conspiratorial teenagers.

## How Do We Write Sex? Let Me Count the Ways

One of the most common things I seek in a story is more sex—or, in some cases, any at all. More stories than you might expect are submitted to the *Herotica* series without a single paragraph of explicit sex written in. Sometimes the writer has never tried to write a sex scene, but is able to do so when encouraged. Others simply refuse—making me wonder just how they've interpreted the title *Herotica*.

Considering the abundance of erotic anthologies currently on the market, these writers aren't totally off base—some of these collections contain nary a naughty word. I used to maintain that there was no difference between the terms *erotica* and *pornography*, but I find I must yield to the inevitable. It's not that erotica is classier than pornography, or that porn objectifies and exploits while erotica is egalitarian and sensual, or any of that gobbledygook that the prudish invoke to justify whatever it is that excites *them*. In fact, it seems to me that with the growth and permutation of this literary genre, we're running out of words to describe it. Erotica and pornography aren't enough anymore: we're going to have to expand our language to encompass the growing varieties of sexual literature. The words we invent, though, shouldn't become labels that confer moral judgment. This is a practical matter, much like the Eskimos' need for a multitude of words to describe snow.

If *Hustler* is pornography and *Herotica* is erotica, it seems to me that we need a new term for fiction that talks about sex but is not explicit—perhaps "erolit" would do. Erolit would include those works that talk about sex and sensuality but are not as explicit as pornography or erotica. Personally, this kind of writing doesn't stir *my* juices—but it does serve a purpose. It's another form of sexual communication and another blow to sexual repression.

As noble as this purpose may be—and I do believe it's noble—the *Herotica* series is not erolit. We have made a conscious decision to be sexually explicit. I do not believe that heat has to be sacrificed for light—in fact, I think the two go together like thunder and lightning. I want an erotic story to hit me over the head with an unusual perspective—but I also want it to take me on a good hot ride.

The stories in this collection do just that. As always, they're wildly diverse—but one theme that popped up in this batch is the influence of cultural background on sexual response.

In "Fish Curry Rice," for instance, after we've been treated to an exquisitely detailed picture of Indian customs regarding the behavior of women of marriageable age, we see the narrator flouting them:

I swept my tongue across his nipples, and they wrinkled and reddened. I struck them again and again until they were purple and
bulging. The twin ridges of his ribs rising over his sunken stomach
signaled the breath held in anticipation. I bit a nipple. He turned
his dilating eyes on me, struggling to focus, pleading, laughing,
challenging me to arouse him further.

In America, where race relations seethe with fire and ice, a
white woman reflects on her attraction to black men in "In the
Mood":

> These lovers left her with sensual memories of black skin on white,
> black cock entering pink pussy.

In "Sauce," a decidedly hip no-nonsense butch who thinks
she knows everything is surprised and seduced by a Southern
belle:

> Oh, she *was* a southern woman, in the best sense—slow, so slow.
> Play all the nuances, taste every subtle flavor, savor the textures. So
> I held steady while Veronica crept over me like a big voluptuous
> cat, rubbing and almost purring into my ear, teasing me, easing me
> to her magic bed.

And in "Dragon Cat Flower," a sexually experienced Chinese
woman is transported, by making love to a Chinese man for the
first time in her life, to a part of her ancestry long forgotten, as she
discovers her totem animal:

> With him inside me now, I thrashed freely, my long spine curving
> and twisting as we continued through a heavenly sky . . . curving
> like wisps of smoke, flying upon the air, dragons . . . I flexed my
> claws and held even tighter to him then, feeling my power.

Reading these kinds of passages, it's easy to forget that not so
many years ago the notion of women writing at all was scandalous,
and any woman who dared do so was subject to ridicule. Even
now, in some quarters, a woman who dares to write the words,
ideas and acts contained in these pages is at risk of ostracism or

worse. I can't honestly say what Virginia Woolf would think of women's erotica, but I have no doubt that she would respect *Herotica* authors for having "the courage to write exactly what we think."

—*Marcy Sheiner*
*Emeryville, California*
*April 1996*

## Joan Leslie Taylor

❦

# The Knitting Circle

At the knitting group we talk about many things, but our main topic is always sex. We've been getting together on Tuesday nights to knit and talk and laugh, and sometimes cry, for almost five years. We are all well above the age of consent, how shall I say? We are women of *un certain âge*. Not one of us looks to be the sort of woman to sit around telling tales of hard cocks, wet cunts, and orgasms that shake beds.

It all began the year Susie was knitting sweaters for her twin grandsons, and Emily decided to knit an afghan for her mother-in-law. Knitting takes full charge of your hands, but leaves your mind pretty much free; just sitting home alone, click, click, click, knit, purl, knit, purl, can be decidedly dull, so Susie and Em started getting together. Then Lenore heard what a good time they were having, so she bought some yarn and started coming over, too. I think they asked me mostly because they all have husbands and they liked the idea of coming to my house where there was no man lurking about so we could be wild and silly.

That's when the sex stories started. I had just broken up with a very fine lover named David. The sex had been terrific, but he'd been a jerk in all other ways. It was a relief to have him out of my hair. I just wished I could have kept him in my bed. Susie, Emily, and Lenore just drooled to hear me tell how David and I used to make love all night long, with him lapping away at my cunt, his gigantic hard cock in my mouth, him on top, then me on top, such wonderful gymnastics. I'd get hot just telling them about it, and they all sat there rapt and looking like their pussies were dripping all over my chintz furniture. They never wearied of hearing about David, but eventually, great sex or not, I got tired of talking about a man I disliked.

"Oh, tell us again about the time you went to the Olsons' barbecue and David brought you to orgasm in the hot tub, right under the noses of all the guests!" Lenore gestured with her knitting needle as if it were a baton and she were conducting the orchestrated ensemble at the Olson barbecue, me and David in the steamy, swirling water, David's finger up my cunt, the laughter and chatting of the slightly inebriated guests wafting around us in waves that seemed to make David's finger twirl and thrust with symphonic genius. Yes, it had been a particularly fine moment, even if that had been the same week David borrowed my car and left me stranded for hours, no warning, no phone call, no apology, and no gas in the car when he finally reappeared.

"Enough already. You've heard that story at least three times. I'm sick to death of David. Not another word. I want to listen to someone else's hot story."

At first they all protested that they were just nice married ladies with boring husbands. Well, yes, they did "do it," but there was nothing to tell. Susie flushed as red as the sweater on her needles, and Emily fidgeted so nervously in her seat that it was as if David's errant finger had lodged itself in her pussy from so much telling. She kept her eyes on her afghan, scrutinizing the stitches as if they were intricate lab science requiring all her concentration, but something in the way she always pronounced her husband's name made me think that she would definitely have tales to tell, tales worth listening to. So I pressed her.

"Emily, tell us about Derek. I bet he's really good in bed." I paused to give her time to bring the image to mind. She shifted again, and let her hair fall across her face, hiding her expression.

"We promise we'll never breathe a word outside this room."

"Yes, Em, do tell," crowed Lenore. I knew that for all her enthusiasm she would be a harder challenge. She probably had the most active sex life of any of us: a robust-looking husband who adored her, plus, I've heard on very good repute, a sometime lover at her office. I think the deception of an affair made her reticent, but I knew she wanted to talk, too. But not yet. First Emily.

With only a little more coaxing Emily told us about Derek and how they'd send the kids to his mom's sometimes on Sunday afternoons, then give each other massages which started with almond oil and ended with enough bodily juices to keep the two of them slipping and sliding, moaning and panting, fucking and sucking, and Emily coming all afternoon. Derek's forte, above and beyond being able to give a terrific massage, was endurance. Ah, we all sighed, as Emily whispered in a breathy little voice about how he could make her orgasm over and over again. How the best ones were after Derek had been slip-sliding his cock in and out of her wet, pulsing pussy for an hour or more.

"I'm afraid I'm slow to warm up," she said apologetically, "so it's a good thing I have Derek who can go and go . . . and go . . ." Her voice trailed off in a sigh.

"Who warms up as quick as most men?" Susie interjected. "No one, I think. Not really. There's pretending to be hot and ready, oh, just a little lubricant, but good loving takes a patient man." Susie sounded like she was giving a Marriage and Family Life lecture, but she'd opened her mouth, so we teased her stories out of her, too. Then we got Lenore talking about her husband and after that her lover.

The weeks and months went by, the needles moved steadily through the yarn, and we talked and talked. We branched out from the present and delved into the dim past of wild youthful flings and into the fantasies of the man next door, the mechanic at the garage, the brawny young hulk who came to repair the roof. Pretty soon more friends began to show up on Tuesday evenings. Some of them didn't even knit. Ruby crocheted, and though she was no sweet young thing, but a slightly overweight, fortysomething, twice-divorced secretary, she always had at least two or more men panting after her. Samantha was a quilter, very healthy, very New Age, with children in their twenties still "finding themselves" while she footed their bills. She was always going off to some sort of festival or workshop at one of the power places of the earth, and coming home with tales of SNAGs (you know, Sensitive New Age Guys) we all wished we had around to adjust our chakras. Delilah brought yarn and needles the first time she came, but we all snickered to see the number 12 poles she had, along with a skein of baby-fine pink yarn that had the well-weathered look of having been in a drawer for a long time. She couldn't knit any more than I could do brain surgery, but we loved having her appear each week and pretty soon she gave the pink yarn back to her sister. A country-music star wanna-be, she had the clothes, including a whole wardrobe of Wonderbras, and the hair and the walk down pat, but she was still working on the singing part. She probably had the tamest sex life of any of us, but she made up the naughtiest tales of late-night rendezvous with cowboys in leather vests and very tight pants bulging over swollen members, throbbing to get into her sateen leggings.

One week a new woman came, a widow who had showed up at Lenore's law office after her husband died, for help in handling some trust documents. Lenore didn't really know her, but she said there was something about Olivia that made her want to find out more about her.

"She's extremely sexy but in a subtle way," Lenore told us. "If I were a man I'd be absolutely in love with her. She's older than we are, I guess about sixty, but the way she looks makes me think sixty is the perfect age we're all waiting to be. I don't know how she managed the last couple of years while her husband was so sick. She did everything for him, and I guess he had a pretty awful time at the end. After I got her trust straightened out and I knew she wouldn't be coming anymore, I asked her if she knitted or anything."

Olivia was as beautiful and fascinating as Lenore had led us to imagine. She was tall, with such gorgeous silver-gray hair falling in drifts about her face that it made me want to stop dyeing my hair instantly. Her eyes looked green, but I later noticed that they changed hue depending on what she wore. I found myself studying her clothes, but they were nothing special: a well-worn turtleneck over a denim skirt, a simple vest, and silver earrings. She made everything she wore seem unique and very wonderful. I made a mental note to get my denim skirt out and see if it still fit, and I wanted a vest exactly like hers. I didn't think she noticed me staring at her, but then she turned and smiled at me.

Olivia didn't say much that first week. I wondered whether Lenore had told her what the knitting group was really about, but she seemed as fascinated as the rest of us with Ruby's excited report of her latest date with the stockbroker who liked to do a striptease for her, starting from the full three-piece suit and slowly, excruciatingly, getting down to his leopard bikini skivvies.

"He's so good at it," Ruby squealed. "The way he bumps and grinds. I've never seen a man enjoy his own body so much. It makes me want to touch him, but he won't let me lay a finger on him, not until the end."

They'd both be so hot by the time the leopard undies (or whatever tiny sexy garb he chose for the night) were revealed that Ruby swore she ripped them off his buns and grabbed his cock, which sprang out fully extended the moment it was released from its spandex leopard bondage.

"Once he's naked, he almost forgets his own body and positively devotes himself to mine. He doesn't even notice that I need to lose fifteen pounds. He oohs and ahs over my fleshy thighs, buries his face in my belly, and oh, how he loves my breasts," she crooned.

I glanced at Olivia, and in the half-smile that flickered across her lips and the fluttering of her long thin fingers as she smoothed an invisible crease in her vest, I saw that she was remembering a man who had loved her breasts like that, too.

Later in the evening, after all of Susie's butterscotch brownies were gone, even the crumbs, Delilah told an unbelievable tale of what happened when the bag boy at the Safeway had helped her load her groceries. Samantha whispered behind her quilt square to Olivia that it was just pretend. We all loved Delilah and indulged her stories, but, like Samantha, I didn't want Olivia to think we were overaged teenagers chasing baggers at Safeway. I wanted her to think we were wonderfully sensual, sophisticated, sexy women.

The next week I noticed that both Susie and Ruby were wearing vests, and Delilah and Samantha were wearing denim skirts. I was wearing both, with a turtleneck. By then Olivia was wearing a pale blue tunic over black knit pants that made me feel dowdy in my denim skirt. For women the late forties and early fifties are like a second adolescence, with all the awkwardness and uncertainty of being neither young nor old. I could imagine myself being ninety, wrapped in a shawl, very frail and extremely wise, but I was having trouble with being middle-aged. I wasn't ready for the shawl yet, but I had given up short skirts when the blue lines etching my thighs became too obvious, and I stopped wearing anything with a waist when my once slim midline expanded to meet the other excess flesh appearing on my body. Olivia was the first person who had made me think that perhaps my attempts at trying to stay young-looking were not only doomed, but missed the point. Olivia didn't look young; she looked beautiful.

The needles were clicking, but no one was saying much. I think we were all wishing Olivia would speak, but it didn't seem quite right to just say, So, Olivia, tell us about your fabulous sex life. After all, she was a recent widow and probably wasn't even thinking about sex.

"That must have been very difficult for you, caring for Ed," Lenore began.

"Illness is never easy, especially terminal illness, but Ed was such a dear and we had such a sweet relationship that I never minded taking care of him." Olivia spoke with such warmth that I think we all envied her Ed. I know I did.

My last boyfriend had been yet another jerk who'd treated me badly, and he wasn't even very good in bed—too selfish and with about as much sensitivity as an anteater. How I wished that just once I could have a man I would think of categorizing as "such a dear," and I realized that for all the sex I'd had, I knew nothing of what Olivia called a sweet relationship. But I knew it was what I'd yearned for.

"Tell us about Ed," I said, reaching into my bag for a new skein of yarn.

"It's hard to describe someone I've known most of my life," she began. "Do I tell you how he was when he was eighteen and I was not quite fifteen, and already smitten with him? It wasn't that he was particularly handsome, but he had such a way about him, as if he'd just discovered something that was more fun than anyone could imagine and he wanted to share it with me." She paused and took a deep breath. "Or do I tell you how he was when he was old and sick and just holding hands was all he could do?"

No one answered her. The needles *click-clicked* on. Olivia cleared her throat. I felt tears building in my eyes.

"You probably think that sick people don't have sex lives, but it's just like everything else in the face of an onrushing illness: harder to attain and more precious by the day." She paused and reached for a tissue. I could see the long months of caring for Ed, the tiredness, etched on her face, the loss welling up in her eyes.

"Only a short time before he died," Olivia continued, her head held high, "there was one Sunday that I would not trade for being twenty again, even with a dozen suitors."

"Would you tell us about it?" asked Samantha.

"Well, it's not a very sexy story, not what you're used to." We all nodded yes, that we wanted to hear her story. "Because it was Sunday there were no nurses coming, and no home health aides. It was just Ed and me. Even though the aides usually gave him his bath, he asked me if I would for a change. I ran the bathwater, checking the temperature, filling the tub just the way I knew he liked it. I brought him into the bathroom in his wheelchair. As I undressed him, I started to really look at him. Even though he'd lost quite a lot of weight, he was still a good-looking man. Suddenly I wasn't giving an invalid a bath. I was involved in a sensual dance. Steam was rising from the bathwater. Neither one of us said anything, but we seemed to be breathing in unison. I slipped off his shirt and ran my fingers across his chest. He raised his hand to my hair, and I felt such desire rise in me." Her voice wavered, and then she was quiet.

I held my breath, silently urging her on.

"Wheelchairs are very awkward," she continued, her voice stronger again, "and never more so than in a small place like a bathroom. I slid his pants down his thin, thin legs, letting my fingers linger on the soft downy hair on his calves. Ed and I used to dance together, but now the best dance we could manage was getting him into the tub without his falling. He put his arms around my neck. Embracing him around the waist, I lifted him and pushed the wheelchair aside. His breath was hot on my neck. As if we were dancing once again, I turned, still holding him tightly so he faced the tub, then lifted one of his legs into the water, then the other. I always held my breath at that point, for fear his weak legs would give way too soon and he'd slip in too fast. That Sunday he settled into the water perfectly, with a sigh that seemed to come from both of us. I smiled to see his long, naked body stretched out in the tub, his genitals bobbing gently in the warm water. I remembered the first time I'd ever seen Ed naked, more than forty years before, when I'd never seen even a picture of a naked man. I'd seen my little brothers in their bath, but that was all, so seeing Ed the first time was quite a shock."

"Was that on your wedding night?" Susie asked.

"Oh, no. Ed and I used to go for very long walks up into the hills outside town. We knew we would marry and spend our whole lives together, so we didn't wait for the wedding." She blushed, as if we might not approve.

"Please go on about Ed's bath," Emily said. "If you want to," she added hastily.

"Well, I sat down beside the bathtub and began washing Ed. We were both smiling, and Ed was looking right into my eyes. I felt shot through with love and desire and sadness. So many years I'd loved this man, and never more deeply than at that moment.

"My blouse was becoming damp, sticking to my skin, sweat trickling down between my breasts. 'Liv, why don't you take off your blouse?' he suggested, with the most wonderfully lascivious look in his eye. I scooted out of it feeling like an eager schoolgirl with her beau. 'There, that's better,' he said, reaching one hand weakly towards my breasts. I leaned forward and kissed his forehead while he caressed my breast. When he reached the nipple, I felt myself begin to breathe heavily. In recent months we hadn't had any real sex. Affection, yes, but I think we'd both become so consumed with taking care of his body that it had ceased to be personal or pleasurable.

"I resumed washing him, moving down his chest, toying with his nipples, which were very sensitive as always. Even his armpits felt sexual as I slid my soapy fingers up under his. I moved down towards his legs, and he said, 'Don't forget my balls, Liv.' " She had tears in her eyes. Someone handed her a tissue, and we all waited.

"It's so silly, really. Ed and I probably made love thousands and thousands of times over the years, but when I think of him now, what I remember is his balls in my hand that Sunday. The soft, soft skin on his scrotum, the tiny hairs, the always, to me, mysterious feel of his testicles. How fragile they are, and so vulnerable hanging exposed like that. We think of women as being the soft ones, but how delicate the skin of the scrotum is. 'I love your balls,' I said, that was all, but there was nothing else to say. For a long time, I continued to hold his balls in my hand, examining the pink skin, feeling the wonder of this treasure. With my other hand I held his penis, which was the more dear to me in its softness. All the medications Ed had to take . . . it had been a long time since he'd been able to have an erection, but holding Ed's wonderful penis in my hand, I saw its beauty, his beauty really, as I never had before. When a penis is hard and we are awash in seas of hormones, we see only its function and miss its perfection. 'How I love your hands,' he said. And how my hands loved him.'"

In the sweet glow that fell upon us when Olivia finished her story, I looked into the faces of the women in the circle, and suddenly I thought about my mother and her friends, and her mother and her friends. We had thought we were so modern, my friends and I, and so very wild, as if we were the first women ever to love sex. Maybe we were the first to share our stories, but we probably weren't the first to send the kids off to a mother-in-law so we could enjoy a lusty Sunday afternoon, or to be secretly turned on to repairmen, or to lovingly fondle a sick husband's balls.

Listening to Olivia tell us about Ed's bath, I finally understood that my mother and her mother, and even her mother's mother, had been sexual women, living out their desires and finding perfection as Olivia had in the ordinary moments of loving and caring. What stories they could have told.

*Catherine M. Tavel*

# Letter from New Orleans

Turning up one block and down another, I was surrounded by seductive fragrances. The sugariness of homemade confections emanated from Laura's Original Praline and Fudge Shop on Royal, the sweets themselves staring out from their doily-covered pedestals. The ruby heat of crawfish beckoned from a Decatur Street restaurant window while the essence of spicy red beans simmering nearby invaded the air near the Praline Connection. And I was lost.

As if by magic, I found myself sitting at a table in the Acme Oyster House, the worn white tiles comfortably familiar beneath my feet. Hands folded on the freshly wiped plastic checkered tablecloth, I watched one of the skilled shuckers across the room behind the aluminum-topped oyster bar. The graceful movement of his fingers as they mastered the flat, dull-edged knife, the soft flick of his wrists as he placed each open mollusk on the dented platter, were as soothing as the caress of a long-lost lover.

With the shucker's masterpiece finally set out before me, I lifted the first half-shell to my lips and sucked the meat. It lingered briefly at my teeth, then slid down the back of my throat, cool as a mouthful of jism is hot. One by one, I raised each oyster to my lips. One by one, I swallowed them, engulfed by the clean, chewy taste of the sea. One by one, until the entire dozen was gone. But I needed more. Something different.

A netted basket of crawfish soon took the place of the empty oyster shells. They were boiled to a brilliant red, almost the shade of an engorged cock tip. (Yet nothing is quite that color.) I grabbed one, snapped off the head and squeezed the tail, exposing its delicious chunk of flesh. Gingerly, I grasped the niblet between my teeth. My mouth exploded with the taste.

I was vaguely aware of being watched as I chewed and sucked and licked my meal in sheer delight. A man at a nearby table met my gaze. He said nothing, yet insinuated everything with his penetrating brown eyes. I kept snapping the heads off crawfish as he sank his teeth into a golden, soggy, Po Boy hero. The hot juices from the boiled decapods streamed down my elbows. I wiggled my tongue into their tiny hollow cavities, extracting as much fire as I possibly could. When I finished, my lips and tongue were burning, tingling with Cajun spice. The next time I glanced up, the handsome diner was standing beside my table.

"It's been a pleasure eating alone with you," he said, his intense caramel brown eyes piercing my skin. He moved to leave.

"Wait," I told him.

"No names," he instructed as we walked toward Jackson Square.

"What should we call each other, then?" I ventured.

"You look like a Beth," he said simply.

"And just what does a Beth look like?" I prodded.

He thought for a moment. "Sweet, fragile. That's what I think I'll call you. Beth. You can call me anything you'd like."

I was intrigued; I had grown weary of boring, predictable, button-down types. But was this man certifiable or safe? I could end it right here or . . . "Peter," I told him. "I'll call you Peter."

Peter and I chose a quiet bench in Jackson Square, past the easels of artists who did charcoal renderings of tourists, past the painters who sold watercolors of local scenes, past the fortune-tellers with tarot cards stacked on snack tables. The heat from the bench's wooden slats crept up through my body. I tried my best to mask my arousal.

It turned out that Peter was visiting from New York. A fire-fighter by trade, his Cuban-Irish heritage explained his exotic good looks and his wicked smile. His body was thick and strong. Staring at his sturdy hands, his solid fingers, I couldn't help but wonder what his cock looked like.

We stopped for reinforcements at the Cafe du Monde: strong chicory-laced coffee and sugar-coated *beignets*. I suppressed a strong urge to lick the sweet powder from Peter's lips. During a stroll along the banks of the Mississippi, we managed to tag along with a walking tour of blue-haired old ladies who welcomed us as if we were grandchildren. An hour into the tour Peter whispered, "I'm hungry."

"But we just ate," I told him.

When the group turned the corner, Peter pressed my back into a wrought-iron fence fashioned of cornstalks and morning glories. The bold outline of his cock etched into my thigh. "Did you ever notice," he said, "that life in New Orleans revolves either around food or fucking?" The crassness of his words sliced right through me, making my pussy throb. I was surprised at myself. How could I be falling for such a ruffian?

"Come on," Peter said, grabbing my hand. "I know the perfect place."

Before I knew it, we were on, of all things, a bus. Not a cab, not a horse and buggy, but a cranking, clanking city bus. We bounced along Canal Street into a residential section that smelled faintly of magnolias. It was a neighborhood of old but well-kept houses with misty front gardens and towering trees whose roots cracked up through the sidewalks. Peter pointed out Mandina's, a simple-looking establishment on the corner.

Across a bare Formica-topped table, Peter and I shared our appetizers: pungent crab cakes for me and spicy gumbo for him. I thought I'd melt when I fed him a forkful of my entrée and caught a glimpse of his tongue running across his lips. My blackened catfish was meaty, juicy and hot. His shrimp *étouffé* was equally delicious. We washed all this down with another cup of robust chicory coffee and a slab of bread pudding. I felt as though my mouth had died and gone to heaven—that is, until Peter kissed me under a moist orange blossom tree outside Mandina's.

As the tip of Peter's tongue gently moved from side to side in my mouth, my knees grew rubbery. He caught me around the waist and held me closer, tugging on my lower lip with his teeth. My nipples sprung erect as I pushed against him. The warm honey began to flow between my thighs as his now-hard prick carved into my belly. He could have taken me right there on Canal Street, but instead he pulled away, looked into my eyes and asked, "How do you feel about Boozoo Chavis?"

Just off Tulane, there's an amazing juke joint called Mid-City Bowling. The locals refer to it as "Rock and Bowl," because that's exactly what you do there. Amid the crashing spares and strikes, you can score some of the hottest music in town. There's a small stage, a dance floor, plus a full-service bowling alley. Culture mixed with crass. Sort of like Peter.

That night, Boozoo Chavis and his zydeco all-stars rocked us with accordions, washboards and spoons. Some people did the two-step and drank themselves into oblivion, while others opted to bowl ten frames. Frosty bottles of Abett's, the regional brew of choice, enhanced the amorousness of the evening. Peter and I clumsily attempted the two-step, but wound up grinding in the crush of bodies, getting lost in a sea of sloppy tongue kisses.

"My hotel's right around here," Peter told me as we stood shakily on Carrollton Avenue. A goodwill store named Thrift City was to our right, industrial buildings and a large looping highway to the left.

"You're kidding," I said.

"I'm staying at the Bayou Plaza," he admitted rather proudly. Beneath the highway was a network of buildings painted a wan, sickly beige. The hotel must have been something in its day, but now the term *fleabag* came to mind.

"I'm staying in the Quarter," I told Peter.

"Why doesn't that surprise me?" He grinned and took me by the arm. "You'll love it."

The pool in the Bayou Plaza's courtyard was unfilled and moldy. The elevator, with its worn carpet, had a distinctly musty smell. Someone had left a crawfish on the emergency call box. Peter laughed and stuck a cigarette butt in its mouth.

Inside Peter's room, both double beds had a distinctly fucked-out look, unmitigated by the chenille bedspreads. As soon as the door slammed shut, Peter pinned me to the faded wallpaper. My mind was pleasantly fuzzy from the Abett's. Peter rubbed against me as his tongue sought to unravel me. My breath came quickly and my clit throbbed without even being touched.

Holding my wrists to the wall, Peter slid my jumper down past my shoulders. My nipples were straining against the lace cups of my bra, itching against the scratchiness. Peter drew them into his mouth one by one, urging them alive. He ground his face from tit to tit, biting softly on my nipples, then yanking them away from the globes with his teeth. He opened my thighs and maneuvered one knee between them. Breathlessly, I rode it.

He pulled away from me and fell to his knees. I noticed that my pussy had left a dark wet spot on the leg of his wrinkled khaki pants—it made me feel that much more decadent. As he unfastened the buttons on my jumper, it fell to the carpet like a discarded flower. Then Peter tore the panties from my hips. Suddenly exposed to the air, my cunt felt both hot and cold at the same time. It was soon covered by his mouth.

Peter parted my pussy with his lips so that my clit stood out proudly, defiantly. He sucked it hard, looking up at me with those wicked candy-coated eyes. I was swooning with the mere thought that I had a big, strong, handsome man I barely knew on his knees in front of me, licking my cunt as though his life depended on it. That alone was enough to send me plunging over the edge, but I held it in. When I could take no more, I pushed him onto his back on the tacky carpet.

My pussy tasted sweet on Peter's kisses. I lapped away the juices, simultaneously unzipping his pants. Tucked into his BVDs was the most perfectly formed cock I'd ever seen. Smooth, slick, bevel-headed. At the base, a hairy, heavy sac with balls ripe as plums. I buried my nose in his honey-colored pubes, and his hips bucked uncontrollably as I slid my mouth up and down along the shaft. I swirled my tongue around the head, flicking the dew of pre-come from the tip. Then I took his balls into my mouth and pursed my lips around them. Every time I felt his body surging, I stopped. When this became too much for him, Peter scooped me into his arms and eased me onto the garish bedspread. It felt rough against my skin. We tore off what remained of our clothing and I lay on my back, legs spread, cunt lips slick with anticipation.

Wordlessly he turned me onto my hands and knees. The fine hairs along my spine sparked with electricity. His balls slapped into my clit with each thrust. I felt myself growing softer, warmer, closer with each movement. Peter kissed my shoulders, my neck, a potent mixture of tongue, teeth and lips.

"I want to fuck you on the balcony," he slurred.

I was shocked. "In public?"

"It's three in the morning. Everyone else is asleep."

"This is New Orleans," I told him. "No one ever sleeps."

Still, the thought of being taken out in the open like that intrigued me. When we reached the sliding glass doors, I noticed that they faced Tulane Avenue, shadowing the Ponchartrain Expressway. Cars and trucks buzzed by in the night.

"Any problem with this?" Peter checked as he bent me over the eighth-story balcony railing.

I smiled over my shoulder. "No problem at all." Rain splashed from the inky sky. The breeze was cool. As Peter rocked from hip to hip, swirling into my pussy, goose bumps covered my flesh. My hungry body clung to every inch of his cock. Lightning flashed in the sky, followed by a distant explosion of thunder.

"Scared?" Peter asked.

"Just cold," I said.

Peter grabbed a handful of my hair. He tugged it so hard that my eyes rolled back in my head. "I think you're lying," he snarled softly into my ear. "I think you're terrified. I can feel it in your body. I can feel it in your cunt."

It was true—I was terrified. I was being fucked on a balcony eighty feet above civilization. The streets below were desolate. If I screamed, no one would hear me. If Peter suddenly decided to slip his fingers around my neck and choke the life out of me, no one would see. He could kill me and easily get away with it. I barely knew this man, didn't even know his real name. He could be a pervert, an ax murderer, a serial killer. This episode could be a pattern for him, his "thing." He could do this with countless other women. I could just be one in a faceless string of others.

Fear crept over my body like a deep chill. I could taste it, like cold, flat metal at the back of my throat, like a gun being held there. Fear oozed down the inside of my thighs.

Fear aroused me: the unanswered questions, the shreds of doubt, the pinpricks of danger. Just the thought that something terrible might happen. It probably wouldn't, but . . . My breath came in ragged chokes. I was helpless. I wasn't responsible for my actions. If we got caught . . .

"Your heart's beating as fast as a sparrow's," Peter whispered, his hand cupped over my breast.

"That's because I'm scared," I moaned weakly.

When Peter bit the back of my neck, I could feel him smiling. "Scared of what? That I'll hurt you? That someone will see?"

"Everything," I said.

"Do you want me to stop?" he asked.

"No," I told him. "I like it."

I grasped the railing with both hands as Peter held onto my ass cheeks and pumped. Mist dampened my face. Thunder boomed, closer this time. Peter wedged his dick deep in my cunt, as far as it could go. One hand pinched my nipples, while the other massaged my swollen clit. Lightning flashed and I started to spasm. Just as I began coming, Peter lifted my feet off the balcony's cement floor. He bent me forward, tipping me further into the abyss. I felt as though I were swirling, falling, floating. "Please don't let go," I begged.

"Of course not. At least," he said wickedly, "not until after *I* come." He, too, was caught up in the moment. "Imagine how you'd look, this bare, broken little body in the alley of this decrepit place," he murmured. "They'd never even know it was me. Could be anyone, anyone."

The railing carved into my stomach. I bowed my head and began to climax strongly, battered by sensations, sounds and emotions. Again, Peter grasped a handful of my hair. Now he was holding me by a mere clump, with just one arm loosely wrapped around my waist. I could fall. I could die.

"Lift your head, Beth," Peter cooed. "I want them to see you. I want them to see me fucking you. I want them to see you come." My legs trembled in midair as my pussy shuddered. I screamed my orgasm into the night. Seconds later, I felt the knob of Peter's cock swelling inside me, spewing ribbons of white froth.

We stood there silent, motionless, for a few moments. Lightning flashed and broke the magic. "I can't believe you made me . . ." I gasped.

"Made you? I thought you wanted to," Peter said.

"Well, I did, but . . ."

We ran inside, giggling to relieve the intensity, dripping with each other's juices. My skin was splotched red from the cold. Stumbling into the bathroom, we turned the jets in the tub until the water gushed steamy hot. We jumped into the shower, rubbing warmth into each other's flesh. It was odd; we didn't speak, really, just smiled and scrubbed. I felt embarrassed, dissected, exposed, vulnerable, extremely naked. In a perverse way, I liked it. Liked being manipulated. Being out of control. It was strangely liberating. But what was Peter thinking? That I was a whore? Was I like all the others, or was I special? Would I ever see him again?

Peter turned off the shower and jostled me out of my mounting hysteria. When we stepped out onto the cold tiles, he grabbed a towel, got down on his knees and dried my legs, my feet. He worked his way up to my spattered ass. Then he looked into my eyes. "Hi," he said.

"Hi," I responded.

"My name is Danny," he smiled.

"And I'm Melissa," I told him.

"Melissa," he repeated. "What a beautiful name."

# Felice Newman

❧

# Box
## A meditation on virtual sex and lesbian cock

My jeans are worn white where my cock fills out the old denim. I've taken off my shoes, my shirt. I don't have the body I wish I had, but I have both more muscle and more flesh than you.

You are naked, stretched out on my white sheets exactly as you described yourself to me: tall and too thin, with lots of dark curly hair falling in your face, and hips that poke out from your body like wings on a starved bird.

I unbuckle my belt and pop the top button of my jeans. I put the head of my cock near your sex, but I do not enter you. This is not what you expect. I am a control freak—just like him—but with a difference: I've got your pleasure in mind. When I don't bang away at your cunt, you don't know whether to be grateful or worried. I laugh.

You are so wet that you slide onto my cock, and I ease inside you just enough so that the muscles ringing the opening of your vagina contract around me. You don't understand how this cock can seem to belong to my body. Your wetness sucks me in, and I whisper in and out of you so softly that I might as well be lips nibbling your flesh, but I'm not.

This you *really* don't understand.

When you want me to fuck you harder, you rock your hips against mine, wrap your legs around my thighs, and tighten your grip.

BOX                    275

I know this because you tell me, "I'm holding on so hard that I'm leaving white marks on your upper arms and shoulders." And then you ask me to fuck you harder.

My fiber-optic cock is not what Nicholson Baker had in mind when he normalized phone sex for the HIV-panicked superstore patrons of middle America.

Lesbian cock *is* virtual reality. It is the woman so pleasured who assigns meaning to the act. That thing is real only if she thinks it is.

By phone, that *thing* achieves virtual virtual status.

How much of this affair was about phone sex—and how much about sex with a straight girl; in this case, a *married* straight girl with two children and a big, useless hump of a husband?

I am fascinated by the fascination of straight women for lesbians. I love flirting with them in odd public places, like movie theater restrooms. "Wasn't that a great movie?" I say, rinsing my hands after pissing for at least three minutes upon exiting *Sirens*. These beautiful, anonymous women respond to me in a way I find weirdly delightful. Not sexually, not quite sisterly, certainly not as man and woman, but nothing like the way they respond to each other. Straight women read my difference on such an unconscious level they are unaware they are blushing—or even that they have been flattered.

My latest straight-girl fantasy concerns a woman I happened to pass on a stairway at the gym. It was my first day at my new gym, The Temple of the Body. She was going down and I was going up. I glanced from her face to the surprise of her magnificently developed shoulders and biceps, and she grinned. My friends made much of it and even half-convinced me to question my original assessment of her non-queerness. Since then, I have worn out my own rewind, fast forward, and pause buttons on that moment on the stairs.

And just tonight I found myself salivating over a young woman with pouty red lips. The lovely length of her was squeezed into a tight white knit dress, complete with cleavage and slit up the side. Oh, how I wanted to cover the soft mound of her belly with my warm hand!

But I'm getting ahead of myself. It was a year ago this month, while perusing sound bytes of sex on the telephone, that I stumbled across a woman who said she was looking for conversation with another woman. I liked her voice, which I can hear even now. Dry, a little throaty, soft. No giggles, no silly dime store porn, no *Penthouse Forum* or Hollywood pseudomasochism. Not even *Desert Hearts*.

She quietly stated her business, not affecting a desire for more than she really wanted, which she was willing to state clearly, seeming unaware that most people find it necessary to dress up their desires a bit.

I jumped at the chance to leave all pretense at the cineplex and get down to it with this ostensibly straight woman who had chosen this moment in late winter to own her desire for another woman.

So I had a brief phone sex affair with a woman who was married to a man who raped her when he came home late at night, after closing the gas station where he worked and the bar where he drank. How a sex ad in the local arts and culture weekly was supposed to ameliorate this situation I never got, except maybe that to this woman any small change in routine looked like salvation. When I asked her why she placed an ad in the girl section of the personals, she chalked it up to the lesbian affair she'd had in college years before, an event she reported as being as inevitable as SATs.

Later, she told me she was looking for an all-girl remake of her previous phone sex experience, her only other such experience, she hastened to assure me, a heavy breathing session with her husband's best friend, who answered the only other ad she swore she ever had placed. He said B-movie macho things about big cocks and never recognized her voice.

Lesbian phone sex, she thought, would be just like that.

It's late and cold in my bedroom, a deep blue room with French windows that face a street lamp on the block behind my house. Distant railroad tracks rumble as a train passes. In the front of the house there is a steady stream of traffic until about midnight and then an odd quiet.

"I can usually talk after ten when my kids go to sleep," she says. "He never gets home until late, at least twelve-thirty, sometimes

BOX 277

later. Sometimes he comes home wanting sex. I figure I might as well. He could really hurt me. It's easier this way."

I'm sleepy, only half-listening to her talk of children, husband, children. "It's easier this way," I hear her say, and then my brain works backwards: "He could really hurt me." The blue of my bedroom walls darkens as something passes between my house and the street lamp. For a second I think the shadow is me sitting up in bed.

"He's raping you," I say.

"Well, no. Not really."

I push the comforter from my shoulders and stare down at breasts, abdomen, thighs. My palm rests on my belly, a not-so-small fleshy mound cradling a hard muscle underneath.

You are naked, stretched out on your suburban white sheets. "He never gets home until late, at least twelve-thirty, sometimes later," you say. I picture your small nipples, your long neck, your flat stomach, the little patch of tight black curls between your legs, the bony feet hanging off the end of the bed. I doubt he ever really touches you, and even if he does, you never get his attention.

I draw a nipple into my mouth and suck gently as you speak. "He never gets home until late, at least twelve-thirty, sometimes later. Sometimes he comes home wanting sex."

Nothing he does to you can be called *sex*. This is sex, I say, and I give you my teeth. I hear you suck air, and I bite down harder. This is sex, I say, and I wet my fingers with you.

You laugh. "I figure I might as well."

I close my eyes: now I have you stretched out on my white sheets, your slender wrists pinned under my weight. I'm straddling you, thigh upon thigh, my belt buckle working a dent in your soft white belly. You buck, try to throw me off, and I do slip, only to land knee to cunt, pinning you more resolutely to the bed. You push. I push back. I push back again and again, and you heat up in spite of yourself.

You don't understand how you can be so wet for me. I unbuckle my belt and pop the top button of my jeans. This is not what you expect: I put the head of my cock near your sex, but I do not enter you. I am a control freak—just like him—but with a difference: I don't believe you owe me this sex, which I will now take from you.

I do require a level of response your husband can't be bothered with. When I don't bang away at your cunt, you don't know whether to be grateful or worried. I laugh.

You don't understand how you can be so wet for me, how I can slide into you so easily. When I want to fuck you harder, I rock my hips against yours, entwine my feet with your legs, and tighten my grip. I've got the base of my cock pressing into me, my clit is hard as a rock, and I'm going to fuck you until I come, and you will drown me. This you *really* don't understand.

I know this because you tell me: You don't want this sex. You don't want to hear this wet sucking sound you make. You don't want to feel the muscles deep inside you lock onto my cock. You don't want anything like this at all.

Am I trying to make this "real," or am I trying to make it hot? How much of this story would anyone believe? Did her husband "really" rape her? Did I? Was she "really" married? Did we "really" fuck? Is it "real" if we made it up together? Is it a lie if I make it up now, all by myself?

I think of boy porn: *His cock straining, yearning to be free of his jeans* . . . My cock is an uncomfortable absurdity in my pants. Who taught me to do this? I am straddling my own erection, driving to the bookstore to meet you.

Is anyone born knowing how to have sex? Not me. That's what I'd been thinking as I turned onto the bridge on the way to the bookstore. Such a beautiful early spring day, a drama of clouds, light and dark, moving quickly downriver. How did I know how to strap it on, what to say, how to feel? Where did I learn to move behind this cock?

We meet by the queer porn rack. Two men flip through hunky magazines. They lean back on their heels so that their hips angle forward, accentuating those little bulges in their carefully worn jeans. The room smells like testosterone, leather and new books.

I walk up to the boy porn rack and select a magazine with a brutally stupid name, like *First Hand*. I am wearing this winter's outfit: black boots, jeans, jacket, red hair.

I spot you at the girl porn rack. You are wearing a doe-brown

BOX 279

leather coat with fringes on the arms. You pick up *On Our Backs* and then *Bad Attitude*, pretending to read rather than look at the magazines.

Now I am having trouble remembering this part. I stand next to you, your hips several inches higher than mine. I touch your elbow, my fingers make sparks fly off the soft leather, and you turn to me. Or, I approach you from behind and touch your neck—you get a rush from my chilly fingers—before showing you my face. Which way did it happen? In any case we don't kiss, or talk.

We left the bookstore and beat a path back to my house, where we burrowed into each other in my room, the deep blue room, the French windows, the street lamp, a scene set. My hand curled inside you, the afternoon getting lost as late-winter shadows darkened the room. We had sex standing up by the porn rack, no one came, or we both came very quietly, quickly. Finished, we wiped fingers on jeans, zipped up and said good-bye. We never got to the bookstore at all. We exchanged letters. No letters, but a last phone call. Or not even a phone call. Nothing. You died. I can't imagine how you would have survived. Really, the weekly newspaper is no shelter, the personal ads no savior. What could you have been thinking?

What could I have been thinking?

It's late. I close my eyes and slip two fingers inside myself, which satisfies nothing but certainly heats me up. Here I am in my bedroom, a deep blue room with French windows that face a street lamp behind my house. Railroad tracks several blocks away rumble as a train passes. In the front of the house, there is a steady stream of traffic until about midnight and then an odd quiet. I let the pillow gently cradle the phone receiver against my ear.

"I can't stay on long, somebody's waiting for the phone—"

You tell me you left your useless husband, then moved to Ohio where you hooked up with a lesbian who beat you until you wanted to kill yourself. You call to tell me this and more—how you landed in a psych ward in Tennessee, lost custody of your kids, hit the road with nothing but your stash.

This isn't what I had in mind. I dig my ear deeper into the pillow.

"Then there's my girlfriend in Ohio. She used to come in drunk from work."

I am watching deep blue shadows moving along the ceiling. Somewhere a truck slowly passes by. Then the room is still, empty of sound—except for the wet suction of my fingers pulling in and out of my cunt.

"She gave it to me real bad. They had some mean ladies down in Tennessee. But nobody busted my shit like that girl in Ohio."

I stop breathing for a moment, hold my fingers deep inside.

"Guess she wanted some, like my man. Like you—"

I laugh, turn over onto my back, open up now for my hand. Sing a low moan into the receiver.

"Guess you want some now."

I close my eyes: now I have you on your knees, your ass spread wide. My belt flies through the loops of my jeans. The next beating you get is from me, I tell you, and I can hear your breathing change, know you are waiting for me to hit you, waiting for me to fuck you.

You are naked at the foot of my bed, your knees stretched open, your fists curled around pieces of my white sheets. My belt is an acrobat.

"It's easier this way," you say.

Your thighs are stretched wide, I have fistfuls of your dark curly hair gathered up like horse's reins, and my belt is performing somersaults on its way to meet your skinny ass.

"Do you think I'm crazy?" you say.

I smell your sex. My belt drives a path across your ass cheeks and, hungry girl, you rear back to meet me and open even wider to catch my belt between your damp thighs. The street lamp catches your moisture, the train passes, your skin is so soft, bone so close to the surface. I raise a welt from one blow even as I deliver the next.

Now I want you. I pop the top buttons of my jeans, loop the belt around your shoulders like a harness, and pull tight as I sink my cock between your cheeks, sliding into your cunt which is so wet I fall into you.

BOX                                    281

I fuck you for every night your husband has left you alone, and I fuck you for every night he hasn't. And when I want to fuck you harder, I rock my hips against your ass, entwine my feet with your legs, and tighten my grip on the belt around your shoulders. I've got the base of my cock pressing into me, my clit is hard as a rock, and I fuck you mercifully, crazily, selfishly, until I come, losing my grip on the reins, until you come—finally, rising up, you grind your ass against me, fistfuls of my sheets in your hands. I sink my teeth into your neck to hold on, and whimpering, finally, you come.

*Cecilia Tan*

# Dragon Cat Flower

The only people who believe in totem animals are those who know their own. Totem animals. A few years ago I wouldn't have believed in them. My Caucasian side would have explained them as genetic memory or some other pseudo-science, and my Chinese side would have taken on faith that we embody inner animal spirits. Either way, it sounds mystical and distant. But really, they're very close—just under the skin. So close you can stumble upon them like a predator in the night.

Like that first time with Jeff. One night we were in bed, making love. We usually made love on Thursdays because he didn't have to teach until the afternoon on Fridays and my weekly department meetings were over with by Thursday. I'd been thinking we'd have a kind of quick one, though, so we could get some rest—boy, was I wrong. I was holding his back against my chest and nuzzling his neck when I had the urge to sink my teeth into his shoulder—and I did. But instead of the usual "ow!" he snarled and arched back against me, a black panther growling and trying to twist out from under me. We wrestled then, a passionate struggle that heated us up like two sticks rubbing together, until he ended up on top of my back, clinging with the claws of his hands and biting me on the back of the neck as his cock nudged at my pubic fur begging entrance. I lay still and let him enter me—he edged his way in while his shoulders and jaw and hands froze rigid like stone. Only his hips moved the first few thrusts. Then I clenched my muscles tight and he mewed, his cock taking control now and moving faster, his hands flying loose and his head thrown back. *Is this what it's like for she-panthers?* I thought as the rhythm built up inside me.

Our lovemaking had been energetic before, but this was an animal passion beyond the neatness of human words like *love* or *sex*. In fact, I stopped intellectualizing after that and melted into the flow of fucking and rhythm and found myself growling and yowling with him as the pressure of his weight on me ground my pubis into the futon and brought me to a shuddering climax, and then another as he doubled his speed and came, too.

Afterward, it took him a few minutes to regain speech, to return to the reality of his graduate student apartment in Evanston, Illinois. He looked around his bedroom as if it were a strange environment, when really it was about the most normal place you can imagine, secondhand furniture, piles of books alternating with piles of laundry. He shook himself and said, "Wow. That was intense."

"You okay?" I rested my head on my arm and stroked his shoulder.

"It was like I went deep into the panther mind, and I saw and smelled and felt everything differently. I could feel the fur and the claws."

So could I, almost. I'd done my master's thesis on mammalian sexual behaviors and knew more about cat sex than anyone should. Having sex like wild animals could certainly be a nice change of pace once in a while, I thought.

"It was fun," I said, thinking it sounded encouraging.

Jeff gave me that little annoying frown of his and said, "It wasn't fun, it was *transcendent*."

We didn't last long after that. He became absorbed by his search to find out more about his panther "self," reading books on shamanism and mysticism, and he kept pushing me to "discover" my own cat.

"My panther wants a mate," he'd whisper through a growl while we fucked, and I did feel rather feline sometimes, but also almost birdlike, like a flying creature brought down by the hunting cat.

Other times I felt so powerful that I could twist him onto his back. All these random things, wings, claws, teeth, a snakelike tail . . . it was fun, but not *transcendent*. I decided he was sex-obsessed and stopped seeing him. Maybe, I thought, I should just look for someone I can have a normal, intellectual conversation with. When an offer from a behavior studies lab in San Francisco came, I took it as a good opportunity to move on. I'd be working with the old standby, white rats. My parents (one an orthopedist and one a general surgeon) were thrilled. I put all the baloney about totem animals in the back of my mind.

I was lonely at first, I'll admit, but I kept to myself until I settled into my routine at the lab. I could manage being alone, I thought. But I would find myself walking down a busy street in the evening, Chinatown, the Haight, wherever, prowling, hunting, hoping to make a catch. I'd go home when I realized it, thinking to myself, who's sex-obsessed now? I missed the intimacy and contact of warm skin. But much as I hoped things would change, I didn't expect it when they did.

I'd spent the weekend moping around the apartment, ordering takeout and not even venturing into the hallway. Sometime Sunday evening, I mustered up the energy to check my mailbox. As I shut my door behind me, I heard the clicking of the locks in the apartment next to mine. Out came a sheaf of jet-black hair, long and straight and slightly damp, and then the head that swung it as a booted foot shooed a cat back into the apartment, and a leather-jacketed, jean-clad body slipped into the hallway, pulling the door shut.

*Must be the next-door neighbor,* I thought. I'd heard the low hum of music from his apartment, but this was the first time I'd seen him. The jacket was emblazoned with some kind of animal, and I absently wondered if he was part of some rock band or Chinatown gang, or both, or if there even were such things. He was slipping his key into the lock as I went past him to the stairs. Then I heard him curse softly and open the door again. A furry something ran under my uplifted foot and down the stairs. His cat. I ran after the little beast hoping no one would come into the vestibule just then and caught up to him by the mailboxes. My black-booted neighbor came tromping down after. I picked up the cat, a smoke-gray beast who looked like every inch of him had been dipped in ash, but no, he was just that color.

I turned towards my neighbor. "I think this is yours?"

Now I got a look into my neighbor's face, broad and brown, with dark eyes so much like mine, the dark flat lashes of an Asian face. "Thanks," he said as he transferred the cat into the crook of his leather-covered arm. The cat clawed at his sleeve, but he didn't act like he noticed. "I'm Jon."

"Marilee." We were both staring at one another. He was the most attractive man I'd seen since I'd moved out here. And to think he lived right next door.

"Nice to meet you."

"Yeah." We stood there a moment longer, while my pulse rate climbed. Then he hefted the cat and smiled. "Well, gotta put the kid to bed before I can go out." And he turned back up the stairs.

I got my mail and passed him locking his door again as I went back to my place. "See you around," he said as I shut the door.

I read a book for an hour and watched the news before I got into bed with nothing better to do than sleep. I was thinking maybe I'd get up a little earlier, get in to work sooner, but as I lay there I knew I wasn't going to sleep right away. I replayed the exchange by the mailboxes in my mind. Did I imagine that he had a slightly sweet smell? Not the alcohol tang of cologne, but something else. If not for the cat I would have shaken his hand, smooth and brown, but instead I only felt the slightest touch as we handed the cat off, a mere brush that nonetheless felt alive with energy. I wanted to touch his face, and I wanted to feel that black waterfall of hair going down his back.

Sigh. I held my pillow to my chest and my eyes tight and imagined. He was probably hairless or nearly hairless all over, skin smooth and delicious . . . and yet the image that kept popping into my mind was of those catlike eyes. He was sleek, and intelligent, and slightly hungry. I hugged the pillow until my arms started to go to sleep and then I rolled over on my back and the rest of me went to sleep for the night.

In the morning I was still thinking about him, like I'd had a dream that I couldn't quite remember. It seemed to me now that when we had met, his eyes had a slight dark glow, like an old ember. And the sweet smell. Almost like smoke, I thought. I'd never made love to another person of Asian descent before. I'd grown up thinking that my father was just about the only Chinese man in the States, as he was certainly the only one I ever saw much of until I went to college, where I dated bland white middle-class boys like Jeff. It had never occurred to me to think about the ethnic blood of my lovers, it didn't seem important. But right now everything about Jon seemed important to me, every last detail. How his fingernails were slightly overgrown, how his lips looked dark. I preoccupied myself with thoughts of him until I left work early.

He knocked on my door that evening. As I stood in the doorway looking at him, still in the same jeans and boots, a tank top, his jacket gone, I decided the interest-attraction-chemistry that I'd thought I felt last night wasn't just wishful thinking on my part.

He stood there, wordless and calm.

I went with him to his place, where our courtship maneuvers commenced. We learned enough about one another to be polite, and then he put me in his bed to demonstrate some Chinese massage techniques he had mentioned.

He lit incense and candles while I took off my clothes, and then began the massage. His hands seemed cool at first, reminding me of a doctor checking for fever, and maybe I could say I was a bit feverish, melting into his touch. He was saying things but I wasn't really listening, about how ancient Chinese medicine was based solely on touching the outside of the body to fix what was wrong inside. My father was a doctor, and Chinese, I told him, but I didn't think he ever did anything like this.

His laugh was musical and quiet. "What about your mother?"

"American," I answered, and sighed as his fingers reached the knotted muscles in my lower back. I breathed deeply as I sank into the softness of his featherbed and felt the warmth of his breath on my neck. This kind of closeness was what I had missed.

Nimble fingers played over my sides, enticing me to turn over so he could search my stomach and throat and thighs for soft places. And then the kisses began, under my chin, on my forehead, my eyelids, my lips. As he broke away, I looked up into his eyes.

They seemed to glow as the candles flickered around us and turned his skin gold. I drew in another deep breath of sweet incense and felt myself buoyed up like a cloud of warm air, as if the futon had become a cloud rising in a golden sunset sky; my hands fluttered up like birds to dart into his hair and encircle his neck as I drew myself up to him or him down to me—there was no gravity in that floating state, no up or down—and we rolled one over the other. As he wound around me and I around him I breathed smoke and we spiraled higher. My conscience nagged me once, "What's happening?" but I was eager to hear his reassurances as he hushed me with a golden finger, drawing stripes around my eyes and across my cheeks and telling me not to worry, to relax. I started tasting him, and my tongue stretched impossibly long as I searched out his secret places, and he mine.

The first growl came as one of his legs fitted between mine, our circling of each other drawing in to a tighter and tighter spiral, and I sank my claws into his back. The motion of his leg pressed up against my desire. I had a flash of it then, an image I had seen somewhere before lighting up the inside of my eyelids like a slide, a sinuous twisting body rising up like a skirl of smoke . . . the dragon emblem on the back of his leather jacket. Now I saw it clearly. What had looked like a shadow when I'd hurriedly glanced at it the night before I now saw was a second dragon, entwined with the first.

One of his fingers slipped into the hollow between his thigh and mine and over the edge of the wet cleft of my mons. He nipped at my chin. I pulled on his generous hair and his back arched away from me and his dark nipples stared at me like icons from a Taoist temple. I used my extra-long tongue to trace up the center ridge of his breastbone, up his chin, and again found myself looking into those eyes, saw myself reflected there and felt the spinning begin anew. He closed his eyes and kissed me, and I closed my eyes too as his other leg insinuated itself between mine and I fell into the tumble and spinning again. I hooked my legs around him and drew him into me as the spiral grew as tight as it could, and we were bonded into one animal.

With him inside me now, I thrashed freely, my long spine curving and twisting as we continued through a heavenly sky. Now the vision expanded, to the black and gold body entwined with mine, to the feeling of the wind lifting us up as we mated, to the sound of our two wordless voices mixing, to the sensation that we were two alike beings, long and curving like wisps of smoke, flying upon the air, dragons. My awareness opened like a bud blooming as he moved in me, and the room fell away to nothing, and the city below was like one giant temple festival, with incense burning and small human voices chanting. And still we rolled on through the sky, trailing thunderclouds, as I rode him and he me, the feeling of his flesh where it went in and out of mine like the point of perfect balance, like the vortex around which the whole universe rotated.

I flexed my claws and held even tighter to him then, feeling my power. When I'd played at being a cat with Jeff I'd been nosing around the edges of a primal energy, tied to the balance of nature by its raw animalism. But now I felt the surge of ancient power, of something so simple that it was science and magic and religion all at once to my ancestors, a people I had never known. They did not divide up the world the same way as the Europeans or the Native Americans, and they assigned the supreme powers of all animals—the flight of birds, the predatory strength of the tiger, the grace of the snake, and a wisdom beyond man—to one creature who was never captured, never seen for more than a glimpse beyond a distant storm cloud.

*This is as it should be*, came his voice rolling out of the sound of distant thunder, as he breathed sweet smoke from his nostrils into mine and we rocked together like tides cycling on the shore. Like my tongue, his penis seemed to elongate as he stretched away from me and then swooped in a long slow motion, never seeming to come fully out of me, as though separation were not possible now. And again he pulled away and I pulled him in, inch by inch, over and over in a rhythm as slow as the turning of the world, the cycle of ancient seasons.

My orgasm built in intensity, radiating from the point of balance between us, rippling through me, along my skin, through my mind. I could see the clouds but feel the tangled sheets under us, feel my wings stretching into the sky but also the clenching of his buttocks under my spread fingers as I drove him deeper and I pushed myself into the heart of my coming. The vortex seemed to spin faster and I clung to him, my loins on fire and the flickering of starlight and candles in my eyes, the taste of his sweet smoke on his lips as I shuddered and shook and felt myself begin the long fall from the peak of pleasure. I opened my eyes.

He cradled me tight against him with one arm as he propped himself up with the other and breathed another puff of sweet smoke into my nostrils. We rolled to the side, and his finger again found its way between us to the balance point, to begin the rise again. My second orgasm was quick in coming, and I closed my eyes again and pressed my cheek to his chest. With every throb of my clit it seemed we swooped past another cloud. For one moment my brain remembered that I was supposed to be at the lab in the morning, and surely two orgasms was enough? I roared as my body soared on another wave of pleasure.

My plain white rats could wait. I had discovered a whole new animal inside myself. I clamped my mouth to his, ground my lips hard against him, and the pleasure went on.

## Christine Solano

# Walls of Fire

His tiger eyes invaded the thin layers of my silk blouse as easily as a hot iron. I could feel the glow touching my breasts. He smiled. He could see every part of me the way a blind man sees, by instinct. Our heat was melting the thick glass window that separated us, rendering it almost useless.

I swallowed, pretending all this wasn't happening, that we really were just having a conversation about poetry. "So what have you been working on, Jesse?"

He laughed his big, easy laugh, the laugh that meant: *I know you're trying not to lose your cool, and it's okay. Whenever you're ready, baby.*

"Something special," he said.

"Haikus?"

"Hell, no. Sex poetry!" He laughed again, delighted with himself and with the sight of me fidgeting on the hard plastic chair and swallowing my juices. My cunt was throbbing. But I wasn't ready to give in. I was here on a serious mission, not to get sucked into phone sex, San Quentin–style.

"What happened to the series of haikus you mentioned in your last letter?" I asked sternly.

"I'll send them to you to critique, as soon as I can manage, ma'am," he replied with an ironic smile. "But don't you want to hear my sex poem? I spent the whole morning learning it by heart, so I could recite it to you."

My ear started tingling, so hard was the heavy receiver pressed against it. The phone was old, and the noise of the other visitors around us reverberated in the cold, hard room. Glancing at the guards in their booth, I hesitated. They seemed preoccupied with their coffee and gossip. I never knew how much of our conversations were listened to, or even recorded.

Three times now I had come to visit Jesse in San Quentin, which the inmates call "The Belly."

Each time I came bearing the banner of "literary mentor to the rising young star of prison poetry," determined to insist on sober, earnest conversation.

But he had interspersed all his letters with giddy kisses ever since I'd made the mistake of sending him a photo of me in my most romantic summer dress, and on each visit, he succeeded in manipulating and seducing me, until I practically kissed the imprint of his fingers on the heavy glass that separated us. Still, I hoped to eventually convert this madness into some kind of friendship, and this gorgeous, crazy, sex-starved black hellcat into a responsible and respected poet.

"Go ahead," I said. *Make my day,* I thought. *Titillate me, until you've driven both of us bonkers. As long as you keep writing, keep creating, something, anything, powerful, beautiful, sad or lovely, out of this hell you're living in.*

His pink tongue shot out and licked his lips. I imagined it flicking over my clit, and a quick, hot flash shot up my belly. *Breathe,* I told myself, *breathe and relax.*

"I wrote this poem last week, when the weather was so hot, I couldn't sleep." He half-closed his eyes, groaned, spread his legs and scratched his long, lean thighs in an overt act of exhibitionism. I tried not to look, not to imagine.

"All I could think of was making love to you, baby." That smile again.

*He's not going to get to me,* I swore to myself.

"Then that freaky thunderstorm hit, and the poem came to me

like . . . lightning!" Jesse giggled, pleased with himself as a kitten on a tree. *All right, all right, get on with it, Jesse.*

"Close your eyes," he whispered. I sighed, but obeyed. It wasn't a bad idea, anyway, listening to him with my eyes shut, avoiding his gaze, his noticing the widening of my pupils and seeing it as an open door. His voice was gentle, soft like the steps of a Siamese cat walking down your spine.

"I haven't come up with a title yet," he said. " 'Sexual Healing' would fit nicely, but I don't want to steal from a brother. Here it goes." His voice became serious, articulate, as he changed from prisoner to poet:

> *Last night, I watched the thunderstorm,*
> *Embraced in heavy, sleepless air—*
> *Lightning struck against the sky*
> *Until it split wide open.*
> *Then came the rain, its smell of earth.*
> *I held my face against it.*
>
> *One night, I saw your eyes in mine;*
> *You smiled behind the looking-glass;*
> *Fingerprints showed on my skin*
> *Like medals won in battle.*
> *Remember what we're fighting for.*
> *I'll see you on the far side.*
>
> *Some night, I'll dance your breath away*
> *Within the echoes of your soul*
> *Recognizing what once was*
> *You might just find the secret door.*
> *For what are we, but dreams of gods*
> *In sleepless, heavy nights.*

I let out my breath. "But that's beautiful, Jesse."

"Yeah? You really like it?"

"It's different from everything you've written so far. But it's really good."

"You've been such an inspiration." His golden-green eyes turned liquid. "I love you, Chrissie."

I bit my lip, trying to suppress the tears that filled my eyes.

"I love you too, Jesse."

He had done it again. He knew how to push my buttons. But I couldn't get mad at him—he was just trying to stay alive, stay sane while knowing that "by the will of the people" he might be executed next year—or next month. Jesse had never killed anybody. His biggest mistake had been to be born in the wrong place, the wrong color.

My thoughts and dreams about Jesse became more and more entangled. In the past, I had forbidden myself to fantasize about him, but at night, I would be overcome by dreams that left me hot and very bothered. So I switched tactics, hoping that with a bit of unrestrained fantasizing and masturbating, his shadow would leave me in peace at night. Instead, visions of his tall, muscular body leaped at me from everywhere—while staring at the screen of my word processor, while talking to a black student, or while looking across the bay toward the harsh lights of San Quentin.

San Francisco is a city filled with exotic odors; now they started to haunt me. Everything took on a smell of sex; over a plate of spicy Thai food I would suddenly imagine fresh, male sweat; walking down Clement Street, the scent from all the ethnic restaurants would mingle in my mouth and leave an aftertaste of semen on my tongue; passing by a bakery, the fragrance of fresh bread would remind me of the aroma of my cunt.

At night I lay awake, my eyes too tired to read. Listening to the forlorn sound of the foghorns in the bay, I would think of Jesse in his cold and comfortless cell.

"Jesse," I whispered, "can you hear me? Can you feel me holding you, keeping you warm and tight?" In the dark, I could almost see his eyes glowing just a few inches away from mine. Sometimes, as I drifted into sleep, I could feel the light touch of his hand on my thighs, his lips on the nape of my neck. Then the dreams would come.

He had talked about his dreams so often that mine began to resemble them. "If we can both dream the same dream, we'll be together," he once said. "No one and nothing can separate us in our dreams."

It was certainly true that my dreams had become more and more realistic, to the point where I dreamt orgasms that shook me into wakefulness. One night, I slipped into the dream he had written after I'd sent him a picture of me steering my dad's sailboat. In Jesse's dream, I would be waiting just outside of San Quentin, down by the beach, the *Santana* gently rocking on the smooth bay water behind me. I would see Jesse stepping through the East Gate and walking down towards me, a big smile splitting his face. He would blink into the sun and put on his cool Malcolm X shades. He would wear the clothes I had sent him: tight denim jeans, a white shirt, a black leather jacket. He would be so beautiful.

"You take my breath away," I whispered in my dream. His arms didn't want to let go of me. "I'll never let you go, never, never."

The boat was anchored a hundred yards away from Angel Island. That's as far as I had been able to steer it, before Jesse had taken off the last of my clothes. The initial hug and kiss lasted forever—or a couple of minutes, I don't think either one of us could have said. His hands and lips hadn't left me for a moment, while I tried hard to keep some measure of concentration on guiding the boat. I wanted to get us to the first cove on the east side of the island, the first place where we would lose sight of San Quentin.

At last, I could drop anchor, and seconds later his fierce tongue in my mouth made me spread my legs, and we both tumbled onto the deck. I was burning brightly from all his touches, from all the hot, wet marks that his lips had left on my body. I needed him with an urgency that left no space for niceties. I pinned his arms down as I mounted him and felt his hot, hard cock slide into me. His eyes rolled up in his head.

"Oh God, no, yes, please, Christ!" he gasped, his fingernails clawing into my thighs, his back arching up. My legs, my cunt, grabbed him tight as he screamed and turned me around to pound his cock into me while holding me with one arm against his smooth, sweat-sprinkled chest. I bit into his shoulder and he exploded, howling, shooting hot come into my cunt and flashes of bright light through my brain. The sky above us was blue, but for a moment, it seemed red with our passion.

He buried his head between my breasts. I kissed his neck, felt a warm tear falling on my skin, laughed out loud, felt the sun on my skin like a blessing. The wind caressed our faces, our bodies. We gazed across the water, at the distant San Francisco skyline pointing its fingers at God. And at that moment the dolphins appeared.

I woke up to a gray and misty morning, the mournful foghorns still echoing in the distance, my bed cold and empty. My body ached and my head was heavy with the wine I had drunk last night. For a whole week, my mailbox had been empty, empty of any news from Jesse, any of the white envelopes with the familiar red postmark of the state prison. Who was Saint Quentin, anyway? What did he do to deserve the dubious honor of having this hell named after him? What a fate for a saint—having his name crown the letterhead of the document that one day would tersely name the date of my lover's death.

Whatever crimes Jesse had committed when he was twenty-one years old, his twelve years in the belly of the beast should have been payment enough. Instead, a barbaric nation felt they needed to kill my gentle, thoughtful poet.

When I came home late that night, after a long and exhausting school board meeting, I did find a message from Jesse in my mailbox. Some time ago, I had sent him a box of postcards. They were full of cheerful, bright images, meant to bring a little sunlight into his airless cell. One of them was a photo of a school of dolphins, sailing through the water, some jumping into the brilliant, sunlit air. He sent that one back to me, with another poem.

*Dreaming with Chrissie*

*Light ripples on the water*
*Announced their leaps a beat before*
*They jumped with their*
*Amazing grace*
*Into the sky—*
*Fell back into the sea and*
*Cleared the shadow of our bow.*

*Their joy was all around us;*
*Their bodies like a song the wind*
*Once whistled in its childhood.*

*And when they left*
*They left us,*
*My lover, in a trail of light,*
*With ripples on the water.*

Jesse and I *had* been dreaming the same dream.

## Kelly Conway

❧❀❧

# Mind Fuck

There is nothing unusual in the still morning air. I hear the same brown wren that I hear every dawn, taunting my little spotted cat, making a mess of birdseed shells on my porch. The same annoying voices assault me from my radio alarm clock, a pair of deejays who find themselves far more amusing than I do. There is nothing different about the emptiness of my king-size bed, sheets rumpled, my blue down comforter thrown to the floor in the middle of the night. There is no reasonable explanation for the uncertainty that shrouds my senses as I open my reluctant eyes.

My coffeepot does its magic. I have the timer set so the coffee's ready by the time I stumble into the kitchen to search blindly for my favorite mug: painted with Van Gogh's orange and purple irises.

I'm not much for routine, but my little cat is. I have to sit with her for at least half an hour to fulfill her snuggle requirement before I can go to work. My office is a mess, but this environment suits me fine. My desk looks exactly like I picture the inside of my head—cluttered, filled with little notes that I can't seem to throw away, stacks of notepads containing information that's no longer useful, crumpled paper littering the floor around the trash can, the aborted poems.

I am a writer. At least, I like to think that I am. I still feel like a fraud when the words "I am a writer" come to my mind—the sentence feels good on my tongue—but I only say it aloud when I am alone.

I smooth out the folded paper that I have been coveting in the back pocket of my overalls. "Writers sought," says the notice, "for an anthology of lesbian short fiction."

As a rule, I don't comprehend the writing of short fiction. I am a novelist. Short story writers amaze me—how can they say so much, with so few words? Maybe they have more control over their characters than I do. Mine defy me, laugh at me when I try to end a chapter, and continue on even after I've turned off the computer. I never know what I'm going to wake up to, who they'll have become in the middle of the night. They don't invite me to the plot parties, or even to the wrap.

My computer blips cheerily when I turn it on. I find WordPerfect and open a new file, determined to write a short story. But the voice of the solitaire game that comes with this Windows program is louder than my own. It screams to me whenever I see an empty screen.

After losing several games, I realize that I can't really write unless a muse is present in the room. Joni Mitchell? Too depressing. Indigo Girls? Too intense. Nanci Griffith? Too distracting. Joan Baez? Works for me. I load "Diamonds and Rust" into my CD player, and return to the dreaded blank screen.

Now seems like an appropriate time to change the marquee on my screen saver. The bookshelf holding my dictionary, thesaurus, essentials of English grammar and poetry handbook is looking mighty dusty. And why haven't I alphabetized them by title yet? Anything to distract myself while an idea takes root. It feels something like prolonging an orgasm—you know how some women, when giving face, will stop just at the crucial moment, and then begin again when they sense that you're ready to kill them? It's kind of like that. I feel an idea taking root, building, my hands tremble, I feel light-headed, then choose that moment to do anything else but write.

Ah! Saved by the doorbell. I am certainly not expecting anyone. I am too lonely for friends. My neighbors see me as the resident queer, and avoid me accordingly. This distraction comes at the perfect time. Solitary masochism wears thin quickly. It's much more fun to be annoyed by a stranger.

When I open the door, the woman on the steps is not the expected Jehovah's Witness, is not selling an all-purpose cleaner, is not a kid pandering candy with a song and dance about staying out of gangs. It is a woman who looks exactly like a bit character from the sci-fi/fantasy novel that I'm in the middle of writing. She's barely more than a sketch, but I have a lot of plans for her.

I drink in her leather jacket, the knife sheath attached to her thick black belt, her steel-toed boots, the silver in her short black hair, her black t-shirt, sleeves rolled up to show arms muscled with experience, the gray eyes that know every embarrassment I suffered in elementary school. Although I am a born-again femme, having recovered from the androgyne ideal bestowed on us in the seventies, I'm not usually inclined to swoon. I swoon. She catches me.

"I'm Lee," she whispers, hot breath striking my neck like fangs. "You wrote me. You've been dreaming that I'll show up on your doorstep one day and fuck the taste out of your mouth. I'm here. Deal with it."

"You're not real," I say, backing up. "I did not write you, you wrote yourself. And besides, I'm perfectly happy with my vibrator." You know you're in trouble when you start taunting your hallucinations.

"See if this is real, sweetmeat," she says, pushing me into my living room, kicking the door closed, undoing the clasps of my overalls, and pulling my shirt over my head.

"Ah, that feels pretty real," I say, trying to sound casual. Her kiss loosens my muscles, and I fall against her hard body. Fuck it. Who cares if it's real, old acid kicking in, or a nervous breakdown? She's packing. This is too good to pass up.

I hear the unmistakable click of her knife snapping open. Before I can scream, gasp or swoon, she slices through the back of my panties like they're whipped cream. How rude. These are my favorite panties, red lace with no elastic around the legs. I thought they were easy access but apparently not easy enough for my impatient apparition. Still, I don't care if they're ruined or not, I just want her to get at what's inside them.

There are few sounds as sexy as the unzipping of a pair of tight black jeans. It rips through the silence of my living room and wetness pours down my leg. By now I'm totally aroused—whatever the hell this is, let it last until I come. Lee grabs me by the nape of my neck, pulling the fragile hair just enough to let me know she's serious, but not hard enough to cause real pain. She bends me over the back of my couch, leaving my ass in the air, the slice in my panties exposing my pussy, my feet off the ground. I assume that she's going to fuck me, but no, she's got to taunt me first.

"You want it, don't you?" she hisses.

I do, but I refuse to answer a figment who speaks to me in that tone of voice. I ignore her, thinking about what it will feel like when she fucks me. She yanks me back to my feet, twisting my hair around her hand.

"I said, you want it, don't you?"

Why the hell do butches always ask this question? I should think it was pretty apparent that I wanted it. I nod yes.

She pushes me to my knees, digging her strong fingers into the back of my neck. I am eye-level with her crotch. I must admit, the view is not bad, but I'm not too crazy about this position. It seems a bit submissive for me. This is not the way I wrote her: she's supposed to be gentle. I haven't written any scenes where she's a top—yet.

Lee reaches inside her unzipped jeans, pulls out her cock, and forces my head back. "I want you to suck me. You can do that, can't you?" she asks. I shake my head no. I'm pretty freaked out. I thought blow jobs were a boy/girl thing.

"Okay, then, I'm gonna tell you what I want you to do. Stick out your tongue," she commands. I comply. She lays her dick on my tongue and holds it there. "Move your tongue a little bit, not too much. Just get it wet." I try to do exactly as she says. "Okay, a little more. No. Don't touch it." She pushes my hand away. "Now, don't move. Wet your lips. There, that's it. Stick out your tongue again."

I feel embarrassed, kneeling before this stunning butch apparition, my overalls around my ankles. I'm used to being somewhat suave in sexual situations, but this creation has me tongue-tied—literally.

She lays her dick across my tongue again, her eyes fixed on

mine. A moan escapes me and I am mortified. I am trying so hard to remain cool.

"Okay, baby, get it wet, then take the head in your mouth, just a little bit."

This is the first time I have heard anything even remotely resembling tenderness in her voice. I do as she tells me, surprised at how much I like the way this feels, wanting to please her. I savor the head of her cock, licking in a circular motion. I hear her breathing become more pronounced, so I draw a little more of her into my mouth. She starts rocking a little, sliding in and out, gently. Why does this turn me on so much? What the hell is going on here? I suck harder, moving my head, trying to get her all the way in. She pulls me away, winding my long brown hair around her hand again.

"Not so fast. I told you just a little. Now lick it."

I move my tongue up and down the shaft of this sweet dick of hers. It's hard to be smooth without using my hands, but I lift her cock with my tongue and move my lips around the head again, keeping my tongue stuck out as far as I can. Holding still, not wanting to make any mistakes, I wait for her direction. None comes, so I just sit there. Finally, she pulls my head towards her and thrusts hard against the back of my throat. I almost gag, but hold it back.

"Suck," she demands.

I want to say, "Okay, baby, I'll do anything you want," but I just keep quiet and do as she tells me.

"Take it easy, not so fast," she cries out, moving faster into me. I tighten my lips around her dick and work my tongue. Her movements become more and more erratic, she moans till she yells, and rips herself away from my lips.

This is all too weird—I mean, I'm on my knees in front of someone who isn't even real, and I'm so turned on that I can't stand up. I think about the outline for an erotic novel lying in my desk drawer. While there is no character sketch that resembles Lee, the femme narrator talks a lot about her butch top who loves to get blow jobs. I have no idea where this outline came from, and no recollection of writing it.

"That was great, baby." Lee's voice interrupts my thoughts. "Just how I like it. You did that really good."

I stare into her eyes and watch her soften. There's something incredible about the way a butch looks when she's just come— that slight hint of vulnerability in her eyes, when for a moment the walls are down. Lee reaches for my hand and pulls me to my feet. I wrap my arms around her neck—the first full body contact we've had—and am startled to find that she feels solid, real, not like a hallucination at all. "I wanna fuck you now, baby," she whispers softly. "Will you let me fuck you?"

I'm not ready for her to go gentle on me just yet. "Have *you* ever done that?" I ask, challenging her butch pride. "Have *you* ever had a woman's cock in your mouth?" I know this will piss her off, but it's worth it to see that dangerous look come back to her eyes. There's a part of me that wants her to make love to me the way I wrote it in the sci-fi piece, slowly and sweetly. But there's another part that wants her to shove that dick through the slice in my panties, to fuck me till it hurts.

"What the hell are you saying?" she snaps. "For that I just might not fuck you at all." She pushes me away from her. "Fuck you! Goddamn smartass femme," she mutters, shaking her head. "Get on the bed, on your hands and knees, and pull your panties halfway down. Wait there for me. Think about how you talk to me. I might come in and beat your ass, I might fuck your undeserving little pussy, or I might just leave you hanging."

I debate with myself; do I want to obey this strange character? My hesitation, however brief, makes her madder. She shoves me to my knees again, roughly. "Pull your panties down, right now." I pull them down a little, look up at her and smile.

"More. Don't make me do it for you."

I push my panties down around my hips and wait.

"Now, crawl," she says. "I want to see your ass moving in the direction of the bedroom."

I move slowly, on my hands and knees, till I reach my room. I hear no movement from the other room as I settle on the bed to wait, my ass high in the air. I close my eyes, listening intently for any indication that she is approaching. None comes. I have never been a patient person, hate waiting for anything. As I lie there in the silence it occurs to me that since I wrote her, she should do whatever I want her to do. I try to draw her to me, creating images of her coming through the door, finding me posed as she told me to be, and stroking my ass gently, kissing the back of my neck. "Come on, Lee," I think as loudly as I can. "Come on in here, I'm ready for you."

Nothing happens. I remember the feel of her cock in my mouth. I loved that. I want to feel it again. But nothing happens. I imagine her pushing the tip of her delicious cock into the wet opening of my pussy, picture her eyes closed in pleasure as she fucks me. Still, nothing happens.

After several eternities Lee appears, looming in front of me, a perfect vision of what a butch top should be. She kneels in front of me on the bed, undoing her belt. It must have worked, I think. She came back for another blow job. But she only removes her belt, and doesn't undo her jeans.

I recoil as the leather lands across my ass for the first time. "Do you like that?" she asks.

I am too shocked to answer. I just shake my head no.

"Do you have any more smartass questions for me?" she asks as the belt slams against my cheeks again.

I cry out, confused. She's my character. I should be able to get her to fuck me the way I wrote it. My ass gets warm and starts to tingle. What really boggles my mind the most is that this feels good.

"Ouch," I yell, to see what will happen.

"Be quiet or you'll get worse than this," she hisses, snapping the belt hard against the top of my thighs. She rotates the places where she strikes—just when I think it hurts too much, she moves to another tender, previously unspanked spot. I moan, unable to stop myself. She pulls out her dick and sticks it in my mouth. "I said, keep quiet."

I suck her as each glorious lash brings me closer to the edge. It's starting to hurt, but in a really good way, and I am grateful for the distraction of her dick. It's impossible to remain quiet; I scream as she expertly flicks my rigid clit with the smooth black leather. She comes before I do, with a long deep sigh.

Lee stands and walks around to the end of the bed. "Your ass looks really sweet in that shade of red," she says, laughter in her voice. Her soft hair rubs across my stinging skin as she covers my ass with light kisses. Her strong tongue probes my asshole and I flinch. No one has ever touched me there, and I haven't written about it, either. She steadies me with a gentle hand as she licks my crack up and down, over and over, until I cry out. She smears a thick lubricant, still cold from the tube, all over my anus. I stiffen, terrified that it will hurt if she fucks me there—yet I want it.

She enters me slowly, with just her finger. I want more. Her dick bumps against my clit as she slides her finger in and out of my ass. This is too good. I am dizzy, think I'm gonna pass out, it's so good. She squeezes more lube onto her cock and gently eases the head into the one place I have never been fucked. I collapse, letting my shoulders take all my weight as she fingers my clit, fucking me harder and harder until the air goes black around me, and I come harder than I've ever come before.

The phone rings. The telephone is the bane of any writer's life—it only rings when you're on a roll. Lee reaches over, switches the ringer off and turns the volume down on the answering machine. She pulls the knife out of its sheath and absently cleans her nails, reading what she thinks she has written. I'm watching her from inside the monitor. I enjoy the look of surprise, then concern that crosses her face as she reads. She's so funny, thinking she can write. I do all the writing. She might wear the strap-on, but I'm the femme who runs the computer—been living in here since she bought it, kind of like a genie, I guess. I laugh as she discovers the story of a bottom, written in first person, on her very own computer.

I want her to submit this somewhere, so I'll let her use a pen name. She won't want her friends to think she's switched. I'll make her use my name. We all know the bottom runs the fuck.

# Serena Moloch

## Casting Couch

### The Job Applicant (Trixie)

I'm so nervous about this interview. I really want this job.

Let me go over it all again. Why I want the job: I'm interested in getting into film and video production and I'd like to learn from the ground up, producer's assistant would be perfect. Why they should hire me: I'm organized, responsible, learn fast, and . . . what was the fourth, oh, right, *responsive*, I'm responsible *and* responsive to my employer. Previous experience, two years as personal assistant to an executive director. Why I left that job: tricky, but stick to the standard answer, no more room for growth. I just hope Gillian wrote me a good reference, like she promised. Typing speed, 80 words per minute . . . I certainly did Gillian enough favors, a good letter is the least she could do for me in return. Oh, I'm tapping again, I have to stop that. Should I go fix my hair? No, better stay here. Do I have copies of my résumé? What time is it? Early still. Ten more minutes to go.

### The Boss (Jane)

As soon as I saw her file, I knew she'd be perfect. With its royal blue letters leaping off a mauve page, her résumé was eye-catching in a vulgar way that suggested initiative coupled with inexperience.

She was underqualified for the position I'd advertised, and I'd be sure to let her know that, so she'd be even more grateful to be hired and even more eager to please. Furthermore, some suggestive phrases in her former employer's reference interested me. Trixie was "a model assistant who never hesitated to provide any service asked, even if that meant helping in ways that some might construe as more personal than professional." She was also "devoted and solicitous."

Trixie must have worked pretty hard, I thought. I leaned back and imagined using that wonderfully ridiculous name in a variety of situations. Trixie, come in here, I'd say over the intercom. Trixie, sit down and take a letter. This is my assistant, Trixie, I'd tell people. Trixie, get me a drink. Trixie, lie down . . . Trixie, take off your clothes . . . now mine . . . very good, Trixie.

I sighed and let the chair come forward again. Too many years of reading scripts had fostered a bad habit of associating names to types and spinning off into little fantasies. Sure, I saw Trixie as a ripe peach, with big round eyes and nipples to match, traipsing her luscious ass around the office in a tight skirt, eager to please. But Trixie would probably be more concerned with her paycheck than with me. Or she'd be all too interested in her effect on me, if the past week's interviews were any indication.

The applicants had been very good-looking, and perfectly competent for the job, but they were all actresses eager to break into the business, and it was obvious they had only their interests in mind and not mine. I had certainly been offered a variety of services.

I didn't enjoy remembering what had frankly been a tiring and unpleasant series of encounters. Jill had stared at me oddly until she finally got up the courage to make her move, opening her blouse and fondling her very beautiful breasts while maintaining intense eye contact. "Do you like my titties?" she asked, and I said, "Yes, I like them, Jill, but I don't like you. Thanks for coming in today."

Then there was Pamela, a redhead in spandex. She was quicker than Jill. After two questions about her secretarial skills she walked around my desk to stand directly in front of me, then lifted up her skirt and started to play with herself through some very transparent underwear. "I could really show you a good time," she whispered as she probed her pussy through the silk. "Not now, Pamela," I'd said, "and not ever."

Lenore had a more sophisticated appearance but an even less subtle approach; as soon as the door was closed she came up to me, got down on her knees, and started tugging at my pants zipper. "Tell me what you like," she said, and though I enjoyed imagining what her tongue might do to me, I wasn't interested; I quoted *All About Eve* to let her know why: "I'll tell you what I like, Lenore. I like to go after what I want. I don't want it coming after me."

Maybe Trixie would be better behaved.

### The Interview (Trixie)

Oh, no, the receptionist is telling me to go in, and I just slipped my shoe off, okay, got it, here I go, now she's calling me back, oh, great, I left my bag on the chair, good work, Trixie, all right, review the four points, learn fast, organized, responsive, and responsible. No, responsible and responsive.

"Oh, what a nice office," I hear myself saying. Stupid, stupid, not a good way to begin.

"Yes, I like it very much," she says. "Have a seat. No, no, on the chair, not the couch. I save that for more informal occasions. Well, Ms. Davis—or can I call you Trixie? Yes? Good. Trixie. Why don't you tell me what you like about the office. Why do you find it nice?"

This is a funny way to start an interview, but she's the boss. "Well, it's very comfortable." She's staring at me. Maybe she's checking out my analytical skills. "The colors are warm and there's a mix of office furniture, like your desk and all those filing cabinets, and then furniture that's more, um, cozy, like the couch and the bar and the mirrors."

She's smiling, that's good. What's she asking now? Oh, okay, normal questions, typing speed, my qualifications, why I want the job, why I left my last job. I think we're getting along well. She's very attractive—forties, sharp suit, pants, very short hair.

"You know you're not really qualified for this position, don't you, Trixie?"

I blush, but remember to hold my ground. "I may not be right now, but I'll work hard and . . ."

"But I'm going to hire you anyway," she interrupts. "Because I can tell that you'll be amenable to training, and that you have the makings of a truly gifted assistant. You had a very special relationship with your previous employer, didn't you? Gillian Jackson?"

Now I'm blushing even more, because the way she mentions Gillian makes me nervous. "We got along very well and I really enjoyed working with her."

"And she enjoyed you. She speaks highly of you and mentions qualities that I've been seeking as well: your ability to help her relax, to devote yourself personally to her needs, never to fuss at unusual requests. If you can provide me with the same attention and if you don't object to some supplementary training now and then, you'll have no problem with this position."

Why do I feel that she's saying more than she's saying?

"Can you start tomorrow morning? Good. Ten o'clock, we're not early birds in this line of business. Any questions?"

"I was just wondering what your specialty is here. The notice just said Top Productions, film and video."

"That's a very good question, Trixie, and in fact we do have a specialized focus, but why don't you and I discuss that in the morning. And, Trixie, please call me Jane."

### *The Job (Jane)*

Trixie's first day turned out to be a busy one: in the morning, a casting call, and in the afternoon, a wrap. With any luck, the day would reveal some significant gaps in Trixie's knowledge and skills that would require the kind of extra training session to which she had so readily assented during the interview. Ah, but I was letting myself get carried away again. I can't help but experience the world in cinematic terms, and from my first view of her, her voluptuous body straining as she frantically tried to put her shoe on, Trixie struck me as a complete ingenue in whom sweet awkwardness and powerful sensuality existed side by side. In another era she'd have been the script girl in glasses who saves the show by shedding her spectacles and becoming a beauty just in time to replace the ailing star. Perhaps she could replace one of my stars today.

Dreams, idle dreams.

She arrived promptly, wearing a red wool suit.

"Trixie," I said sharply. "You mustn't wear red to the office. It's very becoming on you, and I'm sure someone has told you it's a power color, but it's too loud and doesn't give the right impression."

"I'm sorry." She looked hurt and anxious. I tingled.

"Try black or gray or brown. Not blue, though—too corporate. Now, look. You should keep track of these things on a list. You have paper? Write down, 'I will not wear red to the office.' That's right. And that goes for your nail polish, too. Stick to clear. Now, I know we were going to spend the morning getting an interview, but the day is packed and you're going to have to jump right in. This morning we have a casting call. You'll sort the files and run through the audition scene with the actresses. Okay? Tryouts start in fifteen minutes, so go through those folders. The scene is in that binder over there."

I watched Trixie bustle, gathering her materials, somewhat ill at ease because I'd criticized her outfit. I sat behind my desk and scanned budget sheets, looking up occasionally to enjoy her growing discomfiture as she began to understand just what it was we were doing. She looked so sweet when flustered. Perhaps she *was* the assistant of my dreams.

### The Job (Trixie)

I was glad to be involved right away in the details of a casting call, but nervous about running through scenes. Oh, well, I thought, the actresses will probably be more nervous than I am. I opened up the first file, Rochelle King, and looked at her head shot— stern, unsmiling. I flipped to the next shot and nearly yelped, because there was Rochelle in a black leather corset and thigh-high boots and nothing else except for studded bracelets all over her arms and a whip in her hand. Her breasts spilled over her corset and her legs were planted wide apart. Was she trying to show off her body to get the job? I wondered if I should warn Jane. I looked up, but she seemed busy.

I went through Rochelle's résumé next. She'd done a lot of movies, but according to her résumé they were all "pornographic feature films, with female casts with an emphasis on bondage and discipline." I wasn't sure that *Taming Lola, Slut Punishment* and *Put It All in My Pussy, Now!* were the proper qualifications for this role. Maybe some of the other actresses had more appropriate experience. I opened the next file, and the next, and the next, and they were all the same, scary women in leather wearing all kinds of whips and chains. Some of them even had their noses pierced. Three of them stood out, though: Rochelle King, Vampi Calda, and a woman called Mike.

Maybe the scene is some kind of comic sidebar, I thought, with a bit part for a dominatrix. I turned to the scene to check it out before the run-through. But when I started to read it, I couldn't believe it. This was no sidebar, and we weren't casting a bit part. And there was no way, no way I was going to be able to run through this scene.

"Trixie? I'm ready to call in the first actress."

### The Run-Through (Jane)

"Trixie," I repeated, "let's get the show on the road. What's the matter?"

"Um, Jane," she stumbled, "could I talk to you before we begin?"

"Sorry, we really don't have time. Later. What's in the files? Who looks good to you?"

"I'm not sure, but I pulled these three."

I looked at the files. For an innocent, she had quite an eye for experience. "Very good, Trixie. Two of these actresses are my top choices for the part, and in fact we're beginning with Mike. If she reads well, we'll just hire her."

Trixie looked even more troubled. "Is that okay? What about the other auditions we have scheduled?"

"Trixie," I said sternly, "we don't have time for questions like that. I've been in this business for ages. If I say we can do something, we can do it. Where's that list of yours? Go get it. Write down, 'I will not waste time contradicting Jane.' Great. Terrific. Now tell Mike to come in."

### The Run-Through (Trixie)

How was I going to run through this scene?

I trudged to the waiting room and got Mike, who looked tall in a leather trench coat and high boots.

"Mike, hello," said Jane, shaking her hand. "How've you been? Working hard or hardly working?"

"Working hard, Jane, working hard."

"What do you think of our script?"

"It's nice," Mike said. "I like it."

Nice, I thought, about as nice as being caught in a shark tank. I bustled around while they chatted and ignored me.

"Are you ready to run through the scene with Trixie, Mike?"

"Sure," she said, and took off her coat. I'd expected her to be wearing leather, but she had on a white t-shirt and black jeans. Metal chains dangled from her pockets.

"Trixie," Jane said. Something in her voice reduced my resistance. So I'll look like a fool, I thought. At least the pay's good.

I sat down opposite Mike.

"Okay," said Jane. "Let's review the plot up to this point. Mike's character, Big Red, works as a jail warden in a female prison. We've seen her on the job, restraining and disciplining various prisoners, helping the doctor administer exams, humiliating her favorites by making them do their exercises naked and pee in public. In the scene right before this, we watched her break up a gang bang. The problem is, she got all turned on by the woman she was saving and couldn't do anything about it. So now she's getting a drink at her local bar, which moves into a fantasy sequence about the prisoner she rescued. Okay, let's start reading. Trixie, you're the prisoner, obviously, and Mike's the warden. I'll read the bartender's lines."

I crossed my legs and opened my script. My lines were highlighted in yellow.

"Hey, Big Red, what can I get you tonight?" read Jane.

"Double bourbon on the rocks."

"Coming right up."

"Okay," Jane said, "so now we do some business to indicate fantasy mode, and when the fog clears, Big Red sees the luscious piece who only hours ago was being viciously humped by five bad girls. She walks over to her."

"Hey," Mike said, looking straight at me, "I thought I told you to stay in your cell."

"I didn't feel like it," I said, using my finger to hold my place in the script. "I wanted some air."

"Who cares what you feel like?" Mike's voice was as sculpted as her arms. "You do what you're told. You especially do what you're told when I tell it to you."

"What if I don't want to? It's a free country, even in jail."

"Hah! You've been spending too much time in the library. You're in my jail, and you'll do what I say. Or I'll let everyone else do what they want with you, and believe me, it won't be pleasant. You didn't like those women putting their hands all over you, did you?"

"It wasn't so bad," I read stiffly. The directions said I should be pouting, but the way I saw it, they were lucky I was doing this at all. "At least they're prisoners like me, not some nasty pig guard."

*Whack!* Jane made a smacking noise by clapping her hands together, hard. "Okay, so in the scene, Big Red slaps the prisoner and then we move into the action. Why don't you two play it out in front of the mirror so I can see more of the angles?"

I stayed glued to my chair. "I thought this was a reading."

Jane smiled. "It's a run-through. I have to see how actresses use their bodies. Don't worry, Trixie. Mike knows what she's doing, and you just have to stand there. After all, she's the one who's auditioning, not you. Unless you'd like a part!"

"No!" I said. "Um, Jane, could I talk to you for a minute?"

"I don't like to break the flow of a scene," she said.

"Only a second?" I wheedled.

"Okay," she sighed. "What is it?"

I looked at Mike. She was smiling pleasantly. I wanted to ask her to leave the room but didn't feel I could. "Is there any way, do you think, that I could just read the lines sitting down?"

"Trixie," Jane snapped, "where's that list we were keeping?"

"On your desk," I said nervously.

"Get it."

I did.

"What does it say?"

"I will not wear red . . ."

"No, not that. The next thing."

"I will not waste time contradicting Jane."

"Right. Now underline that. Twice. Now write down, I will not make Jane repeat herself. Okay. Now get up and do the scene, for God's sake."

I felt totally humiliated. Mike held her cool smile. I heard Jane say, behind me, in a kinder tone, "I know you haven't done this before, and that it may be embarrassing. But it's just a scene, and we're all professionals here. Okay?"

"Okay," I said.

So we continued the run-through. There actually wasn't much for me to do; I guess this movie was a star vehicle, and Mike was the star. After she supposedly slapped me, she pulled my arms behind my back and pushed me up against a wall, telling my character what an ungrateful cunt she was. "I think you'd better show me some gratitude," she said. "I don't think I'm going to give you a choice about it." Then Mike got to show off how quickly she could get me gagged and bound in a bunch of devices. Still holding my arms behind me, she snapped cuffs around my wrists, tied my arms together near the elbow with some ropes, gagged me with a scarf and put a chain around my waist that she connected to the cuffs at my wrists.

I kept telling myself we were all professionals while Mike read her lines and ran through simulated sex movements. At least I still had clothes on.

"Who's the pig now?" she asked, while she stood a couple of inches in front of me and pretended to grind her hips into me. She looked really convincing, her body strong, her movements lustful, her voice charged and powerful. I even felt myself getting caught up in the scene, wondering how I looked.

"Are you my little heifer?" she grunted, and kept up her air-grinding. "Are you my little sow?" She whirled me around and pushed my hands onto the sofa. Now I could see myself in the mirror. I looked like a cross between a prisoner and a trussed-up farm animal. A twinge between my legs took me by surprise, but before I could focus on it a stronger sensation took over. Mike had taken some kind of whip out of her bag and was whacking the seat of my pants. It stung like hell.

Luckily Jane intervened. "Whoa, Mike, hey, it's just a rehearsal." Mike stopped. Thank God.

"Sorry, Jane," she said. "Got a little too into the scene."

Sorry, Jane? I thought. I'm the one getting my ass whacked.

"Why don't we just skip ahead to page forty-five," said Jane.

"Where I take the gag off and force her to go down on me?" Mike asked.

"Right," said Jane.

If you'd asked me twenty minutes before whether I'd even read that scene, never mind act it out, I would have said no. But I'd crossed a line. Maybe it happened when I saw myself in the mirror; I was excited now.

"Have you learned your lesson, you little bitch?" Mike barked. "You ready to show a little gratitude?"

"Yes," I read. "Let me show you. I'll do whatever you say."

According to the script, Mike was supposed to bring me to my knees, force me to open her pants with my mouth, lick her clit, and then, as the script put it, "etc." But Mike was doing something different. She was pushing up her t-shirt on one side, exposing a breast, and pushing my mouth towards her nipple. "Go ahead," she said, "show me what you can do. Suck on that."

Something about the authority of her voice and the authority of that brown, pointed nipple made me forget myself. I leaned down and took it into my mouth. I'd barely closed my lips around it when Mike yelled "Hey!" and shoved me halfway across the room.

"What's the deal, Jane?" she yelled, pulling her shirt down.

I was confused.

### The Run-Through (Jane)

"I'm sorry," I laughed. "Trixie's new. She just got a little carried away. She didn't know that it's impolite to touch an actress during a run-through. Did you, Trixie?"

Trixie looked mortified and stared at the ground.

"Say you're sorry, Trixie," I said, more sternly.

"I'm sorry," she mumbled, still looking down.

"Not like that. Like you mean it."

"I'm sorry," she said, only a little more clearly. Mike stood with her arms crossed.

"Trixie, you've offended one of my best actresses. I think you're going to have to show how sorry you are a little better than this."

She looked up, flushed. "What do you want to do? Whip me? Throw me on the floor and teach me a thing or two? Or maybe I should kiss her feet?"

"Those are all fine ideas," I said coolly. "You pick."

She was mad now. "Or maybe I should read my little list while Mike holds me down and you spank me, since I've been *such a bad* girl."

Mike spoke up. "Hey, Jane, I'm out of here. I'll call you later about the contract." Out the door she went. Trixie and I were alone.

### The Training (Trixie)

I don't know what made me say all those things, but I meant them. I was quiet with Mike gone, silently daring Jane to make it all a joke now that we were alone.

She sat down behind her desk and said, "Well, Trixie, what will it be?"

I remained silent.

"I think we're both agreed that you're in need of some correction. You've made several mistakes this morning and it's best not to defer our discipline and training session too long. Since you don't seem able to decide on what your punishment should be, I will."

I felt nervous, excited, unreal. The boss and I were about to go over.

"Take your list, Trixie, and put it on the desk."

I did.

"Now pull up your skirt and hold it up."

I did. My body blushed, my pussy contracted, and the blood rushed to my clit.

"Look down at the list and read it out loud, over and over again. Don't stop, and don't look up."

I did. I read, "I will not wear red to the office. I will not waste time contradicting Jane. I will not make Jane repeat herself." While I read and held my skirt up, I heard Jane rustle around in her drawer. What was she doing?

She got up and came around behind me. Her arm snaked around me and removed the list. "I think you have it memorized by now, Trixie. Keep reciting, but put your hands on the table and your ass in the air."

I tried to do it right, but she had to push on my pelvis and spread my legs apart to get me in the position she wanted. Then she grabbed my pantyhose and ripped them apart from the waist down. They floated free of my legs and settled around my ankles.

"Keep reciting," Jane said. "Your punishment will only get worse if you stop. But if you absolutely can't take it anymore, start saying, I will not type letters to my friends on the job. Got that?"

"Yes," I said, and hastily resumed, "I will not waste time contradicting Jane. I will not wear red to the office."

*Whack!* Her hand landed where my butt cheeks met, and my skin heated up. *Whack!* again! She spanked one cheek, then the other, hard. I almost collapsed onto the table, and I lost track of my place in the list.

"What's the matter, Trixie? Did you forget your orders? Maybe this will help you remember."

A barrage of slaps on my ass, even harder than before, vindictive but controlled. My skin felt crisp and burned. I imagined the marks of her fingers on my butt and my pussy got electric. I felt completely out of control even though I knew I could make her stop. I liked the feeling. She was the boss and I was a bad, bad girl.

"I'm going to spank you ten more times, Trixie. Keep count now. If you mess up we'll have to start all over again."

*Whack!* "One," I gasped.

She made me wait, then dealt me another enormous slap. "Two," I said, wondering if I could make it through eight more. But after teasing me by making me wait a long time for a few more vicious wallops, she dealt the rest of my punishment out rapidly, then undid my skirt and pulled it down around my ankles.

"Turn around, Trixie," she said. I did, but I was too embarrassed to look at her. "That's right, Trixie, don't look up. I'm the boss. I'll look at you." She put her hand under my chin and raised my face. I made sure to keep my eyes averted. "I'm going to undo your blouse now, Trixie. I want to see what you're hiding from me." Her hands were warm, her fingers deft, and as she exposed my breasts, I worried about my pussy. It was getting so wet I thought my juices might drip down my thighs and onto the floor.

Her hands cupped my breasts and her fingers teased my nipples. "Nice," she said, "very nice." Her voice had gotten sweeter, but it still commanded. She moved over to the couch and lay down. "Come here, Trixie." I went to her, my movements hampered by the skirt around my ankles. "Get up on the couch, between my legs." I did what she said. "Open my pants." I started to, but was alarmed when I felt something big and hard in her pants. "Take it out," she said, and I did—a long, thick, and very lifelike dildo. She reached under the couch and brought up a condom. "Put it on," she said, "with your mouth." I was clumsy, but I did it. The condom was lubricated, so when she told me to start fucking my tits with her dick, the dildo slid right between them. She groaned as if she could really feel every inch of it. "Suck it," she said. "Get it in your mouth." I moved my chest up and down on it, feeling the friction on my breasts and enjoying it when my fingers occasionally rubbed my nipples. I lowered my mouth onto the head. I sucked and licked it enthusiastically. I moaned and sighed. I felt crazy, and for a second panicked, when I realized that anyone could walk into the office and see me there, naked except for the torn hose and disheveled skirt that held my feet together.

"Oh, that's good," Jane said. "That's it, really put your head into it. Show me how sorry you are that you did your job so badly. Show me what a good slut you can be." She fucked my breasts and mouth some more, then pulled away from me. She got up and rearranged me so that my skirt was completely off and I was kneeling on the couch and looking straight into the mirror. She got behind me.

"I want you to see what you look like when you get fucked," she murmured in my ear. "That way you'll learn your lesson even better." She explored the entrance to my pussy with her dick. "Spread your legs, you bad thing." I moved them. "That's right," she said, "show me your pussy." She edged the dildo in more. "The boss is going to fuck you now," she warned, and pushed it in hard and deep. My pussy swallowed it up and I started moving against it.

She moved with me, working it in and out, watching my face in the mirror. She grabbed my hair and pulled my head up and back. "Watch yourself get fucked," she hissed. I saw her, still perfectly dressed in her executive clothes, knowing that her dick was lodged inside me. I saw my face, tense with arousal, my flushed neck, and my heavy breasts. I felt something change and realized that Jane had put her fingers between the dildo and her skin and was stroking her clit. "You're going to make me come," she told me. "Do you want to come, too?"

I nodded. In the mirror, I saw her stare at me.

"Please," I said.

"The boss comes," she smiled. "The assistant doesn't."

"Please," I begged. I pushed my pussy onto her dick even harder, but I needed my clit touched.

"Why should I?" she asked, stroking herself more and more.

"I'll be good," I promised, "so good. I'll make you come all the time. I'll fuck you whenever you want, and your clients too. I'll give you blow jobs at lunch and a hand job with your morning coffee. Just please, please let me come now."

"All right," she said. "Touch yourself."

And I did, digging my fingers into my clit, hard, thrusting myself onto her dick. In seconds I was coming so much that I didn't even realize until after that she was coming at the same time. I sank into the couch and she collapsed on top of me.

When our breathing and heartbeats got back to normal I realized how awkward the situation was. She was mostly dressed, but I felt ashamed of my partial nudity and my exposed, reddened ass. If I can't see her, I thought, maybe she can't see me, and so I stayed face down even when I felt her get up.

"Trixie," I heard. I turned my head. "Trixie! Sit up!"

I sat up. Jane looked perfectly composed. Her pants were closed up.

"Button your blouse. Put on your skirt. What kind of a spectacle are you making of yourself?" She smiled as she spoke.

"I don't know what we're going to do with you." She took her wallet out of her pants. "Here's some money," she said, and as I struggled into my skirt, I saw that she was giving me $200. "Get yourself some new stockings. And keep the change. Consider it a disability payment—I'm assuming you might have some trouble sitting down for the next two days."

I took the money and smiled back. My first day at work was certainly turning out nicely.

"I hope to see you again after lunch," Jane said. "I think we could work very well together."

"I'd like to come back," I said. "And I'm sure you'll do everything you can to see that I do."

Jane looked puzzled at first, then cleared her throat. "Hm, well, yes, certainly, of course. It's clear that we should be paying you far more than the initial salary we settled on. You're so much more qualified than your résumé suggested. I'll have the new contract drawn up and you can sign it when you get back. How does that sound?"

"Beautiful," I said.

And then I took a very, very long lunch.

## Jolie Graham

❦

# Drowsy Maggie

It was an unusually warm spring day, the day before St. Patrick's. Music rippled through the pavilion—the Irish Festival was under way. Maggie, who had no idea if she had any Irish ancestors or not, drifted through the crowd, seemingly carried forward by the swirl of music. Booths bedecked in green offered a tantalizing array of handicrafts, most not even remotely connected to anything Irish. *What's Irish about Southwestern jewelry?* Maggie wondered, as she paused by a display of earrings, bracelets and necklaces studded with sky-blue turquoise. The ear cuffs were interesting, though, and one caught her eye—a gray metallic figure of a tiny nude man with a full erection.

He was perfectly proportioned, perfectly shaped. She turned him over in the palm of her hand. There was the delicate hint of musculature along the legs, back and buttocks. One leg was drawn up and one stretched down. His hands were positioned to clasp the earlobe. She tried it on and peered down at the little mirror. It looked like he was either climbing the edge of her ear or trying to fuck it. Either way, the ear cuff was very comfortable; he fit her body perfectly, and Maggie was acutely aware of his penis pressed against her skin.

The girl at the booth sold it to her cheaply, advising her that it would need no polishing if she wore it regularly. "I used to wear one all the time, but when I took it off, it got all tarnished," she said, handing Maggie the change.

Maggie thanked her and went looking for a beer. It really was unseasonably warm for March. Ah, Guinness on tap—she sipped the creamy stout and looked about for a place to sit. The chairs in front of the bandstand were taken, as well as all the cafe tables, so she sat down on a concrete ledge under a tree.

She closed her eyes, feeling a familiar tingling in her body, thinking about a man—not any specific lover from her past—but some vague male figure pressed close to her, breathing in her ear all sorts of deliciously carnal things he wanted to do with her body. After a few moments, she opened her eyes, squinting at the brightness, half surprised to find herself alone under the tree. *Boy, the beer really went to my head fast,* she thought, smiling foolishly.

The music reeled through her body. She unfastened the top two buttons of her blouse, pulled her shirttail out and tied it up like a halter so she could feel the breeze wind around her belly. I *really* should get something to eat, she thought. A hot dog. Very Irish. She felt giddy and strangely self-conscious eating it.

Maggie absently reached up and fingered the buttocks of the ear cuff, sliding it up slightly higher on her ear, then back down into its original position. The penis felt hot against her ear, and for a moment all Maggie could see was a thick hot cock rubbing between her legs. She shook her head, then brushed the crumbs of the hot dog bun off her blouse. Her palms swept across her breasts, noting how tight and hard her nipples were. She was glad she hadn't worn a bra.

When he slipped into bed with her that night she wasn't surprised to feel the growing warmth, the heat of his body. She rolled over on her back. In the darkness she could see his face, illuminated by moonlight from the window. High, delicate cheekbones and an aristocratic nose were combined with a strong jawline and cleft chin. Shiny black hair tumbled down to his shoulders. He wasn't at all like the boyish, blond-haired, blue-eyed Adonises who usually populated her dreams.

She could feel his hot erection pressed against her. She slid her hands around his narrow waist. Maggie liked the way his hip-bones felt in the palms of her hands. Gray eyes, soft and open, not dark and distant, looked her full in the face. Then he leaned down and his lips brushed her neck. A hand burned on her stomach, then between her legs.

She spread her legs and gave herself over to him. His mouth sucked deeply and continuously on her breasts. But at the same time she could feel his head between her legs. She writhed, sweating, beneath the covers, lifting her pelvis. Gently, softly, his tongue probed the folds of sensitive skin, stroking her clit. His breath was like steam against her vaginal lips.

Then he was kissing her. She held his beautiful, distinctive face between her hands. His hands were large; they cupped her shoulder blades as his penis moved within her. She was still kissing him, opening her mouth, her whole body tightening.

Maggie cried out and awoke. Her body shook as waves of warmth rushed over her in quick succession. The sheets were tangled and soaked with sweat—just as if it had all been real. She fell back on the pillow, breathing hard. The moonlight illuminated the room. She was alone. As she slowly sank back into sleep, she thought she heard a voice, low and warm, whispering endearments. Then, quite distinctly, she heard "I love you" breathed softly into her ear.

On St. Patrick's Day Maggie awoke feeling great. She showered and dressed in shorts and a halter. The little naked man still clung to her ear. He was not dislodged by sleep or shower and still gleamed dully despite the soaping.

The festival was already in full swing when Maggie arrived, the crowd even larger than the day before. There was *ceili* dancing on the center stage and storytelling on the corner. The ground beneath her feet seemed to vibrate with the energy of the music.

It was a couple of hours before Maggie realized that she was looking for *him*. She caught herself watching the crowd, looking quickly from face to face. She got a lot of smiles, but none of the men were him.

Somehow she managed to snag a small table near the band-stand, where she drank her beer and ate a tiny cup of Irish stew. She sipped the Guinness slowly, closed her eyes and slid down in the chair, her legs slightly apart beneath the table. The sun warmed her upturned face, but her body was already warm from some other, closer fire. Her shorts were damp and she felt sticky all over as if she had been smeared with semen. That was what Maggie thought about as she listened to the music and her beer grew hot. Smeared with semen. Her body pulsed.

Before long her dreams carried her away. He was there, beside her. In the murmur of voices she could hear him speaking, but could not quite make him out. Unconsciously, she touched the tiny nude man who clung to her ear and caressed her so persistently with his cock. She felt a large warm hand trail down from her ear, across her neck to her breasts. Hands massaged her breasts, first outside the halter, then underneath. Rough palms flat against her swelling breasts, her nipples like two pearls in his hands.

The band was playing "Drowsy Maggie," a tune she recognized from the day before. It started off slowly, then got faster and faster . . . a sticky penis in her hands, between her legs. The table and the crowd had melted away. She opened her mouth to receive either his tongue or his prick. She was thirsty and sweating. Faster. More. All over me.

The song ended with a crash, leaving her feeling naked, dripping, aching for some cataclysmic release. Maggie opened her eyes, her mind reeling more from desire than from the half-finished cup of beer.

He stood about ten feet away, his hands thrust deep inside his jeans pockets, his erection following the line of his zipper. As soon as her eyes met his he walked over and pulled a chair up close to hers.

"My name's Nick," he said, leaning towards her. As his two palms moved up her damp thighs, Maggie stared. A figure of a woman was wrapped around the outer edge of his ear, of the same style and color as her ear cuff.

His hands pressed the seam of her shorts against her clit. It was obvious that his fingers would have been more comfortable inside the shorts. Inside her. It was all Maggie could do not to rip her halter off and screw him right there on the chair while the beer flowed and the band played merrily from another time zone.

Unsteadily, Maggie stood, clasping his hand. Nick was tall and broad-shouldered, with tousled black hair and intent gray eyes. Without a word, they strolled languidly hand in hand through the pavilion, out the west gate, across the parking lot, and across a small street into the cool deep green shade of the park.

Kneeling in a thick patch of clover, she unzipped his jeans and tugged them over his ass, her hands trembling so badly that she was grateful not to have to deal with his underwear as well. Nick stretched and pulled off his shirt with one motion, sinking into the lush green bed. Maggie's halter and shorts, along with her drenched and twisted pair of panties, made a small pile of abandoned clothing next to his.

As she sank into the green beside him, the music rang in her ears. Silently, they removed the matching ear cuffs from each other's ears. As Maggie examined the female figure, she wondered, *Is this me?* The woman's legs were spread, knees bent, and her feet as well as her hands had clasped the edge of Nick's ear. She was slightly bent at the waist so that her ass stuck out noticeably. Her hands were positioned much lower down than were the male figure's. Turning the figurine over in her palm, it struck Maggie that the woman looked like she was reaching down, as if she had been frozen before her hands quite made it between her legs. Her rounded breasts had snuggled around Nick's ear. She looked like a woman caught at the peak of arousal, her whole body wild with unreleased sexual tension.

Nick was far less interested in the nude male figure. If he recognized himself in the design, he gave no sign of it. Wordlessly, he handed it back to Maggie.

Dropped into her open hand, the little man suddenly gave a start, then leaped onto the female figure, violently taking her from behind. Maggie and Nick gaped in amazement.

"They're magnets!" he exclaimed. The little man's outstretched hands, which had clasped Maggie's ear, now grasped the female's nipples. His penis was up between her legs, and her hands, which had been reaching achingly for herself, now grasped his cock. One of his legs was locked over hers.

Maggie tentatively tried to separate the figures, but when she could not, she laid them aside on the pile of clothes. They were bound together by the primal force of magnetism; they were one.

Maggie reached out and stroked Nick's hairy balls. His hands covered her breasts as she slid her fingers around his penis. *Smeared with semen,* she thought as she stroked him. He pushed his tongue into her mouth. They thrashed around in the clover, groping and mouthing each other until he sprayed her belly with come. As if reading her mind, Nick smeared the liquid all over her breasts, rubbing his thumbs slowly over her nipples until Maggie cried out, gasping, her body stretched tight with desire. The music swirled faster through her mind.

As her clit began to throb, Nick—erect again—thrust into her from behind. He rubbed his hands over her breasts, then between her legs as he pushed deeper into her. Maggie came, legs trembling. She raised her buttocks to meet his hips once more before finally sinking, exhausted and spent, into the clover. He had fucked her flat into the ground. The image of the two figurines locked together forever in an eternal fuck drifted through Maggie's drowsing mind.

## Winn Gilmore

❧

# Celia and the Bed

Celia snaked the black 450SLC into the tight parking space and, with one long, black-gloved hand, switched off the ignition. She checked her electric black mane in the rearview mirror, then smiled. Perfect. As always. She caressed the door handle, opened the door, then slid her long legs out of the car. She smiled again as her tight black leather skirt slid up her naked thigh. Suddenly she shivered, both from the promise of what lay ahead and from the excitement of her thighs sliding together. She was wet already.

*"Buenas tardes, señora,"* the salesman crooned as she entered the bedding shop. He bowed not out of professional courtesy, but to better guide his greedy eyes up the leather-clad woman's long legs.

She lifted the razor-sharp toe of her left shoe toward the bowing man's face. *"Señorita,"* she hissed between clenched teeth.

The man jerked up. Celia slipped off her gloves with the sweet grace of a lover's licking tongue, her eyes darting hungrily around the store.

"Ah, yes." A tough *mujer*, he assessed. He shifted into a tone of frigid professionalism. "How may I help the *señorita*?"

"I am in search of the bed," Celia replied in English.

The salesman smiled condescendingly. His bedding shop was a favorite of teeming Americans leaving the rigid United States in search of the "exotic, magical Mexico" promised by the tourist packages, so he had a reasonable command of English, though his intelligence prohibited him from letting them know that. They preferred his faked attempts at English that limped along like a bumpkin trying to stroll in Givenchy shoes.

But this woman was surely no North American. She was as dark as he. No, darker. Her ancestry burst through her honey-brown skin and radiated a simple, honest beauty that the exotic-seeking North Americans could never achieve, no matter how many days they basked piglike in Mexico's sun, drinking margaritas and sloshing on expensive tanning oils.

She's no better than me, he thought angrily. Then, with a curt nod, he corrected her. "You don't mean you are searching for *the* bed, *señorita*, but for *a* bed."

"*¿Perdone?*" she asked. Her yearning eyes had already swept over the gaudy, more popular beds. She was about to give up when, like a wet tongue, her eyes flicked over a deceptively humble bed tucked around a corner. Celia could only make out one curved, dark wooden leg peeking out enticingly from beneath a silk cover, but a fine sheen broke out on her upper lip. She licked the sweat. "*Repite, por favor,*" she begged, placing her right hand over her thudding heart. "What did you say?"

The salesman drew himself up taller and repeated, "You mean that you are looking for *a* bed, not *the* bed."

Celia dismissed him with a flip of her wrist, eyes stripping the partially hidden bed of its simple, yet ample covering. "No, I know exactly what I mean, *hombre*. *Yo quiero* the bed. I will know her when I see her." *This must be her*, she prayed, as her nipples tightened and pushed out against her scarlet silk shirt. It called like a demanding lover, long lost but never forgotten.

The man shook his head despairingly. *¡Qué pendeja!* Some people! Try and teach them something, and what *gracias* did you get? The doorbell chimed "La Cucaracha" as other customers, Americans, entered the shop.

"Go ahead," he mumbled to Celia. "Look around. My assistant will be with you *en un minuto*."

His tightly bound buttocks rushed up to the Americans. "Good afternoons, sir and ladies," he fumbled falsely.

The foremost Americana glowed with anticipation and nobility. Nodding appreciatively at the salesman's attempted English, she sighed, "Ah, Mexico!" She clasped her abundant arms around her peeling breasts and smiled. "Where else can you get such good service? And such goods?" she asked, looking knowingly at her friends.

The salesman hid his grimace, then continued with his sales pitch. They were, after all, *gringos*. "Should you like to see my most popular bedding pieces?" he asked, showing all of his well-formed teeth. "Adapted from the ancient Mayan culture which was ruling the country centuries ago." The Americans' eyes lit up. Fawning, they followed the salesman.

The conversation drifted to Celia like underwater murmurs in a bad dream. Mesmerized, she meandered through the bedding shop, drifting through the maze of unclaimed beds towards her bed, *the* bed. It was partitioned off by fabric-covered particle board and it begged—no, demanded—that she share herself with it. The engrossed salesman didn't cast so much as a glance her way.

She took each step slowly, trying desperately to ward off the hunger propelling her towards the yawning bed. It sprawled before her like an insatiable lover who'd strap her in a deceptively soft grip and love her till she screamed. It was her bed, all right. With neither headboard nor footboard, it called as had no other in a long, long time.

But she had to resist for as long as she could. She stopped at a gaudy bed fringed in red velveteen, with mirrors stationed above that watched down like a god's huge eye. She inhaled deeply and closed her eyes. The smell of fresh cloth, unhampered by that unmistakable odor of love, filled her quivering nostrils. She pulled in deeply, the silk shirt softly caressing her tender, hard nipples.

Her breath came in ragged gasps as her flesh strained against the top button, and her long nails scratched and dug into the top of the mattress. She squeezed her thighs together to lock in the delicious ache demanding that she go to her bed.

Celia stole a glance at the salesman, who was still trying to coax his Americans into a sale. She clamped her teeth over her lower lip and bit down. Hard. She pinched her right nipple. *Apúrate.* I can't wait much longer. Her pussy gave a responding twinge.

More Americans entered the store, and she overheard the sales-

man apologize, "I'll be with you in some seconds, please. I am
sorry, but my help is not in yet. She will soon be here." To under-
score his apology, he popped in a Flora Purim tape. Americans
loved her, he'd learned, and many thought she was Mexican.
Weren't they all the same?

As the music pulsed against the store's walls and bounced back
into the room, Celia smiled. Reverently, she placed a hand on one
bed and gasped when she felt the music's vibrations running
legato through the fabric. She walked on, putting one foot carefully ahead of the other, sliding her hips in sync with the music to
intensify her pussy movements.

Breathing heavily, she turned the corner behind which lay her
bed. Still trembling, Celia moved tentatively towards it. Finally, it
lay a mere three feet from her, begging her to jump on top, to bury
her screams and juices in its fresh, virginal self.

Feigning indifference, she turned from her bed and leaned over
the more flamboyant bed beside it. Her leg brushed against her
bed as she bent over the other, and she buried her face in the covers. *I can wait no longer,* her brain and pussy screamed. But she
held on as she ran both hands over the bed's every inch. Flora
shouted and murmured wordless fucking noises from the cassette.

Her breasts echoed the desire rising from her pussy and her
very center like the heat from her own Pelenque earth. Celia sat
and turned slowly on the bed. The music cascaded over her like a
mountain stream gone mad, coming over the ground and flooding
the parched earth, intensifying until there was only herself, sound
and the bed.

Oblivious to the salesman and his customers, Celia kicked off
her shoes, wriggled the tight black skirt over her full hips like a
gorged boa climbing out of its skin, and stood naked before the
bed, *her* bed. The ache consumed her, and her entire body was
ashiver. She offered herself to the bed like a virgin to the gods:
naked, hungry and trusting. She squeezed her eyes tight as she
mounted the simple yet voluptuous bed.

With her long fingers she caressed her tongue, then painted
hieroglyphics on her taut breasts. She squeezed her nipples and
moaned, her smooth brown skin sinking into the silk covers and
soft mattress. She snatched off the top cover, then found her slick

pussy. She sighed as she pulled the silk sheet between her wide-spread, kneeling thighs as Purim's voice and Airto's drums dragged her back to the forest. Spreading her thighs and pussy juices over the titillating covers, she growled. Her ass waved high above the bed, and Celia ripped off the remaining sheets. She sat up and yanked off her shirt. Then she sank her nose, teeth and body into the body of the bed. She rolled over and sucked in the smell of her hair and the naked bed.

"*Buenas tardes, señorita,*" a contralto whispered, seemingly part of the music.

Celia's eyes shot open. Before her was a widespread pair of dark, beautifully curved, strong legs. Her eyes traveled up to rest on a tight red skirt barely revealing a pulsing Mound of Venus. Her eyes darted up to the interloper's face, which sneered down, disdainful yet understanding.

"*Qué en el mundo* can I do for you?" the voice asked. She smiled, and Celia's brown face turned darker as blood rushed up from her pussy. She clasped her sweaty, juice-soaked legs together and pulled the sheets over her naked body. Struggling for some tidbit of control, she looked imperiously at the woman standing before her. "Are you the help?" she asked.

Slowly, the woman pulled the fingers of her right hand through her short, curly black hair, refusing to be intimidated. "I guess you could call me that. *O lo que tu quieras,*" she said. Her long face murmured of Dahomey and Maya, and she flashed her impossibly white teeth at the woman on the bed. "Can I help *you?*"

"No," Celia said, despite the tremor which ran through her body. "You cannot help me, *hermana.*"

Oblivious to anything but the Americans, the salesman's voice boomed from the rear of the store. "*¡Marta! Ven para aca y ayúdame. Hay americanos aquí, y esa mujer,*" he said, indicating Celia, "*no tiene nada para nosotros. ¡Ven aca ahora!*"

"*Ayy,*" Marta groaned as she headed for the front of the store. But she does have something for me, *hombre.* For you, *no.* But for me, *sí.* Still, she waited on the Americans.

Celia quickly forgot about the simpering salesman, his delight-fully arrogant helper, Marta, and even the Americans as she re-sumed making love to her bed. She didn't overhear the man's joy when the Americans left him with a traveler's check to cover the inflated price of the bed they'd bought. She didn't hear the saleswoman's sarcastic contralto faking happiness for him. Didn't hear the salesman leave the shop in the assistant's hands, promising to return after *siesta*. Didn't hear the woman lock the door behind him. Didn't hear her crank up the music; didn't hear her stride to where she, Celia, was. But she did hear her say,

"*Now* I can help you, *señorita*." Marta gazed hungrily down at Celia writhing on the bed. She shucked off her clothes and Celia moaned, between gasps, "*No! No es posible. No te quiero! Solo yo!* The bed *es mia.*"

"But who do you think brought it here for you?" Marta asked gently, and, despite her passion, Celia found herself rolling onto her back, legs and pussy open wide for the stranger.

"*Sí, es la cama*"—Marta put a foot on the bed—"*y yo soy la camarera*" and slid a hand down her now-naked torso. Then she lay atop Celia and kissed her deeply.

Rivers opened in their veins; oceans flowed between them. They streamed together, Ochun finding Yemaya.

"*Ayy, cielo,*" Celia cried as Marta flowed down to her thighs. She grabbed the woman, whose wide, wide mouth and sinuous tongue danced around Celia's clit. Marta moaned delectably and rotated her supple body so that her sex was an irresistible oyster taunting Celia's hunger. Celia wrapped her arms around Marta's thighs and ass, pulling herself up to her pussy. Starving, she buried her face in the woman's sex.

But the searing passion was too much for Celia. She rolled over to present her small, puckering anus. Marta sniffed, then licked the opening. Celia moaned, screamed and buckled as one slim finger slid inside. "*¡Ayyy! ¡Mi cama! ¡Mi cámarera!*" she yelled, coming all over her bed and her woman.

Dressing shakily, Celia smiled lazily at the woman sprawled on the bed. "And when can I see you again?" she asked, trying to sound casual.

Marta grinned omnisciently, then licked her fingers.

"You never know," she said. "*Quizás mañana.* Or maybe never again."

Celia looked at her, already wistful. She smeared the love juices across her face and through her wild hair. Then she picked up her things and headed for the door.

In her Benz, she started the engine and headed home. The next bedding shop could wait. At least until tomorrow.

*Michele Serchuk*

❧❀❧

# Leash

Amanda and I were sitting in my living room after karate one morning, reading erotica, feeling each other out. Not literally. We were talking about bondage, the excitement of the forbidden. Fine in theory, but when she asked me if I liked being dominant or submissive, I froze. Couldn't say the words, didn't know her well enough, choked on shame and pride. I got out some words about power play, the erotic tension built in switching roles and the transfer and exchange of power. All true, but I didn't own anything directly. We went on to safer topics.

Sunday afternoon, a few weeks later. Amanda sashays up the stairs, her libido reaching the fifth floor while her feet are still on three. She wanders about, losing clothing matter-of-factly. Well, yeah, it's not like we've never changed together before. Forbidden fruit, dancing sprite turns naked around the room. Shows dark against white walls, cocoa-sleek, fuzzy and wild. She's happier without clothing, wants you to see her body. I know the feeling.

"Look what I brought," she says. Amanda brings toys. A leash and collar, black leather strip twirling out of her woven pouch. She stands sassy in the middle of the white floor, showing me what she's brought to play with. "I have another one at home with spikes, but I didn't want to get too intense, you know?"

"Oh, yeah, right. Cool. A leash." And what the hell am I going to do with a leash? What's proper leash protocol? I don't want to say this is new to me, appear unsure of myself. Death before embarrassment, you know. My first impulse is always to act cool, a bad habit I'm trying to break. From inside my cool I'm trying to think, to gather myself. I'm more than a little intrigued, but something about this still makes me squirm.

So, what is it about this leash thing? It's this object-thing and I want to conceal it, deny it. I don't want to deal with its existence. More than any silk scarf or bathrobe sash tied tightly around my wrists, this object embodies my fascination and lust for power play, those words, dominance and submission. Object of ridicule, subject of snickering jokes at pathetic degenerates, shame I didn't think I owned. Vestiges of someone else's puritan values lurk, and I feel a flash of political indignation. Scarves are garments until the moment they become bondage; that leash and collar has no other purpose. I want to touch it. I want to hide inside.

That object in Amanda's hands is confession and I am remembering my grade school jump rope made of stretchy, orange rubber tubing with white handles. I am remembering the thrill I got tying my ankles together in my dark bedroom at night when no one was watching. I was too young to know that heat flash as sex, only old enough to know it was "bad," to know better than to tell anyone, ever. I'm thinking of all those spankings my Barbie dolls got. I'm thinking I don't want to think about this now. I just want her to kiss me.

I move into her arms. We begin exploring each other, steamy and soft. Who is she, I wonder, and how can I please her? I've forgotten the collar, lost in her skin, in her curves. Something in her lies sleeping and I want to wake it up, see her on fire, feel her passion. I glide over her, inhale sweet spice, taste salt.

Amanda makes whimpering, cooing noises as I slip fingers into her. Her inner walls suck me inside. My fingers explore, touch the hard dimple of her womb as I push in deeper. I feel her slick and warm against my thigh as she rides me, fingers between my legs, stroking me. I float, riding lazy waves of sex-thrill.

I have forgotten her toy. She hasn't. It's in her hands again and I refuse to say hey, wait, I'm a leash-virgin. She gives it to me. What the hell do I do with this? Nice girls don't play with leashes and feminists don't tie people, other women, up. Funny, I don't recall these thoughts being quite so loud when I played this way with a man. I don't know if it's the leash/scarf thing or a gender thing; my hormones are racing and I'm not certain why I'm doing this, but I can't back down, and, truthfully, I can't resist the challenge.

I hold her down and slip the collar around her neck, moving her body forcefully, feeling her size and my strength. My robe is by the bed and I slip the sash out of the loops, grab her hands and bind her wrists. Her pleasure is obvious, incites me to give her more, her movements and noises showing me the way to be this person, to dominate her. She squirms as I run the leash down between her breasts, between her legs and yank it hard, up her back. Pinning her to the futon, I pull the leather tight. I wonder how the sharp tugs on the collar must feel and imagine the deliciousness of being trapped. Her ass twitches back and forth as she rubs herself against the leash and I tentatively spank her a few times with the looped handle. It makes loud, satisfying, slapping noises. I do it again, more forcefully this time, and watch, fascinated, as she twitches harder.

I am whispering to her, nibbling on her, watching her get hotter and hotter. My hands run over her body, moving her as it pleases me, catching her head, pulling her in to kiss her, spreading her thighs to expose her clit. I want to make her come. Remembering how she liked being penetrated, I fuck her, not exploring like before but pushing, thrusting, filling her. Her response is immediate and fierce. She cries out and gives herself to me, wet and open. I have four fingers in her, see her juices shiny on my knuckles. Her moans come wilder and louder and she rubs herself back and forth over the black leather leash, swallowing half my hand, as she comes.

We sit up laughing and I untie her hands. I'm beginning to surface, not sure where I've been, not even sure if I'm back yet. But she's not done, she remembers my words about role reversal and power play needing to go both ways. The leash and collar are in her hands again and her impish eyes are fixed on me. "Your turn," she says.

Amanda is reaching for my neck. Politics and pride scream in my stomach as a heat wave engulfs my cunt. I can't move. No, I don't *want* to move. I want to struggle; I feel our near-equal strength as we wrestle, knowing she has to win. She has me, slips the collar around my throat, jerking my head back by my hair. It feels dangerous and forbidden. She tightens the collar almost past the point of comfort; blood pulses at my temples from the rough pressure at my throat. I move over to give myself air, relaxing my guard; she has me, pulls me where she wants me, flat on my back. She wants my hands, I see the sash and hold out my wrists even as I pretend to be able to fight. She ties them so tightly that the only way to make it not hurt is to bend my elbows with my arms stretched out and over my head. I have never felt so helpless. Slowly I recognize that there is nothing I can do, that she has to please me now. I lie there, wrists aching, and luxuriate in the realization that I am hers and the pleasure now is mine. She has a dildo in her hand as she moves in over me. I'm your captive, I think, do me.

Amanda's eyes sparkle. Her hand twists in my hair as her gaze travels over my body. My breathing sounds ragged in my ears; I am waiting for what comes next. Her body pins me down and her thigh is hot against my crotch. Nothing comes next. I am waiting. Amanda is staring at me.

"You like this, don't you?" she asks. Her voice is soft, low and in complete control. I buck upwards and grind against her hip.

"That's not an answer. Tell me. I'm waiting."

I can't speak. I am choking from deep inside. The words are stuck in my chest somewhere and I cannot say anything. I wonder what I had been thinking when I started flirting with her that morning on my sofa. I remember feeling so daring; I don't think I had believed this would actually happen.

Amanda tugs on the leash and my mind bounces back to the present. There is no place to hide. I can't move my head to escape her hot brown stare, so I close my eyes. I am conscious of myself inside my body and of each passing second. The moment becomes very long and I silently beg her to resolve it for me.

"I won't be the fall guy for you, girl. You'll say it. Watch." Amanda gets up and leads me to the window, keeping the leash short and tight. We look out over the rooftops, onto streets bustling with Sunday Chinatown commerce.

"Who are you afraid of? Them? You afraid of what they'd say? Or is it your friends, hmm? Afraid they wouldn't approve of your politics?" Amanda is stroking my hair, her warm breath in my ear. She hasn't let go of the leash. It's beginning to get dark and lights go on in the building across the alley. I can see my neighbors watching TV and preparing dinner. I stand naked, collared, peering through the thin curtains.

"Amanda, the neighbors . . . they'll see." I sound ridiculous. Amanda laughs, delighted. She swings me around to face her; the look on her face is pure evil. She reaches over, flicks on a lamp and yanks on the curtain. The flimsy rod falls easily out of the brackets. We stand framed in a pool of light over Canal Street. Amanda holds the leash and collar tight in one hand as the other snakes around and strokes my clit. Her teeth tease at my ear. My knees get weak and suddenly I don't care about my goddamned neighbors, the women at the karate school, or anyone else for that matter. I want her to fuck me and I don't care if the whole damned world knows or what anyone thinks about the way that I want to be fucked.

"Make me come. I want you to. Please." I'm having trouble with words but I am speaking, after a fashion. She's laughing, loving this. Her hands are getting rougher, her teeth biting down on my neck, leaving red marks on my skin. I can see our reflection in the window; I imagine the shoppers glancing up and noticing the glint of light off the thick, shiny collar, suddenly realizing what they are seeing. I imagine them going home hot and bothered, thinking about us later with husbands or girlfriends or maybe jerking off in the dark, alone.

"I want them to see you fuck me. Fuck me." I am screaming it to her. At this rate they won't have to look up; they'll hear me.

"Stay here. Touch yourself. And don't turn around." Amanda unties my hands and kisses me, practically sucking the breath out of my mouth before she leaves. Her footsteps pad across the floor and I hear her rustling around in that bag of hers. I lean against the window frame, put one foot up on the sill and stroke myself.

The leash is hanging down my back, gently swaying. It brushes over my ass and I rub harder as I look out the window.

Amanda is suddenly back at my side grabbing the leash and twisting my nipples. Something hard and rubbery is pushing at my ass—she has fastened the dildo on with a harness. A harness. Oh God, do women really use those things? I've seen one before, but it was hanging on the wall at Ye Olde Local Sex Shoppe, not on a lover. I want to see it but she won't let me turn around. She has one hand on the leash and the other across my chest as she forces me back against her. Her hips are powerful and thrust the rubber cock deep inside me. I scream as I ram into her. She staggers backwards, regains her balance, then pushes me up against the window. I lean forward, holding tight to the frame. The glass is cold against my breasts, her breasts soft against my shoulder blades as she fucks me with deep, hard strokes. The sensation is deliciously perverse. Her long, sensitive fingers stroke my clit and my legs begin to shake. Heat spreads out from my belly and I can no longer stand. Her strong arms hold me up as I scream and tremble in front of the window. We fall to the floor and lie in a sweating, quivering heap. I put my head on her shoulder and let her soothe me to sleep.

It's early evening and she has left hours earlier; I am out walking in the world. Her spicy aroma is still rising off my body. The breeze blowing my hair across my face carries the perfume of her sweat, unchecked by Secret for Women. Her smells are so loud in my nostrils, I can't imagine that anyone who sees me doesn't notice. They don't. Each waft of scent triggers a visceral memory. People see and hear me from so far away, I feel like I'm in a bubble waiting to land. My smile is full of secrets as I turn the corner for home.

*Adrienne Rabinov*

# In the Mood

Allison sat cross-legged on the bed, coffee cup in hand, wearing one of the white terry cloth robes provided by the hotel, watching Grant dress for his business meeting. He looked bright and shiny from his morning shower. "Downright perky," she told him, smiling fondly. The morning newspaper lay strewn about, mostly read by now.

"What are you going to do with yourself today?" Grant asked.

"I don't know. I feel deliciously irresponsible. I think I'll hang out at the pool. How late is your meeting supposed to go?"

"I should be back around three o'clock. Why don't we meet at the pool bar then?"

"Okay," she responded, standing and kissing him, remembering with pleasure their lovemaking that morning and the night before. "Have a good meeting. I'll be thinking nice thoughts."

"Stay out of jail," he said, smiling as he left her.

She took a leisurely shower, carefully shaved her legs, and trimmed her pubic hair. She slathered suntan lotion over her body instead of moisturizer, paying special attention to those parts of her that rarely saw the sun. She dried her hair and put on makeup.

She was amused at herself, so carefully preparing for a lazy day sweating in the sun. It reminded her of the time that a friend, watching her in the office ladies' room, had said, "I don't understand why you put on lipstick before lunch. You just eat off your lipstick anyway." To which another, more astute friend responded in her sexiest Southern drawl, "But you never know—she might meet somebody she likes along the way."

Perhaps she would meet somebody she liked today. She was certainly in the mood.

Allison's attention turned to the weighty consideration of whether to wear her black bikini with the gold trim or her coral tank suit with the iridescent sparkles and the high-cut legs. She tried both on, considering her reflection carefully and assessing her comfort level in each.

She looked out the window at the pool below to check out the early crowd—mostly young families, who she knew wouldn't even notice her as they fussed over their small children. There were also some single women, dedicated sunbathers who were in no worse or better shape than she. "What the hell," she thought, opting for the bikini. She pulled her black beach shift over her head, shrugging it over her suit, slipped into her sandals, grabbed her book, sunglasses and other essentials and headed down to the pool.

Allison pulled up a chair at the far end, giving her a view of the doorway from the hotel where she could monitor everyone's comings and goings. She put down her bag, stood by her chair and lifted her dress over her head, remembering the lover who had told her that he could tell a lot about a woman's sexuality when he watched her strip down to her bathing suit. Some sat down first, effectively hiding while they stripped off their coverups. Others stood proudly. The same man put a lot of faith in the theory that women who wore ankle bracelets were hot, and Allison still wore the one he'd given her. She hadn't needed him to tell her to stand tall while she stripped, though. She liked showing off.

An attractive young couple were just arriving at the pool. The only unattached men were two young pool attendants whose cocoa brown skin contrasted sharply with their hotel-issue polo shirts—cute, but too young. She scanned the windows and balconies across the way. A young girl leaned on a railing on the second floor, wiggling with childish excitement as she called to someone inside. A kissing couple was visible a floor above and several rooms down. Great day, she thought, smiling, breathing in the fresh air and congratulating herself on having taken this beautiful sunny day off. She sat down on the chair, leaned back with her hands clasped behind her head, elbows out, and stretched with pleasure.

Before too long, Allison was fully engrossed in the most recent addition to her library of women's erotica. The quality of the writing pleased her. The stories were rich with imagery, emotion and imagination, as well as sex. The specific fantasies of the writers did not all appeal to her, but there were many that did, and the dampness between her thighs was not all sweat from the sun. "Allison, you're a horny bitch," she thought.

A shadow fell over her, and she looked up to see one of the handsome young pool attendants standing at the foot of her chair, checkpad in hand. His eyes took in her body from toes to face with bold appreciation. "May I get you anything?" he asked politely.

She considered him lazily for a moment and then verbalized her request for spring water, please. Allison watched his cute buns as he walked away to fill her order, thinking, "Maybe he's not too young." She laughed out loud at herself.

Distracted, she set down her book and scanned the scene again. Some families were packing up, getting ready to leave the pool and go to lunch. On the balconies now, close to where their room must be, a single man surveyed the pool. A nicely shaped black man, she noticed. Tall and muscular-looking in shorts and t-shirt. Fantasy material. She paused, wondering idly if he was alone and what he looked like closer up.

A few minutes later, the hotel door opened and a tall, handsome, very virile-looking black man stepped through. "Be still my heart," thought Allison as she recognized him as the man she'd noticed on the balcony. He looked back at her, deliberately smiled and slowly walked around the pool, maintaining eye contact with her as he made his way around chairs and other sunbathers.

Finally he stopped in front of her, inclined his head politely and asked, "Is this chair free? May I join you?" Allison smiled her "yes," invited him to sit down, offered her name. His was Warren, he told her, and stripped off his t-shirt. She watched with appreciation— strong muscular chest and belly, broad shoulders, slim waist and

smooth, hairless brown skin. He watched her closely as he stripped
off his shorts. Flash of white underneath, oh my God, he's wearing
a small white bikini.

As her visitor lowered his body into the lounge chair beside
her, he turned towards her and began to talk. Rich, deep voice;
easy grace. Her body responded deliciously as she talked and
flirted with ease.

She's here on pure pleasure, she tells him, with a friend who is
working but will return later. Engrossed in their conversation,
they are startled by the return of the pool attendant with the
spring water she's ordered. Warren takes in the look she and
the waiter exchange, the way the young man touches her hand as
he delivers the drink. He chuckles knowingly and reaches over for
his wallet. He hands a tip to the attendant, effectively dismissing
him while claiming possession of her. To Allison, he says simply,
"You're dangerous, lady."

As the afternoon wears on, talk becomes more intimate. "Have
you ever made love to a black man?" Warren asks.

"Yes," she answers, then hesitates. Should she continue? She's
had two black lovers. One, half Italian, had delicious dark honey
skin and a football player's body; another was black as licorice and
smaller, with an exquisitely sculpted body. Both were quite beautiful; both provided her with long-lasting erotic memories. The
first one taught her about her submissive side, simply and definitely. All it took was this—he held her arms loosely but authoritatively away so that she could not touch him while he made love to
her. She remembers being helpless to do anything but receive
pleasure. The thought of his teasing still excites her.

The second lover was the first man ever to masturbate for her—
to stand hot and naked before her, stroking his hard cock while
she watched. It was her first real experience with voyeurism, and
she felt scared of his quiet smoldering challenge for her to reveal
more of herself.

These lovers left her with sensual memories of black skin on
white, black cock entering pink pussy. She recalls these images
and feels a stirring as she tells Warren about these men. He listens
quietly, then rolls to his side and reaches over to stroke her hip in
a move that seems involuntary and at the same time deliberately

erotic. Her nipples harden and she finds herself moving her arm to lightly stroke this man's face and neck just once. He is closely shaved, his skin warm and smooth as fine leather. She feels a catch of pure lust in her throat and chest. He takes her hand and brings it to his lips. "What are we going to do about this?" he asks.

Allison considers the question, maintaining direct eye contact. There is serious heat going on here. "What time is it?"

"Two."

"Let me change clothes and let's meet in the bar in twenty minutes. We'll talk more about it there."

Warren is waiting at the bar when she arrives. She buys him a drink and begins to tell him, simply and directly, what she would like. She blushes slightly as she risks his rejection while inviting his participation in her fantasy. She tells Warren in a multitude of ways that she desires him. She leans towards him, her voice lowered, her eyes teasing, and she touches him lightly. He looks at her steadily as she speaks. He does not interrupt. She wonders what he is thinking and how he'll respond.

When Allison has finished her proposition, Warren stands, reaches out, pulls her to her feet. He lifts her to him, his strong hands on her ass. She is pressed against him, stretching to reach his mouth for his slow, deep kiss. Out of the corner of her eye she sees that Grant has entered the bar and is watching. He smiles, a little nervously she thinks, as he takes a seat further down the bar, behind Warren. She signals to him with a quick wave, pulls back to look into Warren's face and asks, "Am I right to take your response as a yes?" He sits down on the barstool, looks into her eyes and takes both of her hands in his, pulling them to his chest. He reaches out and lightly caresses her breasts. Then he grins and gives her nipple an insolent pinch. He pulls her hand to his mouth and moves it deliberately down to press against his crotch. He says yes.

Heat floods her face. "We'd better get out of here before we disgrace ourselves," she says, then tells him to wait just one minute.

She approaches Grant, who watches her intently. They read devilishness in each other as he pulls her to him for a kiss. He looks at Warren, who is watching them. "Do you want to fuck him?" Grant asks. She says yes loud enough so both men can hear.

Out in the lobby, she stops and introduces the men. "Grant, this is Warren, Warren, Grant." Grant suggests that all three go up to their room.

Allison undresses Warren as Grant watches, casually leaning against the wall. She's swept up in touching this beautiful man's body. As she unbuttons his shirt, she moves her hands over his chest, drawing feathery-light circles on his buttery-soft leather skin. She brings her mouth and fingers to his nipples as she draws his shirt off his back and pulls it from his arms. Her hands move down to caress his belly. Warren arches his back and moves against her hand, urging it lower.

Allison's attention is on Warren's eyes—she watches his response as she reaches into his shorts to fondle him. She releases his cock and gives it several upward strokes, feels it hardening, watches the lust grow in his eyes. She takes the weight of his testicles in her hands and squeezes gently. His pubic hair is thick and wiry; his cock thrusts hard against his shorts as he moans.

Pressing his shoulders against the wall, she kisses him, then lowers her hands to his waist. She unbuttons, unzips and lowers his shorts, stroking his buttocks and genitals. Allison drops to her knees in front of him, and takes his cock in her mouth. She draws him deeply into her mouth with slow easy movements, one arm stroking his ass and thighs, her other hand holding the base of his hot black cock.

Grant is watching; Allison deliberately does not look at him, though she can see him in the mirror where she watches herself sucking Warren. She uses her hands and mouth together, moving more urgently. Warren leans back and lets her take him.

She senses Grant moving behind her but does not stop her attention to Warren's body. She is sucking deeply now, hands on each of his muscular thighs, thumbs stroking his testicles as she moves her mouth up and down his shaft. Her body is tense with excitement, her ass sways involuntarily. She feels her sundress being lifted from behind, a soft breeze of air playing across her naked ass and wet pussy. She moans in response to the strong hands kneading her ass, spreading her open, touching her asshole and vagina with teasing fingers.

Grant lowers his mouth to her spread pussy, eating her and rubbing her juices over her ass with his fingers. She wriggles against him in pleasure. Warren watches the three of them in the mirror with obvious enjoyment. He strokes her face possessively, sensually, then wraps his large hands around her head and thrusts his cock into her throat. They move in hot rhythm together, Warren's hands pulling her forward when he thrusts, Grant's mouth luring her backward when Warren withdraws.

Warren suddenly pulls completely out of her, and simultaneously Grant stands up, touching her naked shoulders as he rises. She sits back on her heels, looking only at Warren, deliberately teasing Grant. But there is more to this, she knows: She has always wanted to give Grant the pleasure of watching her make love to another man with full abandon. She is not asking for permission this time. She is hot, very hot, and does not know what will come next, but whatever it is, she wants it. Looking at Grant might break the spell, might prevent her from giving herself freely.

Warren reaches down and swoops her up onto her feet. Two hands move in front of her and two behind her as both men cooperate in undressing her. Grant bends to unfasten the ankle straps on her sandals, his fingers caressing her instep. Warren unbuckles her belt and throws it aside. She is wearing nothing now but the sundress, and her nipples are almost painfully sensitive, their hardness jutting against the thin fabric. Warren reaches under her dress and smoothes his hands up her thighs as Grant lifts her dress from behind and runs his hands up her ass. Together the men lift her sundress over her head. Warren drinks in her body with his eyes and his hands. He bends his head to her breast, suckling greedily, setting her on fire.

As he'd done in the bar earlier, Warren presses her body hard against his. This time, free of clothing and in private, she responds as she was tempted to do in public—her arms around his neck, she raises herself, wraps her legs around his waist and slides her sopping wet pussy down onto his big shaft. Leaning back, her arms extended, she rides him hard. He lifts her up and down on him with ease; her swollen clit rubs against him with every movement. Her orgasm begins to swell, heat rising from her groin to her belly, her chest and then flooding her face as she screams her pleasure.

Warren moves, with her still clinging limply to him, and falls towards the bed. She sprawls on her back as he leans over and kisses her deeply. She catches a glimpse of Grant watching—his pants now off, shirt unbuttoned and hard cock in his hand. Warren moves down between her legs and toys with her pussy. He strokes her wetness, spreads her wide with both hands and watches with enjoyment as she squirms. She wants more. He bends his head to her pussy and tastes. She lifts his face, forcing him to look at her. "Fuck me," she moans. "I want to be fucked again. I want to be fucked hard."

"You do, do you?" Warren asks, but ignores her pleading. He moves up alongside her, leaning on one elbow as he looks down at her face and toys with her clit and her open pussy with his free hand. Smoothly he thrusts three fingers into her; she responds by bucking against them, low growls emerging from her throat. "Look at this," he says, kneeling beside her. "This pretty pink pussy wants cock, doesn't it? You like to fuck, don't you, Allison?"

He has her at his mercy. He is purposely teasing and she is embarrassingly out of her mind with lust. When he finally begins to fuck her again, he does so deliberately and slowly, lifting her ass in the air and drawing her to him. She cannot bear it, he is controlling her movement, the angle at which he holds her keeps her clit out of contact as he pumps slowly in and out. She writhes in his hands as she desperately tries to grind against him to satisfy her want. Warren stiffens; she sees in his face and hears in his sounds that he is going to come without her. Hot, wet come fills her, drips out of her throbbing pussy, spilling down the crack of her ass as he withdraws.

Warren chuckles. "I think it's your turn now, Davis," he says. "I think the lady is ready for you. Would you like me to hold her for you?" And there is Grant, standing at the end of the bed, his eyes hot for her, stroking his cock. "Do you want to be fucked, Allison?" he asks. "Has your black lover made you hot for me?"

Through the haze of her passion, she thinks, "But I never told Warren that Grant's last name is Davis." And suddenly she knows she's been set up. This "chance meeting" by the pool had been prearranged. She likes this—somehow it sets her free. A small explosion goes off in her head. She reaches for Grant, pulling him close, whispering hotly, "Beast—I've been had, haven't I?" He grins in acknowledgment. Warren also grins, in collusion with Grant.

Heat, even more intense than before, floods her body. Warren moves quickly behind her, kneeling and lifting her up so that her head and shoulders are propped against his chest and belly. He takes each of her breasts in his hands, kneading them, pinching her nipples.

"God, I'm hot," she moans. "I need you in me, Grant. Take me. Fuck me hard while Warren holds me."

Grant kneels between her wide-spread legs, and she catches his hard cock in her hand. She guides it towards her and rubs him up and down against her wetness, her juices mixed with those of another man. Grant thrusts hard into her and lowers himself to bring his mouth down on hers, crushing her with a deep passionate kiss, devouring her tongue and her mouth at the same time. Drawing back, he looks at her and says, his face and voice hot, "Tell me that you love me, Allison."

That little explosion goes off in her head again—surrender. Her arms and legs wrapped tightly around him, she bucks wildly, gripping his cock with her cunt, feeling Warren's heat behind her as she and Grant move together against him. "I love you, Grant. Oh, God, yes, I love you." Drowning in emotion and lust, moving hot and hard with him, she comes in long shattering spasms. She holds on, continuing to fuck him, determined to take him with her. Finally, his cries mingle with hers as he shoots into her.

"Beast!" Allison says, smiling at Grant fondly and with no small wonder as he collapses warm and solid against her.

*Karen A. Selz*

# The Hobby Horse

A fragment of passing street conversation had haunted Becky all the way home. A man and a woman were arguing but not angry. "It just won't work," the woman had said. It was the voice of fact, allowing no dispute. Was it always so clear when something was over, Becky wondered as she unlocked her apartment door.

Shaft, Becky's aging tomcat, sauntered out of sleep on the couch as she turned into the entrance hall. He was talking to her in cat: "Glad to see you. I love it when you smell like outside. Did you know that I'm out of canned food?" He trotted off to demonstrate the last point. Would she follow, please?

The kitchen was lit by the few broad threads of late-afternoon sun that wound through the partially closed Venetian blinds. Becky put out more food for Shaft and decided to let the morning dishes wait a little longer. She checked her answering machine while she crunched on a carrot; there were only two messages. A computerized voice reminded her about a NOW fund-raiser at five dollars for potluck and a discussion of reproductive rights in Pennsylvania, and there was a "just saying hi" message from her friend George. David hadn't called.

So that's how it was. She couldn't feel too hurt. After all, she was the one who had suggested the separation. Living together just hadn't worked.

Kicking off her shoes, tying back her hair, Becky was glad to be alone. Maybe when you got past thirty your habits were just too set, too hard to overcome. What got in the way of love then seemed not so much the improbability of finding someone to love, which would be enough of an obstacle, but more the unwillingness to accommodate another object in your life.

The escape from her stockings felt good; so did the cold water on her face. Shaft had eaten his fill and joined her, sitting in attendance on the bathroom counter, watching her with seasoned disinterest. He was a good companion—thick, languorous and swaggering in the way of male cats. Soundly convinced of his many perfections, he was a braggart and a bully, but always happy at her coming home, always in her bed when she woke up.

It had been a rough day at work, leaving her tired and unfulfilled. The week was only half over. And she *had* really expected David to return her call. Altogether a good day for a ride on her horse.

She fell easily into the ritual. Rose oil rubbed hard into her skin. Sitting on the edge of the old porcelain tub, she let her hands work smoothly down the length of her legs, her fingers finally interlacing with her toes. Next the arms, circling each elbow carefully with the thumb of the opposite hand. She pressed with slicked knuckles down her abdomen, her hands splitting before her mons and then lifting to her breasts. Round, happy breasts, she thought. Nipples large and pointed upward. She felt the weight of each breast and thoughtfully rolled each nipple between her fingers. They really were very nice.

Standing again, she oiled the small of her back, arching her spine and planting her feet against the force of her own hands. Her buttocks, slightly upraised, were next to receive her attention. Then, bending at the waist, she slipped her hands down her legs a second time. Exhaling, she stood up.

But what to wear? To look inconspicuous, to make it to the roof without arousing the curiosity that might produce spectators. She put on her old terry cloth robe and, to feed her developing excitement, nipple clamps and a g-string. But then flats, not heels. Dropping her keys into one of the robe's deep pockets, she headed for the roof.

Just as she was opening the door of the stairs that led to the roof, Mrs. Eisley from 4B looked out through the chain. "Damn," Becky whispered to herself.

"Oh, it's you, Becky. I heard some noise."

"Yes, Mrs. Eisley. I'm sorry to bother you. I have to get a few things out of my storage area. I'll be quieter on the way down."

Mrs. Eisley paused to consider the explanation, and then, with a nod so slight it might have been Becky's imagination, the door closed, followed by the sounds of three locks being secured in sequence.

Up one flight of stairs she stood on the tar paper and gravel of the flat roof terrace. It was almost evening. The light that still fell was soft, and the slow whir of the domed roof fans lingered in the humid air. Becky turned left from the stairs and walked past four stalls in the concrete block storage structure. At the fifth she stopped, fished the keys out of her pocket, and struggled with the partially rusted padlock.

The cinderblock storage space was small and damp and usually ten degrees cooler than the outside air on these summer nights, a rooftop haven that felt subterranean. A single naked lightbulb hung from the ceiling, dim, forty watts. Becky had wired a plug off the line that fed the light. A cord dropped from the side of the bulb to the middle of the room, then snaked under an opaque plastic sheet.

The tarp hid her secret machine, her conduit to peace, her horse. Nobody else knew about it. When she had given David the keys to her apartment, she had neglected to provide the extra storage room key.

The idea of the horse had been with Becky since she was fourteen or so, but she had had to wait until she had graduated from college, until she had an apartment to herself, to build and keep her beast in private.

The horse was, in fact, her greatest yield from high school industrial drafting class. She was proud of the design. Sturdy, electronically and mechanically simple, and tailored to a specific purpose. She could build a better one now, a more efficient horse with more flexibility, a more sophisticated machine. But that would take time and money, and this one had become an old friend. It would be unkind to replace it. Becky smiled at the ease with which she could project feelings onto machines, especially the ones she made, and the relative difficulty she had empathizing with most human beings. Some people might be forever outside of her understanding.

Becky closed the plywood door and untied her robe. For a second or two she worried about being interrupted. She always had this moment of concern, but in the five years she had lived here no one had bothered her. There had not been even a close call. No one who didn't have building keys could even get onto the roof. Only seven of the twelve apartments were occupied this time of year, and nobody was going to come through a closed door looking into her storage bin at six-thirty on a Wednesday night. She removed her open robe and hung it over a bronze hat rack just inside the door.

Becky took a step into the room and in doing so crossed almost half of it. She pulled up the plastic and folded it neatly along its creases, then laid it on top of a liquor box full of once-read books.

The horse's anatomy had three main parts. An old, now quite stained Western saddle, with an eight-by-fourteen-inch rectangle cut through its concave seat, was bolted onto a perforated metal frame that resembled a hobby horse except for its dual top bars and a shelf that sat twelve inches from the underside of the saddle's seat. The shelf contained the horse's innards, its working parts, two small electric motors. Each, through a nest of gears, drove a single piston up and down through a rectangular housing set into the horse's back. Attached to the front piston was a dildo, straight, stocky and friendly. The back piston drove a silicon butt plug. A newer model might have pitch and yaw, might have joysticks instead of the side-by-side rheostatic throttle levers that were attached where the saddle horn had once been.

Becky checked the throttles to zero and flipped the toggle switch on the shelf. The little engines hummed like a hundred bees. Becky mounted the horse. She had built it so that her feet rested flat on the ground, even when in a full gallop.

The throttle levers, similar to but smaller than those used to control boat engines, fit nicely in the curl of her right hand. Her right arm, crossing in front of her, put a slight tugging pressure on her chained nipple clips. She eased the left lever up slightly, then down again quickly. As she did, the rear piston slid up three inches and stopped. There was no hurry. Pushing her g-string aside, she repositioned herself, letting the plug slide smoothly into her oiled anus. Then she held back, like she always did when everything was in place. With the humming vibration of the desperate little disengaged engines, with the heat in her spine, with the ticklish pushing of the plug spreading into her consciousness, wiping it clean of other thoughts, of thought generally, she counted to fifty, curling her bare toes against the cool concrete with each number she pronounced.

At the count of fifty she pushed the right lever forward slightly. The dildo peeked up through the saddle back. As it entered her she tensed, trying to hold it in. It was a rigged game. Playing against herself, teasing herself, withholding from herself and then delivering richly and abundantly unto herself.

She let the dildo work slowly, methodically. Rubbing back and forth at the pace of her pulse. Filling her with tentative strokes against the plug that already filled her. She pushed the right lever forward again. The rate of successive penetrations increased, forcing the beating of her heart. Becky tensed against the worn sides of the saddle. The horse was driving her in a cold fire.

When the static charge was sharp and spreading, when orgasm hovered, she pulled back on the right lever, stopping the horse in its tracks. Becky held her breath, lingering at the edge of the chasm. Counting again. When the first wave had passed, she tweaked the left throttle with such a practiced hand that she extended the butt plug to its maximum height inside her.

A shiver ran through her. Now for the finale, she thought. She took the chain between her nipple clamps in her teeth and threw both throttles forward. The horse shook slightly, coughed and stopped. The overhead bulb flickered and died. But while the light recovered almost immediately, the horse did not.

"Shit! Shit! Shit!" Mechanical failure. Her machine had never left her in the lurch. Well, once, years ago, but she had fixed that. She sighed and dismounted gingerly, with a gurgle and a pop.

On first inspection the machine looked fine except for the fact that neither engine was running. A power surge? A short? Maybe a problem with the line. Circuit design and repair had never been her best subjects. For all her hard work she had gotten a B in Introductory Electronics.

The electrical connection to the horse seemed intact. Tracing the line up to the ceiling, she could see no breaks nor feel any hot spots. A more thorough examination would have to wait until tomorrow, when she could bring more light and the proper tools.

Becky climbed onto another box of books to unplug her miscreant beast. The lace g-string stretched grudgingly against her swollen vulva, igniting tiny sparks in her back and neck. She would take care of that in a few minutes, downstairs, with one of her conventional battery-operated devices.

Straining, she could just reach the ceiling. It took no small effort to pull the plug, and it wasn't until the moment it came free from the socket that she registered the breeze. It was slight but noticeable against her bare bottom, hot and soft like a breath. And she could feel someone there, behind her, in the doorway.

She turned before she had time to consider the possibilities, and there, not three feet from her, was David. His face had taken on a most unusual expression, one she had never seen before. He looked baffled, maybe upset, certainly surprised.

Becky looked down at her manacled breasts and soaked g-string, her pedestal of books. She looked at the horse, unplugged and uncovered. And somehow she didn't feel ashamed of these disclosures.

"I'm sorry," David stammered. "I came by and Mrs. Eisley said you might be up here. I mean, I didn't mean to . . ." He made some vague and abrupt hand motions. An erection was obvious under his thin summer slacks, his body bold where his speech was faltering.

"Come in. Close the door." Becky's voice was steady despite her excitement. She stepped down from her box, meeting him halfway. "You're the only other person ever to see my machine," she said.

He didn't reply but reached out a hand, tracing her stomach and breasts in the air an inch or two from her skin. His eyes followed his hand in a kind of worship. He kneeled in front of her and in the same motion clasped his arms around her hips, pushing his face onto the flat space below her navel and above the g-string. His hold was tight, compressing. He mouthed inaudible words.

The heat and pressure melted Becky at the knees. Flowing through David's arms, she joined him on the cool concrete floor. His eyes were open but unseeing as he buried his face in her neck, then pushed his nose and chin along her shoulders and under her right arm. Becky whimpered, tugging on David's clothes, covering his face and neck in a cascade of kisses. They were new together, honest and fierce.

Becky made short work of David's clothes. A button tore and flew across the room, unnoticed. She wanted to climb onto him. To be climbed onto. To occupy and be occupied. His erection was large and strong as she closed her mouth over it. He lifted her, turning her gently. Pushing aside the g-string, David immersed his face in her vulva with the almost involuntary rocking of his head. Oscillating up and down along the banks of her labia, his tongue and lips found her clitoris and pulled hard on it. She nursed hungrily on his penis, swirling her tongue along its underside and along the ridge of its head, tugging rhythmically at his buttocks and balls. They were growling and humming and tearing, and just when it was unbearable, impossibly close to orgasm, they disentangled and Becky mounted David.

Above him, facing him, she pinned his arms above his head, her hands locked to his. "Slow," he whispered with each breath, like a prayer. "Slow."

Soaked and stinging with salt and juices, Becky rocked slowly, rolling her abdominal muscles once with each forward thrust of her hips. Lifting David's captured right hand to her mouth, she gnawed on his knuckles as she pulled and pulsed against him. Her rocking was faster, harder, and more tenacious.

David was gasping out almost-words, unrecognizable syllables of their own shared language. Biting and rubbing, body and body and body. Becky's cycles grew still faster and larger until she could press no further. David was pushing up against her onslaught, clenching every muscle, until they both exploded and collapsed, folding into each other.

They stayed like that, he still inside her, as they became slowly aware of the cold, unyielding floor, of the dank air, of muscle cramps and bruises that would no doubt appear in a day or two. Becky laughed a big, deep, open laugh for no particular reason. She swept the matted hair from David's forehead.

David smiled weakly. "Did you know that there's a fuse box outside?"

"No, I can't say that I remembered that. How 'bout we go downstairs and you make me some dinner?"

## Marcy Sheiner

❧

# Under His Thumb

It's 1963. My parents and older sister Jackie are in the den of our split-level suburban home watching Ed Sullivan, when suddenly I hear a great commotion. Jackie is squealing like a pig, my father is booming his refrain about "you stupid kids," and my mother is telling both of them to shut up, she can't hear the TV. These precise sound effects have occurred twice before in the history of our family: First when Elvis appeared on Ed Sullivan, and again when the Beatles made their debut. Both times I scurried downstairs to witness history. Tonight I do so again.

Five skinny, scruffy British kids with long greasy-looking hair are banging on instruments and mewling with untrained vocal cords. The lead singer, with his thick snarly lips and defiant fuck-you posture, immediately captures my attention. He is not overtly sexual like Elvis, and he isn't "cute" like the four moptops. But Mick Jagger touches something dark and rebellious in my little teenage soul.

Having recently discovered masturbation, I retire to my room, flop face down on the bed and, bunching the covers between my legs, hump furiously against them while imagining Mick Jagger's thick snarly lips on mine. I come.

\*    \*    \*

It's 1973. I'm living in Manhattan. My sister calls from her respectable marital abode in Westchester to say that hubby Kevin, who's an ASCAP lawyer, has scored two third-row seats to a Rolling Stones concert at Madison Square Garden. Kevin, a folkie who thinks the Stones are raucous, has volunteered to stay home with baby Joey. Am I available?

The thought of seeing Mick from a distance of merely three rows gets my pussy tingling. But the concert is to take place on the very same evening as a strategy session for a pro-ERA march, of which I am one of the organizers. My feminist comrades, who despise the Rolling Stones for their sexist lyrics and attitudes, know nothing of my fondness for them; I hide their albums, especially the one with the unzipped fly, whenever they come to visit.

A moral crisis is upon me. Jackie calls every day, saying she cannot hold out forever, soon she'll have to ask someone else. She considers me mad with my anti-Stones brand of feminism and reminds me that the band is part of the cultural movement that has led me to seek liberation in the first place.

"Listen to their liberating lyrics!" she sputters.

"Yeah?" I challenge. "Name one."

"Well, there's . . ." I hold the phone patiently and picture Jackie rummaging through her record albums, desperately seeking a feminist message. At last, success: "She comes in colors!" Jackie shouts triumphantly.

Of course, I relent. (Was there ever any question?) The day before the concert I tell my comrades that my sister and her husband have been called out of town on an emergency and I must go to Westchester to babysit my nephew. What could be more sisterly?

From our vantage point, third row center, I can see every gyration of Mick's pelvis, and a definite hard-on bulging beneath the fabric of his torn jeans. He has, of course, matured from the barely restrained bad boy of Ed Sullivan days into the bony steel-eyed fiercely energetic performer he will remain throughout his long career. Some call him androgynous, but when he clasps his hands behind his head, purses his pouty lips and thrusts his pelvis into our faces, I respond to raw animal masculinity. When Mick struts and frets like a peacock, I feel as if he's inviting me to fall before him as before an altar, to unzip his pants and pour all my love and lust upon the center of his manhood. Is he not my idol? Is this not the ultimate meaning of idolatry? I want to be under his gaze, under his cock, under his thumb.

Jackie screams incessantly for the duration of the concert, but I remain silent, mesmerized. My cunt is palpitating. My nipples are so hard I'm afraid they'll push holes through my t-shirt. I wonder if Mick can see them. I hope so.

When I get home there are urgent messages from feminist comrades on my answering machine: There was some sort of ideological split at the meeting, and my presence, according to one caller, could have averted it. Twinges of guilt do not prevent me from flopping face down on my bed and positioning my hand so that my thumb presses against my clit while two fingers snake into my cunt. I imagine Mick's lips exactly where my hand is. I come.

It's 1983. I am living in Woodstock, New York. It is common knowledge that the Rolling Stones are in town recording an album at a nearby sound studio. It's drummer Charlie Watt's birthday, and rumors fly that the Stones have rented out a local nightclub for a celebration.

I go into overdrive: first I call a friend of a friend who waits tables at the club to confirm the rumor. Then I call Jackie, who leaves Joey and his sister Lucy in the care of the ever-patient Kevin and drives up from Westchester. That night we stand freezing in the parking lot along with several other hopeful groupies, watching with dismay as town hotshots, invited by the club's owner, file smugly inside. When the president of the bank enters, Jackie loses it. "The Rolling Stones come from the working class!" she shouts. "*We* should be in there, not the president of the fucking bank!" I am afraid I may have to sedate her.

A limo pulls up and Keith Richards, wearing a silver jumpsuit with the zipper open to the navel, steps out. Five of us immediately surround him. One woman asks how he's enjoying the mountains; another asks if he's dined at our four-star Chinese restaurant. Jackie ignores all sense of propriety: She demands that we, as loyal fans and common folk, be granted entry to the party.

"You want to go to the party, d'you?" Keith asks, seriously considering the request. "Hold on, luvs, and I'll see what I can do." At the door he tosses his head towards us and tells the bouncer to "Let the five chicks in."

We hear murmurs of uncertainty, a consultation with the club's owner, a protest and then, unbelievably, Mick Jagger's authoritative voice: "Keith says to let the five chicks *in!*"

As we file in, Mick, resplendent in black tuxedo, greets each of us with a kiss on the hand. (In retrospect, he was probably bored to death by all the doctors, lawyers and bankers, and thrilled at our arrival.) I am the last one to enter, and after he kisses my hand, I do not let go.

"Thanks for inviting us," I say.

"Would you like to dance?" he asks, looking me up and down.

I am so stunned that I enter what can only be described as an altered state, akin to a drug high. People and objects, especially Mick, become blurred, almost surreal. In a daze I dance to one song after another, sometimes with Mick, sometimes with Jackie, whose envy is assuaged when Keith whirls her onto the dance floor. At some point a cake appears and we sing "Happy Birthday." Slowly the party winds down and the club empties out. Mick and I are among the last to leave.

Soon we are in a cabin, or a country inn, or maybe even a trailer, deep in the woods. An antique dresser topped by a huge round mirror faces a big brass bed. An armchair sits at an angle in the corner. Mick seats me in the chair and pushes buttons on a tape deck, simultaneously ripping off his jacket, tie and shirt.

The slow bluesy sound of "You Got to Move" fills the room as Mick, wearing only his pants and undershirt, faces the mirror. He begins moving to the music, his narrow hips swaying. He rubs his hands along either side of the growing bulge in his pants, up and down from waist to groin. He purses his lips and inhales deeply. His eyes are glued to his own image in the mirror; I wonder if he's even aware of my presence.

He mouths the words to the song, puts a hand behind his head, and struts back and forth between the bed and the dresser. He opens wide his legs, knees bent, and does a few pliés. The bulge in his pants quivers. He unzips his fly and pulls out his long, smooth ivory cock. It's a lovely organ—but more importantly, it's attached to someone about whom I have been fantasizing for two decades. A famous man, a superstar, one of the icons of our time. To be so close makes me dizzy, brings a lump of emotion to my throat.

Mick is oblivious to my reaction. "Ooooh!" he whispers, exhaling sharply and closing his eyes. Lovingly he strokes his erection.

I press my hands between my legs, my cunt aching like a wound. Is Mick planning to fuck me or himself? Will he let me suck his cock? Abandoning all pretext of decorum, I fall out of the chair and crawl on all fours towards him. Mick opens his eyes.

"Just what d'you think you're doin'?" he taunts, his lips curling at the corners.

"I want to suck you," I gasp.

He laughs, or rather, he makes a sound commonly called a laugh but which is too full of cruelty to be categorized as mirthful.

"And just who told you you could do *that*, li'l chippie?"

"Please," I beg. I choke on the lump in my throat and tears threaten to spill from my eyes. "Please let me."

Mick laughs again, waving his cock at me. He stops his dancing to remove his remaining clothes. I am awed by the sight of every rib, every bone, visible beneath his translucent skin. A blue vein zigzags artfully down his right arm. He moves closer and sticks his cock right under my nose. My tongue darts out, but Mick jumps backwards in a hasty two-step.

The song has changed to "Brown Sugar." The pace of his dancing picks up: naked, he gavottes around the small room, clutching his member, ignoring me.

I rip off my clothes, hoping to capture his attention with my naked body. I do. He dances towards me, and when the song ends and the tape player clicks off, he stands still, his hands on his sharp hip bones, his hard cock aimed straight at my mouth.

I reach out and run my forefinger up and down his silky shaft, around the smooth crown. Am I really touching Mick Jagger's naked cock? Curiously I hold it, study it. It could belong to any man. But it doesn't—and that makes all the difference in the world.

Suddenly I am overcome with terror: talk about performance anxiety! He's probably been sucked by the very best in the world. I resolve to give the blow job of my life.

I bend forward and plant kisses all over this prick that millions of men and women have fantasized about. I caress the head with my lips. I take my time licking it from base to crown, pausing to take each of his balls into my mouth and gently suck on them. I return to the head and take him in, relaxing the back of my throat so I can get it all down.

His hands exert pressure on my head, his thumbs pushing hard against my temples. "Atta girl," he whispers hoarsely. "Oooh, you suck it so good. All the girls wanna suck my dick, y'know that, dontcha baby?"

Indeed I do; that's part of what makes this so very thrilling. Cunt juice runs down my inner thighs. I look up, nod emphatically, keep on sucking.

"But only you get to suck it t'night. That's cuz you're such a good li'l cocksucker."

I feel blessed, grateful and powerful all at once. Mick keeps talking for a few more minutes, his voice becoming softer and softer, until at last he is silent. I open my eyes and gaze up.

Mick Jagger's famous lips are hanging loose. All the muscles in his face have slackened. His eyes are covered with a gauzy film. With a rush of pride I realize that I am responsible for reducing this wound-up bundle of raw nerves to a purry little kitten. My cocksucking skills are such that I have tamed the beast. For a moment I'm afraid I'll faint, but it's just a momentary swoon.

Mick falls backwards onto the bed, his skinny legs hanging over the edge. I follow, not missing a beat: If this is what he wants, then this is what he'll get—I'll do anything to keep him interested in me. I lick and sniff his balls. I squeeze his ass. I rub my tits over his cock. A drop of pre-come appears on the head, and I wonder if he'll deign to fuck me or if he wants to come in my mouth. I take the risk and climb up to straddle his thin hips. He does not move.

I gaze down and see the pretty girl in him. I recognize her easily—I've seen her on Mick's face countless times, when he's singing a tender love song, or caught unawares by some shrewd photographer. She's the girl who saves Mick Jagger from crude macho, the girl who enables my generation, with all our faith in androgyny, to tolerate his excesses of masculinity. I run my hand over her impossibly delicate cheekbones, her vulnerable Adam's apple, her hairless chest. Mick whimpers, sounding for all the world like a woman. I plant tender kisses all over her face, her ears, her erect little nipples. Then I reach down between her legs.

Suddenly Mick's energy switches into high voltage, and he's a man again. His face tightens, his lips purse, his pelvis thrusts and his cock jabs into me. He is all hardness, fury, insistence.

"Yeah, give it to me, girl, gimme your cunt. All of it. Uhh. Uhh."

He's a blind, grunting animal, his hands gouging the flesh on my hips as he moves me this way and that, his cock seeking, searching—for what? The ever-elusive satisfaction?

"I'm gonna come in you, girl. I'm gonna come soon. Are you ready for it? Huh? You ready for my come?"

"Yes," I gasp.

"Yeah, all the girls want my come. They scream for my come, you know that, dontcha? And I'm gonna give it to *you. Now.*" He grunts, and his whole body stiffens as his cock erupts inside me. I press my clit against his prominent pubic bone and I come too, the walls of my cunt contracting around his gushing cock. I come, honest to God, in colors. Trembling, I collapse onto his wiry body, and then I do cry, hot tears all over his neck and chest. All the frustration of so many years watching and wanting Mick Jagger comes pouring out of me. So many years fantasizing about him, feeling teased by him yet never believing I'd really have him, are in my sobs. The orgasm that released my cunt has opened my heart and tear ducts as well.

Mick strokes my hair comfortingly. "There there," he murmurs, "it's all right now, y'know. You're an all-right chick."

Hours later (or is it days?) I find myself back in my own living room. The world is no longer blurry, but my brain is fuzzy. Did it really happen? Did I really make love to Mick Jagger, or was it just another fantasy? A hallucination? I grope inside my panties; they're very wet. *Something* must have happened.

\* \* \*

It's 1993. My boyfriend Jonathan and I have spent the evening watching the Rolling Stones' Steel Wheels Tour on pay TV. Now I'm face down on the bed; Jonathan is fucking me from behind. Despite hours of stimulation in several different positions, I have been unable to reach orgasm. I turn my head and say in my sweetest pretty-please voice, "Sing to me, honey."

Jonathan chuckles, clears his throat and sings something to the effect that I can cream all over him.

He's got a velvet voice, not so belligerent as Mick's, but it works. I imagine myself onstage, on my knees, sucking Mick Jagger's cock while he looks down at me and the audience applauds. I come.

*Stacy Reed*

# Sabrina

Sabrina first caught me eyeing her during English, when we were seniors in Mrs. Cornet's class. Sabrina wore makeup like a mask, and she wore it well. It didn't seem at all insipid that she matched her eye shadow and nail polish to her outfits. With her almond-shaped olive eyes and her tan calves, she struck me as inaccessible and otherworldly. Her ease, her social prowess, her calm floated above me. I slid my eyes—touched with matte-brown powder and black mascara, as usual—guiltily to the floor. She'd noticed. Limply I turned to Mrs. Cornet, cheap red hair dye streaming down her jowls in the late spring's hanging heat. In the temporary buildings we giggled collectively.

Since our last names both began with *C*, we were assigned the same homeroom. Each morning, Sabrina read a new romance or science fiction novel with covers of grossly endowed heroines held at the waist by either an earnest lad clad in white or a cancerously tanned sword-wielding hulk. Like Sabrina herself, these covers drew me inadvertently. They reminded me of dog-eared copies of *Cosmopolitan*—the kind I always flipped through, criticizing the objects of my fascination until I contemptuously abandoned them. But there was something seductive, tempting in those glossy pages: images of worlds far from mine. I considered

my hypocrisy as I continued checking Sabrina out, like the harem
of boys that surrounded her.

She bleached her mousy brown hair white and won Most Beautiful every year. Her two best friends, Nicole and Michelle, were
cruel and stupid, but very pretty. Nicole was sunny, her cropped
hair dyed lemony. Michelle was very tall and wore no cosmetics
but deep red fingernail polish and matching lipstick. Her eyes, like
Sabrina's, were green, but Michelle's hair hung in black spirals
around her bare face. Mostly they fucked college guys, but occasionally a senior would capture one's attention.

All three were in my gym class. Though I tried to impose myself on their tight trinity, I invariably sat on the bleachers alone. I
knew I could never glide through life as inauthentically, but I
wanted to seem like them, to laugh as thoughtlessly. My envy
melted with admiration as I watched them shoot baskets accurately, their teeth white as chalk. When Sabrina occasionally turned
to wave, an effortless throw of her jeweled wrist, Michelle and
Nicole would swivel behind her like the anatomical models in
science lab. Pivoting inward at some invisible joint, they'd smirk.

One week while Nicole and Michelle were out sick—they had
both caught a bronchial infection from some guy they'd gotten
wasted with and fucked—Sabrina came to me during gym as if
we had been friends since kindergarten. Relieved from my soli-
tude, I did not protest. Her unabashed approach seduced me and
soon I considered myself her friend. I began to believe it when
she told me—in confidence, of course—about the time Nicole got
so shit-faced she wet her bed. Our eyes rolled in disdain and met
at mid-arc.

When Sabrina and I became friends I learned that she brought
a different dime-store novel to school each morning not because
she was flaky, but because she went through several a day. She'd
spend every class reading, candy beneath her desk, and then skim
entire texts before finals. Straight A's. After we'd been friends long
enough for me to venture so delicate a question, I turned to
Sabrina and asked, "Why do you read nothing but junk?" She
scrunched her hair and looked away. "Diversion," she answered.

From what, I wondered. Boredom surfaced in her eyes and I

stared, mesmerized. They were as glassy as a pool at dawn. She lowered her lids. We finished our lunch in silence, ruminating. Is she thinking of me? Is she thinking? I wondered if these were her thoughts as well.

For eight months before he left for college, I clung to my boyfriend Victor fiercely and blissfully. During this monogamous recess I introduced Sabrina to Victor's best friend, Jason. Though Jason was one class his junior, he joked with Victor provocatively, as a peer or even a superior would. Sabrina admired Jason's irreverence and soon became his girlfriend. Having more in common and to compare, Sabrina and I were soon as thick as Jason and Victor.

How big is it?

He comes too soon?

Do you swallow?

We'd find nooks in the school theater where we'd meet to eat our lunches (candy, chips and soda), reapply makeup and skewer our boyfriends. Once I asked Sabrina if she supposed they talked about us. She told me that guys didn't talk about sex to other guys unless they were lying. I realized she was probably right and felt simultaneously insulted and relieved. Was Victor ashamed of me? Protecting my reputation?

Often I spent the night at Sabrina's house. After watching *The Shining* while we ate Chinese carry-out and drank Pepsi, I resolved to disclose a secret to impress and shock her. I would see if she'd match me, see just how close we were. I chewed my cashew chicken slowly, pondering my attack.

"Victor ejaculates prematurely," I said in a low voice. Sabrina covered her mouth, her face contorting monstrously, her carefully lined lids wide. I continued for full impact, "He says it's my fault because he was a virgin when we met but I wasn't. For about five months he lied to me about girls he'd fucked." Luxuriantly I twisted my hair, savoring my relentless betrayal. Having already disposed of all boundaries, I finished, "The only way he's ever made me come is by going down on me. But he's very good at it."

I'd revealed gossip that could easily whirl back to Victor via Jason, depending on Sabrina's character. Romantically I imagined my exchange with her a test, a possibility to either form a water-tight bond with this veiled and pedestaled idol or to kill my relationship with Victor. I didn't care which.

Sabrina confidentially placed her hand on my lower thigh and said earnestly, "I've never come." She was eighteen and had already slept with about a dozen guys. "I thought Jason was gonna make me yesterday, but he came first. Seriously, I knew something was gonna happen—I could tell, you know—but then he just stopped."

Since she had matched my confidence with an equal one, I grew bolder. Realizing what my question could lead to, I asked, "Do you ever masturbate?"

The very word made her giggle wildly, but she answered candidly. "I've tried. Do you?"

"I know how," I replied vaguely, my voice softer now. I studied her slack-jawed profile in the blue television light and admired her.

"Show me," she whispered.

"How to get yourself off?" I reddened inadvertently and hoped the lights in Sabrina's living room were low enough for her not to notice. Hadn't I wanted her to watch me for once? Had I not been maneuvering us to this point? I resisted the urge to claim sudden illness, walk home, call Victor. I looked at the object of my infatuation, now more vulnerable than I. Never would I have this chance again. "Do you really want to see?"

"Yeah." She kept her hand on my leg and stroked my hair. I could smell her, a bouquet of hairspray, soap, lotion and sweat. Though my panties were wet, I argued that her parents or her little brothers might see. After she assured me that no one would ever know, I leaned against the sofa's arm and let Sabrina push up my nightshirt. "Show me," she insisted. Fearful that I'd lose her camaraderie, I acquiesced.

I said nothing, only did it. Pulling aside my cotton bikini panties, I watched her face apprehensively as she hunched down on the sofa, looking frankly at my cunt with the distanced appraisal of a physician. This remoteness soothed me. It implied that the experience was on a wholly different plane from the one on which we made out together with our boyfriends in Victor's blue Chevrolet; it didn't seem like cheating, really. The instant the thought of

Victor occurred to me I felt contemptuous mockery of him, guilt pulsing below.

I dipped my middle and index fingers into my pussy and slid them back to my clitoris. Surely Sabrina must notice I'm already wet, I thought. This probability excited me further, and I began tracing my clit slowly, teasing myself to extend the session for Sabrina. I imagined what Victor's reaction would be if my indiscretion got back to him. Sweet betrayal swept through me, nearly getting me off. I paused, sliding my finger around my ass, tracing the orifice lightly, regaining my bearings.

What if she touches me, I wondered. The prospect simultaneously scared me and fueled my desire to divulge my most secret sexuality to Sabrina, a girl I recognized as ultimately opportunistic and hollow. How far did I want this to escalate? Eventually I felt disappointed that she had no intention of participating—and I dared not ask her to. I began rubbing my clit vigorously, eager to come.

"How will I know when it happens?" Sabrina asked.

"You'll know," I whispered. Conversing with her didn't distract me. The exchange aroused me further and reeled me closer to orgasm.

"Will you tell me?"

"All right," I answered.

Sabrina spread my legs wider and commanded me to "Go ahead."

Her tone stripped me of my defenses. Obligingly I pressed my pelvis into my fingers as I gazed at Sabrina. The last time I had masturbated with a girl I'd been thirteen, nearly six years ago. Memories of Sharon and me hugging pillows between our legs and moaning in her single bed returned to me unbidden, and I spat out "Now" through clenched teeth. Sabrina watched my pussy, and I came longer than I did when Victor licked me, as long as the best times when I'd been alone.

Sabrina sat up. "It doesn't work when I do it like that," she said.

Blissful, I lacked empathy and wanted only to sleep. I'd shown her, hadn't I?

The next morning Sabrina and I awoke vinelike and embryonic. Hastily she withdrew her thigh from between mine and pulled her arm from beneath my head. Masturbating, I listened to her shower. By the time she emerged from the bathroom, fully clothed, I was dressed. We spoke politely about midterms as I gathered my things. At breakfast we chewed our pancakes too cheerfully and bantered with her brothers. When my parents rang the bell and I saw the relief on Sabrina's face, I realized that we'd transgressed some unspoken contract; we'd betrayed our boyfriends and were too ashamed to admit it, even to each other. We'd have laughed for days had we cheated with boys. Loss briefly caressed my heart, but I couldn't muster regret.

I never told Victor about the last night I spent with Sabrina. If she told Jason, either he didn't mention it to Victor or Victor held a good poker face. Nothing ever got back to me, but that could have meant anything.

Because of my own actions I recognized in others the capacity to deceive. I could only speculate as to what Victor and Jason kept between themselves. Whatever it may have been, their friendship eroded after Victor left for Tulane, and then Boston University accepted Jason. I went to Chicago and Sabrina took off for UCSD. Sabrina's and my respective relationships with Jason and Victor hiccupped along until distance and arguments eventually snuffed out the little life that still jerked beneath escalating animosity.

Four years later and two years into my marriage, Sabrina called. "I found your number through Information," she said. "I thought I'd say hi."

"Can you come over?" I asked.

"In a New York minute."

When she rang I was reclining naked on the daybed.

"Come in," I called. She entered and complimented my decor. She smelled slightly of citrus and wore a white silk dress that let the light through. She looked radiant.

"Come here," I implored. I'd been toying with my nipples, thinking how sweet a fuck she'd be, but I was nonetheless taken aback by the depth of my attraction, unfaded by time. My marriage hung in tatters, but this relationship had survived unfrayed.

"How are you, Sabrina?"

"Well. I've progressed to action," she said. Eager to give her the opportunity to demonstrate, I grabbed her hair in my fist and pulled her to me. Her lips parted and she moaned as I traced them with my tongue, tickling her gums and finally invading her mouth. She unpried my hand and ordered me to turn over. Lightly she traced my buttocks, spreading my legs to press my outer labia. My hard clit hung down and she pinched it between my lips and her index and middle fingers. She held my pussy against her palm and her wet finger slid up my ass. After she manipulated me for several minutes, my cunt's spasms drenched her rings.

I rolled over and sighed helplessly as she pinched my nipples. She opened my legs and regarded me as she had in high school. I felt a wave of déjà vu, but it passed.

She lowered her head to my straining pelvis, spread my labia and paralyzed me with her tongue. She licked my asshole and lapped at my inner lips and tongue-fucked my gushing pussy until I begged her to suck my clit. She held my lips apart as I pulled her long tresses back to watch. The sight of her pink tongue leisurely tormenting my clit made me even hotter.

When Christian walked in, he said nothing. He stood and watched, his thick cock seething beneath his trousers. This could have been Victor, I thought. He made no move to interfere. Sabrina ruthlessly flicked my clit, quickly and diligently. She wanted this and so did I. I should have stopped her, but it was too good. Watching Christian made it better.

"Who's your friend?" my husband asked. He showed no agitation, slowly removing his coat as his dick swelled.

I could barely speak, but from his demeanor I sensed a chance for redemption. "Sabrina," I said as clearly as possible. "From high school."

"What are you doing with my wife?" Christian asked, shoving his fingers into my wet, desperately clutching pussy. He began tickling my G spot and I whimpered. He pressed into me until I came so hard I ejected his fingers, ejaculating all over Sabrina's lovely face. Christian stood and licked his agile fingers slowly, staring at me. "She tastes good, doesn't she?" he asked Sabrina. When she didn't answer, he pulled her blond hair back and kissed her slicked face. "Now lick her pussy some more."

Sabrina obliged, lapping softly at my recovering cunt. In one fluid movement Christian released his prick and pushed up her dress. He pulled aside her panties and groaned as he penetrated her. He held very still, reaching around Sabrina's waist to pinch and massage her clit. Since I knew his touch so well, I could sense each teasing caress from the changes in her rhythm and the strength of her breathing. I could see his arm moving, jiggling her clit until she came. My cunt muffled her cries slightly, but the sound drove Christian mad. He held her steady between my legs as she continued lapping my entire pussy, from the vulva up to the clitoris, circling it, teasing, then sucking hard. He pulled back a few times before he came, his chest flushed, his forehead damp. He withdrew from Sabrina and swiftly buttoned his chinos.

I felt a peculiar mixture of jealousy, insult and pride in both my husband's and my friend's sexual nonchalance. I still couldn't determine Christian's stance. He was unpredictable. That's why I'd married him.

I broke the silence. "I'm about to come, Christian."

"Don't," he commanded.

"I'm sorry, baby," I moaned as orgasm swept through me like electricity. I bucked beneath Sabrina and she latched on more tightly, sucking me to a third and fourth climax. Minutes passed before I could address Christian.

"Let me suck your cock, baby."

"I'm leaving you," he announced.

"Don't be so sentimental."

After he'd packed for a hotel, Sabrina and I toasted my autonomy. I knew we'd finally resolved our unspoken conflict by consummating our attraction. Closure settled between us and I opened another bottle of port.

I didn't see her again for three years. I didn't get her number and she never called. Our long separation was interrupted last week when I saw her reading Stephen King at an outdoor cafe. Her wavy hair had grown to her waist and she'd draped her breasts with a low-cut jacket. I fought a desire to bolt and calmly crossed the intersection.

"It's been a long time," I said.

"I'm married," she answered. A diamond teardrop, at least two

carats, weighted her left ring finger, a gold band bracing the exhi-
bition. Her fuck-me red lipstick glistened in the sun.

"Of course, I'm divorced," I said.

"Of course. Would you come over for dinner Thursday?"

"I'd love to."

## Ginu Kamani

❧❦❧

# Fish Curry Rice

I can hear my aunt's voice through the wall again, matchmaking.
In Bombay, conversations on the telephone are always louder than
in person.

"See, this girl is very stubborn. She will never come to your
house to meet your boy. But we're going to the club for lunch tomorrow, so why don't you just drop by? That way all of you can
take a good look at her. I tell you, she's quite silly. Insists she has a
boyfriend in America and is not interested in anyone else. Well,
we'll soon take care of all that."

Matchmaking. The favorite hobby of idle adults in India. Sen-
tencing each other's children to a fate worse than . . . .

"How many times have I said to myself, It is an absolute curse
having good-looking girls in the family. Better if my niece were an
ugly duckling. Then we could take care of her right away without
fuss. But once they become aware of their looks, these girls just
lose all their sense. Then *we* have to run around trying to fix them
up with someone decent! Thankless job, I tell you."

I couldn't move. I was fascinated by the way my aunt was ignoring all my unique qualities and treating me like a commodity. I
knew I would go to the club for lunch with her the following day
and I could almost predict the fortyish couple who would drop by
the table: the man with tired eyes, whitening hair, restless to move

on to his tennis game; the woman plump, with perfectly sprayed tresses, chiffon sari and diamonds, unwilling to acknowledge my presence until my aunt introduced us. Then her eyes would turn on me and her lips would part and she would say with perfectly rehearsed surprise, "Oh! So *you're* the daughter of Jamini! We've all heard so much about you. But don't worry, only good things."

She would giggle on cue, pull up a chair and commence an endless session of gossip with my aunt, from which I was pointedly excluded. The man would look around, spot one of his men friends and excuse himself in a hurry. I would watch my aunt's friend glancing at me from the corner of her eye. The bearer would arrive with our lunch and I would grab my usual plate of mutton samosas and finish them off before my aunt had even started on her soup and toast. The two older women would watch me eat with fascination.

"Eating fried food is bad for your figure," my aunt's friend would admonish sharply. "You should give all this up now, while you still can."

"Oh, don't worry," I would retort with one of my stock replies. "I'll go to the ladies' room in a minute and vomit it back out."

"What a sense of humor this one has!" the friend would gasp, suitably shocked.

"Just wait." My aunt's voice would rise as she adjusted her sari over her bulk. "After you get married, you'll never be thin again."

"Actually," I would yawn, "I was a lot heavier before I started having sex. Steady sex in a marriage should do wonders for me."

By this time the friend would be quite insulted and draw my aunt into another long cycle of gossip. I would close my eyes and lean back in the rattan armchair, drifting to the hoarse chugging of a dozen ceiling fans, the clink of glasses and silverware. I'd hear excited shouts from the cricket field and the sharp crack of the bat. These were some of the oldest, most familiar sounds embedded in my consciousness. The effect of hearing them once again was hypnotic.

"If only your parents would come to their senses, they would realize how important it is to fix you up with a nice boy. But even they had their heads turned after living in the States all these years. Believe you me, one word of encouragement from your mother and I would be dragging you all across this city to meet boys. At this very moment, I have at least thirty boys who would agree to you, sight unseen. What's the harm in at least meeting a few of them? Other girls aren't fortunate to have me for their auntie. You're an attractive girl from a good family with a university degree and a green card. Who knows, you might even decide to move back to Bombay if you meet the right man."

I make a list of questions for my aunt: Will you let us use your house to have sex? Will you introduce me to your gynecologist so she can put me on the Pill? Will you rent us your other apartment so we can live together for a couple of years? Can we borrow your vibrators?

My aunt's cook, Ramesh, was an utter sensualist. His food was so delicious that each mouthful entered my body like some ethereal nectar. I could barely stand to chew it. One night when I was alone in the house, I asked Ramesh if he had ever cooked fish. He said of course, many times, but not in this house. He said he had a special fish curry that he used to make for his previous employer, a Swiss engineer who lived in Bombay for three years. I asked if he could make it for me and he nodded. I was surprised.

"What, here?" I asked, laughing. "In this pure vegetarian household?"

He nodded again, said, "No problem" in English, and left the house. It was dark outside. Where would he find fish at this time of the night?

Ramesh returned in ten minutes with a thick filet of *surmai* in his hand. He had begged it from the Muslim cook on the seventh floor. I stood there with my mouth open, as excited as a little girl. Ramesh was shy, and after a few minutes of pretending that he was alone in the kitchen, he turned to me blushing and asked if I wouldn't prefer to sit in the living room until the curry rice was ready. I said, No, I had to watch him. And, I said to his burning red neck, he had to join me in eating the meal. At that he giggled and stammered: "No, no, *memsahib*, how can I, you are not yet married, it will be a shame on us."

The fish curry was astonishing, its flavors as distinct, yet as blended, as a rainbow. I took two bites of the curry rice and, without realizing, started to cry. Ramesh stood at the far end of the kitchen, watching me eat my first few bites, to be sure I approved. When he saw my tears, he approached me nervously. "It is too much chili, *memsahib*?" he asked anxiously. "Shall I give you a little yogurt?" I took control of myself and wiped away the tears of joy.

The gift of his curry was profound. After years of eating fish fingers in America, my body was overwhelmed by the real taste of fish.

I resumed eating. I inquired whether Ramesh was from Goa. He smiled broadly and said yes. "Don't you drink *feni* with your dinner?" I asked. "Let's have some."

He shook his head sorrowfully. "*Memsahib*, very sorry, but this is not possible. If I drink in this house, I will lose my job."

"I understand," I said. "Where can I get some for myself?"

"No problem," he said in English. He walked into the adjoining servant's room where he unrolled his bed every night, came back with a bottle of clear liquid, plucked a teacup off the drying rack and poured out a small amount. He handed it to me, still grinning. "Very strong, *memsahib*!" he warned. "Only for sipping."

I took the cup from him and drank the liquid in one gulp. The burn down my throat was smooth, and filled my face with heat. Ramesh watched me with open mouth and rapidly shifting eyes.

"It's very good," I acknowledged, and held out my cup. "One for me and one for you," I said, motioning Ramesh to get himself a cup.

Ramesh shook his head. "Sorry, *memsahib*. I am happy for you, but it is not possible for me."

"Call me Renu." I smiled at him. "When you call me *memsahib* it feels like you're talking about someone else."

"Want to come with me and get your hair done? You have very little imagination, I think, always leaving your hair open like that. Just collects dust all day. My Chinese hairdresser is very good. She'll show you some tricks. And while we're there, I'll tell her to fix your blackheads. You really should get them removed before it's too late. And also that hair on your chin looks like a nanny goat. There are only two or three of them, but my god, how vulgar! What will people think?"

"Do Indian men really care about my blackheads?" I teased my aunt. "I think it's just an obsession for Indian women. None of my American boyfriends ever notices such things."

"That's exactly why I'm telling you not to waste yourself on an American boy. Leave them for those girls who aren't so eligible. Americans will marry anyone, you know. Comes from not having a sense of their own history. Mongrels, all of them."

To do or not to do Indians, that was the question. I had more than a month to go in Bombay. Could my aunt really rustle up an interesting man for me? To be or not to be sexual around my relatives, that was the real issue.

"Okay. Find me someone. But no virgins. And no anatomical illiterates. And no chaperones, meddlers or parents, please."

My aunt looked at me in shock—she couldn't believe I'd said yes. She smirked with ill-concealed victory, then broke into a triumphant, generous laugh.

"You naughty girl, there's nothing wrong with virgins! In fact, it's a blessing because you can teach them exactly how you want it. Just don't brag about where you got all your experience."

Ramesh and I began a series of nightly trysts. He cooked me fish—one piece was enough to satiate my craving—and then watched me eat. It took me close to an hour to eat the single piece of fish and the bowlful of rice. The flavors were so intense, so overpowering, that I had to stop after each mouthful and let my quivering taste buds settle into some semblance of calm. If I took two bites in a row, my stomach felt unbearably full, as though I had eaten well beyond my limit and would burst.

After that first night, Ramesh saw that conversation was not the right accompaniment for my meal. Instead, he settled down on his haunches and stared at me with intense fascination as I ate. I might as well have been a child or an animal, given the ease with which this normally deferential, barely literate employee entered into my space. If my aunt had seen the two of us together in the kitchen, sitting so intimately on the bare floor, she would have suspected the worst—that I had lost my mind and become the cook's lover.

Never in my life in Bombay had I been able to look a male servant in the eye without overtones of power, dominance, cruelty,

indifference. But every mouthful of Ramesh's fish became a whirl-
pool flooding my entire being with ecstasy. I was too dazed to be
bothered with the codes of domestic hierarchy. With great difficulty I softened my moans of pleasure into mewing sounds, which
Ramesh took as a signal to bring out the *feni*, surreptitiously presented in a teacup.

"Haven't you found someone yet?" I asked my aunt impatiently.
She looked at me with tired eyes. She'd been on the phone non-
stop for the past few days. Quite a few of the thirty "sight unseen"
prospects had moved to the United States for postgraduate studies. Several others were engaged to be married, or close to it. Two
families with Gandhian roots were morally and ethically opposed
to green card marriages. And word had gotten around that my sister had divorced her Bombay–born-and-bred husband. His unhappy family had put out the word that the girls in our family
were fickle and bossy.

Ramesh's fish was having an explosive impact on me. The curry
rice seemed to wander off the normal digestive route and lodge
instead in my groin, creating a slow burn. I hungered for contact.
Bombay was unexplored sexual territory for me, still connected in
my mind to the trusting dependencies of childhood.

I asked Ramesh about the men in the apartment building. He
was incredulous that I wanted information on servants, drivers,
watchmen and janitors, as those were the only men he knew. But
he answered my questions with great gusto. Who were the most
handsome? Who bragged about being the most virile? Which of
them were married, which had girlfriends, who visited prostitutes? Ramesh had an astonishing range of information about most
of the domestics—apparently these men let their guard down
around the sweet-natured cook. Ramesh related these stories to
me with the childlike trust I associated with a prepubescent boy. I
was surprised to discover that he was married and had three children in his village, whom he saw perhaps once or twice in a year.

One night after an exquisite meal of several kinds of spiced roe,
I told Ramesh that Big Memsahib was searching out a husband for
me. The cook's eyes lit up and he broke into a grin. In a rush of

sentences he congratulated me, blessed me with good luck and fertility and shared his conviction that I would be matched to a very good man. Seeing my skepticism, he stopped smiling. "Bad thoughts will hinder the process," he gently scolded.

I looked hard at Ramesh, wondering whether I could trust him with my deepest desires. His youthful face stared back at me, still glowing with the news of my impending matrimony.

I put his hand on my forehead and told him to feel the heat. He admitted that my skin felt feverish. I nodded slowly and added that I felt the same fever burning in my groin and placed my hand meaningfully over my pubis. Ramesh did not understand at first, but then his mouth fell open. He lost his balance and fell forward, almost landing in the remains of the food. He sprang up and brushed himself off.

"You think only men feel a burning between their legs?" I asked sharply.

Ramesh coughed nervously, then began laughing with his hand clamped over his mouth. "*Memsahib*," he said, smiling, "the truth is that if you take a lover from among us poor servants, we will definitely lose our jobs. But if you don't care whether we work or starve, then surely someone among the servants is senseless enough to say yes. Do you want me to ask around?"

Ramesh's words were like a slap in the face; I felt the sour taste of shame in my mouth. Is that what I had seriously been contemplating? Did I expect reciprocation of my sexual urge from men who were in constant fear of being sacked, humiliated, abandoned?

"I didn't make myself clear," I said. "I don't want anyone losing their job, least of all you. So just think very carefully before you do anything. But if there is a *sahib* in the building—unmarried, good-humored, a decent person—who might be alone, just the way I am, then perhaps you could mention to one of his servants that Big Memsahib's foreign-returned niece is in town for a while and likes to have company in the evenings."

Ramesh nodded and cleared the plates. He disappeared into the back room and returned with two teacups of *feni*. Without a word, he placed one cup in front of me and took the other in his own hand.

"*Chin-chin,*" I murmured, and tapped my cup against his in salute.

"You can use my bed," Ramesh offered before draining his cup in one gulp.

"I just don't know why I'm having such bad luck finding someone for you. When you need them, these dashing Romeos disappear into the woodwork like cockroaches."

In a week of hunting, my aunt had found no one. She was beginning to despair. She had lost her appetite. In the past, there had been nothing easier than finding partners for her stable of youngsters.

"I wish your mother had told me openly about your sister's divorce. Honestly, I could have saved face and at least come up with *some* bloody excuse, even if it was a complete lie, who cares, in this city it's all about appearances. It's one thing for you children to have forgotten our Indian customs, but I can't understand what happens to women like your mother when they move abroad. Do they get amnesia or what?"

"My parents supported her divorce. They're quite wonderful that way. If any of us kids are in trouble, they rally around without judgment."

"What a waste, I tell you. Those two were good for each other, really good. The problem was that they waited too long to have children. You have to know how to work a marriage!"

Divorce was a sore topic for matchmakers like my aunt. They took personal offense at the inability of couples to muddle along through life.

"Anyway, Renu darling, there's still hope for you. I've sent your horoscope to be matched through a computer service. Only thing is, the boy may be of a family I don't know. If someone turns up, naturally we will do a full investigation on him. These days you can hire a detective at very decent prices—it's almost become routine, you know, with these caste-no-bar marriages happening all over the place. Personally I can't imagine being married to anyone besides a Gujarati, but youngsters these days seem to have quite the imagination that way, probably comes from reading too many novels. Oh, look, there's someone at the door."

My aunt's bulk blocked the doorway and I couldn't see over her shoulder. There was a brief tussle at the entrance and then she dragged in a protesting young man carrying a ribboned box of sweets. His name was Nemesh Shah, said my aunt, and he was a distant cousin. He looked no older than nineteen or twenty. He shook my hand firmly and introduced himself as Nemo. He said he was just passing through and his mother had sent him with the sweets, and no he really didn't want any tea and he had to get going to the club. I asked Nemo for a ride to the club and he assented.

We drove in silence, Nemo in front with the driver, me in the back. Once at the club, Nemo visibly relaxed. As we signed in, a group of Nemo's friends greeted him with resounding back slaps and cheery hellos. They looked older than Nemo. I studied his face more carefully and saw lines at the corners of his eyes. He was older than I'd thought.

"This is Renu. She lives in my building. She's visiting from the States."

All smiles, the friends began walking toward the tennis courts. I placed my hand on Nemo's arm, signaling him to hang back for a minute.

"I didn't realize we're in the same building! Auntie just said you were a distant relative."

"Oh, that's an old joke, you know, how we're all supposed to be 'related.' Your parents and mine are old friends. We must have met when we were kids."

"So did my aunt call and tell your mother that I was in town?"

"No, no, not at all. The servants were talking, and I overheard them discussing you. Your chap Ramesh is always up there chatting with our cook Hassan."

"You're the ones with the Muslim cook? But . . . but you're Gujaratis!" I sputtered.

Nemesh laughed. "My mother is a Bohra Muslim. Hassan is from her father's village. He's a fantastic cook. Even if the religious fanatics descended on us, the family wouldn't part with Hassan."

Nemesh's laughter brought a mischievous sparkle to his eyes. His smile was brilliant, open, lingering. I looked at him in astonishment, and he stared back. Fast work on the part of Ramesh— here was the *sahib* of his choice. I felt the thrill of the chase engulfing me.

"You . . . you must be circumcised!" I blurted out before I could stop myself. Nemo, who had just turned away to follow his friends, stopped dead in his tracks.

"I've heard about you foreign girls being bold, but honestly, this takes the cake! How would you know?"

"Servants these days know everything." I chuckled. "Isn't Hassan a barber as well as a cook?"

Nemo slapped his forehead in mock distress. His lingering smile proclaimed a sweet challenge.

That night Ramesh and I had an urgent *tête-à-tête*. I congratulated him on his quick work, then interrogated him about Nemo. How old? Not sure, somewhere between twenty-three and twenty-six. Work? Family business, garment manufacturing. Marital status? Single. Series of girlfriends the family had trouble with, and Nemo *sahib* was too obedient to go against his parents' wishes—but too passionate to miss any sexual opportunity. Hassan had often turned over his bed to the *sahib*. Very good lover, according to Hassan, very satisfying to his women. Girls begging not to be sent home in the morning. Some mornings sleepy *sahib* even came to breakfast with the girl's juices on his unwashed face, and mother holding her nose tightly, saying not to eat fish so early in the day. Mother prefers nice Jain Gujarati girl for her son, even though she herself is Muslim. Boy has brought home all kinds—Hindu, Muslim, Parsee, Christian, foreign. All leave Hassan's bed with big-big red bug bites. For the first time I noticed that Ramesh himself had red marks on his arms and neck.

"Who else has been sleeping in Hassan's bed?" I asked, pointing at the bumps. He blushed and turned away but seemed pleased to have been caught. "Hassan is my best friend," he whispered confidentially.

"Darling, I have the most exciting news! Two very nice boys are coming from the suburbs, one for lunch, the other for tea. The lunch-*wallah* is just back from an assignment in Delhi. He's quite shy, so you'll have to do your best to draw him out. Normally, of course, these boys would come with their mother or someone, and are not used to having to speak for themselves, if you know what I mean. But these two are willing to try. The tea-*wallah* actually lives in the U.S. and, surprise-surprise! is in town looking for a wife. He lives in Detroit or Denver or Delaware or something."

My aunt looked quite relaxed as she chatted about the boys from the suburbs. I knew she felt tremendously relieved at having drummed up some hopefuls. Ramesh was preparing another one of his master meals in the kitchen, and the wonderful smells had us feeling slightly tipsy.

"I'd like to invite Nemo over for the day as well, if you don't mind," I said. "He's easygoing and comfortable with everyone, and that way the two guys won't feel like it's us against them, okay?"

"Hmmm. That's not a bad idea, Renu. Why didn't I think of it? That Nemo, isn't he darling? He's going to be quite a catch one of these days when he grows up. They're all so sweet until a certain age, and then, I don't know exactly what, but something happens."

Lunch-*wallah* turned out to be a fashion photographer, just as shy as my aunt had warned. The ubiquitous Indian mustache sat dark and thick over his lips, and his round face was made even rounder by comically oversized glasses. Mohan photographed mostly teenage boys from the suburbs who were hoping to make it big in modeling. He had brought along his portfolio and passed it to my aunt, who quickly immersed herself in the semi-nude shots of airbrushed hopefuls. She murmured and clucked over each provocatively posed boy, and even took down the names of a few of them.

Mohan asked me a series of questions about life in the States, but before I could answer he interrupted me.

"You have such a straight nose!" he stated emphatically. "You should consider modeling."

The doorbell rang and I excused myself to answer. Nemo stood at the door, his wet hair hanging in a curled bunch across his forehead. I tried to read his face, but like every good Indian, he had on his social mask. He sensed the impatience in my eyes and produced a bouquet of flowers from behind his back. He held my gaze warmly, effortlessly, like an old friend. Ramesh's cot and mattress swam into my mind's eye. Just that morning the cook and I had fumigated the cotton bedding and set it out in the sun. It would be baked dry and clean, ready for a post-lunch respite.

Nemo's arrival caught Mohan by surprise. He did not like surprises. He thawed a little when I introduced Nemo as my distant cousin, and further relaxed when he saw the flowers were meant for my aunt. Finally he smiled and commented on the family resemblance. Ramesh brought out the food, and my aunt and I attacked it in silence.

As expected, Nemo put Mohan at ease, and the two men chatted up a storm through Ramesh's glorious lunch. As happened after every meal by Ramesh, I sat in stunned silence. Mohan grew more animated, his voice rising higher and higher, making him seem like a twelve-year-old. At one point my aunt looked at me inquiringly, and I shook my head in a definite No. She nodded agreement and winked at me.

Mohan had an appointment right after lunch, so he left in a hurry. As the door shut behind him, my aunt sighed with a mixture of frustration and relief. She declared that she needed a recharge before the next one arrived, and retired to her bedroom for a nap. Ramesh cleared the table and brought out cups of *feni* for Nemo and myself. He announced that he would be gone for many, *many* hours, buying food for the evening. Ramesh was nothing less than a genius.

There is no greater aphrodisiac for me than having a man open himself up to my probing, revealing himself with subtlety, honesty and wit. The *feni* proved to be just the right lubricant to bring out Nemo's eloquence. He was surprised more than once at my questions, but he spoke with ease about his family, his girlfriends, his work, his dreams. I asked questions that I knew would provoke laughter. His response brought the heat to my face and I knew he could see the flush. We reached for each other's hands at the same moment, our fingers greedily entwined on top of the table, our bare feet hotly entangled beneath. I leaned over and fed him *feni* from my mouth. We melted together at the lips, rolling the strong liquor around, allowing it to blister our palates and tongues. Like divine Indra exploding under his mythical burden, I felt a thousand vagina-eyes swelling and surging along the length and breadth of my skin.

*   *   *

Ramesh had left his bed tidy and turned on the fan to keep out flies. There was still much left to be said between Nemo and myself, but the dialogue now would be wordless. He sat on the mattress with his back against the wall and I sat on his lap with his hands under my clothes. With shirts unbuttoned, our erect nipples prodded each other's skin, sizzling like hot coals on ice. Like the slowpoke game of childhood, where each contestant "raced" to be the last one to the finish line, I set the pace for the slowest, most unhurried arousal.

I swept my tongue across his nipples, and they wrinkled and reddened. I struck them again and again until they were purple and bulging. The twin ridges of his ribs rising over his sunken stomach signaled the breath held in anticipation. I bit a nipple. He turned his dilating eyes on me, struggling to focus, pleading, laughing, challenging me to arouse him further.

Nemo's hungry gaze was thrilling. Not since childhood had I felt comfortable enough to drown in the gaze of an Indian man; not since viewing those open-shirted, sardonic actors whose posters used to line my walls. Searing eyes, fleshy pink mouths, chests thrown back with the promise of unending embrace. But this was no movie star in bed with me. I felt more and more like I was making love to a beloved companion. We must have met as children and perhaps even snuck an embrace or two in a dark corridor.

Nemo curled his legs around my back and rolled me over. Finding my armpits unshaven, he rubbed his nose in the soft tangles. The thousand vagina-eyes coalesced into the throbbing recesses under my arms and between my legs, and soon we were wrestling on the bed. The drops of his musk scent spread slickly over me as we stroked together in the hot afternoon breeze. I spread apart his lips to get a look at his tongue. Out it came, dangling over me like the hood of a cobra. I grabbed at it with my teeth, but he moved down, down, winding and coiling his tongue around and between my thighs, the slow full burn of a heated rope climbing inside me, opening me wider and wider. My thighs stretched to their limits, and I tucked my feet under his chest as my legs began to tremble. His tongue braved the currents like a homing salmon climbing the steep rapids of my desire. I felt my breathing begin to stall, felt the rush of blood humming in my ears, heard my mind command, "Inhale!" but the tongue hammering out a Morse code on my aching, stretching skin signaled a different demand, and there was no breath to be had because my nose and lungs and mouth and arms had all rushed down and were pushing up from under his tongue, pushing up a molten iceberg of immense proportions through the tightening mesh of his strokes and like snow yielding to water, his pressing tongue melted into the tunneling wave of my heat, which finally erupted through the roof of his mouth. My screams shot through the ceiling and down the shuddering walls, scattering into the skyscrapers of Bombay.

At five o'clock Ramesh knocked and cracked open the door just enough to announce it would soon be teatime. I was dozing and oozing, too aroused to actually sleep. I sniffed the odor on Nemo's fingers and brushed against his distinctly fishy mouth. Nemo couldn't possibly settle for an arranged marriage either.

I remembered the way the lines around his mouth hardened with anger when he'd told me how he had allowed his mother once, just once, to "bring a girl home." It was maddening. The parents were pigs, disgusting, selling their daughter like the newest gadget from Hong Kong. The girl couldn't even look him in the eye—or anyone else, for that matter. She was a Bohra girl, so beautiful . . . fifteen, maybe sixteen. Nemo was so upset, he took her father by the collar and told him to get out of his house. He was horrified at their expectation that he feel excited by this young chit of a girl. He asked his mother whether she was planning to pimp his younger sister the same way. Nemo had mimed a hard slap across the face, and I'd winced in sympathy.

It didn't end there. Nemo had become "eligible." Complete strangers found some excuse or other to parade their daughters in front of him—at weddings, movies, even right there in the building while he was waiting for the lift; he started taking the stairs because of them. He dreamed of running away to some country like the U.S., where no one would know him, where no girl would be dragged in front of him, where no parents would dare shower their filthy money on him.

\*   \*   \*

Tea-*wallah* introduced himself as Nick. "Short for Nikhil?" I asked blandly, and he smiled sheepishly. He'd been born and raised in the U.S., and every member of his family had a practical Anglo nickname for their traditional Indian appellations: Jay for Jayant, Vicki for Malavika, Candy for Kundanika, Sid for Siddhartha. Nick was a software programmer being actively recruited by a company in Bangalore. He hadn't been back to India since childhood, and was here to check out the scene.

Nemo sat beside me, the fingers of his left hand trailing secretly along the inside of my thighs. He seemed to know a lot about software, and soon Nick and he were heatedly debating the merits of various accounting programs. I let my head rest against the back of the chair and closed my eyes. Nemo's fingers were like tentacles of dry ice, alternately scalding and freezing the surface of my skin. He felt the trembling in my muscles and dug deeper in acknowledgment.

Ramesh brought out the fragrant ginger tea and an assortment of crisp patties and cutlets. Two he placed directly on my plate, and I knew without being told that they were fish patties. I asked Nick whether he was vegetarian, and he said he was. "Too bad," I said, popping one of the patties into Nemo's mouth. An uncertain smile hovered around my aunt's lips as she registered this sudden intimacy. Propelling food into the mouth uninvited was an accepted Indian custom, but generally reserved for relatives and intimates.

It would be just a matter of time before I told my aunt that Nemo and I were lovers. However conservative she appeared on the surface, she cherished her confidential relationships with her nieces and nephews. We all confided in her, and she maintained our trust without exception.

After a while, Nick forgot that he had come to see me, so animated was his conversation with Nemo. My aunt and I excused ourselves from the table and retired to the swing on the balcony.

"The things you don't find out about young men until you have to deal with them alone," sighed my aunt. "Usually, when the boy comes to see the girl, it's us oldies who do all the talking, you know. This rule of yours of not allowing parents to accompany their sons is turning out to be a social disaster!"

My aunt paused. "You really should let me take you to the hair-dresser, Renu. I'm sick of seeing your hair flying in all directions. How many Indian women do you see roaming around with their long hair open?"

"That's the first time you've ever referred to me as a woman. Up to this point I've always been a girl. What happened?"

My aunt looked at me as though I were daft. "Honestly, darling, you find the most unusual ways to torture your old auntie." I took her hand in mine and massaged her fingers. Her eyes took on a faraway look and she sank back against the padded silk of the swing. "Well, if all goes well you'll be married soon. It's hard to re-main a girl once you're married."

"You know, Nemo isn't nearly as young as you think."

"Hmmm . . . ." My aunt exhaled pleasurably as I pressed the ball of her thumb. "It's his Muslim blood. Makes him look more childish."

"He's just two years younger than me, you know, twenty-five."

"He's that old?" My aunt looked at me lazily. "I suppose I'm al-ways confusing him with his younger brother."

"How come Nemo didn't make it onto your list?" I whispered. My aunt's arm tensed and she drew away.

"In the old days, we were all families of equal standing. It didn't matter whether we were Muslim or Hindu. Not anymore."

"You know," I said, choosing my words carefully, "I'm not really looking for a man to marry at this point. I love you and was curi-ous to see who you'd pull out of your hat, but I don't think I'm des-tined to be married anytime soon."

"Hunh!" she snorted. "That's what they all say, until they tie the knot. Then they wonder how they managed to live so long with-out it!"

"But honestly, Auntie, is it the sex or the marriage that people find so thrilling?"

She rolled her eyes and swatted me on the arm. "You know you can't ask that around here. Most have never had the one without the other."

"But I have, and so have my sisters and most of my cousins. You know that."

My aunt lashed at me with the loose end of her chiffon sari. "You youngsters think you'll end up in fairy-tale marriages because you've slept with a few horny men? You're wrong. Eventually you'll come to see the error of your ways. We're from a different generation—duty first, and all that. We hardly even knew that sex was something separate from marriage. We've all been brought up in terror of it."

She sprang off the ornately decorated metal swing, which jangled with the sudden movement. Her eyes betrayed her hurt.

"You obviously don't understand that an old woman like me would be forgotten like a rusted nail in the wall if I didn't find some way to keep myself in the picture. At least I make the effort to get to know all of you. I do a decent job, all in all."

I took her hand and kissed it. "I understand all that," I said gently. "But I'm talking about me. Things have changed, and you know it." My aunt turned to go, but I held onto her hand. She sighed, and tilted my chin upwards.

"I don't want to know," she whispered. "Do what you must do, but please be discreet. *I don't want to know.* All I can say is, don't ruin your chances for the future. You might just change your mind."

Inside, the two men stood up and walked towards the front door. The visit was over. At the last minute Nick remembered my aunt and me and turned to wave good-bye. Nemo graciously saw him out the front door, then staggered back to the couch and flopped down with a thud.

My aunt whispered to me under her breath, "Isn't he the cutest? You may think it's all your good luck, but it's not. I told his cook Hussan that you were in town and that you needed a little company. You owe me one." She wiggled her bulky hips at me and blew me a wet kiss.

I gasped. My own aunt setting me up for an affair? I felt the knot of anxiety tightening in my stomach. My aunt's eyes darted hungrily over Nemo, taking in his languid limbs and his fatigue-softened lips. She rubbed her abdomen and sighed.

"Ramesh, oh, Ramesh," she called. "Where are you hiding, my love? I wonder if Ramesh has learned anything useful from that boyfriend of his. Don't know what it is, but these days I feel like eating fish."

*Susan St. Aubin*

❧

# Glory

The five months Evelyn spent at cooking school, she never learned a thing she didn't know. Béchamel sauce? White sauce? How to parboil vegetables and cut them up for hors d'oeuvres? She'd learned all this, and more, from *her* mother, who wasn't even a particularly accomplished cook. Where were those guys in her class all those years when her mother showed her how to stir a sauce creamy smooth, or how to boil an egg in salted water so the shell wouldn't crack? Everything seemed new to them, as though they'd never thought about how food got to the table. With each tip from Gregory, the instructor, they smiled at each other, licking their lips and sometimes even stroking each other's backs. Evelyn felt invisible. "They're all gay," whispered Charlotte, the other woman student.

They weren't, of course. Laurent wasn't. Evelyn felt there was something promising in the way he stared right through her rather than around her like the others did. Laurent's reasons for ignoring her had nothing to do with disinterest—he was a serious student. Evelyn admired the way his knife molded radishes into roses or tulips and carrots into birds—unlike the others, he went far beyond Gregory's limited skills. He told Evelyn he'd worked in restaurants in France. She was charmed by his accent and his long brown hair, which he was required to wear in a net just like Charlotte and Evelyn.

She liked to watch his hands as they scraped and sculpted vegetables—sinuous, long-fingered hands that seemed to blend with the paring knife they held. In her head she made a film of those hands all over her—caressing her hair, her shoulders, her ass. She ran it frequently to alleviate the boredom of her days at school. In this private movie, Laurent's fingers noodled her clit and buttered her cunt; then he ate her like a creamy pudding.

Charlotte wrinkled her nose when he walked by, but Evelyn found his scent erotic. She thought of him whenever she picked up a garlic press or sliced a lemon in half with one of the school's cheap, dull knives. A lemon garlic dressing with a hint of fresh pepper, that was Laurent. Her mind wandered to him several times a day, but to Laurent food was just food, and his concentration on that was perfect.

There was only one bathroom upstairs near the experimental kitchens where classes were held, though the restaurant downstairs, where the advanced students practiced their skills on the public, had the usual men's and ladies' rooms.

"We're all boys up here," Gregory told Evelyn and Charlotte on their first day, "or we *were*." He forced a smile at them. "But we *need* more female chefs, and of course we must have them."

"Chefs and chefettes," one of the boys said, wriggling his fingers above his head as he spun around once on his tiptoes, like a self-propelled top.

Charlotte stared at the floor while everyone laughed.

"They're disgusting," she told Evelyn later in the bathroom, where they crowded in front of the small mirror over a rust-stained sink, combing their hair.

In this bathroom were two stalls and a small rusty urinal, which Evelyn thought was a sink until Charlotte, who had three brothers, set her straight. She'd never been in a men's room before, and wondered how men felt about peeing in public like that. How could they stand next to each other, as her boyfriend Hal described it, looking straight ahead, never down or to the side? Since this urinal was for two people only, Evelyn realized the guys must often use the stalls—on their breaks, they went in three and four at a time.

Charlotte wore more makeup than Evelyn had ever seen on a person offstage. Her eyes were outlined in black and circled with shades of silver, blue and green, like a tropical bird's. Charlotte told her the thick eyelashes she applied every day were made of real mink.

"Did you ever think of doing something with your eyes?" Charlotte asked her.

"What do you mean?"

"Makeup," Charlotte answered. "Here—I could lend you this." She handed Evelyn a pot of green gloss. "Put some on your lids. It'll bring out the color of your eyes."

"Not my style," said Evelyn, handing back the gloss. She told Charlotte she was thinking of getting her hair cut short and adding more piercings to her ears—one more in each lobe, and another on the side of her left ear.

Charlotte opened her mouth, speechless. She was easily shocked. Evelyn loved to walk down the street with her after school and pick out some innocuous man feeding quarters into a parking meter, then whisper in Charlotte's ear, "See that guy? He's gonna turn around with his dick out, what do you bet?"

Every time Charlotte would gasp, and then say, "Oh, you!" when Evelyn started to laugh. As they walked back to the kitchen, Evelyn thought she'd get a silver ring through the top of her ear just because it would be such a treat to see Charlotte's reaction.

When they picked up their spoons she said to Charlotte, "I saw a guy last week who had a real demitasse spoon hanging from his ear. I could have one made into an earring."

"You *wouldn't*," gasped Charlotte. "The weight would pull your ear out of shape."

Laurent stood on Evelyn's left side, muttering to himself in French as he scraped the side of the bowl in which he was beating eggs for a practice omelet.

"What?" Evelyn asked, thinking for a minute that he spoke to her, perhaps about spoon earrings; she recognized a French word, coming back to her from high school. *"Cuiller,"* she thought she heard. "Inferior utensils," said Laurent. "Inferior everything in this place. It is impossible."

That afternoon Evelyn left early for her break and found Laurent still at the bathroom mirror combing his long red-brown hair.

"You're here too soon," he said.

"I couldn't wait." She held the door open.

He shrugged. "Come in. I don't mind. Not if you don't. Of course, that Charlotte, she would be shocked if she's right behind you, eh?"

Evelyn smiled and came all the way in, letting the door swing shut behind her.

"Don't worry," he said, "I'm finished. But look." He walked into one of the stalls. "Have you seen this?"

She stuck her head into the stall.

"Go into the next one," he said. When she did, she saw Laurent's finger wiggling through a hole just below her waist. Around and around went the finger, side to side. Laurent bent down and put his eye to it. She watched the brown iris surrounded by viscous white, an eyeball cut off from a human body. She put her finger to the hole, and Laurent's eyeball jerked away.

"Hey," he squawked.

She ran her finger around the edge of the opening, which was neatly cut and filed smooth.

Laurent leaned against the door of her stall. "You know what goes on in there?" he said. "You know what this is for?"

"To watch?" she asked.

"Yes, there's a good view. But there's more."

Laurent came into her stall and stuck two fingers into the hole beside her fingers.

"What is almost this big?" he whispered in her ear. "A cock! He sticks his cock in."

His long vowels and *s*'s lingered in her ears. "You see?" he said. "It's for more than to watch. The glory hole, they call it. Glory!" He laughed through his nose.

Evelyn felt his smooth warm fingers against hers in the hole. She heard the restroom door open; she heard Charlotte suck in her breath as the door closed.

"I was just leaving," Laurent called, withdrawing his hand. When he was gone, Evelyn shut the door to her stall and sat down.

The restroom door swung open again and Charlotte came in, slamming the door to the other stall.

"That guy's got some nerve," she said. "What on earth was he still doing in here?"

Evelyn felt no obligation to answer; stalls were private. Beside her, Charlotte sniffed, flushed, and stood up, snapping the elastic of her underpants and tights as she pulled them up.

At the sink she said, "*I* wouldn't have stayed in here a second with him."

Evelyn tried a Laurent shrug. "He was just combing his hair."

"Hah," said Charlotte. "You can see a lot in this mirror."

"He wasn't looking at the mirror. You saw us. We were looking in the stall." She waited for Charlotte to ask what they were looking at, but she put her comb back in her purse and left Evelyn alone at the mirror.

The next day the hole in the stall seemed larger. Was someone working on it, or was vigorous use eroding the metal? When she ran her fingers around the edges, it felt freshly cut and not quite so smooth. By Friday the hole was even bigger, and edged with slick gray electrical tape. As she sat on the toilet, Evelyn slipped a fist through—a tight but not impossible squeeze. She moved her hand around and stretched her fingers into the next stall, feeling the smooth tape against her wrist.

Charlotte was alone at the mirror, fixing a false eyelash that had almost slipped into her soufflé that morning. Evelyn withdrew her hand, leaving her fingers on the edge. Charlotte rinsed her hands at the sink, then came into the stall. Evelyn heard the lock click and Charlotte's sigh as she sat down, making the toilet seat creak. Her urine hissed into the toilet bowl. Evelyn pulled her fingers out and put her eye to the hole. Charlotte was just standing up; her rump flashed pink and white as she pulled up her lace-trimmed underpants and brown tights. Evelyn watched Charlotte's long skirt roll down over her tights, and watched her smooth herself with her hands, front and back, and slide open the lock on the stall door.

When Evelyn stood up and opened her door, Charlotte was at the mirror combing her hair. "Better hurry," she said. "We've got one minute." Evelyn washed her hands, then ran them wet through her hair and pulled her hairnet back on.

The next morning Evelyn stood beside Laurent at the long counter as Gregory rapped on his lectern with a wooden spoon, calling the class to order.

"Today is soufflé day again," he said.

Laurent muttered to Evelyn, "Every day is soufflé day. These people never learn, so all we do is soufflé, soufflé." He did a shuffling dance in place. Gregory rapped with his spoon again, and began the lesson.

"How you break the eggs does matter," he announced as he hit them sharply against one of the two metal bowls before him, separating whites from yolks with one hand.

Laurent matched his deftness while the others shrieked and laughed, dropping eggs to the floor, smearing their arms with yolk, and getting bits of eggshell stuck to their noses and eyebrows. They beat the yolks first, then the whites, then both together.

"When I have my own restaurant," Laurent told Evelyn, "I'll call it *Chouette*."

"What's *chouette*?" she asked.

"It's a wonder, fine, super," he said, stopping to wave his hand. "It also means 'owl.' Intelligence. An intelligent nightspot. I want the world's most famous night restaurant. I want to be known for that glory."

"Mr. Gagne," Gregory said, "your eggs have fallen. You cannot stop beating a soufflé in the middle like that."

"Do owls lay eggs?" whispered Evelyn. "You could just do omelets and soufflés out of all sorts of unusual eggs, like owl eggs. Or duck eggs. Chinese restaurants use duck eggs."

Laurent snorted. "Oh, I'd do more than eggs," he said. "This would not just be some soufflé cafe." Once their soufflés were in the ovens, the boys left for their break. Laurent stayed behind, as he often did, going into the bathroom between the men's break and the women's.

"Mr. Gagne, Mr. Gagne," Gregory would say, "you'll have no break if you don't leave now," and he would go.

Evelyn began slipping out early, just as the men were coming back. Their instructor glared, but what could he say? She could be ill, she could have her period; blood could be running down her legs. He wouldn't want to ask. She never again caught Laurent in the restroom as she planned. Sometimes he was just on his way out and would hold the door open for her with a smile, but more frequently he was nowhere in sight.

"Do they ever *do* anything in there?" she whispered to Laurent once as they passed each other. He held the restroom door open and leaned his head in after her. "No, mostly looking," he answered. "Giggling. There's no time. What can you do in ten minutes?" He let the door swing shut.

Although Evelyn liked a man who would scorn such a short time frame, she could think of a lot to do with Laurent in ten minutes. Her mind was a projector through which she ran images of herself and Laurent in the restroom stalls.

She imagines that when she sticks her fist through the hole, smooth against the padded sides, it collides with something soft— the flesh of Laurent's ass. She presses further until her hand is out the other side, the sides of the opening slipping against her forearm, the hole itself like a living, breathing beast against her arm. Her fingers search, feeling the smoothness of Laurent and the muscles beneath the soft surface. She's looking for hardness, for a penis, but she doesn't find it; he's standing with his back to the hole. As he bends over, she feels his muscles tighten and stretch.

What do the boys do in ten minutes? This, she thinks. She pulls her arm out of the hole, licks her fingers, puts it back. Her wet blind hand feels the soft hair on his ass, glides down the crack, pushing in, curious as a cock probing, sliding against the skin as her fingers enter him, smooth as a tanned deer hide.

She pushes further—two fingers, three. He moans. She stops. Does he like this? Hate it? Hate her for treating him like a faggot, like a girl? Would he push her hand away, like Hal did once when she reached one hand back there while he was balling her? No hands allowed, he'd whispered. But this time it was all hands.

What would she run into up there? What if she got shit in her fingernails, or even pulled out a turd? She makes herself think of a chocolate soufflé, light, fluffy, creamy sweet. We take it in our mouths and nobody finds that disgusting. We slosh it around our teeth, over and under our tongues; we swallow the glutinous, liquefied mass, we lick our teeth, we take another bite.

She has four fingers and the tip of her thumb up Laurent's smooth hole, the flesh tight yet yielding as she pushes. Imagine each bit of chocolate soufflé as it glides down the esophagus, its coolness passing through the chest and into the stomach where the milk and eggs and nutrition of it are absorbed, leaving behind the unnecessary brown fluff that floats down and is squeezed through the tubular intestines, down and out.

Evelyn thinks of peristalsis as her hand, breaking through a tight ring of muscle, pops into a thick softness. She moves her fist up and down. Laurent bends towards her, moving himself on her hand, until, with a shout, he slides away.

At the sound of the bathroom door swinging open, Evelyn pulled her hand out of the hole.

"Evelyn? You there?" Charlotte came into the next stall, slamming the door.

"Yeah, right here." Evelyn put her hand down to her cunt and twisted her fist around in its wetness. Two fingers up herself, three—she was slick enough to get her whole hand in. It was different from the way she imagined Laurent's ass—moister and more spacious. Half her hand was in, but she couldn't reach all the way up.

She waited for Charlotte to peek through the opening, but she still hadn't noticed it was there. Instead, she chattered about some guy she was going out with who had this tiny tattoo of a rose on his left earlobe that looked just like an earring. "It's the neatest thing you ever saw," said Charlotte.

Evelyn felt like yelling, "Hey, I can't come unless you shut up," but that might push Charlotte beyond the edge of mere shock. Breathing carefully, she moved the four fingers in her cunt around in circles while her thumb kneaded her clit like a small biscuit. She thought of dough rising, mysterious and white inside her, stretching her with the force of its growth until it popped like a pale giant bubble, rippling away from her.

She pulled her fingers out and wiped them off, then flushed so Charlotte wouldn't wonder what she'd been doing in there. At the sink they washed carefully because they were kneading dough for rolls and had been instructed to keep their hands clean and free of oil, or the bread wouldn't rise.

Back in class, Evelyn stood beside Laurent, smiling inwardly at the secret trip up his ass he'd never know about. All he seemed to care about was *Chouette*, and perfectly beaten eggs.

*Aurora Light*

❦

# Playing for the Camera

Suzi kept after me. "Come on, Calla, this is a way to make some money for tuition, food and rent."

We're college seniors. Suzi is my roommate. We were discussing our disastrous financial situation in the tiny kitchen of our studio apartment. The rent was due in four days and we didn't have it. Suzi had a lead on a part-time job posing for amateur photographers, which actually meant horny guys who wanted to take pictures of pretty young gals in sexy outfits and provocative poses.

"It sure beats working at a fast food place. The pay is better, much better. And we'd only have to work three nights a week."

"What if Jeff finds out?"

"So what if he does? He doesn't own you. My boyfriend doesn't mind; actually Tony's the one who told me about the job. I think the idea of me posing for a bunch of other men turns him on. Tony says the man who owns the studio is sixty-five and won't give us any grief. And the men aren't allowed to touch us, only look and take pictures."

Finally I agreed, and the next night we went to the studio. Lorenzo, the owner, showed us to the dressing room and told us to pick out costumes and be ready in half an hour. There wasn't much variety—Victoria's Secret–type lingerie and some swimsuits.

I'm a big girl, five-nine with a forty-two D-cup bosom, flame

red hair and sea green eyes. I put on an electric blue swimsuit cut
down to my navel and high up the hips. With extra mascara, eyeliner, glossy lipstick and long rhinestone earrings, I looked, Suzi
said, trashy but hot.

Suzi, a petite, perfectly proportioned blonde with blue eyes,
chose a black string bikini and four-inch stiletto heels. Nervous,
but excited at the prospect of being ogled by strangers, all male, we
went onstage.

The carpeted stage was brightly lit. The rest of the studio was in
semidarkness, so we couldn't see the men clearly, which eased our
nervousness—but we could hear some comments: "Check out
those tits on the redhead!" and "Oh, Jesus, that blond babe has a
dynamite ass!"

Later, after the picture shoot, Lorenzo said we did okay for the
first time, but we had to heat it up. The customers liked the models to jiggle, wiggle and look like they were enjoying their work.

The second night Suzi and I really got steaming, giving the customers plenty of boobs and bun shots. At the end of the session
Lorenzo was pleased. He had a request—two of the men wanted a
private photo session, with us in the nude, and we would be paid
double the usual rate. Suzi and I hesitated for a second, then nodded yes.

We had decided to pretend we were posing for a high-class
men's magazine, and we'd get naked via a striptease, an old fantasy of mine. We came onstage wearing thigh-length negligees over
sheer white teddies, garter belts, lacy stockings and spike heels.
Five minutes into the hour, the moment of truth arrived.

When Lorenzo put on a cassette of stripper music, what had
been fantasy suddenly became real. I gave myself up to the moment. Erotic images flooded my brain, bringing a tingle to my
breasts and a surge of moisture to my pussy.

Concentrating on the insistent beat of the music, I began my
strip with some bumps and grinds and a spread-legged squat, wanting the men to see my crotch, more revealed than concealed by
the wisp of silk between my legs. A wild wantonness inside me
was awakened by calls to "Take it off! Take it all off!"

At first I did everything slowly, unfastening garters, rolling down
stockings, twirling them around and pulling them back and forth

between my legs, then tossing the stockings out to the men. I took the top of the teddy down one shoulder strap at a time, exposing my breasts, leaning forward to make them jiggle. Increasing the tempo, I pranced around, gyrating, before pushing the teddy down past my hips and stepping out of it. I heard their cameras clicking like mad.

I felt totally vulnerable, and that, in some inexplicable way, increased my excitement. I felt the men's hot eyes devouring me, and I knew their cocks were hard and fiercely aching to penetrate me, to possess me. For an instant I wondered what it would be like to be endowed with that demanding, pleasure-hungry appendage. Suzi was lying onstage naked with her legs up in the air, showing off her dimpled ass and the hairless pink lips of her pussy. I lay down beside her and did some rapid hip thrusts that brought an appreciative "Whoa, babe, you're hot!" from one of the men. The voice sounded oddly familiar.

I whispered to Suzi, "I think Jeff's out there."

"I'm pretty sure the other one is Tony," Suzi whispered back. "Let's pretend we don't know it's them."

A wicked gleam in her eyes, she started caressing her pert breasts and swiveling her trim hips. Slowly, I stroked my pussy, then raised one moist finger to my lips and sucked it. The guys went wild.

"Oh, I'm so hot and wet," I said breathlessly. I wasn't acting. My whole body felt meltingly warm and blushing. "Why don't you boys come up and join us?" I teased.

With embarrassed grins Tony and Jeff came up onstage, major erections bulging in their trousers. Laughing, Suzi and I quickly stripped them of their clothes. I'd never been naked with another couple, but I was so hot and horny that any shyness I might have felt vanished.

"Where's Lorenzo?" Suzi asked.

Tony shrugged. "Maybe he left."

I didn't say anything, but the thought of Lorenzo lurking around somewhere watching us, getting a stiff pecker and jerking off, gave me a wicked thrill.

"Pretty Woman" was playing. We started dirty dancing, which is super-sexy when you're nude and the guy has a hard-on. In an instant my pussy was sopping wet. I felt as though all my senses were exquisitely, almost painfully alive.

Soon Jeff and I were on the carpet giving each other some serious head. Out of the corner of my eye I saw Tony humping Suzi. Watching them, it didn't take long for me to come. Seconds later I heard Suzi cry out in orgasm.

The guys were still hard. Suzi looked at me and I knew what she had in mind. I agreed to switching partners with a nod. The guys were more than willing.

Then Tony confessed that he had a video camera filming everything. A part of me couldn't believe that I was doing, and enjoying, these outrageous acts—but another part of me reveled in the feeling of power and freedom. Knowing the camera was filming us made the sex even more sizzling.

Jeff and Tony switched places. Tony was really hung, with a thick, blue-veined cock and hairy balls. I spread my legs and his impressive prick homed in to my scorching pussy like a heat-seeking missile. I clamped down on his dick with my vaginal muscles squeezing and releasing as he fucked me relentlessly, grunting with each stroke. I came twice before he jetted steamy come.

Suzi and Jeff were doing a sixty-nine, making lewd slurping sounds. I saw her ass jerk as she came. Jeff's cock was halfway down her throat when it erupted. Suddenly things turned into a free-for-all, with lips and tongues, cocks and cunts coming together, parting, forming new, more complicated combinations. My blood and nerves resonated with a wild, electric music.

Watching Tony go down on Jeff, and seeing Jeff's reaction, gave me a rush that almost made me come. When Suzi started eating my pussy I really went nuts. Fiercely she licked and sucked every inch of my slit and clit. "Oh, yeah," I urged. "Right there. Don't, please don't stop." Then a ragged "Uuuuuuhhhhh!" as my cunt spasmed.

Then it was my turn to taste Suzi's cunt. Her pink pussy lips parted under my probing tongue. It was my first time eating a girl. I felt what she was feeling, and my cunt pulsed with shared pleasure.

The guys cheered us on from the sidelines. Suzi grabbed my hair and pulled my face tight against her burning pussy, chanting,

"Oh God, oh God, yes, yes," then coming in convulsive waves, creaming my mouth and chin.

Exposing myself that night to the eyes of the camera and the hot eyes of Jeff, Tony and Suzi was physically and emotionally liberating. Now, whenever I'm making love, playing the goddess, bitch, savage or slut, a part of me is always playing for the camera.

*Carol Queen*

# Marilyn

Kitty and her lover rarely leave the house—they're usually too busy rutting like weasels. When they do go out it's almost always to unusual events of the "urban night creatures" variety, like orgies and SM parties. The way they dress (in black, naturally) frightens tourists. He almost always wears black leather. Kitty can usually be found in rubber or lace, but this time it's black velvet, the tiniest strapless dress with lots of visible flesh, her tattoo hung like a moon (well, it is a moon, with a serpent twined around it) on the upper slope of one breast. And she wears tall high-heeled, thigh-length black suede boots.

Tonight's event is not an orgy. Tonight they're going to an ordinary party, given on behalf of a slightly wild gay organization. Kitty and her lover are there to hand out condoms, and maybe cruise a little.

The place is swarming with drag queens, mostly the thoroughly tasteless, never-mistake-her-for-a-female-in-a-million-years type that Kitty particularly appreciates. How can you possibly worry about what kind of woman you are, surrounded by these fabulous creatures? That one over there is more feminine than Kitty will ever be. This one has hairy legs and a beard. Hanging around with drag queens takes all the angst, Kitty thinks, out of being a girl.

The queens are wearing everything but the kitchen sink. On

them it looks like clothing, even though a lot of it isn't. One of them wears a slinky dress made of bubble wrap. Another one's outfit is mostly tinfoil. On them it is amazing, eccentric, gorgeous *couture*. If the little old Latina clerks at Thrift Town could see to what use those nice young men had put their purchases of chiffon curtains, old lace antimacassars, and size-eleven silver Dream Step pumps, they'd have a fit. And eyelashes! Pounds and *pounds* of eyelashes.

Among them Marilyn stands out like a star. Well, because she is. It's Marilyn Monroe, whom scores of drag queens have courted and precious few have possessed. She is impeccable: tasteful yet sexy peach satin gown, that unmistakable face, even—it would appear—her own hair. She's lost a little weight, but it looks good on her. Oh, those long satin gloves. Oh, that birthmark. Oh, that sweet little pout.

She gives a breathy little laugh when she comes close enough for Kitty and her lover to offer her condoms. She tries to demur. Kitty's lover pulls out all the stops.

"Oh, but you must," he says. "Such a lovely lady must have so many opportunities to use them. You know you can't depend on most *men* to take care of these things. Unless of course there's someone waiting at home . . . ?"

Marilyn blushes, lowers her (not-too-heavy) eyelashes, shakes her head. Apparently she's between husbands at the moment. She opens her clutch and gazes limpidly at Kitty's lover as he murmurs further niceties and stuffs a handful of rubbers inside.

Of course Marilyn falls for him, so tall and handsome, his gentility such a contrast to his scary leathers. She gets flustered and has to run off and have a couple of drinks before she gets up the nerve to come back and flirt. When she returns she carries the peach satin gown gathered up in one hand so Kitty's lover can admire her legs—which he does.

The devil is cruising Marilyn Monroe! Kitty can do nothing but stand back and watch, amazed and amused. She's always been hot for Marilyn Monroe, and this apparition has her salivating. The knowledge that she could travel up the silken legs and find a cock curled under the peach satin makes Kitty's clit hard.

Marilyn Monroe's cock! At the thought of her lover making that journey, gently unveiling her, the touch of his hands making Marilyn's cock stiffen against the lace, Kitty rubs her crotch surreptitiously against the back of a chair. Meanwhile she watches the two of them flirt.

Now, Kitty's lover doesn't do men very often. Sometimes he'll play around when he and Kitty are at sex parties or when Kitty occasionally brings another guy home. But his heart isn't really in it—well, maybe it's his dick that balks. Still, he isn't so straight that he won't run with a promising flirt, no matter what the gender.

But Marilyn isn't flirting with Kitty at all—no lesbian blood in this starlet. Kitty's lover is going to be on his own with Marilyn, and Kitty is dying to know how far he'll take it. And licking her chops at the thought. On one of Marilyn's runs to the powder room Kitty puts her lips close to his ear: "Baby, Marilyn wants you." And Kitty wants to watch. Really she wants to turn this femme boy Marilyn into a lesbian, but she knows that's out of the question. A certain kind of gay man could no more imagine having sex with a woman than your average citizen from Dubuque could picture making it with a gibbon, and that's the sort of boy Marilyn is.

It's a shame to be this close to Marilyn Monroe and know she could never in a million years be persuaded to go down on Kitty. Reportedly Marilyn herself (that is, the original) did plenty of that sort of thing with Lily St. Cyr. But Kitty can generate plenty of orgasms on her own just thinking of her lover's strong hands closing around the slender arms in the elegant satin gloves, pulling Marilyn to him . . . those wide eyes and little moans of acquiescence, oh, it just makes Kitty want to squeal.

She draws in a sharp breath of delight when Marilyn returns, a slip of folded paper showing white against her chest where the real Marilyn Monroe would be spilling cleavage and this Marilyn sports, instead, perfectly formed ersatz breasts. Kitty knows what's on that piece of paper, and laughs silently as Marilyn pulls it with a flourish from her bodice, hands it to Kitty's lover, suffers a moment of helpless shyness, and, making a quick excuse, hurries away again. Kitty laughs aloud as her lover unfolds the paper. Of course it's a phone number, and the name written next to it isn't Marilyn, it's Dirk.

Back home Kitty is still laughing, this time because her lover is flustered and a little abashed. He doesn't know what to do about Marilyn. No—he knows just what he wants to do about *Marilyn*, but he's at a loss over how to relate to *Dirk*. Had he led her on? he asks. He certainly had, Kitty tells him. He wants to respect Marilyn's flirtatiousness, Dirk's courage. Maybe he should send roses to make it up to her? Not unless there's somewhere specific you *want* to lead her, Kitty teases. To bed, for instance.

"On second thought," she says, "why don't you lead her right over here?" Kitty wants to see it. She wants to see Marilyn's impeccably made-up face go soft as her lover clasps the tender neck, kisses the painted mouth, caresses the peach satin over the faux breasts. She wants to watch him run his hands up Marilyn's slim thighs, the dress rustling as it's raised. The hard cock straining under the sexy lingerie, and his hands on it, freeing it to spring up, ready for the careful tongue of Kitty's lover to tease it delicately up and down. Would her lover's cock be hard by then, aching for Marilyn's perfectly painted boy-lips to sink down on it, leaving a little gleam of lipstick in their wake?

Kitty wants to watch so badly she can taste it, wants to see Marilyn's eyes fill with that yielding, that womanly giving over of resistance that's so precious in the eyes of a man. She wants to see her lover grinding against Marilyn, rubbing his cock against the satin of the torn-off dress, wants to see the wet spots of his pre-come on the shiny peach-colored cloth. Then she'll roll over, ass raised, hips bucking in desire and thrusting back hard against Kitty's lover: Marilyn wants to get fucked.

"Give it to her, honey." By now Kitty is saying this out loud, telling the story in gasps as her lover's cock thrusts into her deeper and deeper, making her cry out and catch her breath. "Baby, I want to see you fuck her ass right now!"

She'll reach for condoms and lube, roll the rubber down the length of her sweetheart's shaft, slick it up so he's ready; she wants this sight more than anything—his cock opening Marilyn slowly, sliding in, pumping his hips to get it all in as he holds her by the shoulders and Marilyn arches back and takes hold of her own ass cheeks, pulling them apart. Sinking in deep, pulling back and riding. Her cock's rubbing against the sheets with every thrust, and Kitty knows that soon her bed will be scented with Marilyn Monroe jism. At that thought, Kitty comes.

Now Kitty and her lover are fucking like the sex pigs they are, in each other's arms writhing and grunting and growling, and the story is over for the moment; talking about Marilyn has gotten them into pure rut again. Kitty's fantasies now are past plot and coherence, and anyway, she couldn't force herself to narrate anything, no matter how sexy, because her lover is fucking her so hard she's almost screaming. She is all breath and cunt and her hands where they touch him. It's too bad Marilyn is missing this, though for the time being they've both forgotten her. She'll come shimmering back into consciousness when the fuck is done. Maybe she'll become a regular fantasy companion, or even . . . .

Who knows? After all, they *have* Marilyn Monroe's phone number.

## Blake C. Aarens

❦

# Get on Your Bikes and Ride

Friday. The last long, hard day of a long, hard work week. Finally over. Irene lunged off the elevator and practically ran down the corridor to her apartment. She didn't even see the cobwebs in the corners, didn't give a thought to calling maintenance. She wanted in. To her own little sanctuary. She wanted out. Away from the rest of the world.

Keys in her right hand, Irene unlocked her apartment door and tried to keep the mail from falling out of her left. Her briefcase, hanging from a strap on her shoulder, insisted on bumping against her thigh. She nudged the door open and slipped inside. Leaned back and let the sound of the lock clicking shut bring the beginning of a smile to her lips. She let everything drop—everything, that is, except the mail. That she went through one at a time, flinging envelopes across the room when she saw what they were. PG&E bill (fling!). The public television station asking for money again (fling!). A letter from her mother. That one almost landed in the fish tank.

Suddenly she stopped flinging envelopes, because in her hand she held the brand-new Honda motorcycle catalogue. Irene's slight grin became a full, gap-toothed smile. The rest of the mail slipped from her fingers and was left in a pile at the front door.

Catalogue in hand, she made her way to the bedroom. She

stopped to stare at and straighten the Georgia O'Keeffe print on the wall. Between the image of the dark iris—a stylized pussy with charcoal gray lips and a burgundy clit—and the anticipated thrill of the motorcycle catalogue, Irene's cunt was already throbbing. She set the catalogue on her pillow, positioned herself in front of the full-length mirror, and assessed her image.

"Not bad," she said, grinning. "I'm not a teenager anymore. But then again, I wouldn't wanna be."

Licking her lips and blowing a kiss at her image, Irene began to slowly strip. For herself. First she unwound the black silk scarf from her throat and smelled the thick scent of jasmine oil she'd massaged into her skin that morning. She pressed the silk to her face like a veil and breathed deeply, then let go and watched as the scarf drifted slowly to the floor.

She unhooked the black belt from around her waist and pulled it slowly through the loops at the sides of her red blazer. A snake retreating through the grass. She flicked the leather at the catalogue on her pillow, snapping it against the glossy paper. Like a tease. Like a tamer. Irene threw her head back and laughed. She knew exactly where this was going.

Next, she unbuttoned her blazer and shimmied it off her shoulders. She folded it neatly at the foot of her bed. Watching in the mirror as she unbuttoned the shimmery fabric of her white blouse, Irene spread the fabric apart and blew kisses as the caramel-colored curves of her cleavage came into view. She bent her head and kissed the hills of her breasts, leaving burgundy lipstick marks. She stretched her arms to the ceiling and watched her tits rise with the action. Slowly, she unbound the coil of her dreds and shuddered as the springy locks fell to her shoulders. Irene grinned slyly at herself in the mirror and pulled the catalogue to the center of the bed. She opened to the first page.

A Gold Wing SE. The sight of that pearl green touring machine brought back memories. Of big-hearted, broad-shouldered Cody. A big butch of a woman with laughing eyes and the steadiest tongue in the state. Memory was in Irene's fingertips as she wet them and dipped them into the cups of her bra to pinch and pull at her nipples. She squeezed her breasts together, then flattened them close to her body and thought about all those rides when she'd press her tits against the broad expanse of Cody's back. Irene closed her eyes and inhaled, recalling the rich, oily smell of Cody's leather jacket.

Rubbing her thighs and ass through the fabric of her short black skirt, Irene relived the slow rumble of the big bike as it vibrated the cheeks of her ass apart. Straddling that bike on long trips had made her walk bowlegged for days afterward. And easier to get at, Cody used to say. Irene took a wide stance and jiggled her hips to simulate the vibration.

But Cody and that enormous machine of hers were more than Irene was ready for right now. She stopped herself just short of coming and went back to her reflection in the mirror. She peeled her shirt the rest of the way off. Unzipped her skirt and slid it down her legs to the floor. The sound of the wool against her stockings made her purse her lips together and sigh. She held onto the bedpost and stepped daintily out of the circle of fabric. She reached down and turned the page.

Dirt bikes. And memories of Darlene. Her affinity with the machines reflected in her sex—their high-pitched whine like the sound of her coming, her rough-and-tumble fucking like spewing gravel when she'd hit a rough spot. And the coming she'd treated Irene to—like taking flight at the crest of an unexpected hill.

Darlene would come home from the races covered with dust. She'd strip in the hall and drag Irene into the bathroom with her, rolling around in the tub 'til they were both covered with mud and sweat and each other's come. Muddy handprints down her throat and across her breasts. Long, sticky streaks down the inside of her thighs and wedged in the crack of her ass. Irene shuddered with a mixture of lust and joy. She squealed with delight recalling the rough, raunchy times they'd had. But Darlene was long gone, probably at this very moment tumblebugging some sweet young thing who'd never been with another girl before.

Irene turned to the center of the catalogue. Her breath caught in her throat. There it was. A black Honda Shadow. The bike Layla rode. Layla. The woman who currently rode Irene. This was what Irene had been waiting for. She grabbed the black lace hem of her half-slip and pulled it up and over the brown contours of her body.

This picture brought back memories of the past as well as anticipation of times to come. The rubbed leather seat she couldn't wait to be straddled over, again and again. The name "Shadow" on the black fuel tank in deep violet script, Layla's favorite color. And the chrome polished so bright you could see your reflection in it. The sight of the tassels hanging from the handlebars made Irene blush. She remembered the time Layla had pulled them off and whipped her with them.

Trembling with body memories, Irene turned from the image of the pretty black bike to her own image in the mirror. She turned her back to the glass and looked over her shoulder. High-heeled pumps made her calf muscles tense. Black silk stockings covered her legs, the seams in back like the lines of a treasure map. Leading upwards. The tiniest black lace g-string covered little and served only to frame the cheeks of her ass. Twisting at the waist, Irene admired the demi-cup bra that made her breasts stand up and out and barely hid her nipples.

Irene turned to face her reflection again and hunched her shoulders. The bra straps fell. She reached inside the cups and pinched her nipples again, pulling her body away like she sometimes did with Layla. She slid her hands between her legs and encountered the wetness of the world. She was so ready.

Irene unhooked her bra and pulled it off her arms. Ass in the air, she bent and rested her tits on the picture in the catalogue. She rocked and rolled on the image of the Honda, pinching and pulling on her clit with her right hand, burying the fingers of her left deep inside. She came like that, mouth open, cunt open. Heart. Open.

When the spasms finally stopped, she rolled over onto her back. She kicked her heels in the air and laughed out loud. She painted pictures on her thighs with her own juices. Eventually she curled up on her side and fell asleep.

Layla found her just like that. All but naked. Grinning. Dreaming. The motorcycle catalogue still open to the center page. Layla put her helmet on the floor quietly and peeled off her leather jacket. She sat down slowly, taking time to let the mattress adjust to her weight. Her eyes glazed over with fierce love as she watched Irene dream. She moistened a finger between her full lips, then reached out and flicked one of Irene's nipples. She grinned at Irene's moan and sigh and fidget. Suddenly she pinched the nipple hard. Irene's eyes fluttered open with her sharp intake of breath.

"Someone's been looking at the Honda catalogue," Layla teased.

Irene giggled, snatched up the catalogue and tossed it onto the floor.

"Never mind the catalogue," she said. "Why don't you fuck me?"

"Let me smell you," Layla said. Her eyes had that greedy look in them.

Irene rolled over onto her back and spread her legs wide. She grabbed Layla's short afro and held her face just inches from her cunt. Layla made a noisy business of breathing deeply.

"Damn," Layla said, lifting up to look Irene in the eyes. "You're dripping."

"Are you thirsty?"

Layla grinned and nodded.

Irene arched her back; Layla slid her hands beneath Irene's ass. She lingered there to cup the cheeks, to feel the warmth of her lover's flesh, then dove her head between Irene's legs. She traced the contours of Irene's cunt; she ran her tongue between the inner and outer lips, sucked on the hard little clit. She listened with satisfaction as Irene sang sensation to her with sighs and groans and finally, when she could come no more, with tears.

Irene pulled Layla up her body. Buried her face in Layla's neck and licked her there, tasting the salt of Layla's sweat. "I love the way you love me," she whispered.

"I'm not done," Layla said. And she rose up off the bed and began to undress.

## Michelle Stevens

❦

# The Appliance

Bonnie's in the bathroom crying again. It's the third time this week. I ask her why. She says because she's sad.

"Mad?" I ask.

"No," she says and slams the door on my nose.

We fought about it again. This time we were in Denny's. She was halfway through her Mexicali Combo when I brought it up. Next thing I knew, we were back in the bedroom, and she was dangling it in front of me like a dirty sock.

The Appliance. Her name for it, not mine. Personally, I think the word *appliance* is a little too literal, too Montgomery Ward. But I can't think of anything better. I mean, how do you describe 900 volts of sheer pleasure?

"It's not what you think," I said to her. "I . . . I was using it for my back."

She looked at me with that sad, sad look. "Why do you lie to me?" she asked. Then she started to cry.

It's been like this since the beginning. Literally, since the first night we met. I was lonely, had just ended a six-year marriage to a man. I'd never been with a woman before, never even kissed one. Everything I knew about lesbians I knew from Katherine Forrest and Rita Mae Brown.

Saturday afternoons, while my husband watched TV in the den,

I'd lie under the comforter in our bed, flipping through the pages of *Curious Wine* while I jacked off with his Radio Shack three-speed massager. I never could handle the highest speed.

When I finally got up the courage to tell him I was gay, he didn't know how to take it. "So you have sex with women?" he asked lasciviously.

"Not yet," I said.

"So how do you know you're gay?"

"I just do," I told him.

In the end, he was pretty good about it. For his anguish, he got the car, the condo and a hot new girlfriend who was willing to do all the wifely stuff I hated—like cook. I got the cat and an old electric back massager he vaguely remembered getting for Christmas.

Months later, lying on the futon in my crappy little apartment, I spent a lot of nights wondering how I could've been so stupid. Telling my well-meaning, well-paid husband I was *gay*? I didn't even *know* any lesbians! What had I been thinking? Why did I have to go and make my life so hard? I mean, sure it was a loveless marriage. Sure I was lonely. But not *this* lonely.

I stared at the ceiling, thinking about what an idiot I was. I'd toss, I'd turn and, finally, I'd pull out my only friend. It lived at the foot of the bed. As I envisioned all those beautiful heroines and perfect lesbian love affairs I had read about in books, the gentle hum had a magical way of keeping me company.

Finally, six months after my divorce, I saw a flyer at the bookstore while I was picking up a copy of *The Well of Loneliness*. The flyer advertised a coming-out group at the Gay and Lesbian Center. I wrote down the information in the sleeve of the book and promised myself I'd go.

The night of the group, it took all my courage and two glasses of wine to walk through the door. When I finally went in, I was relieved that no one seemed to notice me. I found a chair in a corner, sat down and tried my best not to make eye contact.

Then it happened. Across a crowded room, I saw her. And I knew.

She was sitting in a chair in the opposite corner, trying her best not to make eye contact, either. I don't think she saw me at first. She was all alone. This tall, lean, butch, beautiful Molly Bolt, Stephen Gordon, Lane and Diana all rolled into one. Yes, indeed, she was the heroine in every wonderful lesbian story ever written. She was the woman who'd been holding me all those nights while a vibrator buzzed under my sheets.

I don't remember how I got to the other side of the room. I don't remember how we got to my apartment, either. All I know is, pretty soon we were two naked women lying on my living room floor. I'd had no idea that skin could feel so soft, that hands could touch so lightly, that one tongue could be in so many places all at once.

"Maybe we should go to the bedroom," I whispered.

Bonnie chuckled. "Yeah, I guess hardwood floors can get pretty hard."

She got up. She was naked. Standing above me. The street light through the window made her skin glow. She was like an angel. A six-foot large-breasted angel. And she was heading towards my bed.

When she pulled back the comforter, it was lying right there, extension cord trailing to the wall. Long. Plastic. All three speeds. She raised an eyebrow. I blushed.

"It's been a long time, and I . . ."

"It's okay," she grinned. "I understand. Every single girl needs her appliance."

She picked it up and tossed it on the ground, where it landed with a loud thump. She pushed me down on the futon and started doing those amazing things with her tongue again. It felt good, as good as before—but in the back of my mind, I couldn't help wondering if the fall had hurt it.

The next morning I sent Bonnie off to work with a stale french pastry and a long french kiss. Then I called in sick to work and crawled back into bed. Even if Bonnie couldn't be there, I was determined to make the best night of my life last a little longer.

Lying on the threadbare sheets, I thought about her soft skin. The way her back curved. How her hair had tickled my breast.

When I came back to reality, I was comforted by the familiar hum of my Radio Shack massager, singing between my legs as usual. Thank God for nonbreakable plastic.

In the weeks that followed, I spent a lot of time in my bed. And on my floor. And once in the stairwell, when Bonnie couldn't wait for me to open the front door. We did it constantly. We did it every-where. We did it every which way. Her on top. Me on top. Three comforters on top so the neighbors wouldn't hear our screams.

In those rare moments when Bonnie and I weren't together, I found myself thinking about her constantly. Her stomach. Her hands. The weight of her body on top of me. It drove me crazy. All alone, I stayed in the bed, the vibrator humming away, the electric meter spinning.

A few months later, I surfaced for air. I had run out of sick days. My boss wanted to know why I was so lethargic at work. I still loved Bonnie madly. I still wanted her constantly. But I was tired. Some nights, I just wanted to sleep. Bonnie, on the other hand, was a jock. She ate too many Wheaties. She still wanted to do it every night.

"I can't, I'm too tired," I said, as she licked my neck.

"You didn't want to last night, either," she said.

"I'm just not in the mood." I rolled over and put a pillow over my head.

"You were in the mood to use the appliance," Bonnie said.

I sat up. "How did you know that?"

"I just know." Bonnie shrugged.

"Did I tell you?" I was confused. I only used it when she wasn't at home.

"You use it every day," she said matter-of-factly. "Usually more than once."

"How do you know that?" I asked. I was starting to get suspicious.

"The other woman always knows," Bonnie said. Then she rolled away from me.

There was a deadly silence. One of those active silences, where you have to work hard not to say anything, where you can't possi-bly fall asleep.

Finally, I turned to her, spooned her from behind, ran my hand through her hair. "Just because I use the appli . . . the massager, it has nothing to do with you. I'm just tired tonight."

Bonnie just sighed, and we fell asleep.

Three days later, I sat quietly fuming at the kitchen table, star-ing at the front door, waiting for my beloved to come home.

"What did you do with it?" I hissed when she finally walked in.

Bonnie smiled. She found this amusing. "You're addicted. Tough love. I hid it."

"I am not addicted!"

"Ooooh! Denial. Classic, classic, classic," she said as she hung up her coat.

"I'm not denying anything. I'll be the first to admit I like it. Give it back."

She laughed at me. A pitying, condescending laugh. Then she pulled it out of a bag in the hall closet. I was holding it again. It was in my hands. Thank God. Thank God.

A few nights later, no matter what Bonnie did with her magic tongue, I just couldn't come.

"Honey, you must be getting tired," I whispered. Gingerly I suggested we use the massager.

"You like it better than me?" Bonnie asked, defensive.

"No, I like *you*. I like you a lot. I just don't think your neck can hold out much longer."

"It's that damned appliance," she yelled. "It's making you insensitive!" She got up and started to pace. "You're addicted to the vibrator," she said ominously. "This is your first lesbian experience, honey. You don't understand the danger. Lesbians get addicted to an appliance, then they can't have real sex anymore." She took a deep breath for emphasis and warned, "If we stop having real sex, we're eventually doomed. Don't you understand? It's inevitable. If you don't stop using the appliance, *we will break up!*"

The thought of losing Bonnie frightened me. I handed over the massager, begging her to keep it safe.

A few days later, after consulting my old library of lesbian literature, I took Bonnie to dinner. To discuss.

"Joann Loulan says a vibrator can't make you insensitive to human touch," I said between bites of my Dennyburger.

Bonnie put down her fork. She looked me in the eyes. "Are you going to bring that up again?"

"I have to," I said. "It's bothering me."

"It's bothering you because no addict likes having their drug taken away."

"First of all," I countered, "using a vibrator is a perfectly natural form of sexuality. Secondly, my using it has nothing to do with you. And third," I added, "I don't like to be told what to do."

"I didn't tell you what to do."

"You threatened to break up with me if I didn't hand it over," I yelled. "You've been bugging me about it for weeks. You're trying to control my life."

Bonnie looked away, deadly quiet. She was trying hard not to cry.

"Let's go," she whispered.

"The waitress didn't bring the Colossal Fudge Sundae yet."

"I'm not hungry."

The car ride home was like a funeral with no guests. She stared out the window, her face turned away so I couldn't see the tears.

By the time we got home, she wasn't crying anymore. She went straight to her dresser and pulled the appliance out of the bottom drawer.

"Here." She held it out with the tip of her fingers.

"Uh, maybe we should talk about this," I tried to reason.

"I don't want to talk about it anymore."

"But if you're angry . . ."

"I don't want to talk about it. I don't want to see it. The issue is dead," she said flatly. When I didn't grab the massager, she let it drop to the floor. Then she turned on her heels and walked away.

I followed her, almost tripping over the appliance in the process.

"It's not that I need it," I said.

"I don't care."

"I don't even have to use it."

"I don't care."

"It's just an issue of control."

She walked into the bathroom and shut the door on my nose. And that was the end of it.

Until the next day. Saturday. She was out playing softball. I was busy in the bed. Over the hum of the vibrator, I distinctly heard the rustle of keys at the front door. I was able to turn it off, but there was no time to remove the evidence.

"Oh, hey," I mustered brightly as she walked into the room.

"Hey," she said back as she sat down next to me. "What are you still doing in bed?"

"I'm, uh . . ."

"Sick?" she asked. She leaned over and put her hand on my forehead.

"No, just resting. I thought you had a game."

"I couldn't concentrate. I hate it when we fight."

"Me too," I said as I carefully sat up to give her a kiss. I kept one hand on the vibrator, which was dangerously close to her thigh.

"I'm really sorry," she whispered. "I just don't like those things. But, you know, it's your life, and as long as I don't have to see it, well, I guess out of sight, out of mind."

"Great," I mumbled through my plastered smile.

"God," she went on, as she stood up and took off her jeans, "I've really missed you. This whole thing has been really draining."

She crossed over to her side of the bed, pulled back the sheets, and crawled in.

"Oh . . . you're naked," she said.

"Yeah, well, I, uh . . ."

"Hmm." Her hand cupped my breast. "I like this. Easy access."

She moved closer and started to suck my neck. I didn't know what to do, so I just lay there. Enjoying it. Her magic tongue moved from my earlobe to my collarbone. Her magic fingers squeezed my nipple. Before I knew what was happening, she was climbing on top of me.

"Ow!" she screamed, as her weight came down on my body. "What is that?"

Her hand fished underneath the comforter. It resurfaced with an old Radio Shack massager. Three speeds.

Oh, God, I thought, here we go again.

Bonnie just sat there for a while, on top of me, staring at the appliance. She rolled it around in her hands; she moved the switch up and down, testing out the different speeds.

"You do it naked?" she finally asked.

"Sometimes."

"Show me," she said. She rolled back over to her side of the bed, propped her head up with her arm and lay there, waiting.

"Is this some sort of weird reverse-psychology thing?" I asked.

"No. I just want to see what it is you like so much."

She nodded for me to get on with it, so I lay back down, fluffed the pillows for a while, checked to see if she was still watching. She was. I'd never done it with someone looking at me before. I didn't know if I could.

I closed my eyes. I turned on the vibrator. Low speed. There was that familiar hum.

"This is no fun," she said. "I want to *see*." She flung back the covers, so I was just lying there naked, holding a big plastic appliance to my private parts.

"I don't know if I can do it like this," I whined.

"Oh, please! You do it seven times a day! Go on."

So I did. I closed my eyes and tried to concentrate. It was disconcerting but kind of exciting, knowing that she was right there. Watching. The vibrator started to feel good. I started to rock back and forth. Next thing I knew, there was a hand on my neck, stroking my hair. Then a magic tongue on my nipple, licking, licking.

I grabbed the back of her hair and pushed her face into my breasts. Her breath, her cheeks felt good on my skin. I took her hand, the one stroking my hair, and brushed it across my face. I took her middle finger and licked it. Slowly. Up, down. Feeling the wet, the warmth. I put it in my mouth and sucked hard.

Suddenly, she was covering me. Her face to my face. Her breasts to my breasts. We were sharing the vibrator. Me underneath. Bonnie on top. We were in rhythm, she and I. Rocking, sucking, back and forth to the hum. Then the familiar wash came over us. We screamed at the same time.

When I came back to reality, when sound and sense and the world came back, I realized she was giggling. Her brown eyes peered at me over my breast.

"What's so funny?" I asked.

"You never told me we could do a threesome!"

# *Julia Rader*

# Thirst

What is it about him that I'm sitting here inches from the telephone, forehead cradled in my palm, praying it won't and craving for the ring? The heat of the summer night carries the smell of salt through the open windows. It's been a whole year, but memories flash like last night's movie. More than anything, it has to do with the way he taught me how to suck cock. (Not technique. They taught me that a long time ago.)

I see myself in the bedroom where we lived together near the foothills of the Rockies, in a suburb outside Denver. In a dark basement I make out the vague shape of his body. I'm wearing a stiff corset—it squishes my breasts together and pushes them up with underwires. I don't have any panties on and his hand is making slow circles on the cheeks of my ass.

Inside his briefs, his cock bulges. I can see it perfectly even in this dim light. In his other hand is a glass of ice water. He shakes the glass close to my ear. He wants me to listen to the sound of the tinkling ice cubes.

"Are you thirsty, baby?" It isn't like he wants to know. He's suggesting thirst, creating and building it—like going for an afternoon hike in the woods, the way the waterfall sounds in the distance when you've been walking upstream to find it, and you first hear the crashing water. Even if you've walked a long way, you're suddenly not tired anymore. The sound itself charges you with energy, beckons you on.

He moves the glass of water down to his crotch and rubs himself there. His hand on my ass moves up to my head. He pulls my face down to his still-hidden cock.

"Umm . . . can you smell that . . . are you thirsty, baby?" I let out a small moan, and he quickly pulls my head away, giving my ass a sharp slap.

"I didn't say you could drink yet. I might spank you if you suck it."

I get confused. I don't know what he wants. I look at him. He pulls my head back down and resumes the slow circles on the cheeks of my ass, the sound of tinkling ice cubes close to my ear.

"Can you smell it? What does it smell like?" I moan again, and this time I open my mouth and make contact, soaking through the fabric with my tongue.

"That's right, I know you're thirsty. But if you don't stop I might have to spank you."

I continue to lick him, until he slaps my ass, harder this time, and the harder he slaps me the more I want him to keep on doing it. When he stops spanking I stop sucking. He still has the glass of water in his hand and rubs it against my face, close to my mouth, then down to his cock, rubbing it all over.

"Are you thirsty?" he asks again.

"Yes," I say.

"Don't you want to take these off me so you can drink? Don't you need to suck?"

My hand reaches out to pull off his briefs, but he pulls away and I get confused again. He continues to back up, several feet away. The tinkle of ice turns mean. Suddenly I'm scared.

When our sex transcends playacting, time and space converge into a laser-beam focus of the immediate. Now, abandoned near the foot of the bed, I see childhood monsters baring ugly fangs. My lover is the devil, and physical union is a sick joke intended to own and pervert me.

I can't help it, I break down and cry, I'm the stupid, trapped baby and I can't help it, please don't hurt me leave me alone I'm scared.

He puts the glass down and comes close to comfort me. He unhooks my corset so that I'm naked, strokes my belly and face, and lifts my breasts up one at a time to kiss the soft skin underneath the folds.

I'm happy again, allowed to touch and please him, and I reach down to pull off his briefs. He puts his hand on my cunt, makes soft, slow circles on my clitoris so that when I finally get to see his naked cock I'm all the more aroused.

"Maybe you want to drink cock water. Do you want some cock water?"

"Yes." His cock brushes my throat. My nipples have gone hard and tingle. He gets up onto his knees and hands me the glass of ice water. He dips his cock all the way in and leaves it there for a minute. Seen through glass, his erection looks bigger. He takes it out and tells me to drink.

"But you know what happens when you drink cock water, don't you? You go crazy and you have to suck."

I'm drinking now, icy liquid and the knowledge of his secretions.

"Drink more . . . drink it all up. There you go, that's a good girl . . . and now you're crazy. You *have* to suck."

He pulls my face down to his cock again. "Can you smell it, baby? How does it smell now that you've drunk the cock water? Suck."

He chants the word, putting me inside of the craving to suck him; my throat opens wider than I thought possible. He thrusts deep inside and I want it. Want this getting fucked all the way down the back of my throat.

"Suck, suck, suck." I'm being force-fed as he guides my head up and down.

And then he begins to spank me, hard. His flat hand stings the surface of my bottom, hard and fast. The blows keep rhythm with my head bobbing up and down. Inside my throat his cock keeps on pushing, deeper and faster. I smell and taste his dripping semen, and feel the electricity shoot between my legs. My bottom's burning and the whole world is on fire and I've learned to love the devil, and surrendering to my destiny is all the safety I'll ever need and the flames shoot up, hot liquid down my throat and I'm coming and I'm drinking, I'm gratefully coming and drinking.

When the phone rings and I hear his voice, I know it's starting all over again.

## Sonja Kindley

❧❀❧

# Tame

I opened the door of a moving car. There was no choice. The windows were glossy with spit, a man was barking at the wheel, sputtering, brutish. I remember the high pitch, the jerky driving, my silence like gasoline to his flame, the thought that I could die because lovers kill lovers in scenes like this. There was no choice. His words clattered like castanets: He said I was pathetic, I heard "prophetic," and then I heard nothing but my lungs, my chain necklace sliding up and down my belt buckle, the shriek of a branch-snapping wind in the woozy black night. I opened the door. I hissed, Stop the car, Steven. And Steven, Mr. Hyde, put on the brakes.

He said, You get out of this car and it's fucking over.

He said, Jude, get back in the car.

He said, Nobody's going to want you like I do. I'm sorry I said some mean things, you're not sociopathic, now come back in the car.

Please, he said, with a broken sound in his throat.

But I cut loose anyway. I knew that trick.

So it's midnight in the Kwik-Mart, my shimmery stockings are wild with runs, thin ladders threading up my calves, my eyes are dry and dusty with mascara flakes, and I am reading dog-eared pop mags like all the other midnight waifs. The man behind the counter—bald, porky, and oddly moist—watches me as if I will slip candy into my purse. When he's not staring at me directly he is watching the silver ball in the corner, then he glances at *Saturday Night Live* on the little Goldstar TV on top of the popcorn machine. I want to go up to him and say, You've got the wrong girl, Mister. I'm a fucking secretary to the CEO of a Fortune 500 food brokerage firm. I could buy you. But I'm frightened by this, I'm frightened that I really am a fucking secretary, not a euphemistic "assistant," let's get real. Every day I take a memo it hurts my pride; when I try to appease Nick Martinetti's temper it's like swallowing his come, it's so vile, my sweet good-bye is me wiping my lips, murmuring, Delicious.

My heart shudders, then beats like a gerbil's; I lose the rhythm, tense up, then find it again. I am aware that I started out beautiful and became hideous at some point this evening, at some point things snapped, my creamy skin cracked, my teal silk dress started smelling sour, like old milk.

Tonight something scratched my brain, ripping zipper-swift to my heart. Steven sneered, You are Teflon Woman, everything rolls off your back—would you just be fucking honest for once. I said, I am sick of your verbal abuse, feeling certain of the definition for the first time. And he retorted, You don't have a clue what abuse is, Jude. Have you ever been shoved down the stairs by your drunk 200-pound father? Don't talk to me about abuse—you had the safe childhood, I didn't.

At the stoplight I was going to sock him. But I couldn't. I can't hurt people, everything drives inward, caustic, searing. It stays in my gut and burns through my pupils. There are so many things I've never done. I ache, flimsy.

When the man seems transfixed by a car commercial I tuck a small pack of Tic-Tacs into my I. Magnin wool coat. To assure him of my integrity, I go up to the counter and ask for Virginia Slims, though I don't smoke. He smiles at me, sweating. He asks me where my boyfriend is. I tell him he's in the parking lot waiting for me to decide how I'll break my twenty, knowing that Steven is long gone.

On the TV there is a skit about a chubby, flannel-wearing androgyne named Pat whose questionable sex is the source of endless jokes and futile attempts to crack the mystery. The man behind the counter is interested in this, and watches it while he makes change.

He says, You just know that's a lady. But they keep on going. Ha ha—it's still funny. The fanny pack, stuff like that. I mean, on TV it's funny, but in real life you like to know what side of the toast the butter's on.

He trusts me now because I bought something. I am shocked that deceit is so easy. It makes me sad.

Take you, for example, he says. You got the dress, the high heels. I can tell what you are.

Thank you, I say, with a miserable smile, putting the cigarettes in my purse with the Tic-Tacs.

Have a good night, hon, he says.

Tonight I am a runaway, a pissed secretary, a thief. He cannot tell what I am. These high heels are scuffed and my wrist is still pink from Steven's grip.

Understand this was not the first time Steven erupted, but it was the last time I could take it. As Dr. Jekyll he was sweet, humble, and brilliant. He wanted to call me "muffin," he was full of cringe-provoking terms of endearment and sappy sentiments; this made him happy. He liked the brat in me. He was intimidated by my cleverness. He liked my skinny ankles and fluffy red hair and the tricks I would use to get him hot. And I liked his fucked-up childhood, academic musketeering, Buddhism, and the way he would whisper what he wanted to do to me as we'd walk down the sidewalk past all the corporate shitheads and how, as we stood against a stone wall by a Dumpster, he would delicately lift my skirt, watching me closely, reading me, our lovemaking a muffled quake, opening and closing, little breathy wings, the only time I could let myself trust him.

He would break things. He would never touch me that way. I got a call from my brother, he thought it was an ex-lover, he punched a hole in my wall. You'd think a bright woman like me would get a clue. You'd also think an assistant professor of philosophy at a famous private college would be more emotionally refined. Because he was smart, wrote lovely letters, and atoned for his tantrums, I let it all slide for three months. Until tonight: the wrist burn, prisoner in his car, suicide drive. If he hadn't braked, I would have jumped.

I'm getting ideas as the coffee hits me like shock therapy, and they have to do with Frankenstein. I want to be the doctor *and* the monster. I want to take parts of myself—my skeleton, my musky voice, these dimples—and create an alter ego. Tonight I believe I could do anything because as of this moment, I am abandoning my former life of the 5:30 alarm, Martinetti's scowl, StairMaster, Crystal Pepsi, and Steven's insanity.

The radio in this all-night diner is playing Muzak of Billy Idol's "White Wedding," which I find sinister. Hey little sister, what have you done?

I am attempting to smoke. As soon as the barbershop opens this morning I'm going to be sitting in that chair, hair's going to fall, I want a fuzzy scalp and stunningly groomed eyebrows, 'cause if you saw me you'd know something was beating inside, gerbil-time, and things aren't always what they seem.

Where did I come from? Let me describe it in objects: a mansion, two parents; a trailer house, one bitter mother. A stepfather, a TV that grew larger with more channels every Christmas, a secret canister of pot in my pink bedroom, a scholarship to a famous college. A palpitating heart, eager thighs, a cruel streak. A fishbowl of dollar bills, bartending tips, my only savings account.

But this is the new Jude, ready or not, and where I come from is just a stack of singed newspaper clippings.

Oh this city, my reeking hutch, creepy-crawly and deafening. I see everything at night. The turkey bone, gristled and chomped, lying mid-sidewalk as a cannibalistic threat. The disease slathered bumpy and red over some faces, the saggy butts, the mildewed sleeping bags. Voices skittering down slimy alleys. Men who speculate at the cost of my cunt, then turn outraged when I give them the glassy eye. I hate this city, there are no lovers, only stern, squalid fuckers.

The barber didn't want to cut my hair. Too pretty, he said, but money is money, and now I am a duckling in need of a beret.

I dip into a boutique, startling the gentle proprietress, all of my secretary charm chucked out the window. I manhandle the wool suits, seeking the strongest fabric, the sharpest style. There is a rich burgundy suit with black velvet retro buttons and cuffs, it looks killer-chic on my petite, wiry body, it is mine with the flick of a credit card. Black beret, leather gloves: I am evil, evil.

Noon at the Greek Cafe, a collective Sunday morning listlessness: solitary youth and sexed-out, latte-slurping couples with the classifieds. It may be the worst time in the world to pick someone up, but there appears to be one person who wants to go against the grain.

To my right at the window seat there is a woman who has just borrowed the sugar from my table. It was not so much the reaching over, the polite murmured rhetorical question (May I borrow this?), but the grin that followed, a grin that showed her cards then snatched them up again, a grin that wagged, I know your type. And I felt a surge, a sudden panic—she knows my type?—and a gratitude so fierce I almost lunged forward.

She is a silky-haired, kohl-rimmed Cleopatra in white, black fringe brushing her eyebrows, bronze lips in motion, following her mind as she sips and speculates. She looks like she is used to controlling people and having them adore her; she looks bored but satisfied with that role. She may be someone avoiding fame.

We are trying to photograph each other in a series of quick, furtive glances. Or perhaps I am the furtive one: Whenever I look over she has those dark, knowledgeable eyes on me, and I flutter, turn away. It occurs to me that this is the first time in my life I have felt desired by a woman, and the first time since I lost my virginity that I have felt so humble, incredulous, and glaringly naive.

Panic rolls in like an unwelcome guest on my driveway, cranking up the terror-rhythm: evacuated brain, blood loss, the grip, the release, the dizzy lurch. I'm thinking, What if, what if. What if I pass out right now. No one knows me. What if something bad happens. I am not so brave.

Cleopatra leans over and says, You're white as a ghost—what's wrong?

Suddenly I am girl to her woman, abandoned kid, not what I wanted, but right now all I want to say is this: I fled, my hair is gone, please take me home.

I tell her that I'm having second thoughts about my new look.

She studies me. But it's gorgeous, she says. Your high cheekbones lend themselves well to that pared-down, glam look. The only thing missing is your skin color. Can I buy you some hot tea? Chamomile?

I let her buy me some tea, and as she wends her way to the counter I begin to place her age, her story. Late thirties, forever bisexual, artistic, solitary, beach cabin, bare feet, purples, whites, deep blues, graceful hips, gemstones, rings, no wedding ring, and now she has moved into the seat next to me, and I thank her very much.

I'm a little disoriented, I explain. Within twelve hours I have wiped out everything—the lover, the job, the look—and now I'm just sitting here contemplating my next move.

Have you changed your name?

I could, but I won't. It's still Jude.

Jude. It makes me think of Judas. But I am always looking for dark connotations, that's what I do. My name's Corinne.

A pretty, hardly threatening name, I conclude, feeling my color return.

She asks me where I come from and I give her the list. I do not mention being a secretary because I want her to think I am a drifter, an adventuress. But she guesses that I worked in an office and seems attracted to that fact, if only for the irony.

She murmurs, It all makes sense. She says, Jude, you're in shock.

Yes, I say, feeling my nerves rustle again, ready to freak.

She stares at me.

I think I've met you before, she says. Or you remind me of someone. I used to dance. My stage name was Cassandra. At Monique's? That classy joint? You remind me of this woman who used to come every Friday and watch me critically, solemn in the corner, always wearing this equestrian get-up.

It wasn't me, I say, But I like the thought.

My eyes surf from shoulder to shoulder, calculating curves,

imagining her jiggling and not liking that image, then replacing it with her winding slowly and sensuously around a pole.

Why do I remind you of her? I ask, adjusting my chair closer.

Corinne lets a smile glide across her face. Because you're a self-conscious watcher on the verge of implosion, she says. And I mean that compassionately.

So it's compassion, then, that leads me to her house in the hills. I am mild as a calf, following her upstairs, mute, warm, touching smooth stained oak, peacock feathers, cream-colored membranal leaves. She knows I haven't slept and advises me to take a bath and crawl into bed. She says she will either be gardening or reading in the living room.

It is as though a fire has been snuffed.

Her towels are velvety crimson; essential oils in blue glass vials line the windowsill. I am afraid that if I climb into this black tub of steaming lilac water I will melt to my marrow, or sleep until I have absorbed the bath like a plump golden raisin. I am only half-conscious; stranger things have happened.

In my dreams there is violence. I am in the car with Steven, his nostrils are flaring, he is wearing a man's version of my burgundy suit, I am screaming, Stop the car, stop the car! as we thunder down a graveled hill and then I realize there are no brakes. We smash into a tree, unhurt. He begins to cry. I urge him not to cry because it scares me. I start to cry, too, and then he turns indignant and says, You're not supposed to!

You don't have to wake up, a voice says.

I'm in a dark room under heavy blankets, naked. I move my sleepy body toward the voice. She says, I'm here if you need me, Jude.

I need you, I mumble.

What?

I want you.

There is a pause and then I hear the bed creak and her breathing beside me.

I wonder if you know what you mean by that, little girl, she says, stroking my fuzzy scalp.

What do you think I mean? I ask quietly, tingling.

You are so pretty you make me sad, she whispers, her hand suddenly tightening at my nape. And I want to kiss you, but there's something wrong, I don't want to steal anything, it's like I could just reach through your skin and pull out your heart.

I don't care, I say. Corinne, you brought me here.

Don't trust so easily, she says in a voice that tells me it has started.

Shadows and slithering drapes, two female bodies confined within four sweating walls. I can smell her aroma—spicy, acidic—and it stirs me. I am spacy from desire, where is she?

Put your hands above your head, she says.

Like angel wings they rise up, only to be bound swiftly with a sash. No childish knot, it is tight, hard-core.

You're going to get what you asked for, my Cleopatra leers. I saw it in you, I knew what you wanted.

But my heart, my lungs—they are frantic, shallow, frenzied. They don't match the beat between my legs, the liquid pulse. I would beg her to tame me if I didn't think she knew that already.

Hands on my legs rubbing circles on my skin, around my belly, across my collarbone. Fingernails suddenly grind into my arms. She has me high-strung, soprano-sexed. Just as I begin to melt she tightens her grip, bruising me. She murmurs words that make me yield: open, beautiful, good.

I want to tell her something, I want to warn her that I am a hard come, to not work on me as if I required work—Corinne, I want to say, I'm the impossible knot, a sexual glutton, I could be wound up forever and still crave more.

Don't even try, she says, smearing me, teasing.

A heavy wave inside glides downward, pooling at the base of my spine.

She says, You are a child, you are unformed, you are my creation, follow this rhythm.

She kneads a pulse into me, her palm is warm, she breathes into my ear, and we begin to merge, it is so dark in here, my hands are bound, my blood is rushing, she is so strong, overwhelming, hot cloves, vapors, breasts kissing breasts, what else is there, where else should I be except underneath this woman, echoing, undulating, my edge sanded smooth, gerbil-heart put to sleep.

It is like waking up from a bad dream and realizing conscious life is no better.

In the morning I prowl through her house looking for explanations, reasons why it had to be her, the one who opened me. Her books are all philosophy, Eastern religion, Renaissance art. There is no junk food in her kitchen, nothing harmful except red wine. Her apparent sincerity frightens me. Where is the danger, I want to demand. I am cranky. I am tired of being such a pussy, succumbing to other people's wills. I want my hair back. I want my virginity back. Corinne made me come; I want that back, too.

Time is running out and there are always tricks. In any enclosed space I risk imprisonment. Hey, I know the power trip of the driver, the knot-tier, the one who nurtures.

I count to ten. I walk backwards, erasing the night.

She had wiped my melt on my cheek like a gash, triumphant when it was over. You're exorcised, she declared.

What I'm saying with my fleeing is: Not even close.

# karen marie christa minns

❧✺❧

# Sauce

When I heard the sobs outside the stall door, I knew I was trapped. Shit! I flushed again, hoping she'd get the message—like, split already; maybe somebody's sick.

I come from a long line of mannered people. We don't ignore children, sick animals or crying women. I cleared my throat, giving her a last chance to save face and escape into the lobby. The ladies room at the Port Theatre is way too cramped to pretend one hasn't noticed the kind of tears this woman was manufacturing. I kept my head down, washed my hands, cursing under my breath at the lack of soap and the shred of towel. Still, our eyes connected. A millisecond of light and shadow, but it was enough. She gulped, swiped at her puffy eyes, then spoke.

"I feel so foolish, but I just can't bear the death scene."

"Excuse me?" I turned in resignation, my fingers still dripping from the sink.

"When Ruth dies." She gulped back more sobs. "I know this is ridiculous, believe me, I don't usually do this sort of thing, crying in public rest rooms, speaking to strangers out of the blue."

I handed her some sheets of toilet paper, peeling them off my fingers as carefully as I could, given the circumstances.

"It's just that I'm new here and this film . . . I grew up in Georgia . . . and today, with the rain, God, you must think I'm crazy!"

The woman attempted a smile. It came out crooked, and just a wee bit snaggle-toothed.

I think it was the snaggle-tooth that got me. Or maybe it was the gray rain drumming over our heads. Maybe it was my own embarrassment at seeing this film again, for the third time—a matinee, no less, during the week, sneaking off work. I'm not the sentimental type. I didn't want this woman to get the wrong idea about my own misty-eyed wanderings in the bathroom.

I took a good, long look at her, feeling invited, sort of. She was five-nine at least, in plain leather pumps. Her hair was pulled back into a French knot. Dull-gold ear posts and a plain gold band on her left pinky were the only jewelry I could see. A tan trench coat swathed her down to her slim ankles. A touch of makeup; some eyeliner, smudgy now and rose lipstick. Maybe no lipstick. She looked as if she'd been chewing her lips, instead of popcorn, in the dark. Her hands were long, thin, the nails trimmed and un-bitten. Maybe this crying jag wasn't in character. She smiled again. Her teeth were very white and only a little snaggly in front—that sexy country look, not enough for braces, but enough to let you know she hadn't had them capped. She held out one of her long hands.

"My name is Veronica. Thank you for not calling an usher." Her accent betrayed her Georgia roots. She'd been working on losing it, though. "I work at the university. I'm a translator."

"Oh." I blushed, caught cruising. The pause implied I should supply my own name. "I'm Emily. Emily Maple." I took her soft palm.

"You write! I've seen some of your work. I like your column in *Coast Tide*. Actually, it's the only part of the paper I read. How did you convince that paper to let you do a liberal column?" Veronica dabbed at her reddened nose. The shift in focus gave her more steam but knocked the wind right out of me.

I wasn't exactly a closet case, not by a long shot, especially these days with my new haircut and leather jacket. Still, it *was* a conservative town. The local paper was trying to live down accusations from mostly university people that it was racist and sexist, and I was the token tidbit thrown in the direction of the school. She was right, I was an anomaly and I walked a careful line. Showing up at a semi-queer (albeit whitewashed) film in the middle of the day wasn't exactly living safely. Another good reason to hightail it out of the theatre before the credits rolled.

I stuck my hands in my jacket pockets, not knowing where else to put them.

"Emily, look, I feel like I owe you . . . I mean, this is so awkward. Could I buy you a cup of coffee? Parting in the ladies' room seems kind of abrupt."

The door opened. A stream of gray-haired women filtered in, some of them, too, dabbing at runny noses.

Suddenly Veronica took my arm and more or less guided me into the lobby. The final strains of the soundtrack flowed around us. We rode the edge of the sound outside, into the rainy afternoon.

I took her to my truck, running ahead to gallantly open the passenger's side. It was pouring now and the cold fingers of rain assaulted us, collars to coattails. Still, I kept my smile clamped on. Veronica, with the grace of a dancer, skirted the wider puddles, unfazed by the downpour. She climbed gingerly into the Toyota, pulling her skirt down carefully and smoothing the raincoat over it as she sat.

I let the engine heat up for a few moments. The rain on the roof sounded tinny and sad. Outside, everything was dove gray, that particular soft color that seaside towns are swathed in during storms. We were fogging the windows with our breath.

The air between us seemed colored by pearls, softened somehow. I began to relax. Veronica unbuttoned the top of her coat. She smiled, noticing the color in my face rise again. I could smell the clean, pure scent of lavender as it escaped from her clothes.

The pulse in my neck, then lower, began to change. A quick hot drum between my legs; a recognized, memorized beat. It was both embarrassing and exciting. Shit, for all I knew she was some married lady with a cop husband and two kids at home. For all I knew she was a sociopath who picked up dykes all across the country at matinees just like this one. What better trap than the PG-13 version of a queer novel? The thump in my lap calmed down. I felt sweat mix with cold rain against my back.

"Emily," her voice cut across the sudden glacier forming between us, "am I making you uncomfortable?"

"What?" I looked ahead at the fogged-in windshield, not wanting to meet her eyes.

"My apartment is right down the beach. I make terrific espresso. Look, I don't know how to say this without it sounding exactly like a line, but I can't face a loud coffee shop right now, and I really don't want to walk alone into a cold apartment. This is not the right thing to do, especially in California, but, well, how about if I show you some ID or something?" Veronica flashed the snaggletooth.

I tried my ultra-butch cool. "Maybe you're the one who should be worried." Had absolutely no effect. The woman sat back, comfortably laughing.

"Turn left at the light, Emily."

I did.

Veronica took my jacket, hanging it up to dry. I sank into an overstuffed chair by the bay window. She flipped on a CD of Bach, filling the space between us. My writer's eye pulled all the details into focus. I forgave her the fake southwest-by-the-sea furniture after catching the row of diplomas on the wall—either extremely convincing forgeries or she was who she'd claimed. I preferred to believe the latter, especially after she emerged from a back room. She stood in the living room doorway, her hair down, a full wave of gold around her shoulders. The skirt and blouse had been replaced by a shell-colored camisole and very faded Levi's.

"You look striking, sitting there in that light," she said. "I love rain in the late afternoon, it's like an early twilight."

That familiar cousin, "the thump," began somewhere in my lower belly and moved south fast. This was going much faster than a first date. Maybe the critics had truly underestimated the effects of that film.

I ran my fingers self-consciously through my rain-slickened hair, ruing the day I'd decided to be daring and have it boy-cut. Veronica came over to the chair, sitting on the arm, looking long and slow, watching me from above. Reading my mind or my bemused expression, she said, "Don't you realize how much I like the way you look?"

Shitfire! This woman was nothing if not direct. Maybe it had something to do with being a translator. She reached down, taking both of my hands. I just knew there was no coffee involved. She led me towards the back room. Behind us, Bach dimmed and was finally lost amid the rain sounds. We came to an open room. Her room. Her bedroom.

Candles. Many candles. The scent of melting beeswax and her perfume filled the air. It wasn't cloying, though, only clean and warm, breathable but somehow denser than regular beach air—like ether, maybe. Amber and gold suffused everything. Even our skin seemed burnished. The silver-blue day had been bathed in gold dust. Warm. Suddenly all of the cold, wet melancholy of the cinema and our first hour together dissolved. It was as if we'd entered a different time.

The furniture added to the atmosphere—an antique four-poster bed and a dressing table with a huge oval mirror attached. The coverlet on the bed had been pulled back. Fresh pillows primped and plumped crested the puff of mattress. I knew if I sat I'd sink—but sitting wasn't really on her mind.

And then I saw it. A mason jar, covered with a muslin cozy on the lid, filled with the oozing comb of a beehive. It was just a wee bit creepy, too planned for my taste, but I had to admit the cool shiver it elicited was kind of delicious in its own way. I half-expected river sounds, lightning bugs, cool bluesy spirituals to emerge from the closet.

"A gift, honestly, from an old, very sentimental friend back home," Veronica said. "Come on, Emily, could you resist?" She slid behind me, leaning slightly into my butt and the small of my back. Her breasts brushed against the thin chambray of my shirt. I felt the hard tips of her nipples rise at the touch, and my own responded. Corny or not, contrived or not, all of this was having the desired effect. I was on sensory overload; Veronica was terminally homesick; it was a gray, cold evening, rainy and sad, both of us alone; and she was beautiful.

"I've been reading your columns in the paper for months. Always figured we'd meet someday . . . this is such a small town, really. Never expected it would be like this," Veronica breathed into my ear.

"Did you know I was a dyke?" I could scarcely breathe. Every muscle in my body ached. I wanted to turn, jump her bones, ravish her on that pristine, ruffly candy box of a bed, pour honey in all the crevices of her luscious body, hear her talk about my column through all of that. But my mind . . . she was snagging at my mind. Oh, she *was* a Southern woman, in the best sense—slow, so slow. Play all the nuances, taste every subtle flavor, savor the textures. So I held steady while Veronica crept over me like a big voluptuous cat, rubbing and almost purring into my ear, teasing me, easing me to her magic bed.

Still behind me, her vulva now rubbing against my ass, her hands circling my shoulders, pinning my arms to my sides, more of an insinuation than a hold, she cupped my breasts but didn't let go, only stood, behind, still moving, and judging the weight of each breast as if this was the most important thing in the world. Her tongue traced the inside of my ear, hot and almost as wet as she was making me in other places.

"Haven't you always wondered," she breathed jasmine, she breathed fire into my head, "haven't you wondered what it must have been like, I mean, for Idgie and Ruth? That first night in Idgie's parents' house, after she'd rescued Ruth from her terrible husband? Everyone home, all asleep somewhere in that great southern gothic, and knowing exactly what was happening down the hall? And they finally together after years apart, the door closed and locked and safe, the world outside and only them inside?" Veronica raised her long, slim leg and gracefully brought it up between mine.

The wet fire drove like a hammer into my clit. I was hard and melting and I could not speak. She was going to kill me with her voice, her touch, her smell.

"Emily," she continued, caressing my neck with her lips, "their first night together, their wedding night, the way it should have been from the beginning. Idgie would have to somehow explain how she'd come to so much knowledge about making love . . . and then, Ruth, the only sex she knew was from her husband, so her hunger for Idgie would be tempered with the knowledge that there could be danger in so much need."

I felt the rumble-burn and throb in my crotch, my lips blood-heavy, swollen with the wet fire she'd lit, pressed into the now too-tight seam of my jeans. She raised her knee and pressed harder, then released, making my legs go weak, making me actually stagger towards the bed, my head swimming with her words.

"In that room, together, Ruth older, terrified, on fire for the first time in her life. And Idgie, this young butch rebel, she knew, she knew what to do, but never, never with someone she loved." Veronica turned me around to face her, to look deep into her sea-green eyes and go under. "I think in that quiet, green-scented, night-filled house, behind that locked door, those women would have burst into flame."

Veronica unbuttoned her camisole. My heart filled my throat as her breasts were freed. Her skin seemed illuminated, filled with the light that permeated everything in the room. Her mouth was slightly open, slightly smiling. Her breathing was shallow, fast and very hot. Her look pulled me in close—hunger hypnotizes, and I was her captive. Her hunger matched mine. It suspended us, beyond time, beyond geography. This wasn't California and it wasn't the twentieth century. We were outside of any given space, somewhere deep and old and far more gentle than where we actually lived.

My cunt was reaching meltdown as she slipped the camisole from her shoulders. Slowly, achingly, she opened each button on my work shirt, never taking her eyes from mine. Her fingers were educated in this maneuver; I smiled, thinking of all the butch shirts that had tumbled at their touch. She frowned again as if she could read my mind.

"You're wrong, you're very wrong, you know. Don't believe me. Don't believe this is different. I'll just have to show you."

As if in slow motion, she danced us down, moving the cambric fabric of the shirt across my breasts, chafing the nipples raw, and then licking them, making them ache even more at this tease.

"This night, this night is what I think happened." Veronica's mouth found mine as she raised the shirt and slid it and my arms over my head on the bed. Her tongue filled my mouth with the taste of peppermint. Again and again she thrust, her body now on top of mine on the comforter and pillows, her tongue creating the cadence.

A moan caught in my throat. This was almost too much. I tried to pull my mouth back, gasping for air, but this only exposed my neck to her lips, her teeth. Her tongue slid back to my ear, darting, quick as one of Idgie's charmed bees; I swear even her voice held a kind of buzz, a whispered but incoherent promise, the words finally unintelligible, unimportant. Perhaps language was her passion, but for now, mine was more primal; mine was flesh. Touch. Flame.

She pushed down and into me from above, straddling me with her weight, crushing the length of me with her long body and legs, holding my arms over my head, my hands still tangled in the cast-off shirt.

I was open, open and pressed, beneath my clothes—except for the shirt, I *was* still clothed. Delicious—I knew I could call off the surrender, could pry her away, peel her from me, but I was giving in, giving her this, and it made me laugh even under the fire, this stunning dare she was pulling off. Delicious shock, this femme riding me, wild, making me undone, taking my control, bucking and rolling and pressing me down, pulling flame from us both as she rose and sank and rose again. The sodden seam of my jeans bit into my clit more than I could take, so fast, we were moving so fast, but she wouldn't relent, not even allow the release of my cry.

"Sssshhh . . . remember . . . this would be all that Ruth would know, this hard, fast heat and ravage. And Idgie would be shocked and silent, they'd both have to be silent. The family was so close, all around them, now, sshhh." Veronica smothered me with her sandpaper whisper. Her searing lips brushed mine, sending another set of scalding waves over my skin.

Still. Be still. Had to fight everything that was natural in my response, in my soul. Fight all I thought I knew about myself. Keep my hands tangled and over my head, my legs wide and throbbing, my center molten, open to whatever this woman, this glorious, golden stranger had in store. Like Idgie, maybe this *was* my first surrender.

I closed my eyes. She was right. It had to be true. The movie, the book, here, in her bed. She knew every stroke, all the moves to get to the heart of me.

She pulled up and off and doffed her jeans. I lay motionless, watching her creamy body emerge from her clothes. I felt the rush of cold and hot air as she stripped my pants over my ass, then the press and burn as she thrust herself toward me, keeping my legs only wide enough, now, for her hands and face, keeping my ankles as tangled as my wrists, keeping me tangled and tied to her.

"All I could have known I would have learned from a man."
Veronica's voice was harsh and sharpened with the quick breaths
she inhaled. Almost a hiss. For a moment I was afraid. But then
her hand—that perfectly manicured, sculpted piece of awe-
inspiring woman, that hand that I'd watched for hours, dabbing at
tears, moving a wisp of hair gently back, buttoning and unbuttoning both her clothes and mine, caressing my face, my lips, my
breasts, caressing her own sex in between stroking my rock-hard
clit—that hand now paused and then slowly, unrelentingly, opened
me in a way that I'd never allowed anyone, in the way that I had
opened many women. And she watched my eyes, my mouth, my
body in the way that I'd watched when I'd felt my hand curve and
slide and flower inside the deep secret folds of my lovers.

Again and again, farther than I thought I could take her, she
took me, coaxed me, opened and split me and then pulled the
scream from me, coming like thunder, sparks from my gnashing
teeth, from my eyes, crying like some raging animal in heat, she
took me, pressed hard and deep and upon me, and she came too,
shuddering, calling my name out, elemental Eve, unbound, the
hidden warrior behind the Southern belle, all Amazon shock troop
and ripe love, all lace cast off and animal revealed. She called my
name as I came to her, totally undone, as surely Ruth and Idgie
must have come, each to the other, after so much longing, so many
years.

We held each other, recovering, sipping the cool mint tea she'd
made fresh. I was in awe: so long in California, jaded, not quite
Republican; I thought I'd seen or done it all.

Fat chance. Leave it to the South.

Veronica leaned over on one elbow, her lips glistening with the
fresh tea. She kissed me slow and full, full of soul and the taste of
green herbs and ice in summer. She sent shudders through me.

Not a stranger anymore, but still, a translator. I smiled through
our kiss.

Then I rolled on top of her, making her drop her tea to the floor.
Before she could react I slipped one hand to my lips, shushing
her, and with the other, I reached up and over us for the mason jar
with the flowered lid. For the honey.

# HEROTICA 6

*Again, For Marco*

# Acknowledgments

*Thanks to the powers-that-be for being right;*
*to Shar for seeing me through yet another collection;*
*to Leigh for her persistent efficiency;*
*and to all the writers who showed me new ways to be*
*sexually creative within committed relationships.*

# Introduction

When the powers-that-be first suggested that we center the sixth *Herotica* collection around a theme, I went wild with ideas: Sex in Uniforms. Chicks with Dicks. Hairy Heroines. Orgies. Said powers considered all my suggestions and then came back with their own: Committed Relationships.

Huh?

It was a theme, they said, that would appeal to the large number of women seeking erotic fiction to share with their lovers. Women were looking for stories that would serve to enhance their sexual relationships with long-term partners — stories that might give hints on how to keep the home fires burning beyond The Seven Year Itch, Lesbian Bed Death, kids, careers and hectic schedules.

The *Herotica*® series is known for being eclectic: in fact, *Kirkus Reviews* noted that the stories in *Herotica 5* "have little in common with one another beyond their use of explicit erotic material." The comment was neither unkind nor inaccurate: The *Herotica*® books have always contained a mix of raunchy and romantic, hard-core and soft. I worried — unnecessarily, as it turned out — that the seeming confinement of Committed Relationships might lead to a homogenous collection that would be anything but eclectic.

Although in my personal experience sex has always been better within the safety of a committed relationship — as trust builds so does my willingness to expose my quirks, fantasies and desires — my professional experience has been quite the opposite. Having edited two previous *Herotica* books, screened fiction for *On Our Backs*, and taught sex writing, I thought I'd pretty much seen how erotic writers handled this subject: They'd invariably set up a hot scenario in a hotel or bar or dark alley, and in the end would deliver the "surprise": "It was actually my husband/lover/girlfriend giving me the best birthday present of my life!" Hell, I'd even written those kinds of stories myself.

I also worried that I'd be deluged by flowery paeans to heterosexual monogamy, and that the sex would read like a romance novel. I fully expected it to take years to accumulate enough hot quality stories to constitute an anthology.

I was in for an awakening when, months later, I sat down with a box of 200-something manuscripts, reached inside, and pulled out "Neighborhood Round Robyn," the first story in this collection. I laughed out loud reading this clever tale of a suburban housewife innocently causing a chain reaction that arouses and transforms the whole neighborhood; I was amazed that a story revolving around an ordinary heterosexual couple managed to convey an almost pansexual sensibility.

I reached into the box again — and came up with "The Album," a story of genderbending and fantasy play between two long-term partners. Talk about pansexual sensibility! "We've acted out a lot of our fantasies," says the narrator. "We've been girlfriends and boyfriends. We've traded genders. We've done bondage and S/M in exotic scenarios. But it's always been just the two of us. When we're brutally honest with each other, we need and want the security of monogamy."

By this time I was thoroughly jazzed; I picked up a third manuscript and sat transfixed by the heartbreaking — and taboo-breaking — "Mourning the Peasant."

I'd read just three stories and they were all in the "Yes" pile, an unprecedented occurrence. I went for a walk and ruminated on this unexpected development.

I am prone to a psychological process that shrinks refer to as "globalization:" I tend to draw vast philosophical conclusions from a small sampling of information. On the basis of these three wildly different and unique pieces of fiction, my overactive mind began spinning an entire philosophy about the role that love, commitment and longevity play in peoples' sex lives. I realized I should not have been surprised to find creativity and hot sex permeating stories about committed relationships: Such partnerships do, after all, provide the stability that enables people — particularly women — to explore their sexuality within the context of safety and security. As the narrator says in "June's High Holy Day," "This trust was a big deal. I'm really not inclined to put myself in vulnerable positions; in fact I've only done so with June, and only in our most intimate moments."

That committed relationships can provide deep and satisfying sexual experiences should not have come as a revelation. As I said, this has certainly been my own personal experience — I'm more likely to share my most elaborate, secret fantasies with long-term lovers rather than with one-night stands.

And the stories in this collection aren't only about couples sharing fantasies, but about acting them out. Now, this is fiction, and we don't know what, if anything, is based on real experience — nor does it matter: The point is that these writers are able to imagine and portray sexual relationships in which committed partners have as much or more fun than bed-hoppers. They don't make the assumption that diminished passion is the inevitable price we pay for comfort and companionship. They don't think that sustaining a life-enhancing partnership and fucking like slut bunnies are mutually exclusive.

Of course, not every story in my pile of manuscripts was wonderful — there were those that didn't fire my imagination and/or libido; there always are. But by the time I'd finished reading through the stack, I had a respectable "Yes" pile.

Admittedly, some of these stories employ the old "Surprise, I knew him all along!" ending, but that was inevitable. And, yes, many of the stories are romantic — another inevitability — but let's face it, a healthy dose of romance is a turn-on to most women. There are more birthdays and anniversaries celebrated within these pages than in previous *Herotica*® collections, an interesting commentary on commitment. And a couple of the stories deal with the death of loved ones.

I think what surprised me most, though, was an expanded idea of commitment. In "Three Note Harmony," the bonds of friendship are tested and strengthened. "Blue Moon Over Paradise" gives new meaning to what we think of as loyalty. In "Always," the practice of "managed faithfulness," as the narrator calls it, leads to a loving extended family. "Mourning The Peasant" pushes the boundaries of "committed relationships" beyond couplehood, beyond marriage, beyond the traditional nuclear family.

These stories remind us that committed relationships aren't always about couplehood, even when we're talking about sex.

### Keeping Sex Alive

So how *do* women keep sex alive in committed relationships? Various self-help books give advice such as playing gimmicky board games to open avenues of communication; exchanging elaborate candlelit massages; spicing things up now and then with an X-rated video; greeting hubby at the door wrapped in cellophane, as the Kathy Bates character did in *Fried Green Tomatoes*. Not one story in this collection relies on those clichés. Rather, they delve into real life experiences, where sex is an expression of abiding love, loyalty or acceptance; they show sex as a tool of discovery, comfort and renewal; they employ sex as a vehicle for working through "negative" feelings like anger and grief. Even those that are strictly about reviving a failing sex life or keeping a good one going are rooted in the dynamics of the relationship. The characters in all these stories test, stretch and deepen their connection to one another through sex. Put that cellophane back where it belongs, honey — on leftovers!

### Genderbenders, Pansexuals, and Switch-Hitters

One of the things I like about editing the *Herotica*® books is that when it comes to sexual orientation or preference, we're an equal opportunity series. Every collection has contained a mix of heterosexual, lesbian, bisexual and transsexual stories. As the narrator says in "Three Note Harmony": "Chocolate Chip Cookie Dough. Cherry Garcia. Macadamia Nut Brittle. Which to choose? Isn't it ironic that we're allowed 31 flavors of ice cream, yet only one flavor of sexuality?"

It's notable that this collection boasts five stories I'd call "pansexual," that is, they don't fall neatly into any of the above categories. In "Neighborhood Round Robyn," people with diverse erotic proclivities are aroused by everyone else. "Three Note Harmony" involves a woman and two men, while in "Always" it's two women and a man. "Being Met" and "The Album" are about couples who do "genderfuck," that is, switch gender identity through the use of props or merely attitude. Even two of the ostensibly heterosexual stories, "Snooping" and "Simple Gifts," involve reversal of stereotypical sex roles.

Could it be that, as a society, we're becoming more flexible with regard to gender identity and sexual orientation, that we can slip in and out of roles with the flick of a leather whip? If we choose to look at cultural trends through the prism of women's erotica — as good a prism as any — we find that the species *is* becoming more fluid in this area. True, women who write erotica are a special breed, and those who write cutting edge sex comprise an even smaller group; but while it's always a minority who explore the far reaches of consciousness and behavior, the rest of the culture does crawl along behind. Witness the popularization of S/M, now openly promoted on billboards where a cheery dominatrix pushes Altoid mints as delivering a pleasurable kind of pain. Would such an ad have come into being without the work of Pat Califia and other S/M pioneers, people most mint-chewers have never even heard of?

Similarly, the dialogue around gender fluidity has been pushed forward by the emergence of a transgender movement. Transsexualism is fast becoming the movie flavor of the month. Intersexed people are beginning to make noise: Trust me, you'll be hearing a lot more about this group in the near future. I foresee a time when people will be able to be female for a day, a year, a decade, and then be male, whether it involves surgery and hormones or merely a change of clothing. I don't expect it to happen in my lifetime, but I do expect it to happen.

## Gender Identity and Fiction

One of the writers' conferences in an online service I subscribe to is called "Writing the Opposite Sex," a topic in which fiction writers discuss the ways that women write men and vice versa. In all my years of editing erotica, I've always been able to tell when a story came from a man using a female pseudonym. Not so this time: I actually had to ask one contributor who'd used initials for her full name to indicate her gender, despite the fact that her characters were lesbian. Similarly, one of the stories in this collection is written from a male point of view. In this case I know the author personally and can vouch for her gender — but I'm not so sure it would be obvious on a cold reading.

This question of writing as the opposite sex is one that's plagued fiction writers since time immemorial, probably since Lady Murasaki penned the first known novel. Male writers seemingly had no qualms about drawing female characters or even writing as women: Sometimes they hit the mark, but more often they failed dismally. Before the Third Wave of feminism, women frequently wrote under male pseudonyms simply to get published. At the height of the women's movement, there was a burst of energetic fiction from women, often portraying men rather badly as they released a minefield of anger; at the same time, men were criticized for daring to presume they knew how to write from a female perspective. Here in the so-called post-feminist era, we're all calming down a bit, and recognizing that, just as a skilled writer must be able to write about characters who inhabit other times, places and cultures, so too must we learn to write about those who inhabit bodies different from our own.

Erotic writers seem to be moving in that direction — we're all getting better at this. We're getting better at imagining ourselves in one another's shoes, or rather, bodies and minds. Through reading and writing about sex and sexual relationships, we're learning more about how the opposite gender feels and thinks.

I'll go even further and say that writing sex, because it's so charged with intensity, has the potential to teach us a great deal about characterization in fiction. College writing classes and workshops might benefit from the experience and skills of erotic writers. They might even use erotic writing exercises as a way of teaching their students the potential of imaginative experience.

## Eclecticism Rules!

So here we are, having chosen a theme, and *Herotica 6* ends up being an eclectic mix after all. Some stories are good old-fashioned jackoff material, while others are complex pieces of literary fiction. By offering a variety of stories, we represent the wide range of women's sexual desires and imaginations. Readers of erotica tend to skip around anthologies, to dip and choose and return to old favorites. By remaining diverse, we offer something for almost everyone — and, not so coincidentally, spark new ideas and notions of what is possible and permissible in bed.

And to think that all this came from that humdrum theme of committed relationships.

*Marcy Sheiner*
*Emeryville, California*
*October 1998*

# Mel Harris

❦

# Neighborhood Round Robyn

Robyn Pearson could not think of his mouth on her body without emitting a little pleasure-filled gasp. It could come at any moment — at the supermarket, driving to work, or getting her hair done. Once it had even happened at the dentist's while she was having her teeth cleaned. The dentist kept asking her if anything was wrong, but all she could do was blush and shake her head. The lingering kiss she'd given her husband Cliff as he'd left for work that day had promised more to come. Ten years of marriage, and she still fantasized about him every day.

Today was her day off and she just wanted to lounge by the pool. The pool had been the selling point for her and Cliff when they'd bought this house six months earlier. They loved swimming, especially skinny-dipping, but they'd had to put it off until they could get a privacy fence erected. It was too easy for their water play to get out of hand; they'd barely made it into the cabana the last time they'd had a late night swim.

Robyn changed into her "tanning" suit — an old, faded two-piece that was stretchy and comfortable — picked up a novel and a mug of iced tea, and headed for the pool. As she positioned the chaise lounge for the best sun, she noticed construction noises coming from the Harolds' house across the street. Shading her eyes for a moment, she watched the handsome construction worker putting the finishing touches on the new sunroom.

Marge and Harvey Harold had a beautiful two-story home and were quite well-to-do, but Robyn wasn't envious. She'd seen Marge Harold wandering around, drink in hand, looking lost and lonely. And she rarely saw Harvey home until late at night. Robyn turned her attention to smoothing suntan lotion over her exposed skin. Satisfied, she lay back on the lounge and picked up her novel.

Derek Collins lifted the piece of redwood siding onto the outer wall of the Harolds' sun room and nailed it in place. He'd be glad to finish this job. Oh, the Harolds were polite and all, and the job certainly paid well. But the hungry look Marge Harold gave him when she thought he wasn't looking made him uneasy. Right now, he was enjoying the relative peace and quiet of the morning. He never saw Mrs. Harold until after lunch; she was probably sleeping off her hangover.

Derek picked up another piece of redwood and laid it out on the sawhorses. Glancing up he saw Robyn Pearson, across the street, getting ready to lie by her pool.

He sighed. It had been some time since he'd been with a woman who really enjoyed herself. Trying not to be too obvious, he continued to watch the sunbather as she stretched out on the lounge and settled back to enjoy her book. Robyn Pearson was the only interesting person in this neighborhood, what with lonely Mrs. Harold and her strange neighbor Perry who lived next door.

Perry Traynor's house was situated just to the right of the Harolds' new sunroom, and he often came out to chat with Derek. Perry was friendly enough — a little too friendly for Derek. He seemed to have that same hungry look in his eye as Mrs. Harold. Derek shook his head. "I guess everybody's got to be some place," he thought. Mostly he just wanted to finish this job and get paid. He returned to measuring the board on his sawhorse.

Perry Traynor sat at his desk in his short silk robe, his head in his hands. He'd been sitting there for nearly an hour trying to come up with an idea for a story he was supposed to write for a gay men's erotic magazine. It was due tomorrow. He wasn't particularly thrilled to be writing those kinds of stories, but it paid the bills and allowed him to stay home to work on his novel. He was going to be a great published author someday, but right now he needed a story, and every idea he'd come up with so far was so . . . *routine.*

Perry stared listlessly out the window in front of him and saw Derek Collins lifting a board into place on the Harolds' sunroom wall. Perry had engaged Derek in several conversations over the adjoining fence, but he could tell that Derek was strictly hetero and only making polite talk with him. Oh well, it didn't hurt a guy to try. He watched as Derek stood at his sawhorse — but Derek seemed thoroughly engrossed in something across the way. Perry followed Derek's gaze until he saw Robyn Pearson settling in by her pool. "No wonder you can't concentrate on your work, Tool Man," he muttered.

Robyn would certainly keep Derek's attention better than that lonely Mrs. Harold. In fact, it seemed to Perry that Robyn Pearson was the only person in this neighborhood who was really happy. Not like that poor Tracy Parks across the street — she came out of her house just long enough to retrieve her mail, and she never looked up or said hello. And no wonder with that husband of hers, Dick. Dick-less was more like it, Perry thought. He could tell from the bruises and occasional swollen lip on Tracy that her husband knew nothing of a tender touch.

Perry sighed again. Well, Derek was a pleasant distraction for him. "If I can't work, I might as well enjoy the scenery," he thought to himself as he sat back in his chair and watched Derek work.

Tracy Parks stood in front of the open refrigerator. She was supposed to be fixing the lunch Dick had ordered her to make before he'd left for work. She leaned over and rummaged around in the vegetable bin — enough for a salad with a sandwich. She took out a head of lettuce and tossed it in the sink. She didn't want to feed Dick Parks lunch, she wanted to feed him poison. A cucumber, two small carrots and a zucchini followed the lettuce into the sink.

Just that morning, she'd decided she was going to leave Dick tomorrow, right after he left for work. She'd had enough of his coarse, disgusting behavior. He treated his truck better than he treated her. He never let her out of the house, even with her girlfriends, always suspicious she'd hook up with some guy. She turned on the faucet, picked up the head of lettuce and slammed it on the counter. Grabbing the core, she yanked it out and threw the lettuce back in the sink to drain.

She knew she wasn't Einstein, but she was decent and hard-working, and she knew she could do better than Dick Parks. She started peeling the cucumber. Maybe she wouldn't even hook up with a guy; she'd had enough of men. Maybe she could find a guy who wouldn't want anything from her except companionship. A guy like that Perry who lived across the street. She knew he was gay, but she saw the sweet way he served coffee to his friends who occasionally slept over. He'd even waved and said hello to her once, but she'd looked away and quickly retreated to her house.

Tracy picked up a carrot and started peeling it furiously as she thought about her escape from Dick. Maybe some day, after enough time, she would find a man like the one Robyn Pearson had. Now *there* was a husband. She saw the way Cliff Pearson looked at his wife and the way he held her before going off to work. She saw the flowers he brought home, too. She threw the carrots into the drainer and picked up the zucchini to scrub. Some day . . .

Robyn put down her book and reached for the mug of iced tea. The sun was definitely doing its job. She took a long drink of tea. Condensation from the mug dripped onto her breasts and ran down her cleavage. God, that felt good. Reaching into the mug, she fished out an ice cube and rubbed it along the length of her cleavage. When that cube melted, she retrieved a couple more and popped them in her mouth briefly before removing them and slipping one in each cup of her swimsuit top. She then got another and slid it into her bottoms. As the ice melted, the cold water trickled down around her nipples and through her pubic hair, finding its way to what Cliff referred to as her "Secret Ridge." Robyn made a mental note to have Cliff do this to her next time.

Still smiling, she lay back and closed her eyes. The reading and the sun had made her sleepy.

Derek was carefully measuring the last piece of redwood for the sunroom when a movement in Robyn's direction caught his eye. Looking up he saw her take a long drink from a mug, beads of water falling on her breasts. His mouth watered from his own thirst and he stepped behind the Harolds' fence. He knew he shouldn't be watching, but his eyes were riveted to Robyn as she smoothed an ice cube over her skin.

His tool belt tightened uncomfortably, and he realized he was swelling. He adjusted the belt, but the swelling continued as he watched Robyn slip more ice cubes into her top and then into her bottoms. He groaned as she patted that last cube just where she wanted it. What he wouldn't give to be that ice cube! Her lazy smile told him she was thinking some very pleasant thoughts.

Derek shifted his jeans, his zipper biting into him, but the more he adjusted, the harder he got. He lifted his tool belt, rested it on his hip bones, then carefully unzipped his jeans. His penis, eager for air, strained at his boxers, and he quickly freed himself from them as well. He looked down at his one-eyed buddy, now waving wildly in the air.

"Jeez, has it been that long?" he wondered aloud. "Pretty soon you're going to jump out and find it on your own!" He reached down and quieted himself with his hand, focusing on Robyn again. By now she had drifted off to sleep, the wet spots dark on her suit where the ice had melted, her nipples pulled taut from the cold.

Robyn shifted and rolled onto her side. Derek's penis jumped in his hand as she revealed the curve where the back of her thigh met her buttock, that tender, dark highway to heaven where her bottoms nearly disappeared. It was the tastiest morsel on the buffet, as far as he was concerned. His buddy was doing its dance in his hot hand, and he knew it wouldn't be long now. He was just trying to hang on . . .

In her upstairs bedroom, Marge Harold stirred. Her head felt like it weighed fifty pounds and her throat felt stuffed with cotton. She went into her bathroom, washed her face and brushed her teeth, avoiding the mirror. Finished, she returned to the bedroom. At least she could swallow now. Sitting at the vanity, she picked up a brush and ran it through her hair. She saw that she still had on the green silk nightie and sighed. She'd intended to seduce Harvey last night, but it had gotten later and later and she'd had too much to drink while waiting for him. She sighed again, and wondered if Harvey stayed at work so late to avoid her. It wasn't that he didn't love her, or so he said. But he was always working.

There was that time, years ago, when she'd made dinner and taken it down to Harvey's office. He'd been surprised, and she'd made him part of the meal. She rubbed her belly remembering the mango and fresh peach she'd eaten off him, finishing with that incredible chocolate mousse that she'd served to his delicate waiting tongue. Marge sighed again. That had been so long ago.

She stood up and went to the window that directly overlooked the new sunroom. She'd hoped the work would have taken a little longer, but she knew from Derek's attitude that he wasn't anxious to linger. Noticing that the hammering and sawing were strangely absent, she wondered if he was through. He'd ring the bell when he was, she concluded, and went back to brushing her hair.

Perry ripped another sheet out of his typewriter and crumpled it in frustration. Three sentences and it was already *dreck*. He threw the crumpled sheet on the floor. He had to get this finished. He picked up another sheet and fed it into the typewriter. As he was adjusting the paper, he happened to notice Derek. Perry's eyes widened. Leaning forward, he rubbed them and looked again. At first he thought Derek was relieving himself in the bushes, but he quickly realized that Derek Collins was holding an erection in his hand. And what a beauty it was, glistening in the sun like the muscles on his delicious back. And that waving thing it was doing. My god, it had a mind of its own!

Perry soon felt himself pulse and, as he looked down, his cock poked out of his robe. He stared at it and it waved back at him. "Oooh, Junior," he cooed, "I'm gonna put you to good use. Just like Hammer Boy and his tool."

Perry giggled and slowly ran his hands down his thighs and then back up again, stopping at his erection. He watched Derek's hand moving along his flushed shaft, sliding it slowly up and down, all the while keeping his eye on Robyn.

Perry looked over at Robyn, but all he could see was the gentle mound of the back side of her hips. He returned his gaze to Derek, who appeared to be having a hard time keeping a grip on himself. Perry's erection pulsated. "You must be looking at something very special, Derek," he crooned.

Tracy had just finished peeling the carrots and was reaching for the zucchini when she looked up and saw Perry Traynor through the open window of the den, sitting at his desk. Something strange was going on; she squinted to get a clearer view. Suddenly her mouth dropped open. In Perry's lap stood a sturdy erection. Perry leaned back in his chair and rubbed his hands up and down his thighs, coming to rest on his penis.

Tracy shut off the faucet, realizing she'd practically scrubbed a hole through the zucchini. Quickly glancing around the kitchen, she spied a barstool and dragged it over in front of the sink. She unfastened her shorts and slid them to the floor along with her panties. Climbing onto the stool, she perched herself, looking out the window. This was one show she wasn't going to miss.

Perry was still in the same position, his hand moving more quickly now. Tracy propped her legs up on the sink, hooking her heels over the edge. Keeping a clear view of Perry, she reached over and picked up the freshly peeled cucumber. It felt cool and delicious sliding in. She tensed her thighs and waves of pleasure ran up her legs and into her belly. By now, Perry was leaning back in his chair, his robe open. His intense concentration and the rippled flexing of his abdomen excited her even more. She slid out the cucumber and reached for the zucchini, which was longer and slightly swollen at one end.

Derek knew that it would only be a matter of seconds before he would be adorning the Harolds' shrubbery. With his free hand, he braced himself against the fence, still staring at Robyn. She shifted slightly, but it was just enough to cause her right nipple to pop out of her top — as if he'd reached over and freed it with his own fingers.

It was all he could take. Derek's abdomen tightened in spasms and he shuddered violently as he spattered the shrubbery and fence, spraying the Harolds' azaleas.

Perry gasped as Derek leaned forward against the fence, giving him an even better view of his full staff. Perry's own erection strained in his hand. That prickly hot rush in his thighs told him he was close on Derek's heels. He pushed apart his robe — no sense in staining good silk — and emitted a long, low moan as he watched Derek lean forward, legs braced, buttocks tight, and erupt all over the Harolds' fence.

Perry reached down with his free hand to cup and massage his velvet pouch, now rippled and tight. "AARRRagghhhh," he cried, falling back in the chair as he shot come all over his thighs. In his intense pleasure, he didn't notice he had leaned back so far that the chair was falling. He landed on the ottoman behind him, which fortunately softened his fall as he continued to orgasm.

The zucchini had been the right choice. Tracy moved it inside her, bringing herself to the edge, Perry's action furiously spurring her on. She spied the peeled carrots and braced her heels firmly on the sides of the sink. Taking the small carrots in her free hand, she slipped one on either side of her tumescent reed, the fresh coolness and the friction causing it to swell. Slow firm strokes with the carrots brought her dangerously close to the edge of that wonderful chasm of pleasure.

Suddenly she laughed out loud. She'd take a vegetable over Dick any day! Just then she saw Perry lean back, reach down, and squeeze himself as he shot into the air. Tracy slid the zucchini part way out and then, in one last stroke, the carrots gripping her clit, she gave the final push over the edge, the zucchini bucking wildly. Oh, how she loved her greens.

Upstairs, Marge Harold had finished brushing her hair. Curious as to why she still hadn't heard anything from Derek, she went over to the window and pushed back the drapes. Where was he? She was about to turn and go into the shower when she gave one last look directly below her window. "My god," she whispered as her hand flew to her mouth. Derek Collins, gleaming erection in hand, was coming all over her redwood fence.

She watched as Derek waited for his erection to go down enough to fit back into his jeans. Straightening himself, he picked up the last board from the sawhorses and nailed it to the sunroom wall.

Marge inhaled sharply; she hadn't been breathing. Without thinking, she picked up the phone and dialed Harvey's office. She tapped her foot impatiently, waiting for his secretary to connect her.

"Hello — Marge?" Harvey sounded surprised. Marge rarely called him at the office.

"Yeah, Harv, it's me," she said breathlessly. "Listen, I've been thinking about bringing you dinner at the office. Something delicious."

"Marge, is everything okay?"

"Oh yeah, Harv. It's more than okay. I was just thinking

about you and the last time we had dinner at your office . . . remember?"

"Mmmm," Harvey moaned softly. "Do I remember? I didn't know you could do so much with chocolate mousse."

Marge giggled. "Well, wait 'til you see the menu tonight."

"I'm looking forward to it. Can you be here by seven?"

"No problem. And Harv?"

"Yeah?"

"I've missed you, and I want to make up for it tonight."

"I can't wait," Harvey breathed softly into the phone.

Perry giggled at himself; feet in the air, erection spent. What a trip! He rolled over, stood up and picked up his chair. Straightening his robe, he sat down and began typing furiously.

Tracy sat there, her heels still hooked over the sink, her legs trembling. As soon as she was able, she got up and put on her panties and shorts. She was slicing the last of the cucumber into the salad when Dick walked through the door and growled, "Where's my lunch?"

Setting the bowl down on the table in front of him she said sweetly, "I've made you a sandwich and here's a nice salad to go with it. The dressing's already on it."

"Salad? Goddamn rabbit food," he grumbled, but he picked up a fork and began to eat it anyway. Tracy quickly turned her back and began washing the dishes.

It was a moment before Robyn realized that something was blocking her sun. Sleepily she opened her eyes and smiled. Cliff was standing there. He reached down and stroked her exposed nipple with his finger. "Looks like one of your girlfriends is winking at me," he said.

She rubbed her eyes and laughed. "The other one wants you

to visit her, too," she replied, holding it up for him.

Cliff looked around. "I wish we had that privacy fence up," he said. "I'd slide the lounge over and let you slip right out of that suit and into the pool."

"Mmmm . . . then what, Mr. Pearson?"

"Well, Mrs. Pearson," he said, sitting on the edge of the lounge and wiggling his finger into the leg of her bottoms, "you'd just have to let me surprise you." Cliff looked around again."Hey, what about that guy over at the Harolds'? I hear he's pretty good with a tool. Maybe I can go over and talk to him about building the fence."

"I don't know," Robyn replied. "I think he might be done. I haven't heard a sound in quite awhile."

# Mary Anne Mohanraj

❦

# Season of Marriage

She was dizzy with the smoke. The traditional wedding had lasted almost three hours, and the heat and oil fumes from the glowing lamps had combined to make Raji feel queasy. There were kids running around all over the place, dressed in vibrant colors that hurt her eyes. And the chanting. It went on and on and on in incomprehensible Sanskrit.

Raji knew no Sanskrit — she even spoke her Tamil with a New England accent. She was suddenly homesick — for America, for Connecticut, for forests and hills and snow and people you could speak your mind around without treading on some custom you didn't understand. She hungered for cold pizza breakfasts and frozen yogurt lunches, for slumber parties and stolen dates and the friends who had covered for her. Despite the cold heart and the pain that had driven her to this wedding in the baking heat of New Delhi, America was home. And it was too late to go back.

She was married now. The wedding reception was ending, and it would soon be time to leave with this seemingly kind stranger, to go to the house of his mother (whom Raji already disliked), to go to his bed. And all her American casualness about sex, the casualness and experience she had counted on to see her through this ordeal, was suddenly meaningless. She was scared. Why, oh why had she agreed to this?

The answer to that was easy: because she hadn't cared anymore. After she'd found out about Jim and that other girl; after all the broken promises and shattered dreams, it just didn't seem to matter. In the midst of the heat and incense a wave of brutally clear memory washed over her.

They'd just collapsed, Jim on top of her, as he always insisted. He was crushing her with his weight. Raji managed to roll to the side, and then turned to gaze into his eyes, still amazed that this gorgeous man would really want her.

"You were wonderful," Raji said.

"Uh huh." He was still panting, but in a very sexy way, she thought.

"Jim?"

"Uh huh."

"I love you."

There was a disconcerting pause. Before, he'd always responded, "I love you, too." Now, he said nothing for much too long.

"Ummm . . . " Jim said.

"Yes?" she asked, eagerly.

"I should probably tell you something. Now don't get too upset, okay?"

And he proceeded to tell her about Sharmila. Also Indian. Raji remembered her from biology class last semester. Drop-dead gorgeous with unfairly huge breasts. Sharmila, whom he'd been sleeping with for three weeks. His conscience had finally kicked in. Or maybe he was just bored with Raji, and this was the easiest way to make her break up with him. Which she, of course, did.

Looking back, she realized how stupid she had been. Not in dating him, but in caring so much about somebody who had obviously cared so little. She had gotten so worked up about what she had seen as the ultimate betrayal that she had sunken into a black fit of depression during which she had let everyone else make decisions for her. She'd ignored the advice of her friends, both Indian and American, and decided that maybe her parents were right, after all. Maybe American men really were slime. Maybe she'd be happiest with someone like herself.

So she'd agreed to meet some Indian men, and the next thing she knew she was flying to India to meet this man Vivek. And he was gentle. And kind. Rich and generous: He'd given her a lovely ruby and pearl necklace the day after they met. And though she'd only known him for a few days, her parents thought he was very suitable and his parents liked her and it was suddenly all arranged and they were asking her and she said yes.

Now she was remembering all the sweet guys she'd grown up with and wondering where they'd gone. She was finally shaking off the depression that had lasted the four months since Jim; suddenly she knew that she'd have been happier with an American she understood rather than with this stranger from a strange land that she'd left when she was six. Still, it was too late. She was married, and though she could probably get a divorce, Raji wasn't the sort to give up on anything that easily. A divorce would mean that she had failed . . . again. Not to mention that a divorce would break her mother's heart. Her dear, scheming, conniving, thoroughly manipulative mother. Sometimes Raji couldn't figure out whether she loved or hated her mother. Not that it really made much difference at this point.

Her silence was noted by Vivek, who asked her in his perfect, if heavily accented English, if she felt all right. Raji was touched that he had noticed — Jim would never have noticed if she were quiet; he would have been too busy talking. She nodded to Vivek that she was okay, then stood with him as the interminable reception finally came to a close. He gave her a tentative smile; a sort of 'buck up' look that was heartening. Raji wondered what this shy and probably virginal man would think of an experienced American. She'd find out soon enough.

The women took her to the bedroom and helped her undress, giving her fragments of advice in broken English as they helped her into a flowing white nightgown, incredibly demure and perfectly opaque. Raji barely heard them, caught somewhere between tears and laughter. She waited patiently, allowing them to dress her as they chose, and then lead her to the crimson-draped bed. One woman, who Raji thought was her new sister-in-law and recently married herself, touched Raji's shoulder before she left, kindly. Then they were gone.

Vivek appeared, ghost-like in the doorway, dressed in flowing white to match her. He walked toward her silently, carefully; a hunter afraid of startling some strange, wild creature. Raji was determined to try to make this marriage work, and so she smiled, slightly trembling. Vivek returned her smile tentatively and reached up to touch her cheek. His hand was not damp and sweaty as she had feared, but warm and dry, as if lit by some inner fire. He had not touched her before this, in all the days of wedding preparations during the short month since they had met. Even when placing the gold *thali* wedding necklace around her neck, he had taken care not to touch her. She was suddenly grateful for his gentleness: stepping boldly towards him, she stretched her slim brown arms to encircle his thick neck, surprised to find that he was shaking too.

Vivek was not very handsome, but was sturdily built, with hair thicker and richer than hers, and deep brown eyes. Raji had thought them dull and calf-like before, but suddenly she was not so sure. There was a hint of laughter in those eyes, and a sparkle of intelligence. Of course, he was a doctor (nothing else would have satisfied her mother), and so couldn't be entirely stupid. Now, with her hands locked behind his neck and her delicate body inches away from his, Raji found herself bemused, not sure what to do next, or how fast to go. He solved that problem for her.

He placed his arms around her waist, gently. Tilting his head, he kissed her. She was startled, not at being kissed, but at being kissed by him, and she stiffened in his arms. He raised his head questioningly. "Is this not customary in America?"

"Yes, yes it is. I didn't think it was here."

"We are not as ignorant as you Americans assume. We do watch movies, after all."

Now Raji was sure that he was laughing at her, as he leaned down to kiss her again. Despite his claims to knowledge she was fairly sure that kissing was new to him, and so responded gently to the firm pressure on her lips. They kissed chastely for long minutes, until Raji daringly opened her mouth and touched her tongue to his lips. He broke away for a moment, plainly startled, but then returned to kissing her with enthusiasm, opening his own mouth and tasting her lips, her teeth, her tongue. She tilted her head backwards, hoping he would get the hint, and he did — kissing her cheek, her nose, her ear, tracing a delicate line along her cheekbone with his tongue. He went slowly, and Raji stood still, eyes closed, feeling him touch her. This was new to her — this gentleness, this seeming reverence. She had enjoyed sex with Jim, but it had always been hard and fast, a summer storm — quickly started, quickly over. Vivek was twenty-five, years older than Jim had been, but he smiled with the wonder of a child. Raji felt an odd constriction in her chest.

Continuing to explore her chocolate skin, Vivek slid slowly down her neck. Shivers were racing through her now, and Raji tried to hold still, wondering how long she could act the shy virgin, how long it would be before her impatience broke through. His kisses were abruptly stopped by the laces at the top of the gown, and he froze and locked her eyes with his. Raji slowly reached up and, almost teasingly, pulled free the tangled white ribbons and laces. Vivek undid them completely, sliding the white fabric off her creamy brown shoulders, continuing the slow kisses that had fallen as cool rain but now began to burn. Despite a ceiling fan, the room was stiflingly hot to a woman raised in New England winters, and Raji began to sway, dizzy with heat and unexpected passion. Vivek caught and held her, as the gown slid from her bare body to pool on the green-tiled floor. Cradling her against him with one arm, he pulled aside mosquito netting and drapes with the other. Picking her up, he gently deposited Raji on the bed and pulled the sheet over her. All this happened so quickly that Raji had no moment in which to become embarrassed in her nakedness before this almost-stranger, this husband. And then he was undressing too, undoing the wrap of white fabric and climbing in to sit beside her, pulling the mosquito netting around them.

"Are you all right?" Vivek asked.

"Yes, I think so. Are you?"

"Of course I am. I'm a man."

Laughter again, from both of them this time, which trailed away into silence. He looked suddenly vulnerable, Raji thought, as he sat there naked and cross-legged on the wide bed. The silence grew more and more awkward until Raji finally raised herself a little on her elbows, letting the sheet fall down to bare her curving breasts. She puckered her lips for a kiss. He laughed again, and suddenly he was swooping down on her in mid-laugh, slipping his broad hands around her fragile frame. Raji began drowning in a hail of fierce kisses and caresses. In the lamp-lit dimness his hands explored what he could not see, curving to surround her small breasts, which fit neatly into his palms. He fumbled a little, sometimes touching her too softly, sometimes too fiercely, but always kissing as she arched into his touch.

Vivek slid his hands down her stomach, across her hips, gently pushing apart her trembling thighs. She stiffened, remembering what she had not told him, and opening her eyes wildly searched for his, until he, looking up, caught her trapped gaze.

"Don't be afraid." he reassured her, though his voice was trembling. "I'm a doctor, it's all right." He smiled again, inviting her to share the joke. Raji wished it could be that easy.

"I'm not afraid, it's just . . . there's something I need to tell you."

"Shhh . . . don't worry."

Vivek smiled at her confusion, and leaned down to kiss her, at the same moment entering her. Raji was suddenly so hot, so wet and ready for him that she thought she might scream. But remembering his despised mother in the next bedroom, she buried the sound in her throat and only moaned, softly. She curved up to meet him as he began long, hesitant strokes which stretched through her long-neglected body, giving her the attention she so desperately craved.

The world blurred for Raji to a haze of cloudy netting above, lit by the lamp glow and measured by the rhythmic movement of this man, her husband, inside her. Some time during that long eternity it began to rain outside their window, but the thunder and lightning couldn't begin to match the pleasure racing through her. He began pounding faster and faster to match the storm, and came suddenly. Raji was caught in a moment of purest frustration underneath him. She opened her eyes a few seconds later to see his concerned face above her.

"That didn't work very well, did it? I'm sorry," Vivek said.

Raji remembered the numerous times Jim had left her frustrated without even noticing. She decided not to think of Jim again — he didn't deserve to intrude on this, her wedding night. This man, her husband, was thoughtful, considerate. She could have done much worse. Raji smiled up at him, feeling warmth unfold within her. "Shhh . . . it's fine. We have lots of time to practice. But there are a couple of things I don't understand."

"Ask," he said, smiling gently.

"Well, for one, why is it still raining? I thought storms in India were short."

"Usually they are, but this one will last a while. It's the beginning of monsoons, remember? It will be storming for the next three months."

"Oh. I knew that."

Raji had the distinct feeling that he was laughing at her again. Vivek smiled brightly at her, rolling her towards him to rest in the crook of his arm. The storm raged more fiercely outside, no doubt churning the dirt paths to mud, soaking the very air and making it hard to breathe.

"Want to ask one of the harder questions now?" he asked.

"There's just one more. Now you know that you didn't marry a virgin. Do you mind?"

She closed her eyes and clenched her fists against the answer, suddenly wanting desperately to make this gentle man happy, especially happy with her.

"I knew from the beginning. Your mother seemed to feel I had a right to know what I was bargaining for," he said quietly.

"She told you? How could she? She didn't even know . . . " Raji was caught somewhere between anger and relief. Vivek chuckled.

"You would be surprised what mothers know. Mine really

isn't so bad; she's just not looking forward to my leaving with you, so she's a little irritable."

"Leaving?" Raji was now completely confused.

"For America. Lots of work for doctors there. The problem in India is that everyone who can become a doctor does so. There aren't enough jobs. I've been hoping to live in America for a long time, and I could hardly expect my beautiful American wife to be like the innocent girls of the villages here. Not that many of them are really that innocent." He grinned down at her then.

Raji didn't return his smile, suddenly troubled by a depressing possibility. Maybe he had married her only for her citizenship, so he could get a visa and emigrate to America. She had certainly heard of plenty of arranged marriages where that was one of the prime requirements — a spouse with American citizenship. Raji tried to ignore the thought. If it were true, it was too late to do anything about it now, and he had certainly acted as if he wanted her and not just a ticket to America. She didn't want to believe that the man who had been so sweet to her could be so mercenary.

Vivek appeared troubled by her silence. "That is," and he was suddenly hesitant, "if you want to go back to America."

"If I want to?!" and Raji started laughing, smothering her doubts. "Oh, yes. Yes, my husband. Soon, please."

"Soon." he agreed, smiling. "I already have a job offer there, actually. As soon as I get my work visa we can go. I just wanted to make sure that was what you wanted, too."

Now she knew that he could have gone on his own, that he had wanted her and not just any American. Now Raji was free to care for this man beside her, and to acknowledge to herself just how much she longed for apple trees and miniskirts and rollercoasters. India had its own strange beauty, its passion and mystery, but she was an American at heart.

Vivek touched her cheek then and said, "Shall we try that again? My mother will be very upset with me if you continue to be so quiet. She will think that I have been too rough with you and that you are crying."

Raji held herself still for a moment, looking up at the face of her new husband. He was such a mass of surprises. Then suddenly she rolled over so that she was lying on top of him. Raji kissed him wildly, ignoring his startled eyes. She stopped for a moment to tell him, "You're about to find out just how rough American women can be," before she returned to teasing him unmercifully, rubbing her small breasts across his smooth chest. Vivek responded with renewed passion, pulling her close so that her pointed chin rested in his hands and her hair fell forward, veiling their faces. Raji finally left behind all thoughts of mothers and matchmaking, allowing herself to go spiraling downward with her husband, losing herself in the touch of sweat-slick skin on skin.

Any sounds they made were soon drowned in the pounding of the monsoon storms.

# Shelley Marcus

🌿

# A Little Slip

"I've really got to get to the office early this morning, hon," I told Karen, pulling out of her embrace and getting quickly out of bed.

"No problem," she answered.

"This budget has been driving me crazy," I said, more an excuse than an explanation. "I have to finish crunching these numbers and send the damn thing out to the head office by the end of the day. I won't be able to concentrate on anything else until it's done."

"I understand, Joan. Don't worry about me," Karen said lightly, but I knew I'd hurt her feelings.

My timing can be shitty sometimes. What did Karen want? Just to have her lover show a little affection on the morning of their first anniversary. So what did I do? I jumped out of bed as if the mattress was on fire.

I'd been truthful about the budget. It just hadn't been the whole truth. Well, if I couldn't be honest with Karen, at least I could be honest with myself. And the whole truth was, I was starting to feel trapped. Karen and I had been together, really together for a whole year, something I wouldn't have thought possible. I'd always enjoyed playing the field too much. There were too many beautiful women out there to even think about tying myself down to only one.

Then I'd met Karen. The sex was incredible between us, and after a few months of dating we stopped seeing other people. Karen was the one who brought up the subject of moving in together, and I'd finally agreed. I suppose I just lost my head. Hell, I was in love. You know what that's like. Everything is so perfect that you'll do anything you can to make the other person happy.

And I wasn't twenty anymore. I really think getting older is harder when you're gay, and the thought of having someone there to get old with me was kind of appealing at the time. I only wish I'd known then how hard it was going to be giving up all those other women. Some people are marriage material, and I've always known I wasn't one of them.

I swore I wouldn't cheat on Karen while we were together, but she has no idea how close I've come in the last year. One of these days I know I'm going to see some cute young thing, and I'm not going to be able to stop myself.

I felt guilty about the way I'd acted with Karen, so I was determined to make it up to her. Do it up right. I'd take her out for a fancy dinner, maybe to a show, and then when we got home we'd really celebrate. All I had to do was get through the day.

I finished the budget in record time, called down to have the kid from the mail room pick it up, then went on to something else.

"Come in," I answered the knock on my office door, but I didn't bother looking up from what I was doing. "This needs to go out tonight," I said, indicating the overnight mailer on the corner of my desk.

"Yes, ma'am."

I lifted my head at the sound of the voice, unmistakably female. I had been expecting Jimmy, the high school kid who was working in the mail room for the summer, not the young woman who stood before me. I didn't know her, and she was someone I would definitely have remembered meeting.

"Are you new here?" I asked.

"Yes, ma'am," she answered, but there was mock respect in her voice.

I put her age at nineteen, but she looked younger in the jeans and denim jacket she wore. Our dress code is fairly strict, but working in the mail room she would have been cut some slack because of the physical nature of her duties. She reached down to pick up the envelope and her jacket opened, revealing a tight, white T-shirt, her small firm breasts, unencumbered by a bra, clearly outlined under the cotton. Her blonde hair was cut extremely short, and she wore no makeup.

Her whole appearance cried out Baby Butch, but I've seen straight teens dress the same way, so it was difficult to be sure. Perhaps it was just wishful thinking. Wishful thinking I shouldn't have been indulging in, not when I had a lover at home with whom I was about to celebrate an anniversary.

"What's your name?" I asked.

"Zoe," she answered lazily. "I just started today." She had looked me straight in the eye when she'd said her name, then shifted her gaze directly to my breasts.

So I hadn't been wrong, I thought. Even more reason not to keep her here any longer than necessary. "Well, welcome to the company, Zoe," I said hastily, "and please make sure that package goes out tonight."

"Yes, ma'am." The phrase was beginning to annoy me, so I was happy to see her leave and let me get back to work.

Preparing the last quarter report figures kept me occupied all afternoon, and I'd all but forgotten Zoe until the end of the day when she knocked on my office door and invited herself inside.

"Yes, Zoe?" I asked, not bothering to disguise my irritation with the interruption. I made a mental note to talk to Human Resources about teaching new employees proper office etiquette. "Is there something I can do for you?"

"No, ma'am. I just wondered if you needed me for anything else."

"No, thank you, Zoe. If I do, I'll call for you." The denim jacket was gone now, and before I could stop myself my eyes went to the naked breasts under her T-shirt.

Zoe caught me looking, and a small smile crossed her lips. "Are you sure there's nothing I can do for you, ma'am?"

The question would have been easier to answer if she hadn't been standing there brushing her fingers across her breasts as she asked it. I'd never seen a sexual move done so blatantly and yet so innocently. This mating dance had the expected effect. Soon my nipples were as hard as hers, but luckily mine were camouflaged by my blouse and the lace bra I wore under it. I was having more trouble concealing the other signs of excitement this little show brought out in me. My damp panties would remain my little secret, thank God, but I was sure Zoe could see the blush rising in my cheeks.

The moment Zoe saw my face she knew she had me. "That's what I thought," she said, answering herself, and in a moment she was across the room and in my lap, kissing me with wild abandon.

"Zoe, we can't," I protested, pushing her away. "Someone will see."

"It's safe," she informed me. "Your secretary's already left for the day."

I didn't take much convincing, especially once Zoe lifted up her T-shirt and displayed her breasts. I had them in my hands a moment later, reveling in her soft skin and her young, firm muscles.

While I stroked her breasts, Zoe opened my blouse and unhooked my bra, pulling it down and freeing my own, much larger breasts. We stood there, fondling each other, and then Zoe pushed me back down into my chair and lifted my skirt.

I didn't protest when she knelt in front of me, spread my legs, and lowered my panties down around my ankles. With the eagerness of youth, she attacked my pussy as if she'd never seen one before. What she lacked in technique she made up for in enthusiasm. She brushed my outer lips with her mouth, then sucked them in and out before slipping her tongue inside to find my swollen clit. It felt incredible. Karen is a wonderful lover, but having this cute young thing, almost a perfect stranger, eating me in my office was a total turn on for me.

I heard the sound of a zipper being undone, then felt the movement of Zoe's arm against my leg. She had unzipped her jeans and was fingering her pussy while she worked her mouth on mine. Soon she was moaning into my flesh, her voice vibrating inside me. "That's it, baby," I coaxed breathlessly, "just a little harder."

I came first, shuddering against my chair, but Zoe used her free hand to keep me joined with her. A minute later I felt Zoe's orgasm as she screamed it into me.

Suddenly the door opened and Karen strode into my office. "Hi, sweetheart. I hope you don't mind my dropping in, but I thought maybe we could go out to dinner." She stopped short when she saw us. Startled, Zoe stood up and turned around, her T-shirt still pulled up to her neck and her jeans down on her thighs. "What the hell!" Karen exclaimed.

"Karen, I can explain," I began. "It's not what it looks like." As if with my blouse open and my tits hanging out it could be anything but what it looked like. Especially with Zoe half-naked between my legs. Realizing I couldn't talk my way out of it, I looked into Karen's shocked, unbelieving eyes and admitted, "I'm sorry, Karen. I don't know what else to say."

I had expected yelling and screaming, maybe even tears, but suddenly Karen's expression changed. She smiled. "There's only one thing to say. Happy Anniversary, darling." At my bewildered look she nodded at Zoe and said, "I don't have to ask if you liked my present."

"Your present?" I asked, completely at a loss. "You mean you arranged this?"

"Of course. I'm not stupid, Joan. I could tell you were getting antsy, and that sooner or later there would be a little slip. I figured if it was going to happen anyway, I'd make sure I picked the when, the where, and especially the who."

"I don't believe this," I uttered, still not sure she was serious.

"Believe it," Zoe said, pulling down her T-shirt and zipping up her jeans. "I guess you were surprised, huh?"

"Surprised doesn't even begin to describe how I feel."

Karen came over and put her arm around Zoe. "And now that you've had your fun," she told me, "Zoe and I are going back to the apartment so I can have mine."

"You — and Zoe?" I gasped.

"Why not? After all, it's my anniversary, too. I think it's only fair I get as much pleasure out of the gift as you have, don't you?"

I watched, dumbstruck, as Zoe and my lover walked out the door. Then a second later Karen poked her head back in to add, "You're welcome to join us if you like."

I hastily arranged my clothes and headed for the door. I may have to rethink this monogamy thing. It could work out — with the right partner.

Laurel Fisher

❦

# Snooping

Momma always told me not to snoop. Nosy people find out things they'd rather not know. I didn't mean to, really. It was an accident. The computer system at work had crashed. Everyone went home at lunchtime except the poor woman stuck trying to fix it. When I got home, I tried to call a friend, thinking this would be a perfect day for a long, late lunch with a margarita or two, but the line was busy.

I changed and wandered out to the backyard to sunbathe instead, and a daydream washed over me: this would be one of the days my husband has time to come home for lunch.

My tall, strong, demanding husband. His view from the kitchen window would be my nearly naked bottom. He'd come out, kneel over me, fondle my ass. Tracing the outline of my bikini, his fingers would slip underneath to the wetness of my daydream.

He'd pull the fabric aside and tug me up to my knees, entering me abruptly, urgently . . . Suddenly I realized that the only heat I was feeling was from too much sun. I wandered back into the house, picked up the phone, and hit the redial button.

"Hello, can I help you?"

I hesitated a moment. Maybe a friend was answering the phone for her? Maybe she was in the bathroom? You can't get a wrong number with redial. Can you? "Um, yeah, is Lisa there?"

"Hold on." The phone thunked on the desk. "Hey, is Lisa around?" I could hear the voice in the background. "She's in the dungeon." The dungeon? What in the world was Lisa up to?

"You wanna tell her she's got a phone call?"

"You wanna get fired on your first day? Don't ever interrupt a session, airhead."

She picked the phone back up. "She's busy. Can I take a message?"

"Uh, I'm not even sure I have the right number. Lisa Sewall? 555-6284?"

A squeaky, inane giggle tickled my ear. "No way, hon. You aren't even close! It's Lisa Smith and 555-9447."

My heart was racing as I scribbled the number on the pad by the phone. I stared at it a moment in shock, not comprehending at all what had just happened, then tore off the top sheet and tucked it in my pocket. I nearly jumped out of my skin when my husband, Sean, spoke behind me. "You're home?"

"The system at work crashed. I've been outside."

"Who were you calling?"

"Lisa. It was busy." Oh hell, he must have heard me talking. "I mean she, um, wasn't home." He had a strange look on his face. I realized he must have made the call. But where? And why? Here I was standing in a string bikini right in front of him, and he was looking everywhere but at my body. The body he usually can't keep his grab-ass damn hands off of.

"Is something wrong?" I asked, uncertain.

"No," he grunted, a man-grunt, and walked away.

He fixed a sandwich. When he came back into the room, he apologized. Said he was having a crummy day. When he headed back to work, I did what any scared, suspicious wife would do: I snooped. There was a copy of the local *Nasty News* in a stack of magazines on his desk. It wasn't really hidden. When one of us goes to the liquor store we pick one up, just for laughs, to read the articles and giggle over the swingers' ads. Easy to do since we had each other. Or so I thought.

I flipped the pages. There it was, staring out at me in inch-high letters, the phone number I had accidentally dialed that afternoon. 555-9447*555-WHIP. It was for a fetish club. A dungeon. But why did he have to call them? I'd let him tie me up in a heartbeat.

The photo wobbled and swam in front of my eyes, and I was spreadeagled on the bed, wrists and ankles secure, blindfolded, gagged. My nipples tightened under his harsh fingers. I refocused and eyed the trio of luscious women in the grainy photo. Suddenly I couldn't breathe. Maybe it wasn't a what.

Maybe it was a who.

How important was this? Was it just a passing fancy, or could it destroy my marriage, take away my man, my life's mate? I thought we belonged together forever. He'd said he did too.

We were different from all the others. From all the statistics. What if it had all been some sappy illusion?

I always tackle a problem head on. Well, sort of. I tend to research it to death first. I suppose it's a way for me to take charge again, or maybe it just gives me a way to avoid the issue until the time comes for the inevitable confrontation. I needed to really know what he might be looking for. The public library probably wasn't going to be much help. Going through the paper again, I found a store that catered to leather people.

The clerk found me wistfully fondling a cat-o-nine tails (actually it was more like nineteen — I counted). He asked me if he could help, I took him at his word. Poor guy, I'm sure he didn't want to hear about my marital woes. I asked him outright what happened at those dungeon places. Kindly he pointed out to me that sexual contact wasn't allowed there, because that would be prostitution. That would be illegal. So being there wasn't actually cheating. If Sean had even been there. Then he told me that those clubs had mostly dominatrices. For submissive men.

Oh dear. My strong, take charge, utterly alpha husband? I could submit to him any day of the week, any hour of the day. But be his Mistress? It was becoming increasingly clear that I didn't know him as well as I thought. Hell, nine years and I didn't know him at all. I left with a book, a rented video, a handful of boot laces, a brass ring, a nice shiny pair of handcuffs, and trembling hands.

I barely had time to skim the book, but I could see that it was wonderful, incredibly informative about things I'd never dreamed people did to each other. Or themselves. I managed to thread the laces through the little brass ring and wrap a half lace into a handle during the movie, but it was tough to concentrate. I kept finding myself kind of distracted. Okay, very distracted. Less than five minutes into the movie, when the Dominatrix made her big strong co-star lick her boots, I started to squirm. I watched in horrified arousal while she poured hot wax on his nipples and a few other interesting places. By the time she let him sniff her panties, I was drenched.

I practiced swinging the leather laces on the couch until I could control just where the strokes were landing. Not that I was actually gonna hit him with it. Just trail it sensuously over his body. Maybe a few gentle swats. Unless he was cheating. If he was cheating I was going to beat the crap out of him and throw him out on the street naked. I shook my head. I couldn't think about that now. I was going to handle this rationally. No teary accusations. I hoped.

I got the cattails going in a nice figure eight, running the strands through my free hand as I reversed directions. The feel of the leather sliding through my fingers was very stimulating.

And the snap! I quivered each time the strands smacked a surface.

The book said you should always try toys on yourself first.

Hesitantly, I swatted the tender skin of my inner arm. Youch! I tried it again, more gently. Then harder and harder, until I was looking in fascination at bright pink skin. The hall clock chimed. It was almost time. I stashed all my new toys and a pair of black heels under the couch. Tearing through my closet and underwear drawer, I settled on a lacy black bra and thong panties, the only things even close to sexy lingerie that I owned. If only I'd had enough money for that leather teddy with all the zippers. I heard the front door open and shimmied into a loose sundress that buttoned up the front.

Sean was home. A sudden dose of reality pierced my arousal. I'd almost convinced myself this was just a kinky seduction game. But it wasn't. My marriage might be in very serious trouble. What if I couldn't give him whatever he wanted from that place? Whoever he wanted? God, what if he'd already done something I could never forgive? I couldn't swallow when I saw the fresh red rose in my crystal bud vase. I felt like my heart was lodged in my throat. Sweet? Or guilty? I wondered.

He tried to kiss me, but I dodged his mouth. I blurted out a question. "Are you happy here? With me, I mean." So much for subtlety.

Sean looked surprised. "Aw, honey, you know I love you. And I'm sure if you would just hold still you could make me happy pretty quick," he added with a wicked grin.

I sighed inwardly and tried again. "Is there something new you want? Or maybe someone?" I asked outright. But he wouldn't give.

"Nope." His look was wary. Then lecherous. "Why, do you have a new fantasy to try out? How 'bout we go to dinner, and you can tell me all about it."

I shook my head and stomped out of the room. I'd never caught him in a lie before. Was it a little lie or a big lie?

Maybe he'd already been to the dungeon. Maybe lots of

times. My insides were trembling. When I regained enough self-control not to burst into angry tears, I came back. He was working out, bare-chested. Push-ups. He always followed the same routine, so chin-ups on the bar he'd rigged in the coat closet doorway would be next.

I had an idea. A very bad idea. But I did it anyway. I was hurt, I was scared and I was just plain pissed off. I reached under the sofa cushion for the handcuffs. I could almost see the printed words in front of me. "Never play when you are angry." Well, I wasn't playing. I wandered across the room with the cuffs behind my back. He gave me a thoughtful look.

"I'm almost done. Then let's go have dinner and talk."

I shrugged. "Sure." Damn right we were gonna talk. I waited until his back was turned and he had started his first set of chin-ups. He didn't even hear the metallic rattle over his grunts and growls. I stretched up, rubbing my body against his back as I flipped one loop around his wrist and the other around the bar. He let loose a lusty laugh and pressed against me, then realized exactly what I had done. He gave an experimental tug at the bar as I backed away. He turned and tried to grab me just as I got out of range of his long-limbed reach.

"What the hell do you think you're doing?" he demanded. "I'm not in the mood for a game."

The noise I made was most unladylike. "Not with me, anyway."

"You can tell me what the hell is going on any minute now." His voice was quieter, dangerously quiet. He was really not very happy about this. I could be in big trouble when I finally let him down. But it was too late to turn back now.

"I know about the dungeon."

He stared at me. I could almost see the wheels turning in his mind. How much did I know? "Damn. You heard me on the phone, didn't you?"

"Maybe I followed you there. Maybe I found a receipt."

"No!" His response was explosive. "You're bluffing! I *never* went there. I called them. Once. You can't believe I would go there without you."

"I *believe* you called them. I *believe* I gave you more than one chance to tell me about it. I *believe* you promised me you would tell me, up front, if you ever wanted anyone else!"

"I don't want anyone else. I didn't do anything."

"Not yet!"

"C'mon, I just called them. Let me loose."

"Nope."

"Whaddaya mean 'no'?"

"Just tell me what you wanted. Or who you wanted." I snapped open the paper. "Which mistress? The bleached blonde here? Or the dark-haired one with the big tits? Which fetish? Were you gonna have her dress you up like a woman? Or play horsey? Or what?"

"Damn it! I was just curious. I didn't do anything wrong!"

I took a deep, calming breath to keep from screaming at him. "I just want to know what you were thinking when you called. Whatever it is that you'd rather pay for than ask me to do for you."

He sighed and leaned his forehead against his captive arm. "I don't want to talk about this."

"I guess you don't want loose tonight," I tossed back. "Whose picture turned you on?"

"None of them!"

"Fine. If you really expect me to believe that, then tell me what you wanted. A mistress? A slave? Cross-dressing? Diapers? Pain? Humiliation?"

"A little pain, and a little humiliation, okay? Now let me down." He was blushing hard, but he looked me straight in the eye.

"But not from me."

"I wanted to rent the space, not rent a woman. For us. Read the damned ad again. They rent space by the hour."

"If that's true, why haven't you mentioned that particular yearning to me?"

"I didn't think you would enjoy humilating me," he answered wryly.

I unbuttoned my dress, slowly, and shrugged out of it. I turned around and bent over at the waist to pick it up and toss it out of the way. I felt the thong back of my black lace panties stretch into my crevice. "Maybe you just think I'm not tough enough, or sexy enough, to abuse you."

I could see a twitch of response in his jeans. "I never said that. I was embarrassed. I didn't know how to ask you to . . . to . . . " I cocked an eyebrow and waited. "I was embarrassed," he finished lamely.

"You hurt me. I thought you wanted someone else. Maybe you do."

"No," he said gently. "Never."

I chose to believe him. The fear and the anger flowed out of me. Most of the anger, anyway. Frankly, I needed to hold on to a little bit to carry this off. I stretched up against him to unlock the cuff that was looped around the chin-up bar. He closed his eyes and shook his arm a bit to get the blood flowing properly again. He reached for me, but I pushed his hand away.

"Do you want to finish this?" I demanded.

He studied my face. Shut his eyes for a second. "Yes."

I turned him around, clicked the dangling cuff around his free wrist. Yanking at the waistband of his jeans popped the buttons free. I shoved the jeans and his boxers down around his ankles.

"Your safe word is *blue*."

"My what?"

"My what, *ma'am*." I reprimanded him.

"My what, ma'am?" His tone was insolent, his grin wicked.

"Don't dis' me, or we stop right now. Your safe word. If you're nervous, use it. If you're scared," I taunted. "But not just because you don't like what I'm doing. This is my game, and you're here to please me."

"Yes, ma'am." His posture was straighter, his tone more subdued, but a touch of insolence was still there.

"I think you should be on your knees by now, slave." He turned to face me, his cock rising steadily. Kicking his ankles free of his jeans, he knelt at my feet. I stood before him, stance wide, hands on hips. He looked appreciatively up at my breasts, until I popped him lightly on top of his head. "Eyes down." His big blue eyes took the long route, checking me out all the way down, so I grabbed a fistful of thick brown hair and forced his head back.

"I don't think you're taking me seriously, lover," I sneered. "You fucked up. Bad. I gave you two chances, and you lied to me twice. You need to be punished." His eyes widened, then dropped.

"Yes, ma'am." When I was sure he'd finally gotten the message I let him go. Bending over the couch, I slid my feet into the black patent stilettos I had stashed underneath it. Hoping I looked high-class stripper instead of a kid playing dress up, I minced around the room lighting a few strategically placed candles and turning out the lights. His eyes followed me warily. In a slightly strangled voice he asked, "Ma'am? You're not going to . . . "

I contemplated his slowly wilting erection. "No, wussy boy. I'm not gonna use the wax on you. These are just for light. This time."

His erection returned, pointing to the ceiling. I stood, propped one foot up on the coffee table, and crooked my finger at him. He started to stand, but I shook my head. "Uh uh.

Stay on your knees." He waddled over to me on his knees, his cock bobbing and swaying. I struggled not to laugh at him.

"My shoes are dirty. Clean them." His expression was quizzical. "Oh darn. You're all tied up. I guess you have to use your tongue." I pointed at the shoe.

With the tip of his tongue he touched it, hesitantly. Within seconds he was lapping at it. Then he was worshiping it with broad, flat strokes. He covered every inch of the shiny blackness, paying special attention to the spike heel. He did such a beautiful job, I had to reward him. I turned around, bent over, and let him kiss my ass. He did that nicely, too.

I pushed him down over the coffee table, face pressed into the cold, polished wood and pulled out my last toy, the square black laces. Lightly I traced the line of his spine, from the base of his neck to the spasming pucker of his asshole. He didn't realize what was tickling him until I delivered the first light lash on his balls. His sharply indrawn breath and the quick move to get his restricted hands off his bare bottom encouraged me to go on. I took my first full swing at him. He gasped and flinched when it connected. I used light flicks to work out a steady rhythm, then settled in with a comfortable left cheek, right cheek that left him squirming and grunting, but not complaining.

When his light cream skin had turned a fiery pink I let up. I turned his head by his hair and asked if he was okay. "Do you want me to stop?"

"No, ma'am. Please, ma'am."

I laughed. "Are you begging?"

"Yes, ma'am. Please don't stop now."

I fondled his balls, gave his cock a long stroke with my hand. I found a long string of pre-come at the end of it. Getting as much of it as I could, I offered it to his mouth. He only hesitated for a second before he eagerly sucked his own fluid off my finger. "What do you say?" I demanded.

"Thank you, ma'am."

I rewarded him with a stinging shot at his shoulder. He recoiled slightly; he'd been expecting another slap on his ass.

I worked his shoulders for a while, left, right, left, right, until the skin color matched his bottom. I aimed another one down there, but this time he flinched too hard. The tender skin had finally had enough. I lightened my strokes considerably, fondling his balls again, and occasionally aiming a very light slap at the tightly wrinkled skin there. "Had enough?"

His answer took a little longer this time. "Yes, ma'am."

"Straighten up then. And turn around." I rested one foot on the coffee table again. This time I presented the crotch of my panties to his face. "Lick me." He settled back on his heels and tentatively reached out with his tongue, wondering what I would allow. Light licks up the sides, then the center swollen button. He tugged at the slick, silky fabric with his teeth, but I popped him on the head.

"No teeth." I ordered.

He went back to work with his tongue. He wiggled it under the elastic, moaned when he tasted my arousal. Ahh, his tongue felt sweet on my bare skin. Too sweet. I had to make him stop. "No. No skin. You can only taste me through my panties."

He whimpered. Then he lapped at the silky fabric with a vengeance. His flat tongue massaged and rubbed, then the tip teased and tormented until I couldn't take anymore. I pulled away with a shudder. My foot hit the floor and I turned my back to him. I straddled him backwards, wiggling my ass in his face. Dropping slowly to my knees, I pulled my panties to the side and guided him into me. Entry was slick and easy. I'd been needing him for hours. I eased onto the very tip of his rock hard cock. He thrust forward, forcing me onto all fours. I pulled off.

"Hold still," I demanded. "I'm fucking you. You are not fucking me. If you want to be inside me, don't move a single muscle. You're nothing but a dildo to me," I lied. He groaned, but held perfectly still.

I backed onto him again. I moved back and forth on the end of his cock, not allowing full penetration, with a slow, steady rhythm. When I heard his breath quicken I pulled free again.

I tucked his erection down between my thighs, and rode the smooth velvety hardness with my swollen clit. "Please, ma'am," he whimpered. "Please, please, please," like a mantra.

Then I guided him inside me once again, clear to the hilt this time, in one smooth motion.

I rested there for a long moment, not moving, just filled with him. My fingers circled my clit in an involuntary motion. I simply couldn't wait anymore. The swift contractions of a powerful orgasm took me by surprise, robbing me of the last shred of control I had left. I rocked back and forth with long strokes. His back arched as he did his best to meet me. Groaning with desperate need, he thrust his hips as far forward as they could go. I could feel the jerk of his cock, trying to strain upwards, demanding release. I clenched my muscles tightly, milking him for all I was worth.

"Oh, God." His words forced themselves through his tightly clenched jaw. "Ohh. My. Gawwwd." He pushed into me, short quick lunges, all he could manage in his awkward position. When he was finished, in danger of toppling over and taking us both down, I pulled free, collapsing on the floor. When I could move again, I crawled over to the couch and leaned against it. I pulled my panties back into place to catch the flow of spent lust. Sean moved clumsily toward me and lay his head on my breast. "I love you," he murmured.

"I know," I whispered, fumbling for the key to his handcuffs. "I just forgot for a minute."

# Maria Mendoza

❦

# Mourning the Peasant

*To Wes, for all the belief*

You read the eulogy out loud as if you are a cheerleader on heroin. It feels good to get the words out to the congregation and yet, your soul is somewhere else, perhaps dreaming. The words come out of your mouth clearly but you cannot feel your tongue move. You cannot feel your body in that long, black dress and matching heels. You cannot feel the stream of sweat that trickles down your right inner thigh. But, in any case, your words are nice and they are causing everybody at your father's funeral Mass to cry.

*And your arms —*
*We will miss holding them.*
*And your smile —*
*We will miss receiving it.*
*And your heart —*
*We will miss feeling it.*

Before the last stanza of your eulogy, you want to cry and you search the congregation for a safe face. You see the face of your father's long-time lover and friend. Laia. She does not smile at you or encourage you to get rid of the sob in your throat; rather, she gives you a wide-eyed blank expression of openness and possibility. You understand. You let your tears flow but you keep your voice coherent. You keep your voice alive by imagining your father patting your back lovingly while you read at the podium. You imagine the smell of his skin and cologne, the smell of soft leather mixed with Grey Flannel. The scent strengthens you and carries you through the Mass and the graveside burial, as you shed your gentle tears.

After the burial, Laia, the Vinnifieds and you have a solemn tea on the patio of Laia's house. Everybody looks both tragic and perfect: all dressed in black and struck with downward eyes and mostly closed lips. Laia's maids scurry about diligently, making sure that everyone has enough cucumber sandwiches, popovers and various teas. Many kiss you as you sit, cross-legged, sipping mindlessly at your cup of Oolong. You either respond to them too vividly — flailing your arms around dramatically — or too passively — sitting still and pretending they had not kissed you at all. Throughout the tea, Laia either stays at your side or watches you from a close distance. She holds your hand, wipes your tears, helps you to freshen your makeup in the kitchen bathroom and wards off relatives who give you too many encouraging words. Laia is like a peregrine falcon, stalking moving prey that mindlessly scurry about in an open field. She is like a lioness, proudly raising her head above the pack to view the savannah she owns while keeping safe watch on you, her beloved cub.

Dressed in a black, flowing pantsuit and a Vivienne Westwood headpiece with an attached half-veil, Laia is a striking sentinel for your mourning soul. She is tall, nearly six feet, and very strong (lots of volleyball with your father on Galveston Beach and countless hours biking at Memorial Park). Her appearance is not so much beautiful as it is dignified. Now, her narrow eyes watch you as you nod your head at some cousin or aunt.

You catch her stare, you smile at her and wave with your

small fingers. She sets her tea down and blows you a kiss through her veil. Your soul stirs and you do not know why. You simply smile and return to the umpteenth conversation about what your father was like and your raw confessions over what you miss most about him. Basically, you tell relatives what they want to hear: how God will watch over your father, how the time was right and how he would reconcile things with your mother in heaven. Yes, you tell them the words they want to hear, family mourning talk.

You can barely speak without tripping over small sobs here and there but you simply look at Laia and this is so sufficient that you do not have to imagine your father's scent again. Once, when putting down your fifth cup of tea, you scan the faces on the patio. All are Vinnified faces. Nobody from your late mother's family. You have not seen a member of the Lopez family since your father divorced your mother when you were seven, except at your mother's funeral, five years later. Not one Lopez had informed you or your father about her death: You learned of it from your father's casual reading of the obituaries in the Sunday paper. It was an awful way to find out. You were twelve, just discovering your newly tender nipples and necessity for training bras. You had not even formed your theories or outlooks on death. All you knew was that it could not happen to anybody in the family.

The Lopezes hated your father not because he was an evil man, a lecher or even a swindler. It was because he divorced your mother on the grounds of spousal abuse. The Lopezes accused your father of insanity and called you a spawn of insanity for having defended your father both in court and to their faces. The Lopezes insisted that he was overreacting and that it was not possible for a woman to abuse a man, that it was not in a woman's nature to hurt or destroy anything or anyone. But you had seen that it was.

Now you do not think, "I have lost my mother and my father," but rather, "I have lost my father and his first marriage partner." You create safe distance between your mother and you. You build the high, stone wall. You tear your flesh away from her womb and think of your existence as having been fashioned by the grace of nature, despite the fact that, during your teenage years, your father pleaded with you to forgive your mother.

You help Laia and the maids clean up after the tea. Laia takes her headpiece off and twists her hair into a loose bun. Your makeup is tired from the tears and the vain powdering. In silence, you collect the tiny porcelain cups and saucers. Now and then, you eat a few untouched finger pastries left on tiny plates. Laia hums to herself as she wipes off tables and sweeps off debris, using a damp washcloth. Mahler's "Tragic" plays from the intercom above the patio. Today has been a sad day for you but you clean up as if you were getting your chores done before an outing with your father. You clean up with forced alacrity and precision, your fingers moving quickly, your stride relaxed and sure. But at the end of the patio cleanup, you go to the kitchen. Your eyes fall heavy on its floor tiles. You outline the pale, paisley shapes with your eyes and you feel disgusted.

Laia places her hands on your shoulders and presses her lips to your forehead.

"It's late, do you want me to run a bath?"

Still looking at the floor, you answer in a small voice.

"Yes, make it hot."

"Music?"

"Yes."

"Incense?"

"Please."

She gives you another kiss — this time, near your mouth, and walks away. You watch her body slice through the air calmly.

"Laia."

She turns around, headpiece in her hands.

"Um-hmm?"

"Thanks for being great today."

"I didn't do anything you didn't," she says gently. She turns away from you and resumes her walk down the long corridor, its walls flanked with mini ionic columns.

You take your shoes off in the kitchen and wiggle your blistered toes. The tiles are cool underneath your feet, but you decide to venture onto carpet, into the television room. Sighing, you pick up the remote control on the black leather couch and point it at the television. You press the button with your thumb as you pose yourself in front of the screen like a stiff effigy. Images. All you see are images: montages of kissing, fucking, home shopping channels, Hollywood films, cartoons, cooking shows and Congressional hearings. You stop abruptly on Channel 32. *The Firebird*, a classic ballet, is painted in front of your eyes.

Your father loved dance as much as you do, and you remember the many ballets the two of you attended together. You remember him coming to all of your performances, from when you were Clara in *The Nutcracker*, all the way to your first contemporary ballet with your university's dance department. *The Firebird* now makes you feel useless. You wonder who will watch your performances and who will buy drinks for the whole company after every performance at the nearby campus bar.

He helped bandage your toes before every *pointe* class. When you were sixteen, he refused to let you cut your hair short, for fear that it would make you less eligible for casting in principal roles. He was raving mad when he saw boxes of Ex-Lax fall from your bag as you climbed into the car after class one evening. He knew exactly what many dancers did to keep themselves thin. For five hours that man griped you out mercilessly and you sat there, your belly hungry and raw, your body 15 pounds underweight, your gaunt cheeks sucked in from crying. He didn't know whether to hit you or hug you as you sat there in perhaps what was one of the most pathetic states of your life. He finally squatted in front of you and looked into your pink face.

"I'm getting a nutritionist for you and a counselor and you are not going to pull this bulimic shit behind my back."

You had burst into tears, throwing your little arms around his neck. You felt his body soften as he, too, wept, his arms around your shaking body.

You force yourself to cease this memory process. You lay down on the floor, in front of the 52-inch television, and continue to watch *The Firebird*, starring Maria Tallchief as the principal. Dance seems so far away from you right now. You can't even think about rehearsal and costume fittings. You can't think of calling Lyle, a boy from the department whom you started to date only one week before your father's sudden death from meningitis. You close your eyes and moan lightly, drifting into an evening nap.

You dream.

Your father is barefoot, wearing the costume of a peasant. An orchestra plays beneath him. A saggy cap lies atop his smoothed-back, chocolate-colored hair and he has a ridiculous grin on his face. You are dressed like a tulip. Daintily, you approach your father *en pointe*, your arms reaching out to him. Your body is fragile, yet strong. Your footwork is careful and precise.

Your father prepares to run to you but before he can take off, a large, white ribbon shoots down and pierces his costume, ripping his pants. It wraps itself around your father's manhood, which becomes erect.

You scream.

You wake up crying and as you rub your eyes, look up to the ceiling. Laia stands over you, her arms crossed. She is in a terry cloth robe, her hair wet and long around her shoulders.

"Was it a bad one?"

You nod and sit up, still rubbing your eyes like a small child. She bends down and rubs your upper back. The black gabardine fabric of your dress itches against your skin.

"Go take your bath," she says.

"Thanks."

You let her hug you from behind, then you rise, turn off the television — cutting off the end of *The Firebird* — and wobble to the bathroom.

The dress falls from your body easily. You rip off the garter belt and tear away the black stockings. The front hook of your bra has left a pink indentation between your breasts. You unsnap it and ease your arms out of the silken straps. You stand in your panties, in front of the wall, its expanse covered with large, square mirrors that are all connected to each other. Behind you is the large square bathtub, its top carved into the shape of a shell.

You sigh at your small breasts, take off your panties and walk backward into the tub, all the while watching the triangular curve of your pubic hair and the slight sway of your breasts in the mirror. You step into the mountain of bubbles carefully, your eyes closing, your nostrils filled with the scent of jasmine incense, your ears caressed by François Couperain operettas. The water is hot and forgiving.

Laia and you are curled into opposite sides of the huge leather couch in the television room. You sip from cups filled with warm milk. It is night. You are both exhausted. You pick at a plate of leftover finger pastries on the coffee table.

"You're going to be wide awake tonight if you eat that many," Laia chides.

"No, I'll be fine," you say, as you shove the fifth pastry into your mouth.

"Does the department know that you won't be coming in next week?"

You nod, finishing off the sixth pastry. One more to go.

"Is this going to change the casting for *Apollo*?"

"I never wanted to be a muse anyway."

Silence. You know she is staring at you with sad eyes but you dare not look at her. You stare into your empty cup.

"More warm milk?"

"Please."

She stands up, takes your cup and breezes away into the kitchen. You stare at the television screen and hallucinate momentarily, seeing Maria Tallchief make her way across the stage of corps dancers. Laia comes back humming and gives you a newly warmed mug of milk. You murmur thanks and gulp it down twice as quickly as the first cup. It tastes like childhood and this makes you almost share with Laia a story about your father's excellent homemade cocoa that he usually made during Christmastime. You decide against it. You stand up quickly, make your way to the immaculate kitchen, and place your mug in the sink, along with the plate that is decorated by one uneaten strawberry-filled triangle.

You and Laia ascend the staircase together, hand-in-hand.

"It was a good service. You read well at the Mass."

"I was scared."

"I know, but you pulled it off. He would have been proud of you. Well, I should take that back. He was there, I'm sure. He was definitely proud of you."

"Thanks."

She pauses and squeezes your hand.

"Honey, I wish I had had the privilege to give birth to you."
You stop at the top of the stairs. A maid whizzes by carrying
a bundle of towels. You let go of Laia's hand and look at her.
Her face is so tired, yet strong.

"You know, I was really scared reading up there," you say. "I
didn't think that any of them knew what the hell I was talking
about. It made me angry that they were all crying. I didn't
think they were stupid but I don't think they were crying for the
right reasons. I think Uncle Jack and Aunt Marty cried because
the funeral had cost so much. I think the other relatives cried
because they were worried about Dad's company going to shit.
I don't know but these are my opinions. I'm sorry."

"No, it's okay. Anger's healthy. I think they really loved your
father. I had my own conclusions — I know that they weren't
comfortable with me. They weren't comfortable that I had
guardianship of you above your own blood relatives. I'm not
even a family member."

"But everyone respects you."

"No, everyone is scared of me, honey. There's the difference.
They see me as a replacement of your mother, a substitution.
To them, I'm part human, part bitch. That's okay, though. I've
gotten over it through the years and I know that they understand what I had with your father and what I have with you."

She grabs your hand again and continues.

"He was a good person. I love him so much. He didn't deserve
this and we can certainly say that we didn't need to go through
this pain. But these things happen and I think that there were
some genuine mourners in our family today. Even those who
we felt were ignorant in their mourning were really genuine in
their way of handling pain, especially your Aunt Marty. I really
don't think the funeral's price tag was the cause of her tears."

You shrug and bury your body into hers. She wraps her arms
around you. Though she is nine years older than you — thirty-

one — you feel that her body is much like yours. A year after you met her, you stopped hating her. You became comfortable with hugging and kissing her, feeling her safe body encouraging yours. Now, at the age of twenty-two, you feel as if you were fourteen again, safe within the confines of her chest. Now, you can feel a new sob developing in your throat. You can't bear another exhausting wave of tears but this is difficult because you can smell the lingering scent of your father on her — a hint of Grey Flannel. You squint your eyes and dry the beginnings of tears on her robe, coughing, pretending to clear your throat.

When you break from her embrace, you see that she is the one crying. You see that she has let her guard down for the day. Her tears are quiet and they fall from her eyes in steady showers. The overhead light of the hallway ceiling casts small shadows under her nose and eyelashes. Even when she cries, she looks unbreakable.

You kiss her cheek.

"You know, Laia, I don't think that you would have wanted to give birth to me."

"Why?"

"I weighed eleven pounds!"

You both laugh and you wipe away her tears with your fingers. She holds your hands upon her cheeks. She kisses the insides of your palms and returns your hands to your sides. Your body shakes.

"Goodnight, lovely." She gives you another hug. This time, it is quicker. She turns away, twisting her hair high above her head and placing it over her left shoulder. Her body swims in light and darkness as she floats between the beams of the tiny, overhead lights. You walk the opposite direction and turn right into a connecting hallway.

"Night." Your voice is small but you are sure it gets to her before you hear the huge double doors to her bedroom close firmly.

The sheets are cool and heavy on your naked body. Your new bedroom is vast and filled with darkness. You light a small candle on your night table and say a small prayer. You blow out the candle and thump your head into the king-size pillow. You close your eyes. Shortly thereafter, your telephone rings. You pick it up and force a half-friendly "Hello." It is Lyle. He wants to know how you are and expresses how much he wishes he could have come to the funeral. You tell him it is late. He tells you that you never go to bed before midnight.

"Please, Lyle. I need to sleep. It's been a hard day for me. We'll talk tomorrow."

It is as if he does not hear you, for he asks if you are coming to rehearsals next week and reminds you about costume fittings next Wednesday. You tell him, once again, that you need to sleep. You accidentally call him a bastard. You apologize. He says that he understands and will call you tomorrow. You thank him, hang up and return to your slumber.

Again you are awakened by nightmares of your father's body, this time being slowly dismembered. You feel yourself falling, but before you hit bottom, you wake up. Dried tears and fresh tears have painted your face. It is hard for you to breathe. You sit up, feeling the taste of stale milk in your mouth. You wobble upright and feel for your robe at the foot of your round bed.

You make your way to Laia's room. The hallway seems larger now and the lights are dimmer. The velvety carpet underneath your feet feels as if it will give way at any time. You open the doors to Laia's room and close them behind you. She is awake. She looks at you from behind Salman Rushdie's *The Moor's Last Sigh*. The grand halogen lamps at either side of her headboard boast a dim setting. She takes off her glasses, puts down her book and gives you a strange stare. She is engulfed in the huge, black mosquito net that forms a canopy over her bed, which is round like yours, but much larger. The black satin sheets make Laia look as if she were floating in a sea of crude oil. She is naked.

"What's wrong?"

You do not answer. You simply burst into tears and make your way into the familiar bed that you used to sleep in during your father's business trips when you were younger. The bed accepts your shaking body. You do not look at her eyes but merely move to her lap, which is covered, waist down, by a single sheet. She says nothing but plays with your sweaty hair and massages your forehead.

You mumble something about the nightmares. Laia listens with no interruptions or questions. When you finish, she turns your body around so that you are looking at her face bent over yours. Grabbing a Kleenex from her nightstand, she wipes your face.

"I'm really going to miss him, Laia." You cry, ruining her clean-up job.

She takes the wet Kleenex and throws it onto the floor. She encourages you to climb underneath the covers with her. She turns on a small, white machine on her night table. A soft sound of waves pours from it.

"Do you like that sound?"

"Yes," you reply, wiping snot from your nose.

She hands you a fresh, pink Kleenex and you both lay on your sides, knees bent, in fetal position. Your faces are close to each other and you can see that, in one of her hands, a new Kleenex is curled within her fingers.

Carefully, you begin to talk of your father. The conversation lasts two hours while the ocean plays obediently from the white box. You do not cry, nor does she. While Laia speaks, you notice the opening and closing of her pink mouth and the flash of her eyelids as she now and then turns to look at the circular top of the mosquito net. Halfway through the conversation, you notice her breasts push from the top of the black sheet. She does not notice, nor does this bother you.

There is talk of his love for your dancing. There is talk of his love for Laia's knowledge of foreign affairs and Lebanese cooking. There is talk of his screening all the men you have dated. There is talk of his helping Laia get over her tragic cocaine spree. Talk of how his former marriage partner abused him and, to a great extent, you. Talk of his excellent taste in clothing. Talk of his ridiculous fondness for golf.

After the conversation, you lay closer to each other, noses together. You cough, covering your mouth, and ask her a difficult question.

"Do you miss the way he touches you?"

A vast silence falls over her body. You can see it caress her face, arms, breasts and legs. She gives you a stare that is not angry but stunned. She answers with forced coolness.

"Of course I miss the way he touches me. And you? I can ask you if you miss his hugs?"

"Yes, they were big hugs. They were safe ones. I liked the way he would always open the car door for me when he dropped me off for school when I was little."

You pause, then say, "Laia, if I ask you for something, will you get mad?"

"Ask me, honey."

The words seem inane. They do not make sense in your head and yet they want to come out — like a baby that has to leave its mother's womb. You go over the question in your head, searching Laia's eyes for the courage to deliver it with your mouth. But she cannot give you her strength now, for she lies silently, awaiting your query.

"Show me," you finally whisper.

"What?"

"Show me."

"Show you . . . ?"

You whisper even lower.

"Will you show me the way he touched you? That's my question. God, I just want to know."

She laughs. She laughs loudly, turning onto her back and kicking her legs underneath the blanket so that you get glimpses of her naked body through the flapping sheet. This absolutely devastates you, her laughing, and you turn away from her. You do not have the strength to stand up and run to your own bed. You do not have the strength to scream, "Stop." So, you resort to the only action your body can bear. You let the infinite storehouse of tears flow from your eyes.

Laia's jig ceases. This makes you cry more. You are afraid of what she will say or do. You are afraid that she will offer to call up your old psychiatrist from the divorce era. You are afraid that she will give you a kiss on your shoulder and dismiss this as an act of post-traumatic syndrome.

Then you feel her arms around your waist, folding over your robe's tie. Your body shakes crazily and you want her to make you forget about the next day, or even the next minute of your life. She buries her head into the back of your neck, using her nose to lift your hair away.

"Alectra."

Your back arches and her hands move to the inside of your robe. She kisses the back of your neck softly, in small spurts. Your breasts face the knowledge of her hands — fingers pinching gently at your nipples. Her naked thigh moves carefully between your bent legs until you can feel the strength of her quadricep beneath your sex — the purple silk of your robe is the only barrier.

The smell of her behind you is consuming. She moves like a lioness or a python around your body, her fingers and tongue performing foreplay as if you were a delicately strung harp. Her breathing is careful and she does not move quickly. Her slowness creates a fire in your belly and you turn your body to her, facing her eyes which are drunk with ecstasy.

"Show me," you breathe, "show me how he kissed you."

Laia kisses your forehead, moving to your eyelids, cheeks, jawline, the corners of your lips. Yes, of course. This is exactly how your father would approach a kiss when making love to a woman. You tease each other with your lips. It is clear that Laia has control of everything that is taking place. You do not try to usurp her but simply reflect to Laia her own strength.

She closes her lips over yours. Your limbs fumble for her legs as her tongue bathes the insides of your mouth. You drink from her as if she were giving you an elixir for all the pains, all the mishaps in your life. Her kiss is both masculine and feminine, both overwhelming and yielding. You cry in her kiss and she pulls back momentarily, wiping your new tears, but she knows that more will follow. She returns to kissing you and your mouth receives this reunion wholly, as if one second of absence were an eternity of separation from that kiss.

Laia feels your hunger and she feeds it. But you, too, feel her mourning, her longing. Though you had asked her to show you her father's art of lovemaking, it now feels as if she and she only were on you — body upon body. You thought that you wouldn't feel as much loss if you knew the sensual side of your father, the part of him you never witnessed — but you feel more loss now, more distant from him than ever. You slap away the emptiness inside you, throwing your arms around Laia.

Bumping your nose with her elbow, she rolls herself on top of you, sitting up. Carefully, she undoes your robe and lets it fall at your sides, unfolding your body as if it were shedding a silk exoskeleton. You say nothing.

You reach up with one hand, cupping the side of her face. As in the hallway, she dips her mouth into the palm of your hand. She licks the fullness of your whole hand, licking each finger with such fervor that it feels like your hand will catch on fire.

She guides your well-licked hand to her breasts. Your fingers pass over them as if you were playing a piano made of fragile keys. She moans lightly, lifting her chin to the ceiling. You break free from her guiding hand. With both hands, you explore her torso, her ribs, the flatness of her belly. Her every muscle is softly defined. Your fingers dig into the contours of these muscles. Laia smiles down at you, approvingly.

Your hands then dance to the top of her pubic hair. Such soft downy hair! You stop and look at her eyes again. They are wet and open. She nods. You let your fingers flow beneath her mound. She tilts her hips up and toward you. You find the sweet mound, placing your two index fingers on it. She tells you not to be too quick. You nod, massaging it slowly. She wails as if she were a forever ringing bell. Her scent is strong and clean, a mixture of honey, musk and flowers. She leans back on her elbows, giving up her sex to you like a willing sacrifice.

The more you rub her mound, the harder she moans. She does this beautifully, from deep within her belly. Slowly, her hips move up and down, teasing your face and your fingers. She looks down the length of her body, into your eyes with a gaze that says nothing but is full of possibility. Your fingers wash her inner lips and you bend your head into your chest, blowing forward into her dark, moist sliver. She gasps, grabs your wrist with one of her strong hands. You both shed tears in this pleasure.

She turns herself over, so that the front of her hips is on your face and her own face, its flushed breath and mouth, are over your sex, which by now is rich with wetness and yearning. Her knees are at the sides of your face. You take caution in this position, breathing lightly on each other's inner thighs and knees. You run the tip of your tongue over the expanse of her soft down. You inhale her deeply. You are each a mass of starvation and mourning.

What happens next is not a product of mutual pain but of celebration — a joyous screaming with the body when none took place at the Mass. A shout for love, when it would have been inappropriate to do so at the tea, in front of somber family faces. A crying from the deepest parts of Laia and you, when the discreet dabbing of tears was not sufficient for either one of you today.

With heavy sobs, you approach each other as if you were women who had been denied the gift of touch, as if you had once been bound, hand and foot, and then beaten for your openness to the possibility of touch. Now all the tenderness and grace in that room spill over your body and hers.

You plunge your tongue into her moist flower. Her head arches up to the heavens and you feel this and plunge again. Through your tears, you search her chasm like a doe that thirsts for water so badly, that she will pierce the barren earth with her raw tongue for any drop of moisture.

Laia returns your affection, eating fully from your sex, madly burying her hair and face between your legs. This is a cleansing. This is a dance of comfort, closure and truth.

Arms, legs, faces, breasts and bellies take up the expanse of the bed. You consume her fully, as if you had no choice, as if taking of her with your mouth were more vital than air or food. She consumes you as if she were not human, but made purely of desire, a bound sack filled with arms, lips and legs, all aching to burst from her pores.

You find each other's peaks and this brings you both to a more urgent rhythm. She introduces her fingers to join her tongue's lovemaking. You gasp for precious air and suckle her with your mouth, driving deeper into her musky cavern.

"Alectra! Keep it like this," her voice pleads.

You obey, grabbing her ass and pushing her sweet heaviness into your face, shutting out all outside air and the dim light of the halogen lamps. She responds by lightly biting your swollen nodule, which sends preliminary waves of joy throughout your lower body.

You wrap your legs over her, your knees crossing above her head. She does the same, giving your wet head leverage with the backs of her full calves. Heavy sobs, moans, gasps and screams. The mosquito net nearly gets pulled off by the random movements of your bodies.

Suddenly, Laia's hips writhe upward and then crash down fiercely on your face. She is sobbing endlessly, grinding her sex deep into your mouth. You welcome her spasms by thrusting your tongue even harder inside her, your pink, deft muscle moving back and forth quickly. She screams your name, not even tending to your sex, and this alone — the simple bellow of your birth name — makes you come shortly after her.

Your back arches, as does hers — two cats in heat, two cats enraptured by instinct. The waves rush through you like a fiery liquid, more potent and more rhythmic than the recorded waves from the small white box. You swallow her honey. It is heavy and numbs your mouth; its sweetness is unbearable. You taste her pain and sacrifice. You taste all of her, in copious amounts.

She dismounts you and laps the rivers of fire between your legs like a grateful kitten. Her hair is stuck to her face in strategic pieces. Her eyes are closed, the lashes fluttering quickly. Finally, she opens her eyes and throws you an amorous glance and cleans off your swollen vulva with gentle strokes. Her tongue is pleasing and warm. You throw your arms over your head and breathe deeply. The smell of sex. The smell of two placated women. You smile reverently and speak.

"You're like a mother lion."

"Oh no," she warns coyly, bringing herself up to your face. "This was not an incestuous pity fuck, Alectra."

You open your eyes. She has pressed her face into the nook of your underarm. You hold her. It feels weird to have her poised below you.

"I know this wasn't incestuous. I've never thought of you like a mother. You've always been something more to me than that."

She kisses your chin and you continue.

"I said you were like a lioness because that's how you move: You're cunning and sexy and definite."

Laia thanks you and throws her leg over your belly. She is exhausted.

"God, I miss him so much," she says, near sobbing.

"It's okay. Laia, you're gonna be fine." You kiss the top of her head, smelling the strong wave of your own sex.

You both lay there, speechless, for an uncertain amount of time. A soft, gray light filters through the windows by the bed. Dawn. In silence, you feel her body relax, giving in to sleep. She snores slightly, her face still pressed up against your right breast. You hold her close to you and refuse the barrage of questions that try to make their way into your mind. You do not need to answer them. They mean nothing now. Your body . . . it feels cleansed and broken. A new vessel. The top of the mosquito net looks down at you. Its long netting forms a loose cage around your bodies. A womb. A black, translucent womb. You move slightly, sensing the wetness all around you. Laia wakes up, asks if you are okay. You tell her to go back to sleep and she gives in to slumber once again. You love her so much.

Soon, your eyes close and you, too, are slave to sleep. You hold onto Laia loosely and in your unconsciousness, the movie screen starts again. A tunnel. A short, dark tunnel that smells of gardenias and honey. Harmless bees zoom to and fro in this tunnel. You stand at one end, which is illuminated with a blue light. You look to the other end. Your body feels weightless. A cello plays loudly. Two figures at the other end, the opening also illuminated. One looks like your father because you recognize the peasant clothing, especially the hat. At his side is a woman dressed in an empire-waist dress and a large headpiece, on it, an attached veil that goes over her face. Under the veil, the woman also wears a black mask over her eyes. Her lips are painted white, matching her dress.

Your father waves at you slowly, the bees dancing around him. He blows you a kiss with both hands. He turns around to walk into the brightness behind him. You want him to look back but he does not. The sounds of the cello fade as he disappears, and the woman walks toward you slowly, removing her mask.

Joan Leslie Taylor

❧

# The Rose Velvet Chaise

It all began with the old-fashioned chaise longue, left behind
in the rental cottage by a vacating tenant. The first time she
saw it with its ornately carved dark wood and its worn velvet
upholstery, Frieda felt compelled to recline on it and stretch
out her long limbs. She had only stopped in to check on the
cottage, to see what needed to be done before a new tenant
moved in. But from the moment she sat down and ran her
fingers along the silken old wood, and sank into the firm but
comforting upholstery, something inside her opened wide,
and it felt as if she'd just taken her first real breath in a long,
long time. The scent of an unfamiliar perfume rose from the
chaise; a hint of floral, with undertones of a Southern summer.

She found herself remembering the June day fifteen years
ago when she'd first set eyes on her husband Blake at a Bolivian
guitar concert. When her gaze fell upon him several rows below her and in the next tier to the right she'd felt an alteration
in her body. Suddenly her skin had seemed so permeable she
was sure she heard the strains of the guitar through her pores.
And when something made him glance up at her, there was
that feeling of opening wide within. She could scarcely bear
the intensity of his dark eyes upon her, but neither could she
look away. It was as if he were touching her. The feeling was
definitely sexual. She felt his eyes, not just on her skin, but

deep inside her. Her face felt hot and her vagina convulsed. A voice in her head told her to get control of herself, pull away from those eyes, and not leave herself open to the intrusions of a stranger, but she'd been drawn to this handsome man with dark eyes and prominent eyebrows, sun-golden skin, and a way of moving his hands that made her see them on her skin, moving up her bare legs.

Blake had courted her insistently. He was so romantic that Frieda fell quickly in love with him. Never had she known such a sensuous lover. He didn't just fuck her and roll over like all too many of the pretty boys she'd known. He took delight in her body, caressing her with his fingers and tasting her with his tongue, whispering endearments in her ear. They made love everywhere: in beds, in cars, on couches, and hidden in the sand dunes with the sound of the ocean pounding in their ears. Their passion had carried them to the wedding and beyond. Blake was as attentive as a young husband as he'd been during their courtship. He brought her flowers; they dined with candles and soft music. And they made love.

As the years went by, though, something changed. Frieda could not name what had been lost, but she was often overcome with a longing that filled her with sadness and confusion. She had a wonderful husband — smart, successful, good-looking — so why was she longing?

Lying back on the velvet chaise, she looked around the small room. There was something comforting about being here. An enormous sigh fell through her like water. Weeks and months and years of tension fell from her. She was at home.

There would be no more tenants in the little cottage. It was now hers. Her heart beat rapidly. Still on the chaise, she looked around the empty room watching the dust motes in the morning sunlight streaming through the dirty panes of French doors that led to the deck nestled under tall trees.

"A little paint . . . " she mused. "Maybe a small rug."

Frieda was a mystery writer. She had four titles to her credit, each a tightly written whodunit, cleverly constructed and satisfying to her small but growing coterie of fans. Blake, a brilliant consultant who flew all over the country straightening out computer glitches and designing whiz-bang systems, had set up one room in their spacious contemporary home for Frieda to write. Because she could not stay put at the enormous teak desk with its cunning compartments for pens and paper clips, he bought her a laptop computer. She roamed restlessly from room to room, for awhile perching uncomfortably on one end of the L-shaped leather couch in the living room with its soaring beamed ceiling and a wall of glass facing out on more view than Frieda could bear to see while she wrote, then moving to the glass and stainless steel table in the breakfast room, and later outside to what seemed like acres of redwood deck surrounding the house. It was a testament to her talent and skill as a writer that roving about the house like this Frieda was actually able to turn out a book a year. Blake kept adding technological marvels to her office, but Frieda could write no more than a paragraph within its confines.

Blake had also devoted his ingenuity to their bedroom. From a concealed panel on his side of the bed, he could control the lighting, change the piped-in music, roll back a screen above the bed to reveal a massive mirror arranged to reflect the action on the bed, or even set the whole bed or a selection of sex toys vibrating. He had assembled a world-class collection of erotic videos which he and Frieda viewed on the wide-screen television with speakers so realistic and precise that Frieda often imagined that the actors — panting and groaning, sucking and licking, thrusting and sliding — were right there in their king-sized bed with its black satin sheets.

Frieda and Blake had sex nearly every night when Blake was

not off in some distant city tweaking someone's computer. Blake was ardent and had the staying power of a much younger man. Frieda was more than willing. They pursued passion in every possible position, in every mood, and every way.

While Blake lay back and watched an erotic video, Frieda would caress his entire body, the fragrant massage oil letting her fingers, hands, and arms glide across his well-muscled flesh. He worked out using the latest high-tech equipment so he had not gone to fat, and was, if anything, more beautiful with each passing year. She liked moving her hands on his body: his firm chest, his broad back rippling with muscles, and his long muscular legs leading to his beautiful genitals, waiting like jewels for her fingers. Frieda wished she could caress Blake's cock and balls with the same leisurely care as she did the rest of his body, but every night at her first touch, his cock sprang into life and the massage was over. He'd slip two fingers into her moist and ready pussy, and before long they would both be at fever pitch, the sounds of the actors on the screen background music to their own groans of pleasure.

Yes, Frieda knew, Blake was still a good lover. He always made sure that she came, and he knew just how to bring her to the peak of arousal and then with the slightest movement to orgasm. Yet after Blake had turned off the video, dimmed the lights, silenced the music, and lay beside her fast asleep, Frieda would feel a distant longing for something she could not name. Many nights she left the king-sized bed and wandered the big house, roaming from room to room just like she did during the daytime, with a restless gnawing hunger.

That very day she first came to the cottage, she swept the worn hardwood floors and brought her laptop computer across the courtyard that separated the main house from the small rental. The moment she sat down upon the velvet chaise and began typing she knew that a change had occurred. Her feminist sleuth, Amber Queen, always so clever and efficient at ferreting out crooks and murderers and spotting clues the high-priced private-eyes overlooked, began behaving in ways unheard of in the four previous volumes. She showed up at the crime scene in a low-cut dress of flowing gauze in a rosy hue. What had become of her tailored suits in earth tones, much like the ones that Frieda wore? Amber smiled warmly at the police sergeant as she removed her sunglasses with the rose-colored frames that matched her dress. And she wore perfume with a hint of magnolias. By the end of the afternoon a tall dark stranger with brooding eyes had shown up. Frieda was breathless.

Later, preparing dinner in her own kitchen with its many labor-saving appliances, she looked out the window toward the little cottage and sighed. She could not wait to find out what Amber Queen might do next under her fingers on the keyboard. Or to feel that opening, that rush of excitement that came upon her whenever she settled upon the rose velvet chaise.

In the next few days she painted the walls of the cottage pale pink, the color of peonies she remembered from her grandmother's garden. She poked around antique shops until she found the perfect little rug, a small round table of the same dark wood as the chaise, and some lace curtains. She stopped at a boutique, not at all the kind of place she ever shopped, and bought a dress, all roses and peonies and camellias on the softest, sheerest cotton. Frieda had never worn anything with such a revealing neckline and so many flowers. As she handed the clerk her credit card, she added a pale pink shawl, so romantic and feminine she blushed.

She spent every day in the cottage, contentedly writing, following Amber Queen as she and the dark stranger solved the mystery of the cry in the boathouse. This was no longer just a mystery, but a romantic tale of seduction. The tall, dark stranger laid his hand upon Amber's arm, and then on her thigh. Frieda's heart pounded as Amber raised her lips to kiss the stranger. She was so aroused by the scene on her computer screen that she had to set the computer aside, lay back on the chaise, and give in to her rapidly accelerating arousal. Her body was hot, her skin reaching out, each pore longing to be touched. She ran her fingers down her neck and across her chest, wondering what it would be like to feel the fingers of a stranger upon her skin. The idea sent a wave of heat through her. Excited and frightened all at once, she unbuttoned the flowered dress and let her fingers find her breasts.

How soft and voluptuous her small bosom felt to her finger-tips. Whose breasts were these anyway? Who was she, this woman undulating on the rose velvet chaise? Frieda's breath came in short pants as a wave of longing swept over her. Who was she longing for? *Close your eyes and see,* she whispered. The tall dark stranger appeared. He floated above her, his brooding eyes upon her, his sensuous lips reaching to kiss her, his fingers reaching to touch her. The scent of summer flowers filled the air.

Inspired, she reached for her computer and her fingers played on the keys as excitedly as they had on her breasts. It was a certain moonlit night — she saw it all — as Amber and the stranger forgot about clues and culprits and lay in each other's arms in the gazebo. Amber sighed. Frieda sighed. Amber moaned with desire, and Frieda's vagina contracted. Frieda watched the stranger's fingers move up Amber's leg, beneath her dress. . . . Whatever would her editor say? *The Cry in the Boat-house* was nothing like any of Frieda's previous books. Months ahead of schedule, Frieda mailed off the completed manuscript.

Blake, who read only technical books and periodicals, inter-spersed with an occasional science fiction title, was proud of his wife's writing career and gave her articles about the latest computerized tools used by police departments, so that her stories could be up-to-date and authentic.

"So now that you've finished your story you can take a break, right?" he asked her. "You could meet me in Rio," he added, running his hands down her buttocks and drawing her to him.

"Oh, I don't know," she stammered, thinking of the little cottage, but moving instinctively to Blake's hands. "I've got an idea for the next book. I must get it down before it slips away."

"I'm not leaving for another week. Please think about it," he said, his hands in her pants as he led her to the marvelous master suite with its automated love controls. "Is that perfume I smell?" he asked, burying his face in her hair and inhaling deeply. Frieda blushed as if she were with not Blake, but a stranger.

Day after day she worked away in the cottage, which continued to acquire furnishings and always had fresh flowers in an antique vase. She loved the old rocking chair she'd found at a garage sale. And the French drawings of nudes took her breath away, the subtlety of line calling up pleasure in her every time she looked up from her work and saw them. She lived with Blake, whom she loved dearly, in their wide beautiful house, but more and more the cottage was her home. Frieda had very casually mentioned to Blake that she was using it as a writing studio, which had surprised him, but he did not question her. He respected her work and did not intrude.

On the morning Blake left for Rio — an enormous computer network in snarls would require several weeks of his attentions — Frieda entered the cottage, already missing him. She could still smell him on her skin, and the memory of their early morning lovemaking sent a thrill, shot from her throat right down to her pussy still slippery with Blake's come. Every night that week he had begged her to come to Rio with him, but something in her would not let her leave the cottage.

In the glare of morning sunlight, she felt unbearably lonely, and she could not remember what had been so compelling in the little cottage. Amber's adventures suddenly seemed silly. What was the point of endless clues and dark strangers who came in the night and disappeared before dawn? She wanted Blake. But not Blake. She missed her husband of fourteen years, but, she realized, she missed him even when he was not flying off to Rio or Brussels, Miami or New Orleans.

Blake was so competent and so successful that their life, like their house, had become too big, too reliable, too elaborate. She missed the intimacy and excitement of when they had first come together.

Her hands trembled and her eyes clouded. Despite the warm sun, she shivered and wrapped herself in her pink shawl. Without turning on her computer, she curled up on the velvet chaise, a teacup in her hand and tears sliding down her cheeks. Longing rose in her. The soft folds of her flowered dress comforted her. Birds twittered in the trees outside. A slight breeze tickled her calves. She raised her skirt to let the breeze touch her thighs. It felt like Blake's fingers, but without massage oil. "I miss his fingers," she thought, "his fingers touching me, just to touch me, not part of a massage." A cry escaped her throat and she was suddenly weeping. "I want his hands on me without music, only wind and bird song!" she cried to the air between sobs. She slipped off her panties and let the wind tickle her longing yoni. "Oh, my dear sweet Blake," she whispered.

"Frieda?"

His voice at the door startled her. How could it be Blake here now in the cottage? But there he stood in the doorway, his white shirt open at the top, setting off his tanned face and revealing his strong neck. His dark eyes ran across her supine form draped upon the velvet chaise.

"Blake?"

He walked into the cottage and stood silently looking down at Frieda, her flowered dress in disarray about her waist, her cheeks wet with tears, and her pussy open to the wind. He did not say why he was not on his way to the airport. She did not ask. She reached one languid hand toward him. A sensuous half-smile on his lips, he held just the tips of her fingers in his two hands and looked into her eyes. She felt her whole being flow into her fingertips. He raised her hand to his lips. His mouth on her fingers brought a low moan from her throat. He moved his mouth along her arm, kissing each spot of skin as if he had never touched her before. Her skin bloomed under his warm breath as he moved his mouth toward her shoulder. Each kiss, each caress of his fingers on her skin sent tingles throughout her body. Each cell of her body wanted Blake's touch.

He opened her dress but did not remove it. Taking the fabric of the skirt in his hand, he let the cloth move through his fingers. He knelt beside the chaise and lay his face on her belly and reached under her, grasping her buttocks in his hands. He made no move to touch her moist vagina, as if his face on her stomach and his hands on her ass were more than any man could want. Frieda continued to moan softly, hungry for his touch. How had she lived so long without his mouth on her belly? She was overcome with the need to feel the length of him against her.

She put her arms around him and drew him to her. Deftly she opened the buttons on his white shirt and touched his fine chest, his dear stomach. She opened his belt, pulled down the zipper, and pulled him hard against her, belly to belly. Only the wind touched her pussy as they lay breathing together as one. Blake's mouth found hers and she eagerly opened her lips to him. His tongue filled her mouth, caressed her teeth, and reached toward her throat. She opened wider and wider, wanting to swallow him, dissolve all space between them. Her tongue moved eagerly across his teeth and met his tongue. Saliva ran on her face where tears had flowed before, before Blake had touched her.

His mouth moved down her neck to her breasts, her nipples erect and rising to meet his kisses. She arched her back and he slipped his arms under her, encircling her in his embrace. She buried her face in his chest, heard his heart pound loudly. This was Blake and not Blake, more than Blake.

Their bodies moved together, their breathing becoming faster, urgency building, their clothes dropping to the floor. She slipped out from under him, and he lay back upon the chaise while she touched his whole body with her hands and her eyes. Her fingers that had danced across the keyboard now wrote stories on the skin of the man she loved. He was her stranger and no stranger at all. She filled her hands with his marvelous cock and balls, brought her mouth to them, ran her tongue across each familiar and amazing centimeter of flesh along the length of his penis, felt the exquisite softness of the skin on his balls, rolled the mysterious inner jewels between her fingers. She knew Blake's penis almost better than parts of her own body, but there on the velvet chaise it tasted new and astonishing to her. It swelled in her mouth, pulsated against her tongue. She lifted her face and beheld this beautiful organ so wonderfully, perfectly suited to slide into her depths.

Without a word, Blake rose from the chaise and lifted her off her feet. He held her in his arms, gazing intently into her eyes, then lay her back upon the rose velvet chaise. Hungrily she drew him to her and let his penis slide into her like silk. Home,

Frieda thought. So perfectly home, his penis sliding in and out, stroking, caressing, remembering all the years of their loving. Her body moving, contracting and releasing, loving and reaching, together belly to belly, penis to vagina, cock to cunt, the breeze caressing their skin, the birds singing louder and louder matching the mounting crescendo of their bodies moving toward the peak of a new mountain.

I don't want this to ever end, she thought, willing their bodies to hold back from orgasm, tears springing into her eyes at the thought that too soon it would be over — but like a small craft nearing the edge of a waterfall, she was helpless to stop or slow the force rushing toward orgasm. Letting go of the last shreds of her customary care and control, like her heroine Amber, she surrendered. They had never in all their years together orgasmed at the same time, but there on the chaise in the little cottage with the lace curtains wafting in the breeze, an orgasm that had grown in them all the years of their marriage bloomed and burst into that little room with a cacophony of bird song outside.

They lay together silently, not moving, his penis now a quiet creature in her pussy overflowing with his come. She held him tenderly to her, loving the unmoving weight of him upon her, not wanting him to rise and leave. The loneliness of the morning cast its shadow on her.

"Come to Rio with me," he whispered in her ear, visions of lush tropical vegetation, the wild colors of parrots, and the scent of deep-hued jungle flowers in his voice.

"Oh, yes," she said, smiling, her fingers stroking his back and the first lines of a Brazilian mystery forming in her mind.

# Nancy Ferreyra

❦

# After Amelia

Amelia's perfectly round mouth tugged at my nipple. Being passed around to so many strangers had stressed her out and she was suckling hard to calm herself, squishing her nose into the soft flesh of my breast and bumping her little fists against me. I stroked her head, smoothing wisps of brown hair. "Oh honey, it's okay. You're gonna go home with your Uncle Diego and Aunt Isabel soon." My brother and sister-in-law had agreed to take Amelia overnight so Miranda and I could spend some time together. We had booked a room here in this swanky hotel, planning to get "reacquainted."

I looked out over the patio railing at a glorious view of the San Francisco Bay, trying to imagine what the night would be like. After all these months, how would we begin? Before Amelia, I'd been able to seduce Miranda with a sultry stare and an intentionally exposed breast or shoulder. Her eyes would lock into mine and a flush would smarten her cheeks. I took great pride in my ability to penetrate my lover's reserved sexual nature and coax her into having sex almost anywhere. One of my most impressive coups was when I enticed her onto the balcony of a highrise where we were attending a community fundraiser. Once I had sparked her passion, she would not stop until we were both satiated.

But the baby had changed our lives so dramatically that

those lustful encounters were only dim memories. It seemed that neither of us had the energy or interest at the same time. It made me cringe to imagine us turning into an old married couple who only had scheduled sex on Friday nights or Sunday mornings.

I was responsible for initiating lovemaking tonight — Miranda had made it clear that she wasn't willing to risk being rejected again. But for the first time, I was unsure how to interest her. Now that my breasts were exposed six or seven times a day, the sight of them didn't have the same effect: When Amelia nursed, Miranda looked on with loving tenderness, nothing else. Twice, after the baby had dozed off while nursing, I'd caught Miranda eyeing my breasts where Amelia's puckered lips lingered an inch from my nipple. I had pulled Amelia close, pressing her temple against my sternum, Miranda's favorite place. Both times, Miranda had stared for a long minute with a look I couldn't identify before turning away from us. What was she feeling? Envy? Longing? Miranda used to nestle between my breasts after lovemaking, while I petted her head. Was she afraid that Amelia had taken her place? Or did she feel left out, thinking that Amelia and I shared a closeness that she wasn't a part of? Introducing this new person into our lives had shaken things up more than I had anticipated.

I wanted to talk about it, but didn't know how. When things were difficult between us, Miranda always brought them up. I tried to resolve things by *doing* something, not talking about it. One evening when Diego and Isabel had taken Amelia, over cartons of pad Thai and yellow curry vegetables I waited for Miranda to broach the topic, but she didn't. When we cuddled on the couch to watch a movie, I pulled Miranda close, cradling her head to my chest to show her that she hadn't lost her place. She sighed and let me hold her for a while before she raised her head to kiss me on the mouth. When I told her I still wasn't feeling sexual, she didn't hide her frustration. Untangling her limbs from mine, she perched on the edge of the couch and looked intently into my face, pulling her thoughts together. Then she told me that although we were still affectionate partners, she missed making love, connecting with me as a lover. I listened carefully, then tried to explain what was going on for me. But all I could say was that my body just didn't feel right, that I didn't want to be touched that way. She told me she accepted that, but she needed me to understand that she was closing down, that it was too hard to want something she couldn't have. She made it clear that the ball was now in my court.

I looked down into Amelia's grey-blue eyes, wide and staring straight into mine. I smiled and stroked her cheek. Releasing my nipple, she clucked her tongue against the roof of her mouth as she swallowed the last bit of milk. She caught her breath and let out a heartfelt sigh. Pressing my lips to her forehead, I was filled with her distinctive scent: a combination of talcum, breast milk and clothes softener.

"Are you finished?" I asked. "Or just taking a break?" I leaned her over my forearm and rubbed her back, trying to coax out a burp.

I buttoned my dress and turned to face the crowd, steadying Amelia's wobbly torso with one hand and pushing the joystick of my electric wheelchair with the other. I scanned the patio, searching for Miranda. Women in strapless gowns and men in linen suits stood in groups of threes and fours, sipping champagne and eating miniature *empañadas* and bite-sized bagels. I spotted Miranda, talking with Diego and Isabel. She was laughing, holding a tall full glass of champagne in her hand. Miranda didn't pay attention to clothes, whether or not they matched, or even if they fit that well. She only cared that they were clean and that she wasn't missing anything important. Miranda's sister had let her opt out of wearing a traditional bridesmaid's dress, so I'd picked out her black tailored slacks and a white sleeveless blouse. The afternoon heat had forced her to finally shed her matching silk jacket, revealing her narrow, rounded shoulders and finely sculpted arms.

I watched Miranda, smiling as she talked to Diego and Isabel. Nodding her head at something Diego said, she tucked her golden hair behind her ear. A couple of inches shorter than me, and lighter, Miranda was nonetheless pretty strong, able to lower and lift me from most places. Before Miranda, I had never been involved with a woman smaller than myself. Poor planning on my part — to fall in love with one who could barely lift me, never mind carry me for any long distance. And while I'd gained twenty pounds, Miranda had lost weight since Amelia's birth. Her lithe, toned body was the product of hours spent at the pool and on the soccer field. I took a deep breath and sighed.

How I missed her body. The feel of her smooth, warm skin gliding over me, her lips and hands roving everywhere, but always coming back to the same sweet places. Mostly I missed her body under mine, her thighs wrapped around my hips, her mouth grazing from one breast to the other while I pushed into her deeply and slowly. When her fingers clutched the small of my back, I would push faster, our hipbones bumping, my cheek pressed against her forehead. When she came, she would roll us onto our sides, pushing the dildo up into her one last time, suckling intently on my breast.

Diego and Isabel walked into the hotel and Miranda turned, flashing me her lazy grin. I remembered a morning about two weeks ago: Miranda had been scampering around the house getting ready for work. She had on her jeans and an undershirt, and was looking for a belt. I had showered and gone back to bed and Amelia was napping. Miranda sat next to me on the edge of the bed, putting on her shoes and socks, and while we went over the day's schedule, I watched her backside: shoulders flexing as she pulled the laces tight on her shoes, the soft curve of her neck. I wrapped my arms around her hips, beckoning her to come back to bed with me.

"They're expecting me at work," she mumbled, glancing over her shoulder.

"Can't you go in the afternoon instead?" I asked.

"I need to come home in the afternoon and bathe Amelia."

We both knew Amelia's bath could wait until evening. Confused, I released her and leaned back against the pillow. She didn't look at me, but kept her flushed face down while she tucked in her shirt and buckled her belt.

When Miranda went into the other room to gather the rest of her stuff, I thought about my body. Of course she didn't want me. Not only had I gained weight since the baby, I was out of shape, the flesh hanging loosely from my arms, around my hips and thighs. My heavy breasts often leaked milk. Maybe that disgusted her. Before Miranda left, she poked her head in, hesitating for a few moments, then slipped her slender fingers from the door frame.

I hadn't really been ready for sex yet anyway. It had been several months since the birth, and I still hadn't gotten back all of my strength. What if I couldn't move the way I wanted to, touch her how I wanted to? What if I didn't respond the same way? I used to like Miranda to fondle and suck my breasts, but now the skin on my nipples was thick and tough; they weren't as sensitive. I didn't know how it would feel to have them touched when we made love.

At times I thought of Miranda while I fed Amelia. On the mornings when Miranda brought Amelia into the bed and curled up behind us, I would be filled with the same sensual

contentment I used to feel after making love with Miranda —
lying under the warm covers with Miranda's arm around my
waist, her soft breath on the back of my neck, and this tender,
perfect little creature feeding from my breast. I didn't know
how to put all of these experiences into words for Miranda. But
I wanted her to know, I wanted to tell her.

Miranda made her way through the crowd toward us, pausing at every third clique to chat briefly, before grinning at me
and moving purposefully in my direction until the next time
she was detained. This was a gathering of her family, and having introduced our daughter to everyone, she was completely
aglow. Her heart-shaped face shone, her grey eyes were bright.
The open joy on Miranda's face as she strode toward us
warmed my cheeks. I looked down at the top of the baby's
head and pretended to be fastening a button behind her neck.

"Hey, how's my angel?" Miranda knelt in front of Amelia
and me, smiling at each of us in turn. When Amelia caught
sight of Miranda's face, she flailed her plump arms, one hand
landing on Miranda's mouth.

"Diego and Isabel went to say goodbye to Laura and John,"
she said, her lips moving around Amelia's chubby fingers. She
took the baby in her arms and stood up. "Then they're gonna
take you home," she said to Amelia.

I looked up and saw Isabel leading Diego by the hand across
the patio. Diego reached for Amelia immediately. "Hey, little
Amelita. Are you ready to go home with your *tío* and *tía*?"

Sensing my desire to hold on to Amelia a bit longer, Diego
and Isabel gently convinced me it was time for them to go.
They assured Miranda and me that we could call if we wanted
to, but that Amelia would be fine.

Diego took a few steps toward me so Amelia's face was next
to mine. The deep baritone of his voice always put her to sleep.
I kissed her cheek. "Bye, bye, sweetie, we'll see you after your

morning nap, okay?" I whispered. Miranda kissed her on the top of her head, whispered tenderly and Amelia was gone. Watching Diego's back disappear, the skin on my chest felt bare. Without Amelia's body next to mine, I felt naked. Although we had spent several hours at a time apart from her, being away overnight felt different.

But it was time to fill the distance that had developed between Miranda and me, I reminded myself. I leaned my head on her shoulder.

Miranda took a deep breath. "How you doin', Trace?" she asked. "Need anything? More food? Something to drink?" She ran her hand down my spine, from the base of my neck to the small of my back. Goosebumps traveled down my arms.

"No thanks." I had eaten more than five of each *hors d'oeuvre* that had come my way. My appetite had tripled since Amelia was born. Miranda pulled up a chair and we sat at a table framed with black wrought iron, covered with a tempered glass top. "Are you having a good time?" she asked.

"Yeah," I said, my voice cracking a bit. I was nervous. I cleared my throat. "It's a nice reception. Beautiful day."

Leaning back, she looked up at the sky. "Isn't it, though?" She looked into my eyes. Her open gaze unnerved and mesmerized me at the same time. "Wow, our first night away from her. She's already four months old. Can you believe it?"

I shook my head and threaded my fingers through hers. "It's been a long time."

"It'll be nice," she said, swallowing some champagne. I leaned my knee against hers under the table and looked into her eyes, raising my eyebrows. We didn't notice Miranda's big bear of a father approaching until he tapped his hand on our table, a benevolent smile on his bearded face. "Hey, you two, we're heading inside for dinner."

Miranda tightened her grip on my hand, grinning up at him.

"Okay, Dad, we're on our way." She pushed her chair out and stood up. "Ready?"

"Actually, I have to use the restroom first," I said. "Can you come with me in case it's not accessible?"

"Sure," she said. Miranda led us through the patio, expertly judging the width of passages and either moving chairs or asking people to squeeze together in tighter clusters so I could pass. She glanced behind her every ten feet or so to be sure I hadn't gotten stuck behind. I followed her, wheelchair humming, through a dimly lit room with plush chairs and brocaded mirrors, into another room lined with toilet stalls. We stopped at the last one with a blue wheelchair sign on it. Miranda followed me into the long, wide stall, its green and white velvet walls completely enclosing us from floor to ceiling.

"You wanna go first?" I offered as she latched the door.

"Okay," she said, unbuttoning her pants. She sat down on the toilet.

"When you dumped our stuff in the room, did you notice if the bathroom was accessible?" Noticing the mirror on the back of the stall door, I adjusted the pads in my bra. Normally I'm small-breasted, but nursing Amelia had given me a bit of a bosom and I was taking advantage of it with a scoop neck dress that showed a little cleavage. Unfortunately, it also showed the pads I had stuffed in my bra to absorb the leaking breast milk.

Miranda tilted her head to the side, her long silver earring tickling her shoulder. "Yeah, it is." She shifted one hip and stuffed a wad of white toilet paper between her spread thighs. "The bed is huge. Looks like a king." She smiled sleepily as if she was lying against the plush pillows right now. Returning her smile, I glanced down at the few blond hairs peeking out from between her legs. She stood up and moved aside, buttoning her pants back up. When we traded places, my arm grazed the front of her silky blouse and I smelled her spicy cologne.

Miranda plopped down in my wheelchair, her eyes on me. "You look great in that dress," she said. "The green brings out your eyes. Did I tell you that?"

"I think you might have mentioned it," I murmured, lowering my eyes to the black and white tiles. After I finished, I flushed the toilet, reached for the grab bar and pushed myself up, my dress falling over my hips, my calves, the hemline tumbling around my ankles. Miranda was standing. Our eyes met.

"Sit back down," I said, my hand on her collarbone. I took a step toward her and she pulled me onto her lap. Sliding my arm around her shoulder, I looked into her clear grey eyes. A few lines creased the edges. "Hey," she said, a grin tugging at the corner of her mouth. She blinked slowly.

"Hi." I tucked a lock of her silky hair behind her ear with my fingertip and leaned my cheek against her temple. When I felt her hand on my hip, I closed my eyes and pressed my lips against hers, soft and sweet. Miranda tilted her head back and we kissed, our mouths tentative, the taste of champagne still on her tongue. Then she ran her lips over my neck, under my ear, and returned to my mouth, darting her tongue between my teeth. I put her palm over my breast to calm my pounding heart. Her fingers went to the top button of my dress and unfastened it, her kisses becoming sloppier, her mouth opening wider.

Miranda slid the top of my dress over my shoulders. She buried her face between my breasts, then planted wet kisses from my sternum, up my throat to my ear. "Hmm, Tracy, I've missed you."

Familiar stirrings gripped my belly, my thighs. "I know," I whispered. "I know."

I craved the feel of her skin. The buttons of her blouse were flat and the openings slippery, so I needed both hands to undo them. She watched my fingers, her chest heaving as I got down to the last two buttons. I tugged on the ribbed, cotton fabric of her undershirt.

"Take it off," I breathed. Clumsily she pulled it over her head. I slipped my hand across her round, firm breasts, catching her nipples between my fingers. Her skin was warm, like mine, from the afternoon heat. She unfastened my bra and stared at my breasts, my nipples just inches from her lips. I breathed deeply, each breath moving them closer to her mouth. Miranda pressed her lips to my throat and slipped the straps of my bra over my shoulders. I wanted to lie on top of her, curl my body around hers so tightly that I wouldn't know where I began and she ended. I opened my legs. My crotch was wet.

Miranda pulled away. "God, Tracy, what are we doing?" she whispered. "Let's check into our room."

But I didn't want to stop. The moment felt too fragile. When Miranda got up out of the wheelchair, I slipped my damp underpants down past my thighs and let them fall to the floor along with my dress. Miranda's fingers halted on the top button of her blouse, a blush coloring her cheeks. Sitting down, I took her hands and pulled her toward me. "I want you to touch me," I said.

She leaned over to kiss my mouth, then my shoulders, pushing me back against the chair. I cradled the crown of her head as she licked a wet trail around the curve of first one breast, then the other, then to my belly, her open mouth exploring every inch. She got down on her knees, her hands on my hips, my closed thighs before her lips. Her fingers kneaded my flesh, trying to spread my thighs apart. Wetness streamed across my middle ribs; my breasts were leaking. I tried to separate my knees, scooting my butt to the edge of the seat.

"This isn't working," I said. "I feel like I'm gonna fall."

"What do you want to do?"

"Let's move to the floor."

She planted a kiss on top of my pubic bone before getting to her feet. I backed the wheelchair away from the toilet and turned the power off, got to my feet and leaned on the velvet-covered wall, while she kicked off her shoes and pants.

"Help me down," I whispered. Miranda pressed her hips against mine and kissed me until my legs felt like rubber. I turned, pressing my back against her sleek skin, and she circled her arms around my middle, grasping her hands in front of me. I bent my legs as she slowly lowered me to the floor. The tile was shockingly cold against my bare skin. I raised my knees and spread my thighs.

Miranda looked me over; she noticed that my breasts were dripping. "You're . . ." she said. She looked from my breasts to my face, then at my breasts again.

"I'm leaking," I said. "It's okay. You can touch me."

"Are you sure? Do you need to pump?"

"No, I'm not full. I'm just . . . excited." I watched her face as she digested this information.

She blinked slowly, her hand playing with a lock of my hair. Then she nodded slightly and cupped my cheek in her hand. We kissed, sweetly at first, our breasts swaying, nipples lightly grazing one another's. Then my kisses became more insistent, pulling her tongue into my mouth, showing her what I wanted her to do to me. Miranda pulled me closer, and traced a smooth path around my thigh, resting her hand just inches from my throbbing cunt.

The floor was hard and cold against the bones in my back, but Miranda's body was warm, her skin hot against my belly, my chest. I ran my fingers lightly over her shoulders, down her spine to the small of her back, while her wet lips covered my throat, my chest. She looked into my face, her eyes dark with desire, before covering my mouth with hers. Wrapping my legs around her hips, I caressed the back of her knee with my foot.

From this position I couldn't really move, or raise my head to see anything. "I want to be on top," I mumbled. She rolled onto her back, sliding her body under mine, cursing when her shoulder hit the back tire of the wheelchair.

Pleased with the new position, I raised my hips above hers, spreading my thighs wide. I ran my fingers through strands of her golden, silky hair, spread out against a black square tile. She cupped my hips in her hands, then squeezed my thighs before reaching between my legs. When I felt her light touch on my bush, I sucked in a quick breath, and pulled her nipple into my mouth. She arched her back, pushing her breasts further into my greedy mouth, while she petted me, first with the back of her hand, then the pads of her fingers. I felt wet and wide, my cunt throbbing, wanting to feel her inside me. "Can I go inside?" she breathed. "Is it okay?"

"Uh huh," I whispered. "I want you to." We moaned in unison when she plunged her fingers into me. I rocked my hips in rhythm with her thrusting fingers. "Is it okay? Am I hurting you?" Her voice was thick and gravelly, her tone distracted.

"No." The fit of her hand in my cunt felt as gloriously thick as usual. "Do I feel the same?" I whispered.

"Yeah," she replied, her voice low. "You feel great." She fucked me slow and strong, her fingers making a clicking sound in my wet cunt. I lifted my body above hers and crawled forward, my knees and palms knocking against the flat tiles. She slid down the rest of the way, the moist skin on her back squeaking against the tile. I felt self-conscious about my stomach, so big and loose since the baby, and looked down to see if it was hanging as low as I imagined. I got a clear view of the top of Miranda's head, her chin turned up as her teeth nipped at my thighs, my belly. She slipped her fingers out of me and took my thighs in her hands.

"Come here," she muttered into my belly. I closed my eyes

and lowered my cunt to her mouth. She pulled back my lips and kissed my throbbing clit. Long, slow, deliberate kisses. Then she glided her tongue inside me, then out, traveling to the tip of my clit. My breath came out in puffs as I rocked my hips against her mouth, heat spreading from deep inside my gut. The palms of my hands were sore and my elbows ached from holding my weight. I was afraid they were going to give out. On the black tile below my chest I saw two little spots of watery milk gathering as it dribbled out of my swaying breasts. As Miranda covered my clit with her whole mouth, her tongue flicking hard and fast against me, I dropped to my elbows, panting and humping wildly against her face. I groaned with each hot flash as it rolled over me. Miranda ran her tongue over me a few more times, then raised her head to kiss my spasming belly. When she slid her body out from under me, I laid my cheek on the floor, my ass still in the air, the puddle of thin, sweet milk sticky against my chest.

Slowly I rolled onto my side, my hip falling against the wall with a thud, then sliding to the floor. Miranda lay down beside me, her cheeks bright pink, little beads of sweat on her forehead. I pressed my lips against hers, tasting the tang of my juices. "Still taste the same," I mused, burying my face in her neck.

"Hmm," she murmured, her voice low and hoarse in my ear. I lay still while she stroked the back of my head. Heat rose from her body; her heart was pounding wildly. She flung her leg over my hip and kissed me, pressing her warm, wet bush against my thigh. Reaching behind her, I traced a path following the line of her cheek.

I cupped my palm around her cunt and stroked her, my fingers getting tangled in her wet, matted hair. Spreading her lips, I squeezed her slippery clit while she planted hot, random kisses on my chin, throat, collarbone. I wanted to fuck her badly, put my hand inside her and make her pant and moan, but I wanted her to be ready, so I held on, waiting for a cue. Finally she pushed her ass away from my leg, toward my hand, and I dipped my fingers into her. Fucking her with only three fingers at first, I pushed them in and out slowly. In the mirror on the back of the stall door, I watched us: her thigh draped over my hip, my forearm pressed into her crack, my fingers hidden inside her.

When she pushed her hips back against my hand I knew she wanted more. Slipping around to her front, I thrust my hand inside her, pushing in all five fingers up to my knuckles. Curling my fingertips around the curve of her cunt, I pulled my hand out some, keeping my fingers inside her. I fucked her this way, pushing my hand in a little further each time until my palm was all the way inside her, almost up to my wrist. She rolled onto her back, pulling me with her, rocking her hips toward mine. I used my bent knee to thrust my hand inside her.

"Oh, Miranda," I whispered, my cheek against her temple. "I've missed you so much." She nuzzled one breast then the other, her mouth still avoiding my erect, throbbing nipples. "Let me take you," I urged. I followed the rhythm of her contracting cunt, thrusting when I felt the pull, so that I could be inside her even further. Clutching my ass tightly, she groaned as she came. Her lips grabbed my nipple, and I moaned, moving my chest toward her face. She twisted her middle, tossing us onto our sides, orgasms rolling over her like waves. With each one, she groaned, suckling noisily on my breast.

Miranda released my nipple and nestled her face between my breasts. I slipped my hand out and wrapped my arm around her shoulder, pressing my lips to the top of her sweaty head.

After a while, she kissed me, the sweet milk still on her lips. I smiled.

She shook her head slowly. "It felt so weird to touch your breasts," she said. "I wanted to, and I didn't want to."

"I thought so," I said.

"How did it feel?"

"It felt good."

"Yeah? It didn't feel wrong? Like I was trying to take Amelia's place?"

"No," I said. "You're my lover, my partner." I didn't think lying on the floor of a public bathroom was the place to reveal to her my sensual feelings about our daughter. We could talk more later. "Hey, we better get back to the reception," I said. "I'll bet they're finished with dinner."

Miranda sat up. "The toasts! I'm supposed to do one of those after dinner!" She looked around for her blouse.

We dressed quickly, checking each other to be sure our clothes were buttoned correctly. When I put my bra back on, I asked Miranda to get clean nursing pads out of my bag. She knelt before me and slipped them into my bra with the same tenderness as when she changed Amelia's diaper. But then her fingers lingered, and she pressed her parted lips against mine. I reminded her that today was her sister's big day and buckled her belt. We left the bathroom, a shy grin on both our faces. Our lives were going to be different for sure since Amelia had joined us — but not *too* different.

Kate Dominic

🖋

# The Album

Kris and I keep a special photo album, one that's just the two of us together. No family, no friends, no professional accomplishments. Just us. Even the wedding pictures in there are strictly personal — me eating the cake from his fingers, him taking my garter off with his teeth, the two of us sleeping naked in each other's arms early the next morning. He actually got up and set the timer for that picture, cuddling back up against me just as the flash went off.

Over the years, we've made a habit of including everyday photos along with the special ones. It's our journal, although the album itself isn't particularly fancy — a plain leather binder with acid-free pages. Whole months can go by without our taking it down off the shelf. Other times, we keep it open on the dresser while we're deciding what to add next. But like any good book, it opens to some pages automatically.

The picture of us at the biker bar is one of my favorites. "Melissa and Her Pet," the caption reads. Just two leather dykes, dressed to kill in black and silver, sitting at a table with the end of a leash barely visible in my hand. It was our fifth anniversary, and the waitress took the picture. Kris' drag was perfect. Not that it doesn't seem strange to call cowhide and chains drag. But he was dressed to kill. The shot doesn't capture the smoky, sweaty ambiance of the bar.

Not quite. But we'd met in a bar, and somehow that made the picture perfect.

We met in one of those dives down on Sunset Boulevard. Kris was fronting a gay punk band from D.C. that was opening for one of the local big names. I walked in the door with my actor friends. As my eyes adjusted to the darkness and my ears numbed to the assault from the speakers, I looked up into the glare of the stage lights — at the most gorgeous human being I'd ever seen. He was obviously a guy. He was dancing in his jockey shorts, and no fake parts ever moved the way his did when he thrust his hips forward. He wasn't hard, just hung.

His chest was very muscular, despite his slender build. I could see his nipple rings move beneath the glitter of his sleeveless Judy Garland T-shirt as he danced. It was his face that really drew me in, though. Kris was truly beautiful, in the classic artistic sense. Soft hazel eyes accented with a minimum of the black kohl outlining obligatory for a punk singer, vibrantly full lips, and delicate bones framed by a cloud of straight blonde hair that just brushed the edges of his shoulders. A thickly studded leather slave collar covered his Adam's apple, and as he pranced around in his shiny combat boots, belting out one indecent song after another, his wicked smile sparkled in his eyes. I blushed when he bent over from the waist, knees locked straight and feet spread wider than his shoulders, and wiggled his ass up against the bassist. The other guy actually moved his guitar to one side so Kris could rub against his crotch. It was obscene and sexy, and I was in lust with Kris from the moment he stood up, vigorously rubbed his crotch, then looked at the audience in mock surprise as the front of his sweaty white jockeys swelled. Damn, that man is an exhibitionist!

Ed, one of the guys in our crowd, sputtered every time he looked at Kris. Now Ed is straight, straight, straight. But he kept shaking his head and saying, "I'm so glad I'm married! If that guy were in a dress, I'd chase his ass until I caught it! Damn, he's beautiful!" Then he'd shake his head and take another long swig of beer.

Cynthia, his wife and my former roommate, just cuffed him on the shoulder and laughed. It takes a lot to faze Cyn. After three beers she took Ed's car keys, then we left the rest of our friends and went upstairs to sit down and watch the show. Cyn was thoroughly enjoying Ed's dilemma. She had her hand in his lap under the table but I could see her arm moving, and she had a really evil grin on her face. Every once in a while, Ed would close his eyes and groan, and Cyn would lean over and tongue his ear while she poured another drink down his throat. She kept telling him he was going to have sweet dreams that night. I figured he probably would if she kept that up.

They were so engrossed with each other I knew they wouldn't miss me if I found some action on my own, so I pretty much kept my eyes glued to the stage, and to Kris, for the rest of the set. Just watching him gave me a major case of the hots, which is frustrating as all hell when you know the guy is gay.

I almost didn't recognize him when I bumped into him, literally, a couple of hours later. The headlining band was setting up and I didn't see Kris come up in back of me to lean against the balcony rail. I heard Ed groan, and when I looked at my buddy, his eyes were somewhere over my shoulder. Cyn just laughed, put her hand over his eyes and pulled him down against her breasts.

"Drunk," she grinned up at the space in back of me.

I heard this really clear tenor laugh behind me. I turned around, bumping into a very solid thigh, and there was Kris. He looked different with clothes on. Same T-shirt, but pink spandex pants and a wide black leather belt. He'd shed most of the makeup, but damn, he was still gorgeous. It took me a second to get over my initial shock at seeing him up close. Then I managed to clear my throat and compliment him on his band's set.

"Cute song about the ice cube blow jobs," I smiled.

"You heard us?" he asked excitedly. Kris is one of those people whose whole face comes alive when he talks. "There weren't that many people here when we played. I was afraid that'd affect the CD sales, but they're really moving."

Cyn nodded him towards the chair where Ed's feet were resting; Ed was passed out, so Kris carefully pushed his feet onto the floor and sat down. The headlining act was starting, so Kris pulled his chair right up next to me and leaned over so we could talk, or at least try to, between songs. It was too loud to really hear, though. When it became obvious he was reading my lips, I raised my eyebrows at him and he just gave me this big grin and pulled back the edge of his hair. He'd put in earplugs. I grinned back and discreetly lifted my hair so he could see I had, too. I think Cyn must have thought we were nuts with how hard we started laughing. It was right then that one of his band's publicity guys snapped a picture of us. It was supposed to have been a pic of Kris enjoying the rest of the show, but the photo didn't fit quite with the band's image, so the guy gave Kris the picture. It's the first one in our album. Kris called it "Fate."

After the show, he asked me out for coffee. We helped Cyn drag Ed to the car and waved them off. Then we walked down a couple of blocks to a little diner and split a piece of pecan pie. Three cups of coffee later, Kris shocked the hell out of me. He was telling me about how the band had started when he stopped in mid-sentence. He leaned over and he kissed me, full on the lips. All I could do was stare at him, stunned.

Kris is straight.

I suppose I should qualify that a bit. Kris is at least as straight as I am. Neither one of us could claim to be a Kinsey 0.

We're both young and horny and we work in entertainment. But our same-sex flings had usually been one-nighters. Anyway, we spent the weekend together, getting to know each other. Yes, biblically as much as anything else. Like I said, we were young and horny, and there's a whole lot of chemistry between us.

On Monday he flew back to D.C., and we started a long-distance romance. His band toured up and down the East Coast, and I landed a series of walk-ons as well as a few commercials, enough to pay the bills. Especially my phone bills, which by Fall were getting pretty impressive, even at night rates.

The band came back out a couple of times over the next eight months. By then, Kris and I were getting serious. That April we discovered that neither one of us had been sleeping with anyone else since we'd met. It's quite a shock to find out you've fallen in love with someone without even realizing it. That night he asked me to marry him. How old-fashioned, huh? And I said yes.

That summer the band moved out to L.A., and in August, a year after we met, Kris and I got married. Ed and Cyn stood up for us.

I have to admit, I'd never realized how much I'd like being married. We're both vegetarians and we can both cook, which probably kept us from starving that first year. But I really think I could have lived on the sex alone. We'd both tested negative, so I went on the pill, and we went crazy with a general frenzy of uninhibited fucking. We discovered we both loved missionary, and we spent hours with his hair and sweat falling down onto my face as he glided into me. There were times we went at it until we were so sore that the only thing that could soothe us was the thick, slippery cream of our orgasms.

We're also supportive of each other's careers. Having two performers in the same family can be a real downfall for a lot of couples. We stuck it out, and during our second year we both started working more regularly, which helped a lot financially. But we also started spending less time in bed together, and more time sleeping when we were there. The sex was still good — comforting and fulfilling, and to this day, just thinking of Kris lying in bed with a hard-on is enough to make me wet. But some of the excitement was gone, along with the frequency, and every once in a while I missed the frantic edge we used to have.

I hadn't realized that Kris was missing it too. It took us a while to figure out that communication is something you have to work at in a marriage. But I remember to the minute when we started talking about our sex life. It was just after our second anniversary, the day Kris called up out of the blue to ask me to lunch. I'd taken a temp job as an administrative assistant at a recording studio so we'd have some extra money for vacation, and he'd been working down the street that morning. At noon, the receptionist called to say Kris was waiting for me in the lobby, and I walked up front to meet him.

I'd gone all the way into the room before I realized the person standing in front of me was my husband. Then, it was a good thing I was too stunned to move, because otherwise I probably would have fallen over from the shock. If I hadn't seen him with scarves tied around his neck so many times before on stage, I'd never have recognized him. Or should I say "her." Kris was wearing a demure Laura Ashley floral print sundress, matching espadrilles, and a stylishly floppy straw hat with a large pink ribbon that complemented the scarf tied loosely around his neck. His, or rather her, hair was impeccably styled, a froth of carefree waves through which she brushed her carefully manicured nails. In short, she was beautiful. And as she winked seductively, each and every one of those lechers I was working with gave her an appreciative once-over as they walked out the door to lunch.

Before I could collect myself enough to say anything, Kris swooped over and embraced me like a long-lost friend, carefully bussing my cheek so as not to mess up her makeup as she whispered in my ear, "Your girlfriend has the hots for you, babe. Play your part. I've got us a hotel room a couple of blocks away."

Linking her arm in mine, Kris turned us towards the door. "Thanks, Jenna honey. You're such a doll."

"Glad to help, Krissie." As usual, the vacuous young lady gracing the receptionist's desk giggled as she spoke. "I think it's so neat when roommates stay in touch. Imagine, after three whole years, you only have one day in town."

Krissie hugged her breast to my arm. "You sure you don't mind covering for Melissa for a couple of hours? We have so much to catch up on."

"Oh, no problem," Jenna replied. "Everybody will be tied up at that finance meeting the rest of the afternoon anyway. Just have her back by 4:00 and they'll never know she was missing."

Jenna twittered, then blushed with pleasure as Krissie handed her a disposable "tourist" camera to take a couple of quick pictures of the two "roommates" together.

As we walked out into the sunlight, Krissie didn't give me much chance to talk. She linked her arm in mine, pressed her bosom against me, and kept up a running, steamy commentary about how nice it was to be back in L.A. where "grrrls" didn't have to worry about having their afternoons interrupted. Most of what she was saying was lost in the whir of the noon traffic, so I just let her lead me down the sidewalk, the light scent of her perfume tickling my nose. Ten minutes later, she swept me into a reasonably nice hotel room where there was a bucket of Chardonnay chilling on the nightstand, the covers were turned back on a queen-sized bed, and the sun streamed in through the gauze privacy curtains of a fifth-story picture window.

I'd gotten over my initial shock, so I turned to my erstwhile roommate and said, "To what do I owe the honor of your visit, Krissie?"

Kris came up to me and gently drew the tip of his finger over my cheek and down the side of my face. "We're getting too complacent, Liss," he said quietly. His fingers were soft and silky as he stroked further along the edge of my neck, making me shiver. "We're too good for that." The finger dropped lower, tracing the outline of my breast, then rubbing slow circles over the nipple. "I want to see the sparkle back in your eyes when I touch you." I could feel my skin reach for him and he smiled as the tip hardened under his touch.

"Now I'm your girlfriend, Krissie, your former roommate who's back in town just for one day, and I want a slow afternoon of the kind of girl-to-girl sex you used to have." As Krissie spoke, she started softly milking my breasts with her enamel-tipped fingers. "I want to get lipstick on your nipples and lick your clit, maybe even make you come all over my face the way you do when I press your G-spot just right with a nice, thick dildo. I brought a couple with me, you know.

"When I'm done I'm going to give you my pussy to play with, Liss. Maybe if I'm really lucky, you'll suck my girly clit. You've never seemed to mind that it's bigger than most grrrls'." She sucked softly on my lower lip as I finally smiled. "What do you say, love?"

I could feel Krissie's "clit" pressing against my leg, and all of a sudden, even though I knew it was Kris, I mean I really knew that, the whole time we were there, suddenly he was Krissie. I was kissing another woman in a way I hadn't for a long, long time, and I wanted her. I mean, my pussy was sopping wet and I wanted grrrl sex like you wouldn't believe.

"Krissie," I moaned, just her name, and I melted into her arms. Then we were kissing, the soft, wet, tasting kisses that usually only two women can share. I took her hat off and buried my face in her neck so that her perfume made even her sweat seem feminine. Salty and sexy and so very, very sweet.

Every giggle was part of the foreplay. Krissie stripped me naked, then stood me in front of the mirror so I could watch her playing with my body. She left pink circles of lipstick around my areolas when she suckled me, her soft hands playing my pussy with her carefully manicured fingertips.

When I tried to touch her in return, she shook her head and touched her sticky fingers to my lips. "This first one's for you, sweetheart," she murmured, shivering slightly as I licked. "Just let me make you feel good."

So I did. I lay down on the bed with my legs spread and Krissie got between them. The soft cotton of her dress brushed against my naked thigh as she nuzzled my breasts, licking and sucking and teasing. When my skin was so sensitized I could hardly stand it anymore, she kissed her way down my belly. Then she settled herself between my legs, took my hips in her hands and lifted me to her lips. It was Kris' strength, yet now somehow feminine as she slowly kissed my labia like she was making love to my mouth. First the outer lips, then the inner ones. And when she reached my clit, she played it like it was my tongue. With infinite patience, she stroked and sucked and nibbled like we were kissing. My whole body relaxed, and slowly, tenderly, Krissie's wonderful, loving mouth drew a climax from deep in the pit of my belly. She laughed, her tongue working constantly as I thrashed beneath her, screaming out my pleasure. When I finally collapsed onto the bed, she lapped the cream of my orgasm off me with her suddenly sandpapery tongue.

When I recovered enough to move, Krissie finally let me undress her. I drew away each piece of her clothing slowly, revealing my lover's body bit by bit. Except for a small triangle above her crotch, she'd shaved her whole body. Everywhere, her skin smelled and tasted of silky, soft peaches.

Krissie insisted I leave her underwear on, though she finally acquiesced to my taking her bra off when I told her how much I wanted to suck on her nipple rings. I reassured her that several of my female lovers had been small-breasted, so she didn't need to be self-conscious. Then I took her nipples, first one, then the other, into my mouth and worked them until she was moaning.

Though she insisted on keeping her panties on, and her garter belt and stockings, I untied the ribbons that held the slit crotch of her panties closed, then worked my lips over her thoroughly engorged and extremely large clit. It didn't take long at all for Krissie to come. She shook in my arms as I sucked her with the same tender intensity she'd given to me.

When she'd recovered, Krissie got out a couple of curved dildos, and we lay side-by-side and brought each other to "G-spot" orgasms that left the sheets soaked. Sated, we curled up and napped, and when I awoke, Krissie was finger-fucking me, not quite fisting me, but almost. I was so hungry for her that I came all over her hand. Again.

At home that night, we started talking, and well, we learned to talk about sex. Not just idle talk, but real communication. We talked about our fantasies, both the things we wanted to do and the things that were best left in our heads. And we've kept on talking — and doing — ever since. We're performers, and, I admit, we're sort of exhibitionists. And we like variety. So we've acted out a lot of our fantasies. We've been girlfriends and boyfriends. We've traded genders. We've done bondage and S/M in exotic scenarios. But it's always been just the two of us. When we're brutally honest with each other, we need and want the security of monogamy. We want to be all the people the other one needs sexually. Luckily, we're good enough thespians that we've been able to pull it off. So far, at least.

I'd be lying if I said it was all easy. Mostly it has been; but the most difficult time for us was pretty much the year we both turned 30. Some people call it the seven-year-itch. All I know is that Kris suddenly got so hungry for man-sex that for the first time, we were afraid for our relationship.

On the night he came home shaken because he'd almost picked up some guy after a show, I figured I only had one card left to play. Now I'm not a man and I've never wanted to be, although I've played one — successfully — on stage. Usually it's Kris who does the drag. But all I could think of was the day Krissie came to visit me at work. She'd been there for me. So I cut my hair really short, changed my clothes, and threw myself into a new character like I was playing for my life.

That's how we ended up in a gay leather bar near Modesto late one night about a week later, me with a slave collar on and Kris in a particularly nasty mood. We'd ridden into town on Ed's Harley, and after a quick stop to get a hotel room, we headed out for the evening. You can see the look on Kris' face in the picture the woman at the front desk took of us as we left on the bike. He was feeling mean and toppish and he was treating me the way he would some trick he'd picked up in an alley.

We were both wearing leather pants and jackets and our old but well-shined black boots, the ones we wear when we're doing heavy S/M. This time, though, beneath the jacket Kris was bare-chested except for a leather and nickel harness that gleamed like his nipple rings, and he had a diamond stud in his left ear. His hair was clubbed back with a leather bootlace and he hadn't been near a razor for three days, so his face seemed dirty as well as unshaven. Like I said, Kris looked mean, and I looked pissed. It's an unusual picture for us. Normally, we're smiling. But not that time. I'd become my husband's untrained little slave boy and was wearing the other earring in my right ear, just above where the leash clamped to the D-ring in my collar.

It was late when we got to the bar. Most everybody else there was at least half-drunk. As part of our characters, we looked pretty wasted too, although Kris had only been sipping at his bourbon and I'd just spilled some beer on my T-shirt to get the smell. I didn't want to get the shirt too wet, because although I'd bound my breasts, they'd still be noticeable if my nipples got too hard.

We were at a table in a dark corner, and I was starting to get more than a little annoyed at how often Kris was yanking on my leash. The room was crowded, and except for the occasional tug, he was ignoring me, trading crude comments with a group of guys around the table. I was getting even more uncomfortable from the rather sizeable butt plug he'd shoved up my ass when we first got to the hotel. He'd said he wanted his boy ready for him, and by midnight the "boy" was real convinced that the plug had stretched his anal muscles wide enough for a truck to drive through. The leather pants held the plug in tightly, and I was horny from squirming against it. Especially after the vibration of the bike ride.

Suddenly, Kris reached up and grabbed a handful of my hair, at least as much as he could of it, and shoved my face down hard against the wet, beer-covered table.

"What the fuck?!" I snapped, barely remembering to keep my voice low.

He yanked viciously on my hair. It didn't really hurt, it was more for show, but it startled me and I yelped. He'd never treated me like that before. He leaned over and growled in my ear, "You need some training, boy. I want your ass, and I want it now!"

I couldn't believe what I was hearing. I felt his hand on my hip, then the slow slide of the zipper moving down the back of my leather pants. I panicked. Shit, we were in a gay leather bar way to hell and gone in the middle of nowhere, and those guys would have killed us if they'd found out I was a chick. I was struggling against Kris when suddenly, I felt a strange pair of hands grab my forearms and slam me down against the table.

"Stop fightin', boy!" the voice snapped. "Your daddy wants your ass, he gets it!"

"Bullshit!" I yelled back, my voice higher than it should have been, but no one seemed to notice.

I jumped and gasped as Kris slapped me hard across the ass. Then the cool air kissed my crack and asshole as the zipper came down the rest of the way, and, mortified, I froze as Kris yanked the butt plug out of my ass. I mean, right there in front of all those people he pulled that plug out and dumped it in his drink! The other guy was laughing so hard the table was shaking, and his friends crowded around to make sure no one would disturb us.

Then I heard the quick tear of a condom wrapper, and the next thing I knew, Kris was bending over me, his weight pressing me hard into the edge of the table, and his thick, hot cock slid up my ass. Right there in the bar, with a good dozen people watching us, he was fucking me over a dirty, wet table.

Now Kris knows how much I like having sex in public, when we act like we're alone but we really know people are watching us. But this was way beyond anything I'd bargained for. Fortunately, my ass was so loose that he slid right in. The others may have thought it was a rough fuck, but he used that butt plug specifically because it was just the right size to get me ready for his cock. And he'd stuffed half a tube of lube up me when he'd put the plug in, so I was slick inside. I still struggled, though. The other guy was holding me down and I was just mad enough that it felt good to fight, especially since by then I was pretty sure the other guy was strong enough to keep me from getting away.

It was odd. I'd never had any rape fantasies. I sure as hell never wanted to be raped in reality. But suddenly, being held helpless while Kris pounded into me brought out a wildness I'd never felt before. I was scared to death those guys would discover I was a chick, and yet all I could think about was how hot it was for Kris to be fucking me in front of all those people. I climaxed from the anal stimulation alone. It was rough and fast, and when Kris was done he just pulled out, stuffed the icy plug back up my ass, and zipped my pants closed again.

I was still gasping when the other guy let go of me and Kris dragged my head up off the table, kissing me so hard his teeth drew blood. I could taste the copper on my lips as he said, "Your ass is mine again, boy, as soon as we get back to the hotel. Now move it!"

The people standing around were still laughing as Kris tossed a twenty on the table for a round of beer. Then he dragged me out the door, threw me on the bike, and took me back to the our room.

It was the most violent night we've ever spent together, and it turned me on incredibly: I knew, at a very fundamental level, that all I had to do was say "stop" and he would.

But I didn't say it. I stayed in character. I argued with him and mouthed off, telling him I'd never submit to him. I wasn't the least bit surprised when he stuffed my shirt in my mouth, threw me over the end of the bed, and whipped my bare ass with his belt until I was screaming. I knew I'd have bruises. It hurt like hell, and he was swinging the belt full out, with the buckle wrapped around his fist and the strap burning into my ass cheeks. But I wouldn't say "stop." I'd never played the part of an untrained biker boy before, of Kris' boy, and I wanted to do it. When he fucked me again, this time without a rubber, he put me on all fours doggy style so he was banging against my sore ass with each stroke, then he reached around and pulled on my clit, "jacking off my little slave boy cock," he called it. And he waited to come until he felt my orgasm shudder through my body.

I cried myself to sleep on his shoulder. My ass hurt, but that wasn't why I was crying. It was just so intense. So raw and violent. We'd brought out parts of ourselves we'd never let each other see before. When I brushed my hand across Kris' cheek, I felt tears running down into his hair. We clung to each other with the strength of those who have fought a war together and won, but now had to live with the knowledge of the demons that lived inside us.

The next morning, our actual anniversary, I fucked Kris with a strap-on. I woke up to find him spooned in front of me, pressing his ass back against me in his sleep. I cuddled against him for a while, listening to the soft purr of his snoring. Then I carefully disentangled myself, slipped out of bed, and got out the harness. I hadn't told him I'd brought it. I just put it on, along with my leather jacket and a motorcycle cap, and splashed on some of the male cologne I'd been wearing on the trip. Then I climbed back into bed, pulled Kris' top leg up towards his chest, and started playing with his asshole.

It didn't take long before he was moaning in his sleep. He was relaxed and loose as I stretched him, stuffing lube up his butt. He didn't wake up until the head of the dildo slipped into him, but then he woke up fast.

"What the fuck?" he grumbled, trying to lower his leg. He stopped only when he felt my fingernails digging into his thigh.

"I'm fucking you, boy," I said, low and mean. I slid my hand over his hip, slapping him sharply when he jumped as I slid further into him. "You're my little pussy boy this morning."

"Dammit, Lissa! How big is that thing? It's splitting me in two!" Kris can be grumpy in the morning, and he was tense as a bowstring. But my butt was still sore from the night before, so even though I stopped moving, I was in no mood to back out.

"Shut up and hold still," I growled. It was hard keeping my voice that low, but I felt I needed to stay in character. "If you fight, it's going to hurt. And I don't want to hurt you. But I am going to fuck you. I'm going to fuck your tight little ass until you shoot all over the bed. So relax, boy." On the word "relax," I pushed in a tiny bit further, hearing him hiss.

Finally, I felt his hips give and he moaned into the pillow. Then his shoulders twitched as his whole body untightened and he shook his head, laughing softly, "Whatever you say, sir. But may I please roll over and stick my ass in the air so I'm at the right angle to take your hard, hot cock? Sir?"

"Okay, boy," I said gruffly, trying to keep from smiling as I slapped his ass again. I let go of his leg, but I didn't pull out. I made him roll over with me in him, and I didn't back up when he lifted his pelvis to put a pillow underneath, just listened to him grunt as the fake dick slid in a little bit further. To tell you the truth, I didn't want him to see how big that latex cock was. If he'd had any idea what I was fucking him with, he would have pitched a fit.

When he was in position, I made him rest his head on his folded arms. "You can drop down and rub your cock against the pillow if you want, but you can't touch it," I said. Then I straddled his legs and pressed a little bit further into him.

I pressed further, and further, leaning onto his back as I moved forward. Sometimes I'd pull back and fuck in and out a few times, to keep him really loose. And on each stroke I'd go in a little bit further. But I still hadn't bottomed out.

That dildo was huge. It was ten inches long and two inches around, and I slid it damn near all the way up his ass.

"Jeez, Lissa. I can feel that thing almost to my throat," he whispered, grinding his hips against me. Then he got real still, and I suddenly realized he was looking in the mirror by the side of the bed.

"You want to watch your ass getting fucked, boy?" I asked quietly, knowing he was going to watch one way or the other. So I slowly and deliberately started backing out of him, not all the way, just until only the head was in him. I could see his eyes getting wider as he watched the monster pull out, then his whole body stiffened as I slowly started pressing back in again.

"Jesus, Lissa! That's too big! Really, I mean it! Stop!" He gasped and tightened hard beneath me.

I froze. He'd said stop and I did, in mid-stroke. But I didn't pull out. Instead, I rested my weight fully onto my legs and massaged his shoulders. "Relax, boy," I said, calmly, still staying in character and hoping he'd be able to drop back into the scene. "It's not too big. You've already had it in you.

"Come on, boy. You want to be fucked. You need to be fucked." I traced my fingers up his spine and smiled as I felt him shudder. "Relax and let me give you what you need. You know I'll stop if you really can't take it."

For the longest time he just lay there, looking at the dildo in the mirror. Tension gradually drained out of his shoulders. I dragged my hand down his back and caressed his lower butt cheeks, where his thighs met his lower curves.

"Give me your ass, boy. You know how much I want it. And I'll make you feel real good." I carefully massaged the tautly stretched skin surrounding the dildo, gently relaxing and stretching him. "Tell me you want it, boy. Tell me so I can fuck you. So I can press your hot come right up out of your ass."

A very long minute later, Kris relaxed underneath me. Then he looked back over his shoulder and laughed shakily. "Okay, sir. But will you kiss me, so I'm not so afraid?"

"Of course I will, boy." I bent over, opening my mouth, and gave him my tongue to suck on. Then I slowly started pressing into him again. He moaned softly as I slid further down. When my weight was resting full on him and I was deep in his ass, he whispered, "Please, sir. Please fuck your boy." I gave him one more deep, passionate kiss, then I leaned back up, grabbed his hips, and started fucking him hard — long, sure, deliberate strokes. He whimpered and twitched beneath me. Then, on one stroke, I moved just a bit differently, pushing down towards the front of his belly just a bit more, and suddenly he arched up and gasped like he couldn't get enough air into his lungs. I froze.

"That hurt, boy?" I asked, holding myself motionless.

"No, sir!" He gasped. "Please, sir. Please," His whole body was shuddering like he was suddenly very cold or scared. Then with a long, low moan, he dropped his head back on his arms and whispered. "Please, sir. Do it again."

Yeah, I grinned. I arched into him, a long, slow glide that made him moan with pleasure, then I pulled back. And when I slid in again, Kris let out a high, keening cry and his whole body shook as I pressed down hard into him. I didn't think he'd ever stop coming as that hard latex dick pressed comeloads of his semen right straight out of his prostate. The vibration of his body was almost enough to make me come. And still he kept shuddering.

When his body collapsed onto his arms, I pulled out. I took off the harness, lay down on the bed and ordered him onto all fours over me. His arms and legs were still shivering as I took his soft, sticky cock in my mouth and let it rest there, tonguing it gently while I slid my fingers in and out of his loose, well-fucked asshole. Then I told him to suck my hard man cock until I came.

"Yes, sir," he whispered, groaning against my hands as he took my comparatively very tiny cock into his mouth. But he sucked and played it for all he was worth, like a good little slave boy. It took me about two heartbeats to come all over his face, and without being told, he dutifully licked the cream from my pussy. When he finally turned around and collapsed into my arms, we both started laughing. We laughed until tears streamed down our faces.

"Damn, Lissa." he choked, shaking his head as he pulled the dildo from the harness and looked at it. "What the hell ever made you think you could get that up my ass?"

I shrugged. "You said you needed to be man-fucked, and this was as 'manly' as I could get!"

Then we were both laughing again. Before we left the hotel, we had the manager take another picture of us on the bike. The album captions say, "Before, and After." And we didn't make a journal entry to go with that trip. We're the only ones who need to know the details. Beyond that, the looks on our faces say it all.

This last picture, "Ten Years," is the one the concierge took of us as we were leaving for the opera in San Francisco last weekend. We decided to reverse genders that night, so Kris wore a glittering strapless gold lamé ball gown with a *faux* fur stole and the most realistic looking costume pearls I've ever seen. He was stunning. I wore a black tux and, as the picture shows, I've finally mastered makeup to show just a hint of a five o'clock shadow.

The performance was wonderful. We didn't even try to talk, just sat there quietly holding hands while the music flowed over us. When we got back to the room, I fucked him with the strap-on while I fingered his enormous clit until he shot all over the bed. And he gave my little clitty cock the most wonderful blow job, licking and sucking in all the right places while he wiggled a finger up my ass. I came like gang-busters.

But this morning, this precise morning, it's been exactly one decade since we first promised ourselves to each other. So we celebrated like any other long-time married couple. We had breakfast at home in our own bed. We took a long, slow sexy shower together. And then Kris climbed on top of me, plain old missionary position, his biceps flexing over me as he took his weight on his arms while he glided in and out, in and out, with all the timing we've learned so well over the years. When I couldn't hold back any more, when I cried out as my orgasm washed over me, I felt the deep, swelling thrust as Kris surged into me, his semen bathing my cervix — so deeply, profoundly satisfying. And so hot my body curled around him.

As I dozed off, I could feel myself smiling against his lips. This time, we didn't take a picture. But over the years I've learned to know Kris pretty well: I have no doubt I'll see a flash in my sleep some time before tomorrow morning.

# Deborah Bishop

## The Portrait

Lily remembered when she'd first wanted Adam to paint her. Not her portrait, as her parents had commissioned him to do, but *her*. Her body.

Her desire for him had evolved in layers along with her image in oils. For three weeks she'd watched him seduce the canvas with color — a stroke of purple, a touch of white, a vigorous rub of crimson — and she'd nearly gone out of her mind with the sensuality of his movements. She had witnessed this mostly from her seat across from him. But once, in the early stages of that first portrait, he'd allowed her to peek around his wide shoulders to watch him work. She'd wanted to seduce him then.

All she could think of was how his artistic brilliance simply didn't jibe with his Dallas Cowboy physique and steelworker's hands: great, clumsy-looking paws in raging conflict with the beauty they created. Now, twenty years later, she still felt that same pulsing awe — an intoxicating sense of surrealism — as she watched him work.

Lily plucked a grape from an antique table and sucked it, contemplating the back of the canvas. She savored a delicious moment of uncertainty. At forty, she was not as firm as she'd been the first time Adam had painted her portrait, but she didn't mind. What she lacked in youth, she made up for in other, more important ways. She was at the peak of womanhood. Strong, sensual, sage. She would do today what she had been too young and shy to do at twenty.

She watched Adam step back from the portrait and felt desire hum through her. Maturity served him well. He was more appealing than ever with flecks of silver at his temples and a sturdiness that magnified his masculinity.

"When will you be finished?" she asked, shrugging her coral straps low over her shoulders. Her nipples hardened against the satin lining of her dress, a prim Elizabeth Taylor remake straight out of *Giant*.

"Today." Adam's sultry eyes, intimate by now with every visible part of her, glanced at the outline of her swollen nipples as if he hadn't noticed. Always reserved. His unswerving gentility made her want him even more.

"So soon?"

"Hmmm, I have a new project to start tomorrow." Adam's voice rumbled in his chest, rich as crude oil.

The sound reminded Lily of stories she'd heard of petroleum thundering through her grandfather's early oil wells and exploding in massive orgasms of instant prosperity. But Adam didn't rumble to an orgasm. Instead, he frowned and pursed his lips. They looked sweeter than grapes.

"But don't you have to varnish it first?"

Adam smiled. "Yes, but that won't be for another six months."

"Right," Lily said, disappointed. She didn't want their sessions to end.

In six months, she'd be back in school working on the MBA she'd abandoned right after Adam had painted her first portrait. She eyed the hard lines of his body and found it hard to contain her longing.

"I need a break," she said with a feline stretch, and flexed her limbs with calculated grace. As she rose from the teal Victorian sofa, her chiffon wrap whispered to the floor behind her in a reflection of her thoughts.

Strip me, Adam. Fuck me.

Adam paused as if to listen and watched the ethereal fabric trail behind her in a coral heap. He cast her another shrouded glance as she approached, and resumed his work. She moved behind him and closed her eyes, savoring the melange of smells: turpentine, linseed oil and, underlying it all, the unmistakable scent of male arousal.

"Do you mind if I look?"

"Not at all. It's finished."

After a final stroke of his brush, he wiped magenta pigment from the bristles and stepped out of her line of vision. His perception of her was shocking. He had captured more than her likeness. Much more. She found it unsettling, exciting. As before, he'd seen through her, painted past her mundane exterior, and turned her inside out. Only this portrait was even more telling than the first. He'd transformed her into a creature beyond redemption: flame blue eyes, skin the color of white heat, hair as black as crude. She was plumper now, but still beautiful.

Did she really look like that? All that sex in one face? And yet, it looked exactly as she felt. Fuck-happy. Unfortunately, the portrait ended at her shoulders. He had passed over her cleavage, her carefully packed breasts, as if too polite to acknowledge them even on canvas, and worked his usual magic of blending his subject into the background. She would have given a great deal to see how he would handle a nude.

Trailing her fingers along the easel in a butterfly caress, she said, "It's wonderful."

He exhaled, his breath warm on her shoulder, his voice rough with something. Lust, perhaps. His burnt sienna eyes sparkled with mischief. "It helps to have a good subject."

"Just a *good* subject?"

He smiled. "Beautiful, then."

She returned the smile, satisfied. "Do I really look that . . . lewd?"

"Is that how you see it?"

"Yes, from the neck up." In a bold movement, she turned on him, letting her breasts rub against the coarse fabric of his shirt. "What happened to my chest, Adam? I look like I have one continuous tit."

He gazed at her breasts, heat flashing in his eyes, then lifted a critical eye to his work.

"Paint my body," she said.

His eyes flickered over the canvas and she knew he was considering its limitations.

"Here," she said, licking her finger and running it between her breasts.

He shrugged. "You're the boss."

When he started to add a strategic stroke of magenta cleavage to the canvas, she caught his wrist. "No. Paint my *body*, not the canvas."

The corners of his mouth lifted in a slow grin. "Oh."

With a swish of fabric, Lily slipped the dress from her shoulders, freeing her heavy breasts, and cupped them provocatively in her hands. Adam's cock ballooned in his jeans. Christ, it was nice.

When she stroked him, he groaned and said, "Lily . . . I don't know if this is such a good idea. Someone might come in."

"Then tell me to stop." Trailing her hands over his belly, she ripped open the hole in his paint-stained T-shirt and sucked his nipple into a hard pebble. He closed his eyes and moaned. Encouraged, Lily rubbed her breasts against his bushy chest. Shards of heat shot from her nipples to her cunt. Surrender flickered in his eyes and he touched her breasts. Lily indulged him a moment before jiggling out of his reach. She wanted to take it slow, save the best for last.

He followed her and she rubbed the ridge beneath his jeans. He closed his eyes and sighed.

"Get your clean brushes," she said.

His eyes blinked open. "What?"

"I said, get your clean brushes. I hereby commission you to paint my body."

At that moment, Lily saw his reserve snap. He pulled her against him, kissing her hard and fierce, and fucking her with his tongue. She sucked it, pretending it was his cock, then pushed him away. Adam stepped back, eyes bright with lust, and removed fresh brushes from his desk. With trembling hands, he slipped them from their plastic cases. Thin ones, fat ones, soft and stiff. Red sable, ox hair and pig bristles. He tested each one against a finger, sable against callous. Lily sighed in anticipation.

She sidled back to the sofa where she wriggled out of her dress. Underneath, she wore only a black lace thong. Adam followed her like a man possessed and, when she bent over to step out of the thin strip of lace, he drew his largest brush over her buttocks and between her thighs. She kicked her clothes aside and spread her legs, arching her back to give him better access. She was like a cat in heat, lifting its rump and tail in invitation.

He teased her cunt, wet with arousal, then grabbed her hips and pressed his groin against her. His swollen crotch grazed her clit and she purred and paused to savor the rolling motion of his hips. Then she scooped up the gossamer shawl and turned away, drawing it around her.

When he reached for her, she massaged his bulge, damp with her juices, and gave a throaty laugh. "No, you don't. Not until you've fulfilled your commission."

"All right. But first I have to apply a bottom coat," he murmured, stroking her buttocks and lowering her to the sofa. He guided her onto her stomach and brushed her from head to toe with light feathery movements. Lily moaned, feeling as though she would explode before she could possess him. He skimmed her back, shoulders and legs with the bristles, concentrating on the sensitive skin behind her thighs and knees.

Adam eased her onto her back, eyes glued to the shifting mounds of her breasts, and ministered to the tender undersides of her arms. He chose a sable detail brush from his collection; featherlike bristles encircled her breasts just shy of her nipples and drifted down her belly and between her thighs, never quite touching her where she needed it most. Eyes closed, she felt him stretch over her and back again, and then felt something wet touch her skin. She opened her eyes to find him squeezing grape juice on her chest.

He dipped his brush in the liquid pooling between her breasts. "You have a beautiful mouth," he said, painting her lips. "Lush. Made for sucking . . . and being sucked."

With a reptilian thrust of her tongue, she captured the bristles. Adam kissed her, pulling on her lower lip. She opened her mouth to receive him and they playfully lapped at each other. Then he broke away, laving the juice between her breasts with his tongue, licking a trail of burning sensation from her belly to her groin. She moaned and opened her legs wider. He painted her there, then licked her furrow from vagina to clit.

"Adam," Lily whispered and sighed, resisting her approaching orgasm. She wanted to make it last. He lifted his head and replaced his tongue with a stiffer brush. Urgency built in her clitoris, inflamed by the masterly movements of his fingers.

Suddenly, it would no longer do. Suddenly, she needed to be touched by something warm and hot, flesh and blood. She tossed his brushes aside and pressed his pigment-stained hands to her breasts. Her nipples puckered beneath the rough skin of his palms. She lay back, ecstasy bubbling in her throat.

"Please," she whispered. "Touch me ... touch me every-where."

"But your commission ... " he said in a teasing reminder.

Snaking her hands over his buttocks, she pulled him to her and buried her face in his crotch, inhaling the smell of desire. "Fuck the commission," she mumbled against his zipper.

He laughed low and sexy.

She fastened her mouth on the hot ridge beneath his jeans, wetting the fabric with her tongue. He grew rock hard beneath her lips and teeth and, when he cupped her head and moved against her, Lily knew she wouldn't have long to wait.

He pulled away, eyes glazed with need, and pressed her down. "I'd rather fuck you than your commission. But I'm honor-bound to fulfill my assignment."

Lily unfurled on the sofa, feeling as luxuriant as a strip of ivory velvet, and opened her legs. "How about just *filling* your assignment," she murmured, "right up to your balls."

"You're almost too hot to handle," he said, pressing against her hand. "Almost."

"Prove it," she said.

With a new intensity in his eyes, he bent to suckle her breast. She moaned deep in her throat and angled the other one at him. Weaving her fingers through his dark hair, Lily drew him the rest of the way down and wrapped her legs around his hips, gyrating against his erection. When he pulled away, his fingers fumbling urgently with his zipper, she followed him up and brushed his hands aside. "Here, let me."

"Hurry," he said thickly.

A moment later, his erection sprang out of his jeans.

"Oh, baby," Lily moaned and slid to her knees.

She tongued the purple head with long lazy strokes and gen-erously lubricated him before attempting to take him in her mouth. He tasted clean and salty and sinful, musky and male. In spite of his girth, she devoured him with relative ease, pumping up and down his length as far as she could go. With concentrated effort, she relaxed her throat and consumed another inch.

"God, Lily!" Adam groaned and pressed her head down.

When he began to thrust, she pulled back and licked him clean. "Enough. I want to feel your hands on me." She rose and pressed them to her hips. "Touch me, Adam. Touch me all over."

Adam responded with unparalleled enthusiasm, touching her breasts and thighs and hips with calloused hands, sparking jets of heat in her cunt. His cock, bobbing hotly between them, was more temptation than she could stand.

"Fuck me now," she commanded and rubbed it between her thighs. It rustled against her curls.

"Do you need it, Lily?" Adam whispered against the corner of her mouth. "Say it. Tell me you need it."

"I need it, Adam," she whispered. "I need it now."

He groaned and drew her back down to the sofa. She straddled him and guided him into her. Her lips stretched taut around his girth, unsheathing her own clitoral erection. He entered her in degrees and she gasped at the sheer sweetness of it. He felt like smooth sunbaked stone.

At first, he held back, pushing her toward fulfillment in careful stages, gently priming her with deliberate thrusts. But her control didn't match his and she wanted more.

"Adam, stop torturing me," she said breathlessly, and rode him with staccato whimpers of encouragement.

In response, he gripped her thighs and pounded into her with hot precision, drilling away at her reserve until he coaxed her closer and closer to the surface. Lily felt the ascent of his balls beneath her pelvis as they crept up his shaft and were slowly absorbed into his groin.

It was too much. She exploded in a crashing orgasm, losing touch with everything except Adam and her throbbing cunt milking his cock. He bucked into her, flesh slapping flesh, with a vengeance she'd never forget. On his final thrust, he held her hips against him and bellowed out his pleasure.

"It's a gusher," Lily panted.

Adam chuckled weakly. Then, after a moment, he nudged her with his hips.

"Lily?"

She lifted her head, heavy with satisfaction. "Yes?"

"Do you really like the portrait?"

"Are you kidding? I love it. It's even better than the first one."

"Really?"

"Yeah." She lowered her head again.

"Lily?"

Grinning, she crossed her arms over his chest and rested her chin on them. "There's more?"

He paused a moment and nodded; words never came easy to Adam. Most of his communicating took place on canvas. He lifted a curl from her shoulder and hooked it around his finger. "I just wanted to say that . . . well . . . these past twenty years have been the best years of my life."

She gave him her most tender kiss. "Me, too. Happy anniversary, sweetheart."

# Michelle Stevens

## Lesbian Bed Death: A Case Study

Don't ask me how it happened. 'Cause if you ask me, I'll have to admit that I don't know. I'm a doctor; I'm supposed to know everything. Right? Four years of med school, three years of residency, all that time being taught, trained to notice the fine details. Listening closely to every breath, every heartbeat, studying every inch of skin for signs of malignancy. I'm a good doctor, attentive. I have a reputation for detecting the elusive symptoms that other doctors miss. And yet, somehow, I didn't see it coming.

I wish I could blame it on subtlety. I wish I could tell you that the clues were obtuse. But the truth is, *I* was the one who was obtuse. I paid little attention to what initially presented as a mild discomfort; left untreated, it quickly grew. General irritability gave way to severe mood swings, marked by anger and depression. By the time I finally realized there was a problem, it was too late, the effects too acute. Untreatable. Incurable. Terminal.

Diagnosis: Lesbian Bed Death.

Like any patient with a fatal disease, I found the prognosis difficult to accept. The first stage is denial. I had plenty of that! For months, Amy would ask me over and over again why we'd stopped having sex.

"What're you talking about?" I'd ask. "We *do so* have sex."

"No, not for a really long time," she said.

"What about that night, you know, in the car?"

"That was four months ago."

"Oh."

Denial was soon followed by anger. Stage Two. Amy wouldn't leave me alone. I knew she was right. And it pissed me off.

"We have to talk about it."

"I don't want to talk about it."

"Well, then, what do you expect will happen? I can't just stop having sex! It's been seven months now. What do you expect me to do? We have to start working on it."

"I don't want to work on it. I don't want to talk about it. Talking just makes me more self-conscious. God, Amy, why can't you just let it be?"

It wasn't until she moved out that I hit Stage Three: bargaining.

"Oh, honey, please please please don't leave me."

"Well, what do you expect me to do?" she asked in measured tones over the line. I was standing at a pay phone in the emergency room during a thirty-six-hour shift. My scrubs were still wet with blood.

"I don't know. Just move back in. Amy, please."

"What's the point?"

"What's the point? You *know* the point. I love you."

"But Kate, we haven't had sex in over nine months."

"Oh, sex, sex, sex! Is that all it's about for you?"

"Obviously not," she chuckled sarcastically, "or I would have left nine months ago."

Then my beeper started going off. Shit.

"Look, Ames, we've been together for *six years*. I mean, there must be some way we can work this out."

"You didn't seem too interested in working it out when you thought I'd stick around forever."

"C'mon, Ames, please."

"Well, what do you have in mind?" she asked, after a deafening pause.

"Marriage counseling, Dr. Ruth books, anything you want."

Then, after a long sigh, "Fine."

She moved back in, and we started counseling. The therapist wondered how we'd met.

"It was our senior year at NYU," I said. "It was the first week of Fall classes, and I had put off buying my books — a dangerous thing to do at a school with 20,000 students. Anyway, the school store was packed. I think every kid at the university was wrestling over the last three copies of *The Norton Anthology*. I was actually doing okay, had every book I needed except for one, the *Gray's Anatomy Coloring Book*. But just as I got to the shelf, I saw this beautiful black-haired girl grabbing the last one."

"She asked me if I was taking her physiology class," Amy added. "And that pissed me off. I asked her why she just *assumed* I was taking some stupid science class. Was it just because I'm Asian?"

"I told her no, it was because she was holding a stupid science book."

"Then I was embarassed," Ames said. "I told her I needed the book for my nude sculpting class."

"Then I told *her* she better hand it over, because being a doctor was clearly more important than being an artist."

"To which I replied that I would *never* give a book to someone so arrogant."

"Then she started walking away. So I followed her and asked her if she would share."

"Oh, I shared all right!"

"Yeah, her phone number," I laughed.

Therapy seemed to be going okay. We talked about that first year, when things were hot and heavy. Amy told her how we did it in the dorm room, in the cafeteria, in the library stacks. Then I told her about med school at Stanford. How we moved to Palo Alto and Amy had to work two crappy jobs to keep us solvent.

"Uh-huh," said the therapist. "And did that ruin the sex?"

"No," Amy said. "The sex got ruined when we moved to L.A., and Kate started her residency."

"I see," said the therapist. "Tell me more about that."

And so Amy did. She talked about my thirty-six hour shifts, her weekends all alone and how we get beeped out of bed. She said that even when I'm home, I'm not really *there*.

"And how do you feel about this, Kate?" the therapist asked.

"Uh, I don't know," I said. "It's kind of all true, but Amy knew this would happen when she decided to marry a doctor."

"Yeah," Amy snarled. "Well, I just didn't think it would be this bad. And besides, being a doctor is no reason not to want *sex*."

"It's not that I don't *want* to," I shouted. "There's just no fucking *time*!"

"You have to *make* time," Amy hissed, in her most self-righteous tone.

And so I did make time. Don't ask me how. But one night, despite the patients, the nurses, the attending physicians, I managed to sneak home early and turn the beeper off. Amy seemed pleased that at least I was trying. We took off our clothes, and we got into bed. We kissed for a while, and I played with her breasts. But when I tried to go inside her, she yelled.

"Ouch!" She wasn't even wet.

"Maybe I should do you," she said.

But I wasn't wet either. That's when we hit Stage Four: Depression.

The therapist said we should start slower. After all, it had been a long time. So we tried a few things — cherry-flavored love oil, dirty videos, Twister — but nothing worked. The magic was gone.

Which brings me to today — our last visit to the shrink, because we told her that we're finally ready to accept it. Stage Five. The relationship is dead. We both know it, and we're calling it quits.

It's good, I guess, how it worked out. The lease was up anyway. And now I can get through my residency without all this bullshit.

The thing is, if this is for the best, then why do I feel so lousy? I mean, when Ames and I broke up, I thought it would be a relief. No more of her constantly nagging me to call her, to come home early, to snuggle with her under the sheets. No more of her skin, or the way she smelled, or the way she would wake me up with coffee when she knew I had an early shift. Jesus Christ, I'm a fucking idiot!

The front door opens. It's Amy. She got some boxes from the Ralph's store down the street. She doesn't even look at me when she walks in. Just heads to the bedroom to pack. I want to talk to her now. I want to go in the bedroom and tell her I think it's a mistake.

But it's too late. And what would I say, anyway? That we ought to go to therapy? Been there. Done that. Besides, it's not just up to me. *She* was the one who started this in the first place. Remember? All that crap about sex, sex, sex.

I grab my own box and head to the bedroom. Amy or no Amy, I'm ready to pack. But when I get in there, she's nowhere to be seen. Not in the closet, not in the bathroom. Where the hell did she go?

Then I notice a little lump under the quilt. The one her mom gave us for our fifth anniversary.

"Ames?" I ask with a raised eyebrow.

"What?" A muffled grunt.

"What're you doing under there?"

"Just leave me alone," she screams.

I know that scream. It's a lot like the one I heard when I told her, five years ago, that I was moving to Palo Alto. Before I asked her to come along.

"Ames?" I venture over to the bed, put one hand on the quilt. "Are you crying?"

"No! Yes."

I pull down the covers to reveal my wife's tear-drenched head. "What's going on?"

"Nothing. Leave me alone."

"What're you crying for?"

"What do you think?"

"I think you look like a big, old, soppy head."

She laughs a little, and I grab for the tissues on the nightstand. They're not there, must already be packed. I crawl into the bed and offer her my shirt sleeve.

"You better not blow your nose on it," I say. She laughs a little again. "Now, what's going on?" She cries some more. I lie my head on her head.

After a while, it's quieter. "I just can't believe this is happening," she says. "I mean, I thought we'd always be together. That's what we said. What went wrong?"

"We stopped having sex."

"Is that all?" she laughs. "Is that why? Seems like a stupid reason after six years of marriage."

"You won't settle for a marriage without sex. Remember?

You need a relationship that makes you feel alive."

"But now that we're breaking up, I feel dead inside."

"I know, baby. I know."

I use my shirt sleeve to gently wipe her eyes. Man, I forgot how black they are. So black you can't even see the pupils. Amazing, the way they reflect the light. When we first got together, I used to stare at them all the time. And her dark skin. Such a contrast to my pale white. I pick up her hand, hold it next to mine.

"Hey, remember, Ames? When we were in college? Remember how we used to just stare at your arm next to mine?"

She smiles, giggles, "I'd never seen such a white white girl! Or such a perfectly straight nose!"

"And *I'd* never seen such big lips!"

"All the better to kiss you with," she teases me with her old line.

Those black eyes are staring right at me now. And before I even know what's happening, they've pulled me in. I'm kissing her. Very lightly. I want to feel the soft, soft mouth. My fingers, by rote, are already stroking the thick, warm hair.

I'm gone now. Lost to her. To it. To us. Everything I do now will be automatic. Ritualized. It will slip on comfortably, like a pair of well-worn jeans.

I will lie on top of her, so she can feel my weight. My hip will press against her stomach. My breasts will lightly brush her breasts. I will pick up her hands, lace my fingers in hers.

I will get a little more forceful then. I will pin her arms down with my own. Quickly, I will part her lips with my tongue because I know she likes to be taken by surprise. She will fight back for a moment — but only a moment. Then, I will feel her body relax. And I will know she has given in.

After that, it will all happen quickly. And slowly. Like there is no time. I will suck on her neck, her ears, the insides of her elbows. Gradually, my mouth will find its way to her chocolate nipples, warm and hard. I will suck on them hungrily, deliberately, as my hands gently cup her breasts. Then, as I suck harder, faster, as I flick my tongue back and forth in steady rhythm, her hips will press into my thigh.

I will let go of her arms then, letting my full weight fall onto her. My fingers will find their way to her face, her lips, then slide into her waiting mouth. My tongue will explore her stomach, her shoulders, the round contours of her breasts. As I bite into the dark, salty neck, she will surely moan. From the pleasure, from the pain, from the sheer intensity of feeling. She will try to pull away, turn her head, anything to stop, slow down, release the pressure. But I will not let go.

Instead, I will suck harder. I will sink my fingers deeper into her warm tongue. I will press my leg harder into her undulating crotch. Neck to mouths to fingers to hips, our bodies will move as one. Moving back and forth, tiny waves to bigger waves to violent waves, until that old, familiar sea finally washes over us.

Then, after a while, after the waves have stopped and the mouths have stopped and it is quiet, she will open her big, black eyes to look at me. She will part those big, soft lips to speak to me. And she will say . . .

"Katie?"

"Huh?!"

I'm startled back to our bed. The one waiting to be thrown in the moving truck. I look around at our nearly empty bedroom. Boxes stacked everywhere. Wow. I guess it's back to Stage Four: Depression.

"Whatcha thinkin'?" Amy asks. She's got a funny smile. One I've never seen before.

I shrug and start to climb out of the bed. I gotta get this over with. Fast.

But before I get very far, Amy's pulling on my shirt.

"Katie," she asks, that same funny smile on her face, "You wanna play doctor?" And then she does something she has *never* done before. *She* pushes *me* down on the bed and sits on top of me. Then, with the skill of a surgeon, she glides her hand through the waist of my jeans.

Prognosis: Very, very good.

# Marcy Sheiner

❦

# The Adventure of Marriage

When I was younger I was what I guess you'd call a swinger. I went to sex parties, did threesomes with men and women, and slept with just about anything that moved. I tried bondage, dominance and water sports. I loved it all. So I hope I won't seem too old-fashioned when I say that what really turns me on now is the ups and downs of my relationship with my husband.

I met Danny in that wild anything-goes world, and we ended up as a fuddy-duddy monogamous couple in the suburbs. I am so in love with this man that the mere sound of his voice gets my pussy wet. When we got married eight years ago, I wondered if sex with just one person would get boring, but I have been amazed to find that we keep discovering new ways to excite and satisfy each other. Everything that happens in our lives and in our relationship seems to get expressed in the bedroom. We have periods of distance, and then the return to intimacy makes our lovemaking feel brand new. We fight and make up and then we fuck our brains out. We go out with friends and something happens to turn us on, and we rush home to merge our flesh.

It hasn't always been this way. Danny, always a great fuck with a terrific body and awesome staying powers, didn't know how to treat a woman outside of bed. He didn't realize that what went on during the day affected what would go on at night. In other words, he was unromantic, self-centered, and insensitive. A perfect example of this behavior came just five months after our wedding, on my twenty-eighth birthday.

When I was a kid I had so many bad, even traumatic, birthdays that now I like to do it up big. For me, getting laid is an essential ingredient to the celebration, as is getting presents, especially from my "significant other."

Well, it turned out that Danny had to be out of town on business for a few days before the big event — but he'd be returning on the evening of my birthday. I wasn't thrilled that he'd be gone during the day, but was looking forward to him coming home in time to fuck me. I spent the afternoon with a few friends, and at 6:30 picked up Danny at the airport.

It had been three long days since I'd seen him, and I could hardly wait to fall into his arms. But when he got off the plane he gave me a distracted peck on the lips and said, "I've been looking for a present for you in airports all day."

"In airports?" I said, stung. "You were going to buy me a present in an airport?"

I couldn't believe he hadn't found something for me before he'd left — and worse, that he was telling me in such an offhand way. During the drive home I figured out that he realized he'd screwed up and felt guilty, but I didn't really give a shit about his feelings — I was too involved with my own. I hurt, and when I'm hurt, I seek revenge.

For the first time since I turned sixteen, I didn't get laid on my birthday — I told Danny that I didn't feel well. The next day I waited for him to give me a present, or a card, or surprise me with a fancy dinner. Nothing. Not the next day or the next or the next.

And so he didn't get to fuck me; every night for a week I coldly declined. Finally he asked me what was wrong. I told him I was pissed that he'd ignored my birthday. He apologized, but I told him it wasn't enough.

"You have to be punished." I slid out of bed and switched on the light. Slowly I lifted my white silk nightgown over my head. I cupped my size 40-D tits in my hands and held them up like an offering of ripe fruit.

"You like to suck on these babies?" I asked.

"You know I do," he moaned.

Gently I released my globes, then slid my hands down to my crotch. I parted my cunt lips. "And you also like to put your hard cock into this warm wet hole?"

I saw his cock rising underneath the blanket. "Damn right," he said happily, obviously thinking that this teasing was a prelude to lovemaking.

Slowly I turned around and stuck my butt out. Danny loves to bite and suck on my ass cheeks.

"And you *really* like to chew on these, don't you?"

He lunged forward, but I quickly evaded his grasp.

"Uh uh uh," I said, turning to face him and wiggling my finger as if he were a naughty little boy. "Only grownup men who know how to treat women get to touch."

I put my nightgown back on, switched off the light, climbed into bed, and turned my back on him. I sensed his hand moving around his dick to relieve himself.

"Don't you dare! If you have to do your dirty business go do it in the toilet."

I don't know if Danny jerked off or not, because I fell asleep. The next day he brought me a fancy birthday card.

"Big fucking deal," I said, tossing it into the garbage. That night I replayed my teasing routine, this time sticking my fingers into my cunt and holding them under his nose to give him an aromatic whiff of what he was missing.

The next day he brought me a box of candy; I fed it to the dog. That night when I stripped I stood above him with my legs apart so he could look up at my bush. He begged me to sit on his face, to let him touch my breasts. "Anything," he pleaded. I laughed and told him when he learned how to behave like a real man, he might be allowed access to my precious body.

"But I brought you a card and candy."

"Fuck you," I said, turning my back on him for the third night in a row.

The next day it was roses. "You're getting warm," I said, putting them in a vase. He came up behind me and pinched my ass. I slapped his hand. "I said warm, not hot."

He groaned as I fell to my knees, unzipped his fly, licked his dick until it was hard, then stood up and walked away, laughing.

The next day he brought me a pair of elaborate dangling earrings and a matching necklace. I took off all my clothes and put on the jewelry, feeling like an exotic princess, and danced for him, shimmying my body in front of his hungry eyes before climbing into bed and turning my back on his hard-on.

"Aw, Chrissy," he begged. "What more do I have to do? How much more money do I have to spend?"

"It's not about money, Danny. It's about you loving me enough to want to show me you do. It was my birthday. I wanted to know that you were really glad I was born." I started to cry. "You hurt me, Danny. You hurt me real bad."

He reached out and took me in his muscular arms. I snuggled closer and rubbed myself against his hairy body. It felt so good after such a long time apart. I cried as he hugged me and stroked my hair. When he turned me onto my back and tenderly kissed me all over — on my breasts, my belly, my thighs, I finally softened completely. When he came to my cunt he ran his tongue up and down the inner lips, pushing deep inside me, lapping up my juices like a grateful puppy. My hurt melted in a surge of arousal.

His tongue spoke eloquently in a language I understood bet-

ter than words. It told me that he cherished me, was sorry he'd
hurt me, and would never do it again. His hands reached up to
caress my tits, and he kneaded my nipples until they grew taut
between his fingers. He blew hot air on my pussy, then took
my clit into his mouth and sucked, making me cry out. I could
have come then, but he released my clit and moved on top of
me, sliding his long hard cock between my aching cunt lips. I
gripped him with all the fervor that came from having gone
without for so long, sucking his hard-on into me. We began
our long familiar ride, spinning to greater heights of ecstasy,
higher and higher, to the final explosive climax. Danny cried
out as his cock began shooting into me, pumping like a piston
and spurting hot come into my steaming cunt. I pressed closer
to him and the muscles deep within me spasmed, squeezing
every drop of fluid from his organ as I too came. Waves of satisfaction rippled through me, heightened by all the emotions
between us.

We've come a long way since then. Last year, on my thirty-
fifth birthday, Danny reserved a room in an elegant hotel
where we spent two days drinking champagne, ordering
shrimp cocktails from room service and, of course, fucking like
lions in heat. He's learned to bring me flowers occasionally, tell
me he loves me often, and make those little romantic gestures
that let me know I am loved. Of course we still have our dis-
agreements, and I can't say he's never hurt me since then—but
our relationship, and our sex, gets better and better. In fact, I'd
have to say that marriage is just about the most exciting sexual
adventure I've ever taken.

Lisa Prosimo

❦

# Blue Moon over Paradise

Sam was tired. He stretched, rotated his shoulders, tried to work the ache out of his muscles. Just a little more work, then he'd stop. A few more bushes, that's all; then he'd call it quits. It had been a long day and he suddenly realized he was hungry.

He gathered the last of the dried brush and carried it to his truck, looked around at the work he had done and was satisfied. Sam liked the hard work, it made him brown and fit. He would buy himself a beer, have a steak for dinner at The Shady Pine, turn in early and be up slightly before dawn, get started before the heat took over. He looked at the dry brush, the dead trees that needed to be cut down. About a week's worth of work still to be done, two weeks in all. Not bad. Good money and a guest house thrown in, too.

As Sam pulled away from the property to head for town, he looked through his rear view mirror at the stately old cabin that stood among the trees. It seemed strange to call that monster house a cabin, but that's the way the townspeople had always referred to the McEnery place. When he was a boy he used to come out with his friends just to stare at the thing. That was in the days when the place had a caretaker, Mr. Jenkins, who stood on the porch and yelled at them to "get the hell off this property before I call the sheriff!" Except for an agent who checked on the house occasionally, the place hadn't truly been cared for in years. Now the owner wanted to come back, and the agent had hired Sam to clean up the brush and remove dead tree branches.

Sam was back home in Paradise, doing a job his father had done, one he swore he would never do, and in a place he had run from years before. Funny how people change, he thought. This place, this work, made him content. San Francisco, the city Sam had called home for over fifteen years, had somehow lost its allure. Without knowing why, he no longer looked forward to getting up in the morning and going to his job teaching at the university. Only gradually did he come to understand that he had stopped caring about political science, political correctness, and politics. He found his mind drifting back to Paradise, wondered what was going on in the woods where he used to hunt and fish as a boy, began to pine for the life he once thought he hated. It seemed so easy to slide back into that life after his father died and he had to come back to put his affairs in order. His regret was that he had waited too long. One morning, his father just didn't wake up, dead of a heart attack. As Sam filled boxes and cleaned things up, he knew he wanted to come home.

Gloria was shocked. They'd lived together for six years, she reminded him. Their lives were good; they had excellent jobs. Why would he want to change anything? She asked him if it was something she'd done. No, he assured her. Nothing. She asked if it had anything to do with her receiving tenure while he had not. No. He just wanted to go home, he said. To do what? she demanded. Clean out brush, take dead branches off trees? She laughed at him, said he couldn't be serious. He said he was dead serious.

"I don't want the life I have, Gloria. I want to do something different. I want to work outdoors, feel the sun on my face. And I hate to be told there's no honor in that sort of work. I know there is."

He watched the tears spring to her eyes and run down her cheeks. She had hurt him by laughing at him; now he had hurt her. "I won't go with you, Sam," she whispered. "I can't."

He had come back to Paradise alone, and for a time he felt hollow in the place where she had been. But he filled his days with work, and more work, grateful that people still remembered his name and were willing to employ him. One morning he woke up to find the void had filled in much the same way a wound grows new tissue. He was scarred, but the organism still served.

Sam might have stayed in town at the house that now belonged to him, but he chose instead to return to the McEnery place, to the little guest bungalow that had come with the job. He liked being in the woods, and close to his work. All he had to do after waking up was wash his face, put on his clothes and get on with it.

When Sam pulled onto the property after his trip into town, he saw a Lincoln, long and black, in the driveway. The downstairs windows of the main house were open, the curtains drawn back to let in the evening breeze. It was just slightly past dusk. He peered up into the sky. There would be a moon tonight, almost full, cool and bright. He went into the house, dropped onto the bed and fell asleep almost immediately.

Sam awoke to the howling of a coyote, forgetting for a moment where he was.

Light from the moon spilled across his skin, parched in the hot night, and he tossed for only a minute before admitting he could not fall back to sleep. He sat up, reached for his jeans, thought better of it, and went out onto the porch. There was no one to see him naked and he wanted his body to catch what little air that moved. He sat in the shadows, hidden under the canopy, watching the moon hang upon nothing as he breathed in the clean sweet air he hoped would act on him like a sedative. If he didn't get enough rest, he would be worthless come morning.

The bright circle of the moon stood against the big house and Sam noticed the French doors on the upstairs balcony were open. The room was black, but the light picked up the sway of the soft gauzy curtains, tinting them a pale blue. A figure emerged from inside, female, wrapped inside a white sheet dyed moon blue, too. She leaned over the railing and sighed, the sound making its way across the expanse to the little bungalow where Sam sat in the darkness. From the way she moved, he knew she was young, between twenty and thirty, he would guess. She stepped away from the railing, threw her head back and shook out her hair. She let go of the sheet and it fell to the floor. Sam moved forward just a bit, to get a better look. The woman stretched her arms out to her sides as far as they would go and sighed again. The moon's radiance tinged her body and Sam could make out the curve of her hips, the contour of her breasts as she moved slowly, like a cat gauging its surroundings. She sat down in an old rocking chair, the only piece of furniture on the balcony; propelled herself forward, then dropped back. Forward and back in a steady, almost hypnotic cadence. She rocked for a few minutes, her head back, her arms hanging loosely over each rest, her feet planted on the floor. The moonlight caressed her shoulders, her breasts, her belly. Slowly, she shifted her body, leaned into the far side of the chair, brought her arms over her head and slipped one leg over the armrest. She shifted again, moved her pelvis closer to the edge, stretched her leg as far as it would go. Her body draped the chair like a shawl as she continued to rock back and forth.

Sam moved toward the light, just short of the end of the black that shrouded him. He monitored his breath, sure that if he had heard her sigh, she would hear his breathing. A concentrated warmth caressed his groin. The porch groaned under his weight and he moved back a bit, just in case she might follow the sound. But she wasn't paying attention to the night. She brought one hand down to her face, placed her fingers in her mouth then drew them out. She altered her position another fraction, moved her hand over her vulva and slipped her fingers inside.

Sam heard her soft, quiet, "Ah . . . ," almost a gurgle, as she rocked into her fingers. The old chair squeaked in protest, but she pushed it relentlessly as her fingers moved faster and faster. The woman's body jerked upward, seemed to devour her hand, and she moaned; moved her head from side to side. She kept the steady rhythm going, became one with the chair, and as she rode herself to climax, she let out a loud cry, a sister sound to the coyote.

Sam felt the woman's release, saw her body relax into the old chair. He envied her, wanted part of her climax. He could have reached down, brought himself off, but the thought repelled him. He didn't want to share the act without her knowledge or consent; that had never been his style. He'd been trapped into watching her, compelled to see it through, and now he was suddenly ashamed, felt like a Peeping Tom. Quietly he retreated out of the shadows and went back into the house.

They walked toward him, the woman and the old man. The man's body bent slightly, his legs bowed, his hands, one on the woman's arm, the other holding a cane, twisted like the bark of a tree. Sam left off bundling the dead branches, straightened up, pulled his handkerchief out of his pocket and wiped the sweat from his brow. "Morning," he said.

The woman's face was passive. In sunlight she was beautiful: long black hair, clear brown eyes, flawless skin, full lips; a little past thirty, he decided. He took her in with one glance, careful not to let his eyes linger too long. If he had seen her any place but here, would he have known her as the woman who presented her orgasm to the moon? The man smiled in Sam's direction, but couldn't see him, he realized. Sam extended his hand, placed his fingers lightly over the man's. The man grasped Sam's hand and shook it. "I'm Justin McEnery. Leah tells me you've been working non-stop all morning. Says the place is starting to shape up," he said, his voice gravelly, but warm. "Just wanted to let you know I appreciate it."

"You're quite welcome, Mr. McEnery. And thank you, sir, for the work. My name is Sam Warner."

"You a local boy?" asked McEnery.

"Yes, sir."

"I'm a local, too. Been a long time." He sniffed the air. "Place still smells the same, though."

"Yes, I guess it does," said Sam.

While Sam and McEnery talked, the woman, Leah, hung back quietly, not once looking at Sam directly. She kept her eyes on McEnery when he spoke, but looked into the sun or past the trees whenever it was Sam's turn, and yet he knew instinctively that she was acutely aware of him; was sure she felt, as he did, a certain type of current pass in the space between them. Could the old man feel it too, Sam wondered? Blind men can see things sighted men can't.

"Well, we'll leave you to your work," McEnery said. He turned away from Sam and he and Leah started to walk back to the house. "Oh," he said, stopping suddenly. "Come dine with us tonight. Our housekeeper won't be here until the end of the month, but Leah is a wonderful cook. Take pot luck, Sam."

The old man's invitation astonished Sam, and he was even more surprised when he heard himself accept the bid.

Digging in his closet like an awkward teen, Sam considered what to wear to dinner at the McEnery's. Finally, he settled on a pair of jeans and a fresh white T-shirt. They were in the woods, for God's sake, what else should he wear? And what should he take over there? The four beers from his remaining six-pack? Hardly. His one and only bottle of wine, which he'd already opened? No. He settled on a bouquet of wildflowers for Miss McEnery's table.

Leah answered his knock, the same passive expression on her face. "Good evening," she said, and he noticed that in spite of the absence of a smile, her voice, full and rich, was welcoming. Sam handed her the flowers.

"They're beautiful," she said. "I'll put them in some water."

You're beautiful, Sam thought, as he followed Leah into the dining room.

The table was set informally, stoneware instead of porcelain, and he was glad. He and Leah sat across from each other, while McEnery sat at the head of the table. They made small talk during the meal, which was simple, but good, and he noticed that McEnery didn't eat very much. But he drank constantly, downing two glasses of wine to every half glass of his and Leah's. Each time his glass was empty he drummed his fingers against the stem and Leah replenished his wine. And as the old man spoke, his words crowded in on each other until they were just a series of vowels and consonants sticking like glue to his lips. Sam had to lean in to make out McEnery's sentences.

"LivedinSanFranciscotoolongSam.Gladtobebackhome."

"Yes, sir. So am I." Sam explained that he had lived in San Francisco, too.

Leah said very little, almost nothing to Sam, but she was very tender with the old man. At one point she served him a fork full of food and murmured in a little girl's voice, "Daddy, you need to eat more."

Sam wondered if Leah were McEnery's only child, if she had come back from another life in order to care for her father whose health was obviously on a downward spiral. There were a lot of questions he would have liked to ask, but these people were his employers.

"My dear . . . I think I'm tired."

"Yes, of course," said Leah. She looked at Sam. "Would you help me take Mr. McEnery to bed?"

Sam jumped up. "Certainly," he said.

They stood on either side of McEnery, guided him out of his chair and walked him to the bedroom at the back of the house. The old man was nearly asleep on his feet and Sam wondered how she could manage getting him to bed alone every night, since Sam was sure by the way McEnery had tapped his glass and she had filled it, that his heavy drinking was a ritual.

Sam took the old man's shoes off and helped Leah slip his shirt over his head, then he discreetly left the room. Leah soon came out and quietly closed the bedroom door. "Thank you, Sam."

"No problem," he said. They stood for a moment against the wall in the hallway, looking at each other. Sam felt that strange current flow between them again, same as it had that afternoon. He was awkward, his hands and feet suddenly big and clumsy.

"Well, I'll see you out," Leah said finally, and Sam realized he was being dismissed. At the front door, she said, "He wasn't always like this. It's just been the last couple of years. Before that he was so vital . . . He grew old overnight. The blindness is from diabetes."

"Diabetes?"

"Yes. I know what you're thinking. The drinking. I can't stop him."

She said the words defensively and Sam was startled. None

of this was his business. Why did she feel she had to explain anything to him? He opened his mouth to speak, but she had opened the door, stepped out, and he followed. "Good night, Sam," she said, and before he could say a word, she stepped back inside and closed the door.

Sam walked to the bungalow. He was full of food and wine and a vague feeling about what had actually taken place between Leah and himself. She had been neither rude nor friendly, simply perplexing.

That night, from his window, he watched the moonlight play against the open French doors, just as it had done the night before. But Leah didn't come out and after a while Sam left the window, sank down onto his bed and entered a dreamless sleep.

Leah came out of the house and walked down the driveway to the mailbox. Sam stood in the clearing not more than a hundred yards away and knew she had seen him. He almost waved to her, but stopped himself when he realized she had no intention of acknowledging his presence. She had served him dinner the night before, this morning he was not worthy of a greeting. She came up the drive clutching the mail in her hand, looking at the face of each envelope as she walked up the steps and back into the house. He resolved not to care that she had snubbed him, even as he was conscious of the desire that stirred him.

Toward the end of his work day, as he was cleaning up, Sam turned and there she was, standing before him with her arms folded across her breasts. "He wants you to come to dinner again," she said, a soft contempt in her voice.

Her manner puzzled him, brought up an anger he didn't understand. "He made you come out here to ask?"

"Yes."

Sam sneered at Leah and bowed in an exaggerated fashion. "Well, m'lady," he said. "Please convey my regrets to Mr. McEnery. Explain to him that I have another engagement." He turned away. Now it was his turn to act as if she didn't exist.

He attacked the brush and the leaves and branches furiously as he thought how glad he would be when this job was over, when he could get away from this exasperating woman and her dying, drunken father. He told himself that over and over, as he put his tools away, as he scrubbed the grime from his body, as he sat on the porch and drank his four remaining bottles of beer.

No food in his stomach, lightheaded from the beer, Sam wasn't sure what he heard coming from the big house. A crash, glass breaking? Then Leah's scream. He ran across the small meadow that separated the two structures and threw open the door.

The old man sat at the dining room table, same as he had the night before. Leah stood holding her hand before her. Sam noticed a broken glass on the table and a smashed wine bottle on the floor across from where she stood. Above the shattered bottle, wine, red as blood, stained the white wall.

"Sam. Please tell Leah I'm sorry." The old man had tears in his unseeing eyes. He looked up in Leah's direction. "I'm sorry, my dear. I would never hurt you. Sorry."

Sam picked up a napkin and wrapped Leah's bleeding hand. The cut wasn't bad, but her body trembled as if she were in shock. He settled her into the chair, then turned his attention to the old man.

"I didn't mean it, Sam. What did I do?"

"I don't know, sir," said Sam. "Let's worry about it tomorrow. Right now, we'll get you to bed."

The old man nodded, allowed Sam to lead him to his room. Leah sat in the same spot where Sam had left her, still trembling as she stared at the white cloth that covered her hand. Sam gently pulled her out of the chair and slipped his arms around her, whispered against her hair, "It's all right."

After a few moments her body relaxed against him and she began to cry. "I can't. I can't do it anymore. I can't watch him . . . "

"Sh . . . sh," he crooned, his voice low, soothing.

Sam swept Leah up into his arms, surprised by how light she was. She rested her head against his shoulder as he carried her up the stairs. He knew which room was hers. Sam sat Leah down on the bed, went into the bathroom and gathered what he needed to dress her hand.

"It will heal in a few days," he said when he had finished. "Now you need to rest."

She hadn't said a word during the time it had taken him to care for her wound. Now she grabbed for his hand. "Don't," she said softly. "Please don't go."

Sam hesitated, then stood up. Leah reached out, her arms encircled his waist, she drew him to her, buried her cheek against his belly. Her touch inflamed his groin; the warmth spread over his legs and up to touch his nipples. He felt his knees grow weak, felt his penis harden against her face. She ran her cheek along his erection, traced with her chin its outline inside the denim. She looked up at him and Sam read the hunger in her eyes, and more. Longing, sorrow, loneliness. He reached down and ran his fingers lightly over the outline of her lips. Leah grabbed for Sam with her teeth, nibbled at the tips of his fingers, sucked. Sam's breath stuck inside his throat. He had never wanted a woman more than he wanted Leah.

She undid his belt while she watched his face. Sam closed his eyes, concentrated on the sound of leather slipping out of the buckle's grasp, the tinkle of metal on metal, the sound of his zipper opening. He felt keenly the soft flesh of her hands, one covered by a gauze bandage, as they stroked his hips slowly, pulled down his briefs and freed his cock. Leah reached beneath him with one hand, caressed his heavy sac, while with her other hand, guided him inside her lips. He moaned, felt her mouth on him, hot and wet as her tongue slipped over and around his shaft, licking lightly, but thoroughly, making him harder, pulling the skin on his balls taut. Sam was aware of the moonlight spilling into the room, the pitch of their breaths, the moist, light clicking of Leah's mouth as it slid over his cock, taking him in deeper and deeper. The room became a tiny world of sensation. Nothing outside existed. He moved inside her mouth, in and out slowly, and with each inward thrust she sucked him soundly, relaxed her lips as he withdrew, then sucked again, pulled, coaxed, called up his essence. And he felt it rising, almost there, almost there inside the perfect rhythm of lips and tongue, intense and absolute. He groaned, pressed forward, bounced on the balls of his feet as he surrendered his orgasm to her in a jolting burst of light.

Sam fell to his knees, his strength drained. He looked up at Leah sprawled across the bed, her eyes closed, her chest rising and falling. He pulled his clothes off and joined her. He caressed her cheek and she opened her eyes. "Sam," she said, reaching up to touch his face. He kissed her, a deep, probing kiss, exploring with his tongue her taste and his own. "I knew this would happen," she said. "That's why I didn't want you around."

"Are you sorry?"

She sighed. "No."

Leah's face filled with wonder, fascination, and him. She looked vulnerable and so incredibly beautiful his heart melted. He bent over her, scooped her into his arms in a gesture of protectiveness. This time the passion exploded in his heart and he made a conscious effort not to cry out his joy. He wanted to tell her that she had made him feel as no other woman had ever made him feel, but all he could say was, "Leah."

She pressed against him, her need pressing through the thin cotton of her dress, her skin hot, firing his skin. He laid her down, lifted the dress over her head, slipped it off her body and dropped it to the floor. She reached for his hands and moved them to her breasts. Her eyes closed and a sigh left her lips as Sam kneaded the firm flesh, made tiny whorls around her nipples with the tips of his fingers. Leah shuddered beneath him, whispered his name, grasped his hair in both her hands and brought his lips down on hers. She sucked his tongue, his lips, his chin; kissed him until he gasped for breath. Sam pulled his mouth from hers and rested his head against her breasts for a moment, then let his tongue roll slowly over each mound, flood the nipples before drawing them, one at a time, deeply into his mouth. She cupped her breasts, squeezed them together as he kept sucking her rock-hard nipples against his tongue. He buried his face inside her bosom, breathed in her warm scent, planted moist kisses in the valley between her breasts, licked and kissed his way down and over the soft slope of her belly; felt her smooth, silky legs under his hands. He placed his palm over her soft curls, slipped his finger into her wet cleft and pressed gently on the delicate folds at the mouth of her vagina. She arched into his hand as if a bolt of electricity had entered her body, and Sam felt the energy from that shock leap into his. He pulled her lips apart and met the mouth of her sex with his mouth. He savored her wetness, drew her juices against his lips. He sucked and licked, ran his tongue into the deep crevices and over her sensitive clitoris. Her body jerked up, rose to keep itself fastened to Sam's mouth. He was lost in the taste of her, the soft warm slickness of her. He wanted to go deeper, deeper, drown inside her womb. Leah clutched his shoulders, thrust into his face, abandoned herself to his ministrations. She cried out, and he could hear the tears in her voice, their force rising up from her cunt and into her throat; spilling over her lips. "Oh, Sam . . . Ahhhhhh . . . ," she groaned, and he felt the impact of her orgasm wash over his tongue in a baptism of their spirits.

Sam lay with his head against Leah's belly as she ran her fingers through his hair. The glow of the moon bathed their bodies like a gentle lagoon. He dipped his tongue into her navel and she sighed. "Let's never leave this bed, Sam," she said.

"Okay."

He thought about the old man asleep downstairs, and he was a little ashamed for being grateful that McEnery had been too drunk to have heard them. This was the first time he had ravaged a man's daughter while he was a guest in the man's home. Perhaps he should have been more ashamed, but he wasn't. He had Leah under him, the taste of her still in his mouth. He was smitten.

"I wanted you the minute I laid eyes on you, Sam."

"Me, too."

"Yes? That day in the garden?"

Should he tell her about the night before that day in the garden, when he'd seen her on the porch in the moonlight, say that he'd begun to want her then? No. He decided to keep that his secret for now.

"Yes. That day in the garden," he said.

She rolled out from under him, scurried into the crook of his arm, laid her hand upon his chest. "There's so much I should tell you, Sam, about the way things are . . . "

He gently covered her mouth with his hand. "Shush," he whispered. "Not tonight."

He had discovered in making love with her a different kind of appetite, a hunger that pervaded his being, a desire to possess her, not in a way that smacked of ownership, but a blending of her soul into his. His discovery did not come in a series of thoughts, but through an arrangement of emotion as he kissed her, touched her, moved inside her. He, over her, she, over him, his hands holding her torso steady as he thrust his cock up into her again and again. His penis deep within her, Leah shuddered over him, and he shared the impact of her orgasms, first one, than another. "Please. I don't want you to stop. Don't ever stop," she whispered. To hear her speak, to watch her face as she came thrilled him so, as if her orgasms leapt out of her body and into his. Sam cried out as the energy poured out of him to fill her, and still it was not enough. He wanted to melt further and further into her, blot out the bed, the room, even the moon, everything except the soft cries that spurred him on to reach her center, the place where he wished to mark her, stamp her his, the way a wolf marks its territory. Again, over her, his chest shaking and heaving, her arms around his back, drawing him close, fusing to him, her tears flowing free, warm against his skin, attentive to each other's desires, with an absence of self-consciousness or judgment. Sex and love, pure and beautiful and committed.

The tides cannot resist the moon, and like them, Sam could not resist the pull on his body, the drawing of his being toward the house where somewhere inside, Leah stood. Was she making breakfast for her father? Folding laundry? Thinking of him? Would she come out of the house if he willed her to?

Leah, Leah, like a buzzing in his head as he hacked the brush, freed twisted vines, and uncovered smothered walkways. "The mail man was here. Come out and get the mail. I want to run my face along your legs, your thighs; I want my tongue to taste your skin again." The sun stood high in the sky, the sweat trickled down Sam's body in rivulets, and he trembled with desire.

The door to the big house opened, Leah stepped out, her

arms wrapped around two jugs, one with tea bags floating around inside, the other filled with clear water and ice. She set the tea on the porch, came down the stairs and walked toward him, the ice tinkling against the glass jug like wind chimes on a breezy day.

"Hi. I brought you some water. Thought you might need to be refreshed."

"I do need to be refreshed," he said, drawing her to him. "Come inside the bungalow with me."

She laughed. "Sam, I can't. He just woke up a little while ago. I gave him his insulin and some breakfast, but I've got to watch him."

"I know," he said, but he was pulling on the skirt of her dress, walking backwards toward the bungalow. She followed, weakly protesting, laughing and shaking her head.

Behind the door he kissed her, took her tongue into his mouth like a starving man, held her to him so closely the sweat on his body stained her dress. She pulled away, looked up at him helplessly. "My knees are weak," she said. "My head is light. See what you do?" He kissed her again. "It's so good," she murmured against his mouth.

"What is? Which part?"

"All of it."

"What's the best? The kissing; the touching. Licking. Fucking."

"Yes, yes, yes, yes." She pulled away from him, looked deeply into his eyes. "Trust."

"What?"

"I trust you. There's nothing I wouldn't do for you, wouldn't want you to do to me."

"Wilder and wilder?"

"Yes," said Leah. "Wilder and wilder."

She pushed him up against the door, climbed on top of him;

he grabbed her, dug his fingers into the soft flesh of her ass, kissed her mouth as if he hadn't kissed it in a long, long time. Such a rich, juicy mouth. He opened the buttons at the top of her dress, peeled the cloth aside, and took her nipple between his lips. Leah wound her hands into his hair as his busy mouth worked. His strong arms lifted her high, turned her so that her back was to the door; and his head disappeared under her dress, to the sweetness of her cunt with its soft black curls over deep pink folds. He savored the smell of her; the taste of her, heard her moan above him. Heard her say, "Sam . . . I want you inside me."

He brought her down; they stood toe to toe, her breath coming in gasps against his chest. She looked up at him. "Sam . . . please . . . "

He turned her around and gently pinned her arms with his hands. "Bend over, Leah," he said. "Put your hands against the door."

She did what he said. He moved closer to her, threw her skirt over her back, bent to kiss the soft flesh of her ass. He brought his arm under her, slipped his finger inside her moist lips; she was hot and wet and he spread her juices along the crack of her ass. She moaned in anticipation, spread her feet wider apart, drew closer to him.

He rested his hands on her hips. "Do you trust me?" he whispered. She turned her head, nodded. With one hand he undid the zipper on his jeans, let them fall. He pulled on his aching cock, drew out the moisture at the tip and spread it over the head, then with his hand, guided his cock into her tiny hole. He pushed slowly and felt her tense around him. "I don't want to hurt you, Leah. I want only to give you pleasure. If you want me to stop, I will."

"No . . . I want this," she said.

"Relax," he said. "Take me in. You do it, move against me. I won't move at all until you want me to." She arched slightly, moving him further inside her. She moved again, then again, inching her way over him until she had all of him. "Good," he said. He brought his hand under her again, stroked her dripping lips and Leah began to moan, moved her hips back and forth against him.

"It's so good, Sam. Do it with me, move with me now."

"Like this?" he asked, pumping in and out of her slowly.

"Yes, like that. Don't stop."

His balls were so full, he wanted nothing more than to explode within her, but he held off, took her lead, kept pushing in a steady rhythm until she could take no more, cried out that she was going to come. Her muscles tightened around him as she began to spasm, and at that moment he drove two of his fingers deep inside her cunt. She shuddered, lost control, and in her excitement almost broke away. He quickly grabbed her hips, drew her back, slammed against her, meeting the end of her orgasm with the beginning of his.

She went limp under him and he withdrew. He turned her around and tenderly kissed her eyes, her ears, her lips, her neck; whispered his love to her.

"Sam, I've never done anything like that before."

"And?"

"It's quite amazing."

"That it is," he said.

Her eyes clouded over. "I wish I could stay here, make love with you all afternoon, but I've got to get back."

"I know. But tonight, when he's asleep . . . "

"Yes."

He held her face in both his hands, kissed her lightly on her smiling mouth. "Go on, go take care of your father. I'll see you later."

The smile on Leah's face dissolved, she stiffened and pulled

Sam's hands away from her face. "What is it?" he asked. "What's the matter?"

She searched his eyes. "My God, you don't know," she said.

"What?" He was suddenly afraid.

"Justin isn't my father. He's my husband."

Somehow he'd heard the words, understood them before they formed in her mouth. He's my husband. My husband. My.

His dimension had shifted. Paralysis ebbed around his body; Leah's, too, for neither of them moved. He forced himself to break their silence, an act of will.

"What have you done to me, Leah? What kind of game are you playing?"

She started to cry, and in a broken voice, "No game, Sam. No game."

"You fucked me, Leah, with your husband asleep in the bedroom right below us. Jesus Christ, you called him, 'Daddy!' I don't fuck other people's wives!"

Leah moved her hands over her ears. He lunged for her again, grabbed the sleeve of her dress and it came away from her shoulder with a cracking sound.

"Sam, please don't."

"Please don't," he repeated, lifted her and carried her to the sofa, flung her unceremoniously onto the cushions. "Now, you tell me," he said, his face close to hers, his voice terse. "Why me? Because I was here? Because I was available?"

How many dawnings had he experienced in his life, that time when the light goes on and everything is crystal clear? Here was another fountainhead of truth, one he had no stomach for. He had pronounced this woman his simply because he had wanted her, because they had made love flawlessly. Why had he believed that's all it would take to give him the right to her? He could picture her, his Leah, rounding her back over that twisted old man, bringing her hips to his with a deliberate sway, fucking him. The image sickened him. But why should it? He was the interloper here.

Leah sobbed into her hands. She looked like a child who has just been scolded for touching something she should not have. What did he look like? Did he look like a man guilty of touching something he should not have? All at once, he was tired. "Jesus, Leah," he said quietly. "I run a tree service, not a stud service."

Leah took her hands away from her face, wiped her eyes on the skirt of her dress. "It wasn't like that, Sam. I swear."

"He invited me to dinner, he sent you looking for me. He lined me up for you, isn't that true, Leah?"

For less than a moment, she hesitated. "Yes . . . but, you've got to listen. Please."

I should tell her to shut up, he thought. Tell her I don't want to hear what she has to say. I should throw my gear together, get the hell off McEnery's property. I have no claim to McEnery's property. But he sat watching her, wanting to hear, and fearing what she might say.

"I married him when I was nineteen. I've always called him 'Daddy;' it started as a little joke between us."

Sam felt his gut wrench. He turned his face away from her, but he couldn't block out her words.

"He was wonderful; we had a good life together. For a long time, he was a young man. Nearly thirty years older than I, but young in so many ways." The wistful sorrow in Leah's voice forced Sam to look at her again.

Fresh tears stained her cheek. "He hates being sick, says he wishes he had the courage to end his life, even begged me to help him. . . . " Leah rose from the sofa, went to stand before the window. The sun was high in the sky flooding the small room with a scorching light, yet she shivered, wrapped her arms around her middle, drew into herself. "I couldn't do that and he stopped asking." She turned to look at Sam. "And I couldn't do the other thing he begged me to do. It seemed as though everywhere we went, the ballet, the opera, out to dinner with friends — there was always someone — even in the pitch black of his blindness — someone he would pick to pair me to. A colleague of his, a business acquaintance, a waiter . . . It's the reason we came here. I'd hoped in the quiet of these woods he would forget, stop bringing it up, just let me be there for him, let me comfort him until he died in peace." She sat down, began to reach for Sam, but stopped. "You've got to understand something, Sam. It was good for us, for me. He wanted that for me, still. But I never . . . until you."

Jealousy and guilt lay on Sam's stomach like a bad meal. It had been good for them, for her and the sick old man, when he wasn't sick and he wasn't old. She peered into his eyes. "I can't apologize for that," she said. "Did you think I came without a past, Sam? Does anyone? Do you?"

"No," Sam whispered.

"He's dying. I love him and I always will. But I love you, too. Is that wrong? Is it wrong for him to want a second chance for me? Is it wrong for me to take it? Tell me, Sam. If it's wrong, I'll walk away. You won't have to."

Sam's quiet breathing filled the room. Finally, he took a deep breath, looked through the window at the sunshine. "Have you ever noticed that sometimes there are two full moons in a month? A blue moon. It doesn't happen very often, but it does happen."

Leah's brow wrinkled in confusion. "What does a blue moon have to do with this, Sam?"

He smiled. "Nothing, really. It just came to me when you talked about second chances. I know about second chances, Leah. About starting over."

Sam stood up, gently drew Leah to her feet. "Do you still trust me?

"Yes, Sam. I trust you."

"Okay, then. Go take care of him."

Leah opened her mouth, but no words came. She nodded and left the bungalow and he watched as she walked to the big house, opened the door, and went inside.

Sam stood on the porch of the little house, picked up the gloves he had been wearing earlier, put them on and gathered his tools. That afternoon he would begin to clear away the dried brush atop the higher peaks.

Diva Marie

❦

# Simple Gifts

"How's my little girl this evening?" I inquired upon entering the room. He was positioned in the exact manner I had instructed him: all fours on the floor, face down into the pillow, ass sticking in the air behind him.

He raised his head slightly to answer somewhat breathily, "Fine, Mistress."

*His voice only gets that seductive air when he's in lingerie,* I thought to myself. The items I wore were of a more aggressive kind: a tight-fitting, black patent leather teddy with garters, shiny black stockings, thigh-high patent leather boots, and lace gloves.

My red hair fell partially around my face as I bent to fix one stocking, and I caught him peeking at me from the corner of his eye. "Enough." I said, slapping his upturned ass. "You will get a full view of me later."

"Yes, Mistress." He raised his head.

"Turn your head away from me. There you go. I can hear you without you raising your head." I lifted my booted foot, and placed it on his ass. "Tell me how you felt in the lingerie store today, when you knew the clerks were laughing at you."

"Embarrassed, Mistress. But I admit, I liked it, too."

I removed my foot. "I, for one, loved it. Of course, you do realize there will be more shopping trips like that one?"

"Yes, Mistress."

"You'll get used to them after awhile. Pretty soon, you won't think twice about picking up a girdle on the way home from work," I teased, and gently kicked at his behind.

I moved a wardrobe mirror from its place behind the bedroom door to the other side of the room, positioning it so he could see himself. "Look at that pretty picture. Do you like it?"

"Oh, yes, Mistress."

"Good. I want you to watch everything from this angle, in this mirror." I moved behind him and picked up my gift, the one he had crafted just for me, just for tonight. "It's well-made, slave. I might even reward you twice for making it." He didn't reply verbally this time, just shivered.

The harness was made of fine black leather, accented with silver studs and spikes. It fit perfectly around my waist and through my legs. I saw the alternating emotions in his eyes as he watched me pull it on, his fear and his arousal. *Which feeling feeds off which?* I wondered silently. "Have you ever in your life played with a woman in a strap-on harness?"

"No, Mistress, and definitely not one with such a big cock attached."

I nodded — this was a big one. Looking it over, I estimated at least eight inches in length, and two inches around. I knew he'd never taken as much in his life, and the thought of using it on a near virgin caused quite a flow in my crotch. "This is your last chance, slave. You can get out of this now, with no retribution from me. Are you ready?"

"Yes, Mistress, I'm ready."

Slowly I walked around to face him. Each step sounded menacing on the hardwood floor. "Look at it," I demanded, and pointed to my cock. He raised himself off the floor. "Worship it."

Without hesitation, he took it into his mouth, rocking his body back and forth while he moved his lips over the full length.

I grabbed his hair. "You like to suck my cock, I can tell. Take more of it." I shoved his head down onto the dildo, one, two, three times, then pulled it out. "You're good at giving head, too," I smirked.

"Thank you, Mistress," he grunted.

I walked back to a position behind him. "Watch the mirror," I hissed. "Don't close your eyes, and don't look away."

I knelt behind him while I spread lubricant over the shaft and head of my new cock. I lifted it up to his asshole, and pressed down on his lower back to move him into position. Very slowly, I inserted it.

It seemed to take forever, I wanted inside him so much, but I knew he couldn't take it any faster and still enjoy the experience. He gasped only once, when the head slipped inside him. I was proud of him for being so quiet, and for watching my cock's progress in the mirror without flinching.

Once inside, I reached around his abdomen and pulled him onto my lap as I leaned back onto my legs. He was sitting directly on top of my strapped-on cock; it was entirely inside of him. He groaned when I began to move him up and down, and each time I deliberately pulled the shaft out a little further with each stroke. Soon we had a rhythm established, and I knew he wouldn't be able to contain himself much longer.

"Pull your clit out from under those panties, girl. Stroke it while I pump your new cunt. You've got thirty seconds to come, or don't bother."

I was foolish to have given him such a long time. He came in what seemed like a microsecond, and once he started, it didn't feel as if his muscle spasms would stop. Finally he relaxed. "Lie down on the floor," I said, and I removed my cock.

While I detached the harness, I soothed his ass with a little more lubricant. Then I slid my body up next to his and situated myself in his arms.

"You can take care of my needs when we wake up in the morning," I whispered as I kissed his cheek. "Oh, and happy anniversary."

"Can you believe it's been four years already?" He smiled.

I couldn't. But I was already wondering what to get him next year.

Red Jordan Arobateau

❦

# Prince Valiant, Queen Serena & the Peepshow Palace

Serena. Of Mediterranean descent. Her face was wide and full, framed by dark curly hair. Her eyes wide with a greenish hue. Big face. Dark white skin dotted with black hair on her arms and legs. Stocky. A peasant body.

Valiant. A medium-sized butch. Sandy brown hair. Freckled face.

Valiant had not always led such a tame life as she had since this marriage. She'd once been the center of attention, a butch-around-town. But she'd met Serena when she was no longer a baby butch, already worn out from chasing after gals. She was quite ready to be settled and a loyal husband.

They were poor, landless, of the vagabond class. Physically Serena looked ambiguous; she usually wore ladies' pants or tight-fitting jeans upon which she'd stitched some fancy design — embroidered flowers, rainbows. She wore peasant blouses with frills and ladies' boots — though tough, shit-kicking boots — a femmy kerchief over her wild black hair, and a jacket to wrap herself in as a defense. One might think she looked like a strong amazon female and let it go at that — but when she was with Valiant, which she usually was, it was obvious what the two of them were: Queer.

They lived on the third floor — a walkup — of the Avondale Hotel. Dank. Worn carpet. Dusty walls of corridors and stairwells colored beige, no paint in years. A few faint veils of cobwebs showed it was not attended to very often. Theirs was a large room with a makeshift kitchen at one end, a tiny bathroom with sink, toilet and shower stall made of metal rusted into the floor. A kitchen table and chairs sat in the middle of the large room, with a bed set in a corner.

Valiant and Serena had worked for a few seasons for upper middle-class people, even some rich ones, as housecleaners, but they kept losing jobs — Valiant was convinced it was because they were gay. Now, with only a handful of gay guys left to work for, they earned only $150 a week. They'd purchased a broken down car four years back when the jobs had been plentiful. And they didn't live entirely in a depressing, starvation fashion — but not very well either. They were always living on the edge, with never enough money. They'd not paid rent in several places, moving from apartment to apartment, finally coming to rest in this furnished room with a bath and what passed for a kitchen. When Valiant thought about her happy childhood it all seemed to fit — like a penance of sorts — maybe she was finally being forced to share the misery of the majority of the world's people.

At least they had no dependents — not a cat or a dog or even a plant. Footloose and fancy free. And their relationship was full of hugs, love, tenderness and real sex. Serena was no occasional woman — she was a 24-hour, 365-days-a-year woman. She was Valiant's wife.

They'd been married seven years and shared a body language. One would start a sentence, forget what she was saying, so the other would finish the sentence for her. They enjoyed the same TV programs, the same food.

Nights Valiant took her burden of sex to Serena: clit held in her hand, pussy lips squeezed between two fingers, the dripping juices of her vagina. She sought out her lover and her hot loving, and they fucked each other's pussies. It was one of the high points in their relationship. They were not hand-holding lesbians, nor were they spinster sisters. They did nasty, wet, bodily-fluid-exchanging real sex.

Valiant was the more passionate, always inspired to take her wife, to investigate the scent, the heat and eroticism of a woman. Serena's stocky peasant build was sturdy enough to bear up under the full weight of her lover's butch body.

Though they were in love, Valiant still needed to soothe her depression and add zest to their sex life. She did it like this: She was a regular attendee of the Peep Show Palace.

Valiant and her friend Devon ducked and dodged traffic and pedestrians as they walked through the city streets, past multimillion dollar car dealerships, large corporate offices, huge modern skyscrapers, toward a row of grubby residential hotels which still survived in the shadow of the silver and gray towering giants. Homes for the mind-damaged; or for starving seniors; drag queens and kings; other creatures who didn't fit in anywhere else.

The two butches entered a building and descended into the netherworld of the sex industry. The dark interior. Ads for girlie videos, porn, flashing lights all colors of the spectrum, advertising GIRLS!

They turned into the lobby, hands stuffed inside their trousers, sweaty fingers clutching their carefully hoarded green one dollar bills. It was dark inside. Glitzy lights in a galaxy dotted along the ceiling. Music piped in from the center showroom flooded the Palace with the pounding insistence of a masturbatory jerkoff. Mindless men stumbled through the Palace, in and out of booths that showed fuck videos, all in a heightened state of sexual arousal. The place was full of them.

Once in awhile other female customers graced the place—curious giggling Asian coeds with their boyfriends spilling over from nearby Chinatown; lost tourists; dykes like Valiant. None stayed very long. There were no other females today; they were the lone adventurers in a sea of milling men waiting in front of a row of doors, a neon sign over each one flashing "Occupied" in red, or "Vacant," in gold.

They mingled in the dark with the men walking around waiting for a booth, staring up at the signs over the doors waiting for a golden flashing "Vacant" to appear. Finally they got two booths side by side.

Valiant stepped into the tiny coffin-tight cubicle. With a whiz the machine ate up her dollars and the metal screen slowly lifted. For a few furtive minutes of bliss she watched pink and tan nude flesh. Women gyrated in front of her, their legs spread, wearing disinterested looks.

The flesh pit pulled Valiant in, soothed her soul. She lost herself in that comfortable dark hideaway, and experienced the high-powered big-money environment. Some deep dark animal lust, not simply of sexual gratification, but of conquest, enabled a spiritual release by melding her erotic force with a nude pink stranger behind glass.

Five dancers strut. Awesome. As a team — all that beauty, all that power. Nude on high heels, hair coifed, some with pubic hair shaved. Tits bouncing, pert nipples, backbones erect, heads held high as if they'd trained in finishing school with a plate on their heads. Smiles full of sparkling teeth. Four whites, one tan-complected African-American. Bored straight ladies undulating slowly, not wasting too much energy, pacing themselves, like race horses, for a full six-hour shift.

Valiant fed dollars, and then when the green stuff ran out,

quarters, into the slot to keep her window open and view the nude girls. She wound up spending all the money in her pocket, bankrupting the household budget for the week. Just to see inside the glass-walled cage of carpeted pink walls and mirrors the warm, naked bodies, the soft hot thighs, the pubic hair as the girls opened themselves up with their fingers; to see pink pussy lips and vulva humping up and down, riding the air.

The peep show dancers thrust their pelvises forward and back, butts jerking, humping in giant arcs, tan and pale skin; they sashayed nude on top of their tall high heels, making devouring arcs, humping air. Strutting on their high heels before mirrors sparkling bright as a drag queen's sequins.

Soon a slender young girl slid down the pole. Valiant got hot in her cubicle. Through the glass she and the girl shared a physical intimacy; the dancer worked her slim hips and tits tantalizingly, while Valiant got hot, blood racing to her clit. Erotic closeness of the dancer pumping, grinding her pussy in the direction of Valiant's face, inches away. Her pale white stomach downed with fine blonde body hair; moist pussy inches away, but separated by glass.

After viewing nude girls Valiant's soul would be at peace, a bridge having been built out of herself into another, leaving her body with a vague tingle of horniness which was not at all desperate, but pleasant, exciting, and expectant — knowing she would fulfill that lust at night with her accommodating wife, Serena.

Valiant's underpants were soggy. Yes, she would take her hot lust and her love embraces and kisses home to her wife that night — or maybe the next, if Serena was too tired, simply put Eros on hold, then summon it up once again, those erotic images, the heightened sexual energy from recent memory of the Peep Show.

From a cubicle around the side of the showroom a shutter slid down. A broke dyke stumbled out from the high tension erotica into the dark hall; hands jammed into the pockets of her sports coat, she looked like a little man walking hurriedly over the red carpeted lobby, and out.

"This drives me crazy," Devon said when they got outside. "Tits and ass. You're lucky you got Serena to go home to."

When Valiant came to bed in the wee small hours of that morning, Serena awakened. "What took you so long?" she murmured. "Do you want to make love?"

"Yes, my queen." She lifted Serena's nightgown, fumbled her pussy folds to find her joy spot.

"My prince," Serena cooed. "Prince Valiant." She lay back on the sheets.

Valiant knelt at the fragrant flower, probing the sweet fleshy folds. With her thumb she stroked Serena's curly wet pubic hair over her vulva, then bent to kiss her thighs. The tip of her tongue licked over her wife's thighs, then flicked, pink, into her pussy. With each forefinger of both hands she smoothed aside the pubic hair and parted the pussy folds. From Serena's viewpoint, Valiant appeared to have twin mustaches on either side of her nostrils as she went down on her. Valiant savored her lover's salty taste.

Once Valiant's mouth was pressed fully upon Serena's sex, her hands reached up and groped for her breasts. As she fondled her tits, squeezing the nipples between her forefingers and thumbs, suddenly she stopped. Her mind had gone blank. The bed stopped its motion.

"What are you doing?" Serena asked in an exasperated tone.

"I thought I was making love to you." Valiant paused in mid-lick, glancing up, her eyes round, questioning. The rest of her body lay like a lump under the covers.

"Well, it seems like you're just fumbling around. Your mind's not on what you're doing."

"Uh . . . I'm sorry," Valiant said sheepishly. In truth, she'd suddenly been struck with pangs of guilt for spending their money at the Peepshow Palace.

"Well, come on. I'm ready," said Serena, slightly pissed. She lay, thighs spread wide, extending her legs, one foot pointing to the right, one to the left, ending in twinkling red nail-polished toes. Her pale white butch squirmed on top of her. In the meeting of their pearl clits, the rub of their hooded cowls, in the hot pussy of her lover, thrusting with urgency, Valiant sighed, "Queen Serena."

"My Prince Valiant," Serena cooed.

Lying between Serena's sturdy thighs Valiant rode her fast as her muscular arms supported the weight of her torso and her white hips began grinding round and round. Their clits became firm and hot, moving together nestled in their mashed-together vulvas, and Serena moaned, a low, guttural warning. Valiant ceased her movement, reached out and grabbed a pillow to put against her wife's face.

"We have to be quiet," she whispered.

"I don't have to!" Serena shouted, pushing the pillow away. "I can scream all I want."

But Valiant couldn't forget about what other tenants might say when she had to face them in the halls the next morning. Once before, during a passionate bout of Serena's sex-satisfied screams, someone had knocked on their door asking if everything was all right. And on another occasion, the manager had informed her to please keep their voices down in the future.

Still, Valiant kept up the passionate pounding of her lust.

"Ohhhhh! Ahhhhh!"

"Serena, please. People will hear," Valiant pleaded, her hips stopped in frozen mid-motion, the palms of her hands sweating.

"I don't care," Serena screamed, tossing her head from side to side. "I'm not ashamed."

Serena humped her hips, jostling for better clit contact, and the two resumed the rhythmic motion of their union. Fire. Fire between their legs. Melting fire. Melting liquid fire. And they were coming.

Serena's passion-rocked cries cut loose to fill the room and echo down the dusty halls of the Avondale Hotel. Faster, faster Valiant pumped, her white ass gleaming in the moonlight. She came with all the frustrations in her soul, pounding out along with her lust all the anxiety and repression she faced daily, all the effacing of her real self.

"Ah, fuck! Ah, fuck!" Even Valiant cried aloud now as her loins melted, a molten shock of orgasmic fire shot through her body and the muscles of her hips and legs and back and arms shuddered.

Sweat poured into the sheets. The dark wild-haired woman cut loose, her voice rising in a second orgasm of even greater intensity, shattering the night stillness, "Ah you butch, fuck me. Fuck me. Ah!"

Finally they collapsed and drifted into sleep. Moonlight shone through the glass.

# Susanna J. Herbert

❦

# Three Note Harmony

Chocolate Chip Cookie Dough. Cherry Garcia. Macadamia Nut Brittle. Which to choose? Isn't it ironic that we're allowed 31 flavors of ice cream, yet only one flavor of sexuality?

Vanilla.

Man-to-woman, cock-to-cunt, sex-to-sleep.

Not that smooth, creamy vanilla isn't wonderful. But imagine how dull life would be without the occasional dollop of Fudge Ripple. As a girl, my experience with boys was about as exotic as a swirl of Tastee-Freeze. We would "court," we would grope, we would long for more, virginities firmly intact. Both dates and desserts were sweet snacks for an uninitiated palate. How fortunate that time has taught me the infinite joys of a lavish sexual feast.

Derek and Reg began playing together at seventeen. Guitar, that is. Only guitar. Derek left East London for Chicago when his father died and his mum ran off with a sailor from Liverpool. "Reg," short for Adam Reginald, was a Windy City native, raised on Pete Townshend and Willie Dixon. When they met sparks instantly flew. Brought together by an intense love of music, coupled with a passionate, tenacious drive to succeed, their relationship was equal parts Lennon/McCartney and Ali/Frazier.

Derek was tall, wiry and, in his own words, "an insufferable bastard." His thick, semi-sweet chocolate hair was never combed and his dark, scowling, scoundrel's eyes could bore through cast iron. No pretty boy; still, women were attracted to him like bees to clover. His somber sexiness stemmed from a lightning-quick wit, uncanny talent with a Stratocaster, and the world's sexiest ass.

Reg had the radiant face of a fallen angel; a mischievous meld of metallic blue eyes, silky blonde curls and a smile that could melt lead. He was Adam after the first bite of apple. His shoulders and biceps were hard and chiseled, his torso reminiscent of Athenian sculpture. He possessed an intellect as singular as his body. Derek would often complain, "One guy can't 'ave everything! If his cock is longer than two inches, there's no bloody God!" Divinity notwithstanding, Reg had a throbbing eight-inch penis that stayed up all night.

Fortunately, Reg wasn't obsessed with his looks — in fact, he was delighted when, during an argument over a new lyric, a hard right from Derek broke his perfect nose. Or maybe he was just thrilled that the uppercut he shot back knocked Derek on his ass. Did I mention they were best friends?

Derek likes to remind me that he and I connected first. I had graduated from Northwestern, a copywriter who struggled each night to create The Great American Novel. I lived in a tiny flat off Davis Street which, in the '80s, was still a deal. Derek was my part-time neighbor, since he was banging the girl next door. They fucked loudly, and I knew how he came before I knew who he was.

Finishing Chapter Nine would often take a back seat to enjoying the porn soundtrack that wafted through my walls: "Christ, love! Grab me cock! Yeah! Suck it!" Her squeals of ecstasy made me crazy with wonder. What the hell was he *doing* to her?

As they fucked, my hands spent less time on the keyboard than on my aroused body. As her moans grew louder my hands traveled, caressing each spot I'd want a lover to kiss, nibble or suck. I was completely swept into their erotic current.

I would softly stroke my outer lips, feeling the slippery, hot wetness ooze from within. My clit would emerge, hard and hungry, eager to be teased by my thumb. I used my fingers to mimic his cock, letting her moans orchestrate exactly when and how deeply to penetrate. As I probed deeper, I would thrash about, breathing in short, moist bursts. When I came, I'd try not to scream. I had lost my virginity to the vanilla boys, but none of them had fucked me with the fervor and relish of this nocturnal fantasy.

Arriving home late one night, I was drawn to the most hypnotic, soulful guitar I had ever heard. When I reached the third floor, a disheveled lump in worn black leather sat in front of my neighbor's door playing a Gibson, surrounded by shards of broken glass. Blood trickled from a gash over his eyebrow, but he seemed neither to notice nor care.

"You're cut!" I stammered.

"She chucked the mirror at me," he replied calmly. "Got any tea?"

Twenty minutes later, a bandaged Derek was sipping chamomile ("Bloody piss!") and we were engrossed in the first of endless discussions about life and love. Things were finished next door and I was the only one upset about it. He had merely lost a place to crash. I was losing an incredible source of interactive entertainment, years before the invention of CD-ROMs.

I didn't let Derek know about the wall-to-wall intimacy we had shared. Truth was, I couldn't believe this intelligent, complex and sensitive man was the Fuckmonster from Apartment 3. That night he slept on my couch, but never ventured into my bed. Instinct told us we were destined to be friends. That alone was pretty damned precious.

Derek slyly played matchmaker when he invited me to see their four-piece band at an underground club in New Town. I was blown away. Too pure for punk, too much mettle for metal, after six years of sweating blood, they were on the verge of greatness. Derek's lyrics were cut-glass poetry, and Reg ripped them out as if emerging from a frosty mountain stream into a wildflower-covered mine field. One look at Reg and I fell instantly in lust, unaware the combustion would later forge the love of my life. Afterwards, the three of us walked to the lake, sat on the rocks, and talked and laughed as if we'd known each other for years. Derek was clearly pleased.

It began in the back seat of Reg's beat-up '73 'vette, Derek at the wheel. As we rattled north on Lake Shore Drive, going far too fast, Reg's hand moved to my bare thigh and caressed the flesh between my skirt and stockings. Our first kiss was a swim in a soothing pool that seemed to go on for days. My hand was on his crotch (Did he put it there? Did I grab it?) and the size of his hard-on made me gasp. Reg loved to kiss as much as I did, and he augmented tender touches with quick, unexpected bites to my neck. The heat was overpowering. I couldn't let him go, yet I wasn't prepared to make love in the back seat of a moving vehicle, my new pal in the driver's seat. I didn't do such things. Or did I? Before I could decide, Derek called out, "Look 'ere, Reg, don't be a bastard to this one or I'll kick your ass. She's awright. She's got a brain — and killer tits!"

Derek dropped us off at their apartment, and left to meet his flavor-of-the-moment. Once inside, we quickly shed our disheveled clothing. We faced each other — so closely his breath tickled my skin — but didn't touch. We swayed, my nipples caressing his smooth, hard chest, his arms running down my back, his hands squeezing my ripe ass. We couldn't stop touching each other, exploring new and enticing terrain. He fed me his fingers, ten tiny cocks, connected by an equal number of minuscule cunts. Every nerve ending became sexual. We fell onto the bed and kissed and kissed as his cock throbbed against the outer lips of my pulsating cunt.

He adored my breasts with sweet kisses and soft sucking, squeezing each nipple between his forefinger and thumb. His tongue moved like a hummingbird's wing, down to my belly. Slowly spreading my legs, he lightly tickled my inner thighs as his lips explored my cunt. I rocked. I gasped. I may have died, traveled to Venus, or recited Yeats in a Celtic tongue. He brought me to the brink, again and again, knowing just when to stop and when to begin. The feeling was like running naked from a sauna into a fresh snow bank. My senses exploded in orgasm.

I was starving for his cock. Veins throbbed from every angle, crying to be licked and sucked. I swallowed the shaft and ran my tongue around his undulating balls. He threw his head back and yowled. I wanted to ride him to climax, but there was no stopping either one of us. As he called out my name, he came deep into my throat. Spent, we held each other. Heartbeat to heartbeat, he traced my face with his finger and said, "Derek was right. You are special."

I asked, too casually, "Does he always get you women?"

"Don't insult yourself. Or me," he said sharply.

"Let's rest." I said. "I want you inside of me. Maybe later."

"What do you mean, later?" He rolled on top of me, and we rocked in a dozen combinations until well past dawn.

Three years passed. Reg and I were in love. We all shared a place, although Derek — who chewed up and spat out women like sticks of gum — rarely slept at home. A record label had shown interest in some of the band's demos. I sold some fiction. It looked like we'd soon be able to afford to stock the fridge without stealing food from wherever they were playing. Things couldn't have been better, but Derek was suddenly behaving cold towards us in the club and distant whenever he actually came home. Repeated attempts to talk were met with stony silence. We tried logic, humor and threats to break through. Nothing. Finally, frustrated, Reg called him an unfeeling asshole. Derek shoved him, hard. Reg hit the table with such force, dishes smashed to the floor. Unhurt but stunned, he pushed Derek back toward the wall.

I'd seen them yell and roughhouse like schoolboys when arguing about their music, but never with this level of fury. I pulled them apart and Derek stormed down the hall, shouting, "Piss off, both of you. It's over."

When I got to his room, he was throwing clothes into his backpack.

"Derek, what the hell is going on? This is insane."

"Leave me alone."

"Goddammit! Why are you lashing out at us? We love you."

"Bullshit."

"What's 'bullshit'? You're my best friend."

"Not anymore. Don't want your friendship." Cut and dried.

That stung. We were *comrades* who'd been through everything together, good and bad. We'd painted each other's rooms, nursed each other's needs, ripped apart and praised each other's work. Hurt and furious, I snapped, "What have I ever done to deserve such fucking coldness from you?"

He spun around, silencing me with a piercing stare. "I'm in love with you."

I lost all composure. "We . . . can . . . work it out. . . . "

"No, we can't." He spoke quietly, without apology. "I'm in love with 'im, too."

Absolute silence. My mind was spinning through a montage of memories we three had shared. There'd always been women on the periphery — women who Derek happily pushed away before they got too close. Still, I never would have guessed this. When I tried to speak, he cut me off.

"I didn't plan it, but that's how I feel. You're the only people I care about in the fucking world. And you've got each other. And I'm thrilled for you. But it kills me. So, I'm going." He was crying. Fearless Derek. I put my arms tightly around him and felt my own tears fall.

"Why didn't you tell us?"

"Are you insane? 'Oh, by the way, I know I've always been straight, but I fuck boys now, as well as girls, pretending they're you.' He'd never understand."

From the doorway, Reg broke the silence. "I understand."

Reg entered. Together we clumsily held each other. I wept like an idiot, afraid I'd come between their friendship, afraid ours was over. Slowly, silently, the energy shifted. Derek tenderly ran his hands through my hair, again and again. Reg kissed me, and licked the salt from my cheek. I closed my eyes and felt a new pair of lips brush mine: Derek's. Reg squeezed my shoulder, urging me to continue. I kissed my dearest friend. He was urgent, a bit rough but soothing — like raw velvet. His stubbled cheek gave me goosebumps. I felt lightheaded, as simultaneously Reg ran his tongue along my neck and behind my ear.

Together they undressed me, then removed their own clothes without any physical contact. For now, I was the conduit for their sexual energy. Nothing was said, unusual for the three of us. Not that things were silent. We'd touched upon a new language.

I cupped my hands and squeezed my full breasts together. Each man chose a nipple to explore. Now Derek was the gentle one. The hot, moist kisses from his soft lips offered a thrilling contrast to Reg's more insistent sucking. The dual sensation was so intense, my knees buckled. They slid their arms through mine, to keep me upright. Suddenly, we were face-to-face-to-face.

No one moved. No one dared breathe. Our eyes mirrored a mixture of excitement, tenderness, and sheer panic. Reg, who had never touched a man sexually, looked shaky. Derek was clearly fascinated, but didn't make a move. I took the lead, playfully gliding my lips to Reg, to Derek, to Reg and back again, each kiss subtly maneuvering their faces closer together. Then I stepped back. Reg gasped, not quite silently. Derek had never looked more vulnerable. Hands glued to their sides, they tentatively brushed their mouths across each other, a precarious nuzzle that longed to become a kiss. At last, their lips relaxed into a yielding embrace. It was a bit awkward, but genuine. Neither quite knew where or if to touch. Arms stirred, then froze. It was sweet. It was hot. And it grew hotter. Much hotter.

I had never been turned on by gay porn, but this was the most erotic dance I'd ever seen. They clutched at each other, simultaneously reaching for me. Transfixed, I felt two hearty erections nudge my thighs. Wild with emotion, I dropped to the floor and went for their cocks.

Derek's was smaller, but magnificently thick and uncut. Reg's shot straight out, swollen and glorious. I squeezed the torrid, turgid flesh, sucking one throbbing head, then both. The taste was sweet, then salty; scent of soap and sweat. Delicious. Above me, I watched them bite and kiss, listened to them moan.

I was soon on the bed with Derek's tongue at my clit. Reg looked on, methodically stroking himself. I purred in ecstasy, remembering the Fuckmonster from Apartment 3. I tried not to explode, but the way Reg watched us — along with Derek's singular skill — set me off. Reg kissed me as *he* wildly came. There were more tears, now of joy.

Derek hadn't climaxed. He was ecstatic, but I felt we had to go to the next level. Reg knew my thoughts and looked nervous — but hard. I got on my knees and rubbed my ass against my lover's crotch. From behind, Reg plunged slowly into my cunt. Derek slid beneath me, took his wondrous tongue and touched my clit. Licked and fucked. A bolt of electricity shot through me. Why had no one told me such sensations were possible?

As much as I didn't want Derek to move, I nudged him toward the hungry cock ravaging my pussy. Reg froze for an instant, then realized there was nothing to fear. Each time he pulled back, Derek sucked and nipped every emerging inch of hot flesh. Reg loved it. Derek's cocksucking skills were so dexterous, I was overcome with voyeuristic desire. I thrust my pelvis forward and, before Reg knew it, my cunt was replaced by his best friend's eager, talented mouth.

What a sight! Derek teased Reg as he had teased me, teaching me a thing or two about fellatio in the process. Inch by glorious throbbing inch Reg's cock disappeared into Derek's insatiable mouth. Reg was in another world, panting Derek's name and mine as his pelvis thrust deeper and deeper down his partner's throat. Derek's own cock was rock-hard by now.

I could no longer merely watch the boys at play. I pulled back Derek's foreskin and tried my damnedest to mimic what he was doing to Reg. Through the lust and sweat, Derek looked at me with a tenderness I had never seen in his face before, all the while sending my darling Adam Reginald into another stratosphere. Reg fiercely came, followed a millisecond later by a writhing Derek who, after swallowing Reg's come, rubbed his exploding cock across my body. Both men, competitors in everything, raced up and down my flesh, seeing who could lick the most come off my belly and breasts.

After that, it's difficult to recall exactly who did what to whom. At one point, I tried to get Reg to suck Derek. I remember being massaged by four hands and two cocks. Some time past sunrise, someone cried, "I love you."

Who said it? Who were they talking to? Who knows?

We all said it. We all meant it.

## Shar Rednour

❦

# June's High Holy Day

June says that she has always relied on her imagination to make her gifts special — and let me tell you, what I get on my birthday is nothing like that homemade vase her mom got last Christmas.

Of course I had fantasies before meeting June, but as with so many people, they stayed in my head. Then came June, who thinks that Willy Wonka is real; she won't let me throw her stuffed animals on the floor for fear of hurting their feelings; and she values storybooks more than diamonds.

Sometimes the fantasies simply involve a special pair of eyeglasses or maybe a certain place or certain words, but many times our fantasies involve other people — characters — some with leading roles, others with only cameos — and, of course, a smattering of extras. The extras seem to be the ones who really make the fantasy — and sometimes they're the hardest to find.

I started seeing June almost eight years ago. It wasn't love at first sight but rather love at first *kiss* which came right after staring at each other for fifteen minutes or so. On one of our first dates — after fucking for ages, then eating in bed and drinking wine and all that — I was lying on my back on June's bed listening to Sade when June had one of her bursts of high energy and ran into her closet. She emerged wearing only her dad's Schlitz muscle shirt and a pair of gogo boots. She danced over my face before sitting on it for a few minutes, then disappeared into her closet again, this time reappearing in a *Cat on a Hot Tin Roof*-style slip and vintage high heels. She made me cream: one outfit and persona after another. We laugh about it now, but at the time I couldn't believe how fucking incredible she was and she couldn't believe it was turning me on so much.

None of her other lovers ever got it. Ever got June. Or Jeannie, Elizabeth, Sophia or Endora. Those are just the ones with names — there's also Slave, Bitch, Mommy, and Kitten. Lucky me — I've gotten them all and more. Since June's sexuality is inextricably intertwined with being an object of desire, my turn-on was her turn-on. After all, what's a show without an appreciative audience?

Other lovers had just laughed; they didn't get the boner she'd expected. So when I was thrilled, it was one more way we saw soulmates in each other. Sharing our fantasies and making up new ones became an intricate part of our sex life. What we can't act out we turn into stories. Begging her to "tell me a story" and jacking off as she filled my ears with what my dirty mind had only dared to dance with became my favorite position. She'd dress up as Ginger Grant seducing the professor on "Gilligan's Island," or become the big-breasted wife in a Russ Meyer flick — and she has the closet to do all this.

On date number four we listed all the sex make-believe we wanted to live out. Have we calmed down over the years? Well, we've been sick, unemployed, crazy, depressed, and bogged down with family dramas — so, no, we haven't gone to bed with nasty stories every night. But let's just say the surprises never stop.

For example, she just now sauntered in wearing only a red bra and a tiny, tiny apron.

"Honey, I'm writing." I don't sound very convincing. She's

trying to distract me by *faux* dusting my desk with a feather duster attached to a butt-plug that sits snug in her ass. Help me.

"I am so sorry I didn't get your room clean while you were out!" She wiggles her saucy ass, flips her wild, black hair to look over her shoulder.

"The other maids and I were having such a good time." She's pulling her breasts out of the miniscule bra and pinching her nipples. "Am I bothering you?"

"Sweetie, you know I gotta finish this story," *Fuck,* she's so hot. The anal thing always throws me over the edge.

She has her ass on the desk and is wiggling again. Mommy.

She turns around and her lips are two inches away, "Oh, big business man are you? You didn't put out the 'do not disturb' sign." She blinks big as if *innocennnnnnnnnxxxxx@@@######*

I'm back. Oh shit, I think I got lube on the computer keys. Where were we? Oh, yes, the fantasies. I could go on . . . . But first you need to know about June's High Holy Day — her birthday.

June believes in celebrating birthdays. She celebrates the person, the mom for giving birth, and the dad on his anniversary of a joyous day. For at least a month she celebrates in big and small ways. Her favorite saying is, "Get what you want" and she truly believes that we can all have almost any fantasy come true. Since knowing June, fairy tale birthdays have come to life — both mine and hers. Eight years of real life that's better than a fantasy; make-believe made no-big-deal in our cynical world. Adults forget how to play.

We're lying in bed. Today was her day off, but I worked like a dog. We are feeling sexual but I am not in much of an initiating mood. She taps her finger on my chest. "What do *you* want?" she asks.

"Tell me a story," I say. And she begins:

*You've been told that there's a new gift waiting for you in the
west wing. The tails of your velvet coat swing behind your
tight thighs and ass. The soles of your fine leather riding
boots strike the glimmering polished marble floor assuredly.
You push open the doors and there she is. Long, dark, curly
hair falling around her face, the sheer tunic the servants
dressed her in revealing her curves, her dark nipples. There's a
gold shackle around her ankle that keeps her on the jewel
inlaid solid gold four-poster bed, along with the chains
around her wrists. She lies on piles of silk. The servants have
followed your commands to the letter. She has been bathed in
flower waters, massaged with oil of olives, stroked in every
crevice and cranny. It may be awful that she has been captured and she may always prefer freedom but you know that
she will be treated better here than anywhere in her peasant
world. The servants have fed her berries of delirium, put
smoke to her lips and prodded her pussy, sucked at her
nipples, male and female putting their genitals to her mouth.
To initiate her. As you circle the bed you see the blue and
purple marks on her wrists from fighting. The oils have
soaked through her tunic so that it clings to her, a second
skin.*
*'Wake up, my sweet,' you say.*
*Her eyes digest you. And you, in your princely cockiness, know
that she wants to hate you but you don't look like the monster
she's heard about. Your skin is smooth and hairless over your
hard jaw, your shirt and jacket are open enough to reveal a
chest of smooth muscles and she looks to your crotch but there
your shirt tail hides whatever she is looking for.*
*Her black eyes tighten on you and you swear that she is going
to spit on you, you've seen that look before. Instead she says,
'Bring your cock to my mouth, you do have one? Bring it to
me . . . . Master.' She licks her lips. Oh, if only you were that*

*stupid! You slap her hard across the face then circle back
away from the bed and say, 'Oh, you will choke on all of me
but first let me treat you, yes, to some of the sweet honey our
land produces.' Slaves hold jars of honey above her twisting
legs and drizzle it over her thighs and into the hair of her
cunt.
Two guards, each with a huge black monster dog, appear.
'Have the dogs clean her,' you say. And she screams.
The two well-trained canines jump onto the bed and thrust
their noses between her legs. . . .
How can I explain the orgasm? I explode.*

I know I should be finishing this story but a girl's gotta have
some fun too. June and I are playing hooky. We've called in
sick to work. Please don't tell anyone in San Francisco this —
we'd be embarrassed if they knew we don't go strolling
through the Castro — but we pretend we are tourists and go
down to Ghirardelli Square at Fisherman's Wharf. We hold
hands, moon over each other, blocking out the tourists' stares.
We share shrimp cocktails, little bottles of wine, and a loaf of
bread while sitting on the edge of a pier. We walk, talk, browse
the street artists' wares and make out in doorways.

We leave barely in time to beat rush hour. People are just
beginning the push out of doorways into streets, into people. I
grab June's hand and we jump on a 68 bus which heads down
the length of the Embarcadero. We slip into the last available
seats. Soon people are hovering over us and every space is
taken.

Her hand lies casually in my lap and she does that absent-
mindedly-fingering-your-clothes thing. When she discovers
the hole in the crotch of my pants she says "Honey, you never
did patch these jeans."

"I tried. I gotta get a better patch."

Her middle finger slips through the hole and past my BVDs to my clit.

"Now, now," I admonish, putting my hand on her wrist.

She pushes her hand down and whispers into my ear, "*You are gonna make a scene and we don't want that, do we? Right now it just looks like my hand is resting in my girlfriend's lap —* no one is counting how many fingers are present."

I relax my hold on her wrist and feel her relax her hand again. "Good," she says, then raises her voice for the benefit of any eavesdroppers. "Oh, honey, look at that," pointing to nothing outside the window.

I smile and say, "Wow."

Delicately, just barely, she strokes down the hood of my clit, over and over. The tenderness of just the tip of her finger is such a tease. I grip the bar in front of me as if I were on a rollercoaster that is getting ready to take off. June leans over me, acting like she's looking out the window. Under her breath, into my ear she begins:

*It's the street fair and we are snaking through the crowded streets. I have on a mini-dress and no panties. You have shaven my cunt bald and my pussy lips bulge hard with blood. I am so turned on that I almost come with each step. You tell me that you have a plan and that I will get relief soon. I moan; I am thinking that you are going to finally touch me and not just tease with your hand on my ass. You push me into a stinky booth full of barrels of empty beer cans and an old ice cream cart. I sit on the cart and pull you in between my legs so you'll kiss me. You do. You stroke my thighs and pull at my ass. We're moaning and kissing and grabbing at each other. Suddenly you flip me around and bend me over the ice cream cart. 'You want to be fucked?' you ask me. 'Huh, you need some dick up your cunt?'*

*I gasp, 'Oh yes! Please, please fuck me.' My pussy is so
swollen I think I'm going to die.*
*You hold my elbows and push your pelvis into me. 'You need
some dick, huh?'*

My knuckles are turning white from gripping the bar. "I
don't know how much longer I can do this," I say.

June laughs and says, "Just laugh through it because you're
not getting out of it." She laughs, once again pointing to something out the window.

"I mean it," I say.

"So do I," she says, and moves her action on my clit up a
level, hitting my favorite rhythm.

She continues the story:

*'You need some dick, huh?' you ask.*
*'Yea, Baby, please I really need your dick,' I answer.*
*'Did I say anything about mine?' you say and I gasp, startled.*
*I start to turn my head and you grab me by the back of my
neck and push my head down. 'Don't turn around, Bitch, did
I say you could turn around?' Then I hear you say in a low
voice, 'Pull on up to the bumper, boys, she is wet and ready.
Don't touch my bitch though, you just get to sink your dick
into her.'*
*'No!' I scream.*
*'Shut up, Bitch.'*
*And then sliding up to my pussy is slippery, latex-covered
warmth. 'It's warm and soft, Daddy,' I say, 'not like your cold
rod.'*
*You tell the guy, 'Slam into her.' And he does. His big dick
splits my lips right open and he is scratching the itch I've had
so bad and even though I want a hard fucking I am afraid to
fuck him back for fear of angering you. I know I should just
hold still.*

*'Fuck her harder,' you growl, and he does. He fucks and fucks
and I scream and scream. You watch my asshole as his dick
goes in and out of my pussy. You see my asshole puckering,
begging for your cock . . . .*

"Oh, shit," I moan, interrupting June. I am going to come any
second. I release the bar in front of me to punch the wall of the
bus, then grab it again, "Fuck," I say, under my breath.

"Laugh," June says in a sing-song voice, her finger never
stopping.

The orgasm grips my cunt and clenches all my muscles, "Ha
ha, that's quite a knee slapper," I scream through gritted teeth,
as I come, trapped on an overflowing bus. "Oh, boy, June, what
a jokester!"

You know how your pussy just twitches and twitches with
aftercome? That's what mine is doing right now.

"What are you doing, June?"

She has plopped into my lap and is scrolling down, reading
what I have written so far.

*You've been told that there's a new gift waiting for you in the
west wing. The tails of your velvet coat swing behind your
tight thighs and ass.*

"These are all the times I told you dirty stories," she says,
squinting at the computer. "And this one too?"

*I am going to come any second. I release the bar in front of
me to punch the wall of the bus . . . .*

"Bobbi — that just happened!" she exclaims. "Are you telling
everything?"

"Honey, I'm trying to be realistic." I did wonder how far she was going to let me get, you know, broadcasting our sex life to anybody out there.

"And look," she points. *'Shut up, Bitch.'* It's just all these stories where I'm running a foul mouth and getting you off. At least tell some of the ones where we actually have sex and it's not just me talking dirty."

"Sugarplum," I say, scrolling up to very first paragraph, "what does this say?"

*What I get on my birthday is nothing like that homemade vase her mom received last Christmas.*

*'What I get on my birthday,'* see? I'm just leading up to it."

"Oh," she sighs, probably a little disappointed that she doesn't get to remind me of more of our stories. "Okay. Just checking on you. 'The Nanny' will be on in thirty minutes, the clock in here is wrong so look at the one on your computer." She kisses me, then gets up from my lap.

"I'm going to work. Tell Fran I said hi." She waves over her shoulder and is gone.

You need to know that I am mostly a top, but June knows that I can be a bottom if it's in the service of her pussy. Also know that she likes to confuse her participants, so that just when you think one thing is going to happen, some other twist or tease will surface.

So, it was eight years ago, my birthday. We had been together nine months but weren't living together yet. I awoke to a knock on my door. A young butch in a thrift-store tuxedo and a punky young femme in a flouncy mini-skirt and tap shoes greeted me with their version of "Happy Birthday." The femme threw herself into my arms and planted a big kiss on my mouth. As I stood there dumbfounded with purple lipstick all over my face, the butch slapped an envelope into my hand. Then they were gone. I tore open the envelope and read, *"Be clean, shaven, fed, packing your dick and feeling good by 5 p.m. You'll be fetched. PS: You'll have a mind-blowing time but you must trust me and most importantly trust that I know you.*

This trust was a big deal. I'm really not inclined to put myself in vulnerable positions; in fact I've only done so with June, and only in our most intimate moments. I tried to calm my worries by telling myself that she probably just had a bevy of babes for me to fuck.

I had lunch with my sister and spent the rest of the day getting ready. My emotions were all over the place. I felt nervous excitement at such a fancy date, annoyance that I hadn't seen her all day, horny anticipation solely from not having her in my arms for 48 hours, and trepidation — that whole birthday responsibility thing, thinking she is doing so much and what if I hate it? I don't want to do something I don't enjoy and have to pretend to be happy — I mean it is *my* birthday.

A friend picked me up, smiled, said, "don't worry," and drove us to an obscure Victorian in the hills overlooking the Castro. Once inside, I was left alone until June appeared from a dark corner wearing a robe.

"I love you." She kissed me. I pulled her hard into me and kissed her back, anticipation shoving me into her throat. I wanted to remind her who was boss. I grabbed her ass and slammed her into my pelvis.

Her fingernails went into my neck. "Yoowww! Time to slow down, Big Boy." She kissed me once more, sweetly, but pulled away before I could get crazy again. "Listen to me, I love you. You trust me?"

"I'm not good with surprises."

"This will be one of the most amazing nights of your life but you have to give me total control and know I will use it wisely. It's that or nothing. But don't just say it, you really have to trust me. So?" She pressed into me. Her smell made me swoon.

I took a deep breath. "Okay, you have total control." I pulled her to me tight again. "But remember, I'm trusting you."

"Last thing: nothing will happen tonight that I won't know about. Nothing will happen that isn't okay with me."

"What are you talking about — *I* don't know anything; I hope *you* know what's going on."

She shook her head, which meant I didn't understand. "Kiss me now, you won't be seeing June for awhile."

"What?" My heart fell; I wanted to spend my fucking birthday with her!

She pecked my lips. "Trust me. I said, you won't be seeing *June* for awhile."

I contemplated that clarification as June left me. Minutes passed and then a strong, English-accented voice bounced through the hallway. "Oh, another scummy slave." My friend Jeanie emerged from the shadows.

"Jeanie. What are you doing?"

"It's Salinka the slavemaster to you, you piece of slime. You types think you can just charm your way out of everything. Well, now you're really stuck. Follow me peacefully, or I'll bring in the heavies." She slapped a two-foot long leather paddle in her hands then turned back toward the darkness. Her auburn hair missiled out into short pigtails held by studded leather cock rings; they looked anything but childish. She wore a shiny new leather gladiator skirt and chest harness; thrown over them was a ratty army jacket left hanging open. She came across as some sci-fi post-war sadistic prison warden. I watched her high, round ass as I followed her. Soon I was stripped of everything but my dildo and harness and put into leather shorts and a spiked collar. I begged to keep my boots and Salinka allowed me to wear them.

"Hold out your wrists."

"No, Jeanie, come on, you're not supposed to do that, are you?"

She smiled sweetly, bent down to whisper in my ear as I sat on the floor. "Probably not, it's just for fun, come on, now, don't ruin the surprise." She winked.

I decided to stop worrying and go along for the ride. I held out my wrists.

Jeanie — that is, Salinka — clasped big, real shackles around my wrists. "Hey, Jeanie, these are pretty serious, I —" *Smack.* She hit me hard across the face.

"That was for calling me 'Jeanie,' you filthy worm." *Smack.*

"That was for being such a pathetic asshole that you thought you could talk your way out of the Queen's lair." Her accent had returned and I forgot who Jeanie was. I raged at this slave master for hitting me so boldly when I had done nothing to deserve her wrath.

"Don't ever question me. Get down." She kicked me between the shoulder blades, knocking me down to my elbows with my ass in the air.

"I know you don't like this, but you better take it on your ass or I'll break the teeth out of your handsome little mouth." She paddled me. I wouldn't give her the satisfaction of even a moan.

"I'm getting bored down here. Aren't we supposed to be doing something?" She hit harder.

"You're a smartass, aren't ya?" She kicked me in the shoulder, knocking me sideways, then pulled me by my hair to her pussy. "You want to be a good boy? If you're good then you can have a taste of Salinka. What the Queen doesn't know won't hurt her."

I was ready to go from pain to lust; just seeing her tits shake as she smacked me was driving me wild. I heard June's voice in my head: *"Nothing will happen that isn't okay with me."*

"Oh, please Mistress Salinka. I learned my lesson." I licked my lips.

She laughed. "Oh, don't grovel, my pet. Come here to Salinka's pussy." She shoved my face into her cunt. I wiggled my nose and tongue through her wiry, black hair until I felt the softness of her inner lips with my tongue. I nibbled, bit and licked like a little puppy. Salinka's firm grip on my head never faltered. I let her guide my mouth to the right position so she could fuck my face until she bucked and came in my mouth.

She pushed me back on my haunches. "Let's get you to the Queen before that bitch sends the hounds after me." Clink. She snapped a leash onto the collar.

I crawled on my hands and knees up a flight of stairs, around a winding, dark hallway to a large oak door. Sounds of laughter drifted into the hallway. Salinka kept me still, waiting. She bent down and sneered, "Why don't ya stick ya nose down there at the crack and see if ya can sniff her out, slave. Can ya sniff out the Queen?"

She pushed my head to the floor where a sliver of light, smells and sounds teased me. I *could* smell her and I could hear her full, hard laugh. I wanted to float like a magic carpet under the door and plant myself beneath the Queen's precious feet.

"Sniff, I said!" Salinka's harsh voice shattered my daydream. I scowled at her. She pushed my head down again, holding it there. "Sniff like the dog you are." I sniffed a little; when she relaxed her grip I jerked back and spat at her feet.

"You piece of shit!" *Smack*. It only half hit because I rolled out of her reach. She was grabbing at me when the door opened.

Suddenly I was staring at boots polished so high that I could see my reflection in them. I looked up into the face of a butch in a very upscale guard's uniform. She returned my stare with disdain. "Keep your eyes on the floor."

"Salinka," the Queen's voice echoed into the hallway. A pause ensued and I could feel everyone in the room getting nervous — finally, someone besides me. "Are you having problems controlling the slaves again?"

"No, your Highness. I, no, I . . . "

"Salinka, leave your slave with the guard and approach my throne." Her every word sent shivers down my spine.

"Your Highness, I, yes, your Highness." I heard Salinka's well-worn boots shuffling away from me.

"If this slave's face smells of you she'll be mounting you like one of my Dobermans. Guard, bring in the slave."

"No, ma'am, it's disgusting and filthy, don't, I'm sorry, I'm truly sorry."

The guard dragged me onto a red carpet

"Angelina," the Queen's voice changed to a purr, "sweetheart, put your face very near — but don't touch, my dear, because it *is* truly a filthy creature — put your face very near to this thing and tell me what you smell."

Angelina's name fit — a truly angelic face came into my vision. She had buttery toffee for skin, wore her curls naturally like a halo around her face, and her eyes were the color of a chocolate river. She put her cheek just an inch from mine and sniffed — just as I had at the door. Her seemingly innocent eyes narrrowed as she inhaled Salinka's scent. She curled an eyebrow at me, then moved out of my vision again.

"Your Majesty, she doesn't smell clean. She smells of dank places, a place I cannot name but which has been on my own fingers."

"Angelina cannot tell a lie, Salinka. Unfortunate for you." I appreciated her rhythm of speech: solidly delivered words punctuated by pauses to work our nerves and make us weak. I clung to the sound of her voice, for I still had not been able to see my Queen. "So," pause, "guard, pick up," pause, "this, this *thing*." Pause. "Let me see its face."

They dragged me and dumped me at her feet. I recognized the sleek, muscular lines and the perfectly painted toenails which commanded a pair of red patent leather high heels from behind red fishnet stockings. My first thought was to look up at June, the Queen, but a natural instinct took over and I found myself leaning forward to kiss her feet.

"Outrage!" *Thwack*. She hit the side of my head with a riding crop. "Not only did you violate my property, Salinka, but you didn't even succeed in training it! You pathetic excuse of a slavemaster. You master nothing but your own asshole and now I will master even that."

"No, your Highness." Salinka's voice wasn't a grovel or a plea but a statement. I remembered this was a game and wondered if June was about to cross some line.

"Look at me, creature."

I was immediately brought back to my role.

I let my eyes follow the trail of her crossed legs past the top of her thigh-high stockings, past the meeting of her delicate dark thighs. I noticed that she wore an elaborate gown split open to her crotch, piles of red fabric on each side like curtains that could be shut at any time. This led to a tight bodice, bulging cleavage, the throat that begged of sucking, and my Queen's face, framed by ringlets of hair falling down from a sparkling crown. I looked into her deep, hazel eyes only for a second.

"My Queen." I quickly bowed my head.

"Wrong! Do not address me. Ever. It is *I* who is examining *you*. Lift your head like a good sow."

I did as I was told, indignant that I didn't even seem worthy of worshipping her. That pissed me off. She poked my head side to side.

"It seems to have good bones and teeth. Let's see what else. Lean up on your haunches."

*Yes, this is more like it,* I thought. I leaned back to reveal my specially chosen cock, knowing she couldn't resist it.

"Hung like the court donkey," she said. This witticism brought peals of laughter and I suddenly remembered the voices I'd heard earlier. Quickly I looked around and saw that the room hosted ten or more others, all aristocratically dressed in gowns and tuxedos from various eras.

"Angelina, pull it out, my dear."

The girl gasped but did unbutton my shorts until my pride tilted out like a lowering drawbridge.

"Guards, bring Salinka. Everyone, let's have some entertainment, shall we?"

"Hear, hear!" Fans quickened, cigars puffed, and nails clicked.

"Guards, undo the shackles from the creature's wrists. You know the rest."

Just as my excitement for freedom rose it quickly crashed. The guards released only one of my wrists, then forced Salinka to stand with her back to me. They shackled her right wrist to my right wrist. I knew what they wanted. I grabbed her other wrist before she could wrestle it away.

"Fuck her, donkey. Fuck the filthy Salinka who likes to spoil my goods."

The crowd clapped and shouted with anticipation.

The Queen looked me square in the eye. "You can fuck her right up the ass, donkey, right up the ass."

"Bitch." Salinka's voice brought the applause to a halt.

The Queen slowly rose from her throne, leaned into Salinka's face and spat.

"Test me . . . my Queen," Salinka said slowly, and fought no more.

The Queen returned to her throne and flounced her skirts in the court's dead silence. Then she tilted her head back, smiling evilly. "Guards, prep the meat," she commanded and fell into laughter.

The guards stood on each side of us. One donned a latex glove and poured streams of lube into the deep crack of Salinka's fine ass. One guard pushed a hand into the crevice and worked in the lube. Salinka couldn't help but push back and grind her hips around. I just watched, my inner boner growing as my outer dick bobbed against her flesh, waiting for entry. The other guard rolled a condom onto my dick and shined it up with lube.

"Do it, donkey," the Queen said teasingly. The court chanted, "Do it, donkey, do it."

I teased her hole until she pushed back into me. The head of my dick glistened between her cheeks. *What a big dick for an ass, I hope she can take it*, I thought, as I sank the head into her darkness. "Oh baby," I muttered.

"Oh, yeah, I can take it, donkey, don't hold back. Oh yeah," she moaned, and pushed back into me. My dick slid until my belly pressed against her ass cheeks. I grabbed her wrists and used them like reins as I banged into her harder and harder.

The Queen squealed and yelled, "Look at Salinka's titties bounce as she gets plowed — plowed by a donkey!" and more peals of laughter arose from the court. I faintly registered their heat rising and their clothes dropping as the sounds of sex mixed in with their laughter.

"Bounce those titties, donkey, bounce those titties and plow that ass." I looked over Salinka's straining back into the Queen's face. From the height of her throne she could see everything. She smiled wickedly at me, then tossed her head to the side shouting more orders. "Angelina! My feet. Lick my feet, you precious slut."

Angelina threw herself at the Queen's feet and took up her task. The Queen's face soon softened so I knew the girl's mouth was working hard. I just kept fucking and Salinka kept fucking me back, moaning and egging me on. I grabbed her shoulder and growled into her ear, "Come like it's your pussy. You like me fucking your ass? Fucking your ass like it's your pussy? I bet you can come with my donkey dick up your ass, come like it's your pussy, slave . . . master."

The Queen looked drugged. She took little gasps of breath and watched us through heavy-lidded eyes. Angelina's head bobbed frantically.

"Oh, yeah, that's it, slave, that's it."

"Come like it's your pussy, come for me," I reached around, pinching her nipple with my free hand. She shoved her fingers in between her legs and jerked, coming on my dick. The Queen came too, screaming and writhing in her throne. I groaned from the pressure pounding back into my clit. Five seconds more and I could have come but Salinka pulled away from me and, forgetting the shackles, brought us both tumbling to the floor.

We lay panting; I was totally frustrated. I had a moment to look around and see people in all stages of sex: lapping, fucking, kissing, teasing, coming.

My head lolled to the side. The red-dressed feet stood there.

"Guards, unshackle them and have the maidens bathe the *thing*." I looked up in time to see only her retreating skirts. The guards dragged me from the lust-filled den and shoved me into a candlelit room with a hot tub. Angelina and another ethereal treat welcomed me. Angelina smiled sweetly and motioned me toward the bath.

"How blessed you are to be bathed in the palace. Here, let us help you. This is Dainty." Dainty's raven hair was piled softly on her head, her alabaster skin pale even against the white lace shifts they both wore. They undressed me, guided me into the hot tub, and soaped my back and chest. Then they sank down into the bath with me; their dresses melted into the wetness like clouds. They dropped gentle kisses like flower petals onto my neck, back and chest as their fingers reached under the water, soothing my thighs. Their softness lulled me into an altered state. Finally Dainty kissed me firmly on the mouth. Then Angelina, then Dainty. I turned my head side to side taking in tongues, lips and sweetness of girl. My edge returned, and I faced the two maidens. I grabbed them each by a nipple and took turns biting and kissing them.

"I think I am clean enough, girls, don't you?" I finally said.

Angelina led the way back to the carnal ballroom and Dainty followed. Both of them were now nude and covered in oil. I returned to my leather and had a clean cock again in my shorts.

Sounds of spanking and laughter rang out from the room. I knew the drill this time: When the door opened I kept my eyes to the floor. My clit and heart ached in frustration. I wanted to get close to my Queen the easiest way possible. I was willing to play by the rules . . . for now.

"Approach the throne."

I walked, without looking up, to her feet, where I knelt.

The court shuffled into silence. I wondered where their gowns were now.

The Queen stroked my face with her long, soft fingers. I pushed my cheek into her hand — her touch felt so good, so familiar and comforting. I hadn't realized how much I'd missed it.

She tilted my face up to meet hers and said softly, "You clean up nice." She raised her voice for the benefit of the court. "You have the opportunity to become my personal slave. My *personal* slave. All you have to do is lick my pussy adequately. But if you fail, your head will roll. You have a choice. You can be a slave of the court and keep your head or you can take a chance and possibly be mine. But remember, if you do not satisfy me then off with your head." She did one of her perfectly calculated pauses. "Notice, no others are beside me. No others passed the test."

The entire court stood frozen.

"They couldn't *give* head so they *lost* heads!" She laughed wickedly at her bad joke and the court laughed uneasily with her. How had I missed seeing this wickedness in June?

"Test me . . . my Queen," I said, and a hush followed.

"Your eyes may rise, slave," she said. "Everyone, fuck." She clapped her hands together. "I want to see fucking, now." They did as they were told.

She leaned back into her throne, pushing her hips to the edge of her plush seat. Her mouth curled into a sideways smile as she parted the curtains of her gown so I could see what was mine.

"Approach the throne," she said again, her voice now low and husky.

I crawled forward, reached out a hand to each of her thighs. My senses reported in slow motion. Warmth, softness straining through the sharp lines of the fishnet, then solid as I wrapped my arms around her legs. I pulled her pussy to my face. She gasped. I openly sniffed her moist hair and smelled her come, her sweat. I moved excruciatingly slowly, separating her soft, silky curls with my nose and letting my breath tease her clit. She moaned and writhed slightly. My tongue came down on her clit hood so slowly that I could feel the warmth of her on my tongue before I even touched her. She groaned as my tongue landed. I did full, rough doggy laps up the length of her cunt. She gasped and sank into me further. I tightened my grip on her and let my tongue do the rest. I dipped into her hole to taste the juices that had flowed during her foot-licking.

I pushed my nose into her like a puppy's. I teased and nibbled, tickled her lips with my tongue, and sucked at her clit. When I knew the teasing could settle into a beat, I sank my teeth into the base of her clit and throbbed my tongue with her rhythm. She groaned and writhed, ran her fingers through my hair, guided my head with her hands.

"Oh, God. My slave, my slave . . . " she bucked wildly into my face over and over, pulling my hair, pounding my face, screaming as she pulsed with wave after wave of orgasm.

I was resting with my face against her thighs when she grabbed my face between both hands and pulled me to her. We kissed ferociously and then she jumped on me and we fell to the floor. The Queen freed herself of duty and the whole place became an orgy. I finally got to fuck June until I came — my cock pounding into my clit, her body full in my arms, her screams ripping my ears as sure as her nails on my back.

There's the door; done just in time. I went to answer it.

"Hey, Jeanie, come in, I was just finishing a story. Listen, I couldn't wait to tell you: I reserved a little hut-like cabin on the beach and the curve of the beach at this place even resembles a lagoon! It looks exactly like Gilligan's Island. I already have Gilligan, the Skipper, Mr. and Mrs. Howell. I thought you would be just perfect as Mary Ann . . . if you're interested." I smiled mischeviously.

June's birthday is next month, and she's always had this *thing* about Ginger and the Professor.

Victoria Smith

❦

# First Call

The only rule was that she had to do whatever he said.

Startled from sleep by the ringing phone, she listened to his seductive voice whispering in her ear. "You're my little slut, aren't you?"

She loved to tell him no. It was a game she enjoyed playing, seeing how high she could get him. He loved it as much as she did, as long as she let him win. She never forgot that part, the part about who was really in charge. Whatever he asked her to do, she did — and she did it just for him.

She stretched, fighting off the morning, knowing she could not refuse him.

"Wake up and talk to me, sweetheart. I need to hear your voice. Are you feeling like a bad girl today?"

"No, I'm a good girl . . . a very good girl."

Instinctively, she caressed her bare breasts, rolling her nipples between her fingers. She squirmed as they began to harden.

In that luxurious place between sleeping and waking, she let herself be seduced by his words. It was like floating on a cloud. Lisa loved the sound of his voice, the things he said, the way he whispered in her ear until she ached for him. Her fingers began a downward journey, seeking the moisture between her thighs. As she slid a hand through her silken hair and across her clit, she sighed and spoke his name.

"Mmmm, Carl . . . "

"You sound good, baby. Tell me what you're doing."

She massaged her clit in tiny circles, ignoring his words, lost in the sound of his breathing. If she was very quiet, she could hear him stroking his cock, slow and steady. She closed her eyes and pictured his hand, moving up and down, spreading the wetness along his shaft. She imagined him standing over her, watching her, stroking his cock right above her face. She slipped two fingers into her warm, wet cunt, then brought them to her mouth and sucked them, knowing he heard every little sound.

In his sweetest, most reassuring voice, he said, "I really want you to tell me what you're doing, Lisa. I think — perhaps — you're being naughty. You *are* a bad girl, aren't you?"

He spoke to her like she was a small child, and she sounded childlike when she answered.

"No, Carl, I'm a good girl. You're the one who's naughty. You *make* me act this way for you. Please don't make me tell you what I'm doing."

His voice was sweet. "Are you a masturbator?"

"No." It came out as a whimper.

"I'm masturbating for you, Lisa. You know I am. Please tell me . . . "

"I can't . . . " She was already so far out there that she could barely form the words.

"Say it, Lisa. Tell me what you're doing."

Heart pounding, breathing like a child who'd been crying for a long time, she tried, her voice a broken whisper.

"I'm masturbating, Carl."

"Louder, I can't hear you."

"No, Carl, stop . . . I don't like this game." Lisa took a deep, ragged breath, rubbing herself furiously. She liked to make him wait. She was right on the edge, and ready to fall. Lisa tried very hard to be quiet, but her noises were animal-like.

Carl knew and loved the sounds she made when she came, and his cock grew harder in his hand. He heard Lisa groan as she lifted her hips to meet her searching fingers.

"You're a bad, nasty girl, Lisa. I know exactly what you're doing. I can see you and feel you and smell your fingers. Tell me . . . I want to hear you say it again."

"I'm masturbating, Carl, just for you." Barely breathing the words, she panted into the phone as her body began to shake.

"I want to hear you come, Lisa. I need to hear you. Please tell me what you're doing. I'm on my knees in front of a mirror, stroking my cock for you. If anyone found out, they'd think I was very nasty. You like it when I'm nasty, don't you?" He said it not as a question, but as a plea.

She had him right where she wanted him now.

"I'm not sure if I like it or not, Carl. Nice girls don't talk to nasty men on the phone."

"You like it, Lisa. Don't lie to me. Say it louder. Tell me you're a masturbator."

Trembling, she rode an orgasmic wave. She didn't want to talk, she wanted to listen to him tell her that she was his. She closed her eyes tightly and moaned.

"I'd do anything for you, Carl, anything to get you this high. I'm a very bad girl. I like talking to men I don't know and making them come."

"You're a nasty, naughty girl, aren't you?"

No answer.

"Say it!"

"Yes, Carl, I'm *your* nasty little girl — and I like the way it feels. You like it when I'm a little slut for you, don't you?"

His turn to not answer.

Inside her head she counted, making him wait, as she listened to the incredible sounds he was making.

Carl took a deep breath and started questioning her again.

"You want lots of men to watch you masturbate, don't you? You want them to watch you touch yourself and lick pussy juice off your fingers. You're addicted to this, Lisa. You need it. You need to be listened to and watched. Tell me you're addicted."

"I'm addicted, Carl. I'm addicted to the sound of your voice, to hearing you stroke yourself for me, to knowing you think of me all day long. I like knowing that I can get you off like this, it excites the hell out of me. Is that what you want to hear?"

She was getting closer and closer, getting lost inside herself. But he kept pulling her back, making her wait, making her pleasure last.

"I want you to come for me again, Lisa. I want to hear how wet your pussy is. Let me hear you."

"No, I can't. Not now . . . just talk to me. Tell me what you want me to do."

Lisa knew that Carl watched himself in the mirror, his swollen cock all red and purple in his hand, knew he wanted to come. She could hear it in his voice, he sounded so helpless. They took turns being in control, pushing and pulling each other right to the edge of passion, then stopping abruptly, changing the tone, trading places.

"Are you masturbating for me, Carl?"

"Yes, just for you. Tell me you are, too. Tell me you're touching yourself."

His words came out in one long, forced breath, and she imagined his hand pausing on his throbbing cock while he waited for her answer.

"I love to touch myself for you, Carl. I love the way it makes me feel. I want to lie here all day and feel like this. I want men to watch me, and I want you to watch them watch. I'll do anything you ask. What do you want me to do?"

She was so high now that she could barely stand it.

"Would you like to spank me, Carl? Listen . . . "

*Smack!* She slapped her own thigh, and rolled onto her side. Again, *Slap! Smack!* Hard, across her bottom.

"Did you hear that? Does it get you hot? It makes me very, very wet."

"You *are* a bad girl, Lisa, and I'm going to have to spank you. I'm going to put you across my lap, and then I'm going to spank your little ass for talking dirty on the phone. I know you talk to other men. I know how much you like to tease them, to make them stroke their cocks for you."

She heard the crack of his hand against his own skin.

"You like to make men come for you, don't you? Tell me you tease them." *Smack!* went his hand again, as another orgasm reached out and grabbed her.

"Again, Carl, harder . . . I want it."

"Tell me you're a masturbator."

"I'm a masturbator, Carl. I do it just for you."

"No, you're lying."

His tone was teasing now, his voice hypnotizing. She was completely under his spell.

"Not just for me, Lisa. You do it for lots of guys. I like knowing you fuck other men on the phone."

Her thighs were slick with her juices. She pressed them tightly together and bit her bottom lip. His words poured into her ear, smooth as honey.

"Listen very carefully, Lisa, I'm only going to tell you once. I want to see how many guys you can talk to today, and then I want you to tell me about it. All the details. I like to hear about what you do. Will you be a nasty girl for me today and see how many men you can fuck on the phone? At least ten . . . and I want you to masturbate with a woman, too.

"When we get off the phone, I want you to go online and go into a room and tell everyone what you just did. Tell them you masturbated for me, and tell them you want a lot of men to fuck you and make you come."

"Can I tell them you told me to?" She said it in her sweetest little girl voice. The idea was making her very hot.

"Yes."

"Can I go to a room full of guys and let them all fuck me right there? I want to do it in front of everyone, lots of them watching and stroking themselves. And they can do whatever they want to me."

His breathing had changed again — she had him back on the edge. She was his little whore, and she knew how to get him off.

She moved the phone away from her ear, and held it right above her parted pussy lips. Slowly, she slid her vibrator in and out, raising her hips to meet the thrusts. The sounds were incredible, squishy slurpy slippery sexy wet fucking sounds. As another wave washed over her, she moved it faster and faster, knowing Carl heard her moans in the background.

She knew the power of those sounds. This was the part she liked the very best, a man listening to her sweet wet cunt. Every man she had ever talked to had been totally blown away by it, begging for more. And it never failed to send her somewhere she had never been before, pure feeling and raw nerves mixed into a drug she could never get enough of.

She could picture Carl stroking himself harder, faster, furiously matching her rhythm. Her orgasm rose up and out of her, and she collapsed onto the sweaty sheets, unable to speak or move.

She was his, and she knew the rules. Fuck at least ten guys — plus a woman — on the phone. That would be tough, even for her.

Breathing deeply, Lisa smiled. It was going to be a wonderful day.

Cecilia Tan

❧

# Always

Morgan was always the one who'd wanted a child. Even when I first met her, before we got involved, before we got engaged, always the talk of motherhood with her, of empowering Earth Mother stuff and of making widdle baby booties. I, on the other hand, had always said I would never have children, was sure somehow that I would never decide to bear a child, and yet I had always thought about it, secretly. So when I fell in love with Morgan, and she fell in love with me, and we had a hilltop wedding where we both wore white dresses and two out of our four parents looked on happily, I figured I was off the hook on the parenting issue.

This was, of course, before John, and way before Jillian. But I'm getting ahead of myself.

Back up to the summer of 1989. New England. Cape Cod. Morgan and I are in a hammock in the screened-in porch of her aunt's summer house. The night is turning smoothly damp after a muggy day, cars hiss by on pavement still wet from the afternoon's rainshower, the slight breeze rocks us just enough to make me feel weightless as I drowse. I am on my back with one foot hanging out each side of the hammock; Morgan rests in the wide space between my legs, her spill of brown curls spread on my stomach and her knees drawn up close to her chest. The hammock is the nice, cloth kind, with a wide wooden bar at either end to keep it from squeezing us like seeds in a lemon wedge, not the white rope type that leaves you looking like a bondage experiment gone wrong. Morgan's hands travel up my thighs like they come out of a dream. It never occurs to me to stop her. Sex with Morgan is as easy and natural as saying yes to a bite of chocolate from the proferred bar of a friend. Before her fingers even reach the elastic edge of my panties I am already shifting my hips, breathing deeper, thinking about the way her fingers will touch and tease me, how one slim finger will slide deep into me once I am wet, how good it feels to play with her hair on my belly, how much I want her. With Morgan, I always come.

Imagine afterwards, lying now side by side, holding each other and sharing each other's heat as the beach breeze turns chilly, when I decide to propose to her. I am gifted with a sudden and utter clarity — this is the right thing to do. It has been six years since I came out as bisexual, three years since I began dating women, but something like ten years of getting into relationships with men and constantly trying to disentangle myself from them. It's not that I don't like men. I like them, and love them, a-proverbial-lot. But I've never been able to explain why it is I feel the need to put up resistance, to define myself separately, to have my foot on the brake of our sex lives, with a man. I always do.

But here, with Morgan, the urge to resist is not even present. Maybe it has nothing to do with men versus women, I think, maybe it has everything to do with her. She's the right one. And she says yes.

So we got married, that part you knew. Marriage for us did not mean monogamy, of course — rather we defined it as "managed faithfulness." We had our boundaries, our limits, our promises — but outside dalliances were allowed. When you're happily married, though, who has time or energy for all the flirting and courting and negotiating with someone new? Neither of us did for several years. And that's when John came into the picture.

A raw spring day in Somerville, me in galoshes and a pair of my father's old painting pants with a snow shovel, cursing and trying to lift a cinderblock-sized (and -weighted) chunk of wet packed snow off the walkway of our three-decker. On the first floor lives our landlady, one frail but observant old Irishwoman, Mrs. Donnell; on the second a new tenant we haven't yet met, a single guy we hear walking around late at night and never see in the morning. Hence me trying to shovel the late-season fall, two April-Fool's feet of it, because I'm pretty sure no one else will. Morgan inside rushing to get ready for work, emerging soap-scented and loosely bundled to plant a kiss on my cheek as she steps over the last foot of unshoveled snow onto the sidewalk (cleared by a neighbor who loves to use his snow-blower). She's off to catch the bus to her job downtown as facilities coordinator at the Theater Arts Foundation. I heave on the remaining block of snow with a loud grunt. Perhaps it is my grunt that prevents me from hearing the noise my back must surely have made when it cracked, popped, "went out," as they say.

I am hunched over in pain, cursing louder now and not caring if Mrs. Donnell hears it, when another person is there, asking if I'm all right. His hands are on my shoulders and he slowly straightens me upright. It is the new tenant, wearing an unzipped parka and peering into my face with worry. I tell him I'll be all right; he says are you sure? I say yes but I'm clearly not sure — it goes back and forth the way those things will until it ends up somehow with me in his apartment drinking some kind of herbal tea and then lying face down on his formica counter with my shirt on the floor while his thumbs and palms map out the terrain of my back.

In the theater world a backrub is a euphemism for sex ("Hey, come upstairs, I'll give you a backrub." "Oh, those two, they've been rubbing each other's backs for years.") So you'd think I'd know. But no, there's obviously no way that he could have planned my trying to lift too much snow. No, it was an honest case of one thing leading to another. Maybe a couple of resistance-free years with Morgan had dulled my old repeller-reflexes, and we . . . well, to be specific, after his hands did their magic with my spine, they strayed down to my ribs, and he planted a line of warm kisses down my back. He had longer than average guy hair, straight and tickly like a tassel as it touched my skin. I moaned to encourage him, my body knowing what I wanted before my mind had a chance to change the plan.

Morgan always says I plan too much.

My father's oversized pants slid to the floor and kisses fell like snowflakes onto the curve of my buttocks, feather light, and then a moist tongue probed along the center where it went from hard spine to softness. We got civilized after that, and went to the bedroom. It wasn't until we were lying back having one of those post-coital really-get-to-know-you talks that Morgan knocked on the door. No bus, saw your galoshes on the second floor landing, she explained at her seeming clairvoyance, to which I replied, "This is John."

John always says "How do you do?" and bows while he shakes two-handed when he's formally introduced.

Our first threesome happened right away, that night after dinner fetched on foot from the corner Chinese restaurant. On our living room floor, the white waxy boxes and drink cups scattered at the edges like spectators, the elegant curve of our bay windows standing witness to his hand between my legs, Morgan's mouth on his nipple, my lips on Morgan's ear, John's penis sheathed between us, my chest against his back while he buried himself in her, her tongue on my clit, his nose in my neck, my fingers in her hair, our voices saying whatever they always say, mmm, and ahh, and yes. I didn't know if this was going to be one of Morgan's experiments in excitement, or one of my few dalliances, or one of John's fantasies come true. What it was, which I didn't expect, was the beginning of something more solid, more intricate, and more satisfying than any twosome I had known.

John always buys two dozen roses on Valentine's Day, which he gives to Morgan and me one rose at a time.

Maybe a year later, when Morgan became director at TAF, the three of us talked with Mrs. Donnell about buying the building. The idea hit us at Christmas dinner, at Morgan's parents' house in Illinois, her mother on one side of her, me on the other, John on my other side, and all manner of relatives near and far spread down the two long tables from the dining room into the ranch house living room, in folding chairs brought along in minivans and hatchbacks. Turkey so moist the gravy wasn't needed, and gravy so rich that we used it anyway. Wild rice and nut stuffing heaped high on John's plate, shored up by mashed potatoes, his vegetarian principles only mildly compromised by the addition of imitation bacon bits on green salad. Family chatter and laughter, Morgan's father sometimes directing men's talk at John. Somehow the discussion turned to Mrs. Donnell and her plans to sell the house, and somehow our three hands linked in my lap, under the table, and John announced to everyone, suddenly, that the three of us would buy the house together, voicing the thought that was at that moment in all three of our heads, even though until then we'd never contemplated the idea.

I always clean the toilets and the sinks but I hate cleaning the shower and bathtub. John, who has a slight paranoia about foot fungi, loves to do the shower and tub. If only we could convince Morgan to do the kitchen floors.

If my life seems like a series of sudden revelations, that's because it is. The most recent one was watching Jillian walk her stiff-legged toddler's walk from one side of our living room to the other. I knew then what Morgan looked like as a child, what her exploratory spirit and her bright smile must have been like when she was knee-high.

The night we made Jillian we had a plan. We didn't always sleep together, or even have three-way sex together, but we knew all three of us had to have a hand in her creation. For months we had charted Morgan's period, her temperature. We cleared a room to be a new bedroom and put a futon on the floor, lit the candles and incense (we're so old-fashioned that way) and made ready. Imagine Morgan, her long brown curls foaming over her shoulders, her back against the pillowed wall, her knees bent, framing her seemingly round Earth Mother belly, watching us. John kneels in front of me, naked and somber-faced. I will not let him stay that way for long.

I begin it with a kiss. I kiss Morgan on the lips and then John and we pull away from her. I take his tongue deep into my mouth, my hands roaming over his head and neck, and he responds with a moan. My hard nipples brush against his; my hands on his shoulders, I continue to kiss and wag my breasts from side to side, our nipples brushing again and again. Then I am licking them, my teeth nipping, my hands sliding down to his hips, one hand between his legs, lifting his balls. He gasps and throws his head back. My mouth is now hovering over his penis, hardening in my hand. I reach out my tongue to tease.

Instinct begins to overtake the plan, his hands are reaching for me, he pushes me back, his mouth on mine, his tongue on my nipples, his fingers seeking out my hottest wettest places and finding them. He knows my body well, he slides two fingers in while his thumb rests on my clit.

Morgan watches, her belly taut, her hands clenched in the sheets.

He is slicking his hand wet with my juices up and down his penis, and then he climbs over me, my legs lock behind his back, and he settles in. Tonight there are no barriers between us. I let go with my legs and let him pump freely. If I let him I know he will grant me my secret wish, to make me come from the fucking, from the friction and rhythm and pressure and slap and grind. I am sinking down into a deep well of pleasure, his sweat dripping onto me, as he becomes harder, hotter, faster, tighter, his jaw clenched, and I become looser, and further away. The turning point comes, though, with a ripple in my pelvis, and then every thrust is suddenly bringing me closer to the surface, up and up again, drawing me in tighter, closer, until my wish comes true. I break the surface screaming and crying, and calling out his name, and thinking how good it is to have learned not to resist this.

His eyes flicker in the candlelight as he strokes my hair and jerks out of me — the plan is not forgotten after all. His penis stands out proud and red and wet and the strain of holding back is evident in his bit lip. Morgan's nostrils flare and she slides low on her pillows. I go to her, my fingers seeking out her cunt, my mouth smothering hers, our tongues slipping in and out as I confirm what we already know. She is ready.

I put myself behind her, my hands cupping her breasts, my legs on either side of her, as John lies down between her legs. My fingers sneak down to spread her wider, to circle her clit and pinch her where she likes it, while he thrusts slickly, my teeth in her neck, her hair in our faces, the three of us humping like one animal, all of us ready.

Morgan always comes twice.

There's nothing like a grandchild to bring parents around. So Jillian has six grandparents and none of them mind enough to complain about it. We always have them here for Christmas now, we've got the most bedrooms and the most chairs. Jillian will always be my daughter. John always shovels the snow. And Morgan always says we could make Jillian a sibling — that it could be my turn if I want. I don't know. I just know that I love them always.

# Carol Queen

❦

# Being Met

We've had so many adventures together. It started out as an adventure. I was not looking for you, nor you for me: we were only looking for a story to tell later, a hot night, excitement. Now we tell it over and over again, the story of how we met. Mostly we tell it to each other, because I am your best audience and you are mine.

It was a party, a very particular sort of party, an erotic gathering for wild searching people. I had helped to plan it, hoping for an adventure, hoping that by bringing people together with plenty of latex we might strike a blow against the terrible fear of sex that pervaded so many hearts, the legacy of AIDS. I had only just met you; I'd invited you along.

In a part of town rarely visited after dark we met like a secret society of initiates to faded but still potent mysteries. A San Francisco night, the kind we have here on the edge of the land, with fog swirling between the buildings, shrouding then revealing a waxing moon. There you were, arriving just before me, pulling up before the warehouse whose address I'd given you.

The door of your little car swung open. Your foot hit the pavement squarely, your booted foot, black leathered ankle wound around by a silver chain. It mesmerized me. That was where it started, this wanting you. The silver chain on your black boot signaled me in a language I wasn't sure I knew. The left boot. It meant — perhaps — that you played with mastery, that you would know what to do with this desire that I was not sure how to show you.

We went into the dark building; inside it was light and warm and convivial, like a clubhouse. We worked together to set up the party. You charmed me, taught me a dirty limerick, helped me strew condoms around, looked up my skirt when I climbed a ladder to change a lightbulb; you flirted. How could I tell you what I wanted? Finally you took my hand and led me upstairs.

You smelled like family, from the minute I got close enough to you to touch. I wanted to reach for you, though I'd come to the party only wanting to explore, to be with other people who thought sex was important. But the minute you took my hand I started making plans — that's so dangerous, making plans! — lists of things I wanted you to do, ways I wanted to see you, things I wanted you to know about me, what I wanted to know about you. Where you came from. Why now, why here, when I had lived in this sexy city half my life, why were you here smelling like someone I'd known forever? So I kissed you, just to taste you — taste who you were — and since that second I have never for a minute stopped wanting you. When we are wrapped up in each other now, curled together under a quilt, feeling like we have never been apart, when we take each others' faces in our hands and come together in a kiss, I always feel an echo of that first one, the kiss I knew I'd willingly change my life for. That first kiss from you, with my common-sensical self still shouting, "But you don't even know this man!" I didn't care. I wanted you consumingly, wanted your hands on me, the want coming from a pool of desire so rarely accessed, and so precious, that trying to hold it back would have made me feel dead. You kissed me like you wanted to eat me in tiny, savory bites, you kissed me like we could start to learn each others' life stories there.

I shook as much from fear as from the electricity of that kiss. I was so afraid that I had tumbled off a cliff. That I wanted too much of you. I was asking one kiss to carry so much, and I scarcely knew you, and already my heart was ready to break for losing you. It was crazy, I didn't even have you yet.

I get lost in kisses. I still get lost in yours.

You found us a place to sit, finally, after that kiss that seemed to last an eon. You put me in your lap, do you remember? And pulled long black latex gloves out of your pocket.

"Show me how you like to be touched."

No man had ever said that to me before. No other man has said it since. You asked me to show you and it told me that my pleasure was important to you. I showed you how I like it, how to run your fingers into me and moisten them, to slide the middle finger down over my clit and into my cunt a little, over and over, each neighboring finger on either side of my labia, pressing it all together, fucking me a little deeper each time

When your mouth was not on mine it was next to my ear, whispering. You still talk to me that way when you're making me come. Your words make me as hot as your hands do.

"Give it up to me, little one, little honey, that's right, give it up, come for me, come in my hand . . . "

I had not been looking for you, but I was so deeply ready for you. Your silver chain, the way you spoke to me. The way your kiss made the floor under my feet turn to quicksilver. I wanted your collar the way a straight woman wants a ring. But mostly I wanted you.

For hours we sat and told each other where we came from, the stories of who we were — though it felt to me that we already knew. You held my foot in your lap, stroking it. I remember what we wore, what we ate for dinner when we finally went out. You dripped Thai peanut sauce onto rice while you looked into my eyes and I nearly came. For weeks after that, every minute I was on the edge of a broken heart: "What if this ever ends, what if this ever ends?" That's the salt, falling in love, the salt in the wound. "What if I tell him I love him, what if I chase him away?"

We are both so complicated. I grew up thinking men were another species. I never thought I could learn men's bodies, so I just learned how to fuck. I always loved women, but besides the love, women seemed easier. I trusted my prowess. You were the first man I ever told I was scared. And your sexuality has so many layers. For weeks we didn't even fuck. We explored with our hands and our mouths; we invented games and personas. We told each other our fantasies, our deep arousals.

My pussy is easy. But my fright and heat and shame when you touched my asshole made me tremble. I have been masturbating that way, anally, in secret, since the crazy heat of puberty. But I'm tense and tight and another man tried to fuck me there once and hurt me

Now I know you won't hurt me, so I can divert the fear into fantasy. Sometimes that's what I do. I make up stories, I give my fear a context. Sometimes I pretend I'm you, a boy on my belly waiting to take it up the ass. Sometimes I pretend you've kidnapped me. Or that I'm a gay man in a bathhouse. Other times I'm only myself, and you are yourself, the only man I've ever trusted so much. Showing you that trust, that's what the collar means to me. It proves to me you want me enough to make it into a ritual. It tells me you're going to be focused on me. So many of my past lovers were nervous about my intensity, felt afraid of me. I never feel that from you. I feel like you want my intensity all to yourself, enough to give me the signal, "We are going to be each other's whole world until the collar comes off."

When you say, "You're mine," I get wet. My cunt starts humming and thinking for me.

I know how alone you were, thinking no one else wanted sex as much as you did. I used to masturbate and cry after my lover went to sleep. I used to wander around the house looking for things to fuck myself with. I felt alone, convinced I would never find someone who would want me as much as I wanted them — but it wasn't only *them*: it was the sex, the touching, the smells, getting high on each other. When you tell me how much you want me, that I'm yours entirely, I want to cry — from happiness, now, and because of how sad I used to be, convinced I'd never be *met*.

When you hold me down and fuck me, when you tie me down and pretend I'm your captive, you're proving that you want me and you're willing to show me. When we lie tangled together, holding each other fiercely, eyes locked, murmuring words to each other, your cock thrusting in and in and in, our hips pumping together, I pray the whole rest of the world will learn how to feel this way.

We're floating then. We're in the secret world we found that first night, even though we were surrounded by people.

We're brother and sister, veins running with the same blood. You're my good little boy, touching mommy so sweetly, making me feel so wonderful and loved. You're the best little boy in the world, honey, don't be scared, touch me again right there, oh, darlin', I'll teach you everything. It's how you give your vulnerability to me. Feeling like a frightened little boy. It's the way you fantasize being taken, seduced, letting me be the powerful one. Such a big man, turning into a trembling child in my arms . . . you are so open then, it makes me want to do sweet, forbidden things to you. Riding through the land of dreams with you, where we can be anything for each other, where we have a hundred ways to love each other, a thousand.

Where I have a companion even in the things I thought had to stay secret. Where who you really are is my lover. Through every adventure.

Susan St. Aubin

❦

# The Man Who Didn't Dream

Evelyn the dreamer married a man who didn't dream. Every morning she'd tell Hal her dreams as though she were giving him the harvest of her night. She always had at least one, usually more: dreams of tigers, of sailing through the air, of falling — a circus of images.

"Flying tigers?" he'd laugh. "Isn't that an airline?"

"Well, what do you dream, that makes so much sense?"

"I don't dream," he'd say. "Not since I was a kid."

"What did you dream then?"

"I don't remember."

Sometimes when her dreams woke her, she'd lean on one elbow and watch him in the dim light that showed through the slats in the blinds. She knew he didn't dream as he lay there, gray as a statue, because he never moved and scarcely seemed to breathe. She was active at night: In the morning she often found herself in a ball at the foot of the bed, or on her back when she clearly remembered falling asleep curled up on her stomach. Hal kept the same position all night — on his back, nose in the air, lips unmoving, snoring his half snore that was like the whistle of an interrupted sneeze.

One summer night she watched as he lay unconscious in heat that would have kept any normal person awake. When she touched him, his skin was cool and smooth as marble. She ran her hand across his chest and down his right arm.

She wondered if she could give him a dream. She put her mouth on his shoulder, so much cooler than his daytime flesh that she felt like she was seducing another man. She ran her hand down his side, following it with her tongue. Harold, as he called his penis, lay flat while he slept, as unstirred as the rest of him, dreamless until Hal awoke and willed him to rise and take the form Evelyn called The Herald. Hal was different from other men she'd known, whose cocks had dream lives of their own, pressing her hips and ribs while their owners slept.

Her tongue moved closer, licked Harold, moved away. She took him in her mouth and massaged his cool tip with her tongue; then he stirred, growing and hardening into The Herald. When Hal's mouth twitched at the corners, she let The Herald slide out and watched him loll against Hal's thigh, pulsing as he diminished into Harold.

The next morning when she asked Hal what he dreamed, he said, "You're the dreamer."

"Maybe you don't remember," she prompted. "Maybe you're hiding your dreams from yourself."

"No. I don't have dreams." He wrinkled his forehead. "I don't know if I want to. I don't miss them."

"I saw you smile in your sleep last night," she offered. "I thought you might have been dreaming."

"Could have been a muscle spasm." He frowned. "Maybe I had a headache in my sleep."

"The Herald rose up," she said.

His eyebrows lifted. "Men have erections in their sleep, but I don't think it's part of a dream."

"But there must have been some dream to arouse you," she insisted.

He shook his head. "Not necessarily. It's just a reaction. I don't remember anything. I'd like to remember that kind of dream, but I don't think there was one."

Evelyn began waking every morning at two, as though there was an alarm in her brain that forced her out of her own dreams to watch Hal lie dreamless, a blank slate on which she could create a picture.

A picture of what? What would he dream if she could get inside him? Would he dream about a lover? What would he want? She searched for props. At a garage sale she bought a riding crop — a short wooden stick sprouting worn leather strips from one end. She slapped her wrist with it as she walked down the street. What did people do with whips during sex? Threaten each other before? Spank each other after? Everything she imagined seemed like bad theater.

One night Evelyn knelt beside Hal with her hands on his scalp, her eyes closed, and invented a lover for him, someone who looked like a perfect version of herself, with dark hair cut in a curve along her cheek and tanned honey skin. This ideal self knelt beside him and took over the stroking of his hair, then let her fingers inch down his side, shifting him gently until he was on his stomach. With her palms she kneaded his shoulders like mounds of dough, then moved down to his ass, which she rocked back and forth with caresses. An ideal woman like this just might have a whip hidden at the back of her closet to bring out at the right moment.

He moaned, then mumbled, and seemed to be awakening. When he rolled over, his eyes were open and The Herald brushed her legs. "Hal?" She shook his shoulder; perhaps if she woke him right away, he'd remember a dream. "Hal, wake up, you're talking in your sleep, what are you dreaming?"

With one arm he pushed himself up, then shook his head. "No," he said, "I don't remember any dream. Something woke me, some noise — sounded like a crash somewhere. Something fell, didn't you hear it?"

"No," said Evelyn. "Nothing fell."

"You must have been asleep then."

"Are you sure you didn't dream it?" she asked. What about the woman rubbing your back, she wanted to say. Don't you remember her?

"I heard it," he said.

If she didn't hear a crash, he must have dreamed it. That was a start.

The next night she woke in the light of a nearly full moon. She thought she could throw something to recreate his dream crash, make love to him, and then tell him the next morning it never happened, he must have been dreaming. But what if he couldn't get back to sleep? He'd know he wasn't dreaming, unless she could convince him that not sleeping was also a dream.

She pulled off the covers to inspect his body, under her power, every inch but that brain, the unknowable part of him that refused to dream. She pressed her lips to his jugular vein and gave a light suck, then licked her way down his throat — the Adam's apple, the hollow, then across the chest. She was a mother cat cleaning a kitten, a growling purr low in her throat. She licked him to his toes, which were less clean than the rest of him, salty and slightly musty, like miniature cocks.

When his toes were clean, she paused for breath, then took poor limp Harold in her mouth, sucking and licking him until he was hard, like a Popsicle that would never melt. She willed Hal to dream; she tried to make her brain join with his. Dream this, dream it, she thought, but she couldn't find an opening into his mind. She sucked that Popsicle until The Herald quivered between her lips, becoming warm salt in her mouth. She saw Hal's eyelids flicker and open. Was he awake? No, the lids shut again and his quick breathing slowed. What would he remember?

Since the next day was Saturday, she could watch him all morning before she had to leave for the restaurant where she worked as a *sous chef.* He ground beans and made coffee — she thought the beans smelled rancid, but he didn't say a word. He didn't seem to notice she was watching him. He read the paper and ate an English muffin.

"I dreamed I was licking a yellow banana-flavored Popsicle," she said, "but no matter how much I licked it and sucked it, it didn't go away. I could devour it without eating it, and have it, and still suck it some more."

"That's a cook's dream," he answered. "Food as art, not nourishment. I've always hated bananas, though." He got up to make himself another cup of coffee, scratched one leg with his foot, and yawned. "God, I feel drained this morning."

He went into his study, where toasters with wings floated beside pieces of toast across the screen of his computer. When he sat down he stared at them, shaking his head. "I can't seem to get started," he mumbled.

"It's because you don't dream," she told him. "Maybe you don't really sleep if you don't dream."

"You think I'm abnormal, don't you? You're trying to make a big deal about my not dreaming."

She stood behind him, rubbing his shoulders. "No, everyone dreams. Some people don't remember, that's all."

"Oh, bullshit. You're saying two different things — first you say I don't dream, then you say everyone dreams. Which is it?"

She shrugged, dropping her hands to her sides, and stepped back. "Nobody knows," she said. "There's different theories.

Maybe you don't dream and maybe you don't remember."

"So, what difference does it make?" The toasters and toast were gone from his screen now; lists of words in squares filled it.

"None," she said, but he was no longer listening. She saw a book called *The Psychology of Dreams* under some papers on his desk. She left him, closing the door of his study.

Saturday night she came home late from the restaurant, slid out of her shoes at the front door, and crept into the bedroom, where he was already stretched out like fallen marble. She slipped off her clothes and lay down beside him, then reached under the thin blanket that covered him and ran a hand down the cool flesh of his leg. He didn't stir, but his lips moved.

She felt he must be dreaming. "What do you see?" she whispered.

"Mmmm," he answered, licking his lips.

"Tomorrow you won't remember," she said, stern as a teacher, "so I want you to tell me now."

"Mmmmm," he said.

She sensed he was very nearly awake, so she waited until he began to breathe through his nose in a light, steady whistle. She stroked his arm; he didn't stir. She crept her hand down his side and across his relaxed belly to Harold, whom she teased with her fingertips and draped across her wrist like a fat bracelet until he grew so hard she couldn't bend him anymore. When Hal sighed and stirred, she withdrew her hand again, watching her playmate The Herald soften and retract. This wasn't going to work if arousal woke him. But would he be conscious enough to know he was awake? He didn't wake up last night, but then he was so completely unaware, he didn't even think he'd dreamed. She wondered if a person had to be almost awake in order to dream.

She leaned over him, her mouth open, and licked Harold's tip.

It felt cold, so she blew on him, sucking him into the warmth of her mouth, where he warmed and hardened. Hal's breathing quickened but he didn't move. She slipped her mouth off The Herald and sat back on her heels. Hal's eyelids flicked open.

"This is a dream," she stated.

He stared beyond her.

"A dream," she repeated.

His eyes closed. "You're mine," she whispered.

She took The Herald in her mouth again, sliding him back and forth with her tongue while gently touching his balls with her fingertips. She felt heat rise from him. Again she withdrew and watched. Hal rolled to one side, moving his leg over the thick Herald, and murmured into his pillow. When she nudged his shoulder, he rolled onto his back again, The Herald on guard.

She sat up on her knees and straddled Hal, then lowered herself onto that alert Herald, still clean and glistening from her mouth. Hal opened his eyes and stared. She stared back, not blinking, holding her breath. He ran his tongue over his lips, closed his eyes, and sighed.

"Strawberries," he said.

Evelyn moved up and down, fitting The Herald into herself. She tried to remember when they'd last eaten strawberries. Strawberry shortcake last summer? A tart a couple of months ago? Strawberries weren't a great favorite of hers, nor of his, as far as she knew. They never ate bowls of strawberries and sugar, or strawberries on cereal or ice cream.

She was still until he went into a deeper sleep, when she began to move slowly. Leaning close to his face, she whispered, "Whipped cream. Whipped cream and strawberries."

His tongue flicked at the corners of his mouth.

"With powdered sugar," she said.

He rolled his head back and forth.

She balanced on her knees, touching nothing but The Herald, whom she massaged with her inner muscles. When Hal began to move, she stopped to be sure he was asleep. When he began chewing and smacking, she whispered, "Strawberries?"

He stopped moving his jaws, but didn't answer.

She moved again and he moved with her.

"Mmm," he said, "Mmmm."

He sighed and thrashed but she didn't want to stop; although she thought it might be dangerous to lose control and come herself, the man beneath her was irresistible.

She slowed down, contracting her muscles against The Herald to see how far she could arouse him while barely moving at all. Hal moved his hips faster, driving The Herald into her; he was like a runaway horse with Evelyn bouncing on top. His breathing became so harsh and fast she felt he must be awake, but she didn't care. They seemed to her to be together in another world, neither dream nor reality. She felt her cunt ripple as the pressure of pleasure spread from her cleft to her toes and fingertips.

She didn't want to ride any more, but The Herald wasn't finished with her yet. He churned beneath her, leaving her with no choice but to stay on as he ran. All the time Hal galloped he didn't say a word — his mouth was open, nostrils flared, eyes shut; he panted, and after awhile she began to pant, too. His eyebrows knit together. She wondered when his dream would end, or if it already had; she wondered if perhaps this was his dream or hers. Finally The Herald moved deeply inside her and shook with the effort of his proclamation.

Hal, as usual, was silent; only his quick, deep breathing gave him away. Sweat glistened on his forehead, where his damp hair clung to his skin. Evelyn collapsed on top of him, listening to the slowing thump of his heart. She was sure he must be awake because no one could have slept through that, but soon he began his soft snore. When she was certain he was asleep, Evelyn rolled off and lay on her side.

"Strawberries?" she asked again, but he was too far gone to react.

Sunday morning he said nothing. Harold lay limp on Hal's thigh; she stroked him and still he lay there.

"He's being a nerd today," Hal said, pulling away from her. "Give him a couple more hours of sleep." He rolled over on his side, his back to her.

"Did you dream last night?" Evelyn asked.

"No," he said.

"But I heard you talk in your sleep." She sat up.

He rolled over on his back again. "What'd I say?"

"'Strawberries,' which must at least be proof of a dream about strawberries."

Hal raised his eyebrows.

"You smacked your lips when you said it."

He shook his head. "I don't remember."

"Do you remember anything else?"

"Not anything that's a dream," he said. "I like strawberries. We don't eat them much because you don't like them, right? You're the cook, so you control what we eat." He laughed.

"We'll have them; I'll get recipes."

"We don't need recipes — I like them raw."

Her hands were in fists. "Rest up for tonight," she told him as she got out of bed. "I'll bet you remember some dreams."

He laughed again. "What are you trying to do, control my dreams, too? Bake them in a quiche?"

While Hal was in the bathroom, Evelyn rummaged in the back of the closet until she found the riding crop. She took the smooth wood in her right hand and slapped her left wrist with the leather, twice, hard, with a whooshing snap. He *will* dream, and remember, she promised as she stuck the crop under her side of the bed.

Late Sunday night she woke to find Hal on his back, breathing his whistle that was almost but not quite snoring. The Herald stood upright, a promising sign.

"Nocturnal beast," she whispered into The Herald's eye. "You will make him dream."

She reached under the bed, found the riding crop, and climbed on top of Hal, gliding The Herald inside her cunt, already wet at the thought of the ride to come.

The smooth wood of the whip fit her palm as though she'd been born with it in her hand; the strips of black leather drooped from its top. With a snap of her wrist, she flicked them against her pillow as she began to move up and down on the Herald. She tickled Hal's nose with the leather tips, which made it twitch. If he sneezed, he'd wake up. She moved up and down faster, clutching the riding crop, ready to convince him he was asleep and dreaming. Had he ever seen her with a whip before? No; therefore, he must be dreaming.

She rode him slowly, imagining her steed trotting into an ocean, over the waves, while she bounced on his back. He moved under her now in an independent motion that became so strong she was afraid he'd throw her. She steadied herself with her knees. His heart thumped beneath her, and his eyes were wide open, staring up at her. She brushed the leather fringes of the riding crop across his eyebrows, which made him blink.

"Sleep," she whispered. "You're asleep."

This time he answered, "No, I'm awake."

She raised her whip above his head. "See this? You can't possibly be awake because I don't own one of these. I don't even ride horses. But if you're awake, I'll use it until you sleep." She brushed the leather across his forehead, shaking the handle in his face like a threat.

He closed his eyes and sighed, continuing to bounce her along on his rotating pelvis.

She bent and whispered in his ear, "If you're good, I'll buy you some strawberries for dinner tomorrow."

He licked his lips. "Good."

When she lifted herself up on her knees, he rose with her. She tightened her legs around his flanks.

As they rode together, she whooshed her riding crop in the air over his head. He panted hard and rose until she was sure he'd throw her off the bed, and then with a groan he was still.

She had forgotten herself. Rider without a mount, she'd have to walk. She waited until she heard a faint snore, then stuck the handle of the riding crop into her cunt and walked her fingers down her belly into the swamp of her fur, wet with his jism and her juices.

Her fingers slid around her hard and swollen knob, the key to all the secrets at the center of her body. She pressed on it with one finger while with her free hand she moved the riding crop up and down, letting the leather softly slap her ass. At first she moved in time with Hal's slow breathing, and then faster, leaving him behind as she galloped across hills rippling with grass and lupine and poppies until she dropped, exhausted, into a soft field, where she pulled the whip out and flung it away before she slept.

In the morning he woke early, went into the bathroom, came out brushing his teeth, went back in. She lay with her head under the pillow, peeking at him. Monday was her day off.

He sat on the bed beside her. "Hey." He shook her shoulder. "Pretty good last night. I liked that."

"Liked what?" She lifted her head from under the pillow and stared into his eyes, making herself not blink because only a liar would break eye contact for even a second.

"What you did last night. Getting on top of me like that and waking me up."

"What are you talking about? I went to sleep as soon as I came home."

He smiled. "Come on. Where's your whip?"

She raised her eyebrows. "What whip?" Where had she thrown it? Far under the bed, she hoped. "Are you talking about some *dream*?" Now she was up on her knees. The whip was out of sight.

He shook his head. "I don't think so. It was very real."

"Well, what do you think dreams feel like? Mine are real."

"No, they're not. You fly, you see monsters. That's not real."

"But it always *feels* real, that's what matters."

"Well, this *was* real. Sex is real."

"Sex? Tell me more."

"You were there," he said. "What do I have to tell you?"

"Well, what about this whip? Have you ever seen me with a whip before?"

"No, but just because I've never seen it doesn't mean you don't have one."

"So how long was this whip? Six feet? Did I slash it around like a big black snake?"

He stared at her. "Well, you know, it was this stick with leather strips at the top."

She gazed at him steadily. He looked away.

"Like a riding crop?" she asked. "Like for horses? Do I ride horses?"

"Well, it was sort of like a fantasy." He was smiling at her now. "A dream. Of course. Now it seems like a dream. You could be right."

"Tell me about it," she murmured. "I'd like to share it with you."

"I'm not sure I want to," he said. "It's mine. I might not have another if I tell you about it."

"We could really do it the way we did in your dream," she said.

"Do you want me to dream, or not?"

She lay down again, exhausted from the effort of the past few nights. *All right,* she thought. *The next dream better be his because I can't keep this up forever.*

He put on his shirt, pulled on his pants, buckled his belt. "A dream," he said. "I'll be damned."

Susannah Indigo

❦

# Shadows on the Wall

There was never a problem of trust between us. Yet I promise myself every night that I won't do it. I will not go near that wall. I will light the two tall emerald green candles on top of the upright piano. I will play my music out, trying to let the memory of Jack pass through the dissonant chords and disappear into the shadow of the flames.

I start with "Going Out of My Head." Jack loved it after I told him about winning a fifth grade talent show with this song. I'm not sure it sounds any better twenty years later, but it does make me feel like a little girl again. Before I play, I lift my skirt as he always required, placing my bare bottom on the velvet-padded piano bench. I spread my legs as he liked; I rarely use the pedals anyway. He called me his little girl, he called me his pet, he called me his kitten. "Play for me, kitten . . . dance for me, kitten," he would say.

Most of the lights are off, but the special track lighting that he had installed for me is on. He would often turn the lights toward me playing or dancing. "You're on my stage, kitten. Entertain me. You're all I need. Let me watch you."

I will not go near the wall tonight.

I dress every morning for him, even though he's not here. I look at my closet and see the style he brought to my life. When I moved in, he threw out all my pantyhose and restrictive underthings.

"A body like yours needs to be free, kitten," he said. He didn't touch my dance clothes, since I use them to make a living. He told me the things I should wear. It was control, but he was right, and it was beautiful. My closet is full of short skirts, and thick belts to show off my waist. The colors are mostly black or red, some white, and some emerald green, his favorite color.

I felt him watching me this morning as I got dressed. I slid on black thigh-high stockings, a longish black wraparound dance skirt, and a white silk shirt tied at my waist. I put on the black Chinese pierced earrings that represent the symbol for energy. Jack liked to put my earrings on for me. The first time he slid a long steel post through the tiny hole in my earlobe was one of the sexiest moments of my life.

Next I play "As Time Goes By," my own favorite song. Jack's picture sits on the piano in a brass frame between the candles, but I don't need to look at it. I see him and feel him every minute of the day. His dark eyes and warm smile are emblazoned on my soul. I always teased him that he looked like Sam Shepard, but of course I wouldn't even look at Sam Shepard if Jack was in the same room.

A couple of weeks ago I was playing this song over and over again, and the guy named Michael who lives below me came up to tell me how much he liked it. I think he was a bit drunk, we just stood at my door and looked at each other, wanting to say more. I found him very warm and attractive and I wanted to invite him in. But I couldn't.

I turn the track lights off for now. Jack owned my life for almost a year before the motorcycle accident. It was so like him to be prepared for his death, even though he was only 44. He left me instructions, and I followed them perfectly. His headstone says "While alive, he lived." He trusted me. He is controlling me from the grave and I don't know how to get away from it.

The wall is painted a deep emerald green.

I move to the sofa and try to read, after putting on a Van Morrison song — "heart and soul/body and mind/meet me/on the river of time." When I opened the box of letters full of instructions, I cried. How could he have known? When did he do this? The first letter said:

*My kitten,*

*I'm writing this under a strange and very frightening premonition. I feel like I will not be with you for long, as silly as that sounds as I write it. I suppose it's because of my father dying of a heart attack when he was just forty-five. I guess if you're reading this, my fears are right. I know you can't live without me. I could not live without you. We belong to each other. You are so young and so beautiful. I don't want you to be lost and crying without me. I will always be with you. Feel me on you right now. Touch yourself for me. Close your eyes and run your hands up your thighs just like I would. Thank you, kitten. I've written these letters to be opened one a week. I know you will obey this. I trust you implicitly to do everything that I ask. I don't know how many letters there will be. Do not read ahead for any reason. Your only instruction this week is a simple one. Know that I am with you and that I am watching you. Mourn me with love and respect and sensuality. Do not withdraw from the living. This is what I want you to do: Read this letter every morning for a week before you get out of bed . . . .*

At that point the letter went into great detail about how I was to stroke myself to orgasm for him every night for a week. Where I should sit or lie each night, what I should wear, what I should think about. I never thought I could do it. But I did. With my eyes closed, I could feel him watching. I don't believe in spirits. I don't believe in God or heaven. But yet I follow these letters just as though Jack can see me.

I played the piano at his memorial service. My ass was bare on the piano bench underneath my full black skirt, as he requested. I played "Amazing Grace" for him, and I know that he smiled as I sang the second verse, his favorite, to myself:

'Twas grace that taught my heart to fear
And grace my fears relieved;
How precious did that grace appear
The hour that I first believed

Some days I think of telling the man downstairs my whole story — I know he's a writer, and I need someone to talk to. But I don't.

I turn the lights back on and shine them on the wall.

We lived in harmony. Perfect equals in the outside world, perfect lovers inside our home. We lived a life of what people call "dominance and submission." I can't talk to anyone about it, because people have this image of women in chains and leather being abused. That's not what it was at all. It was about an exchange of power, about our agreement that we wanted to do this, about love and passion and a depth of sexuality I'll never know again.

I arrange myself in the big black leather armchair as he has instructed me to, the same way I did when he was here. I always wear skirts, never jeans. I lift my skirt, spread my legs over each arm of the chair, and relax back. Sometimes we would both just sit and read this way, with me available to him. It was in both of us, a very intense sexuality just under the surface no matter what we were doing. Tonight I lift my black dance skirt up above my hips.

I opened the second letter and it was rather spooky. I found a tape with it. I put it on the tape player as instructed and cried all the way through the first time. Then I rewound it and listened more carefully. There was laughter, he read a favorite story for me, and there was a lot of music. There was also sexual talk, the kinds of words that have always made me blush. Then there was that music, the music that will haunt me the rest of my life no matter what happens. And the instruction to get up and dance for him.

I dance for a living with the Black Oak Dance Project. It seemed to entrance him; he could watch me practice my dance for hours. He would just watch me dance whatever routine I was practicing. Then he started asking more of me. The first time I stripped for him I was buzzed on a couple of glasses of wine. I'm not a stripper, I'm a modern/jazz dancer. It took me forever, and I know by the way he fucked me that night that it turned him on as much as it did me.

The wall beckons me, and somehow I know I will go to it yet again.

After discovering the creativity in my stripping, he moved on. He started to control me as I danced. Not just asking for something, but setting up requirements, usually sexual. At first it was fun and challenging. Then I started to get scared. The control he has over me takes me into a space where I'm flying and completely vulnerable. I don't think he could have known the impact these letters would have on me.

It's been almost six months now. Twenty-four new letters. Sometimes I dread opening them, sometimes I can't wait. The letters have gotten shorter.

The fifth letter started in about the wall. It was something he made up for me one night long ago. It began mildly, dancing in the shadows. He would sit and watch me and often stroke his cock. We would fuck like crazy afterwards, like animals in heat. I don't know what you'd call what we were doing, not exactly dancing, not exactly sex. Just another world, a special moment of power in our own private universe.

I think about Jack so much that sometimes when the phone rings I'm sure it will be him. Yet when I see Michael from downstairs go by my window, I often wish that he would come and save me and make me normal again. I know no man can save me, but that doesn't stop the desire.

I untie my shirt and slide it off my shoulders. The heavy silver heart that Jack gave me dangles between my bare breasts. My nipples are hard. Every time I open a letter now, I half hope it will talk about my future, about the possibility of another man. But he doesn't write of it, and I still dance my heart out for him every night. I rise from my chair, start the exotic Indian music, and head slowly toward my wall.

#5

*My kitten, I'm rather enjoying writing these letters, much to my surprise. If nothing ever happens, we can share them some day and laugh over my silly fears. This brings out my creativity like nothing else ever has, except for the hours I spend painting you. I try to picture you in our apartment alone, without me, reading this, dancing for me, staying sexual for me. I try to think of what you will need. I have several hard things to ask of you, but I also want to take care of you. You know that I left all of my paintings to you, with instructions to keep them in storage for now. We both know how much I love my art, hobby though it is. And we both know the most gorgeous work I've ever done involves you as my model. You also know that James had a standing offer to me to put on a show in his gallery. I not only want you to do it, I want you to be there as the guest of honor. You can do it. You may destroy the hundreds of photographs if you like, but I want the paintings shared. James has the instructions on how I want it done. It's to be called "Visions of Juliana." All you have to do is call him. It's always your choice. Your submission to me was always the choice of your free will.*

What he didn't mention in the letter is what the paintings are.

Naked, half-dressed, stroking myself, lost in ecstasy, on the wall, bent over the chair. He painted them beautifully. I think he painted me through a haze of love, because I don't believe I've ever looked like that in my life. They are all dreamy, massively sensual, and I would die before I'd let anyone else ever see them.

This fifth letter went on —

*I want you to dance on the wall for me tonight, kitten. Do you remember the things you submitted to there? I remember the first night we got past the play of dancing in the shadows. You were like a beautiful butterfly pinned to a board for me. I could have kept you there forever. But nobody else is watching you now, not like before. I know you haven't moved any of the equipment. I hope you never will. Dance for me there tonight. Put your wrists where they belong, the lights as they should be, and see me in the shadows . . .*

I stood before the wall that night as I do now. It's all still here. The glossy deep green paint, the black velvet cords hanging down, the octagonal mirror on the opposite wall, the leather box in the corner. There used to be a dining table in this part of the room, but we moved it out a long time ago.

Sometimes we'd laugh and joke about "our wall." He'd even say we might not do it anymore. But when we got here there was no laughter, there was only music and power and sex. It obsessed both of us after awhile, wondering what could possibly be next. I teach dance and gymnastics to small children in my off-season. How could I ever explain this to anyone?

I press my bare back against the green wall. He would ask me to decorate my body before I started. The leather box holds many choices for decoration, and most of them hurt. My body is still permanently decorated for him, but these are all temporary. I slide my skirt off, leaving nothing covering me but my black stockings. My hands caress my marks: the tiny ribbon-shaped tattoo just above where my pussy hair would be if I didn't still have it waxed off for him. The ribbon says only "kitten." A matching tattoo with his name just above the top of my stocking, on the inside of my thigh very close to my pussy. And, of course, the tiny gold ring pierced through the hood of my clit, the gold ring that shows up clearly in so many of his paintings.

I never thought I'd let a man do any of these things to my body. But each act of marking turned out to be desperately sensual and erotic. He had his friend James come to our home and do each one at different times. Jack would get me high on submission beforehand and then hold me down tightly while James did his work on my body. I remember having an orgasm during the piercing of my clit hood. Jack never let me forget it.

*Go to the leather box, kitten, and choose a decoration for your body. Remove all of your clothing except stockings if you're wearing them. Wait, let me choose for tonight. I want you to put on the gold filigree chain that threads through your clit ring and up over your ass and around your waist. Then put on the nipple clamps that match, the tiny black ones with the matching chain . . . .*

The thing that people miss sometimes from reading things like *The Story of O* is that real S/M is not about force at all. It's about love and power and desire. It's like my ballet training when I was a young girl: It's a tradition of ritual, sacrifice, pain and beauty, all at the hands of another. Jack introduced me to all his devices of power, but I would beg for them if he didn't initiate them. We were like two pieces of an interlocking puzzle — he was dominant and power-driven, and I am submissive and driven by the need to be controlled. Discovering that I could live this way and still be in the world saved my life.

I reach up and slide one wrist through the black velvet restraint. He liked me to do this to myself while he watched. The cords are long enough to give me a full range of motion. He would start the same music every time, give me that look, and say, "Tie yourself up for me, kitten," and I would. Real bondage is in the mind, not the knots.

My other wrist is tied. How can I do this without him? He made me feel safe. I don't feel that way now.

The gold chain around my waist shimmers in the lights. There are other restraints, but I can't do them all myself. Everyone who comes to our home thinks the black cords draping the green wall are a work of art.

Jack forgot one thing, and that's why this is so hard for me: he didn't realize I would transcend reality even without him here. Afterwards I need him to take care of me, to bring me down, to bring me back.

*Remember the things we did there, kitten.*

The night of the feathers. The night of the examination. It all makes me soaking wet to remember. The night he mastered how to lift me off the ground against the wall with the combination of cords. When he said I should be nothing but a work of art and kept there forever. The night his friends came over and he showed them everything. He let them touch me, he let them command me. He never let them fuck me. The pictures. The first night I asked him to take me to the wall. The small black suede whip. The music. The music.

I dance.

This is not something to do alone. I will go mad. I have to stop. I turn and face the wall the way he required.

I love it.

It makes me wet.

My nipples are hard against the cold wall.

I hate it.

I slither against the wall, making love to the wall and to myself as he would want me to.

I miss him. I need him. I need his voice telling me it's all going to be all right, telling me to go wherever it takes me and he will be here to bring me back.

I turn and twist and rub my gold clit ring against the wall and I am coming for him and our love and our past and his power. I start to shiver. No more. I will free my wrists and put my shirt back on and begin to find a way to tell my story. I am alone, and I will learn to live without him.

# About the Authors

**BLAKE C. AARENS** is the great-granddaughter of Hattie and Esther, the granddaughter of Dicy, and the daughter of Cobia. She is a survivor of childhood sexual abuse who writes award-winning erotic fiction. Her work has appeared in *Aché: A Journal for Lesbians of African Descent, Best American Erotica 1993, Penthouse*, and the anthology *Switch Hitters: Lesbians Write Gay Male Erotica and Gay Men Write Lesbian Erotica*. Blake is a working artist in search of her tribe.

"I've always lived partly in worlds 'out there,'" says **EMILY ALWARD**, whose early role model was Wonder Woman. She has just completed a novel, *Shimmer Spell*, set in the same culture as "Honeymoon on Cobale." Her published work ranges from environmental history articles to science fantasy and erotica. Emily currently shares a lakeside house in Indiana with her dog, Bonnie, and two visiting cats.

**RED JORDAN AROBATEAU** has been writing and self-publishing since the early 1970s and is officially on the bookstore shelves with *Lucy & Mickey, Dirty Pictures, Boys Night Out, Rough Trade, Satan's Best, Street Fighter, The Black Biker, Where the Word Is No*, and *The Nearness of You/Sorrow of the Madonna*. She has acquired something of a cult-like following among many working-class dykes.

**CHRISTINE BEATTY** is a transsexual lesbian author and musician. Her recent publishing credits include a collection of short stories and poetry, *Misery Loves Company*, and an entry in *Beyond Definition*, a gay-lesbian-bi-trans anthology from Manic D Press. She is also a staff writer for *TransSisters* magazine, and her work regularly appears in *Tapestry*, the *Spectator*, and the *San Francisco Bay Times* Letters section. She performs with Glamazon, a rock band she formed with her lipstick lezzie lover, Rynata.

**DEBORAH BISHOP** is an award-winning romance writer who lives in southern Indiana with her husband, two stepchildren, and three unruly dogs. When she isn't writing she enjoys reading, gardening, and rebuilding computers.

ERIN BLACKWELL is a Eurocalifornian who went to France to learn about love and was not disappointed. "Real Pleasure" is dedicated to her personal *"prof d'amour,"* Nicole Guenneugués.

CALLA CONOVA, a poet and short-story writer, found that the key to getting published was moving to San Francisco, where the readers are kind, the people are good-looking, and all the dogs are above average.

KELLY CONWAY, a writer and musician, lives in Sacramento, California, with her divine butch and their three ill-mannered cats. You can find more of her work in *The Femme Mystique*, edited by Lesléa Newman; *Mother Lies*; *Write from the Heart, May/December*; and *Lesbian Short Fiction*. When not working on her novel, she's a booking agent whose company, Lavender Underground, produces concerts by women musicians and comics.

BARBARA DeGENEVIEVE is an artist and professor at the School of the Art Institute of Chicago, where she teaches in the photography program. She received an NEA Visual Arts Fellowship in 1988 for her photographic work and in 1994 was awarded another NEA Fellowship, which was revoked by the National Council on the Arts because of sexual content.

KATE DOMINIC is a Los Angeles-based writer who is addicted to sexy stories because they're so much fun. Her work, mostly fiction, has been published under various pen names in various periodicals and anthologies. Under this name, her credits include honorable mention in *Libido* magazine's 1997 fiction contest. A graduate of the University of Wisconsin, Kate considers writing erotica to be her solution to the quandary of "What do I do with an English degree besides teach?"

DEBBIE ESTERS is the happy single mother of one and lives in San Francisco. She works as a health professional and writes whenever she can.

DIVA MARIE is an active, out, happily married pansexual leather player and professional dominatrix currently residing in New

Mexico. When she's not teaching or writing, she can usually be found at national SM/leather conventions looking for virgin boys who need debriefing of any kind.

ANGELA FAIRWEATHER, the recovered wife of several ex-husbands, lives her life as a colorful memoir. She has reinvented herself as the queen of vanilla and belly-dance goddess, and writes passionately of food and sex. She shares her life with abundant friends, a beautiful, adored daughter, and two tortoise-shell cats.

BONNIE FERGUSON of Benicia, California, is completing *The Intruders*, a short-story collection. "Amazing Grace" inspired her first novel, *Bloodroot*, the story of a biracial friendship between two families in the rural South circa 1940. *Vahine*, a novel of the South Pacific, will explore Polynesian taboos and will require leisurely field research.

NANCY FERREYRA is a disabled lesbian living in the San Francisco Bay Area. "After Amelia" is her first published short story. She is currently finishing an erotic novel, *Slip*, about a disabled lesbian's journey of self-discovery through an affair with a married man.

LAUREL FISHER lives, loves, and writes in Denver in the company of one knight in slightly tarnished armor and an odd assortment of critters and motorcycles.

WINN GILMORE grew up in the South, graduated from Smith College, and lives in California. Her writing has also appeared in the magazines *Aché*, *On Our Backs*, and *frighten the horses*; the anthologies *Unholy Alliances* and *Riding Desire*; and the journal *Sinister Wisdom*. She is seeking a publisher for her short story collection, *Trip to Nawlins*.

JOLIE GRAHAM is a West Coast writer and artist presently at work on an erotic novel. She still wears the ear cuff.

C. A. GRIFFITH left New York City and a career as a professional camera assistant and cinematographer for the challenge of writing and directing in Cali.

JANE HANDEL is a writer, visual artist, and publisher. In 1990 she founded SpiderWoman Press, which publishes limited edition artist-designed and -illustrated books and broadsides. She currently makes her living as an art dealer and curator specializing in vintage photography and other works on paper.

MEL HARRIS is a freelance writer who has only recently discovered how much she enjoys writing erotica, especially humorous erotica. "Neighborhood Round Robyn" is her first erotic story based on a favorite fantasy. She has also contributed to *Sex Toy Tales* (Down There Press). She lives on the Gulf of Mexico in Northern Florida with her Miniature Pinscher, Maya.

SUSANNA J. HERBERT's words have lived via TV, films, theatre, magazines and anthologies. Thanks to Marcy Sheiner for her support. "Breaking and Entering" is dedicated to her muse, Hondaki. "Three Note Harmony" is dedicated to the Brown Bear boys, the lads from Shepherd's Bush, and Alan—who is too much of a gentleman to peek at my notes.

SUSANNAH INDIGO is a systems consultant and writer, and the mother of two young boys. Her fiction has been published in a variety of magazines, including *Libido* and *Black Sheets*.

GINU KAMANI is the author of *Junglee Girl*, a collection of short stories exploring the sensual recklessness of Indian women. Her work has been published in *On a Bed of Rice: An Asian-American Erotic Feast* and *Dick for a Day*. She is working on a novel and screenplays.

SONJA KINDLEY's work has appeared in a number of publications, including *Elle*, *ZYZZYVA*, and *CutBank*.

AURORA LIGHT has had erotica published in *Gallery*, *Hustler*, *Pillow Talk*, and *EIDOS*. She is a volunteer for the National EAR Foundation and publishes a poetry review.

JO MANNING's stories have appeared in *Imagine!*, *Fiction Forum*, *Just a Moment*, *Stuff*, *Nocturnal Ecstasy Vampire Coven*, *Romantic Interludes*, *Travel Erotica Anthology*, and *The Star*. An audio book,

*The Prairie Princess and the Sanskritologist*, was released by Radio Books/Redwood Press. She finds writing erotica very liberating.

The only thing **SHELLEY MARCUS** likes more than writing gay porn is reading it, so she couldn't be happier to see the genre flourishing. Shelley is currently single, but is not opposed to seeing that situation change some day. A writer since childhood, she lives and works in New Jersey.

**EVE MARIPOSA** is a poet, drummer, and lover of everything she can sing to. She thanks all the warrior women who have lit her sky with their truth.

**MARY MAXWELL** was raised by wolves. In subsequent years, she has adapted reasonably well to the strictures of civilization.

**MARIA MENDOZA** was born and raised in Texas. A college graduate in journalism from the University of Texas at Austin, Maria's main love is fiction writing. "Mourning the Peasant" is her short fiction debut. She resides and works in New York City.

**MARTHA MILLER** is a Midwestern writer. Her short stories are widely published in lesbian and literary periodicals and anthologies. She writes a monthly book review column for women and has had three plays produced by Mid-America Playwrights Theater. She has recently completed a novel.

**KAREN MARIE CHRISTA MINNS**, author of *Bloodsong*, *Virago*, and *Calling Rain*, is a novelist, exhibited painter, and general adventurer.

**MARY ANNE MOHANRAJ** has published her first book, *Torn Shapes of Desire*. Her work also appears in *Sex Toy Tales* (Down There Press) and in *Best American Erotica 1999*. She moderates the Internet Erotica Writers' workshop, co-moderates the newsgroup soc.sexuality.general, and edits the erotic webzine www. cleansheets.com.

**SERENA MOLOCH** lives in San Francisco. Her hobbies include improving her typing speed and trying on expensive clothing in stores. She has a story in *Virgin Territory 2* and is working on a script for an erotic feature called *Harmony's Party*.

FELICE NEWMAN is publisher of Cleis Press, where she is privileged to work with many cutting-edge authors of erotica. Her fiction appears in *The Second Coming*.

LISA PROSIMO lives in Southern California and entertains dreams of living in Northern California. "I like to think my characters are alive before they enter my stories and will continue to live after they leave." Her erotic fiction has appeared in *Sauce Box Journal*, *XStories*, and Lonnie Barbach's *Seductions*. She has a novel under construction.

CAROL QUEEN's first novel, *The Leather Daddy and the Femme*, was released in 1998. She is also author of *Real Live Nude Girl: Chronicles of Sex-Positive Culture* and *Exhibitionism for the Shy* (Down There Press), and co-editor of the Lammy award-winning *PoMoSexuals*, as well as *Switch Hitters* and *Sex Spoken Here* (Down There Press).

ADRIENNE RABINOV is a business consultant and professor at an East Coast university. She and her West Coast lover, for whom she wrote "In the Mood," think it's a hoot to be publishing their personal pornography.

JULIA RADER loves to make money from sex, especially from writing about it. For her mental health and global unity she makes performance rituals. She's studying to be an Alexander teacher while continuing to work on *The Dr. Angel Letters*, a novel that explains how S/M can save your life.

SHAR REDNOUR wrote *The Femme's Guide to the Universe*. Her short stories appear in *Best American Erotica 1996*, *Leatherwomen III*, and *Once Upon a Time: Fairytales for Women*. She publishes *Starphkr*. Jackie Strano, lead singer of The Hail Marys, is Shar's true love and eternal inspiration.

STACY REED is a Houston writer and editor. She studied at the University of Texas at Austin and danced topless for several years.

Reed has published essays, criticism, editorials, and features, and has reported news. Her erotica appears in *First Person Sexual* (Down There Press). She is currently writing a novel.

**FRANCESCA ROSS** is the pseudonym of a widely published romance novelist. An editor of nonfiction books, she also teaches composition and literature at a state university. She lives with her husband and two young sons in the Midwest and communicates with other writers through computer networking.

"Commuter" is **LISA ROTHMAN**'s first piece of erotica. She is currently working on a collection of short stories about ballroom dancing, the harrowing world of coordinating volunteers, and why dating assistant sous-chefs and computer consultants is probably not a good idea.

**SUSAN ST. AUBIN**'s erotica has been published in *Libido*, *Yellow Silk*, *Erotic by Nature*, *Fever*, and *Best American Erotica 1995*. She believes in her dreams, even when they don't come true.

**KAREN A. SELZ** is an assistant professor at a medical school, where she applies the conceptual and computational tools of mathematical physics to the study of brains and behavior. Sex-positive in her poetry and painting, she found it natural to design a machine that could compensate for and heal interpersonal deficits. Her story "The Hobby Horse" is the first entry in the smut category of her curriculum vitae.

**MICHELE SERCHUK** is a writer, photographer, and performer. Her work has been published in *Bust 'Zine* and *Australian Women's Forum*. She has adapted her stories and poems for the stage and has performed this work at New York's Dixon Place and in the Womenkind V and VI annual theater festivals. Her photography has been exhibited in a solo show at MBM Gallery in Soho and has appeared as cover art for several books of erotica.

**MARCY SHEINER** is the editor of *Herotica 4, 5*, and *6*, as well as *The Oy of Sex: Jewish Women Write Erotica* (Cleis). She writes fiction, journalism, and erotica, and is the author of *Sex for the Clueless* (Citadel).

**VICTORIA SMITH** lives in central California, dividing her time between the desert and the coast. Her stories, poetry, and sexuality articles have appeared in many venues, including *Carnal Knowledge*, *SEXlife*, and *Moondance*. Victoria's current projects include a market guide for writers of erotica, and two novels.

**CHRISTINE SOLANO** is a bilingual and bisexual San Francisco writer, poet, and activist involved in deep ecology, human rights, and the abolition of the death penalty.

**MICHELLE STEVENS** lives in Los Angeles with her wife, Chris, who wants everyone to know that "Lesbian Bed Death" is purely fictional.

**ANNALISA SUID** is a California-based writer of erotic fiction, currently at work on her second and third novels. She dedicates "After the War" to Anne Rice, her inspiration, and to Judy Cole, her mentor and friend.

**CECILIA TAN** is the author of *Black Feathers: Erotic Dreams* and the editor of numerous erotic science fiction and fantasy anthologies for Circlet Press. Her short stories have appeared in *Best American Erotica 1996* and *1998*, *Best Lesbian Erotica 1997*, and many other anthologies and magazines.

**CATHERINE M. TAVEL** lives with her firefighter husband in their native Brooklyn. Their many adventures take them to the tops of active volcanoes in Guatemala, river rafting during hailstorms in Wyoming, and yes, even to perilous wrought-iron balconies in New Orleans. She considers herself very fortunate to be able to immortalize these experiences in print.

**JOAN LESLIE TAYLOR** is a writer and accountant who lives in the woods of northern California with a large dog and a small cat. She is the author of *In the Light of Dying*, a book about her experiences as a hospice volunteer. In *Herotica 2* her story "Double Date" appeared under the name Maggie Brewster.